NAOMI GREENSMITH

THE Dark Heart OF THE Raven

BOOK TWO OF THE LAST LUX TRILOGY

Dear Nanee,
I hope you enjoy
my second book!
Lots of love,
Naomi xxx

Disclaimer
This is a work of fiction. Names, characters, businesses, places, events, and incidents are either the products of the author's imagination or used in a fictitious manner. Any resemblance to actual persons, living or dead, or actual events is purely coincidental.

Cover designed by Joan Culum
joandrawslinks.carrd.co

ISBN:
978-1-7384257-1-6

For Mum and Dad,
you taught me what love is.

Content Warnings

This book contains adult themes, including portrayals of drug and alcohol use and dependence, moderate descriptions of injury, torture, murder, and corpses, themes of grief, references to self-harm and suicide, and non-graphic scenes of a sexual nature, including one open door scene at the start of Chapter 39.

If you have any concerns about the themes listed above, please do not hesitate to contact the author via email or social media for further details. Contact details are provided in the About the Author section at the end of the book.

Prologue

That whole afternoon, he couldn't stop looking at her, unable to believe she was really there. From the moment they met at the college gates and he walked her into town, his disbelief that she had finally agreed to a date gradually bloomed into a tentative hope. Their conversation had started off tense, with stilted rambling about the weather and an upcoming essay, but by the end of lunch in the cramped and crowded café, they were talking as easily as if they had been friends for years, not rivals in more than just the academic sense.

"You're not as arrogant as I expected you to be," she said when their coffees arrived after a meal that he had been too nervous to finish.

"Well, you're not as cold as you pretend to be," he replied, unable to suppress the smile that crinkled his eyes.

She pursed her lips, but amusement still danced across her features. "If I seemed so cold, why on earth did you want to go out with me, Victor Bolton?"

He surveyed her, taking in those forget-me-not blue eyes slightly narrowed in curiosity, the fine fair hair that curved around her pretty face. As her expression softened, a happiness he had never felt flooded him like warm, calming water. "Meredith, where on earth do I begin?"

It wasn't just her classical beauty that had caught his attention, even if she did hold herself with more grace and dignity than most of the young women he had come across at the college. It was her mind that had attracted him, that raw intelligence that had humbled him in the classroom, the witty remarks flung at him to make him feel small, but that had instead filled him with admiration and amusement. It was the way she looked when she thought no one was watching, lost in thought, admiring the beauty of her surroundings. It was the way her nose wrinkled when she laughed, the way she absently curled a strand of hair around her finger when she was deep in a good book, or the delicate way she held her coffee cup as she watched him, her blush deepening with his every confession about why he had fallen in love with her.

By the time he finished telling her, she was avoiding his gaze, trying to prevent the smile that she couldn't keep off her face. "And there I was," she said eventually, when she had regained some of her composure, "thinking you just liked to irritate me."

After the stuffy café, they meandered through the cobbled Cambridge streets towards the river, too engrossed in one another's words to notice where they were going. Their conversation jumped from topic to topic like stepping stones across a pond, ranging from childhood memories to funny anecdotes about lecturers, then to Meredith's summer plans to travel around the Mediterranean coasts with her older brother. Now that he had confessed his feelings, Victor felt braver, occasionally brushing against her arm or placing his hand lightly against her back, and before long she was doing the same. Every contact felt electric, even if they only touched clothing, their eyes meeting and then flitting away. When they decided to sit on the riverbank, he tried not to cringe at the cliché he was enacting as he offered to let her sit on his jacket. At first she refused, but reconsidered when he pointed out that she would get grass stains on her white linen trousers. They talked for what must have been hours, not noticing the rain clouds gathering until Meredith shivered, and they decided to head back to campus.

She took his hand then, and he would never forget the shock that went through him at her touch, and the feel of her cool fingers in his. He met her gaze, making her blush and look away. The first raindrops landed, and they walked faster.

"I'm afraid I didn't bring an umbrella," he said, not having expected the rain. The day had been so warm and sunny.

"Me neither," she admitted, casting a concerned glance at the sky. Thunder rumbled in the distance, awakening the lightning deep in his chest. There was a flash and another rumble a moment later, followed by an increase in raindrops which quickly turned into a downpour.

Victor looked at Meredith, taking in her carefully styled hair, the light lemon and white summer clothes that would do little to protect her from the rain. "Should we run?" he suggested. And there it was, the mischief that glinted in the eyes of the girl who had been brought up never to run, or get grass stains on her clothes, or do anything improper or unexpected of a well-raised woman. And before he could react, she was off, dragging him along by the hand.

He caught up quickly, sprinting along with her, and spotted a bridge up ahead. "There," he pointed, and she sped up, leaving him wondering how she was managing in her flimsy summer shoes. Within moments, they reached the shelter beneath the bridge, both laughing hard. Meredith bent down, her hands on her knees, struggling to catch her breath. Victor panted through his grin, but his heart stopped when she straightened and smiled up at him, looking happier than he had ever seen her. He didn't know what drove him to approach her, to leave behind any inhibitions as he reached out to embrace her with one hand and brush the wet strands of hair out of her face with the other. He took her in, filled with wonder at the light in her eyes and the sprinkle of freckles across her nose, noticing how the raindrops still clustered on her lashes. She wrapped her arms around his neck, coming closer, not taking her eyes off his. His arms tightened around her, and when her nose brushed his, he kissed her and never looked back.

His dreams had been strange, and violent. Almost always violent. But worse than the violent dreams were the tender ones, the ones where his daughter was still a girl, where his wife was still alive, where his family was safe and happy. They were worse because when he awoke, he grieved his losses all over again. His daughter was not a girl, but a grown woman with a heavy burden, and his wife was dead. And perhaps he would soon follow her.

Each time he awoke, he was accosted by pain. His captors had numbed him enough for his Talent to be beyond his reach, but the agony was etched so deep that Veto didn't touch it. They had broken his mind and his bones, extracted every piece of information they could from him, and once they had done that, they broke him some more, just for the sake of it. They only kept him alive to exchange him for his daughter when she finally gave herself up. He hoped his end would come before that could happen.

When he awoke this time, it was to semi-darkness. The lone lightbulb flickered on and off with an electric buzz. He was slumped in a chair, arms tied tightly behind his back, ankles tethered to the chair legs. It was some time before he was able to raise his head, all the while vaguely aware of how his back and ribs ached and it hurt to breathe. When he finally lifted his gaze, he found himself in unfamiliar surroundings, and he was not alone. Through the gloom, a small, dark figure stood before him, leaning against the door that was the only way out of the small room.

A low, satisfied laugh told him who his tormentor was this time.

"Awake at last, Bolton. I don't recall you being such a late riser."

His only response was a cough, which turned into a pathetic splutter as pain wracked through his chest. There was no sympathy to be had from his visitor. Instead, the woman only laughed again, the sound chilling him far worse than the cold lingering in the room.

"They have left you in a state, haven't they? Tut tut, there isn't much left for me to play with."

Victor coughed again, this time hacking up blood. He spat it on the floor, half of it spattering his already filthy trousers.

"I must admit, having you here has been rather entertaining these past weeks. I've come to know you very well, warts and all. As for all your memories of Skye, and Meredith…" The woman paused, allowing herself the pleasure of teasing him. "I always wondered what her death was like. Now, thanks to some talented Telepaths, I know."

"What else do you want?" His throat rasped the words on their way out, his voice sounding foreign to him. As far as he knew, they had extracted every last memory and morsel of information. Aside from keeping him alive to trade for Skye, there was little use left in him.

The woman laughed again. "Why, sweetheart," she said, stepping into the flickering light to loom before him, "I want revenge."

How many years had it been since her trial? Camilla Linden had not aged well. Her face was like a cadaver, the scarlet lipstick and lank red hair contrasting sharply with her pale skin. She was thinner than ever, wearing a tattered purple coat that drowned her tiny frame, and black stiletto boots that did little to enhance her height. Still, having her standing before him sent a fear through Victor that promised worse than anything he had so far endured during his imprisonment. Until now, the torture had been a means to an end. But Camilla needed no reason. She lived to hurt.

She pushed her coat to one side, sliding an ornate knife from amongst an assortment sheathed in a belt around her bony hips. She lifted it to his face, and Victor tried not to tremble as the metal glinted in the meagre light. Biting her lower lip, she ran a hand through his hair. Her touch was a caress, but it sent a horrific shudder down his spine. In her other hand, the knife hovered in front of his face, then she pressed the flat of the blade to his cheek, the metal a cold kiss. As she ran the knife along his skin, he felt the sharp edge bite into him, leaving behind a sting and a wet trail of blood.

"There, there, Bolton." Her voice was gentle, but her hands were not as she grabbed his chin in a vice-like grip, stopping him from moving his face aside. "We're only just getting started."

"I acted in the name of justice," he managed, the words strained.

Camilla scoffed, pushing his head up and back, forcing him to look her in the eye. "As did I. Once upon a time it was legal to execute a man for adultery. In some parts of the world it still is."

Victor was in no state to argue. Prison seemed to have made Camilla even more deranged than when he had prosecuted her for murdering her husband and his lover.

"But it's not just that, Victor, darling. It's not just six years of my life you took from me. You took *her*. We were friends, Meredith and I. I've not forgiven you for poisoning her against me."

It was Victor's turn to be amused as his eyes burned into her. "Friends? That's a strange word for it. She used you,

Camilla. You were her loyal pet. Did you not see that in my memories?"

Camilla's eyes narrowed, and before he could react, she delivered a back-handed slap across his left cheek. Despite her small stature, the force nearly knocked him from his chair. Victor swayed, dizzied, and a cold sensation crept into his eye.

"We were friends," she hissed, grabbing his hair and shoving him upright. "But you destroyed our friendship, and then you destroyed her. Not that she didn't deserve it; she let you turn her into a stupid bitch."

"Don't speak of her that way," Victor snarled, anger burning him from the inside.

She kneed him in the stomach, leaving him grunting against the pain. "I'll say what I want. She's dead, and soon you will be too. And when we finally get our hands on her, your daughter will follow."

"You won't get her," he said, putting as much conviction into his voice as he could muster. "You already know she's thc Lux. That makes her too strong even for you." The news about his daughter's destiny had come from one of his interrogators. He had always suspected after Meredith had been so ready to die, had considered consulting a Seer for the truth of it. But he had feared that truth, and learning it now – now that he was separated from Skye and unable to protect her – made it all the more difficult to bear.

Camilla let out a cackle that made Victor's ears ring. "She wasn't too strong for us last time. Or are you blaming that one on her stupid misplaced loyalty?"

Victor tried not to think about Skye's previous failures, but his terror grew in spite of himself. It was a moment before he recognised the artificial tinge to his fear. Camilla was using her Talent on him.

"Yes, she was susceptible to my influence too. Perhaps not as much, but even the Lux has weaknesses. She is not too strong to fall, Bolton, and she will fall." She pulled his head back again, the cold blade pressed against his exposed throat. Her mouth was close to his ear, her breath tickling his neck.

"No," he whispered, but the artificial fear made him tremble, his breath shaky.

"Yes," she said, licking her lips as the knife cut into him again, just enough to bring forth a trickle of blood. The fear clouded his mind, obscuring the reminder that they wanted him kept alive. And then she brought the knife to her lips, dragging her tongue along the sharp edge.

"I can taste your fear, Bolton," she said, grinning with cruel delight. "And I can taste your pain. It's delicious." Sure enough, every ache, every sting, all flared at her words, sharpening into an agony that he didn't think he could bear much longer.

"Why are you doing this?" he whimpered, hating the sound of his own voice.

"Why not?" She laughed, running her fingers once more through his hair, gentle as a lover, then tightening her grip. And in that moment, his spine was on fire as the sharp point of her knife stabbed him in the back.

PART I

Chapter One

PHAEDRA RONAN

"Are you going to tell me the truth?" came Alessia's cold words from the green velvet sofa opposite her – the same words she had repeated every day since she revealed she had found the hidden photos and documents linking Phaedra inextricably to Ombra Medley.

Phaedra stood in the middle of the draughty lounge, trembling beneath her sister's icy glare, partly from cold, mostly from fear. She was clean and fed, but the rooms Alessia locked her in were poorly heated, with wind whistling through ancient window fixtures at all hours. Castle Uaine was Brydon Marsden's home, but to Phaedra, it was a prison.

"I didn't know she was a Caplinite." Phaedra repeated the same statement that sounded no more convincing than the first time she had uttered it a week ago. And sure enough, Alessia's eyes only narrowed, blue as a winter sky. Barely a flush of anger coloured her delicate features, her lustrous dark hair and high-necked black dress only enhancing her pallor. Phaedra glanced at their uncle Caspar sitting at the other end of the sofa, his matching blue eyes full of concern that echoed Phaedra's own. At least he was their only audience today, along with the two guards who held her sandwiched between them, one of them being her assigned chaperone, Glen Farraday.

"Come on, Allie," said Caspar, turning to face Alessia and resting an elbow casually against the velvet back of the sofa. "Phee came into contact with all sorts of people at her parties, and we were at peace with the Caplinites at the time. Even if she knew this Ombra was a Caplinite, what difference would it have made?"

"My name…" Alessia sneered, after taking a long inhale, "is *Alessia*."

Phaedra shrank at Alessia's reprimand, her reaction to the nickname bringing back memories of her sister's frightening tantrums when they were girls, when Caspar or their father had to contain Alessia's dangerous shadow power with their own. But their uncle only raised an eyebrow as he held his niece's glare, showing no fear. Phaedra wished she could be so brave.

"Ignorant or not," Alessia continued, looking back at Phaedra, "you stole Medley's records from Father's desk. You knew she was involved in the Mason kidnap, and you tried to cover it up."

"I didn't—" Phaedra began, then stopped. She sniffed, looking down at the floor, trying to think of some other lie. Glen's hand on her right arm squeezed reassuringly, and she resisted the urge to look up at him. "She was my friend," she said eventually, taking a deep breath to steady her nerves. "I was scared for her."

Alessia snorted. "You take me for a fool?"

"No, I—"

"Alessia," said Caspar, glancing between them, "Phaedra is young. She's not a soldier or a politician. She hasn't been trained the way you and I have. She was probably just not thinking things through."

"You're not a fool either, Caspar. You know full well she's lying."

Silence followed. Caspar looked at a loss, and fear crept sickeningly through Phaedra's gut. Alessia only watched her with a cruel curve to her lips, enjoying every moment of her fruitless attempts to lie her way out of her trap.

"I've given you a week's worth of chances, Phaedra. Since you can't bring yourself to tell me an ounce of truth, I need to decide what to do with you." She let her words hang, and Phaedra glanced at her uncle, a flicker of fear and shadows darkening his eyes. "Should I lock you up in a proper cell, or save myself the trouble and have you executed as a traitor?"

Phaedra's chest tightened, her breathing suddenly ragged. Glen's fingers twitched around her arm again, and if the two guards hadn't been holding her up, she might have sunk to the floor. She had seen her sister calmly watch their father drink the poison Alessia had planted for him, witnessed her murder him in cold blood. Phaedra didn't doubt she would kill her too.

"Alessia," Caspar muttered, glancing between them again, his face starkly pale against his dark hair and beard. "She's your sister."

Alessia said nothing, only stared at her with that same cold look. Had Glen told Caspar that Alessia wasn't above killing her own blood? Phaedra hadn't had a moment alone with her uncle yet, no chance to tell him exactly why she was afraid of her.

"One last chance, Sister," Alessia said finally, sitting upright on the sofa. "If you can't give me the truth tomorrow and tell me how to find this little terrorist friend of yours, you will meet a traitor's end. Sister or not."

***

The chill wind bit at her cheeks and tangled her hair into knots as she leaned through one of the windows in her bedroom, judging the distance to the ground. The emerald green lawn rippled far below her like waves. She was four storeys up, unlikely to survive a jump unscathed. But if the attempt killed her, surely it would be better than whatever torture her sister had in mind?

She bit her lip as vertigo filled her throat with bile, and withdrew from the drop, shutting the creaky window with a shove. Shivering, she hugged herself and turned back to the room, searching for options. Alessia had taken her phone, so she had no way to call someone for help, or warn Ombra to lie low. She had also forced Phaedra to take Veto to suppress her dark Talent, but her lack of control wasn't suited to fighting her way out of the castle anyway.

Caspar had tried to reassure her, speaking to her through the door and promising he was doing everything he could to convince Alessia to change her mind. But Phaedra had no faith. She knew what Alessia was capable of.

Pulling the blanket off the bed, she wrapped it around herself and sat cross-legged in the middle of the lumpy mattress. She watched the grey sky gradually darken, waiting for Maggie – her father's former housekeeper – to bring her evening meal.

The food never came, but Maggie did, with an entourage in tow.

Phaedra opened her mouth when she saw the pair of maids that crept inside after Maggie's stout frame, but the housekeeper pressed a finger to her lips, saying nothing until the door was quietly shut behind them.

"This is Jemima," Maggie whispered, pointing at a short, pretty woman in her mid-twenties. "She worked for Mr Marsden's daughter, and she's proficient in glamours."

Phaedra stared, letting the blanket fall away and getting up off the bed. "Glamours?"

"She's going to disguise you."

"Disguise me?" Phaedra asked, barely daring to hope.

"Come on, silly goose," said Maggie, beckoning her over. Her hands trembled, and her cropped grey hair was dishevelled.

Phaedra did as she was told, glancing between Maggie and Jemima. The other maid, with straight blonde hair pulled back in a ponytail, started to pick up her clothes and belongings and shove them into a laundry bag. Jemima placed dainty hands either side of Phaedra's face, making her flinch.

"I'm going to make you look like me," she said, turning her face this way and that, lifting her by the chin and peering at her from all angles.

"What?" Phaedra said, staring at her. Jemima's curly brown hair was gathered in a ponytail, and her large eyes were the colour of molten chocolate, with long lashes and perfectly shaped brows.

"We're going to get you out of here, Phee," Maggie whispered, helping the other maid to gather her things. "You need to stay quiet and do what we tell you."

Hope and uncertainty swirled in her tight chest, questions flooding her mind. But all she could manage was a mumbled "okay". She struggled to get a breath down, to form her voice into more words. "Are you coming too?"

Maggie didn't reply at first, and Phaedra tried to keep still while Jemima cast the glamours on her face, muttering the names of the sigils that her soft fingers traced on her skin. "This will last until tomorrow," Jemima said when she was done, running her hands over Phaedra's hair, then picking up a brush and beginning to style it into a ponytail. Phaedra glanced in the mirror above the dusty dressing table. Her blue eyes were replaced with a pair of large brown ones that stared fearfully back at her, and her pinched and pasty face was now a twin of Jemima's.

"Maggie?" she asked as the housekeeper dropped the last of her things into the laundry bag, then finally turned to her.

"Sweetie, we'll only slow you down," Maggie said, taking both her hands. "I don't know where you'll be going, but you need to keep moving until you get somewhere safe."

"But…" Phaedra's fear squirmed in the pit of her stomach as tears glazed the housekeeper's eyes. "But what will happen when she finds out I'm gone?"

Maggie swallowed, then drew her into a tight hug. "Let us worry about that. The most important thing is that we keep you safe."

Phaedra clung to her, trembling and breathing in her familiar scent of clean linen and polish.

"Put these on," the second maid interrupted, handing Phaedra the same pale green uniform that she and Jemima were wearing. Phaedra did as she was told, unzipping her hoodie and pulling on the tabard and slacks. The maid took her discarded clothes from her and shoved them into the laundry bag.

"You'll go down to the laundry room with Sally," Jemima said as the other maid, Sally, handed her the laundry bag. "If she has to refer to you, she'll call you Jem, okay?"

Phaedra nodded, glancing between the three women. "And then what?"

"We'll sneak you outside. Glen is waiting for you in a car," said Sally, sounding a little short of breath.

Phaedra nodded again, her heart speeding up. "Thank you."

"Don't thank us yet," said Jemima, moving towards the door. "And stay quiet."

Phaedra worried at her lip, following Sally as she beckoned her to the door. She opened it a few inches, peeking out to make sure the corridor was clear, then nodded and stepped through. Phaedra glanced at Maggie one last time before she followed. "See you soon?"

The housekeeper only smiled and nodded, a tear running down her cheek.

Taking a deep breath and doing her best not to cry as well, she tore her eyes away from Maggie and followed Sally along the corridor, then through a door that creaked a little as it opened and shut. Beyond it was a spiral staircase leading down, the stairwell colder than the corridor and bedroom, the walls bare brick. By the time they reached a brightly lit corridor full of the mingled scents of cooking and cleaning products, Phaedra's head spun.

They passed the laundry room full of thudding machines and servants chatting as they worked. Next was the kitchen, where staff were wrapping up leftovers, preparing things for the next day, and cleaning up. Sally led her along the edge of the room, heading towards a familiar tall and thin figure in a white chef's uniform.

"Hey Kiaran," Sally said, twisting the end of her blonde ponytail around her finger. "What time d'you knock off?"

"Now, actually," Kiaran replied, looking between them and flashing a smile that didn't quite reach his hazel eyes. "Fancy going for that drink?"

"Love to." Sally grinned, tilting her head flirtatiously. Phaedra glanced around, clutching the laundry bag tightly, but no one seemed to be paying them any mind.

Kiaran beckoned them into a small hallway that led off to a bin store on the left and a break room on the right, where he took off his hat and overalls and dropped them in a laundry basket. He and Sally then pulled on coats, and handed one to Phaedra as well. Figuring it was all part of the plan, she put it on, zipping it up with trembling fingers. Kiaran then led them through a door into a delivery car park. She could just about make out a dark car parked a few feet from the entrance. Her heartbeat began to race again.

"Good luck," Sally whispered, squeezing her arm and nodding towards the car. Phaedra turned around, mouthing a thank you to them both. Kiaran only bowed his head in return, giving her a small smile.

She opened the car door, relieved to see Glen wearing a close-lipped smile in the driver's seat, the green glow of the dashboard casting his stubbly face in an eerie light. "I thought you'd stood me up."

"Shut up and drive," Phaedra replied, shoving her laundry bag in the back seat and sliding in next to him.

"Great to know I'm running off with a gobby pixie instead of the hot laundry maid," he said after she shut the door.

Phaedra only snorted. Beyond the window, Kiaran and Sally were walking towards another car, arms around one another. "D'you think they're gonna be okay?"

But Glen said nothing, turning on the engine and creeping out of the car park, headlights off. His eyes darted in every direction as they made their way to the drive that led to the open road, and Phaedra held her breath, her chest tight with anxiety that only eased once they were finally off the estate.

Chapter Two

ROXANNE SUMMERS

A broken man sat before her. In the weeks since Cameron's death, Oliver Matheson looked like he had aged twenty years. Grey stubble peppered his lower face, his blonde hair was dirty and dishevelled, and his clothing hung loose on his thinner frame. The deep lines on his face and the dark shadows beneath his eyes were evidence he wasn't sleeping. He was also drunk, which became apparent when it took him a moment to meet her gaze as she stood frozen in the doorway.

"Hello, Roxanne," he said eventually, breaking into a mad grin. "Long time no see."

Roxanne's jaw hardened as she studied him. It had been years since she had last seen Oliver face to face. Even phone calls had ceased, giving way to the occasional formal letter when getting in touch became necessary. After a moment of indecision, she crossed Oliver's luxurious dining room awash in tan and periwinkle blue wallpaper. Pulling out a chair, she tried not to breathe in the alcoholic fumes that emanated from him as she sat down opposite.

"It has been a long time," she agreed, clasping her hands before her as she eyed him across the table. "I would ask how you are, but I already have my answer."

Oliver laughed, a drunken, mad laugh. "While we're on the subject of how terrible a father I am, how's our daughter? Did she get along with her brother while he was under your roof?"

Roxanne's stomach squirmed, dread gnawing despite the fact that she had been expecting this turn in the conversation. She wanted to look anywhere but at him, but she forced herself to hold his gaze.

"She's a little shaken by Cameron's passing, but she's putting on a brave face."

"You haven't told her?" He raised an eyebrow, his eyes narrowed and bloodshot. Bright blue eyes, like Cameron's. Like Amber's.

Roxanne swallowed down her guilt. "Why would I? He might have been terrified of *you*, but there was still a chance he would reconcile with his mother. Last I knew, you still wanted to keep *her* in the dark."

"I don't care anymore." Oliver leaned on the table, running a hand over his face. "I'm done with her. I should have left a long time ago."

A long time ago, Roxanne would have been pleased to hear those words. But now she felt disgust for the man she had once loved, and pity for the wife who had kept him from her.

"Well I care, Oliver. I care about Amber's feelings."

"So do I, Rox. Which is why I want to do right by her. I've neglected her long enough. I think it's finally time I met her properly."

"You're meeting no daughter of mine in your state." Roxanne surprised herself by how sharply her words came out. But Oliver only laughed, the harsh sound grating through her.

When he was done, he wiped tears from his eyes and tried to suppress his grin. "You're right, she wouldn't be impressed to discover her father is an old drunk. But I do want to meet her, Rox. If she rejects me, fine, but I want to at least try."

Roxanne glared at him, her teeth gritted. "You've neglected her all her life. Drunk or not, she's already unimpressed with your efforts as a father." She paused, letting her words sink in, and was glad to see him wince. "A private education and expensive gifts may have been appreciated to a certain extent, but throwing money at her is no replacement for a dad."

Oliver's mirth finally dropped away, his expression growing serious, vulnerable. "I'm sorry. So, so sorry. To both of you. If I could tell her that in person…"

Roxanne already felt her fire guttering, her anger backing down at his regret. He had tried, at first. He had visited, done his best to bond with Amber despite the tension between them. She had seen joy and love on his face as he held their baby, had been surprised by it. But then Cameron came along, and when the gaps between his visits became more and more drawn out, Roxanne asked him to stop visiting. As painful as it was, they agreed it was better if Amber didn't know who he was if he couldn't properly be in her life.

"There's just one thing I need to know before I agree to let you see Amber," she began carefully, knowing full well her next question would hurt him. "Why was Cameron so afraid of you?"

As expected, his face crumpled in anguish, and he hunched his shoulders, curling in on himself. It took him a long moment to find his voice, and when he did, it was strained. "I was never violent towards my family, Rox. You know me, I'm not like that. Maybe I shouted – it was hard not to lose my temper living with Sheridan all those years – but I never would have hurt my wife or children, I swear it." He paused, sunken eyes lost in the past as he absently scratched at a dark knot on the table. "You know how timid

Cameron was, and he saw what I did to Ronans' prisoners. So I can't blame him for being afraid I would do the same to him after his betrayal. I hate to say it, but I wasn't the most affectionate father to him. We were too different, had little in common except a Talent for healing. I thought letting him work at the prison would toughen him up and give him a taste of the real world, but I have never been more wrong."

Roxanne silently agreed. Cameron wasn't suited to the brutality of a prison – nor the battlefield. She, too, had made a mistake, and had let this man's son run headfirst to his death. Her eyes stung as her throat tightened, and she swallowed down the tears with difficulty.

"I'll tell Amber the truth, and ask her what she wants."

"Thank you, Roxy." Gratitude brightened his pasty complexion, and he reached across the table as though to take her hand, then thought better of it.

"Don't call me Roxy," she snapped, clasping her hands tighter. She had always disliked the nickname, remembering the teasing way he had used it from the day they had first met.

Oliver smiled sheepishly at her reprimand, but said nothing else. Instead, he laboured to his feet, swayed slightly, then made his way to the drinks cabinet in the corner, grabbing a decanter of whiskey.

"Is that really a good idea?" she asked, an eyebrow raised at his back.

Oliver looked around at her, lifting a half-filled glass to his smug lips and drinking deeply. "No, but you're not going to stop me." He set his glass down, topped it up, then took another sip. "Why don't you join me? It's good whiskey."

Her first response was to refuse, but as she hesitated, she asked herself what harm one glass would do. Perhaps a drink would calm her nerves. "Fine," she relented. "Pour me a small one."

To her surprise, Oliver obliged by pouring her just half an inch, handing her the cut crystal glass carefully. Their fingers touched as she took it, his skin warm against her icy hands, and Roxanne felt the colour rise in her cheeks. Instead of his stupid grin, Oliver gave her a gentle smile as he sat back down, his soft expression reminding her all too well of the moments he had been good to her, when they had time alone and he had let the arrogant façade he kept up for the rest of the world fall away.

"It's good to see you," he said, watching Roxanne closely while she busied herself by sipping the whiskey. The earnestness in his voice caught her off guard, and she met his gaze. There was a twinkle in his eye that she hadn't seen in a long, long time. She couldn't remember the last time he had been pleasant with her.

"It's good to see you too," she said, at a loss for anything else to say. She wasn't being entirely truthful, and she was aware of how fast her heart was beating and how uncertain she probably looked.

"I've missed you, Roxy," he said, growing serious again. "I've missed my best friend."

Roxanne was quiet, searching his face for any sign of the spiteful, sarcastic man she had met just minutes earlier. "It's been years, Oliver."

"I know. And I've been rotten to you. But it doesn't change the fact that I've missed you and I'm sorry for what I've done."

Roxanne hunched her shoulders, sure it was the drink that was making him so apologetic. "You already had a wife and child. You didn't want another family. We made a mistake, but I have a wonderful daughter out of that mistake so I don't regret it for a second."

"And by the sound of it, you've been a wonderful mother to her."

She took a deep breath. "I've done my best." Oliver would never know how hard it had been to raise their child alone. From the get-go she had to set her pride aside and depend on her parents, and as much as it made her sick to rely on Oliver for anything, there had been times when she had had no choice but to accept his financial aid. Those who were in the know about Amber's parentage, or at least had the faintest idea of his background, had always urged her that he had a duty to at least support his child financially if he wasn't there in person, but that hadn't made it any easier for Roxanne to take his money.

"I wish I could have helped more. I was so selfish." He sounded genuinely remorseful, but Roxanne's more cautious side warned her not to let her guard down.

She shrugged again. She wanted to say something harsh, or at least tell him to stop wallowing, but then she reminded herself that his son had just died. Instead, she took a sip of the whiskey, trying not to wince as it burned on the way down. "I *will* talk to Amber," she promised. "But if she doesn't want to meet you, I won't push it."

Oliver's smile of gratitude split his face in two, bringing out a hint of the handsome young man she had once loved. She remembered how that smile used to melt her heart, how she had loved him for years, even after he had betrayed her twice over: first by marrying someone else despite their relationship at university, and then by going back to his wife and abandoning her, pregnant with his child, after their affair a few years later.

"I know I'll never make it up to her, but I want to know her. I want to be in her life some way or another."

"Just promise me one thing," said Roxanne, a thought crossing her mind that struck fear into her heart. "Don't tell

Sheridan. I know you've left her, but her family… I don't want any harm coming to Amber."

"Don't worry. I may despise her, but I don't want to rub my love child in her face. As for the Marsdens, they will never know."

Roxanne held his gaze, anxious to make him understand how important Amber's safety was. The Marsdens were a family Roxanne had long feared, and she didn't want them to seek out Amber as some form of revenge against Oliver for leaving his wife and betraying the Ronans.

"So, what are your plans now?" she asked him, taking another sip of her whiskey and watching him over the rim of her glass.

Oliver shrugged. "What choice do I have? I'm your prisoner, unless you've come to tell me otherwise."

In truth, nobody had decided what to do about Oliver yet. He had surrendered of his own accord, so they had a duty to keep him safe and not harm him, despite mixed opinions on the matter. There were many who wanted to interrogate him, and Roxanne knew how valuable his information would be, but torture was out of the question. And Roxanne had fought against it even more in light of his bereavement. So instead, they had left him here, imprisoned in his summer house with their own guards keeping him inside and bringing him supplies while they decided what to do. Roxanne would tell them to stop bringing him alcohol, although he had plenty here to last him some time.

"Perhaps…" she began tentatively, fiddling with her glass and trying to make herself meet his gaze. "Perhaps you could… work with us?" She scolded herself for her hesitation. Oliver knew she had never been a confident speaker.

He leaned back in his chair, a teasing smile playing around his lips. "Now why would I do that?"

Roxanne's mouth twisted in discomfort, her fingers tightening on the glass. She wanted the ground to swallow her up. "Well…"

"Well what? Just because I surrendered, doesn't mean I'm going to work with you."

She glanced down, scratching a nail against the grooves of the pattern on the crystal glass, then willed herself to look back up at him. "What else is there?"

Oliver was silent, the smile fading. Perhaps she had said the right thing. She waited. But the words that came out were unexpected.

"I loved you, you know. Even at school. And I wanted to marry you. I regret putting my family's wishes before my own."

The weight of their past froze her beneath his gaze. She knew exactly when in their history he was referring to, at the end of university when their friendship transitioned into an awkward, fumbling romance. But Oliver had acted like any young man with the weight of his family's expectations on his shoulders. He wanted her, but he knew his parents would disapprove of him liaising with a lowly commoner. So instead he led her on, toying with her emotions, and ended up proposing to a woman worthy of his bloodline and breaking Roxanne's heart, all the while trying to brush off what they had as a silly university fling.

"Hindsight is a wonderful thing," she said eventually, taking a thoughtful sip and swallowing with difficulty.

"I loved my wife too. Until I realised what a spoilt brat she was." He laughed bitterly, sloshing more whiskey into his glass.

There was a lot Roxanne wanted to say to that. But as always, she held her tongue. She had promised herself long ago that she wouldn't criticise Oliver's wife to his face, even if her opinion of her was far from good.

"I thought she was different at first, you know? She was so sweet, and clever. But when things got bad for me..."

"Oliver," said Roxanne, a little more sharply than she intended, "why are you telling me this?"

Oliver glanced up at her, his tired face caught in surprise. She could see the realisation dawn on him slowly. "I'm sorry."

She paused, and then gave him a tiny smile. "I don't want to talk about the past. It's done. I've accepted it. I've healed. There's no point regretting things we can't undo."

Oliver nodded sheepishly, dipping his head in a way that reminded her achingly of Cameron. "You're right. There's no point regretting. And my children have brought me so much joy..." His voice broke, and he sniffed, hiding his eyes with a hand. When he finally lowered it, he was blinking furiously, avoiding her gaze. "But there's one thing worth regretting, and that's the fact that I abandoned you and Amber."

Roxanne winced, trying not to relive the night they rekindled their old romance and finally came together, after years of avoiding their feelings when they wound up working at the same hospital. She wasn't proud of her behaviour, but she wouldn't change her actions for the world. Oliver's father had just died, his marriage appeared to be about to break down, and he was seriously considering quitting his career. When he came to her, she accepted him with open arms. She had dwelt on the memory of that night for years, and as happy as it may have made her, only time had managed to dull the heartache that came afterwards. No matter what he said now, Roxanne knew he had loved Sheridan back then, and it was guilt that not only made him abandon her, but also leave his job, cutting her out of his life completely. That was, until she had to tell him she was pregnant.

Mentally shaking the memories from her head, Roxanne sat straighter and took a deep breath. "Anyway, like I said, I came here to discuss your… situation, not our past."

He nodded, resigned.

"If you won't work for us, what else are you going to do?"

He considered. "I might retire from all this politics palaver."

Roxanne nodded. "That option is available to you."

He raised his eyebrows. "You're not going to force me to be a tool? Interrogate me for what I know?"

She pursed her lips. "We're a democracy. Human rights are at the forefront of our aims."

Oliver's lip curled. "And yet that doesn't stop you from torturing and executing when it suits you."

Roxanne nodded. "That's a fair comment. Those are actions that I disagree with, but when we're up against the Ronans and the Caplinites, sometimes we have to fight fire with fire."

"But you're offering me a quiet life, if I want it?"

"Yes."

"No sentencing me for war crimes, et cetera?"

Roxanne paused, remembering that she was representing her party now, not just her own interests. "There may be a trial. But it wouldn't be until after the war is over, and your sentence is likely to be a light one. You were acting on orders, after all, and you surrendered at the end of it."

Oliver was quiet as he considered her words. "I suppose that's called 'getting off lightly'," he said eventually, but there wasn't much humour in his voice.

"For the time being you'll remain under house arrest. Understandably, we don't trust you. We'll be keeping a close eye on your family too."

"I hear you have Skye Bolton in your pool of resources now. Why not just get her to Break our minds, then you'll know who you can trust?"

"Because first of all we would have to trust Bolton."

Oliver raised a haughty eyebrow, assessing her so closely that she felt the flush creep into her cheeks again. But then the corner of his mouth lifted in a satisfied sneer. "It's good to know you're not letting the Caplinites push you around."

Roxanne swallowed, tunnelling within herself for the dregs of her courage. "Caplin has tried, especially where you're concerned. You should be glad we're the ones who have you and not them. They'd have torn you limb from limb."

"In that case, my thanks to you. I quite like my limbs."

Roxanne grimaced at his dark humour. As he refilled his glass yet again, she realised it would be best to return when he was sober. She had said what she had come to say, and more besides. Draining her glass, she set it down and scraped back her chair. "Well, Oliver, I'll leave you to... consider." Standing up, she surveyed him, her fingertips braced on the table.

His sneer faded into a soft smile. "Thank you for coming, Rox. It's been good to see you... after all these years."

Her stomach knotted as she tried not to let her emotions show. "Is there anything I can get you?"

He shook his head, running his thumb along the edge of his glass the same way he had once caressed her face. "Nothing. Just... just Amber, if she'll come."

Roxanne nodded, then left, not looking back as she let herself out.

Chapter Three

SKYE BOLTON

She had blood on her hands.

It was there in the moments before she awoke, leaving the image seared into her mind for the entire day, every time she closed her eyes: her own pale fingers, stained with mud and blood.

She saw him too, that innocent young man who had only ever wanted to help people. He had saved her life twice over and lost his own in return. But the memories that haunted her most were his. The memories that had tumbled down their mental connection as he died, every hope and dream and fear, the thoughts of a lost boy who no longer knew where home was.

There was nothing she could do for Cameron now except carry on, determined that his death would not be in vain. But carrying on was difficult when most days all she wanted to do was drink herself into oblivion, trying to forget that her father had been taken from her and everyone wanted something she didn't have the strength to give. But for her father's sake and Cameron's, she pushed away dark memories and fears and dragged herself out of bed each morning, with or without a shot of some drink or other to help her on her way.

"This has to stop, Skye."

Her brother's voice, his warm hands cupping her face, drew her from a deep reverie as she stood swaying in the kitchen, her consciousness surfacing to the here and now through a drunken swamp. When her gaze finally met Dean's, his dark brown eyes were filled with concern. She touched his fingers on her face and wondered how they had got there, how she had not noticed him approach.

Slowly, she pulled his hands away and lowered her eyes to the floor. She couldn't look at him. "I'm fine."

"How much have you drunk?"

"Not enough," she whispered, and turned away, vaguely searching the kitchen for more drink to take the edge off. Her fingers trembled as she twisted her mother's silver necklace.

"Skye—"

"No, Dean." She shrank away from the thoughts that filled his mind and drifted down their connection. Instead of listening to him, she built up her mental wall, blocking him out. It was a defensive mechanism she had found herself resorting to all too often lately. She couldn't bear to hear him judging her for wallowing instead of stepping up to her responsibilities. She knew what she had to do, and she was building herself up to it. She shouldn't have to explain herself.

Dean ran an agitated hand through his cropped dark hair. "Roxanne wants you to join their meetings."

"Caplin is already representing his party."

"They want you, Skye. You're the Lux."

"Well I don't want them."

Dean sighed in exasperation as Skye started opening cupboards. She pulled out items with the pretence of making coffee, when what she was really looking for was the alcohol she knew he had hidden. If it weren't for his thoughts that she didn't want to hear, she could have just jumped into his mind to find his hiding place. Dean knew her telepathy could be a double-edged sword.

"You could at least hear them out. They want what's best for everyone."

"I'm not everyone." She gave up her search and began to make coffee after all. Dean said no more, letting Skye concentrate on her task as she methodically went through the motions. It wasn't until she turned to see if he wanted a cup that she realised he had left the room.

***

"I need your help."

Caplin sat across from her, avoiding her gaze as he finished writing whatever it was that he felt was more important than what Skye had come to say. He hadn't wanted to see her, and if it weren't for the fact that she knew he was going to be at a meeting with the Resistance Leaders at the allied barracks, she wouldn't have been able to corner him. But eventually he gave in, leading her to the sparse office that had been set up for him at the barracks. The furniture was plain and functional, and pine window blinds let in watery light. It was nothing like the lavish office where she had once relayed mission reports, or he had praised her on a job well done.

Finally, he stopped writing and leaned back in his chair, surveying her with apparent indifference. Caplin's posture was languid, with his straw-pale hair swept hurriedly across his head and his expensive grey suit thrown on with the casualness of a schoolboy in uniform. And yet, Skye didn't miss the calculating power of a ruler blazing in his narrowed yellow eyes. A power that had her jaw clenching and her back straightening, ready for a fight.

"I don't know what you want me to do, Skye."

Blood boiled within her, and she counted as she took a deep breath through her nose, willing herself to remain calm. "Let me Break Matheson. And the other prison wardens we hold. Let me talk to them."

"They've already been interrogated. And Matheson—"

"I don't care what Summers says, Matheson knows where my father is. And he's as guilty as Alessia Ronan. The Resistance have no right to protect him."

"They have every right." Caplin's eyes flashed in warning. "And after the stunt you pulled at Ronan Manor, it's a wonder they want anything to do with you."

Skye sank back into her chair, taking more deep breaths. Her head pounded dully and her mouth was dry, a side-effect of all the drinking. The shot of bourbon she had taken on her way to seek out Caplin had done little to curb the hangover.

"We both know why they want me involved, so let's use that to our advantage. I'm not going to cooperate until my father is safe, so if they want me to be their hero, they have to let me see Matheson."

Caplin studied her for a long moment, until he finally let out a bitter, hollow laugh. "You're forgetting that I know how these things work, Skye. I descend from the last Lux. Prophecy or not, there will be a final battle sooner or later. And if you truly are the Lux and Alessia Ronan is the Nox, then she will seek you out, or you will go to her, whether or not you cooperate with the Resistance."

He let his words hang, leaving Skye to absorb them. "So?"

"So I still have a war to fight, regardless of whether you bother your arse to fulfil your so-called destiny. In case you hadn't noticed, we don't have the upper hand, so I need to keep the Resistance on side. And that means respecting their wishes."

Skye's nostrils flared, and her hands tightly gripped the arms of the chair as she resisted the electric power buzzing in her veins. "You can't just leave him to rot."

"Though it grieves me that your father is a prisoner, Skye, we're at war. These things happen."

"He's your *friend*," she hissed, leaning forward, no longer able to keep her temper in check.

"He is, and has been for a long time, which is why he was aware of the consequences of associating with me, of becoming involved politically. As were you when you swore in as one of my Guardians. Which, may I remind you, was a vow you took for life."

"Would you keep the vows you made when you married your wife, if she were in my father's place?"

Caplin stared at her for a moment, eyes widening in shock. And then he laughed, lounging in his chair again. "That is irrelevant and, quite frankly, none of your business."

"I made no vows to my father," she said, her blood rushing through her veins along with her lightning as the pounding in her head increased, "but if it came to a choice between him and you, I would choose him, every time."

A silence followed, and Caplin's face was impassive as he kept his gaze trained on the desk before him. As the seconds dragged on, Skye opened her mouth to say something, but he spoke over her. "I understand you're upset, Skye. You've been through a lot. You're going through a lot. But we have to trust the Resistance on this. When the time is right, I will ask them to let you Break Matheson, but until then—"

She slammed her hand down on the desk, making him jump and forcing him to look at her. "By then, my father could be dead, and you would have another avoidable death on your hands."

But she could see she had pushed him too far. Behind his sharp eyes was a fury that brought her own rage rising to the challenge, and she braced herself for the fight that would surely follow.

"Just who *do* you think you are?" he asked, masking his anger with a voice that was infuriatingly condescending. "I know you're the Lux and you've always had an arrogant sense of entitlement and superiority, but you can't just waltz in here throwing around accusations and demanding things of me."

"Demanding things?" she asked, her hands curled into fists. "What, like saving your friend's – my father's – life? I would have died for you in Blackwater. My father would die for you. But that doesn't mean you should just sit back and let it happen."

But Caplin was shaking his head. "I don't know how many ways you want me to say the same thing, Skye. My hands are tied."

"They're not, and you know it. I know you still hold the Masons that my comrades captured last year. Use them to broker a deal. Offer Ronan a prisoner swap."

"Those Masons don't have the same value to our enemies as your father, even if there are two of them. And besides, while I hold his son, I control Gerald Mason and his small army that remains in former Ronan territory. There is more at stake than you realise, Skye. I'm not playing a game of chess here."

"You're playing with my father's life," she snarled, a crackle of static sparking between her fingers.

But he only picked up his pen again, dismissing her like she was a sulky child.

Skye sat in silence, fighting the lump that rose in her throat and blinking away the sting in her eyes. Once she was sure her emotions weren't about to take over, she swallowed, determined to keep her voice steady. "I don't understand why you won't lift a finger, why you're not even grateful enough for what my father and I have done."

"You were doing your job, Skye. And recently, not very well, might I add."

She had heard enough. She was on her feet, her chair scraping back, and she laid her hands flat on the desk, leaning over him. He didn't shrink back as he raised those indifferent yellow eyes to her once more, and a warning gust swept from him, stinging her face and snapping at her hair. But she blinked only once, leaning closer.

"You will regret this," she promised. Her lightning trembled through her, desperate to get out, to hurt him. But as she saw the amused glint in his eye, she turned away, storming out of the office before she did something *she* would regret.

Chapter Four

ALESSIA RONAN

Alessia seethed as she stood at the window, waiting for the Seer to answer her call. All through the morning the household staff were sent in, one by one, their statements mostly confirming they had no idea about her sister's escape. She had narrowed it down to a handful of servants whose stories didn't quite add up, and to her fury, but not quite to her surprise, most of them had come with her from Ronan Manor.

"You want me to confirm your suspicions," came the lilting voice behind her, making Alessia jump. Biting her lip and taking a deep breath heavy with the sudden scent of jasmine, Alessia turned. The Seer stood in the middle of the room, her customary infuriating smile gracing her lips.

"Do you never use doors?" Alessia asked, unable to keep the bite out of her voice.

Vala's smile didn't falter, and her skirts and long brown hair swayed on that phantom breeze that smelled of death and night-blooming flowers. "I apologise for startling you, dear Alessia."

Alessia narrowed her eyes, but otherwise swallowed her irritation at Vala's insistence on using her first name uninvited. As though they were equals. As though Alessia were not the most powerful being alive. "Tell me what you have Seen."

Vala lowered her head a fraction, her fathomless blue eyes drinking in the light. "I am sorry to say that some of your staff have indeed betrayed you. They smuggled Phaedra out of the castle, and her bodyguard drove away with her. They are heading to Manchester to look for the Resistance."

"*Farraday*," she hissed. She knew she shouldn't have listened to Caspar when he convinced her to let the man live. She should have ordered her Guard to put a bullet between his eyes as soon as the Mind Breaker confirmed his affair with Bolton. "Who helped them?"

Vala hesitated. "The three that the head chef saw leaving the kitchen, and Margaret Mariott."

Alessia froze, her new, icy power creeping through her veins. Of course Maggie had helped her. The woman had practically raised the pair of them. Taking another deep breath and mentally counting to ten, Alessia turned back to the window. She clasped her hands in front of her to keep from hugging herself, frowning at the soggy grounds of the ancient castle. The small, human part of her that hid from her dark powers didn't want to hurt Maggie. Not when she was the closest thing she had to a mother, even if Alessia had refused to let anyone take her own mother's place. But she couldn't afford to let anyone think her weak if she just let people betray her left, right and centre. She wasn't her fool of a father.

Alessia let out a slow exhale. "Why did no one see Phaedra?"

"Jemima Broughton glamoured her to look like herself."

She nodded, the details finally clicking into place. She had her culprits. There was just one more question that she feared the answer to. "Did my uncle put them up to this?"

Vala hesitated long enough that Alessia turned back to her, prompting her with a slight raise of her eyebrows.

"I cannot See if Caspar was involved. But you know he cares for Phaedra. Perhaps more than he cares for you."

Alessia clenched her jaw. The knowledge that Vala likely spoke the truth made it no easier to bear. Caspar may have acted the part of advisor, but deep down, she knew his support of her was only to further his own agenda, whatever that may be. "Then perhaps it's time to cull the traitors from my following."

***

"It has come to my attention that four members of staff helped my sister escape with Mr Farraday last night," Alessia said, standing before the entirety of Brydon Marsden's household staff in the vast dining room. At her back sat Marsden himself, Caspar, Arthur Linden, and General James Pierce. They had all been present throughout the morning's interrogations, and Linden's expertise as Head of Intelligence was essential for unravelling each statement.

The staff remained deathly still as she swept her gaze over them, waiting for her next words. "I thank you all for your cooperation and the statements you have provided. Thanks to the evidence gathered, I confirm that the conspirators are Kiaran O'Flanagan, Jemima Broughton, Sally Peveril—" She paused, and Maggie's face paled as she met her eye. "And Margaret Mariott. Please step forward."

The four of them hesitated, then obeyed. Peveril was trembling from head to toe. Broughton looked like she was about to burst into tears. Maggie glanced at her colleagues in turn, then back at Alessia. Only Kiaran seemed calm, always a man of few expressions and fewer words. Alessia had thought him the perfect example of a loyal and dutiful servant. How wrong she had been.

"By aiding a traitor to escape, you, too, have committed treason. I cannot have disloyal servants roaming around this hideout. I cannot risk you selling my secrets to my enemies. For your treason, you will receive capital punishment."

Jemima Broughton's tears came, bursting like a dam and distorting the laundry maid's pretty features. Maggie swayed where she stood, and Kiaran put a protective arm around Sally, as if he could make any difference. There were several gasps and murmurs, but as Alessia glared, silence fell once more, broken only by Broughton's sobs. What did they expect? Surely they must have known that by helping Phaedra they were putting their own lives on the line.

"Miss Ronan, please," Maggie said, her voice barely above a whisper. She was a far cry from the brisk woman who had commanded her father's army of servants.

"I won't hear it." Alessia refused to look at her, squashing down the regret trying to rise to the surface. "You knew the crime you were committing when you helped her escape."

"Miss Alessia," Maggie tried again, her clasped hands twisting in front of her. "You know what Miss Phaedra means to me. What you both mean to me. I love you like my own daughters. I couldn't stand by and let you hurt her."

Love. What had it brought her, in the end? Only grief. A mother and grandfather both snatched by death. A father who drank himself into oblivion every day until she put him out of his misery. She swallowed down her guilt the way she had done before she watched her father drink his last glass, rising to her full height. "Love isn't going to keep my enemies from the castle gates if Phaedra shows up here with an army. The Nox has no need for love, Ms Mariott."

Maggie gave a sob, and Alessia's eyes slanted to the old woman, the woman who had fed, bathed and clothed her all through childhood, the woman who had tucked her into bed at night. But the memories would not sway her resolve.

"Alessia," came Caspar's voice behind her, and Alessia gritted her teeth, anticipating his next words. "Surely an execution is too harsh a punishment. Imprison them if you must, but given the nature of their relationship with—"

"We do not have the resources to imprison replaceable servants. I have made my decision." And without wasting further words, she raised her hands, shadows rapidly forming between her fingers.

"Alessia, stop!"

She ignored Caspar's shout, releasing two globes of shadow simultaneously. To her fury, the right one was forced off course by Caspar's intervening power, sending it careening into the ceiling. Plaster rained down and caused the servants to scatter and press themselves against the wall. Her other attack hit its mark, colliding with Jemima Broughton's head and sending her crumpling into Sally and Kiaran. The woman's curly hair was matted and dark where she had struck her, a trickle of blood dripping from the wound. Alessia quickly averted her eyes, rounding on Caspar instead.

There were shouts and screams, and the three remaining culprits gathered around Jemima's body, checking her wound and her pulse. But Alessia had eyes only for her uncle, who had vacated his seat with a second handful of shadows at the ready.

"You dare to intervene?" she hissed, meeting his cold glare.

Caspar's hands curled into trembling fists, but whether he shook from fear or fury, it wasn't clear. "Think this through, Alessia. Please. They served Phaedra as much as they served you. They were only doing what they thought was right."

"Then they should be willing to pay the cost," she snapped, summoning her darkness once more. "As should you." And before he could say another word, before he could move, she lunged forward, aiming her shadows straight for his heart.

Caspar's eyes widened as he saw the incoming attack, and he stepped back, quick as a cat, dodging one stream of darkness and sending the second off course again. Beside him, Marsden and the others flung themselves from their seats, putting as much distance as possible between themselves and the brewing fight. Alessia paid them no mind, kicking a chair out of the way as she advanced on her uncle.

With a flick of his wrist, he hurled his darkness at her, and she returned the favour, the two attacks meeting and exploding between them.

"Being the Nox doesn't mean you have to kill everyone," he said, blocking another of her attacks. "You're not Ivor. You don't have to reign with fear."

"Don't speak his name," she snarled, throwing another stream of darkness at him, which he narrowly avoided. "You weren't worthy of being his son."

Caspar scoffed, his expression humourless. "He wasn't a worthy father. He made my life a living hell. Everyone around him suffered far more than he did on his deathbed."

Alessia held her tongue, aware that bickering with her uncle would reflect badly on her in front of such a vast audience. So instead she lashed out with her Talent. He avoided her first hit, but couldn't dodge the second she sent in quick succession. Caspar jerked back with a gasp of pain. Her darkness caught his left arm, shredding through his shirt and leaving behind a charred wound across his shoulder. But he recovered quickly from the shock, returning the attack.

Alessia side-stepped, and they circled one another until Caspar planted himself firmly between her and the traitorous servants. Strands of dark hair fell across his forehead, while a muscle ticked beneath his beard as he panted through gritted teeth. Behind him, some of the staff slipped through the double doors in their fear, while others flattened themselves against the wall. Keeping her eyes on Caspar, she addressed them.

"Those of you who had no hand in my sister's escape may leave. But remember the consequences for traitors. The Nox has no tolerance for disloyal servants."

There were a few whimpers and audible sighs of relief. The servants hurried out, leaving behind only the sound of Maggie's muffled crying.

"Pierce," Alessia said then, letting the shadows pulse in her palm and drawing Caspar's attention. Her general stepped forward, tall and thin, his lined face impassive as he saluted her. "Take the three remaining traitors outside and shoot them. Bury them in an unmarked grave."

More sobs as the blonde one, Sally, clung to Kiaran and buried her face against his shoulder. Kiaran held her tightly, his calm demeanour finally starting to crack.

"Yes, ma'am," said Pierce. If he had any feelings about her order, he hid them well. Caspar, on the other hand, did not.

"Alessia, please," he said, his face sagging with anguish. "You don't have to do this."

"Be thankful I'm not ordering Pierce to execute you too, Uncle," she said, unable to keep the satisfied smile from her lips. "I can't prove whether you were involved in my dear sister's escape, but I don't trust you're completely innocent. Tell me, Ms Mariott, were you acting on my uncle's orders? O'Flanagan?"

But the servants said nothing. Kiaran boldly held her gaze, while Maggie continued to cry and repeat her name, begging her to reconsider. Each plea sent a stab through the armour Alessia wrapped around her heart. A handful of soldiers entered, answering Pierce's call. Without a word, they dragged the three of them up and clamped handcuffs around their wrists.

"Miss Alessia," Maggie said one last time, her voice small and choked.

Alessia met her eye with difficulty, her chest tightening as she took in the tears of the kind old lady who had raised her. Deep down, the lonely little girl who had hidden away in her bedroom wrapped her arms around herself, wishing she could smile and play like her sister had done. If only she had been a normal child, not the horrified creature whose mother had taken her own life. Burying the past, Alessia jutted out her chin and cupped her darkness in the palms of her hands.

"Goodbye, Ms Mariott. Thank you for your service."

Caspar seemed to deflate as he turned towards the servants, watching as they were escorted from the room. He took a step towards them as though to interfere again, but hesitated. His injured shoulder was hunched, and dark blood stained the silvery grey of his shirt. The fourth servant, Jemima, lay still on the floor, with large brown eyes staring blindly into space. Her death whispered like an incessant prickle against Alessia's ear.

"Since I can't condemn you," Alessia said, dragging Caspar's gaze back to her, "I'll give you a choice. You can stay and try to fight me, or you can leave and catch up with your favourite niece. I wouldn't be surprised if you know where she's headed."

"I had no part in this," Caspar said, his face a mask of earnestness.

“Perhaps you didn’t give the orders, but I know that both Farraday and the Telepath who swept his mind are on your payroll. I wonder what secrets the Telepath will reveal if I buy him out? Secrets you’re covering for Bolton’s little pet?”

Caspar said nothing, but a cold sneer played around his lips. Alessia returned it.

“If you want to regain my trust,” she said, letting the shadows in her palms die down a little, “deliver my darling sister to me. Otherwise, consider yourself my enemy, and don’t you dare come crawling back if you want to keep your life.”

He snorted, his own shadows winking out as he closed his hand into a fist. He did his best to hide his pain, but Alessia noted the stiffness in his jaw each time he moved. Her shadows were no ordinary darkness. The average Obscurae would not have harmed him, but her attacks were too powerful even for him.

“Phaedra doesn’t need me as much as you do,” he said, the self-satisfaction evident in his voice. “But I would rather serve her than you. Goodbye, Alessia.”

Alessia struggled to keep her temper in check as she watched him saunter out of the room, opening one of the heavy doors with one hand and letting it swing shut behind him.

Silence fell, punctured only by a series of gunshots beyond the castle walls. Alessia took a deep breath as the haunting sound echoed in her ears and pierced her dark heart. Seconds later, three more voices swept past her, their whispers joining the dead maid still lying on the floor. But she hardened herself against the hurt and guilt pressing on her, pushing the whispers and intrusive thoughts to the back of her mind. She had not forgotten the men who lingered behind her.

“Mr Marsden?”

“Yes, ma’am?” asked Brydon. His narrow, wrinkled face was mild, and his short grey hair was barely dishevelled by his time spent crouching behind his chair. If he was afraid following what he had just witnessed, he hid it with a falsely cheerful tone.

“Send some of your Tracers to tail my uncle. When he leads them to my sister, I want them both arrested and brought to me.”

There was a short silence, and then Brydon acknowledged her with obvious amusement. “Yes, ma’am.”

Chapter Five

DEAN ROSWELL

"Roswell!"

Dean froze outside the barracks canteen, standing to attention as Irvine Sullivan – the new captain of the Caplin Guard – swept down the dingy corridor towards him. The captain was a wiry man in his late forties. His greying hair was immaculately buzzed, and no stubble peppered his narrow face. Though shorter than Dean, he was still imposing in his black uniform, and the crimson epaulettes and Caplin shield were the only splashes of colour on his clothing.

"Yes, sir?" Dean projected his voice as he held a salute, mentally scanning his army fatigues for anything that might displease his captain. Sullivan looked him up and down, but there was only concern in his superior's eyes.

"Mr Caplin granted you compassionate leave in light of your stepfather's imprisonment."

Ordered, you mean. Dean knew full well that there was little compassion in Caplin's actions. Anyone Caplin knew to have links to Skye – from their friends, Sabine and Jacob van Zanten, to her cousin, Lorcan Medley – had been moved to different legions and assigned other duties – duties that kept them away from Caplin and out of his inner circle meetings. Skye herself was still suspended, partly due to the disciplinary that was at the bottom of everyone's list of priorities, but mostly due to her being the Lux.

"I prefer to keep busy, sir. I would like to be of help in some way."

Sullivan continued to scrutinise him, and heat crept up Dean's neck. As far as he was aware, his presence at the barracks was breaking no rules, although his actions weren't entirely innocent. Under the pretence of keeping his body fit by joining drills and killing time in the gym, he had spent the preceding weeks fishing for information from his comrades, searching for something, anything, that might help him and Skye rescue Victor from Ronan's clutches.

"Perhaps we can find something to take your mind off things," Sullivan said eventually, his expression softening a fraction. "We've had an influx of cadets that require a commander."

Dean hesitated. Any other time, he wouldn't have minded training and commanding youngsters – would have welcomed it, even. But right then, with everything going on, that was far more responsibility than he needed.

"How about co-commanding then? I also broached the subject with Sergeant Medley. You two work well together."

Dean forced a grim smile. He didn't doubt Lorcan shared his outlook when it came to being demoted to training cadets. As members of the Caplin Guard, they were sworn to protect the presidential family and inner circle figures, not bark orders at unruly teenagers. It was just another indication that Caplin was subtly trying to quash any potential insurgence.

"I'll consider it," Dean said carefully, hoping his hesitation wouldn't come across as insubordination.

"I expect a decision by the week's end," Sullivan responded with a nod. "Those kids need a strong leader, and we need every fighter we can get against the Nox."

He saluted again as Sullivan moved away, holding in his sigh of relief as he was dismissed. He waited until the captain disappeared around a corner, before scarpering in the direction of the gym where he had arranged to meet his comrade, Ikarus Arrowsmith, for an afternoon sparring session.

Ike was already waiting when he slipped into one of the smaller gymnasiums, his pale face splitting into his customary wide grin as he held his elbow over his head in a stretch.

"Saw you getting an earful off Sullivan just now."

"Not quite." Dean dropped his bag full of training gear just inside the door, stripping off his black jacket and laying it next to Ike's on the bench that lined the wall. The cool air prickled his skin where his vest left him bare, but no doubt he would be sweating within minutes. He extracted a piece of chalk from a side pocket of his bag and drew a handful of sigils on the door, warding the room against eavesdroppers. "He asked if I want to train cadets with Lorcan."

Ike snorted. "Did he give you the same bull about being a good role model?"

"Something like that." Dean unlaced his boots and kicked them off with his socks, then joined his friend on the training mat to begin his own stretches.

"I suppose he couldn't ask Sabine to lead the newbies," Ike exclaimed lightly. "She's more terrifying than a Nox."

"Tell me about it. Half of them would desert before they're ready for battle."

The stretches and easy banter began to loosen some of Dean's tension, and he rolled his neck and shoulders one last time before settling into an attack stance. Ike mirrored him, before lunging forward, then feinting to the right. Dean was ready for him, batting off his attacks with ease.

"So, I hear Caplin's asked Captain Sullivan to hand pick a new Guard," Dean ventured once they were suitably warmed up, his vest beginning to stick to him. "He's not demoting you too, is he?"

Ike jerked away from a jab Dean aimed at his face, his fair hair darkened with sweat. "I'm not officially demoted, but I'm almost exclusively guarding Irma now."

Dean wrinkled his nose. "He might as well have kicked you out. Aside from a potential hostage, Mrs Caplin isn't exactly inner circle."

"Nah, she just has fancy tea parties with her lady friends most of the time. Yesterday she was lamenting how long it's been since she had a ball. It's not like we're at war or anything."

Dean snorted, but in truth, he felt sorry for Caplin's wife. Sure, she enjoyed luxury and cared little for politics, but she was caring and charitable, innocent and ignorant of most of the disagreeable actions her husband committed.

"Any idea who Sullivan is picking?"

"I don't know, but apparently Caplin has Welch Breaking their minds as part of the recruitment process." Ike's brow furrowed in distaste.

"Well, we all know how much Welch hates Skye's guts," Dean said bitterly, recalling the blazing rows Skye had had with Caplin's second Telepath. "If he finds even a hint of sympathy for her in their minds, they'll be off the short-list."

"No kidding. You should've seen the look on Welch's face when he found out she's the Lux. He turned green." Ike's face was a picture of delight as he swung a fist at Dean's side, which he pivoted to block.

"I imagine the green tinge went so well with his strawberry blonde tresses."

Ike snickered as Dean attempted to hook a foot behind his knee, but the Aeres darted away, his airy Talent lending him additional speed.

"I'm sure we'll find out soon enough who our new teammates are," Dean said, circling around his comrade.

Ike grimaced, springing forward with another flurry of failed attacks. "I don't think Caplin wants you back."

Dean raised an eyebrow, but he wasn't surprised. "Has he said as much?"

"No, it's just obvious. But right now he can't afford to officially strip you of your positions. Not if Skye's the Lux. Not everyone likes her, but too many people have their eyes on her now." He side-stepped another of Dean's jabs. "If it comes to picking sides, people are more likely to rally behind the Lux who fights her own battles rather than the man who hid himself away while his people were killed and tortured."

Anger soured Ikarus's pale face, so at odds with the pleasant, easy-going man Dean had long been friends with. But the ugly expression was short-lived as a breeze rippled across Dean's ankles, and before he could react, his feet were swept from under him. Ike's laughter tore through the room as Dean landed face first on the training mat.

"Cheater," Dean let out, rubbing his smarting cheek.

"Ronan's soldiers won't hold back on the battlefield, Deansie. You gonna call them cheaters for using their Talents?"

"Be careful. Next time I spot you wearing metal, I'll have my revenge."

"Don't be a sore loser." Ike held out a hand, amusement still twinkling in his pale eyes. Dean hesitated, then took his hand. But before he could get his feet beneath him, Ikarus's Talent levitated him off the floor, throwing him over the Aeres's shoulder and landing him flat on his back, knocking the breath from his lungs.

More laughter skipped around him as he groaned, but it was cut short as the doors to the gymnasium slammed open. Dean turned his head to see three black-clad figures stalk through the door: their fellow Guardians, Sabine and Jacob, with Lorcan bringing up the rear.

"Are you two layabouts going to do something useful today?" Sabine's voice cut through the room like a firecracker, and she stopped next to the mat, folding her arms across her chest and looking down at Dean with a pierced eyebrow raised. Having regained his breath, Dean got to his feet. Despite their height difference, Sabine still had a way of making him feel small, and he tried not to shrink beneath her scrutiny.

"We're training," Ike replied to his cousin, crossing his own arms with a casualness that made Sabine narrow her golden eyes. "Maybe you should join us. I recall I handed you your arse last time."

Sabine gritted her teeth, the sharpness of her clenched jaw only enhanced by the undercut along the right side of her head. "You're in for a swatting, fly boy."

Her twin, Jacob, tried not to smile, mischief smouldering in his eyes. "As much as I'd love to see you two battle it out, we wanted to run some ideas by you."

"What ideas?" Dean asked, looking between his fellow Guardians. The Caplin raven glared darkly from the black and crimson crests embroidered over their hearts.

"Something that might help Victor," said Lorcan, stepping to Sabine's side. He towered a good head above the twins, with an abundance of freckles and hair coloured a reddish brown in the filtered light.

"We want to commandeer Caplin's prisoners," said Sabine, lowering her voice after a glance at the door. The sigils Dean had drawn held firm. "Offer them to the Nox in exchange for your father."

Dean's stomach twisted with nausea. "You can't be serious. It's way too risky."

"Now's not the time to be a goody goody, Dean," Sabine said dismissively. "Caplin's looking for any excuse to fire us all, so let's take this opportunity while we still can and give him a good reason to get rid of us."

"Execute us, you mean," Dean said quietly. "You're suggesting treason."

"Dean's right," Ike piped up. "Caplin is using Primus Mason to control his father. If he no longer holds sway over the Masons, they could break the ceasefire we have with the former Ronan territory."

"It hasn't stopped Mason soldiers from running skirmishes on *our* territory," Sabine sneered. "I don't know why Caplin doesn't just send the Aeres in to bomb them and be done with it."

"Sabine," Dean warned, her flippant remark turning his stomach, "that's exactly the kind of scenario we're trying to avoid."

"What Sabine is supposed to be telling you," Lorcan interrupted, flashing Sabine an irritated look, "is that there might be a chance for us to ask Caplin to stand down as our leader, if Skye is willing to take his place. And then we can do what we like with the prisoners, and the rest for that matter."

Dean's nausea continued to churn, his friends' suggestions growing more and more absurd by the minute. His mind drifted to the state of his sister that morning, and every day since Cameron's death and the failed attempt to rescue Victor from Ronan clutches. "That's… not really something Skye can take on right now."

"Is she still drinking herself stupid every day?" Sabine asked bluntly.

"How about we don't judge our friends for their coping mechanisms," Jacob said quietly. "We've all been through a lot of shit this past year."

Dean nodded to him gratefully, even if it was no secret that Skye turned to the bottle each time things got too much.

"Let me see her," Sabine ploughed on, pinning him with her golden glare. "I managed to talk some sense into her when she was wallowing over that asshole dumping her."

He cringed. "This isn't like last time. She's grieving."

"What about your mum?" Jacob said, looking around Sabine at Lorcan. "She's inner circle, knows the laws. Hell, she even had a hand in writing them. Reckon she'd have a stab at being president?"

But Lorcan paled behind his freckles. "My mother doesn't have a rebellious bone in her body, even if she's as pissed off as the rest of us that Caplin is letting Ronans tear her brother apart."

Dean's chest tightened painfully, and he turned away, Lorcan's poor choice of words evoking images he had been doing his best not to think about.

"Well done, mate," Ike muttered to Lorcan, then padded across the mat to wrap a comforting arm around Dean's shoulders. Dean could only inhale deep, steadying breaths, fighting the panic welling up in his chest. "It's going to be alright," Ike told him, squeezing his shoulders. "Old Victor's gonna be just fine."

He nodded, straightening. The irony that Ike was comforting *him* when his own father had been killed so recently by Ronans wasn't lost on him.

"We just want to help, Dean," Sabine said, her voice marginally softer. "We know what you and Skye are going through."

He swallowed down another breath, then turned back to his comrades, taking in their sympathetic faces. Lorcan looked especially apologetic. "I appreciate it, really. But let's just hang tight for now. The last thing we need is one of us getting killed."

They all nodded their understanding, and his stomach began to settle. It was hard enough dealing with Skye's unpredictability. He couldn't be doing with everyone else losing their heads – metaphorically or otherwise.

"I still think we should talk to Alma," said Jacob, glancing up at Lorcan again. "She might have some valuable advice."

Lorcan ran a hand through his hair, considering. "Maybe it won't look too suspicious if she invites you all for dinner."

"I'm there." Ike grinned, picking up his abandoned jacket and stuffing it into a duffel bag. "Your cook is better than ours."

"Tell Skye to come too." Sabine's heavy boots squeaked as she prowled towards the door, and she and Jacob threw Dean matching backwards glances. Dean could only grimace. He wasn't sure when he had last seen Skye consume anything that wasn't liquid, but perhaps this would help him drag her out of her rut.

***

Dean dwelled on his friends' insane ideas the rest of the afternoon, his head crammed full of the things he needed to share with Skye. It was a relief when the siren signalled the end of the training day, and he took the portal back to their safe house on Land's End.

The cottage looked like a dark, empty shell when he arrived, with windows boarded up, the garden overgrown, and the perimeter wall crumbling. But when he pressed the medallion hanging on his set of keys to a nook in the low brick wall, the glamour fell away, revealing the tidy, cheerful holiday home that Victor had often taken Dean and Skye to as children, until they grew too old to care for exploring rock pools and swimming in the sea.

He walked up the garden path, previously cracked and half-hidden by weeds under the glamour, but now pristine, having been relayed just a year before the coup. Dean had used his own Talent to do it, and much of the flora in the garden had been planted and coaxed to grow by his own hand. A few late bees buzzed in the flower beds now, and the honeysuckle bush in the corner cast its sweet scent over the garden. The nostalgia for happier, simpler times gripped his heart like an iron fist, and his thoughts went to moments when Victor had shared the quiet joy of gardening with him.

Delaying his return to what would no doubt be a frustrating evening trying to talk Skye out of her binge drinking, he allowed himself a few minutes to check the flower beds. He pressed his fingers to soil and stems, felt for signs of rot or weakness, and called on the gentler side of his Terra ability to give the plants strength. All too often, his Talent was moulded into a weapon for Caplin, but building and growing had always been his passion, a passion he someday hoped to return to. For now, he would keep fighting for his family and for the country, upholding the oath he had taken when he swore in as a Guardian.

Once he was satisfied that the garden, at least, was thriving, he brushed soil off his hands and took a deep breath of the soft spring air, inhaling a tang of sea drifting from the nearby beach. With a last wistful look at the peaceful scene, he pressed the medallion to the doorknob, then unlocked the door with the key.

The sight that greeted him was like a murder scene. Kerry was scurrying around the kitchen with tears in her eyes and her grey hair in disarray, sweeping up broken glass. And on the floor, with her back against a cupboard, sat Skye. Tears and shame were splashed across her face, and she had blood on her hands and bare feet. Around her, the kitchen tiles glistened with shards and spilled liquid. From the fumes that invaded his senses, it was whiskey.

"What happened?" His voice was quiet, but he stared between his stepsister and the housekeeper, incredulous.

Skye said nothing, only wrapped her arms around herself, blood smearing her white shirt.

"She… Skye…" Kerry began, anguish and despair evident on her face as she met Dean's gaze. "Skye had an accident."

And then Skye raised a bloody hand to her face and sobbed.

"Skye, don't," Kerry said quickly, abandoning the broom and crouching next to her, tugging at her wrist. "You have glass in your hand."

"I'll sort it." He crunched across the broken glass that Kerry had been trying to clear, leaning down and hooking his hands beneath Skye's arms. She struggled, but he pulled her to her feet, forcing himself to be firm with her. "Stop it."

"He won't do anything!" she shouted in his face, and he drew back, but held her arms tightly. "What can I do, Dean? Caplin won't let me—"

"Stop it," he repeated, raising his voice a little more. Skye collapsed against him, sobbing into his shoulder. He held her for a moment, stroking her damp blonde hair as she cried. "I'm going to carry you to the bathroom," he said, then continued before she could protest. "I'm not letting you walk across broken glass, Skye."

She finally relented, wrapping her arms around his neck as he lifted her. She was still crying as he carried her through the kitchen, as was Kerry. "Can you bring me the first aid kit?" he asked as he went, and Kerry nodded, tiptoeing through the glass.

In the bathroom, he set Skye down on the toilet, then ran a cloth under warm water to clean her hands. Kerry brought the first aid kit and handed him a pair of tweezers, and he began picking the glass out of Skye's palms, dropping it into an empty soap dish.

"So you found my hiding place?" he said as he worked, head bent over her hands. He cringed inwardly, realising that tucking the alcohol away in the highest cupboard was a stupid idea. The scene played out in his head: a drunk Skye climbing on the worktop to find it, then toppling to the floor, bottle in hand.

"Don't tell anyone about this," she said sullenly. She had finally stopped crying.

"And wound your bruised pride even more? I wouldn't dream of it."

An exhausted smile tugged at the corner of her mouth, but he couldn't return it. He reached for the damp cloth, cleaning the blood and alcohol from her hands.

"Did you hurt anything else?"

"Probably not badly," she admitted, and Dean looked her over, searching for any other injuries. Finding none, he knelt and began to pick the glass out of her feet.

"You're lucky you don't need stitches."

"Yeah…" came her mumble, and Dean shook his head, continuing his task. Eventually, she began to tell him about her day. "I went to Tewkesbury. Figured if they took Dad out of Blackwater, he's probably there."

"Did you find anything?" he asked, his pulse speeding up.

"Nothing. Whole place is empty."

He sighed, his brief hope fading with her words.

"Caplin just laughed at me, Dean." Tears welled in her eyes again. "He doesn't give a shit. The things they must be doing to our dad, and he just doesn't care."

"We'll find him," Dean said, but his words sounded hollow to his own ears. He felt Skye's telepathy whispering through his mind, and worked hard to push away his negative thoughts as he wiped the bloody smears from her feet.

She gave a hollow laugh as she touched on Dean's memories of the afternoon. "I can already tell you Alma won't be up for a coup or releasing prisoners, but have a nice time at dinner."

He kept his eyes on her feet as her Talent continued to sweep his mind, her skin cold to his touch. "You should come. Alma might have other ideas."

"This isn't something we're going to resolve over a tea party." Some of her familiar bite entered her voice now. "But I am starting to wonder why we're all still putting up with Caplin."

The back of Dean's neck prickled. He wasn't sure what was worse: her drunken desolation, or her volatile defiance. "After what you went through to protect him, that's something you need to decide for yourself. But for now, I really need you to stop… this." He gestured to her vaguely, and shame washed over her features again. While she sulked, he pulled gauze and bandages out of the first aid kit, setting about bandaging her feet.

"If I don't drink, I can't stop seeing him. All that blood…"

Dean paused, taking a moment to realise who she was talking about now. Continuing his wrapping, he spoke quietly. "Cameron wouldn't want this for you."

"I know."

"Then stop." He tied off one of the bandages, then sat back on his heels, looking up at her. "I know it hurts, but try using the pain to drive you, rather than shutting it out."

"Sounds like some therapy spiel."

"Well here's another one: you're at rock bottom. Where are you going to go from here?"

She glared, but Dean held her gaze with determination.

"That's what I thought."

They lapsed into silence as he cut more bandages for her hands, Skye's sniffing and ragged breath the only sounds.

"Maybe I should just hand myself in." Her tone was dull, but Dean looked up to see the bleak fear in her eyes.

His own stomach churned, his earlier nausea returning. "Skye, you can't do that."

"Why not? I'm the one they want. I could go quietly if Dad goes free."

Her fingers trembled in her lap, and he enclosed them between his hands, careful not to brush against her cuts. "You're the Lux, Skye. If you hand yourself in, it's game over for the rest of us."

She said nothing, and merely stared into space. Her trembling continued, and he rubbed his thumbs against her cold skin, trying to soothe her. "And besides, where does that leave me?"

She met his gaze, her usually sharp brown eyes glazed and distant. But slowly, she came back to him, his words cutting through her drunken haze, her voice and expression becoming tender. "It leaves you free."

He shook his head, squeezing her fingers. "I don't want to be free if you aren't. I will follow you, Skye. Wherever this cursed prophecy leads you, I will follow you until the end."

Chapter Six

PHAEDRA RONAN

Her long dark hair fell strand by strand into the miniscule, avocado-coloured sink, some clinging to her clothes or floating to the floor. The snips had made her cringe at first, but the more she cut away, the more determined she felt to drastically change her appearance.

The moment she was alone in the bathroom of the rundown bungalow they were hiding in for the night, she let everything she was feeling overflow. The grief over her father's murder at the hands of her sister, Alessia's terrifying rise to power, the fear that she was next to be killed, and the paranoia that she would be found out as a spy… it all came bubbling to the surface, choking her.

At first, it was a hit that she wanted. In the absence of drugs and alcohol, she had held the rusty scissors she had found in the medicine cabinet, her hands shaking as she debated what to do with them. If she cut herself, Glen would notice, and when he was the only person she could rely on at the moment, she didn't want him to think she was crazy and abandon her. So instead, they were the source of her sudden inspiration to attack her hair.

She cut, and cut, her anger slowly beginning to subside. When the last long strand fell and clung to her top, she paused to examine her hedgehog-like haircut, and breathed a sigh of relief. There was no denying that Alessia was her sister. With the same light blue eyes, pale narrow face, and dark brown hair, they looked too alike. But with her hair short and spiky, they now had one less thing in common. She ran her fingers over her head, examining the jagged cut in the mirror. Calmer now, she snipped more carefully, aiming for a style before she cut away too much. Wax would disguise any unevenness, and she would get a dye too – maybe an especially outrageous colour – to further distance herself from Alessia. Once satisfied, she let the scissors clatter into the sink, then dropped her arms to her sides, exhaling and studying her appearance.

She had always been thin, but the new haircut pronounced it. Her skinny shoulders stood out, her cheekbones were more angular than ever, and her neck looked scrawny on her small body. Her tight-fitting black vest showed only a hint of the little cleavage she had, and her ribs were visible through the stretchy fabric. Glancing down, her legs, too, had barely any flesh on them. It was just as well she hadn't been blessed with height the way Alessia had been. She would look like a reed otherwise.

She brushed the hair off her clothes, cleaned up the sink, then braced herself for Glen's scrutiny. Whatever he thought of her hair, it would be better than him seeing her covered in bandages.

He was sitting on the brown, sagging sofa when she emerged, swigging a beer and watching sport on the outdated television set. His demeanour told her he was far from relaxed, but after the crazy day they had just spent, it was no wonder. It took him a moment to acknowledge her standing in his periphery, but when he finally did, he did a double take.

Phaedra waited, watching the conflicting expressions that crossed his face. There was surprise mostly, confusion, and she thought she detected the slightest wince. But eventually, he settled on what he wanted to say and gave her a nod and a slight curve of his lips. "You look good."

Phaedra's face twisted in disagreement. "No, I don't."

"No, seriously, it suits you. Maybe a little tidy here and there, but if anyone can pull off the style, it's you."

Phaedra watched him for a moment, looking for any sign that he was lying to her. When she was satisfied that he was being honest, she relaxed, shoving her hands in her pockets and huffing a deep breath. "Maybe you can help me tidy it up." She made her suggestion sound like a joke, but truthfully, she hoped he could help her.

"You trust me with scissors near your hair? I wouldn't." He grinned, then rubbed his stubble thoughtfully. "Maybe I could do with a disguise too. Reckon I'd suit a beard?"

She raised an eyebrow, taking in his sandy hair, trying to imagine it on his chin. "It might make you look like a bear."

"Bears are pretty tough."

"And cuddly."

He frowned. "Only in storybooks."

"Glen the teddy bear. I suppose some girls would dig it."

He shook his head in mock defeat, then swigged his beer and picked up the remote. Phaedra watched him flick through channels for a moment, then went to the fridge to get one of the beers Glen had bought.

"Hey, I didn't get those for you."

"Well tough, you're sharing." She opened the bottle on the edge of the worktop, then took a long drink, gasping in satisfaction.

Glen grimaced, but she could see he was trying to hide his amusement. "I'm pretty sure you're not even legal yet."

Phaedra laughed. "You're wrong, actually. I turned eighteen in December."

Glen cocked his head. "I see. And how many years before that were you pretending you were already eighteen?"

Phaedra only winked, flopping onto the sofa and folding her legs beneath her as she drank her beer. "Now that we're both outcasts, I can't think of anything better to do than get absolutely wasted."

"You can," he said, flicking the channel to the news. A flaming building flared across the screen, the headline announcing something about looting in Birmingham before it flickered to scenes of more destruction. "I can't get too bad in case someone comes knocking."

"And what are you gonna do if someone comes knocking?" she asked, eyes glued to the images of fire and rubble as an unpleasant taste filled her mouth.

"Find some way to protect you, for a start." She glanced his way, finally noticing the gun sitting on the side table to his right.

Phaedra snorted. "If someone did try to carry us off or murder us, I'm not sure we'd stand a chance. And besides, I can cause more damage with my hands than you can do with that."

Glen turned to study her, but the humour was gone. Eventually, he asked, "What was your Talent again?"

Phaedra's lips twisted. Her Talent had always been a touchy subject. She had never been the best student, and despite the fact that it was her uncle Caspar who had taken it upon himself to teach his nieces how to wield the darkness that the Ronans were famous for, she had never had much control over it. Once, in privacy, Caspar had told her that her power was stronger than Alessia's, which had both shocked and excited her. But where Alessia was disciplined, Phaedra's power demonstrated itself in sporadic bursts and dangerous magnitudes, leaving her afraid to use it and controlling it with sedatives.

"I'm an Obscura," she said, wrapping her hands around her knees defensively.

Glen whistled. "Yep, you win."

"Not really," she confessed. "I'm all over the place."

"Doesn't matter. If something happens, you don't need control, you just need to blast somebody."

She considered his words, picking at what looked like a cigarette burn in the arm of the sofa. "I guess."

Glen drained his beer, then set the bottle down, turning to look at her.

"You could manage that much, right? I've seen Caspar fight, and I hear your sister is adept at her Talent, but that could just be hearsay. What about you?"

She nodded. "I'm strong. I just can't control it."

He gave a satisfied nod. "Strong. Good. That's all you need to be. Have faith in yourself." He got up, crossing to the fridge to take out two more bottles. Opening them, he handed one to her. After draining the bottle in her hand, she swapped with him.

"I'm glad you look like yourself again," he said, sitting down with his drink. "Having you look like Jem was weird."

"Why? Did you two have a thing?"

She didn't miss the way his face flamed as he kept his gaze on the TV. A teasing grin grew on her lips.

"Uh, kinda. We dated for a while."

"Why did you stop?"

He shrugged. "Your dad assigned me to guard the Marsdens when I first started working for him. So we met at Castle Uaine."

"Okay. And then?"

He scowled at her prying, but continued. "Then I got reassigned to Blackwater. And my mum was sick, so I just… didn't have time."

Phaedra wrinkled her nose. "How can you not have time for romance?"

He sighed. "Life gets in the way sometimes, Phee."

Ombra's beautiful, grinning face crossed her mind, and her chest ached for what she had lost. It had been too long since she had last held her, too long since the morning of her father's death. She had treasured the moment they had finally confessed they loved one another, not knowing they were a handful of hours away from being torn apart. "Well, maybe you two will get a second chance." She hoped as much for herself and Ombra as well as for Glen and Jemima.

But his face fell at her words, and there was a haunted look in his eyes that sent dread crawling through her. Dread she had been trying to keep at bay. Because she knew what Glen's old girlfriend and Maggie and the others had risked by helping her. Knew that if her sister found out, they would be in deep trouble. And if they were in trouble, then Caspar could be too…

"Glen… did my uncle ask you to do this?"

He hesitated, his expression unreadable. "When he assigned me to be your chaperone, his only order was to keep you safe. That hasn't changed. But the escape plan… that was Maggie."

Phaedra blinked, the memory of Maggie's last hug and tearful face sending another stab through her aching chest. She prayed it hadn't been their last goodbye. "They should have come with us."

Glen chewed a thumbnail, his hazel eyes darting away. "I wanted to bring them but… larger groups are easier to track. They all knew the risks of being involved with the plan, and they accepted them."

She tried to hold back the tears that welled up, shaking her head. "They should have just let Alessia do what she wanted. They'd be okay then."

"Don't be an idiot," he said, but his voice wasn't harsh. "They care about you. Especially Maggie."

She curled in on herself, staring at the TV without seeing it as she sipped her beer, her stomach knotted with worry. Glen picked up the remote and flicked through the channels for a few minutes, before settling back on highlights of an old football match.

"So," she said after a long silence. "What do we do now?"

Glen took a moment to answer, distracted as the ball whistled past the post, into the crowd. "I don't know. But I don't want to sit around drinking and vegging every day until they find us."

Phaedra took a shaky breath, tipping more beer down her throat. "Well… I guess we could fight."

"Fight for who? The Resistance? The Caplinites? Haven't they both teamed up anyway?"

"I was working for the Resistance."

"I think *working* is an overstatement, but okay." He swigged his beer, his eyes on the match. "So, say we decide to join them, how do we find them?"

"I know where the Resistance headquarters is. I'm sure they'll take us in."

He nodded, his shoulders relaxing a little. "That's a good start. And what about your friend, the Caplinite? Could we call her?"

"I don't have her number." Anxiety and darkness prickled down the back of her neck as she thought of the countless missed calls and texts Ombra had sent before Alessia confiscated her phone. She wished she had told her the truth long ago. Wished she had memorised her number the way she had memorised every freckle on her face.

"Okay, we'll figure it out," Glen said, trying and failing to give her an encouraging smile. "Surely the Resistance won't turn away two willing fighters."

She gave him a weak smile of her own, then glanced around the dank sitting room that looked like it hadn't been decorated in fifty years. "And even if we don't fight, it's got to be better than sitting around in dumps like this place."

"True. We'll rest tonight, get some sleep, then look for them tomorrow. It can't be that hard, we're refugees after all."

"Okay," said Phaedra in a small voice, but she couldn't help but be cynical.

"And hey, you can't complain when I'm sharing my beer with you."

Phaedra smiled and carried on sipping her drink, telling herself to relax.

Chapter Seven

SKYE BOLTON

Once she set her morals aside and flung Caplin's authority to hell, breaking in was too easy. The first set of guards waved her through the gate with few questions. The second lot were a little more wary of her lies, but Skye fogged their minds, knowing full well she was breaking the law that banned Telepaths from resorting to mind control. She then gave each of them a whiff of Veto to knock them out. As for the wards, they were in place to keep Oliver Matheson in. She bypassed them with ease.

He was asleep when she found him, draped over a blue silk couch with an empty bottle of brandy tucked into the crook of his elbow. She stood over him, studying his appearance. He looked like he had been sleeping in a ditch rather than with a roof over his head, and didn't smell much better. He was a far cry from the elegant man in the tailored suits who had tormented her back at Blackwater. He wore a crumpled and stained shirt that was supposed to be white, loose-fitting trousers that had seen better days, and no shoes or socks. His hair was overgrown and greasy, and he hadn't shaved for a while. Beneath his eyes were shadows dark as bruises, and he looked older than Skye remembered him. She supposed it was grief. Funny, she hadn't realised he cared that much for his son.

There was a dining room through the double doors to her left, with a bar in one corner that caught her eye. Glancing down at Matheson and confirming he was still asleep, she went to the bar, studying its contents. There wasn't much left. She chose a bottle of vodka, unscrewed the lid, then came back to Matheson. He snored. She poured the vodka straight into his mouth.

Within seconds he was choking and spluttering. He rolled off the couch onto the floor, the empty brandy bottle falling with him and cracking in two. His reactions were slow, and as he reached out to grab her ankle, she shocked him, the electricity crackling and burning where his face was wet. She then shoved her boot under his stomach and kicked him over onto his back.

"Sk—" he started, but he was still spluttering, staring at her with wide eyes. She knelt, digging her knee into his chest, and carried on pouring the vodka down his throat.

"This is for Jacob."

He choked, eyes watering, hands scratching at the fabric of her jeans as he convulsed. The bottle emptied and she chucked it to one side, before grabbing Matheson by the front of his shirt, lifting him bodily and shoving him back onto the couch. He sat there, the alcohol on his clothes seeping into the pretty blue silk. Then he lurched forward, head between his knees as he coughed and vomited onto the floor. Skye only watched him, taking a step back so his vomit wouldn't spatter her boots.

Eventually, he recovered enough to sit up, slumping back against the couch in exhaustion. He looked up at her with bleary eyes and snot streaming down onto his lips, a shadow of the man who had interrogated her at Blackwater.

"You know why I'm here."

He stared at her with his dull gaze for a moment, then nodded.

"You know where my father is."

Another pause, another nod. He would probably tell her without a fight, but she didn't care. She wanted to hurt him, and her power rose to her fingertips with barely a thought, springing into his body again.

Matheson twitched and jerked. But more satisfying were his gargled screams. She never shocked him long enough to do any lasting damage, and definitely not to kill him. But with each shock, she chipped away at the cold, hard man who had stood by and watched her being burned alive on his orders.

She was no stranger to hurting people, but it had always been a means to an end, a necessary evil that she had learned to numb her heart to. But this was different. He had seen her reduced to her most primal self, broken and screaming, an intimacy she wished to share with no one. Inflicting the same kind of pain and debasement on Matheson filled her with a brutal kind of pleasure, and she savoured every second of it with cold cruelty.

"Please," he gasped finally, his body trembling. "Stop."

She did as he bid her, unable to resist a dark smile. Seeing the look on her face, he began to laugh, growing more and more hysterical.

"Well, look at us." A mad grin spread across his face as she smirked down at him with her arms crossed. "Roles reversed. Does it feel good, Skye?"

"Oh, it does, Oliver."

"I could end it now, by telling you where your father is, but what's the fun in that?"

"That would be no fun at all, Oliver. You don't want to make it too easy for me."

"You mean too easy for *me*."

"Exactly."

He fell quiet, wheezing as his chest rose and fell. "It's lucky really," he said eventually, closing his eyes. "Lucky that Doran wouldn't let me kill you. What would we have done if we'd killed the Lux?"

"Oh, you'd have been alright. You were backing the winning team."

"I don't know about that. I reckon Alessia was just waiting to bump me off."

"I don't think I'd have a problem with that."

Oliver's smile grew. "And what about now? Are *you* going to bump me off?"

Skye laughed. "Oh no, Oliver. I think letting you rot in here is a more fitting punishment for you right now." And before he could say anything else, she went on another shocking spree, watching his eyes roll and his teeth smash against each other.

"Tell me, *Oliver*, can you heal yourself?"

"I can…" he confirmed, looking at the wounds that had spread like blistered roots over his arms, his skin smoking slightly. As they watched Oliver's Healing Talent in action, the wounds gradually faded, like footprints washed away by waves.

"Good. I wouldn't want to piss off the Resistance any more than I have to. Roxanne Summers was adamant that none of us could interrogate you."

"Roxanne?"

"Yeah, the too-soft-for-her-own-good one. I can't see her lasting five minutes if she were your prisoner."

Oliver said nothing, but Skye was preoccupied, looking for something to drink. She spotted a whiskey decanter on the bar in the next room and poured a measure into two glasses. She knocked hers back, refilled it, and carried the glasses back into the sitting room. Matheson hadn't moved. She handed him the other glass.

"Isn't this Ronan's whiskey?" she asked, rolling the liquid around her mouth.

"It is. A Solstice gift."

"A nice gift. That the last of it?"

He nodded, swaying a little, then knocked back the drink. His hand slumped back down on the couch, holding the empty glass loosely. "Is this to numb the pain?"

"No." She swallowed the rest of the whiskey, then dragged one of the dining chairs into the middle of the room so she could sit opposite him. "It's a toast to my father's health. Now, *Oliver*, I'm going to show you how *I* do things."

And with that, she shot out at him with telepathic tendrils, slamming into his mind with a force that made his head jerk back. She began to bore into his mind, peeling away layer after layer as he twisted and tensed and grimaced in agony. His defences were strong, but not strong enough to keep her out in his weakened state. The Break took all of five minutes, but the fountain of information she found within his mind was too delicious for her to leave just yet.

Matheson lay with his eyes closed, his breathing shallow as Skye ransacked his mind. He wasn't unconscious, but she knew he was in a lot of pain, his head laid open and vulnerable as she sifted through. Most of his secrets weren't really of interest to her, although two came floating to the surface, two that must have been at the forefront of his mind. "Amber Summers is your daughter? You and Roxanne?" She let out a shocked laugh, incredulous at the unlikely pairing. "No wonder she's so protective of you."

He scrunched up his face in embarrassment. "Don't…" he murmured, but that was all he could manage, his thoughts saying the rest.

"That's not my business." Regardless, she stored the information away to consider later, in case she ever needed something to hold over his head. Or Roxanne's, if it ever came to it. After today, she didn't doubt the Resistance would be pissed off with her. Moving on, she waded through other thoughts and memories, many of them tinged with pain and grief. She tried to avoid those, shying away from his thoughts about Cameron, but his mind was saturated with him: memories of a small blond boy learning to ride a bike, an argument over a failed class that had a teenaged Cameron trying to hide his tears, and Matheson's pride as his son healed his daughter's broken wrist with the Talent they had worked years to improve.

She paused in her search, swiping at her bleeding nose and blinking back her own tears as grief and guilt threatened to overwhelm her. "He was too good for you. You didn't deserve him," she murmured, her voice strained.

Matheson watched her through half-open eyes, his flare of anger at her mention of his son dulled by the pain, both physical and mental. She knew his answer before he spoke. "Neither did you."

Skye nodded, then bowed her head, giving him another moment's reprieve while she braced herself for more thoughts of Cameron. When she was ready, she continued, more secrets unveiling themselves to her.

"So, *you* were the one who arranged the poison plot." She delved deeper, the truth of Doran's death unravelling: Alessia promising she would get Cameron back in exchange for Matheson planting the poison that both killed Doran and framed her family. And then... sitting in an office with Caspar and the Telepath who Broke Glen, Caspar demanding that the Telepath sweep Matheson's mind as well. She blinked, a smirk growing on her face as she snagged greedily onto his memories. "Ahh, so Caspar did know who killed his brother after all."

Matheson gasped a laugh, his hands trembling in his lap. "Yes, it turns out the Nox underestimated her uncle."

She delved further back, discovering more about the scheme Alessia and Ivor cooked up long before she ascended. “That’s why you surrendered Blackwater when Cameron…”

He coughed, but didn’t reply out loud. She saw the months of resentment towards the Ronans, the belief that they weren’t doing enough to get his son back. And then she saw the argument with his daughter, Lindsey, who accused him of being the reason for Cameron’s death, of scaring him and driving him away. She shrank back from the darkest memories. The depths of Matheson’s guilt and despair were better left unexplored.

By the time she found what she was looking for, the copper tang of her nosebleed coated her lips. She wiped it impatiently with the back of her hand, her heartbeat speeding as she searched frantically through the memory. As it turned out, Matheson’s knowledge of her father’s whereabouts wasn’t as clear as she had hoped. There was no exact location, but what she discovered drained the burning fury from her body, replacing it with freezing fear.

“*Camilla* has him?” Her father had history with Camilla. He was the one who sentenced her to prison time after she killed her husband, and Skye could well imagine what she was putting him through. She had witnessed Camilla torturing people first-hand.

She watched through Matheson’s eyes as Camilla showed up on the morning of the prison break and boasted she had authority to move Victor. She had thrown a warrant on Matheson’s desk and then stalked out to collect her prisoner. Matheson himself didn’t care. He was already bored by that point, already aware that he was on his last life with the Ronans.

“Well, Oliver, it’s been a pleasure.” She sprang to her feet, not bothering to put the chair back in the dining room. “I’d love to stay and chat a bit longer, but I need to have a catch up with dear old Camilla.”

Matheson only coughed, then crumpled on the couch, his face half-hidden in a cushion.

"That's right, sleep it off," she said cheerily. "You'll feel better in the morning." And with that, she left him to it, echoes of his memories deepening her own fear and guilt as they trailed after her.

Chapter Eight

DEAN ROSWELL

"Sabine and Jacob did a bit of digging about the Mason prisoners. They're definitely off limits," said Lorcan, sitting opposite Dean at the breakfast bar of the Medley family home in Arundel.

Dean kept his gaze fixed on the garden beyond the French doors, where countless colourful flowers waved cheerfully in the breeze. Aunt Alma's kitchen was bright, one half of it built from glass interspersed with wooden beams, rather than the brick and thatched roof that dominated the rest of the house.

"I hope that's stopped Sabine from trying to do anything stupid," Dean replied after swigging from his bottle of beer, the previous day's fear over execution rearing its ugly head again.

"She still thinks she's going to persuade Mum to run for leadership, but she's got a shock coming to her if she thinks she can convince High Justice Medley to do anything she doesn't want to do."

Dean smiled in spite of himself, noting the glint of amusement in Lorcan's pale green eyes. "Then I look forward to watching them battle it out over dinner."

"I hope you're wearing armour under that T-shirt. There will be fallout."

They drank in silence, Dean privately dreading the evening ahead. The truth was, he didn't want to hear Sabine and Alma fighting at all, but a brainstorming session had to be better than aimlessly trying to wheedle information out of his comrades until an idea surfaced.

"How have you been, anyway?" Lorcan asked quietly, and Dean realised he had been staring at his bottle for the past minutes, leaning slumped on his hand. He straightened, but his skin prickled beneath his friend's scrutiny.

"I'm… getting by."

"We can talk about it, if you want. What I said yesterday… I'm sorry, it was insensitive." He ran a hand awkwardly through his hair, his thin face pinched with shame.

"Don't worry about it, honestly. It was just a figure of speech." But considering the state of Skye and Jacob when they got out of Blackwater, Dean knew that Lorcan's thoughtless comment probably wasn't far off the truth. He winced, planting his chin in his palm again, the horrific images he was trying to keep at bay flooding his mind.

"Victor's strong," said Lorcan. "He'll make it out, just like the others did."

Dean nodded, but Lorcan's words did little to reassure him. All he could do was keep reminding himself that as long as Skye was free, Victor would live. And if Dean had anything to do with it, Skye would not be handing herself over. There had to be another way to get him out.

"Has your mum been in touch?"

Dean sighed, nursing his beer. "My mother calls twice a week to convince me to move to France with her. Sounds like she's having a fabulous time in her new villa."

"The villa she bought with the proceeds of the divorce from Victor?" Lorcan asked with a wince.

Dean wrinkled his nose. He wasn't keen on criticising his own mother, but in light of everything going on,

Aurelia's actions were tactless, even for her. "The very same."

"I can imagine that's going down well with Skye."

He huffed a humourless laugh. "I haven't told her. The less Skye and my mother have to do with one another, the better. Might be best not to mention it to your mum either."

"Oh yeah, Mum thinks the world of you, but she's never been Aurelia's biggest fan."

Dean returned Lorcan's awkward smile, then shifted to another topic playing on his mind. "Ike mentioned Sullivan also collared you about training cadets. Have you given it any thought?"

Lorcan grimaced. "Can't say I fancy it, especially not when my sister is one of the new recruits."

"Ombra's re-enlisted?" Dean blurted, remembering how much drama Ombra had caused last time she had signed up as a cadet, then promptly dropped out.

"Yup. She thinks that because she did so well at the siege on Ronan Manor, she's invincible."

"And your parents are letting her?"

Lorcan shrugged, looking desolate. "They can't stop her. We'd rather she spend her time sewing garish clothes, but Ombra's determined to help with the war effort."

Dean gritted his teeth. The thought of teenagers like Ombra roaming the battlefield terrified him, another reason why he didn't want to train the youngsters. It would feel too much like raising lambs for slaughter. "Ike's joke about having Sabine train the cadets doesn't sound so bad now. Might scare them all into dropping out."

But Lorcan shook his head. "That might have worked in the past, but this is a Nox war. Caplin will send every soldier who can fire a gun to the front lines. Especially an Obscura like Ombra."

Dean knew what Lorcan claimed was true. Caplin had proven his ruthlessness time and time again. But before he could find words of comfort and reassurance, Alma stormed into the room, eyes flashing behind her glasses, her chestnut hair frazzled.

"Dean, you need to come home right now. Skye—" But before she could finish her sentence, her eyes snapped to a point at the far end of the garden, and Dean and Lorcan both followed her gaze to a hedge quivering in the corner. "What the…"

As they watched, Alma's daughter, Ombra, emerged from the quivering hedge, branches snagging on her patched denim jacket and ripped jeans.

Alma crossed the kitchen in several furious strides, shoving open the French doors. "Just what do you think you're doing, young lady?"

Ombra jumped, then scowled, prowling towards her mother with a face like thunder. The effect was made slightly comical by a couple of leaves stuck in her golden-brown hair. "I thought you were out."

"I just got back. And you were supposed to be staying in. Don't you dare tell me you've been out of town."

Ombra stopped on the patio outside the doors, glancing in to see Dean and Lorcan staring at her. But instead of brightly greeting them like she usually would, she gave no reaction, looking back at her mother.

"I had a lead."

"A lead? On what?"

"On Phoebe!" Ombra exclaimed, then shoved past her mother to come inside. "Hi Dean," she said monotonously as she crossed to the fridge without looking at either of them, taking out a bottle of bright blue soda and drinking straight from it.

"Nice to see you too, little sis," came Lorcan's sarcastic greeting, but his bemused expression betrayed him.

"I told you," said Alma as she snapped the door shut behind her, "if your girlfriend wanted to get in touch, she would."

"She could be dead!" Ombra shouted, whirling to her mother, her usually cheerful face turning pink with rage. "Or hurt, or captured! I have to find her."

"When did you last see her?" Dean asked. In truth, he hadn't known Ombra had a girlfriend, but now didn't seem like the best time to say so.

"The day Ronan got bumped off," she said, tears in her eyes. "I think… she might've got caught up in the bombs or something. I know she wouldn't ghost me on purpose."

Alma huffed, court heels clicking on the tiles as she crossed the room. She was wearing a burgundy trouser suit, and Dean wondered if she had been meeting Caplin. "At least put that in a glass."

Ombra frowned, then lifted the soda bottle to her lips again, holding her mother's glare as she drank defiantly.

"What's her surname?" Dean asked, glancing between them. "I can ask around for you. The Resistance took down a list of dead and missing."

A tear slid down Ombra's cheek, and she turned away.

Alma snorted. "She doesn't know her name. Never thought to ask."

"Stop it," said Ombra, her voice breaking.

"Who the hell goes out with someone for months and doesn't even think to ask their last name? Especially during a gods damned war." Alma's words were a snarl, and with that, Ombra slammed the soda bottle on the counter and stormed out. Dean blinked, watching the soda fizz and spill over.

Alma let out another long breath, then picked up a cloth and began aggressively wiping up the spillage, screwing the lid onto the bottle and shoving it back in the fridge.

"She's been insufferable."

“I… didn’t know,” Dean said, unsure what else to say. With the mess going on with Skye and Victor, he hadn’t taken much notice of anything going on outside his immediate family.

“I wouldn’t mind, I haven’t even met the girl. If you’re that serious about someone, at least bring them home to meet your family.” Despite Alma’s furious tone, tears glazed her eyes, and she let out a frustrated sigh. “Anyway, Dean, you need to come home. Your sister…”

He raised a wary eyebrow. “Has she been smashing bottles again?”

Alma frowned, seeming to struggle for words. “Worse.”

Dean’s stomach plummeted when she didn’t elaborate, and she was already circling the breakfast bar towards the exit.

“Sorry, Lorcan, you and your friends will have to start dinner without me. Mind Sabine doesn’t burn the house down while I’m gone.”

“What’s happened?” Lorcan asked, voicing Dean’s own question. But Alma had already left the room, leaving Dean and her son to exchange a confused look.

“See you later,” was all Dean had time to stutter before he hurried after Alma, his heart in his mouth.

He caught up with Alma in the vast garage, a pair of sleek vehicles housed comfortably in the space – vehicles befitting the Medleys’ status as both wealthy lawyers and members of high society. But she didn’t head for either car, and instead stepped up to a glistening salt and quartz circle, sigils drawn within it in white chalk – protections and directions. She held out her hand for him.

“What’s wrong?” Dean asked, reaching for her hand. Her fingers buzzed with static as they touched, and she herself was bristling with anger and… was that nerves? He rarely saw Alma phased by anything.

“You’ll see,” she said briskly, her hand closing firmly around his as they stepped as one into the circle.

His vision blurred, and a split second later they stood in a different circle, in a different place altogether: inside the shed opposite the safe house Dean shared with Skye and Kerry. Crossing the line of salt, Alma let go of his hand and flung open the shed door, striding over to the glamoured cottage and pressing her own medallion to the gate to let them inside.

Inhaling a bewildered breath, Dean followed close behind as she unlocked the door, leading him into his temporary home. Inside, Kerry hovered near the empty fireplace, her eyes wide with fear, and Dean scanned the cosy sitting room for his sister. But then he heard cheerful voices coming from beyond the closed kitchen door. One of the voices belonged to Skye, her laughter strange to him after so long. Perplexed, he glanced between Kerry and Alma, but neither of them offered an explanation. So Dean strode to the kitchen.

He shoved the door open, finding his sister at the kitchen table with a socialite smile pasted on her face, whiskey glass in hand. Next to her was a dark-haired man in his late thirties, light blue eyes crinkled in amusement and sitting so close that the pair looked like they were about to kiss. When Dean pushed the door wider, the man leaned back in his chair and met his eye, his face familiar. For Dean had seen him countless times on television and in the press, wearing the colours of their enemy.

“Ahh, Skye, this must be your brother,” said none other than Caspar Ronan, grinning up at him as he lounged at the table. Skye glanced at him, also grinning, looking more like herself than she had done in weeks. Dean stood frozen, unable to make sense of the sight before him.

“Dean,” she said, using the tone of voice she reserved for the shallow society events they had been expected to attend before the war, still portraying a charming façade. "Caspar brings such *fascinating* news."

Caspar. Dean knew she had been friendly with the younger Ronan brother, and had played games with him for information that she fed back to their father and Caplin. But to see her sitting with him now that the spying was over, laughing and joking like they were old friends, or even more…

"What news might that be?" Dean finally managed, his voice a growl, his hands curled into fists.

"Alessia Ronan has banished her uncle *and* her sister."

Dean raised an eyebrow. "So?"

Skye rolled her eyes. "So he's going to help us."

"In a manner of speaking," said Caspar, smiling at Dean's sister like a cat contemplating its dinner. Dean's stomach churned, his nails digging into his palms.

"Is that why he's here?" Dean asked, struggling to keep the hostility out of his voice. "To help us?"

"Oh, we thought we'd have a little catch up first." Skye placed a hand on Caspar's upper arm, her touch lingering a little too long. Dean tracked the movement, disgust pooling in his stomach. "Alma won't let him stay for dinner."

"I'm not surprised." Dean levelled his furious gaze on Caspar again. To his credit, Caspar held it, smiling as he raised his glass of whiskey to his lips. Dean's blood boiled.

"Your aunt has been kind enough to let me stay at her own holiday cottage. Skye tells me it has the most incredible views of the lakes."

Dean's eyes snapped to Skye's. *You're taking him to Alma's cottage?*

But Skye only smirked, drained her glass, then stood up, her chair scraping on the tiled floor. "Actually, we should make a move. If we leave now, we'll catch the sunset. It's a real treat." She winked at Caspar. Indeed, the sun was sinking beyond the windows, staining the kitchen with golden light.

Caspar emptied his glass too, setting it carefully on the table as he stood up. He then approached Dean, extending his hand. "It's good to finally meet you, Dean," he said good-naturedly.

Dean only glanced down at his hand, raising an eyebrow. Finally, he said, "It's Mr Roswell to you."

But Caspar only shrugged, smiling and holding up both hands when Dean refused the handshake. "My apologies," he said, then clapped Dean on the shoulder as he passed. Skye only rolled her eyes at him as she followed. "Thank you for your hospitality, Mrs Medley, Ms Saunders," Dean heard him say to Alma and Kerry as he headed out. Neither of them replied.

The front door had already snapped shut by the time Dean left the kitchen. He looked between the two women, who stood rooted to their spots. "What the—"

"Don't ask," said Alma, passing him to enter the kitchen and helping herself to a bottle of red wine in the rack. Kerry silently followed, hurrying to get Alma a glass. "I was dropping off Kerry with supplies when we found her in here with him, no warning, nothing. Said she trusts him."

"How can she trust him?" Dean blurted.

"No idea," Alma snapped, sloshing wine into the glass and drinking deeply, "but if Lady Skye says she trusts him, then I suppose we'll have to trust him too."

But Dean couldn't help but wonder if this was all just a game, a game that Skye had already admitted Caspar liked to play. And if so, he wondered what game Skye was playing in return.

Dean was chain-drinking bottles of beer by the time an equally drunk Skye fell through the door, alone this time.

Alma had taken her leave a couple of hours beforehand, going back to her family and the dinner that Dean was in no mood to attend. Kerry, meanwhile, had long-since retired to her room when she couldn't coax him to eat the meal she cooked.

He glowered at his sister as she struggled but eventually succeeded at securing the door. She then turned to grin at him.

"Evening!" she exclaimed, then stumbled to the kitchen, coming back with an open bottle of beer. Dean glared at her through his own intoxicated haze, but Skye was unphased, cheerfully swigging her beer.

"Are you going to explain or just keep acting like this is a huge joke?"

"Oh, lighten up. Caspar needed a place to stay. I found him a place. And he's going to help us in return."

"He didn't seem too thrilled at the prospect of helping."

She shrugged. "He knows what side his bread is buttered. Right now his priority is staying out of the lovely Nox's way and finding his niece. I can help him with that."

"And you trust him," Dean scoffed.

"I trust him as far as I can throw him. But don't worry, Dean, I'm not stupid. Caspar and I will use one another until we don't need each other anymore."

Dean let out a breath, relieved her relationship with Caspar was just business. Even so, the familiar way Caspar had acted with Skye played on his mind, not to mention the sickening looks they had exchanged.

"You're not sleeping with him, are you?" he asked, the question casual, but with just enough venom to make it clear how he felt about the idea.

Skye narrowed her eyes, her glare challenging. "That's my business."

Nausea roiled his stomach when she didn't deny it. "But he's—"

"*It's my business,*" she repeated, so he dropped it.

The silence dragged on, both of them glaring now, swigging their beer in mutual disgust. At least she had stopped acting like a clown.

"How did he even find you?"

"He had one of my connection rings."

"*You gave him a ring?*" Dean's incredulity only grew.

"I left it behind when Matheson tried to arrest me. Caspar got hold of it."

Dean sighed, things slotting into place. He supposed Ronan's options were limited, but that didn't mean he had to like it.

"Alma is furious," he said eventually, lowering his now empty beer bottle.

"I don't care," Skye snapped. "She can rant and rage all she likes, but if Caspar helps us to win this war and get my father back, she'll suck it up. She knows I'm right. Why do you think she let him stay?"

Dean held her gaze a little longer, but he knew she had won the argument. She always won with him, always got her way. "You should go to bed. You're drunk."

"So are you," she snarled.

"I'm going!" he snapped back, and with that he stood, striding out of the living room and slamming the door behind him.

Chapter Nine

GLEN FARRADAY

"You sure it was this one?" Glen asked, peering through the windshield at a run-down building that looked for all the world like it had been abandoned two decades ago.

"Positive," Phaedra replied, craning her neck to examine the old office block.

It wasn't the prettiest corner of Manchester. Debris littered the streets, graffiti decorated the drab grey walls, and the glass pane of a nearby bus stop had long been shattered, shards still glittering dully on the pavement. Further down the street, a ragged bearded man rummaged through an overflowing dustbin, setting the hairs on Glen's neck prickling. The man had only once looked their way, when they first pulled up opposite the former Resistance headquarters. The poor guy was probably just homeless, searching for any mote of food or source of income after the chaos that had ravaged the northern cities following Alessia Ronan's attacks, but Glen was taking no chances.

"Let's go look." Phaedra lurched into movement, reaching for the door handle as she unbuckled her seatbelt.

"Wait." Glen reached out, pausing her with a hand on her shoulder. She turned back to him, questions in her eyes. "Your sister probably knows the Resistance had a base here. There might be surveillance in the building."

Phaedra hesitated, looking from Glen to the building, then glancing at the homeless man. Her fingers were still curled around the handle.

"Even sitting in the car, we're too exposed. I could come back tonight and have a look around. *Alone.*" He emphasised the last word, noting how Phaedra's face lit up.

"What if you get caught?"

"Can you drive?"

She shrugged. "How hard can it be?"

Glen resisted the urge to roll his eyes. "I was gonna say, if I get caught, drive down south. But if you can't even—"

"Caspar showed me the basics, no need to give me lessons." She scowled, crossing her arms over her chest.

"Alright," Glen conceded, admiring her carefree confidence despite the ugly situation, amusement tugging at the corners of his lips. He glanced at the building again. There was no hint of life beyond the grey windows, and a faded orange poster half hung off the wall and flapped in the breeze. He started the car, the homeless man glancing their way once more. Eager to get away from prying eyes, he swung the car around and left the crumbling street behind.

"What do we do if we can't find them?" Phaedra asked once they were on their way, weaving through streets as derelict as the one they had just come from.

Glen didn't answer, but continued to scan their surroundings as he drove towards the city centre. The road was lined with fire-damaged buildings, broken or boarded-up windows, graffiti depicting every political opinion splashed across brick walls. Resistance and Saoirse Army freedom slogans were most visible, blue and green letters and lopsided silver stars catching his eye. Now and then he caught glimpses of the Ronan purple and gold dragon, or Caplin's raven on its crimson shield. But as he slowed to navigate his way around rubble overflowing from a bombed-out supermarket, a slash of yellow and gold distracted him from the road: the crumbling, blackened wall of the supermarket bore a forked lightning strike, the spray paint glistening in the grey light. But against the background of lightning was a mythical bird painted in painstaking detail, its outstretched wings spanning the smoke-darkened wall in shades of grey and purple and midnight blue – the stormbird.

Glen craned his neck to examine the mural as the car bumped over rubble, unable to make sense of why anyone would bother to paint the Bolton crest in the middle of Manchester. As Caplinites, the Boltons weren't exactly a popular family up north. Beneath the stormbird was a slogan in the same yellow paint as the lightning: *The light in the gathering storm.*

Shaking off his confusion, he glanced forward in time to swerve around a pothole that would surely damage his tires. The last thing they needed was to be stranded in the middle of a city full of potential enemies, and judging by the hints of Ronan symbolism in the graffiti, the place wasn't short of people willing to sell them out to the Nox.

"You said we'll go south?" Phaedra prompted at his lack of reply to her earlier question.

"Uh, yeah." The tension in his shoulders grew as they turned onto a main road that was a lot less deserted than the backstreets. Groups of people loitered on corners or gathered around looted shopfronts, eyes following them as they passed by. Some also looked homeless, while others held themselves menacingly, clutching weapons and flexing hands. His own gun was a solid weight in his inside pocket, but with Phaedra in the car, he didn't dare stop to ask questions about the Resistance's whereabouts.

"Why south?"

Glen turned onto the high street, then slowed right down when he saw their way was blocked. The tram tracks he had ridden on countless times as a teenager had been uprooted and twisted into a barricade, most likely by a Terra. Before the wall of distorted metal stood another group of ragged vigilantes. Their faces were obscured by bandanas and lowered hoods, but Glen felt their attentive glares all the same. Backing up, he turned the car into a side street, glimpsing more homeless people huddled on sleeping bags and stained mattresses stacked in doorways. A couple of dirty-faced kids watched with blank stares as they passed.

"Glen?" Phaedra's voice was shaky, her eyes darting from danger to danger.

"What?" he asked distractedly, catching sight of a civilian approaching in the rear-view mirror. Glen thumbed the button next to the door handle to ensure the car was still locked, but when he glanced back up, he saw the stranger take out a phone and hold it up before him. *Shit.* He sped up, turning a corner and hoping that any photographs the stranger had taken would come out too blurry to identify the car registration. Not that it mattered. They had swapped to a stolen one along the way.

Phaedra was twisted in her seat, taking in the destruction that Glen was desperate to leave behind. She only turned around again once they left the city centre and the civilian presence thinned. The breath she released echoed Glen's own relief. "Why do you want to go south?" she asked for the third time, her words finally piercing his panicked fog.

"If we can't find the Resistance," Glen said, picking up speed as they drove along a canal, "we might have to pay the Boltons a visit." He cringed as he spoke. The thought of seeing Skye again brought up all sorts of mixed feelings he was trying to keep buried deep, but after the risks he and the others had taken to get Phaedra out of that castle, he wasn't going to squander a chance to get her to safety.

"You think your girlfriend can help us?"

He didn't miss the teasing hint in her voice. "She's not my girlfriend."

"But you want her to be."

Glen winced, shooting her a dirty look. "I don't want anything to do with Skye, and especially not Caplin. But they teamed up with the Resistance. If they can help us find them, it's better than driving aimlessly around Manchester waiting for someone to capture us."

Phaedra considered his words, eyes tracking a cluster of youths that sauntered along the road like they owned it. "Do you know her address? Surely she wouldn't stay where anyone can find her."

Glen kept his eyes on the youths too, but they didn't seem to be a threat. "She probably won't be there, no. But knowing Skye, she'll have eyes on the place. It might be the best shot we've got."

"Fair enough." The girl lapsed into silence, watching trees whip by as they left the city behind.

"Maybe we could try your friend, too," he ventured. "Do you know where she lives?"

"And lead my sister to her? Bad idea."

This whole operation is a bad idea. But he didn't say it out loud. His only order was to keep the girl safe. Caspar Moneybags hadn't told him where to go if they needed to escape, and Glen had been so terrified by the threat of execution that he hadn't thought to ask. He knew full well that if Caspar hadn't stepped in when Matheson interrogated him over his affair with Skye, he'd probably be rotting in a shallow grave by now.

"Anyway," Phaedra muttered, still looking out the window, "she doesn't know I'm a Ronan. I used a fake name."

Glen glanced at her, frowning. "She wasn't one of your… spy buddies?"

But Phaedra wrapped her arms around herself, her voice becoming very small. “No. She was my girlfriend.”

He raised his eyebrows in surprise, realisation dawning on him. “Oh… uh… I see…” Suddenly, Phaedra’s actions and anguish made a lot more sense. No wonder she hadn’t wanted to sell the Caplinite girl out to her sister.

“Don’t tell anyone,” Phaedra warned, finally turning her frightened gaze back to him. “I’m not out, and I don’t know what… I don’t know what my family would say about… about me dating a Caplinite.”

Glen glanced between Phaedra and the road, lost for words that she was trusting him with her secret. But eventually, he gave her a tentative smile, eager to put her at ease. “Of course I won’t tell anyone. Anyway, I suppose Caplinites aren’t that bad. And if they are, then we both have terrible taste in women.”

She snorted, elbowing his biceps. “She’s not terrible. She’s… she’s amazing.” Phaedra smiled slightly, drawing her knees up to her chest and looping her arms around them. But as Glen glanced at her again, he noticed her eyes were shining.

“Well then, all the more reason to get you to safety so you can get your girl back.”

She huffed a sound halfway between a laugh and a sniff, swiping at her cheek with the back of her hand.

“But for now,” Glen continued, keeping his tone light to banish her tears and the fear still tugging his muscles taut, “looks like we’ve got a whole afternoon ahead of us. How do you fancy a spot of carjacking and pizza for dinner?”

She looked up at him, an eyebrow quirking beneath her jagged pixie cut. “I thought you’d never ask.”

***

The former Resistance headquarters were empty, and the only scraps of paper left behind were leaflets and invoices for the fake insurance company that had been their front. Glen sifted through them as he moved from room to room, his gun in one hand, a torch in the other. But the rebel party had left nothing useful, no clue as to where they had moved to next.

With a sigh, Glen admitted defeat as he arrived at the emergency exit at the back of the building, finding it ajar and letting in the cool night air. Switching off his torch, he slipped out into a staff car park, weeds growing through cracks and loose cobbles, a lone cat scarpering over a wall. A trio of industrial bins occupied the space to his right, one of them overturned, its contents long torn apart and raked through for anything of value. He considered searching through the rubbish himself, but a prickle raised the hairs on the back of his neck, and he turned. Sure enough, a pair of eyes were glued on him. But it was only the cat, its white fur looming in the shadows of a tree that sprawled over the wall.

Letting out a breath, he headed to the wide gate at the end of the car park. It, too, was left half-open, and he kept his gun at his side as he weaved his way through the back alleys, pocketing it when he emerged onto a dimly lit street. If he couldn't get answers from the silent building, surely someone in this city knew where he needed to go.

The city centre was overrun with more of the homeless and menacing vigilantes he and Phaedra had spotted earlier that day. They clustered around fires, drinking and talking in low voices. The scents of woodsmoke, cigarettes and illegal substances mingled in the air, and Glen pulled up the hood of his sweater as he drew closer. Shoving his hands deep into the pockets of his leather jacket, he clutched the gun, hoping he would simply blend in with the other displaced citizens of the city. At least his accent wouldn't stand out.

He approached a group of half a dozen men huddled in the wide entrance of an old bank. They were drinking beer, and crates of loot were stacked behind them. Eyes marked him across the fire that burned between them, narrowing in mistrust. He took a pack of cigarettes out of his pocket, holding it out. "Trade yer a beer for a ciggie?"

There was a pause as they looked him up and down, and Glen returned the favour, marking faces, ages, demeanours. They were all pretty worse for wear, their clothes shabby, the cloying scents of beer, sweat and cigarette smoke emanating from them. The pinched faces ranged from a youth with chin fluff to the craggy, weather-beaten man closest to him, who looked to be the oldest at around fifty. He was the one who spoke first, turning to a younger man sitting nearest the crates. "Mikey, pass us a beer."

Mikey glowered at Glen, his expression dark beneath his patchy, close-cropped black hair, but he reached into a crate without a word and the group passed along a brown glass bottle. Glen forced a half smile, pulling a cigarette from the box and offering it to the man nearest to him. A moment later, the stranger popped the cap off the bottle and handed it over.

"Cheers, mate."

"Gorra light?"

Glen grunted, tossing his lighter, then swigged the beer as the man lit the cigarette.

"Sit down," said one of the others, the biggest of the group, belly straining beneath his stained shirt. Glen obeyed, pocketing his lighter as it was handed back to him.

"We've not seen you before," said the one called Mikey, a bite edging his words.

"Some lootin' bastards burned me house down last night," Glen lied.

“Ronans bombed ours. Whole fuckin’ street went up in flames,” another grumbled.

Glen nodded, swigging his beer as he surreptitiously eyed his homeless companions. “So the Resistance aren’t doin’ nothin’ to help?”

“Like they give a shit. They’ve scurried off down south to try to win London.”

“Last I saw of the boys in blue, they were teaming up with Caplin’s crows.”

“They’re not here at all?” Glen asked, lighting a cigarette for himself.

“Apparently those two doctors come through with a team of medics every week, but I haven’t seen ‘em meself,” said the man at his side.

“What day?”

“Why, you injured?” Mikey asked, casting his eye over Glen’s abdomen. He drew his knees up, bracing his elbows on them as he drank the beer.

“Sick wife,” Glen replied, thinking quickly. “We lost her medication in the fire and the chemists are all smashed to pieces.”

“You lose yer wedding ring too?” said the one at his side, eyeing his bare fingers.

“Traded it for food.”

The men nodded, but Glen didn’t miss the way they glanced at one another, and the tension built between his shoulder blades. He swigged his beer again, then set it down at his side, bracing his hand against the cold floor within reach of the gun in his pocket.

“What day do the doctors visit?” he asked again, working hard to keep his voice casual.

“Answers’ll cost more ciggies.”

Glen shrugged, offering the older man his cigarette packet again. The stranger helped himself to another and slipped it into his chest pocket.

"Wednesdays, they reckon."

He cursed silently. It was Thursday. "What's the situation with the hospitals?"

"That'll cost ya."

Keeping in his sigh of impatience, he handed over another cigarette.

"The only one still running is on Oxford Road. All the others got looted after the bombing."

Glen nodded. The hospital was as good a place to look as any. Tossing the stub of his cigarette into the fire, he stood, picking up the beer bottle. "Cheers, I'll head there now."

"It's a long walk," said the man beside him, craning his neck as he looked up at him.

"Bet he's got a car," said Mikey.

"He's definitely not married," said the large one, and Glen's heart sank when two of them rose silently to their feet. "He's the one Ronan is looking for."

Glen didn't wait. He swung the bottle in his fist at the man who lunged at him, the glass smacking into the stranger's jaw, beer spurting from it. As the stranger staggered back, stumbling into the fire, the one who had taken his cigarettes jumped on him from behind, wrapping his arms around Glen's neck and squeezing.

Glen dropped the bottle, the glass smashing at his feet as he scratched at the arm pressing against his windpipe, staggering back into the road. But the older man was skinny, his grip slippery. With a tug, Glen dragged him off his back.

By the time he began to back away, panting for breath, the others were on their feet, advancing on him. They all held weapons of some kind: bottles, a crowbar, a cricket bat. But no guns, and as Glen pressed an elbow to his side, he confirmed his own was still safely hidden.

"Give up lad," said Mikey. "Yer outnumbered."

"Tell us where the girl is and we'll let ya go," said the older one, rubbing his elbow where he had fallen.

Glen snorted, raising his fists as he circled towards his exit route.

"We mean it. Keep movin' and I'll set you on fire."

Glen's breath caught as one of the strangers that hadn't spoken raised his own fists, flames glowing hot between his knuckles. He was taller than Glen, his thin face as pinched as the rest of them, murder blazing in his eyes.

He had told Phaedra to leave if he wasn't home by dawn. Knowing her, she would sleep in without him there to wake her. But she had car keys and a full tank of petrol, and could be at the Boltons' by late afternoon if she didn't try to come after him. He hoped the stubborn kid would do as she was told for once.

His hopes for Phaedra were swept from his mind as the six men advanced on him. The Ignis hung back as three others took their first swings, watching, assessing. Glen's fellow Talentless were easy pickings: starving, drunk, probably high. He ducked, dodged, smashed Mikey's nose with a well-aimed hook and plucked the cricket bat clean out of the large man's limp hand, swinging it around to land with a crunch on its owner's head. The man crumpled to the ground like a tonne of bricks, knocking over Mikey as he went.

The Ignis finally stepped forward, a pair of fireballs entering the fray. The old boxing injury in Glen's left knee protested as he fell into a familiar fighting stance, keeping the fire and his remaining enemies in his sight as much as possible.

As the Ignis loosed his fire, Glen dodged away, a loose cobblestone catching his foot and making him stumble. One of the balls of flame sailed right past him, but the other collided with the bat, the dented wood roaring into flame. He almost dropped it, shrinking back, but then he swept it before him, scaring off the two youngest that approached him now. The Ignis laughed.

"Don't matter how the saying goes; you *can't* fight fire with fire."

The Ignis beckoned with a claw-like hand, drawing the fire back to his palm with a hiss. Glen backed up, lifting the charred wood before him with both hands, just as the youngster with the chin fluff brought a bottle smashing against it. Shattered glass exploded between them.

He shoved forward, jamming the bat between the kid's lips. Two teeth snapped loose and clattered to the floor like dropped pennies. The youngster howled and staggered away with a hand pressed to his mouth, but one of his companions soon took his place, and a fast fist to Glen's gut knocked the breath from his lungs.

Another fireball came hurtling towards him. He dropped the bat, thrusting his arms in front of his face. Heat seared the backs of his hands, but the leather sleeves of his jacket took the worst of the attack. Batting his arms against the wall at his back, he smothered the flames as the Ignis and his last standing companion prowled towards him.

"Let's have it, then," Glen goaded, raising his fists to his chin again and ignoring the pressure building in his knee.

The Talentless one came for him first, fists flailing and spittle firing from his snarling mouth. Glen feinted to the left, his knee groaning beneath his weight. The man went to punch his stomach again, but Glen's right fist slammed into his ear, sending his head bouncing off the brick wall. He caught sight of the Ignis's approach from the corner of his eye, and flung out his left arm to pin the Talentless one against the wall, his elbow digging into the soft flesh at the base of his neck. Turning his face towards the Ignis, Glen grabbed the gun in his pocket and raised it just in time to press it to the Ignis's forehead. The man froze, flames sputtering at his fingertips.

"The magazine is fully loaded. Let me go or I'll splatter the cobbles with your brains, *mate*."

The man hesitated, his face barely visible over the fire that still flared in his hands, hot against Glen's exposed skin. And then the fire died out as the Ignis raised his hands in surrender.

"Boss?" garbled the youngster whose teeth he had knocked out.

"Let him go," said the Ignis, backing up a few steps. Glen kept the gun trained on him, his hand steady despite the man he held against the wall grappling at his sleeve. "Anyway, they reckon Ronan is the new Nox. She'll find them sooner or later."

"We'll see." Glen gave a grim smile, backing up and letting the Talentless one slump to the floor, wheezing for breath. Behind the Ignis, Mikey and the older man who took his cigarettes were trying to revive the big guy, while the youth hung back, clutching his bleeding mouth. Eager to put as much distance between himself and his attackers, he kept his gun aimed at the Ignis as he stepped backwards out of the street, then broke into a run as soon as he was out of their sight.

Chapter Ten

ROXANNE SUMMERS

Roxanne stared as Skye Bolton strode into her surgery, clad in her padded Caplin uniform and armed to the teeth. A handgun and ammo bulked out her hips, and knives glinted like a deadly promise in intricately designed sheaths along her forearms and thighs. Roxanne struggled for words, examining the hardness Skye's face had taken on, the hollowed-out cheeks, the sharpness of her bone-structure. But despite the determined set of her jaw, there was fear and uncertainty in the Lux's dark eyes. Her brother stood at her side, similarly dressed, minus the handgun. He, too, looked uncertain, eyeing her doubtfully.

"Why do you look like you're heading into battle?" Roxanne finally asked, her voice a terrified squeak.

"Roxanne…" Skye began, then trailed off, rising to her full height and curling her hands into fists. "I need to introduce you to someone who my comrades would probably pick a fight with if they saw him wandering around their barracks."

Roxanne frowned, glancing between Skye and Dean, waiting for answers. The siblings shared a loaded look, before Skye turned back to her. "I don't know who else I can trust with this, Roxanne. I… need you to promise not to freak out."

"Skye, what are you—"

"Can I trust you to keep quiet?"

She paused, looking between the two soldiers again. They both towered above her, making the surgery feel suddenly small. She tried to remind herself that she had seen the kinder side of them, that Skye had cared for Cameron and worked alongside the Resistance. But after what Skye had done to Oliver, Roxanne knew just how dangerous she could be. Right then, all she could see in front of her was a pair of lethal killers.

Please, Skye's telepathy whispered through her mind, carrying a vulnerability that her voice did not.

Roxanne held her gaze, noting her fear again. Then she nodded, more because she was afraid of what Skye might do if she refused. "Whatever you need to tell me, it stays between these walls."

Skye's mouth tugged up in a failed attempt at a smile, then she looked at her brother again, muttering what sounded like a counter-sigil beneath her breath. As Roxanne followed her gaze, shock clenched around her heart at the sight she saw. Dean's face melted away, revealing an older man with a groomed beard and ice-blue eyes that glittered like the winter sun on hoar frost. Roxanne stumbled back, bracing a hand on the desk, her pulse loud in her ears. Behind her, in a drawer on the other side of the desk, was the gun Devan had given her, uselessly out of reach. But if Caspar Ronan's reputation was to be believed, he could disintegrate her into dust with barely a thought.

"I mean you no harm, Dr Summers," came his silken voice, quiet in the small surgery.

"He needs your help," said Skye, her hard demeanour cracking.

Roxanne could only stare, vaguely aware of her staggered breath, her trembling hands. She curled her fingers around the edge of the desk, trying to steady herself. At the sight of her panic, Caspar took a step back, his hands splayed palm-first in surrender.

"I believe you are already acquainted with my niece, Phaedra. My priority is her safety, and she's missing."

At the mention of Phaedra, Roxanne took a deep breath to settle her trembling. Trying her best to push aside her flight response, she found her voice with difficulty. "What happened?"

"Alessia found out her sister has been associating with her enemies." Caspar glanced briefly at Skye, but the Lux's eyes were trained on Roxanne. "I feared for Phaedra's life, and allocated a trusted guard to protect her. A few nights ago, the guard and some of Doran's former household staff helped Phaedra escape, but Alessia has Marsden's Tracers on her side, so no doubt they will catch up with her soon."

Guilt lodged itself in the pit of her stomach. She had done this. She had put a teenager in danger. "I'm so sorry..." she murmured, barely knowing where to begin. She raised a hand to her throat, her chest tight.

"I don't know how much information Phaedra was passing to you," he said, voice tight with worry, "but I know she witnessed Doran's murder. I also know who conspired with Alessia to carry out the poisoning."

"The anonymous tip off came from you," said Roxanne as realisation dawned on her, her voice barely audible. "We had Phaedra's witness statement, but your information confirmed her story."

"That's right. Phaedra didn't know how much I knew, and I wasn't aware that Phaedra was informing on Doran and her sister either, until I had her guard confront her. I'm afraid such a huge responsibility weighed too heavily on her mental wellbeing. She risked giving herself away."

Roxanne lowered her gaze, a blush heating her cheeks. "I'm sorry... I'm... I'm afraid Phaedra hasn't been in touch. She has a phone I gave her, and phone numbers..."

Caspar nodded, and to Roxanne's surprise, he no longer felt like the threat he had been moments before. He was just a concerned person searching for a lost loved one. "Alessia found the phone. She couldn't bypass the security wards, but she knows it's what Phaedra was using to inform with. I believe they would have headed to Manchester to seek you out. Has anyone from there been in touch with her?"

She shook her head. "We've had no reports, but I'll send a trusted team to look for her."

"Thank you, Dr Summers," he said, bowing his head.

Skye shifted then, turning towards him, worry pooling in her gaze. "There's more. Show her, Caspar."

The man met her eye, his expression heavy with unsaid words. Then he took a deep breath, looking back at Roxanne. "I sustained an unusual injury, a parting gift from my *dear* elder niece. I believe you're a powerful Healer."

Her cheeks heated further, and she glanced at Skye, who was watching her almost pleadingly. "I have the healing Talent, yes. What is your ailment?"

Caspar shifted uncomfortably, vaguely indicating his left shoulder with his right hand. "It's... not healing as it should."

Sensing his reluctance, Roxanne pulled a chair out from beneath the desk, setting it in the middle of the room and gesturing for Caspar to sit down. He did so, then unbuttoned the high collar of the Caplin uniform he wore, removing the jacket. It was only when he took off the T-shirt he wore beneath that Roxanne noticed the difficulty with which he moved his left arm, his face distorted with a grimace. Sterile dressing obscured the injury, clumsily taped into place.

“We’ve tried everything,” Skye said, stepping to Caspar’s side. “Ointments, brews, even sigils. It’s not healing.”

“May I take a look?” Roxanne asked, working to keep her voice even despite the fear that clearly weighed on Skye.

Caspar nodded and leaned back in the chair. Carefully, Roxanne removed the dressing, the white gauze coming away blackened with soot and blood. She stifled a gasp at the wound that festered beneath. A spiderweb of dark trenches marred his skin, edged with bruising and seeping watery blood.

“What did this?” she asked. The wound was like nothing she had ever seen.

“Alessia’s darkness,” he said, gritting his teeth.

“But… aren’t you an Obscurus too?”

“I am. So you’re right in thinking she shouldn’t be able to wound me. But she has.”

Roxanne released her breath, assessing the damage again. “How has the wound behaved since it happened? And when did it happen?”

“Two days ago. And it’s not really changed, apart from the bruises changing colour. The cuts themselves have just become more swollen.”

“Can you help him?” Skye asked, her voice unsteady. Roxanne wondered whether it was concern for this Ronan or fear of the Nox that had toppled her usual resolve. Perhaps both. She had spent a lot of time with the Ronans, after all.

“I’ll try my best. Darkness wounds can be healed in non-Obscurus victims, but this… it’s much worse.”

Caspar met her eye, nodding his understanding. “If there is anything you can do to help, consider me in your debt.”

Roxanne frowned, about to contradict him, but then her earlier fear echoed in her gut. He might be an informant like Phaedra, but she still couldn't trust him. Still, if he was an honourable man, perhaps he would keep his word and repay her by helping the Resistance.

She pulled a trolly full of medical implements towards him, setting about cleaning the wound. Skye still hovered at his side, and Roxanne glanced up at her.

"Make yourself comfortable, Skye. This might take a while."

Getting the message that she was in the way, Skye dropped into a chair on the other side of the room, watching intently. Roxanne did her best to ignore her stare as she set to work.

Despite her misgivings, the swelling reduced and the open wounds scabbed over as she hovered her hand over his shoulder. But the darkness was still embedded in his skin along the edges of the cuts like a tattoo, black against the mottled purple bruising. Caspar peered down at his shoulder to inspect her handiwork.

"I don't know if I can prevent scarring," she admitted. "Like I said, I haven't seen this kind of wound before, but keep the scabs dry and it should at least heal."

But Caspar flashed a relieved smile. "Thank you, Dr Summers. I was beginning to worry I was doomed to walk around with a gaping hole in my shoulder."

Skye crossed the room then, standing over them both to see the injury. Her expression finally softened as she let out a breath. "What now?"

"I should see you daily to continue the healing treatments," Roxanne said, then looked up at Skye. "Is that possible?"

"I can bring him in under a glamour again."

Roxanne nodded. "I think it would be wise to tell my fellow Leaders, at least. Keeping this a secret puts me in a very difficult position."

The pair exchanged an uncertain look. "Can you trust your fellow Leaders?" Skye asked, the edge returning to her voice.

Roxanne paused, assessing Caspar uncertainly. Playing for time, she cut up gauze for a new dressing. She would follow Devan and Darshana until the ends of the earth. But Peter and Nanette? She could imagine what they would say about this, and what they would say about *her* for helping an enemy, even if he had been their anonymous second informant.

"If you meant what you said about repayment," she told Caspar, carefully layering the gauze against his wound and taping it in place, "then my fellow Leaders would trust you more if you can help us in this war. That said, the Nox is your niece. I understand if going against her contradicts your nature as a member of her family."

She could hear Peter and Nanette's voices in the back of her mind, sneering that this could all be an elaborate ruse cooked up by the Ronans. But then Skye was here, looming protectively at his side, the fated enemy of the Nox. Could she have been taken in by this wounded man before her? Roxanne didn't miss the looks they exchanged, some connection based on trust and mutual understanding that she didn't want to begin to fathom. She turned away, pushing the trolly back to the wall and taking some small glass bottles out of a cabinet, glimmering like amber in the harsh surgery light.

"Alessia threatened her sister's life, and promised to kill me if she set eyes on me again," came Caspar's voice behind her, and he stood to pull on his clothing, moving with more ease than before. "As a result, I'm not inclined to side with her in this war. My father was the Nox fanatic, not me."

She mulled over his words as she crossed back over to him, handing him the glass bottles. "This is a tonic to support your body's natural healing. Take one bottle daily after breakfast."

"Thank you." He took the bottles, placing them carefully in a pocket of his jacket. "Regarding Phaedra…"

"I'll instruct the team immediately. How can I contact you to share news?"

"Through me," Skye said, reaching into a pocket. She extracted a small, silver ring, holding it out for Roxanne, who looked at it uncertainly. "When you want to contact me, wear the ring and think my name. The sigil creates a bridge between us to extend my telepathic reach."

Roxanne took the ring hesitantly, holding it up to examine it. It was a simple band, the only decoration being a communication sigil etched on the inside. Clever.

"If I hear anything, I'll be in touch. I hope we can find her."

"I appreciate it, truly," said Caspar, bowing his head. "I will find a way to repay your kindness."

Roxanne tried to smile, then looked back at Skye, but her expression was guarded. *Perhaps if you bring him to the meetings, the others will be more inclined to trust him.*

But if Skye heard her thoughts, she didn't reply. Instead, her tired face morphed into a cold, hard smile, her narrowed eyes glinting. "Thank you for your help." She then looked back at Caspar, inclining her head towards the door.

"Yes, thank you, Doctor," Caspar agreed, his smile much more earnest. His expression was replaced a moment later by Dean's appearance as Skye muttered sigil names and the glamour slipped back into place. The pair made their way out, leaving Roxanne with a trickling uncertainty.

Chapter Eleven

GLEN FARRADAY

"Why have we stopped?"

Glen grimaced, failing to hide his pain from Phaedra as she waited for his answer. "I need a break."

He let himself out of the car, hissing through his teeth as he straightened and stretched his swollen knee. It wasn't unusual for it to ache after hours of driving or a strenuous workout, but he must have strained his old injury during last night's fight. The joint throbbed, the pain building to the point of being unbearable.

"Okay," said Phaedra, hopping out of the car and slamming the door. "I need a pee anyway." She set off across the car park towards the roadside services.

"Wait…" he called out, bracing a hand on the roof of the car and suppressing a groan as his stretch tugged on his tendons. "Don't go by yourself."

"I am toilet trained, you know. Don't need you to hold my hand."

He snorted a laugh in spite of himself, then locked the car and followed her, limping a little. "You know what I mean."

"Can we get lunch? I'm starved." She almost skipped ahead of him, gambolling like a puppy discovering the outdoors for the first time.

"It's not my fault you didn't have breakfast."

"What was I supposed to do? You made me get up at five AM."

Glen rolled his eyes. "I'll be more considerate of your beauty sleep next time your evil sister's minions are on our tail."

"Do you think they have a chemist?" she asked casually, falling into step with his slower pace.

He shrugged. "If they do, I doubt there's much in there. Why?"

"Your hands could do with some bandages, they're kinda grossing me out." She shot him a glance, stuffing her own hands in her pockets.

He frowned at the blisters and angry red burns stinging his hands. "Sorry my injuries are such an inconvenience to you."

She suppressed a smile, which faded quickly. "Seriously though, they look sore. And… I also need something."

He scrutinised her, unsure if he should ask. Sensing his curious gaze, she met his eye again, looking sheepish. "I'm out of sedatives."

"Sedatives?"

"Yeah, for my Talent. I don't have full control, remember?"

He bit back a curse. "Why didn't you tell me this yesterday? I could have asked for some when I went snooping around the hospital." He knew he shouldn't be annoyed, but between the ache in his knee, the sting of his burnt hands, and the fact that he had barely slept in three days, his patience was wearing thin.

"I didn't realise." She stared up at him apologetically, her anguish evident. With her jagged haircut and the exhaustion paling her face, she looked a lot younger than her eighteen years.

He held in a grumble as they neared the double doors into the building, reminding himself the poor kid had been to hell and back these past months. “Let’s see what they’ve got.”

His fingers curled around the gun in his pocket as the electronic doors parted for them. The interior was eerily quiet, until they were greeted by the sound of a gun cocking. They whirled around to see a middle-aged man behind the counter, clutching a rifle in his trembling hands.

“What d’you want?” the cashier demanded, hefting the rifle for dramatic effect.

At Glen’s side, Phaedra drew closer to him, elbows tucked in tightly. He responded by shifting slightly in front of her. “Just food,” he told the cashier, “and medicine, if you have it.”

The cashier scrutinised them, his gaze lingering longer on Phaedra. Glen hoped he didn’t recognise her. “Where are you headed?”

“South,” Glen grunted. “This one skipped breakfast. We just want a couple of sandwiches.”

The cashier sagged a little, the aim of the rifle faltering.

“There are some in the fridge. They’re out of date though. Haven’t had a delivery in over a week, and most visitors come here on the rob.”

“We have money,” he promised. The stash Maggie and the others had smuggled to him had barely a dent in it. “I’ll pay full price, even if they’re out of date.”

After further hesitation, the cashier nodded, jerking his head towards the fridges lining the back wall. Keeping a close eye on him, Glen and Phaedra edged towards the food, slipping between the aisles of groceries to put a barrier between them and the gun.

“Cheese or ham?” Phaedra muttered, her voice lacking her earlier chipperness.

"Whichever is less likely to give me food poisoning," Glen grumbled, filling a basket with the last five soda bottles.

The girl shrugged and dropped two of each sandwich into the basket, then shoved a couple of packets of crisps on top. She then moved towards the medicine aisle. "They only have cold and flu remedies," came her voice from beyond the shelves.

"Anything that will help?"

"Probably not." She came back to him then, concern clouding her eyes.

Glen headed back towards the cashier, walking slowly as he kept his eye on the rifle. Taking his wallet out of his pocket, he drew out several notes and placed them on the nearest shelf. "For the food," he explained, lifting the basket in his hand. "Don't suppose you have any sedatives…? Or Veto?"

The cashier's eyes narrowed, his gaze lingering on Phaedra again. "My sister has a condition," Glen lied, eager to dispel any suspicion. "She gets seizures."

The man nodded slowly, eyes still on Phaedra. "Nearest hospital is in Milton Keynes. But last I heard, it's a war zone. Gets worse the closer you get to London."

Glen nodded. What news he could get his hands on had confirmed as much. "Got any painkillers, at least?" If they were to avoid London, they had about three hours driving ahead of them. He didn't think his knee would last out that long without something to numb it.

"They took everything," the cashier said with a shrug.

"Can I use the toilet?" Phaedra interrupted.

The man only gave a sharp nod, so Phaedra slinked off, leaving Glen in a staring contest that he was only too eager to leave behind once she returned.

Back out at the car, Glen bit off pieces of the stale sandwich as he stretched his leg again, rubbing his knee to dispel some of the pressure.

"Want me to drive to the hospital?" Phaedra asked, chugging from a bottle of soda.

Glen looked her up and down doubtfully. "Sure you can get me there alive?"

She rolled her eyes. "If the food poisoning doesn't kick in first."

***

Phaedra did get them there in one piece, despite Glen's certainty that his out-of-date lunch would make a reappearance each time she took a turn too fast or slammed on the brakes. After two wrong turns, they finally entered the hospital car park, only to find the main entrance barricaded by a gang of youths who glared as they sailed past, all manner of makeshift weapons grasped in their fists. Glen ordered her to turn around, but she bumped into a barrier on the way back out, eliciting a stream of curses from him.

"I thought you had lessons?" he grumbled, grabbing the wheel to steer straight and avoid it happening a second time.

"Yeah," she confirmed, face burning. "One or two."

"One or—?" He shook his head, half incredulous, half bemused. "Pull over here. I'm driving."

Phaedra muttered under her breath as she skidded to a halt in the middle of the road. The car stalled as she shoved on the handbrake, then slammed the door after her. Glen got out a bit more slowly, his knee spasming as he stretched it out, but he hid his pain and irritation with a sarcastic grin as he held the door open for her. "Milady."

She frowned and stuck her tongue out, but slid into his vacated seat.

“Seatbelt on,” he instructed as he firmly shut the door, then limped around to the driver’s side, glancing around for enemy eyes and allowing himself a quick flex of his knee before he got back in.

“I don’t think we’re going to get to the Boltons’ today,” he admitted a short while later, putting as much distance between them and the hospital as he could. “If we can’t get medicine, we should find somewhere to rest.” He ground his teeth, hating that he was letting her down because of his stupid knee.

“I could keep driving,” she said hopefully, her face lighting up.

“It’s not a good idea. The last thing we want is to get pulled over because of your wacky driving. The police still work for your sister.”

She scowled. “The police have more important things to do than pull over dodgy drivers.”

He took a deep breath, turning into a suburb, scanning the houses either side. “I just don’t think we should be drawing more attention to ourselves.”

Phaedra grumbled something inaudible and crossed her arms over her chest. Glen turned into a side street, then pulled over. “Come on,” he muttered, getting out and shoving the door closed. Stuffing his hands into his pockets, fingers around the gun once more, he limped down the nearest alleyway between rows of bungalows.

“Where are we going?” she asked, stumbling after him.

“Home,” he said firmly, turning towards her and briefly pressing a finger to his lips. Looking stricken, the girl shut her mouth as she trailed him through the alleyways.

In the third alley, he found what he was looking for. A broken window gaped, shattered glass lying dusty in the overgrown grass. He carefully pushed the back gate open, beckoning Phaedra to follow. The backdoor hung ajar, and he drew out the gun as he stepped inside, aiming it into the gloomy interior. Phaedra followed closely behind as he moved from room to room, scanning for any sign of life. The place was deserted, the furniture dusty.

"We'll stay here tonight," he announced when they returned to the living room, finally putting away his gun. "I'll go for some supplies. Make yourself comfy and see if you can get the interweb working."

Phaedra raised an eyebrow as she took in the nicotine-stained net curtains that reminded Glen of his nan's house, the chintz sofa and armchairs, and faded fake flowers on the mantelpiece, the leaves more blue than green. But then she flopped down on the couch, picking up the remote to turn on the television. To Glen's surprise, it worked.

Chapter Twelve

SKYE BOLTON

"I should be the one buying you wine," said Caspar as Skye handed him a pair of bottles, already chilled and shimmering golden in the evening light.

"You're not exactly in a position to go strolling into a liquor shop," she replied wryly, glancing around the rustic kitchen. She had always loved the way the sinking sun gleamed across the tiles and drew out the russet tones of the old wooden beams. And the view of the lake beyond the window brought back memories of much happier times spent at her aunt's holiday cottage. Swallowing the lump that tightened her throat, she turned to the cabinet, pulling out a pair of glasses as Caspar uncorked a bottle. "Has everything been alright while you've been here?"

"Everything is working just fine." His tone was pleasant, obscuring the worry and fear she was sure must still be weighing on him. "Please thank your aunt for me, once again."

"I would, but she's still not speaking to me."

His face twisted into a grimace. "I'm sorry for that."

Skye laughed it off, ignoring the squirm of guilt in her stomach. "Oh, don't worry. I should probably have taken her a couple of bottles. She usually forgets grudges when she's outrageously drunk."

"I'll remember that next time I try to win her over."

She grinned as he poured the wine, taking in his appearance. Despite everything going on, he had regained his habitual mask of looking perfectly relaxed, the effect enhanced by his clothing. He wore an untucked linen shirt with the sleeves rolled up, beige slacks and a pair of soft brown loafers, as opposed to the tailored suits and starched shirts she was used to seeing him in. But what struck her most was his hair. Instead of slicked back with styling wax, it was left natural, waves of dark brown instead of black, falling in his eyes. She swallowed, the sight of his casual ease feeling strangely intimate, as though she had caught him in a state of undress.

She glanced away when he met her gaze, gritting her teeth in embarrassment. When he handed her the glass, his fingers brushed hers, awakening static. She looked up to find a mischievous glint in his eyes, and she couldn't help her suggestive smirk as they clinked glasses.

Skye drank the wine greedily, needing a distraction from his proximity. His warmth was just within her personal space, the scent of his woody cologne invading her senses. Slipping away towards the window, she tried to quash the fire smouldering at her core, tried not to think of the memory of his lips against hers.

She wasn't here for him. She had work to do.

"How's your shoulder?"

"Much better. You were right, Roxanne can work wonders."

She let out a sigh of relief, her thoughts drifting back to when she had first seen his wound after she picked him up on the nondescript roadside where he arranged to meet her. He had tried and failed to hide it from her, his shirt bloody and blackened beneath a hastily thrown on coat. She remembered his hiss as she peeled the torn shirt away at the kitchen table of the safe house, his uneven breath warming her neck as she cleaned and dressed his wound as best she could. If Alessia's power could even damage other Obscurae, Skye's odds of winning the final battle didn't look good.

"No news on Phaedra?" She jumped to the next topic, pushing away thoughts of the Nox and their entwined destiny, gripping her glass a little too tightly as she drank.

"Nothing." Worry injected his tone. "I just hope your old chaperone is keeping her out of trouble."

Skye winced as she stared at the sunlight glittering on the lake, her guilt like a knife twisting in her gut. She had thought about Glen more often than she wanted to admit these last weeks. And since Caspar had told her what happened with Alessia, her worry had been niggling away at her, refusing to remain at the back of her mind. She lowered her voice, not trusting herself to hide her concern if she spoke any louder. "I'm surprised you trusted him with such precious cargo."

"He's the only one I could trust." He came to stand beside her, clutching his wine glass. "He's lucky the Mind Breaker who swept his mind is a friend of mine, and since he owed me for keeping my mouth shut, I knew he would do right by Phaedra."

"So you blackmailed him." She narrowed her eyes in amusement, doing her best to push away her guilt.

"It was nothing personal," said Caspar, his own lips curling.

She fell silent, drinking her wine, the cool, crisp liquid easing the tension in her chest as she broached the next topic. "I don't suppose you've heard from Camilla?"

Caspar froze at her side, and then his gaze fell on her, his expression guarded. "Why do you ask?"

She looked up at him, searching his face, her heart racing. If he knew what Camilla had done, if he had been involved at all with her father's capture… "Is she still a friend of yours too, or is she Alessia's pet now that Doran is gone?"

He blinked, then raised an eyebrow, his mask cracking. She let out her breath when she saw a chink of surprise shine through. "Camilla has kept a very low profile since Doran's death."

"She hasn't been in touch with you?"

Puzzlement mingled with his surprise now. "She was at the inauguration, but after the attack…" He paused, sipping his drink as he sifted through memories. "I haven't seen her since."

Skye took a deep breath and looked back at the lake, more of her tension ebbing. "Camilla has my father."

She heard his exhale, and he leaned against the window frame. When she met his eye again, he was watching her, a ghost of a smirk gracing his lips.

"What?"

"This is why you're helping me."

She frowned playfully. "Maybe I just want your company."

He scoffed a laugh, then drained his glass and crossed the kitchen to refill it. "When you Broke Matheson, I assume you got all the gory details about the plot Alessia and my father cooked up."

"Sure did." She followed him, then held out her glass as he topped it up, Oliver Matheson's memories yapping for her attention. She brought the glass to her lips, drowning those memories with the wine.

"I can only assume Camilla was in on it. She'd do anything to stay in the Nox's good books."

Skye nodded, heading through a wide archway into the living room and curling up on one of the two brown leather sofas. Caspar followed, sitting opposite her and setting down the wine on the oak coffee table between them.

"Where can I find her?" she asked, finally cutting to the chase.

Caspar took his time, an ankle rested on one knee as he leaned back against the sofa. "She didn't show up at Alessia's hideout while I was there, meaning she probably isn't keeping prisoners there. My next guess would be Tewkesbury, otherwise…"

"Otherwise?" Skye prompted, already finishing her glass and reaching for more wine.

"Are you familiar with Roswell Manor?"

Skye narrowed her eyes. "Other than the fact it shares its name with my brother, no."

He nodded. "It was part of Vincent Roswell's estate. Most of his assets went back to his family after Camilla was condemned for his murder, but since the manor was already a ruin, they let her keep it."

"Is that where she lives?"

"It's not really inhabitable. I believe she and Vincent planned to renovate it when they married, but the marriage didn't last long."

"And that's where she might be keeping my father?"

Caspar sipped his drink, a line creasing his forehead. "It's possible. Otherwise, she's taken him to Ireland, by which point you want Tracers involved."

"I'm not asking Caplin or the Resistance to lend me Tracers. This is personal."

Caspar watched her drain the rest of the wine into their glasses. Without a word, he went to retrieve the other bottle from the kitchen, uncorking it and setting it on the coffee table.

"Listen," he said, once he was settled opposite her once more. "You're familiar enough with Camilla to know she likes to play games. I get the feeling the reason she took your father was personal too."

Skye clutched her glass, her vision already starting to blur around the edges. The whiskey she had consumed before she arrived probably wasn't helping. Regardless, she drank deeply, trying not to entertain the intrusive images. "She took him for revenge." It didn't matter that Victor had given Camilla a fair trial after she murdered her husband. He had still condemned her to a life sentence in prison. A life sentence that was only overturned when Ivor Ronan planted false evidence in her favour.

"Not just that," said Caspar quietly, pouring her more wine when she held out her glass. "She's luring you in."

Skye froze, the glass partway to her lips. Did she imagine it, or was that fear flickering in his eyes? "What would she want from me?"

He shrugged. "What does Camilla always want? Control. Power. You're the Lux."

She looked away, the title leaving a bitter taste in her mouth, which she washed down with yet more wine. The sun was sinking towards the lake by now, bathing the room in red light.

"Skye?"

She looked back at him. The sunset warmed his complexion, highlighting the auburn tones in his dark hair and beard, and muscle feathered in his jaw as his gaze pinned her in place.

"Whatever you do, don't try to rescue him. It will be a trap. And if you meet her, please, don't go alone."

Something cracked in her chest at his open concern, flooding her with a mixture of fear and gratitude. She could only nod, lowering her gaze to her drink again.

"What about you?" she asked once she had swallowed the lump swelling her throat. "What's your plan once you've found Phaedra?"

He raised an eyebrow at her change of subject, but indulged her all the same. "I honestly have no idea."

She forced a mischievous smile, topping up their glasses. "I think you should help the Resistance."

Caspar shifted in his seat and busied himself with his refilled glass, avoiding her gaze. "I can see that working with the Resistance may become inevitable sooner or later."

"I can understand why you're anti-Caplin, it's in your blood. But the Resistance are running the show right now. You have no feud with them."

"True..." He let out a slow exhale, staring at his knees. "Although going against my family... it's not easy for me, even if Alessia is the Nox."

Despite the stakes, she couldn't blame him for that. Alessia *was* his blood. "And yet you went straight to the Lux when she threatened you," she teased.

"What can I say? I got the impression you liked me too much to kill me." The flirtatious glint from earlier was back in his eyes, and Skye clung to it, eager for a distraction from the doom and gloom.

"You supposed right. To kill *you*, Caspar, would be an utter waste."

His lips parted in surprise as she echoed his own words back to him, words he had once whispered in her ear as he held her in his arms on a crowded dance floor. And then those lips curved seductively as he raised his glass in a mock toast. "It appears our feelings for one another are mutual."

"So it seems. If you weren't so attracted to me, you might still be bored out of your mind playing advisor to the Nox."

His lips twitched. "It's a good thing the Lux doesn't have to be modest."

Skye shrugged. "Believe me, I often wonder whether Vala got the wrong person."

They lapsed into silence, Skye finishing her wine and setting down her glass, then stretching and settling back into the sofa, more comfortably than before. Caspar also finished his drink, not even trying to be subtle as he took in her appearance, his gaze leisurely and lingering like a caress. And she didn't mind one bit as she returned the favour, admiring the sharp edges of his cheekbones and jaw, not to mention the angles of his collarbone just visible in the gap where he had left his top button undone. Her thoughts went back to the night they kissed once more, the way his wandering hand had set her skin alight, sending shivers down her spine. She suppressed a shiver now, biting her bottom lip. She knew she was playing with fire, but the fear of getting burned wasn't enough to hold her back.

"Aren't you tempted?" she asked eventually, catching and holding his gaze in a challenge. "Now that we're no longer enemies?"

Caspar's eyes roamed over her body again, causing her lips to curl in spite of herself. He swallowed, then took a deep breath. "Of course I am."

Sparks prickled at her fingertips, anticipation flooding her. "Then what's stopping you?"

He blinked, his body tensing as he studied her face in what appeared to be disbelief. "Skye…"

But Skye didn't wait. She was done with waiting, with resisting, and the wine in her veins helped her decision fall into place. Getting up, she stood before him, her hands going to the buttons of her shirt, undoing the top one, and then the next, and then the next. Caspar glanced between her eyes and her hands, watching hungrily as she exposed more flesh, goosebumps rising on her skin. When she was done, she let her shirt fall to the floor and approached him, sliding into his lap and straddling him between her thighs.

Her breath hitched as his fingers traced her bare skin, sending a tingle of electricity skittering down her spine. His eyes shuttered, lips parting as she leaned towards him, but then his hands stiffened around her waist, holding her firm.

"Are you sure?" he asked, his voice guttural, eyes searching hers once more.

She raised her hand to his face, brushing the loose hair from his eyes, the weight of his question hanging between them. But alone with him, the voices both inside and outside her mind were hushed. In that moment, in his arms, she couldn't care less who he was, or what family he belonged to.

"Yes," she breathed.

The single word was all he needed, and he finally unleashed everything he had been holding back. She met his lips with the same feverish need, enveloped in his scent, his taste, the feel of his hands caressing her scars with the same reverence with which he touched her unblemished skin.

She had wanted him for far longer than she dared to admit, and it was time to take what she wanted.

***

"So are you going to stop fucking about and get your shit together?" Sabine's voice was harsh, her words straight to the point.

When Skye got back to the safe house the following afternoon, finding only Sabine waiting for her, she knew Dean had arranged an intervention. And as much as she wanted to curse her brother to hell and back, calling in Sabine was a stroke of genius on his part. Or perhaps Sabine had bullied him into it.

"Could we not do this now?" Skye passed Sabine where she lounged at the kitchen table and grabbed a glass out of the cupboard. She then dropped into the chair opposite her friend, avoiding her golden glare as she poured whiskey from the bottle between them.

"Why? Because you have a raging hangover? Because you've been out all night?"

Skye grimaced, knocking back a shot of the whiskey and pouring herself more.

"Don't bother lying about where you've been," Sabine continued, eyeing Skye's crumpled clothing – the same clothing she had seen her in the previous day.

"I wasn't going to," Skye retorted, finally meeting her stare.

Sabine searched her face for a moment, then scoffed, leaning back in her chair and putting her booted feet on the table with a heavy thud. "You've always had shit taste in men, but bedding a Ronan takes the biscuit."

Skye dropped her gaze back to the table, but found herself grinning in spite of herself. She couldn't hide anything from Sabine. "I don't see how my sex life is relevant, but thanks for your blessing."

Her friend snorted. "I hope he was worth throwing away your last shred of dignity."

"Oh, he definitely was," Skye shot back, then poured them both more whiskey, working hard not to let her memories of the previous night fill her cheeks with heat.

"Absolutely shameless," Sabine replied, shaking her head.

"Anyway," said Skye, leaning back in her own chair, glass in hand. "I assume you didn't come here just to judge my shit taste in men."

"Not entirely." Sabine levelled her gaze on Skye. "But it was on the list."

Skye gritted her teeth, waiting.

"Also on the list: stop being such a jerk to your brother."

She winced, lowering her gaze to her glass. "You don't need to tell me that."

"Don't I? Seems like someone had to, since Dean is too nice to stick up for himself."

A handful of half-baked excuses shot through Skye's mind, but none of them were valid, and even if they were, Sabine wouldn't stand for it. "I'll apologise."

Sabine laughed darkly. "You owe him more than an apology, but it's a start."

Skye nodded remorsefully, sipping her drink. "What else is on your lovely little list?"

There was a pause, until Skye looked up at Sabine to see a smile on her purple painted lips, a smile she didn't like the look of.

"You'll go to the meetings with the Resistance."

Skye wrinkled her nose. "Caplin is already going."

"Don't give me bullshit, Skye," she said, tucking a braid behind an ear heavy with piercings.

She tried again. "After what I did to their precious prisoner, they won't want me back."

"You think Breaking Matheson is going to make a difference in the grand scheme of things? Sure, they're pissed off and Caplin got hell for it, but you're the Lux. They need you if they have any hope of winning this war."

"So I keep hearing," Skye said bitterly.

"And since you're getting cosy with Ronan, bring him along too. He might as well make himself useful."

Skye rolled her eyes, lifting her glass to her lips.

"As for the drinking," Sabine said next, eyeing the whiskey bottle between them.

"Oh, don't start—" Skye interrupted, but Sabine cut across her.

"I was going to tell you to take it easy. You don't get to fall apart like you did after our first battles. People are relying on you now."

The words felt like a slap to the face, the kind of slap to make her wake up and see sense. But despite Sabine's good intentions, Skye's rage reared up, thundering through her along with her riled Talent. "You don't get it, do you? What I'm going through—"

"Oh, poor little Lux, no one understands me so I'm going to drink myself stupid and hope my problems go away."

"Sabine—" she seethed through gritted teeth.

"You think a drunk is going to win this war? No one wants another Doran Ronan at the helm."

Skye held her glare, then knocked back the remaining whiskey, setting down her glass with a dull thud. "Don't compare me to the bastard who murdered my mother."

But Sabine said nothing else, merely sat watching her with an irritating curve to her lips. Skye took a slow, deep breath, still holding the glass a little too firmly. Again, excuses failed her. It had been weeks since she had broken into Ronan Manor and found Vala waiting for her instead of Alessia. Weeks since she found out she was the Lux. And she could count on one hand the number of useful things she had done since then.

"I'll leave you the bottle." Sabine set her feet back down on the floor and finished her own drink in one swallow. "But I'll see you at the barracks tomorrow. Seven AM."

Skye let out her breath, eyes following Sabine as she stood and walked past her. When she was almost at the door, Skye twisted in her seat. "Sabine?"

Her friend paused, her back still to her, but she turned her head so she could see her profile. Skye hesitated, studying the studded skull emblazoned across the back of Sabine's leather jacket, and the undercut that enhanced her sharp jawline.

"Thank you," she said eventually, unable to find a better way to sum up the storm of mixed feelings raging in her chest.

Sabine turned a little more, her eyes sliding to meet Skye's. She held her stare for the briefest moment, then the corner of her lips tugged up and she gave her a single nod.

And then she was gone, leaving Skye with a little too much food for thought.

Chapter Thirteen

PHAEDRA RONAN

Phaedra's eyes itched and her fists vibrated with suppressed energy as she sat curled in the passenger seat, trying not to let Glen see the puffs of darkness emanating from between her clenched fingers. She buried her hands inside the sleeves of her oversized hoodie, the dark purple fabric stained with black and beginning to get holey. She sneaked a peek at her chaperone whose hands were equally tight on the steering wheel, his white knuckles contrasting with the angry red of his burns. A muscle in Glen's jaw feathered beneath his tightly knitted brows.

"Is it sore?" she asked tentatively, glancing at his knee. But Glen only grunted, the engine groaning as he accelerated.

They had spent a couple of hours that morning searching for a hospital or pharmacy that wasn't looted or overrun with menacing gangs, before Glen finally gave up in favour of continuing the journey further south. By now, familiar rolling hills unfurled around them, and road signs for towns near Phaedra's childhood home, Ronan Manor, whipped past.

"Do you think if we go to my house, the Resistance will be there?"

Glen bit his lip, taking a moment to reply. "It's risky. Too many of your sister's followers live around here. They might get to us before we can reach the manor."

She nodded, her fists tightening as her shadows surged. With any luck, they would reach the Boltons' house before Phaedra's Talent exploded and Glen's knee gave out.

"What if we make a portal? Do you know any connecting ones down south?"

"Down south in Caplinite territory, you mean?" he replied with a sarcastic edge. "Even if we could get hold of materials, we'll be arrested the moment we step through a Caplinite portal."

She shuddered. "Maybe being arrested by Caplinites wouldn't be as bad as my sister's people finding us."

"It probably wouldn't, but I'd rather not risk being shot on sight before we've had chance to explain. You are a Ronan."

Phaedra wrinkled her nose at the reminder and rested her chin on a knee. She returned to reading the road signs, her chest aching with grief for a past and a father she would never get back. Her childhood had been far from happy, saturated with fear of her sister and grandfather, but Doran had loved her, as had Maggie. And she had taken their love for granted by escaping the house every chance she got.

She scratched her bitten thumbnail against one of the holes in her sleeve, her Talent ebbing and flowing with the tide of memories she fought to keep at bay. Doran had always been disappointed when she and Alessia could never get along, and until Phaedra learned that it was better to just stay out of her sister's way, he had long tried to find activities that he thought they might enjoy doing together. She wondered if he would have been so inclined to get them to build a relationship if he had known it would be Alessia who would kill him.

She took a deep breath, swallowing the tears and darkness that threatened to emerge as the memory of her father's sudden death tumbled into the forefront of her mind.

After what felt like an age, Glen slowed as they approached Reading. Houses with green lawns and pretty gardens sprang up beyond the windows, but as they drew further into the city, evidence of the war revealed itself, and scattered groups of civilians marked their car as they passed by. Reading was on the border between her father's lands and Caplin's, and had long been contested over the past decades.

"We'll check out the hospitals, then get out of here," Glen muttered, taking a turn.

Phaedra nodded slowly, her anxiety and shifting shadows heavy in her chest. She forced down a breath, wishing she knew how to cast glamours like Jemima. Her short spiky hair and the sandy fuzz on Glen's cheeks felt like inadequate disguises. As if reading her mind, Glen jerked a thumb over his shoulder.

"I swiped some caps while getting supplies yesterday. Put one on."

She took a deep breath to quash her riled Talent, then twisted in her seat to rummage in the carrier bag until she extracted a sports cap in a shade of red so bright it made her eyes hurt. She turned it in her hands, wrinkling her nose at the slogan across the front.

"*Football*? You are joking."

He shrugged. "Beggars can't be choosers."

"Worse, it's a Milton Keynes team. Are they even good?"

She didn't miss the flicker of a smile at the corner of his mouth. "You won't catch me cheering them on any time soon."

Phaedra grimaced as she put on the cap, the harsh colour washing out her already pasty skin tone. "Where's yours?"

Glen snorted. "I'm from Manchester. I'm not wearing some southern team's merch."

"But it's okay if I do?" she complained, stuffing her fists into her hoodie pocket.

"You are southern."

She ground her teeth, grumbling unintelligibly as she glared at her ridiculous appearance in the wing mirror. But before she could dwell on it further, Glen turned into a hospital car park.

Unlike the places they had scouted previously, this hospital seemed to be fully functional, with civilians milling around, paramedics scurrying in and out of ambulances with patients, and a handful of police lurking around the door. Phaedra couldn't take her eyes off the police as Glen searched for a parking spot.

"Whose side d'you think they're on?" she asked as he swung into a space.

He killed the engine, then let out a painful gasp as he stretched out his injured leg. "Let's try to stay out of their way until we've sussed them out. If anything happens, or we get separated, meet me back here."

Her darkness roiled, and she dug her nails into her palms to contain it. "Okay."

Glen opened his door, groaning as he laboured out of his seat. Phaedra followed suit, her nerves for his wellbeing only adding to the nausea in her gut. As she shoved the door closed, the metal gave beneath her fingers, and she snatched her hand back. Sooty black dents marred the silver finish of the car, and she rubbed at it hastily. But she only made it worse, the charred metal crumbling into flakes. She cast a fearful glance at Glen, but he was busy stretching his leg, his face contorted with pain.

Keeping their eyes on the trio of police at the main entrance, they fell into step with a forlorn family making their way into the hospital. Phaedra couldn't help but sneak peeks at them from beneath her hideous football cap, dreading the moment when their eyes might land on her or Glen. But another civilian claimed their attention with a complaint about queues, and they slipped inside without notice.

The foyer was crowded, people restlessly queuing to speak to the receptionists, while more police kept watch from corners. Phaedra tried not to look at them, nor at the injured and crying people dotted through the crowd. Instead, she concentrated on Glen, who scanned the signposts listing the departments overhead.

"This way," he said, easily making a path through the crowd as people dodged out of the way of his bulk. Phaedra hurried to stay close behind.

"Where?"

"Maybe the pharmacy will have what we need. I haven't got time to hang around in a queue."

There was a queue in the pharmacy too, and Phaedra struggled to keep still at his side, antsy with anticipation. But as they drew closer to the counter, the words of one of the two pharmacists squashed their hopes.

"Medication is rationed. The doctors prescribe pain remedies for emergency patients only. Here is a list of herbs to alleviate mild symptoms instead."

A disgruntled patient ahead of them began to argue, glaring at the leaflet the pharmacist had handed him. She seemed like a sweet lady, apologising profusely and reminding Phaedra of her late grandmother. But regardless, she sagged at the words, while Glen shifted on his feet.

"Maybe we can bribe them," he muttered, flashing her a weak smile.

But when they finally got to the front, the pharmacist only told them the same.

"How about sedatives?" Glen tried, glancing at Phaedra. "My sister gets seizures."

"What kind of seizures?" she asked, looking at Phaedra.

"Uh..." Phaedra stared, taking in her gentle brown eyes, the pretty chestnut curls cascading in a pile on top of her head. She was probably around her sixties, with smile lines around her eyes. But despite her apparent kindness, Phaedra floundered for a convincing lie, digging her hands deeper into her hoodie pocket. "My doctor prescribed me sedatives, but... we had to leave."

The pharmacist glanced between them. "Then you need to see a doctor here. Reception will take your details and give you an appointment."

Glen shifted again, his arms tense with agitation. "If you can't sell us medicine, do you have a knee support at least? I have an old sports injury that's playing up."

The woman sighed, assessing the queue behind them. "Alright, come to the back, I can fit you with one."

Neither of them hesitated as she beckoned them into a small room behind the counter, though Phaedra was all too aware of the grumbles of impatience at her back. "Wait here," said the pharmacist, closing the door to the public space behind them, then heading into what looked like a stockroom before she shut the door.

Phaedra looked at Glen, but he only shrugged, lowering himself with difficulty into one of the chairs.

"Is it bribing time?" she whispered, hovering near the door. The room was small, with a machine like the one her doctor used to check blood pressure, and some weighing and measuring apparatus.

"I'll try my best."

She tried not to tremble as she stood against the door, her hands in tight balls inside her front pocket. The lady didn't take long to return, but the seconds dragged, their silence crackling with nervous anticipation.

"How much mobility do you need?" asked the pharmacist, laying down a pot of ointment and several packages.

"I need to drive," Glen replied, glancing at the items doubtfully.

"This one then, it's more flexible. Let me fit it for you."

Phaedra's heart thumped in her chest as she watched Glen roll up his jeans while the lady took a seat opposite him.

"Listen," Glen began with a glance at the door, his voice low. "We're trying to get to family down south, but we've seen some pretty awful stuff along the way. What's the safest route to the West Sussex coast?"

Phaedra watched the lady's face carefully as she applied ointment to Glen's knee. The pungent aroma reminded her of childhood sprains and bruises.

"Caplinites still hold territories south from here," the pharmacist murmured. "They've agreed with the Resistance to offer safe passage to Portsmouth and Southampton, where refugees can take ferries into Europa. But from here… I'm afraid you'll have to try your luck with border control, or double back through London."

"Border control?"

The pharmacist grimaced and began strapping the knee support around Glen's leg, her voice barely audible to Phaedra. "Some of the Nox's military managed to keep hold of territories around here. They mostly leave us alone, but I wish they'd gone up north with the Ronans."

Glen's eyes slid to Phaedra, and she took in a shaky breath, imagining soldiers bursting through the door at any moment. "So Ronan's soldiers won't let us out, or the Caplinites won't let us in?"

"Honestly? Tensions at the border are high. Caplin is just waiting for an excuse to obliterate the military presence here, and I don't like to think what kind of trouble that would bring for the rest of us. If you want to keep your sister safe, don't risk it." The pharmacist glanced at Phaedra too, who shrank in on herself at the scrutiny.

"I can't risk London either, not unless the Resistance has managed to sort it out in the last twenty-four hours."

"Things are changing all the time. Last I heard, the Resistance and Caplin set up a portal from Windsor to Portsmouth for refugees. If you can get there, that might be your ticket to the south coast, but if I were you, I'd find shelter around here and wait for this mess to blow over."

Phaedra chewed her lip as Glen glanced her way again, his expression unreadable. After a moment's hesitation, she dared to speak. "And there's nowhere else I can get my sedatives? I have to wait and see a doctor?"

"I think you need to see a doctor anyway," said the woman, scrutinising her again. "You don't look well."

She swallowed down the darkness welling up in her throat. They were already risking too much having the pharmacist peering at her. A doctor would ask too many questions.

"Thanks for your help," Glen said, rolling his jeans back down over the knee support, then bracing his hands against the chair arms as he struggled to his feet. "How much for the support and the ointment?"

"Don't worry about it," said the pharmacist. "You might need your money wherever you decide to go from here."

"Thank you," Glen said solemnly, limping towards Phaedra. "I hope things get better for you too."

"They may yet," said the woman, fingering a protection rune pendant at her throat, the same rune Maggie's finger had traced on Phaedra's forehead countless times as a child. "Gods guide the Lux."

“Lux?” Glen asked, arching an eyebrow as he glanced back at her.

She nodded tentatively, glancing beyond Phaedra to the door as her voice dropped to a whisper. “They say it’s the Bolton girl. She will lead us out of the dark.”

Phaedra’s eyes widened, and Glen’s mouth dropped open. “Skye Bolton?” he asked, incredulous.

“The very same.”

There was a pause, the air heavy with unspoken questions. But then Glen seemed to sag, and he looked back at Phaedra, sceptical. “Take care, ma’am.”

“Gods keep you,” the lady replied as Glen nudged Phaedra through the door.

“She’s deluded,” Glen muttered once they had left behind the glares of angry patients in the pharmacy.

“I thought she was nice,” Phaedra stammered, her footsteps uneven as she kept pace with his limping, glancing around for any sign of police or soldiers.

“Oh yeah, she was lovely, but if the Lux exists at all, it wouldn’t be Skye Bolton.”

“Why not? My sister hates her. It makes sense.”

Glen scoffed. “Maybe, but it sure sounds like some bullshit Caplin spun to keep the Resistance on his side.”

Phaedra didn’t comment, tugging her cap lower as medical staff hurried to and fro. “I don’t think we can see a doctor.”

“No,” Glen agreed, but as they entered an elevator, he examined the buttons, then jabbed for the basement. “But maybe we can steal what we need. What’s the bet *Private* means stockrooms?”

The elevator dinged open, and they exited into a dingy space with three corridors leading off it. To their right were a pair of trollies stuffed with dirty sheets, but the corridors were otherwise deserted.

“Which way?” Glen asked doubtfully.

Phaedra shrugged, then headed down the right-hand corridor, glancing at the doors for any clue as to what lay behind them.

"This one's a stockroom," she mumbled partway down the corridor, nodding to a sign that read *Stockroom 2.0.* Without hesitation, Glen shoved the door open, and she followed him inside.

Rows of shelves were stacked with bottles and boxes of powder, cleaning rags and mop heads, buckets in various colours. "It's just cleaning stuff," Glen confirmed, then headed back out into the corridor.

The following rooms were more of the same, or else stocked full of bed linen, or contained washing machines and dryers that churned noisily, the scent of washing products tickling Phaedra's nose.

Back at the elevators, they peered down the two other corridors. "What if there's a morgue down here?" she asked, the thought both thrilling and sickening.

But before Glen could reply, four soldiers in grey and emerald green uniforms turned into the corridor ahead of them, striding their way. Two clutched guns.

"Better a bunch of corpses than armed guards," he muttered, turning to jab the elevator button.

"It's the Saoirse Army!" Phaedra blurted without thinking.

"No," Glen corrected, still jabbing the button, but the digital numbers above them counted upwards. "They're Mason soldiers."

"Which Masons?" she asked, panic bubbling in her chest as she realised that the symbol on their chests was a hammer and chisel, not the golden harp of the Saoirseans.

"The ones we don't want to run into." He lay a hand on her shoulder, nudging her back the way they had just come. "Walk normally," he instructed, his gruff voice replaced with a shaky whisper. "Head down."

She did as she was told, and Glen's limping picked up speed as they went further down the corridor, his hand between her shoulder blades urging her on.

"You there, halt!" came a shout from behind them, and without warning, Glen's fingers curled around her upper arm as he broke into a run, dragging her with him.

As they ran – Phaedra's trainers squeaking on the dull yellow linoleum – her feet were suddenly running on air, her cap blown off as unnatural wind ruffled through her hair. And then she smacked into the cold floor, her breath and darkness escaping her in a *whoosh.*

Glen yelped, and her panic grew as she saw the blackened floor between them. His leather jacket was torn, exposing a black and bloody scrape along his outstretched forearm.

"Go! Go, go, go!" he cried, his face twisted in agony as he scrambled upright, clutching his injured arm.

"Glen!"

But before his name had left her lips, gunshots rang out behind them. Her darkness shot out before she could think, a dangerous wave sweeping down the corridor towards their attackers and missing Glen by inches. The soldiers yelled and scrambled, and the Aeres that had brought them down wielded the wind to blow her involuntary attack off course. But before Phaedra could see it hit its mark, Glen grabbed the back of her hoodie and hauled her to her feet, limping and grunting as he dragged her through the nearest door.

Machines churned around them, the noise deafening. Glen let her go, heading between the row of industrial washing machines, then took a left at the end of the room.

"Are you okay?" she blurted, guilt roiling and tears threatening. But he didn't reply, and didn't stop, shoulders hunched as he staggered towards a small window high in the wall. It was slightly ajar on the latch.

"Through there," Glen ordered, squatting down and cupping his hands to give her a leg up. "Can you break the latch and crawl through?"

"But—"

"Phaedra, quick!"

She swallowed down her questions and shoved her trainer into his hands. He lurched her upwards before she had barely made contact, and she swayed dangerously before grabbing the bottom edge of the windowsill, her fingers staining where they touched.

"Hurry!" he urged as she fumbled with the latch. The darkness in her hand disintegrated the metal, and she flung the window further open. Behind them, the door slammed open over the racket of the washing machines.

Glen shoved her up further as she grabbed the edges of the window, bringing her foot to his shoulder. She wriggled and squirmed until she was through the window, gravel digging into her hands and knees.

"What about you?" she gasped.

"Take the car and go." He tossed the keys at her, which she scrambled to catch, then shoved into her pocket before her Talent could gobble them up.

"No, I'll wait for you!"

But he was already backing away, shaking his head as his eyes darted around for another escape route.

"Meet me at the car!" she hissed, glancing beyond him, expecting the soldiers to appear at any second.

"Go, for gods' sake!" He drew the gun from his pocket, disappearing amongst the machines. The yells of the soldiers reached her now. With a surge of panic, Phaedra set off along the hospital wall, not even sure if she was heading in the direction of the car park. Gravel crunched beneath her feet, the keys jangled in her pocket, and her lungs burned.

Phaedra stumbled as a gunshot rang out behind her, her heart leaping into her mouth.

She caught the wall for support, rough bricks scraping her fingers, and glanced back the way she came. What if…? For an agonising moment, she teetered in indecision, then forced herself on. Glen would be okay. *He had to be okay.*

The car park came into view, and she let out a strangled cry of relief when she saw it. Between her and the cars was a chain-link fence, but she didn't slow, colliding with it hands first, darkness spewing from her fingertips. Destruction – it was all she could do, and occasionally it came in useful.

She shoved her way through as the fence disintegrated, broken metal snagging at her clothes. She frantically scanned the space for their vehicle, every silver car as indistinct as the next. But then she saw it, her smear of darkness along the doorframe. Hurtling around to the driver's side, she flung the door open, barely closing it before she jammed in the key and turned on the ignition.

But before she could touch anything else, more darkness billowed from her fingertips, coming dangerously close to the steering wheel. "No!" she gasped, curling her hands into fists to smother the black smoke-like substance as it sputtered between her fingers like an angry cat. She gulped down a choked breath, then another, staring at her hands, willing herself to be calm, silently begging her Talent to stop. But it was no use, and as she burst into tears, the darkness continued to funnel out along with her sobs.

"Don't fuck with me now, stupid shadows!" she shouted, uselessly shaking her hands. She then pressed the heels of her hands into her eyes, the darkness rippling uncontrollably through her hair, almost like it was laughing at her. She imagined her sister laughing at her too, that cold sneer making her feel small and pathetic. And then she thought of Caspar, coaxing her to trust her Talent, to treat it like it was part of her, not a separate entity, his voice soft and encouraging. Finally, she thought of Ombra, of how she always made her feel safe, who showed her that their Talents could be something beautiful.

She inhaled a long, shaky breath, lowering her hands. With another breath, she opened her eyes. Wisps of darkness fluttered around her, leaving sooty smears where they landed. The steering wheel bore scuffs, but it was mostly intact, and a dark film coated the window to her right. But for the most part, the dashboard was undamaged, the engine still rumbling beneath her. When she was sure she wasn't about to melt the car's innards into useless dust, she stepped on the clutch, carefully putting the gear stick in reverse.

As she rolled backwards, shouts made her slam on the brake, and she peered through the windscreen to see Glen hurtling towards the car, his terrified face bloody. Behind him, a gaggle of soldiers and the trio of police burst through the throng of civilians at the entrance, flailing guns and raising their hands to summon Talents. Before she could react, Glen flung open the back door and scrambled in behind her.

"Drive!"

Heart hammering, she found the bite and the car lurched back, crashing into the bumper behind them. As she struggled to get it in the right gear, she glanced at the soldiers and police officers storming towards them, her darkness surging once more as they took aim.

"Come on, come on!" came Glen's panicked voice in her ear, drumming on the shoulder of her seat.

Phaedra let out a strangled moan as the gear stick finally ground into place. Stamping on the accelerator, the car hurtled towards the exit just as shots rang out, bullets pinging off the car.

"Are you okay?" she yelled, glancing in the rearview at Glen.

"Head for the city centre," he said breathlessly, ignoring her question.

"What?" She could barely steer the car, never mind follow directions.

"Turn right at the exit, then follow the signs for city centre!"

The exit barrier snapped as she shot through it, bouncing off the bonnet, and she swung the car to the right, barely missing a vehicle coming in the other direction. She swerved to avoid other cars, the engine groaning as she picked up speed.

"Change gear."

But she ignored him, not daring to take her foot off the bite for fear that she would stall.

"Phaedra!"

"Shut up and let me concentrate!"

She spotted a sign just in time and hurtled around the corner, barely missing an angry pedestrian who leapt out of the way. She sucked down another breath as her darkness riled again, humming against the steering wheel and beginning to eat away at the black coating. Finally doing as Glen suggested, she dared to go up a gear.

"Take a right."

"Okay, okay!"

She took the side road he indicated, the wing mirror snapping off as she clipped a lamp post. She sped down the road, then slammed on the brake again as she realised just in time that they had reached a crossroads. The car stalled.

"Left."

She struggled to restart the car, fingers trembling, darkness puffing, more tears streaming down her face. "Glen, I can't."

At her panicked confession, he got out of the car without a word, pulling open her door. Clutching her spurting fingers to her chest, she flung herself into the passenger seat, legs catching on the gear stick as she went.

Chapter Fourteen

GLEN FARRADAY

His knee throbbed, the cuts on his face stung, and whatever the hell Phaedra had done to his arm was agony, but he didn't hesitate as he took over the wheel and merged into the main road traffic.

His breathing eased as he navigated the city centre and saw no sign of anyone giving chase, but he didn't miss the sirens ringing in the distance. Following signs for a multi-storey car park, he swung the car into the dimly lit building, taking the first empty spot they came to.

"Grab your stuff and let's go."

He got out, trudging to the boot and flinging it open. Phaedra scurried to join him, pulling out her bag.

"Where—?"

"We can't stay in this car."

He slammed the boot shut and headed to the exit, every step sending pain jolting up his leg, while his torn sleeve and the strap of his rucksack chafed his injured arm. He led her out into the open again, but kept to backstreets, weaving through them until he saw glistening white marble columns ahead. Sirens continued to screech, heading closer.

"We'll hang out in the temple until things die down."

The round structure came fully into view, graffiti marring the carved flora and fauna that decorated the façade. Glen remembered clearly the last time he had stepped foot in a temple, for Ivor Ronan's funeral. He had spent the entire time sick with the memory of his own mother's funeral, the pain of her death still harrowing two years later.

Avoiding the openness of the front square, they headed for a side entrance. The ornate arched door had been torn from its hinges, probably by someone with a fancy Talent. As they stepped over the damaged threshold, the flapping of startled pigeons made him jump. Behind him, Phaedra's darkness puffed out around her like a cloud. He eyed her uncertainly.

"Maybe stay a few feet away," came her small voice, tears shining in her eyes. He sighed, but nodded, heading between columns decorated with twisted vines into the temple proper.

Stone pews surrounded the central altar in quarter circles, aisles splitting the round space to lead to the four element altars set at the cardinal points. Above the northern altar, beneath a grand rosette window that let in cool light, more graffiti drew his eye. He froze, recognising another stormbird, the colours and detail even more intricate than the mural on the side of the supermarket. Instead of lightning, it was surrounded by a halo of sunrays the way it usually appeared in the Bolton crest. Unable to help himself, Glen wrinkled his nose as his torn feelings for Skye bubbled to the surface.

"Seems that lady wasn't the only one who thinks she's the Lux," said Phaedra, hovering some yards away and clutching her hands close to her body.

Glen looked back at the stormbird, but it was Skye's face he saw in his mind's eye, and a dull ache entered his chest. Not so long ago, he had woken up to her warm body in his arms almost every morning, and had worshipped that body with his own. And as the handful of months they had together drew on, he had come to worship the rest of her too. But his feelings had been stupid, reckless, and wasted. She didn't care for him, not in the way he wanted her to. And whatever the hell she had going on with Caspar Ronan added further salt to his wounds. It didn't help that the cocky bastard had taken the connection ring that had been Glen's only way to contact her. Perhaps they wouldn't be in such a mess right now if he hadn't.

"I still think it's just propaganda," he replied dully, slumping into a pew and leaning his head against the cold stone back of the seat in front of him. He closed his eyes, breathing through his pain as he reached down to rub his throbbing knee. After a long moment, he straightened, easing off his jacket to inspect his latest injury.

"I'm sorry," came Phaedra's tearful voice from behind him. He couldn't help his hiss as he peeled off his hoodie. The torn material of his sleeve was sticky with blood.

"Not your fault," he replied through gritted teeth, inspecting the mess of his arm. More blood oozed from the wound, the damage resembling a blackened burn. "Can you get me some water from the Aqua altar?"

Phaedra scurried off, returning moments later with an ornate silver chalice decorated with blue sapphires. Glen raised an eyebrow.

"I'm surprised thieves haven't made off with that by now."

The teenager shrugged. "Maggie always said stealing from temples bestows a curse."

He gave her a small smile, remembering the prayer Maggie had whispered to him and his co-conspirators during their last meeting, beseeching the Nameless Gods to guide them. If the gods existed, he hoped they had answered her prayer. Hoped Jemima and his former colleagues were safe. "Maybe there's some truth in that."

He took the chalice from her, setting it on the pew beside him and dipping the undamaged sleeve of his hoodie into it. He then began to clean the wound, gritting his teeth again and trying not to make too much noise at the stinging.

"Any idea how to heal this?" he asked, flexing his arm.

"Dad just used to get Matheson to heal people whenever me or Alessia…" She trailed off, hugging herself as her eyes darkened with fear. "I'm so sorry."

He managed a grim smile. "Don't worry about it. You kept those soldiers off our backs. We made it out, and we're alive."

But tears still slipped down her face. "How did you get out?"

Glen lowered his eyes, dipping a clean bit of his hoodie into the water to wipe the bloody cut on his forehead. The memory of the Aeres slamming him into the corner of a washing machine still jarred through his skull. But at least his skull was intact, unlike the Aeres who had ended up with Glen's bullet between his eyes.

"I found the stairwell on the other side of the elevator."

"We went the wrong way?"

He gave a hollow laugh. "Yup."

Phaedra released a breath, leaning against the back of a pew. "What do we do now?"

He flexed his leg experimentally, clutching the cold stone beneath him as the pain flared up his thigh. "I can't drive like this." He met her terrified gaze, tensing as the injury throbbed again. "I'm sorry."

"It's not your fault," she said quickly, her anguish echoing his own. "You got me this far."

But not far enough. Perhaps the pharmacist was right. Maybe they needed to lie low and keep an eye on the news until they were certain where the Resistance would be. Glen rubbed his useless knee again, indecision battling with his fear and failure.

"Let's give it an hour, wait for things to calm down out there. Then we'll look for somewhere to stay tonight."

She nodded, sniffing, then perched on the other end of the pew, rummaging in her bag for the sandwiches Glen had bought the previous evening. She tossed him one, which he ate without tasting, every bite jolting through his aching head. All he needed now was to injure his other arm and leg for a full house, he thought bitterly.

When the sirens finally died down, Glen stripped off his bloodstained T-shirt, tearing it with some difficulty. He then wrapped the torn cotton around his arm as best he could, hoping it wouldn't chafe. After pulling on a clean T-shirt, followed by his burnt and torn leather jacket, he extracted the anti-inflammatory ointment the pharmacist had given him and unstrapped the knee support to slather some on.

"Maybe that will help your arm," Phaedra said hopefully, but Glen shook his head.

"The herbs in this will make me feel like my arm is on fire."

"Oh."

"Do you need any? Are you hurt?" He swept a glance over her, but she shook her head. He sighed, then pocketed the ointment, re-strapped his knee, and unrolled his trouser leg, finally rising to his feet with difficulty. His limbs were stiff from sitting on the cold stone.

"Can we light a candle on the Ignis altar before we go?" Phaedra asked in a tiny voice, shifting on her feet and looking at the floor. "For my dad..."

Glen hesitated, glancing at the southern altar. The candles that usually burned atop the marble carving of a sun were all extinguished, but fresh ones lay in carefully stacked pyramids either side of the alcove, red wax glistening. "Of course," he murmured and followed her down the aisle, stepping through a patch of late afternoon sun slanting through the western rosette window.

Phaedra carefully took the topmost candle from the right-hand pile, peeling old wax from the central candleholder and slotting the new one in place. It seemed she had calmed down considerably: no shadows darkened her hands now.

"Can I borrow your lighter?"

Glen gave her a small smile, withdrawing the battered lighter from his pocket and handing it over. Taking a deep breath, Phaedra leaned towards the altar, clicking the lighter and holding the flame steady until the wick caught.

They stood in silence a moment, staring at the flame as Glen's thoughts drifted to Doran. Whatever anyone said about the fallen conqueror, Doran Ronan had only ever treated him with kindness. He had plucked Glen from obscurity and sponsored his fledgling boxing career, then gave him a job and a purpose after his damaged knee meant he could box no more. And then, to solidify Glen's gratitude and leave him forever in his debt, he had paid for his mother's care, the best doctors and treatments money could buy. But even Oliver Matheson's healing Talent hadn't been able to reverse his mother's disease, and in the end, Doran's generosity went towards the hospice where she spent her final days with Glen at her side. Perhaps getting Phaedra to safety could go some small way towards repaying his unpayable debt.

Glen swallowed the tightness in his throat and blinked back the blur in his eyes, shuddering away the horrific memories of his mother's last days. Without a word, he took another candle from the pile, lighting it from Phaedra's flame and carefully placing it next to hers. The silence continued, and to Glen's surprise, Phaedra slipped an arm around his middle, leaning against him, her eyes swimming as she stared at the candles. He let out a sad sigh, then put his arm around her shoulders, squeezing slightly.

As his mind and gaze wandered upwards, he took in the animal motifs carved into the translucent white marble, all symbols of fire: lions and salamanders, fireflies and a phoenix, and further up, captured in flight and breathing flame, was a dragon. Another shudder went through him. "There's your family mascot."

She followed his gaze, giving him a wobbly smile when she spotted the dragon. "Maybe that's a good sign."

Perhaps the gods were listening after all.

"Come on," Glen said eventually, once the sun had sunk below the glassless window. "Let's look for somewhere to stay tonight."

"Can we have pizza again?" She looked up at him, hope illuminating her pale blue eyes.

He huffed a laugh. "Is that all you ever eat?"

***

By eleven o'clock that night, after an agonising evening seeking out the cramped bungalow they had broken into, Phaedra was dozing on the sofa beside him, her small, skinny body curled into a ball so tight that Glen couldn't believe she was comfortable. He, meanwhile, was uneasily sipping a beer and absently rubbing his knee, the joint still throbbing, and his arm wasn't faring much better. His gun, as ever, was on the arm of the sofa to his right, and the sound of the TV was turned down low so he could listen for any suspicious noises. At the other end of the sofa, Phaedra snored lightly, turned on her back, stretched, then curled up on her other side and went back to sleep. He envied her, but he had to stay alert until it was time to wake her for the second watch.

A tap dripped into the open-plan kitchen sink. A clock that read the wrong time ticked unevenly back and forth. Glen nodded, then awoke with a start as his head lolled forward onto his chest. He cracked his neck, flexed his burnt hands, and blinked several times to try to clear the tiredness. Tilting his beer bottle, he saw he had a mouthful left at the bottom and swigged it down. Labouring to his feet, he entered the kitchen, the small space full of the odour of empty pizza boxes stacked on the worktop. He splashed his face with water from the sink, scratched his sprouting beard, and got another beer. After uncapping it, he went to stand by the window, opening it a foot or so to let in air as he drank.

There was only a slight bite to the night air, and aside from the odd light and the flickering of televisions in some of the windows, most of the surrounding houses were in darkness. Orange streetlights lined the road, and Glen found himself scrutinising the pitch-black patches between them. Every leaf that swayed in the breeze set the hairs on the back of his neck prickling.

He stretched his throbbing knee as he continued to scan the darkness, his breath coming uneasily. After the trail of chaos they had left behind that afternoon, he wished they had gotten as far away from Reading as possible. But with the state of his stupid knee, he wasn't even sure if he could manage the drive to Windsor the following morning.

Shivering – from nerves rather than cold – Glen pulled the window shut and turned his back on it. But as he stepped away, a horrendous crack overpowered his senses. He froze as the glass smashed, shards piercing his head and back.

Glen was falling. As he went, he caught a glimpse of Phaedra rolling onto her back, legs and arms splayed like a spider. And then he was on the floor, his bottle spinning away and spurting beer everywhere. Glass cut into his hands and forearms, and he lay sprawled, winded and bleeding as he tried to gather his jumbled thoughts into coherence. Seconds later, dark shadows leaped into the room.

Phaedra was screaming. Glen finally got to his feet to see her kicking and bucking as two men held her, and he lunged over the sofa for his gun. But someone grabbed his torn T-shirt, pulling him back, the collar choking him. The intruder made the mistake of letting go, and Glen whirled on him, the momentum of his turn making for a cracking punch. But as the man went down, two others took his place, guns poised.

Before he could move, a blast pierced his eardrums and collided with him, knocking the breath from his lungs. He staggered back against the sofa, clutching his chest, unable to make sense of the pain pulsing through him, nor the hot, wet blood gushing from a hole in the centre of his T-shirt. He sank to his knees, blood flowing down his front faster than he had ever imagined.

The second man aimed his gun at Glen's head. He lifted his bloody hand instinctively, whether in a pointless attempt to shield himself or to knock it away, he didn't know.

Phaedra was screaming. The sound was distant over the rushing in his ears, but she was screaming.

And then, just as the man before him cocked the gun, the world shattered.

Chapter Fifteen

PHAEDRA RONAN

Curls of shadow drifted at the edges of her blurred vision, gradually dissipating in corners and escaping into the night. Her chest and limbs hurt, raw and hollow after the force that had just torn through them, and her own sniffles and ragged breathing were the only sounds in the darkness.

Phaedra was afraid, and she was alone.

The telephone receiver that she held to her ear was silent, and she punched the emergency number into the keypad again, leaving behind bloody thumbprints. But no dial tone sounded, the landline caught up in her blast that had taken out a wall and half the roof. Stifling a sob, she let it slip from her trembling fingers, dropping to Glen's side and pressing the soaked towel firmly to his chest again. The hot red flow of his blood had slowed, but showed no signs of stopping.

She dragged the hem of her T-shirt over her face, scrubbing away tears and dust. She hated to look at what she had done to him, but if he somehow survived, then almost killing him would be what saved his life.

Glen murmured something incoherent, eyes roaming beneath his eyelids, and she gave another pathetic sob. "I'm sorry, Glen," she whimpered, pressing both hands to the towel, wondering if she ought to get another one, if there was any point. And it wasn't just the bullet wound. Blood seeped from his ears and nose too, and his head was cut from where debris had rained down on him.

She ought to get help, but she was too terrified to leave him. But surely it was only a matter of time before someone came looking? People weren't likely to ignore what sounded like a bomb going off in the middle of the night.

She tried not to look at the shattered corpses around her, at the remains of the lives she had taken, covered in brick dust and plaster from the blast. She had never killed before. And even though it had been an accident, even though they had shot Glen and probably would have killed her too if they had been ordered to, nausea and self-hatred roiled her stomach, her murderous Talent tingling beneath her skin. She knew Glen had only survived because he had been on the floor, the sofa between them taking the worst of the blast.

Glen mumbled again, which turned into a groan. His face crumpled as his hand lifted towards his chest, then flopped down halfway. His eyelids flickered open, and Phaedra's heart sped up in hope until his eyes rolled back into his head and shut again. The towel she held to him was saturated, a trickle of blood escaping to run down his side onto the carpet.

She hauled herself to her feet, tripping over something as she ran to the bathroom and not daring to look down to see what it was. She brought back more towels, folding one tightly before dumping the soaked one on the floor and pressing the new one to the wound as quickly as she could. She wished she had taken a first aid course. Wished she knew what to do for him other than pressing the towel down as firmly as possible, her hands shaking.

Seconds trickled by, and Glen began to shiver. She had to do something. Anything. She couldn't just sit there. She looked around, registering the cold for the first time, drifting in through the blast in the roof. It was then that she also noticed the glow of headlights beyond the shattered windows, and the knot in her gut tightened when she heard the crunch of footsteps approaching the building.

"Hello? It's the police," came the sound of a woman's voice. "Anyone inside? Anyone hurt?"

The *police*. After all that, they were going to capture her anyway, to do what, she dreaded to think. She looked down at Glen. All colour had leached from his skin, and a slick sheen of sweat coated his face and neck. Perhaps she could make a bargain. She would beg them to help him, in exchange for her going quietly.

Phaedra crouched lower as feet stomped up the front steps, making herself as small as she could, watching the door, waiting to see who would walk through it.

"Anyone there?" came another voice, male this time. "We're coming in, stand back from the door." There was a pause, then Phaedra flinched as the door was kicked in. Two people entered, half squatted in defensive positions, aiming guns and shining torches through the small open-plan space. They spotted her immediately, the torches blinding her, but they lowered them quickly, instead illuminating the distorted heaps of body parts on the floor. Phaedra tried not to look at the grisly state of the corpses, guilt and nausea attacking her again.

The woman approached first, casting a professional eye over Glen and Phaedra, while her companion focused his torch on the surrounding bodies, occasionally nudging one of them with his foot, before he strode to the bedrooms and bathroom to peer inside. "All clear," he confirmed, returning to the living room.

Phaedra squinted in the harsh torch light, gradually piecing together the strangers' features. As the woman knelt beside her, Phaedra took in a blonde braid coiled beneath a flat cap, large brown eyes scrutinising her. Not police, Phaedra realised with a jolt. And with another jolt, she recognised the woman at her side as Lindsey Matheson, her father's Head Tracer – now Alessia's.

"I'll come with you," Phaedra stammered, panic flooding her. After all that, all they had done and risked, Alessia's Tracers had still found her. "Just… just please, help him."

But Lindsey was already leaning over Glen. She checked his pulse, opened one of his eyelids, then lifted the corner of the towel to examine the wound beneath. Phaedra lifted the towel further, letting her look.

"How long has he been like this?" Lindsey's tone was brusque as she shrugged off a backpack and began rummaging through it.

"I—I don't know." Why would Lindsey even care? "Five minutes? Ten?"

The Tracer nodded. "Bullet wound?"

"Yes."

Lindsey extracted what looked like medical implements from her bag, her movements fast as she injected Glen's wound with an unknown substance, then lay some kind of dressing over it.

"What are you doing?" Phaedra blurted.

"It's to slow the bleeding." Lindsey lowered the towel back over the wound, then lifted a phone to her mouth. Warding sigils glistened against the black casing. "Target Little Dragon located. The companion is injured, bullet wound to the upper abdomen. Send ambulance."

Phaedra trembled, the words reaching her through a hazy fog. Were they actually taking her up on her request to help Glen, or was this all some nasty trick?

"Seth? Fetch a blanket from the bedroom, will you?" Lindsey glanced at her companion, then back at Phaedra. "Keep that towel firmly against the wound." Phaedra obeyed, pressing the towel even harder against Glen's chest.

Seth came back, spreading the quilt over Glen, then tucking it into his sides.

"We need to keep him warm until the ambulance arrives," Lindsey clarified, her voice as cool and commanding as ever. She then stood up, peering through the shattered window as she gave further instructions over the phone, half the words coded and making no sense to Phaedra.

"What happened to the others?" the one called Seth asked, standing some feet away as he examined the floor. His hair was dark beneath his cap, black eyes glittering in the torchlight.

Phaedra lowered her gaze to her knees to avoid looking at the destruction around her, tears stinging her itchy eyes. "My Talent… We… we couldn't get sedatives."

Lindsey came back then, casting her narrowed gaze over Phaedra and Glen. "I'll make you a hot drink."

Minutes passed like a whirlwind. By the time Lindsey was wrapping her in another blanket and pressing a cup of hot sweet tea into her hands, the ambulance had arrived, and paramedics relieved her of her towel-pressing duty. She wondered if they were going to the hospital they had escaped from earlier. She didn't doubt the Mason soldiers had reported them, pointing the Tracers in the right direction.

Clutching her cup and blanket close, she watched anxiously as they loaded Glen onto a stretcher, then out of the destroyed bungalow and into the back of an ambulance. Lindsey tried to steer her towards an inconspicuous black car.

"No, I want to be with him!" She backed away from Lindsey, who only nodded, watching as she climbed into the ambulance with Glen's prone body, then shutting the door behind her. After squeezing herself into a fold-down seat in the corner, Phaedra's hands trembled around her cup as the pair of paramedics set to work, injecting Glen with more unknown substances and hooking him up to an IV.

"Boss said you need a sedative," said one of the paramedics once a machine linked up to Glen was beeping rhythmically, and the ambulance was well on the way to wherever it was taking them. The man was older, well into his forties, with grey hair and stubble peppering his narrow face.

Phaedra nodded, holding her near-empty cup tightly. Her darkness was dormant now, spent after exploding from her so viciously, but it was only a matter of time before it recovered and started plaguing her again. "My Talent…"

The paramedic reached for a syringe and a vial of clear liquid. "I can give you a small dose of Veto to take the edge off. It might make you sleepy."

She shivered, inspecting the measure he extracted into the syringe. It would be so easy for him to give her a higher dose and knock her out until they got to Scotland, by which time, who knew what would become of Glen. She hesitated as he approached, eyeing the dose, searching the paramedic's face for any sign she shouldn't trust him. But as she debated, her darkness crept under her skin, sluggish, but still very present. She withdrew her arm from beneath the blanket, offering him the crook of her elbow. Despite his gentleness, the needle stung, but her trembling settled instantly, as did her racing pulse.

"The doctor will examine you and prescribe sedatives," he informed her, taking a seat near Glen. The ambulance tilted as they rounded a corner, and Phaedra gulped down the last of her tea, the sugar like grainy syrup at the bottom of the cup.

The drive felt long, longer than it should have to get to the hospital. Phaedra agonised over Glen's safety, but he didn't mumble or moan now, and his face and body were completely relaxed on the stretcher. Whatever they had given him had sent him into a deep sleep.

"Will he be okay?" Phaedra finally dared to ask, looking at the two paramedics.

The other man, with light shining on his bald patch, tilted his head, studying Glen. "If we can keep him stable until we can get him to a Healer, then yes."

A tentative hope rose in her chest. "How long will that take?"

But the paramedics didn't reply, and despite the Veto spreading its comforting numbness through her limbs, fear quashed the seed of hope. A moment later, the ambulance stopped. Phaedra was all too aware of her ragged breath and the eerie beep of the machine in the sudden silence. Footsteps and voices drifted from outside, too quiet to make out words, and the tension in her chest rose as seconds slipped by without an explanation. Then the doors were flung open, revealing Lindsey and Seth illuminated in the harsh ambulance light. Beyond them, Phaedra could see only blackness.

Seth sprang into the van, and he and the paramedics started to unload Glen's stretcher. Phaedra jumped to her feet, her blanket slipping to the floor. "What are you doing?"

"We can't take him to the hospital." Lindsey's smooth voice pierced the panic and Veto fogging her mind. "I'm sending you through a portal." She reached out a slender hand, but Phaedra didn't budge.

"Please don't hurt him," she cried, tears welling. She glanced around, her sight adjusting to the night blindness. They were on a dark country road, the golden lights of a town twinkling in the distance. Beyond Lindsey, a wide salt circle and four chunks of quartz glimmered in the ambulance light. Were they just going to dump Glen in a field and drag her through the portal? "Take me to my sister, but save him, please. He was just trying to help me."

"Phaedra," Lindsey said firmly, stepping into the van and grabbing hold of her shoulders, "we're not taking you to your sister."

Phaedra stared, shrinking beneath Lindsey's fierce gaze. She had barely spoken to the Matheson siblings whenever they met at family events, the age gap between them too great. Lindsey had always been aloof, but her younger brother, Cameron, had been friendly. "Then where—?"

"Somewhere safe," Lindsey promised, squeezing her shoulders. "Now let's go. We're wasting time and Farraday needs urgent surgery."

Phaedra breathed a shaky sigh, barely daring to believe her. But she was right, Glen needed help. With a glance back at his unconscious form, Phaedra let Lindsey guide her out of the ambulance, then across the tarmac to the portal. Behind them, the three men laboured to get Glen out.

"Go with Seth and the others," Lindsey urged, pressing a comforting hand between her shoulder blades.

"What about you?" Phaedra asked.

Lindsey's face was dark beneath her cap. "I need to clear up the portal and cover our tracks."

She nodded, looking down at Glen on the stretcher, then taking hold of his limp hand. His burnt skin was rough beneath her fingers.

"On three," said Seth, hefting the stretcher as he backed towards the salt circle. "One, two, three!"

Phaedra's feet moved automatically as they stepped into the circle, the dark road and surrounding fields vanishing, replaced by buttery light that made her blink.

Looking around, she could see she was in a garage, and an open door to her left was the source of the light. A curvy body stood silhouetted in the doorframe. As the person's face came into focus, Phaedra cried out, recognising Roxanne Summers. She ran out of the connecting salt circle, flinging her arms around the woman.

"It's okay, you're safe now," Roxanne soothed, stroking her uneven hair. It was only then that Phaedra realised she was sobbing. "Go inside. We need to help the patient."

Phaedra glanced back to see the three men approaching with Glen. She did as she was told and went indoors, finding herself in a bright, cheerful and pristine kitchen. Opposite, a young blonde woman stood in the doorway, her round face wary as she looked Phaedra up and down.

"Come and sit in the living room," said the stranger, a cardigan wrapped tightly around her. She was wearing pink gingham pyjamas underneath. "Mum is going to work in here, it could be messy."

Phaedra glanced around, and sure enough, the table in the centre of the room had paper laid out on it, and surgical tools sat in neat rows near the sink. It was then that it dawned on her, a detail she had forgotten in her panic: Roxanne was a surgeon, and a Healer.

So she obeyed, lingering long enough to see Roxanne guiding the paramedics through the narrow doorway, instructing them to place Glen on the table. When she saw them set him down, she followed the other woman, who was clearly Roxanne's daughter.

Phaedra took in her surroundings as she went, assuming she was in Roxanne's house. It was homely like the kitchen, with little knick-knacks and ornaments, the smell of floral scented candles and diffusers filling the air. The living room that the woman led her into was more of the same, taken up by two cosy-looking sofas in white corduroy, piled with throws and cushions.

"Here, make yourself comfortable," said Roxanne's daughter, and after a moment's hesitation, Phaedra sank into the sofa. "Can I make you a hot drink? Tea? Coffee? …Hot chocolate?"

Phaedra stared around her, then back at the woman. She looked like her mother, with large blue eyes, a bright blonde bob, and soft round cheeks. But although she was smiling faintly, she didn't seem to have the easy, motherly kindness that Roxanne had.

"Um… hot chocolate sounds good, actually."

She nodded, her smile growing a little, but it didn't reach her eyes. "Coming right up. I'm Amber, by the way."

Phaedra nodded. It was a pretty name. "Nice to meet you, Amber. I'm Phaedra."

Chapter Sixteen

AMBER SUMMERS

Roxanne removed the bullet and stitched up the man's wounds in just over half an hour, her powerful Talent seeking out and healing the damage that medical implements couldn't touch. Amber hovered between the kitchen and the living room in anxious anticipation, her heartbeat racing from the late-night interruption to their routine. Her mother hadn't wanted to disturb her, but when Amber awoke to the sounds of running water and Roxanne rushing up and down the stairs, she found her fully dressed and frantically setting up the kitchen for surgery, mumbling about Resistance members needing urgent help.

The paramedics remained on hand to move the injured stranger upstairs to Roxanne's bedroom, leaving him linked up to Veto and a blood transfusion. Roxanne said she would share Amber's bed, but in the end she spent the night between her patient's side and the sofa, checking he was recovering.

As for the girl, Amber made up the guest room for her, trying not to think of how Cameron had been the last person to sleep in that bed, trying not to look at the few mundane things he had left behind: toiletries on a shelf and a pair of trainers beneath the bed, a T-shirt peeking out from the wardrobe door left slightly ajar, and a wonky origami sparrow on the nightstand.

She failed in her resolve not to let Cameron's loss come bubbling back as the sparrow caught her eye, and she picked it up, smoothing out the bent wing, the sunshine yellow paper bright in her pale hand. The dull ache in her chest sharpened, and she tucked the bird into the pocket of her cardigan – a small relic that couldn't begin to fill the space her friend had left behind.

It was strange to remember how unhappy she had been that her mother had invited an enemy into their house. She had grown to care for that enemy, even thought of him as family. But now Roxanne had invited in two more, and Amber trusted the Ronan girl much less than she had trusted Cameron.

The girl was young, terrified, and looked like she had been to hell and back, but Amber found it hard to feel sorry for her, even if she had been working for the Resistance. But she did her best to be kind, gently nudging her awake when she went back downstairs and found her fast asleep on the sofa. The hot chocolate was half drunk and tilting dangerously in her hand.

"But Glen—" Phaedra started. She jumped up and took a staggering step towards the kitchen.

"He's going to be fine," said Amber, taking the mug from her and placing it on the coffee table. "He'll probably be awake by morning."

The girl – Phaedra, she had called herself – studied her with bleary eyes, then nodded.

"You need sleep. The guest room is this way." She led her upstairs, showed her where the bathroom was, and gave her clean towels, "to wash off that blood". She then left her to it, closing her bedroom door firmly and falling into bed.

She slept, but restlessly, eventually waking and realising her mother hadn't come to bed. Rubbing her eyes, she checked the time to see it was still a couple of hours shy of dawn, then drew on her dressing gown and made her way downstairs to check on her mother.

Roxanne was lying on the sofa. Amber was going to tell her to come to bed, but when she saw she was fast asleep, she took a throw from the basket in the corner and turned to lay it over her mother. But Roxanne stirred, and sat up when she saw Amber. She took the quilt anyway, wrapping it around herself.

"What time is it?" she asked, stifling a yawn.

"About four." Amber curled up on the other sofa opposite. "You should come to bed. You said yourself, he's stable, he just needs rest now."

Roxanne nodded, but made no move to follow Amber's suggestion. "I was just… trying to decide what to do. I must have fallen asleep."

"And what are you going to do?" Amber tried to sound gentle, but the words came out more accusatory than she meant. On top of everything going on – Cameron's passing, the recent battle, the brewing war, the Resistance meetings and long shifts seeing to sick and wounded – Roxanne really didn't need the responsibility of harbouring two fugitives.

Roxanne brought her knees up to her chest, pulling the quilt closer around herself. There was no heating on, not for another hour yet when the timer kicked in. "We'll keep them here until he's fully recovered."

Amber nodded, pulling a quilt over herself too, toying with the plaid edge. It felt too soon after Cameron to have the house full again, to have someone sleeping in his bed. Even if she felt sorry for the girl, she didn't want her there. The sooner they left, the better. Her Trace tugged at her as the Nox crossed her mind, and fear rose in her chest at the thought of Alessia Ronan somehow tracking them to their home.

"Amber..." Roxanne said after a moment. "There's something I need to tell you."

Amber looked up at her mother, suddenly alert. If she was choosing the early hours of the morning to tell her, when they were both exhausted and supposed to be asleep, it had to be something big.

"It's about your father. I... I saw him a few days ago."

Amber raised her eyebrows. Aside from gifts for birthdays and Solstice, all tagged with a simple "love from Dad", her father was a resented stranger to her. She didn't even know his name, and as far as she was aware, Roxanne only communicated with him when absolutely necessary.

She stared at her mother, waiting for her to continue. Roxanne took a deep breath.

"I should have told you who he was a long time ago. But... he was married. And... working for the Ronans."

Amber's stomach gave a painful twist. She had known about the married part. Roxanne had told her when she was around fourteen, when she had demanded to know why she had never met him. She had stopped asking questions after that, too upset by the knowledge that she was the product of an extramarital affair. An accident, an inconvenience, at least as far as her father was concerned. But the fact that he was working for the Ronans... she grew cold.

"Why would you go near someone like that?" she asked, unable to imagine it. Her mother, and someone aligned with the Ronans? It went against everything Roxanne believed in, everything she had taught her.

"We met at school, long before he worked for them. We were friends."

Amber sank back into the sofa, her mother's words softening the blow a little. "Why did he get involved with them?"

Roxanne shrugged, her face a mask of despair. "His wife's family are loyal Ronan supporters."

Amber shook her head, unable to comprehend it, unable to get her head around the logistics of it all.

"There's something else," said Roxanne, and she began to cry, wiping her tears with her sleeve. It took her back to Roxanne's desolate grief after Cameron's death, and the sight tore at Amber's insides, sending her heartbeat into an anxious frenzy.

"What is it?" she asked when the seconds dragged on without an answer.

"He… I… I should have told you…" She was crying in earnest now, fishing in her pocket for a tissue. "Amber… he's Cameron's dad."

She could only stare at her mother, stare while the words took a moment to reach her, while she took another moment to make sense of them. Her father was Cameron's dad. Which meant that Cameron… Cameron was…

She was on her feet before she even realised she had jumped up, the quilt sliding to the carpet. She stared at her mother, chest suddenly tight, hands curled into fists. "Why… why didn't you…" she stammered, unable to put into words what she wanted to say. "You didn't tell me," she said finally. "You didn't tell me he was my… he was my…"

"I wanted to." Roxanne dabbed her eyes with the now soggy tissue. "I should have. I just didn't know how."

"How? What do you mean, how? How could you not tell me he was my *brother*?"

Roxanne flinched. Amber's voice was almost a shout in the quiet house.

"All this time, all this time he was here, under our roof, and you *knew*, you knew he was my brother and you didn't say a thing. How could you not tell me?"

"I couldn't. I was so scared he would go back to his mother. I can't risk her knowing who you are."

"I don't care about his mother," she snarled, and Roxanne flinched again. They had never fought, not like this. "I care about the fact that I didn't know he was my brother and now it's too late, because he's *dead.*"

Roxanne only whimpered into the wet tissue, rubbing at her cheeks with her hand. "I'm so sorry Amber, I'm so sorry..."

"Don't." Amber turned away, crossing her arms. Cameron was her brother, and now he was dead. It was bad enough that she had lost a friend, but her *brother...* Questions crammed her head, questions she didn't know how to ask, and would she even want to know the answer to some of them?

"I wanted to tell you," Roxanne was saying, fighting to suppress the sobs. "So many times, I tried to pluck up the courage, or find the right time. But if I told you I would have had to tell Cameron, and that wasn't just my decision to tell him something like that. Your father, he... well... he wants to meet you."

But Amber shook her head, hugging herself while her breath came with increasing difficulty. It was too much. Cameron being her brother, her father wanting to meet her, her mother's lies, it was all too much on top of the grief and the stress. She was so caught up in the panic that she didn't know Roxanne had gotten up until she felt her hand on her back, pulling her in to try to embrace her. But Amber pushed her away. "No!" she shouted in her face, making Roxanne shrink back. And before she could think anything through, she fled, needing to be alone with her shocked and jumbled thoughts.

Chapter Seventeen

SKYE BOLTON

There was no use trying to break her father out. She had known that as soon as she found out who was holding him. Camilla was expecting her, and had probably set up a trap. So instead of a breakout, she accepted the older woman's invitation for "a little chat", as Camilla called it, once she finally tracked her down.

She didn't bother to ask for Caplin's permission, not after their last argument. As far as Skye was concerned, her father's imprisonment was a personal affair, not a political one. Dean didn't try to argue with her either, which meant he knew they had no other option. Instead, he just came with her, knowing that what Skye needed right then was his support, not an earful.

So they waited. Moors stretched wide in every direction, with few trees and shrubs dotting the landscape surrounding the small hill where they stood. It was the perfect place to keep a high security prisoner, with nowhere for an escapee to hide, nowhere for a rescue team to conceal themselves, not without using glamours and the risk of tripping the wards around the place.

Before them was a crumbling manor, one wing already uninhabitable, while the other was half-obscured by scaffolding. Roswell Manor, the old seat of Dean's family, the same family who had disinherited his mother when she became pregnant with a commoner's bastard. The manor had fallen into ruin long before Camilla's years in prison, and it seemed she hadn't bothered to return after her release. Until now.

Skye stared hard at the manor, her telepathy unable to bypass the wards. She wondered where in the building her father was being kept – if he was even there at all, or if it was just another of Camilla's tricks. Did he know she was there, so close? Her entire body was screaming at her to run over there and fight her way to him, but the voice of reason reminded her again and again that it would be a suicide mission.

As if he knew what was going through her mind, Dean reached out and wrapped his arm around her shoulders. "Perhaps she'll offer us a deal."

Skye met his gaze, concern narrowing his warm brown eyes. Taking a deep breath, she leaned into him, his solid warmth softening some of her tension. He had accepted her mumbled apology for her recent behaviour, but the atmosphere between them was still far from the placid companionship they had enjoyed in simpler times. After a moment, she glanced back at the manor, a grim smile curving her lips. "Perhaps, but whatever deal she might try to make with us, I doubt we'll like it."

As she finished speaking, movement caught her eye at the manor. A door opened, and several small figures emerged. Skye reached out mentally, recognising Camilla's mind, obscured as always. Her companions' minds were also hidden by obsidian, probably bodyguards. The woman wasn't stupid. She knew Skye could snap her neck with her strength alone, never mind her Talent. Skye straightened, and Dean let his arm drop as they watched the figures saunter across the distance between them. She had chosen to wait for Camilla well away from the house, refusing to give her the opportunity to trap them. An active portal was already waiting behind them, ready to jump through at a moment's notice should things not go well.

Camilla was sporting a sickly smile long before she was close enough to speak. Skye stood her ground, looking down at her from the little hill she had chosen, her hands curled into fists. She didn't return the smile when Camilla finally drew level with her and Dean, stopping some ten feet away. Skye spared a glance at the men either side of her, and her stomach churned when she recognised Jenkins, the heavyset warden who had been at Blackwater, the man who had set her on fire at Matheson's orders. Skye fought the shudder that threatened to course through her, the tight scars on her back tingling at the memory of the fire that had seared across her skin. Instead, she kept on her mask of icy rage as she looked at Camilla's other companion. She didn't recognise him, but he was older than Camilla, with slicked-back greying hair and a carefully trimmed moustache. He was dressed in a suit, but he had the air of a servant. Perhaps he was her butler.

"It's awfully windy out here for our little gathering, Skye," Camilla simpered by way of greeting, and Skye's eyes snapped back to her. She was dressed in that long, purple coat Skye had seen her wear before, paired with knee-high black boots that had probably not been the most comfortable footwear for walking through the moors in. "Won't you come inside for a hot cup of tea? Or how about a proper drink?"

Skye said nothing, refusing to move. At her side, Dean remained as still as she was. Camilla's eyes fell on him then, and her smile widened, waxy red lipstick stark on her skull-like face.

"How nice of you to bring your handsome brother. It's good to meet you at last, nephew."

Skye's nails cut into her palms. "You don't speak to him." Thank goodness he had no blood of hers, that the relation was only through marriage – a failed marriage to an uncle that Dean had never met.

Camilla laughed. "Well, at least I can look at him." And she did, her gaze roving up and down, slowly. Dean only glared back at her, his thoughts full of discomfort. "I've brought a surprise for you too," she said, gesturing to Jenkins, "I thought it would be nice for you to see an… old friend."

Beside her, Dean's imagination ran riot as he tried to figure out who Jenkins was, what part he had played in Skye's past. Camilla's next words brought his thoughts close to the truth. "He's missed you since you left Blackwater."

Skye refused to look at him again. "Just say what you have to say." It was an effort not to snarl.

Camilla only grinned. "At least let us have refreshments. If you won't come in for them, we'll have them here." She turned to the man in the suit. "Tony, would you be so kind?"

"Yes, madam." With a wave of his hand, a decoratively wrought iron table and matching chairs appeared, covered with a tablecloth and laden with food and drink. Skye raised an eyebrow. Whoever this Tony was, he had a rare and useful Talent.

"Take a seat," said Camilla as Tony pulled out a chair for her, and she settled herself in it as he poured whiskey from a crystal decanter. He then stepped back, level with Jenkins, who also remained standing. There were three chairs. After a moment's hesitation, Skye met Dean's gaze.

What do you think?

Dean glanced at the table. *Why not? Just don't touch the food. Or the drink for that matter.*

Skye resisted the urge to roll her eyes, pulling out the metal chair and sitting down. Dean did the same.

"Pour them both a whiskey," Camilla ordered Tony, who obliged. Static tingled in Skye's fists as he leaned over the table to pour their drinks. "Only the best for dear Skye. It's Ronan's vintage, I still have a couple of barrels left."

Skye studied the glass and the decanter, then looked at Camilla's glass. *Do we trust her, if she's drinking from the same decanter?*

Dean was also going through the possibilities. Eventually, he replied, *Wait until she drinks.*

Camilla raised her glass in a toast. "To start with, here's to you, darling. Congratulations on being the Lux."

Skye reached out for her glass, twisting it absently. "Personally, I don't find that something to celebrate." She lifted the glass anyway, tilting it as she studied the liquid inside. "But it would be a shame to let good whiskey go to waste. So yes, here's to me, long live the Lux."

Camilla gave her a coy, close-lipped smile as she touched her glass to Skye's, then to Dean's as he reluctantly lifted his. It was clear that Camilla knew they were waiting for her to drink first, so she downed the glass, smacking her lips when she was done and signalling to Tony for a refill. Tentatively, Skye and Dean both took a sip, then set down their glasses.

Not bad, thought Dean. *I can see why the Ronans got you drunk so often.*

Skye pressed her lips together as she leaned back in the chair. She studied Camilla, smoothing her features into a mask of arrogance and vague amusement while she waited to hear her out. The obsidian pendant that was keeping Skye out of Camilla's mind was large and cut into a faceted oval, set in a ring of diamonds. Very Camilla.

"Well, Skye," Camilla finally said, lighting a cigarette from a tacky gold case and offering them one, which they both refused with a brief shake of their heads. "Clearly you've figured out that your father is my guest here."

"A little bird might have told me," said Skye, swirling the whiskey in her glass and resisting the urge to glance at the manor behind Camilla.

Camilla gave a small laugh. "And tell me, did the little bird tweet of its own accord, or did it take some… persuasion?"

"Oh, the little bird didn't have to tweet at all. But it had quite a headache after I was through with it."

"Poor little bird," said Camilla, although she didn't look very sorry at all. She took a long drag of her cigarette, then exhaled the smoke as she surveyed Skye. "Back to the matter at hand. I have your father, and you want him back."

Skye held her hateful gaze as she sipped the whiskey, barely tasting it.

"I get the impression you don't hold much sway with Caplin. Even the *oh so persuasive* Victor Bolton seems to struggle to convince him to do anything nowadays, unless it was Caplin's idea to begin with. So I won't bother asking you to talk him around." She took a puff of her cigarette, watching Skye, the smile gone from her face. "But that doesn't mean you're not useful where Caplin is concerned. You might not be able to sway him, but you can certainly kill him."

Skye raised an eyebrow. "I got myself captured, tortured and left to rot in a cell for Caplin's sake. Why would I kill him now?"

Camilla lounged in her seat, then reached forward to bring the glass to her lips with the same hand that still held her cigarette. She didn't speak until she had set the glass back down again. "Was he worth it?"

She wasn't sure if the rage that came bubbling to the surface was real or influenced by Camilla's Talent. For it was the question she had been unable to find the answer to. Was Caplin worth it? Was he worth the pain and the fear and the torture, was he worth everyone's sacrifice? Did Darius die for a good cause like he had believed?

Seeing that Skye had no answer, Camilla carried on. "Think about it. Alessia Ronan is the Nox. The Resistance want a democracy. And you lot want your power back, to the point where you're willing to team up with those… democrats." She wrinkled her nose in distaste. "Say you're successful in your Lux duties and you defeat Alessia. Whatever alliances and promises Caplin has made with the Resistance, he will break them, and things will go back to how they were before. But if he dies… who do you think his followers will rally behind?"

Skye drained her glass, then poured herself another measure before Camilla could signal Tony. She poured some for Dean too. After setting the decanter back on the table, she took a sip before answering. "You think his people would follow me after I murder him?"

Camilla's lips curved. "They will if they hate him enough to want him dead."

Skye, be careful, Dean thought at her side, although he had been silently questioning his own loyalty to Caplin with increasing frequency. And then there were their comrades. Sabine's feelings towards Caplin were clear, while Jacob, Lorcan and Ikarus were open to the idea of Skye taking Caplin's place, even actively encouraged it. But Aunt Alma had warned them against openly opposing Caplin when the political situation with the Resistance was already precarious.

"And what's in it for you?" Skye asked, fixing Camilla with her glare.

Camilla's smile grew as she sucked her cigarette. "With Caplin dead, we have one less enemy. One less pain in the arse sticking his oar in everywhere. If the Nox outlives you, she can continue her work with less opposition. If you end her, and you Boltons come to power, I would rather see Victor as president. Your father is… easier to manipulate."

Skye frowned. "Don't—"

"I mean he has more to lose. Caplin doesn't give a shit about anyone or anything except himself."

She mulled over Camilla's words, as Dean was doing beside her. Killing Caplin went against everything she had worked her entire career for. What was more, as his Guardian, she would be breaking the oath she had taken to protect him. But his behaviour in the months since they helped him escape from Blackwater, and his reluctance to help her save her father had her questioning whether he really was the sort of man she wanted to lay down her life for, and the lives of others she cared about.

"If I kill Caplin, or arrange for his death by other means, my father will go free?"

Camilla's lips were still curled, her eyes never leaving Skye's. "As soon as Caplin is dead, Victor goes free. Or if you deliver him to us so we can finish the job. Either way, you and yours must do all the work. Caplin is hard for us to get to, but if we happen to beat you to it, you'll have to figure out a new bargain."

Skye settled back in her chair again, crossing her legs and resting the glass of whiskey on her knee.

Don't rush into anything, came Dean's thoughts, and she resisted the urge to shoot him an irritated look.

You don't have to tell me that. "How long will you give me to think it over?"

Camilla shrugged. "As long as you like. Either way, your father stays here until my conditions are met." She cocked her head, glancing from Skye to Dean, then back again. "And if anyone tries to get him out, I will kill your father myself. You know I don't give empty threats."

Skye didn't doubt her for a moment. Not with her history. She took another drink, emptying the glass, and when Camilla signalled to Tony to refill it, she waved him away. "How is he, by the way?"

"Your father?" A slow, sick grin spread across her lips, making Skye's stomach churn. "He doesn't take well to imprisonment, put it that way."

Skye willed herself to remain calm, but it took all her strength to stop her from lunging over that table and killing Camilla there and then. But no doubt there were people in that manor who had orders to kill her father if she touched a hair on Camilla's head.

"I can well imagine what you've been doing to him." She uncrossed her legs and braced her elbows on the table, staring Camilla down. "And I have no doubt you've delighted in whatever hurt you have inflicted. But from now on, any torture or mistreatment stops. You won't lay another finger on him, and nor will your cronies. And when he is freed, if I discover that he is scarred or maimed or at death's door, I will hunt you down, and I will return the favour. An eye for an eye." She leaned back, crossing her legs again. "You know I don't make empty threats either."

Despite her words, Camilla remained as unflinching as ever, not that Skye was surprised. "Your demands aren't too steep. You have my word."

"Your word means shit. Before I agree to assassinate Caplin, I want proof my father is still alive."

Camilla cocked her head again, her face an infuriating mask. "What proof do you require, darling Skye?"

"I want to see him. Now." Her heartbeat thundered in her tight chest, and she tried not to get her hopes up that she might speak to him, hold his hand…

"Tony," Camilla called in her saccharine voice. "Take off your obsidian charm and let the Lux take a peek into your mind."

Without a word, the butler removed the shiny black signet ring from his third finger and placed it on the table.

Skye dived straight for his memories, sifting through meaningless ones until she found her father – weak, in pain, barely able to swallow the watery soup Tony had brought him. The sight of him in such a state clawed her insides, and she could already feel the lump rising in her throat as she took in his face – dirt and bruises and matted beard – and how his bloodied clothing hung loose on his bonier frame. But she examined the memory carefully, checking how recent it was, searching for others and piecing a timeline together. She eyed Camilla suspiciously when she came back to her body, but if this was the only proof she was going to get, she supposed it was better than nothing.

Camilla raised a thin, pencilled eyebrow. "Satisfied?"

"Hardly." Skye swallowed down the tightness in her throat. "But I don't suppose you're letting me look in *your* mind."

She snickered, stubbing out her cigarette in an ornate ashtray. "And let you see all my secrets? I don't think so, sweetie."

Skye only gritted her teeth, but beside her, Dean spoke.

"If Skye agrees to your offer, how do we know it's not a trap? How do we know that word won't somehow reach Caplin, and he punishes her for treason?"

Camilla's eyes snapped to Dean again, and as before, her gaze roamed over him hungrily, lips puckering. "Ah, so he does speak… Your uncle was a handsome man, and you have a look of him. But he wasn't half as attractive as you are. Perhaps instead of asking your stepsister to assassinate Caplin, I should request a swap. Her father for you. How about that?" She looked back at Skye. "Won't you share your handsome stepbrother with me?"

Skye was on her feet in a flash, her chair clattering away behind her. But she took only a step before Dean grabbed her around her middle, pinning her arms to her sides and gripping her firmly to his chest. Static crackled as she struggled, but Camilla only laughed, languidly crossing her legs. Beside her, Tony was tense, while Jenkins had shifted into an offensive position, ready to fight.

"Uh oh, it seems I've hit a nerve…" Camilla lifted her whiskey glass to her lips, holding Skye's gaze as she drank. And it was then, as she fought against Dean's hold on her, that Skye recognised the artificial tinge to her fear and anger. Her fury flared in response to Camilla's empathic influence, and Skye bared her teeth, barely in control.

"Don't worry, Skye. I can see dear Dean is too high a price to pay. But if you fail to end Caplin, maybe I'll make Dean the contingency plan." She looked at Dean again, who was still holding Skye tightly, mentally trying to soothe her. "You might be surprised, Dean. Older women are more experienced, especially in the bedroom." She winked.

The vile woman's words made Skye want to throw up. Dean himself was inwardly cringing, but Camilla's influence finally slithered away. Skye stopped trying to prise herself from Dean's vice-like grip, and squeezed his arm in reassurance. *That will never happen, I swear to you. She won't make me choose between the two of you.*

Dean didn't reply as he pushed his own thoughts to the back of his head, finally releasing her.

"Well, it seems this meeting is over," said the woman, and indeed, the sky on the horizon was stained red with sunset, the moors becoming darker by the minute. "To answer your question, Dean, Skye is more useful to me alive and free, at least for the moment. You see, our dear president is new to the role, and while she may be the Nox, she has yet to reveal what her real intentions are. I was friends with her father and her grandfather. I knew I was in good standing with them. But with her? Let's just say I like a comfortable life, and I'm not sure I'll get that with her in charge. So until I've decided which side I'm going to back, the Lux is safe from me." She smiled at Skye, raising her glass to her and then emptying it.

Skye held her gaze. Camilla had revealed much more than she would have expected, but knowing what she knew about Camilla, it was just another form of manipulation. If she was even telling the truth. Regardless, Camilla had the upper hand, so Skye drew herself to her full height, her hands curling into fists again.

"I have as long as I like to decide?"

"As long as you like," she nodded, refilling the whiskey glass herself, "unless we get to him first. But given the circumstances, that will take time and resources I can't be arsed to waste."

Skye nodded. "Then I will think on your offer."

And before anything more could be said, she turned away, taking Dean's hand as she led him through the portal.

Chapter Eighteen

GLEN FARRADAY

He awoke in a cosy bedroom awash in dappled sunlight. It certainly wasn't a bedroom he recognised, full of muted pastel tones and floral designs. The bed he lay in was extremely comfortable, which was just as well, because his body was so heavy he felt like he was anchored to the mattress. There was a dull ache in his chest, which flared each time he breathed in, but other than that, he felt mostly numb, eyelids crusty with sleep. As his senses came further to, he heard muffled voices in the distance, and the clink and clang of dishes.

He lifted a hand to his face, rubbed at his eyes, then pulled away the heavy quilt to look at his bare chest. There, just to the left of his solar plexus, was an ugly dent. But aside from a red tinge to the tissue, the scar already looked years old. Either he had been out for a very, very long time, or someone very talented had healed him.

He remembered being shot. After that, everything was a blur. He was vaguely aware of Phaedra crying and talking to him, prodding him, but she was his last, muddled memory. The fact that he was alive meant he was safe, but had Phaedra made it out with him?

He pulled the quilt away, pushing himself up with a trembling arm. The world suddenly slanted, black stars popping in his vision. He panted, waiting for the stars to fade, then got to his feet.

And promptly fell to the floor.

The impact shot through his hip and elbow, floorboards shaking under his weight. He rolled onto his back, clutching his elbow and sucking in deep breaths, willing the throbbing to subside. Below, he heard the voices change to murmurs of alarm, quickly followed by chairs scraping back, and then rushing footsteps. Well, it wasn't going to be the most dignified return to the land of the living. At least he was wearing underpants.

Three figures burst into the room. He craned his neck, getting an upside-down view of two blonde women. To his infinite relief, Phaedra's peaky face peered at him from behind them.

"Uh oh," said one of the blondes, crouching over him. "You should have stayed in bed. Amber?" She gestured to the younger one, who sullenly approached to help her lift him into a sitting position. He blinked as he leaned against the side of the bed, then blushed. The older woman pressed a cool hand to his forehead, peering into his eyes expertly. She was very pretty, her blonde curls pulled back in a ponytail, her cheeks full and pink, her mouth a dainty rosebud. Glen stared at her, still somewhat dazed. All he could think was that he was practically naked in front of these women. Especially this pretty one.

"Are you hurt?" she asked, casting a look over his body and prompting Glen to pull his knees up to his chest.

"No, I'm fine," he said quickly, although his elbow and hip still throbbed, the pain nauseating. Then he remembered Phaedra. She hovered nervously in the doorway, wearing a knitted cream cardigan and a baby pink T-shirt that certainly weren't her style. "I wanted to know if you're alright."

"I'm fine." Phaedra smiled faintly, hugging herself, her face drawn with concern. "Roxanne healed you."

His gaze snapped back to the pretty woman, his breath catching as he saw her in a new light. So this was Roxanne. He had heard she wasn't the sort of person people expected to lead a Resistance, but *this*… She was even further from the severe matron he had imagined. "Th-thanks," he stuttered eventually, unable to find more eloquent words through the fog clouding his mind.

Roxanne smiled, and his heart fluttered. "Just doing my job," she said. "Now, let's help you back into bed. I'm afraid you're going to have to use some of those muscles of yours, you're too heavy for us to lift."

"Sure," he mumbled, still blushing furiously at his stupidity in ending up on the floor. Roxanne took his arm expertly in preparation to heave him up, looking at the other blonde, Amber, to do the same. Phaedra hopped from foot to foot, getting in the way, but they managed to help him enough for him to get his feet under him. His legs were trembling again by the time he was sitting on the edge of the bed, and Roxanne fluffed the pillows, then fetched another one to prop up behind him. Following her instruction, he scooted across the mattress until he was leaning against the pillows, and Roxanne pulled the bedspread over him and *tucked* him in, like he was a child. He didn't know where to look, what to do with his hands. Phaedra couldn't keep the smirk off her face.

"We'll get you some food." Roxanne straightened and studied him again, as though deciding whether they could leave him alone. "I'll let Phee tell you what happened." And with another pretty smile of hers, she and Amber left him alone with Phaedra.

The girl was watching him as though she were worried he might drop dead at any moment. The cardigan that she had most definitely borrowed from one of the other women was pulled tightly around her. After a moment, she perched on the far corner of the bed, like she would somehow hurt or disturb him if she came any closer.

"I'm sorry," she murmured.

Glen stared at her. "What for?"

"I..." She looked away, and Glen swore tears glazed her eyes. "I could have killed you."

He smiled. "Don't be daft. The bullet could have killed me. The explosion just knocked me out. No different to a well-placed punch really."

But Phaedra didn't return his smile. She was watching him, terror twisting her features. "You didn't see those soldiers. What I did to them."

Glen shrugged, but the movement pulled the skin on his chest taut, and he rubbed the scar to settle the twinge. But then her words registered, her guilt and fear hitting home. They had been her first kills. And before he could stop it, a memory surfaced, a memory that still felt as fresh as the day it happened: a gun in his trembling hands, a stranger bleeding out before him, the realisation that he had made a mistake echoing in his mind like a haunting mantra. His job had forced him to carry on, to push through the fear and self-disgust that overwhelmed him each time he picked up a gun after that, until the horrors he witnessed numbed him to it.

"My first kill was an accident too," he confessed, still running his fingers absently over the dent in his chest. "The guilt doesn't go away... but it does get easier to live with. Just keep reminding yourself they were planning to kill us, or capture us."

Phaedra nodded, staring at the floor, her hands balled into fists. And then she launched into the story, telling him what had happened from start to finish.

"I don't know what you want to do, but... Roxanne said my uncle escaped too and he's been looking for us. That's how Roxanne found out we were on the run. The Boltons have put him in a safe house, and he said I can live with him, if I want to. What about you? Will you come with us?"

Hateful jealousy twisted his gut at the revelation that Caspar had managed to contact Skye when Glen couldn't. As for the idea of living with him… it had been bad enough bumping into him in that huge castle, but *living* with him… "I don't know," he admitted, trying to smile for Phaedra's sake. "We'll cross that bridge when we come to it."

He was saved from further discussion about Caspar by Roxanne's return with a tray of food. Phaedra scuttled out of the way as Roxanne crossed the room, waiting for him to sit up a bit straighter before placing the tray in his lap.

"Chicken soup to help you get your strength back," she said with one of her pretty smiles, and Glen smiled back, the blush already warming his cheeks again.

"Thank you." He glanced down, taking in not just the soup, but also a generous piece of fresh crusty bread, a banana, and a large glass of fruit juice.

"It's nothing," she said, already heading back to the door. "I'll leave you with Phee." She shut the door behind her. When Glen looked at Phaedra, she was smirking again.

"What?" he asked innocently, ripping off some of the bread and dunking it in the soup. He ate it as she crossed the room and resumed her seat at the end of the bed. The soup tasted homemade, and it was heavenly.

"Oh, I'm just laughing at you, the way you're blushing at Roxanne like you're a schoolboy with a crush." She raised her eyebrows, grinning from ear to ear.

Glen frowned, but continued eating, his stomach growling appreciatively. "I was *not* blushing."

She laughed. "If only everyone were as smitten as you are, there wouldn't be a war."

Phaedra was right. He couldn't imagine Roxanne in politics, and definitely not in battle, or commanding armies, or giving orders. And yet she had. She managed a network of spies and had helped to orchestrate the siege at Ronan Manor, had apparently even been on the battlefield. He had always imagined Roxanne to be a cold, hard woman, not this bubbly and kind soul who had a floral bedroom and made chicken soup from scratch.

"I don't know how she's not married," he said, lowering his voice. "She's like the perfect woman."

Phaedra raised an eyebrow again, but this time she wasn't amused. "Probably because no one is good enough for her."

It was the wisest thing he had heard anyone say in a long time.

Chapter Nineteen

ALESSIA RONAN

"The Tracers and soldiers we sent to retrieve your sister have been found dead in a bungalow near Reading. It appears that someone possessing powerful Obscurus powers ended them."

General Pierce's voice was steady as he delivered the infuriating news, but he stood as far away as possible in the small parlour, close to the door, perhaps to slip out quickly in case she decided to turn her own *powerful Obscurus powers* on him. And considering the fury that simmered just below the surface, he was wise to fear her.

"My uncle probably caught up to them, then."

"Mr Marsden's team of Tracers confirmed Mr Ronan is now being sheltered by the Boltons, ma'am. There is no sign of him at the crime scene."

Ice entered her veins at the confirmation that her slippery eel of an uncle had indeed betrayed her. She gritted her teeth, fearing how many of her secrets he might be sharing with the Lux. As for the Obscurus attack, either her uncle had managed to throw the Tracers off the scent, or he wasn't the one who killed the soldiers.

"What about Phaedra?"

"Your sister and Farraday remain off the radar, and their bodies were not amongst the dead in the bungalow."

Alessia blinked, the only show of surprise she would allow. "When you say powerful Obscurus powers, to what extent do you mean?"

Pierce hesitated, his hands behind his back. "It was like an explosion, ma'am. Half the roof had caved in from the blast. The bodies were…"

Alessia raised an eyebrow. "Go on."

"They were… dismembered, ma'am. Even disintegrated in parts."

She clenched her jaw. Phaedra's work then. Caspar wouldn't be so sloppy. Clearly her sister wasn't taking her sedatives. "Keep searching for them. It's not safe for my sister to be on the loose with her lack of control over her Talent."

The general nodded, opening his mouth to assent, when there was a brisk knock at the door. Alessia paused, then called out to come in. One of Marsden's servants entered.

"The Seer is here to see you, Madam."

Through the doorway, Alessia spotted Vala standing just behind the man, blending into the dull greyness of the corridor in her drab clothing. Yet despite the lack of light, her eyes still shone an unnatural blue.

Alessia bowed her head to accept the new visitor, then looked back at Pierce. "You are dismissed, General."

He nodded, then saluted before leaving the room. The Seer swept in as Pierce disappeared from sight, crossing the parlour with a rustle that reminded Alessia of disturbed willow branches sweeping a bed of dry leaves.

"Where is my sister hiding, Seer?" she asked before Vala could even speak.

Vala didn't reply immediately, settling herself on the sofa opposite, smoothing out her skirts and shawls. "I am afraid," she began, fixing Alessia with those too-blue eyes, "your sister is well-hidden and well-protected. My sight does not show her at present."

"Then what use are you to me if you can't even see *the present*?"

Vala's lips twisted into a wry smile, a glint of warning in her eyes. Alessia refused to show any fear in response. "The gods work in mysterious ways, my dear Alessia. They show me what they wish for me to see."

"Then what *can* you tell me?" Alessia snapped, her voice brittle with impatience.

Vala held her gaze a long moment, then sighed, a small, resigned smile gracing her lips. "How about we take a walk, and I will tell you what I do know."

"It's raining."

The Seer let out a laugh like the tinkle of bells. "The castle is vast, sweet Nox. We need not go outdoors to stretch our legs."

Alessia's eyes narrowed in distrust, but a walk wouldn't hurt. She had been sitting in the gloomy parlour all morning. She rose as the Seer gestured towards the door, and a servant opened it quickly.

Out in the corridor, Vala looped her arm through Alessia's, leaning towards her conspiratorially once they were out of earshot of the staff. "Your General Pierce has already confirmed your uncle plots with your enemies. It would have been wiser to kill him, but the damage is done."

"Damage?" Alessia's eyes widened as Vala steered her down a draughty corridor flooded in watery light. "You mean Caspar will march here with Caplin's Forces?"

"No one is marching here. You are safe," said the Seer, breezing along at Alessia's side, as content as though they were taking a stroll in sunlit gardens, not pacing through cold, grey hallways.

"But for how much longer?" Alessia asked through gritted teeth, unable to keep the bite from her voice.

Vala smiled sweetly and squeezed her arm, despite Alessia's flinch. She tolerated the Seer's strange overfamiliarity and clucking, mother hen façade, but whether it was out of fear or simply need, she wasn't sure. "Your enemies have neither the resources nor the courage to march up to Scotland. You will bring your war to them, when the time is right, and many towns and cities will fall to you on the way. You will regain much that has been lost."

Alessia took a deep, steadying breath, comforted by this small promise. Who knew what favours her uncle and Phaedra could call in after their spying, but at least they could keep tabs on her no longer. And after she had rooted out the culprits behind Phaedra's escape, none of the staff would dare to turn on her either. "And the Marsdens, are you sure I can trust them?"

"You can. Brydon was always a cold, unfeeling man, but the Nox of all people can trust him. He is power-hungry, much like other great men we know." She looked like a teenager confiding a secret, and Alessia tried not to bristle as she implied her grandfather was a man like Marsden. But it was true; the Marsdens had long been the Ronans' closest allies, especially since all that mess with the Masons splitting.

"And when can the Nox expect to resume her presidency?" Alessia asked, unable to hide her frustration at being kept locked up like a child in need of protection while her country fell into chaos.

"That is why I am here, actually," said Vala, turning into another wing. "I have been in Edinburgh, working with Brydon's sons. Until you regain control of London, you can hold council from there. They have managed to flush the Resistance out of the Scottish cities, so we know you will be safe."

"Cities are full of people, and people have all sorts of political orientations," said Alessia. "How can you be sure that Resistance sympathisers won't riot?"

"Oh, Andrew and Rupert have already fixed that. They have implemented strict curfews, guards in the streets at all hours, raids taking place daily, neighbours spying on neighbours… I will not lie to you, Alessia. Tensions are high, but there will be no attacks or riots in Edinburgh."

Alessia was not convinced, but it was better than no presidency at all. "Then tell the Marsdens to expect me in Edinburgh at nine o'clock tomorrow morning. We have a war to plan."

Vala nodded, a hint of mischief in those fathomless eyes. They walked on for a few minutes in silence, Alessia already planning the following day, when she could finally return to the leadership position that she and her grandfather had worked so hard to gain. All the while, Vala kept her arm linked around Alessia's, and eventually her voice broke the younger woman's train of thought.

"How are your Talents?"

Alessia walked on, mentally reaching inward to the deadly powers that roiled deep within her. She had never felt so *alive*, her darkness constantly demanding her attention and craving release. She longed to inflict it on someone or something, preferably a battlefield where she could cause mass destruction without having to worry about the consequences. It took a lot of effort and self-discipline to keep herself in check.

"I thought the reserve of power I gained when I came of age would be all there was to it. Instead, my power grows, day by day."

Vala nodded, her amusement gone. "It is a trait of the Nox to come into more power than their minds and bodies can handle. That is why many of them go mad, and the devastation they cause… But they had little guidance. Fortunately, I have taken the liberty of recruiting a trainer for you."

Alessia's head whipped around, scowling at Vala's revelation. "What?"

"He is the descendent of a Nox. It is rare for descendants to be as powerful as this one is, but the bloodline was mixed in quite an interesting way. Fate combined with careful planning brought together Talents that truly complement one another. The man is… quite the weapon."

Alessia felt a spark of jealousy mingling with her distaste at Vala taking it upon herself to find someone to *train* her. As though she wasn't the most powerful being in existence. As though this *man* could somehow match, or even surpass her.

Vala seemed to read the emotions in the frozen mask that Alessia kept on her face. "Do not worry, Lucien is only coming to help you master control of your new Talents. You do not need to build your strength, you have more than enough. You just need to be able to aim it."

Alessia said nothing, only held herself even straighter as she stalked on, turning another corner. Vala – still linked to her arm – kept up easily, almost as though she were floating on a phantom breeze rather than moving her feet. But then she stopped, holding Alessia's arm firmly to make her pause too. Alessia looked down her nose imperiously, waiting to hear what she had to say.

"I foresee a lot of switching of sides during this war, Alessia. Nox wars bring out the best and worst in people, especially once they see how much they should fear you. Many *will* rally behind the Lux, but others will clamour for your favour, especially those who do not share Skye's values. I advise you to consider offers of alliance very carefully, even from those who may surprise you."

She eyed the Seer with a sidelong glance, wondering what secrets she was holding back. But before she could ask, Vala caressed her cheek with cold fingers, placing a chaste kiss on her forehead. Alessia froze beneath her touch, her darkness unfurling like smoke deep within her.

"Until tomorrow, dearest Nox."

Chapter Twenty

GLEN FARRADAY

Glen couldn't believe his own senses as he stood in front of Roxanne's floor-length mirror, but after a few days of her care and healing treatments, his bullet wound was almost completely healed. Only a faint twinge and a patch of shiny scar tissue served as a reminder of his ordeal. The woman had worked wonders. When he said as much, she had waved it off, telling him it was nothing. But for someone like him who was Talentless, it was a miracle.

He pulled on the army-issue clothes Roxanne had sourced for him from the Resistance barracks. The grey T-shirt strained across his broad chest, and the blue trousers were a little snug across his thighs. His own home – the bungalow where he had grown up with his mother – was just within Resistance territory north of Manchester. He hadn't dared to take Phaedra there, not when Alessia would have had eyes on it, but perhaps it would be safe for him to go alone and pick up some of his things. But that was a thought for another day.

Giggles greeted him as he walked down the stairs, and he hovered at the doorway into the cosy living room. Phaedra was on the couch, playing with a cat. The tabby purred in her lap, rubbing its head against her, eliciting a look of pure joy. For a moment, she looked halfway like a kid again, not the terrified husk of a person he had spent the past weeks trying to keep safe from a world that wanted to hurt her.

"Do you want some breakfast?" came a gentle voice behind him, and he turned, spotting Roxanne waving at him from the kitchen. He left Phaedra and the cat to their joyful bonding and entered the sunny room. Beyond the window was a view of a pretty garden and a stretch of fields.

"What do you have?" he asked, feeling too big in the pristine kitchen, afraid to move too quickly in case he knocked over the porcelain cups or the decorative plates on the walls.

"Do you like omelette?"

"Uh, sure." He tried to return her smile, then glanced around to see if he could do something to help.

"Take a seat." She gestured to the table in the middle of the kitchen, where an array of brightly coloured tulips was artfully arranged in a spotted vase. "Tea? Coffee?"

He watched her bustle around, pulling eggs, milk and butter out of the fridge. "Coffee's great, thanks."

While Roxanne put the kettle on, he looked around the kitchen again, taking in the pastel towels and tea cosies, the jars of dried herbs and spices shelved in neat rows, the floral plates and bowls stacked carefully in the cabinets. And the more he took in, the more the doughy weight of nostalgia settled in his stomach, leaving him longing for a past he would never get back. His mother's kitchen had looked like this. A kitchen full of things that he had no idea what to do with, but he would never change a thing because every item had been lovingly chosen and placed by the only person who had cared for him.

"Have you given any thought to what you want to do?" Roxanne asked, bringing him back to the here and now with her cheerful voice.

"I still don't know," he admitted, fiddling with the corner of the placemat in front of him. The harsh truth had lingered in the back of his mind for the past few days, brought up by Roxanne's subtle suggestions that he should join the Resistance. Skye's accusation that he didn't know what he wanted may have been hurled at him as an angry throwaway comment, but she had been completely right. He had spent the two years since his mother's death simply existing, going through the motions as a cog in Ronan's regime. But now that he was free of an employer, he had no idea what to do with his life, where to go next.

"The Resistance could use people like you," she said, finally voicing her opinion clearly.

He grimaced, curling the placemat between his fingers. "I wouldn't make much of a difference. I'm Talentless."

But Roxanne gave him a knowing smile. "Devan Harlow is Talentless. He leads our army. You think he doesn't make a difference?"

He sucked his teeth, scanning his memory for what little he knew about the man whose name he had heard whispered over the years, the freedom fighter who wanted to lead Britannia out of the shadows.

"You know how to fight, how to shoot a gun," Roxanne pressed with gentle persuasion.

"I've not been in battle," he said, but he knew he was just making excuses.

"You'll be trained," she replied as she poured whisked eggs into a frying pan. "People much less experienced than you have been honed into skilled soldiers."

He nodded, lowering his gaze to the tulips before him. Joining the Resistance would be the honourable thing to do, but it meant going against the people he had worked for all his career. He didn't care for politics, but after what Doran had done for him and his mother, it felt like an insult to his memory. Still, Doran's legacy was split, his daughters enemies of one another. After what Alessia had tried to do to Phaedra, supporting the Nox was out of the question.

"Where would I live?"

Roxanne shrugged. "You can live at the barracks. Everything would be taken care of, food, clothing, washing facilities..."

"Would I be paid?" It seemed shallow, in the grand scheme of things, to ask about money. But he hoped to still have his life after this war, and he didn't want to be a bodyguard or a prison warden forever. If he was going to put in time and energy, even risk his safety, for a future where he might be able to live a normal life, he at least wanted something to show for it.

"I don't know the exact details, but I believe there's a small salary for serving soldiers, and a veterans' pension to follow once the Resistance is in power."

His eyes dropped to the flowers again. There was some hesitation in Roxanne's voice, and he was glad she wasn't trying to give him the hard sell by overpromising. The Resistance getting into power was a long shot, and he couldn't imagine the country would be rolling in money after decades of a crippled economy, a coup, and a Nox war.

"If it makes a difference, we're working closely with Caplin's Forces."

He looked up, meeting Roxanne's searching gaze. He wondered if Phaedra had been blabbing about his business. "Can't say I was ever a fan of Caplin." The Resistance he could bend for, but Caplin's policies had only ever brought poverty and heartache into their lives.

Roxanne nodded, thankfully dropping the subject as she turned back to the stove. Moments later, she set a plate with the omelette down in front of him, along with a cup of coffee, milk and sugar.

"Any sauce? Some toast?" she asked, hovering between the table and the worktop.

Heat flooded his cheeks as she smiled at him, and he looked down at the food, gratitude overwhelming him for a moment. "This is perfect, thank you."

She nodded, then settled across from him with a cup of tea. Glen mulled over his dilemma as he ate, trying to concentrate on the simple but delicious food despite the bittersweetness flooding him. When he was done, he set the knife and fork down, absently rubbing his left knee as he drank the coffee Roxanne had made him. He realised the twinge that bugged him now was the first pain he had noticed since waking up.

"I couldn't heal your knee completely – the injury is too old – but I reduced the swelling. Feel free to come to me any time it's bothering you, I can settle it down again."

Glen stared at Roxanne's matter of fact tone. "You... you can do that?"

"Of course. It's better than taking painkillers for the rest of your life."

He flexed his leg beneath the table experimentally. It felt better than it had in years. "I just kind of... got used to the pain. I didn't realise anything could be done about it."

Roxanne's expression was sympathetic, but there was a hint of doubt in her eyes. Before he could change the subject, she asked the question he always dreaded. "How did you hurt it in the first place?"

He shrugged, grunting the lie that came naturally to him by now. "Boxing injury."

She raised an eyebrow. "It must have been some injury. Your whole kneecap was shattered."

He floundered beneath her scrutiny, feeling like a child caught out by his mother. But the truth was too shameful to share. "Let's just say my opponent got a bit carried away."

She held his gaze, pity in her clear blue eyes. But before she could pry further, the door creaked, and the cat entered the kitchen, closely followed by Phaedra. Glen watched the creature cross the tiled floor, then disappear under the table. Instinctively, he drew his chair back, peering under the table to find the cat staring at him.

"Her name is Mischa," Phaedra said brightly, crouching down next to the table to watch the cat. "She wants to say hello to you."

"Uh, hello?" Glen mumbled, moving his legs back as the cat edged closer to him.

Phaedra frowned. "Are you scared of cats?"

"I, uh, no," he said lamely, his cheeks burning. The cat meowed. "I'm allergic."

"You're allergic to cats?" Her eyes widened as though it was the most incredulous thing she had ever heard.

"Oh, I'm sorry. I should have asked you first," said Roxanne, getting up and reaching for a jar that rattled. The cat immediately slipped away, its attention stolen by the treats Roxanne extracted from the jar.

"If you touch a cat, will you explode?" Phaedra teased, a silly grin on her face.

"Explode into itches and sneezes, yep."

"Sucks to be you."

***

Glen was fully healed, and it was finally time to go. They had stayed up late the previous night, he, Phaedra and Roxanne, discussing their next steps. Phaedra was only too happy to go to her uncle, but Glen refused to join them. When she begged him, he had finally admitted that he and her uncle didn't see eye to eye. She snorted at that, but finally, she understood that what she was asking of him would be uncomfortable for everyone. So he accepted Roxanne's offer to join the Resistance instead, and although he wasn't sure where his loyalties lay, if they lay with anyone at all, he was glad of the chance to keep himself busy.

It was with a heavy heart that Glen sat at the breakfast table that early morning, with a bowl of porridge in front of him that he was stirring more than eating. Across from him, Roxanne was eating and chatting away, telling them an anecdote about her mother playing an April Fool's joke on her father by swapping apple slices for potato peelings in a pie. Phaedra sat between them, uncharacteristically animated despite the early morning.

The daughter hadn't come down. They had barely seen her during their stay, and Glen assumed she wasn't happy about their impromptu visit, and had had a disagreement with her mother about it. It was true that Roxanne seemed tense, and her lips twisted in discomfort whenever Amber appeared or was mentioned, but Glen knew it wasn't his business to ask.

When they were finally finished, hurried along by Roxanne checking her watch and saying they had to go soon, Glen and Phaedra washed up while Roxanne went upstairs to finish getting ready.

"So, is this it?" Phaedra asked after a short silence while she stood drying a plate.

Glen couldn't help a small smile at her glum expression. "Why does this have to be *it*?"

She shrugged. "You're going to be a glorious soldier, I'm going to be stuck with my uncle, little better than a prisoner until this war blows over."

Glen looked down at the bowl he was washing, then handed it to her. "Well, maybe you'll need a bodyguard again. Whatever… disagreement your uncle and I had, I think he trusts me. He'd rather I step in if needed, over anyone else."

Phaedra grinned. "It sounds like you almost admire him, despite him stealing your woman."

Glen's stomach twisted, jealousy writhing in his gut. "Did he steal her?"

Phaedra snorted. "I'm no expert, but I think she'd rather tumble with you. Apparently straight women like brave knights with stupidly big muscles."

Glen gave a satisfied smirk. "Well then, according to your expert opinion, it seems it's your uncle who should be jealous of me." He drew himself up to his full height and flexed his pecs, but instantly regretted it when the movement pulled at his scar tissue. Still, Phaedra snorted again and snapped him with the towel.

"Oh, get over yourself," she said, laughing wildly.

Glen was laughing too, and took the towel from her to dry his hands after he let the water out of the sink. After hanging the towel on a hook on the wall, he turned to her.

"You're right though. This might be *it* for a while."

Phaedra nodded, her amusement dissipated. She fiddled with the hem of her T-shirt, the pastel colour definitely not suited to her pallid skin tone. "I know you'll be busy, but try to visit."

He smiled. Although Phaedra would be the last person he expected to be friends with, he had grown fond of the girl and her sassy attitude, like she was an annoying little sister that he cared about regardless. "So you can be a pain in my ass?"

She frowned, swatting his arm playfully. "Shut up. You know you're going to miss me." And then she hugged him, wrapping her skinny arms around his waist and barely coming up to his chest. Surprised, Glen wrapped his arms around her too. Only a month or so had passed since they had met, but they had been through a lot together in a short space of time.

She held him tightly until they heard Roxanne coming downstairs, and then he ruffled her hair. "Right, time to go."

"Hey! I just styled my hair!"

"Did you? It doesn't look any different from before."

She snorted and scrutinised his sprouting beard. "At least I don't look like a bear."

He raised an eyebrow as she ran her fingers through her hair, trying and failing to tidy it. Roxanne had helped her to trim it into more of a style, and she had bleached the front so a blonde streak ran along her scalp. "I'd rather look like a menacing bear than a mardy badger."

That earned him a playful punch to his shoulder.

Roxanne drove them away from her home, along country roads and then into the forest, slowing down and pulling off the road onto a dirt track through the trees. The car bumped and lurched as they trundled along, eventually coming to a closed gate. Roxanne stopped the car and applied the handbrake a few yards from the obstacle.

"Glen," said Roxanne, twisting around in her seat, "would you help me with the portal?"

"Sure." Glen left Phaedra alone in the car and followed the Healer around to the boot, where they extracted a bag of salt and chunks of quartz as big as his fist.

"The place we're going…" he asked as he measured out the steps to set down the crystals in a grid, "does it belong to the Boltons?" His stomach gave a nervous squirm, unsure he was ready to come face to face with Skye playing happy families with Caspar.

"It's the Medleys' place, I believe," Roxanne said as she carefully poured glittering salt between the crystals. She glanced up from her task, giving Glen a searching look. "Skye and her brother live elsewhere."

Glen nodded, ducking his head to hide his conflicted feelings. To his relief, Roxanne finished laying the salt circle, then grabbed a fallen stick to draw direction sigils in the dirt within the circle.

They got back in the car, and Roxanne drove through the circle. The gate and the forest melted into nothing, to be replaced by misty, rolling hills.

For a moment he thought they were back in Scotland, and his stomach gave a backflip. But it turned out to be the Lake District, and he twisted in his seat in spite of himself. The pink glow of dawn was softened by mist, the hills rolling away as far as he could see in tones of purple and grey. He remembered visiting the lakes as a child and had hated it. It had rained the whole time and he had been bored and sick of the mud. But looking at it now, he could see why his mother had liked it. She had been able to see the beauty that he, as a child, had missed.

The car bumped along on the uneven road, and before long, they rounded a corner, then turned up a barely visible driveway, obscured by trees and more mist. The driveway was even more uneven, but eventually the trees gave way to a pretty garden and, just visible through the mist, a thatched cottage. By the time they stopped and Phaedra had removed the seat belt and opened the car door, Caspar was already standing on the doorstep with a huge grin on his face. He looked the picture of health, and his clothing was less flashy than usual – a plain shirt and slacks. No sign of Skye. Phaedra ran over to him and threw her arms around his middle, the pair hugging as Glen and Roxanne got out of the car.

"Isn't this a bit early for you?" Caspar joked as he surveyed his niece, then raised an eyebrow at her hair. "Finally, I was wondering when you would start to rebel."

Phaedra cringed. "I know, it looks bad."

"Oh no," he replied, looking more closely at her hair. "It's great. And an excellent disguise."

Caspar's gaze then locked with Glen's. His expression was unreadable, while a whirlwind of uncomfortable thoughts razed through Glen's mind. Caspar looked away first, turning to Roxanne. "Thank you, Roxanne, for tracking her down and taking care of her. I owe you a great deal."

Roxanne smiled her pretty smile. "It's been my pleasure. She's a brave and incredible woman. More than she knows."

Phaedra was looking sheepish, and descended the front steps to hug Roxanne tightly. "Thank you for everything."

"Any time," Roxanne replied, then pulled away far enough to look at her. "I mean it. Anytime you need me, if you're in trouble, or you need more sedatives, you call or come to me. You have that new phone with all the numbers you need. And I'm sorry I wasn't there for you from the start this time."

Phaedra shook her head. "Don't worry about that. It all worked out in the end."

Glen watched the exchange between the two women, hands in his pockets as he swallowed the lump in his throat. But Caspar moved in his periphery, holding his gaze as he approached.

"Thank you," said Caspar quietly when he was in front of him, reaching out a hand to Glen. There was no hint of the usual smugness on his face. "You protected her with your life, and I am in your debt."

Glen looked at Caspar's hand, then back up at his face. He didn't have to fear this Ronan anymore. He had nothing left to hold over his head, and Glen owed him nothing. Not even a handshake. Still, for Phaedra's sake, he took the man's hand, resisting the urge to crush his fingers.

"I didn't do it for you. I did it for her."

Caspar nodded, shame washing over his face. "I know. But you have my gratitude all the same."

Glen paused, glancing at the two women who watched with bated breath. "Roxanne's right. She's an amazing girl. It's been an honour to serve and protect her."

Over Caspar's shoulder, Phaedra cringed at the formal words, her expression clearing some of his tension. But Glen had one more question for Caspar. Lowering his voice, he looked back at him.

"Did anyone else make it out?"

His face fell, and Glen's heart plummeted with it. Caspar turned away a moment, glancing at his niece, then inclined his head towards the fence, drawing Glen out of earshot. He felt Phaedra and Roxanne's eyes pinned on his back as he followed.

"I'm sorry, Glen…"

Glen blinked. Caspar had never used his first name before, and especially not in that tone of voice.

"Alessia carried out an investigation, found out who helped with the escape. I'm sorry, I know you and Jemima had history."

A hollow pain clawed deep within. He forced a deep breath, rubbing his chest where the dent from the bullet rested. "She's… dead?" he asked, needing to hear it straight.

Caspar's face was grave. He nodded, and Glen half turned away, chewing a nail as the pain in his chest grew worse, unable to help the memories and regret surfacing in his mind.

"She was very brave, Glen. You all were. I won't forget what you've done for Phaedra. And when I get the chance, I'll ensure their bodies are given a proper burial."

Glen swallowed the bitter taste pooling in his mouth. "How did it happen?"

Caspar hesitated. "It was very quick. A head wound. I… I don't think she suffered."

Glen nodded, forcing a shaky breath. "And you… you didn't try to stop it?" He glanced back at Caspar, whose face was strained with regret.

"I did. Alessia and I fought."

Glen waited, raising an eyebrow.

"She won," Caspar said simply, sagging a little. "She's the Nox, Glen, she—"

"We're not on first name terms, Mr Ronan," Glen interrupted flatly, turning away again. He let his words hang, let Caspar realise that his excuses and apologies weren't welcome. Finally, he released a tight breath. "I'll… try to speak to her family. Tell them what happened." The thought of facing Jemima's family… the mother who had invited him for Sunday lunch, the brothers who had drunk with him at the pub… nausea roiled his stomach.

"If there's anything I can do…"

"Sure," Glen said dismissively, eager for Caspar to get out of his sight. "Thank you."

Caspar drifted back towards the house. Glen chewed his nail again, staring at the beauty that unfolded around him, but unable to see it. The world had lost a good person – four good people – all because they had tried to do the right thing while Caspar Ronan sat back and let them do the work for him.

Squaring his shoulders, he turned back to the house, trudging after Caspar. He forced a smile as Phaedra tripped across the garden to give him one last hug. He held her tightly, trying to draw strength from her embrace and ignore the ache that felt like a punch to his gut.

"Don't hurt yourself again," she mumbled against his shoulder, voice strained.

"Stay out of trouble." He ruffled her hair again, then stepped back before she could swat him.

Phaedra went to stand with her uncle on the threshold while Glen and Roxanne got back into the car. He could feel Roxanne's eyes on his face as he struggled to plug in his seatbelt.

"Are you alright?"

"I'm fine," he managed, steeling himself against the grief that threatened to crush him. He looked back at Phaedra through the windscreen, taking in her sad smile and wave. One life for four, and almost his own as well. But thinking back to how Jemima had come to him just days ago and told him Maggie's plan, he knew none of them would have chosen differently if they'd been sure of the outcome.

Perhaps resisting the Nox to protect those in need was worth dying for.

Chapter Twenty-One

PHAEDRA RONAN

Phaedra watched the vehicle until it disappeared from sight, Caspar's arm wrapped tightly around her shoulders.

"Do you want breakfast?" he asked when Roxanne and Glen were gone.

"Roxanne already fed me."

"Of course she did." He was smiling, happier than she had seen him in a long time. "She also had some of your things brought from the manor. I put them in the nicest bedroom for you, but you can choose another if you prefer."

She looked around the cottage, taking in the rich warm wood and brown leather sofas, the floor-to-ceiling windows with views of the lakes. "This is Skye's house?"

"Her aunt's."

Phaedra blinked, seeing the place in a new light, looking back at her uncle. "Alma Medley?"

"The very same," he said, raising an eyebrow.

Butterflies awoke in Phaedra's stomach as she walked upstairs to the bedrooms. Ombra must have stayed here. Which bedroom had been hers? She poked her head into each. There were four in total: one with Caspar's things, one covered in dust sheets, a third with kids' toys in it, and a fourth with her things. She stepped inside, the room bathed in soft light from the open window. The coverlet and curtains were lilac satin, the carpets cream. She opened the wardrobe, finding some of her clothes already hung, still smelling of the soap powder that Maggie and the laundry maids used at home. Turning back to the door, her heart stuttered as she spotted a pair of paintings – one above the bed, another near the door. They were abstracts, the one by the bed evoking a pair of wings with swirling feathers, the other was yellow stars in a purple night sky. Both were signed with the initials *MK*. They were Marina's paintings – Ombra's flatmate and distant cousin. She shivered, sure this must be Ombra's bedroom.

She headed back downstairs, feeling utterly weirded out. How would Ombra feel if she found out her missing girlfriend was squatting in her holiday home? What if she showed up and found her there? How could Phaedra even begin to explain? She would need to, at some point. She wanted to, but she was too afraid to hope she could somehow salvage their relationship. But that was a battle for another day, when she wasn't overwhelmed with so many changes.

She took a deep breath as her trainers creaked on the floorboards at the bottom of the stairs, and followed the scent of coffee to the kitchen.

"Do the Medleys visit?" she asked her uncle, dropping into a kitchen chair as she watched him make coffee. The furniture was old and rustic, but well kept.

"They won't while we're here. I'm afraid Mrs Medley isn't too happy about our arrangement, but Skye wore her down."

She raised an eyebrow, wondering if Glen's suspicions about her uncle and Skye were right after all, but it didn't feel like the right time to ask. "But we're safe here?"

"We're safe." He smiled, pouring coffee into two cups. "I'm helping Skye find her father. And the Resistance have asked me to join their meetings." He set down the coffee in front of her, claiming the seat opposite.

"Do they want you to help them fight against Alessia?"

He grimaced. "It might come to that. I would rather stay out of the whole thing, but it looks like it's the price we'll have to pay for our safety."

Phaedra lapsed into silence, hugging the coffee cup to her as she sipped. After her sister had threatened to kill her, she shouldn't feel anything but anger towards her. But the thought of fighting her, a person she had lived with her whole life…

"What happened?" she asked, her voice small as she met his gaze, "after I left?"

The expression on Caspar's face became grave, and a more nauseating kind of butterfly flitted around her stomach. "I'm sorry, Phaedra…"

The tears came before the realisation fully hit her, her uncle's face swimming before her. She set the cup down, pressing a hand to her mouth.

"Alessia carried out an investigation, narrowed it down to Maggie, Kiaran, Sally and Jemima. I tried to stop her, but… she's strong, Phee. Stronger than I've ever seen her."

She blinked through her tears. "Stronger than you?"

He nodded, and a violent shudder shot down her spine. "And Maggie…?"

He shook his head, his jaw tight. Phaedra crumpled, curling in on herself, sobbing into her hands. After a moment, she felt his arm around her, and she leaned against him, her chest tight as the grief ripped through her.

"I'm so sorry, Phee," he murmured, rubbing her shoulder. "I know how close you were to Maggie."

"I shouldn't have left," she gasped, furiously wiping her eyes with the back of her hand. "It's my fault." She had lied to protect Ombra, only for others to be killed. Maggie and Kiaran were practically her family, and the two laundry maids surely had families of their own who were missing them. How was she supposed to live with that?

"Don't say that," he said firmly, looking down at her. "Maggie loved you. The others wanted to protect you. I didn't even ask them, Phee. They did what they felt was right."

"You didn't?"

He shook his head. "Only Farraday had the order to keep you safe. The others… they just did it because they cared about you."

She hiccupped, and Caspar left her side for a moment, coming back with a box of tissues. She took a handful, balling them up and scrubbing at her face, but more tears came the more she thought of Maggie and the others, the way they had helped her get out of that castle, knowing full well that Alessia would probably find out. And Glen… Glen had asked them to go with them. He had known they weren't safe if they stayed behind.

"Did she hurt you?" she asked, looking him up and down.

A muscle feathered in his tight jaw. "She did. But I'm alright now."

She scrutinised him again. "What did she do?"

He hesitated, then undid the first few buttons of his shirt, pulling down the collar. Phaedra stared at the black bruise mottling his shoulder and half his chest, branching out in thin strands, like roots of a tree. "That's darkness."

He nodded, pulling his shirt shut and buttoning it again.

"Darkness shouldn't hurt you."

"It shouldn't," he agreed. "But Alessia is the Nox."

"So…" she stammered, struggling with the truth. "So no one can beat her?"

He frowned and reached for his coffee, drinking deeply. "It is said the Nox is unmatched in power, except by the Lux."

Phaedra mulled over his words, trying to make sense of them. She had known her sister would be crazy powerful, but she hadn't imagined she would be able to hurt other Obscurae, and certainly not Caspar. "Is it true that… Skye Bolton is the Lux?"

He turned the cup in his hands. "You remember how Ivor talked about a Seer? The same Seer apparently visited Skye. Doran suspected her too. So it seems that yes, she's the Lux."

Phaedra frowned, the puzzle coming together: the fact that the Resistance had teamed up with Caplin, the way everyone suddenly wanted to be friends with Skye. And then there was her uncle. "Is that why you came to her? Because you knew she was the Lux?"

Caspar hesitated. "To be honest, I came to Skye because she was the only person I might be able to trust. Farraday told me what you told him the day of the siege, but I didn't know for sure that the Resistance would harbour us until Skye introduced me to Roxanne."

He fixed her with a pointed stare, and she shrank under his scrutiny, a prickle of her old anxiety creeping across the back of her neck. She knew what was coming next. Knew it was finally time to come clean.

Caspar took a breath. "It seems you owe me an explanation."

Phaedra's fingers tightened around her coffee cup. He didn't speak unkindly, and there was no malice in his gaze, but her guilt bubbled to the surface even so.

"I'm not angry." His expression softened even more, as though he noticed her fear. "I just need to know what's been going on. Why you've been working as an informant, why you covered for Ombra Medley. It seems neither Skye nor the Medleys are aware of your involvement with her. Were you working under a pseudonym?"

Phaedra let out a breath, bracing herself to finally tell the truth, or some of it, anyway. She trusted her uncle more than the rest of her family, but she wasn't ready to admit exactly what Ombra meant to her. "Ombra is my friend. I didn't know she was a Caplinite when we met, and she doesn't know who I am."

He nodded, still watching her closely. "And is that why you were informing on your father and sister?"

"No…" She took another deep breath. Ombra was a forgivable mistake based on ignorance. But the spying… she had known full well what she was doing from the start. "I've been spying for the Resistance since… since Dad told me Alessia would be the Nox."

Caspar blinked, leaning back in his chair, his expression unreadable. She waited as he mulled over her confession, the anxiety now prickling its way down her neck. She lowered her gaze, rubbing her throat.

"You've known since you were fifteen."

She nodded, chewing her nail.

"I don't know whether to be afraid or proud of you."

She looked back up. "You're not mad?"

"Phaedra… I'm in awe."

A blush bloomed across her cheeks as she took in the expression on his face. "I didn't do much. I just fed stuff anonymously at first, then when the coup happened… I knew someone who knew someone, and they put me in touch with Roxanne directly."

"Well, it looks like your bravery has paid off. We need all the allies we can get if we're to remain a step ahead of Alessia."

Phaedra didn't know what to say, and instead lowered her gaze to her coffee, relieved to be safe from her murderous sister at last.

Chapter Twenty-Two

ROXANNE SUMMERS

It was growing dark by the time she walked up her driveway, but her little house was cheerfully lit, welcoming her home. And she hoped it would soon feel like home again, hoped she could clear the air with her daughter.

She had thought about it the whole way home, what she would say now that it was just the two of them again, without the prying ears of people that Amber didn't want in their house. The past days had been agony, with Amber ignoring her and staying in her bedroom where possible, or else replying in clipped tones when she had to. But the worst thing was that she hadn't looked her in the eye, not since that night Roxanne had told Amber who her father was.

Roxanne put her key in the lock with a twist of nerves in her stomach, and braced herself before she opened the door. She was greeted by the smell of cooking, and the rumble in her stomach reminded her she had barely eaten since breakfast. She let her keys clatter in the bowl by the door, alerting her daughter that she was home. The continued silence from Amber made her chest ache. Taking a deep breath for the confrontation to come, she took off her coat and boots before heading into the kitchen.

Amber was laying the table, the oven glowing merrily behind her. Inside it was a bubbling shepherd's pie, the mashed potato topping turning a delightful shade of golden brown. But the sight of Amber's efforts made her feel even more guilty about what she had hidden from her, and the argument that had ensued.

"I expect you haven't eaten," said Amber. It was clear she was trying and failing to keep her voice light.

"I haven't," Roxanne confirmed, looking to see if she could help in any way, but Amber had already done everything.

"Well, it's more or less ready, if you want to wash your hands." She turned her back to her then, grabbing the oven gloves from their hook.

"This is amazing," Roxanne told her daughter when they were both sitting down and Roxanne had swallowed her first mouthful. She put her fork down, looking at Amber. "Thank you."

Amber gave her a small smile, barely meeting her eye, then returned her gaze to her plate. "You're welcome."

They ate in silence, and as nice as the food was, Roxanne could barely taste it. There were too many words weighing on her tongue, and she didn't know where to begin.

"How was your day?" Amber asked eventually, eyes still trained on her plate.

"Productive," Roxanne said after taking a moment to mull over her words. "Phaedra is with her uncle, and Glen has enlisted as a soldier. Peter was dubious, but Devan and I wore him down."

Amber only nodded, and they lapsed into tense silence again, the only sounds the scraping of forks on plates. Amber finished hers, then sat and sipped her glass of water until Roxanne swallowed her last mouthful and laid down her fork. "Would you like more?"

"No, thank you," she said, taking a drink from her own glass. "That was delicious."

Amber gave her another watery smile, then got up, picking up both plates and putting them in the sink. Roxanne got up to help.

"No, don't." Amber turned, sitting back down again. "I want to talk."

Roxanne looked at her, half out of her seat, but when she saw the seriousness in Amber's face, she slowly lowered herself back into her chair. They sat and stared at each other for an agonising moment, until Roxanne blurted, "I'm sorry—"

"No," said Amber, shaking her head and twisting her hands on the table in front of her. "I am. I'm… I'm still angry and upset that you didn't tell me, but I understand. I know you were in a difficult position."

Although Amber's words didn't quite seem like forgiveness, Roxanne's heart filled with relief and pride regardless. Pride at the woman her daughter had become. That instead of falling out over this, she was willing to talk it over and get through it.

"I wanted to tell you, so badly. Not a day went by when I didn't try to figure out a way to tell you, to let you know who your father was, and that Cameron… There aren't many things I regret, Amber, but not telling you about Cameron has been the biggest regret of my life." Roxanne tried not to cry, but she couldn't help the tears that welled and spilled. Amber only watched her for a moment, and then handed her a tissue from a packet in her pocket.

It was a few minutes before she spoke again, waiting for Roxanne to stop crying and dry her eyes. And then she said, "Tell me everything."

They were both crying by the time she was finished, both dabbing their faces with tissues.

"I can't believe he treated you that way," said Amber, scrubbing angrily at her cheeks.

"I'm not proud of myself either," said Roxanne, twisting a damp tissue in her hands. "But I don't regret it. I have you. You've made it all worth it."

Amber nodded, dabbing her eyes again as fresh tears welled. "I don't know how you've done it, taking care of me the way you have done and being… being *you*, despite it all. Despite how he treated you."

"There are worse ways to be treated, Amber. And I had a wonderful support network. I couldn't have done it without my parents. And I couldn't have done it without you."

Amber gave a sob then, and got out of her chair to come and hug her. Roxanne held her tightly, kissing her head. When Amber finally quieted, Roxanne kissed her hair again and said into it, "I think it's time we put the kettle on."

She huffed a laugh and straightened up, wiping her face as she went to the kettle. Roxanne opened the cupboard to choose two of her favourite mugs, large and covered in cheerful flowers. When the tea was ready, they headed into the sitting room.

"So he wants to meet me?" Amber asked when they were both settled under the same blanket, tea held in their laps and a plate of chocolate biscuits balanced between them.

Roxanne had dunked a biscuit in her tea, and was quickly eating it before the soggy part could fall into her cup. "Yes. As you know, he and Cameron weren't close, and he regrets that, I can see he does."

"So Cameron's… passing has made him realise he regrets not knowing me."

Roxanne twisted her mouth, struggling to find the right words.

"It's okay, Mum. He didn't want anything to do with me, but now he feels he should. There's no point in trying to sugarcoat it."

Roxanne looked at her sadly, but didn't try to argue. "He's… he's not the man I was in love with anymore. He's a lot colder. Bitter."

Amber shrugged. "He's been working with the Ronans. I don't expect him to be nice."

"If you… if you decide to meet him, though, I told him he has to… sort himself out. He's been our prisoner since Cameron…" She couldn't say the word, and instead scrunched up her face. "And, well, he's been in a bit of a state."

Amber nodded, sipping her tea. "Part of me wants to meet him. I can't help being curious. But the other part… I just keep thinking, why should I? I owe him nothing."

Roxanne took her hand, her heart aching at the flicker of Amber's anger. "Whatever you decide to do, I am with you one hundred percent."

Amber smiled slightly and squeezed Roxanne's hand. "And what about… what about his daughter? My… sister?"

She saw the hope in her daughter's eyes, the burning curiosity. Roxanne couldn't share what she knew about Lindsey's political allegiance, but she knew she had disowned her mother. What would she make of all this? Would Oliver tell her that she had a sister? A sister she had been at school with? If it weren't for the fact that Lindsey was a few years older, they might have even been friends.

"I think it's better if you ask Oliver about her. It's going to come as something of a shock, finding out she has a sister, especially so soon after she's lost her brother."

"I admired her, you know? At school." Amber gripped her cup tightly, staring at her knees. "She was top of the class. She always had the best marks, won all the awards, became head girl, you name it. I always wanted to talk to her, ask her for advice, but never had the guts."

Roxanne studied her daughter, remembering the shy little thing she used to be. She was still shy and lacked confidence, but she had come a long way from the little mouse that used to cling to her hand at the school gates, terrified of boarding with the other students. And considering the bullying that had taken place, Amber had been right to be afraid.

"Well," said Roxanne, wrapping her arm around Amber's shoulders, "maybe now you will be able to."

She hoped it was true.

Chapter Twenty-Three

ALESSIA RONAN

"It's a pleasure to meet you, President Ronan."

Alessia glowered at the young man bowing before her, his action more like mockery than a sign of respect. He held her gaze with an infuriating curve to his lips, and the way he dressed – in jeans, heavy boots, and a black leather jacket – reminded her unpleasantly of her sister. His raven-dark hair was slick with styling oil, and his unusual eyes were neither blue nor silver nor grey, glinting with unsettling mischief. But what bothered her most was the smell of cigarette smoke that emanated from him, mixed with aftershave.

"I'm Lucien." He straightened, his invisible power rippling around them and filling the small parlour. He stood a good head taller than her, and slipped his hands into the pockets of his jeans with a casualness that made her seethe. Either Vala had chosen this man as some sort of test, or he really was as Talented as she said he was.

Alessia didn't bother with words of welcome. "I understand you are here to train me. How do you intend to do that?" She glared at him, her voice sharp with ice.

The man hesitated, glancing around the cluttered space, at the china figurines that adorned the fireplace, the paintings on the walls and the lace hanging over the windows, doing little to keep out the draught. "We'll need more space, for a start. Perhaps outdoors, if you want to wrap up warm."

"We can't go outdoors."

"If you're afraid of people seeing, I've already cast extra wards around this place. The previous ones weren't quite up to the job."

Alessia raised an eyebrow, looking him up and down again. She herself had cast the previous wards, and Marsden had tested them. "I see," she sneered, already fighting to keep her rage at bay. "Then outdoors it is."

As it turned out, Lucien's first lesson involved "blowing off steam". And she hated to admit it, but it felt good to let out some of her pent-up energy.

She shot towards Lucien with her darkness, the tension gradually leaving her chest with each stream of shadow that bridged the ten-foot gap between them, leaving calm in its wake. Lucien stood his ground across from her, a shield of shadow held between his own hands, absorbing her attacks.

"You're an Obscurus?" she asked, a little breathless with the effort of reining in her power again.

"I'm a Mirror." The shadows fell from his hands like dark liquid, and then a miniature whirlpool twisted between them, promptly freezing over. He clapped his hands together, the ice shattering into glittering frost, then they parted to reveal a flower of flame, which merged into some kind of bird. As the flamebird took flight, it crackled, a shock of electricity forming between his splayed fingers.

Alessia scowled at his showing off. "I didn't think Mirrors existed."

"We're pretty rare," he confirmed, his self-satisfaction making her blood boil.

"How can you produce those elements without being near someone with that Talent?"

He shrugged. "My Talent allows me to absorb other people's Talents on a more permanent basis. But I can only carry so many at a time. The rest of the time, I just mirror whoever is nearby. You, for example."

Alessia pursed her lips, refusing to admit that she was impressed. And deeply envious. She looked away, scanning the grounds for any sign of an intrusion. His wards seemed to be working, which annoyed her more than pleased her after he had condemned her own security measures.

"I hope you plan to incorporate electricity into our training sessions. I fully intend to defeat the Lux."

He smirked his stupid smirk, hateful sparks crackling between his fingertips once more. His gaze was on the lightning, his ever-changing eyes reflecting the bright light. "One thing at a time, Madam President."

"What else can your Mirror do?"

He closed his fist, then slipped it into a pocket. "I can pass Talents to those who can handle them."

"You can give people new Talents?" She was torn between disbelief, envy, and admiration.

Lucien narrowed his eyes slyly. "I can. But the host needs to be strong enough to contain the extra power, and adaptable enough to be able to embrace it and wield it."

Alessia held his gaze, wondering if he was trying to discourage the thought that had crossed her mind, or if he was simply stating a fact. She wondered if receiving a new power was anything like what she had experienced when she ascended. All that extra energy – previously dormant – now running through her veins, eager to tear out of her, to be turned into a weapon. As tempting as it would be to have further Talents, perhaps he was right to warn her of the consequences.

"What about Talentless people?"

"I've experimented with that, yes. Some manage it, others go mad with the lack of control. It's difficult to know how someone will react to a Talent occupying their body if they've never possessed an ability before. It's normally not worth the risk."

She mused over his words, wondering what kind of havoc she could unleash if she ordered him to experiment on her behalf. "Have you never mirrored Vala's Talent to see how the future will play out before you experiment?"

His smirk twisted, his eyes pooling into Vala's unnatural blue. "That's for me to know."

Alessia recoiled slightly, sticking out her chin. And then, without warning, she blasted her dark energy at him, sending a twister of smoky black tendrils heading his way. Her eyes widened when he didn't stop the power that hurtled towards him, until the last second, when a glittering dark wave appeared between his hands and absorbed the energy with little more than a ripple. And then he threw the shadows back at her.

She caught the ball of darkness, the impact knocking the breath from her lungs and forcing her back a step. She raised narrowed eyes at Lucien, whose face was a picture of pure arrogance.

"Perhaps we should start our training by working on your defences, President Ronan."

Alessia hissed through bared teeth as sparks crackled in Lucien's hands once more, and it took all her effort not to attack him again. Instead, she warped her shadows into a shield as lightning thundered towards her.

***

"What did you think of Lucien?" Vala asked later that day, looking far too at home nestled in the most comfortable armchair in the parlour, sipping tea and popping little cakes into her mouth. Alessia sat opposite her, touching neither the cake nor the tea.

"He's insufferable." That said, she did feel much more relaxed now that the edge had been taken off her restless Talent.

Vala's deep red lips twisted into a wry smile. "I thought you might say that. But admit it: he is… unique."

Alessia pressed her own lips into a thin line, refusing to admit anything. Her jealousy over his apparently unlimited power reared its ugly head again. "You said they bred him to have that Talent?"

Vala winced. "*Bred* is such an inhumane word. But yes, I suppose there is no other way to describe it."

Alessia let her gaze drift towards the window, where the sun had made a rare appearance, changing the lawns from dull grey to bright green. "You described him as a weapon. Why haven't I heard of him before?"

The Seer hesitated, taking a long sip of her tea. After she set the cup down in its saucer, she took another moment to answer. "As a descendant of a Nox, he has a price on his head. Nox relatives have been hunted since time began, even butchered as babies, or their pregnant mothers killed. Your family kept you a secret, and killed Meredith Mason so she would keep that secret too. It was the same for Lucien. When his mother was killed, his father feared Lucien would be next, so he entrusted him to me, to protect him. He travels with me, and serves me."

If she were capable of compassion, Alessia would have pitied the arrogant man who had been bred as a weapon. But instead, she only considered how fortunate she was that she had not suffered a similar fate. Perhaps she, too, had been bred in a manner of speaking. Her grandfather had ensured her existence came into being when he heard of Vala's prophecy, after all. But even so, she knew people had cared for her, even if they were all gone now.

Not gone, came a whisper so quiet it could have been the wind whistling through the ill-fitting window frame. *Waiting*. Hair tickled her cheek, and she tucked it behind her ear, swallowing down her grief, pushing away the memory of her grandfather's wasted face against the pillows of his sick bed.

"You came to protect me," she said, meeting Vala's gaze. "Do you intend for me to serve you too?"

There was that wry smile again, as Vala lifted the teapot to pour herself more tea, her hands and wrists as pale as porcelain. "My dear, I am here to serve *you*. That is my purpose."

"Is it true you have assisted every Nox before me?"

She gave a tinkling laugh, then sipped her tea. "If I have, it must have been in a previous life."

But the way she said it sounded too much like a lie. Alessia had read the descriptions, seen the faded illustrations. Vala's face, or at least her name, had appeared in every historical report she had read about former Nox. If this wasn't the same Vala, she was at least a reincarnation.

"I have news of your sister and uncle," she said after a moment. Alessia had to give her credit for the tactical change of subject, because she immediately caught her attention.

"Oh? Where are they squatting now?"

"They are indeed allied with Skye Bolton, and the Resistance."

Ice stabbed at her insides in fear and fury. "*Where*?"

There was a wicked gleam in Vala's cerulean eyes. "Oh, somewhere in the Lake District. They are cloaked and warded, but a good Tracer would have little trouble finding them."

Alessia let her words sink in for a moment, then finally poured herself some tea, leaning back in her chair and sipping it. "I should have executed them when I had the chance."

Vala's lips curled in pleasure. "All in good time. When the Lux loses this war, they will come crawling back, begging for forgiveness. Then you can have your revenge."

She ground her teeth, her patience bristling. "Do you have wind of their plans? Are they plotting against me?"

"I have foreseen that Caspar will meet with Caplin and the Resistance, yes. But what they are plotting, I do not know at present."

She considered this news, trying to decide which of her informants she would be best placing to gather intel about the allies' plans.

"If you foresee anything else, you will share it with me." Perhaps it was presumptuous of her to voice it like a demand rather than a request, but if Vala was truly there to serve her, she was surely Alessia's to command.

"Of course," said Vala with a smile, but there was a tightness to her eyes and lips that suggested she didn't take too kindly to her tone, servant or not. Alessia didn't care. She was the Nox, after all.

Chapter Twenty-Four

SKYE BOLTON

Skye was sick of boardrooms. Sick of the glares and thinly veiled sneers from the people who didn't really want her there, sick of the snide comments and assumptions. It didn't help that Caplin was always there, either acting like she didn't exist or talking her down like she was no more than a servant. It didn't make a difference that she might be the only thing standing between the country and the obliteration that Alessia Ronan was desperate to deliver. If it were up to him, she wouldn't be there. But it was Roxanne Summers who kept requesting her presence, and after her meeting with Camilla, she had finally agreed.

Despite the cold and uncaring demeanour she kept up around most of the Resistance Leaders, Skye couldn't help but feel guilty about bullying her daughter every time Roxanne was nice to her. For all she had done to Amber at school, Skye never would have expected her mother to fight in her corner. The other Leaders mistrusted her, but tolerated her because they knew they needed her. But for the most part they ignored her where possible, and that suited Skye, because she ignored them too. She was content to only speak when necessary, but every so often, Roxanne would turn to her and ask, "What do you think, Skye?" and she would be forced to give an answer.

But today the agenda would be a little different. Because today, Caspar had finally agreed to speak to the allies. Whether or not he would give information remained to be seen, but he had told her he at least wanted to hear what the Resistance had to say, and he would consider offering some advice.

It was with no small amount of interest that Skye waited in the corridor outside the boardroom that morning, with Dean, as always, at her side. She refused to join these things without him there, whether or not he was invited. Most of the Resistance Leaders had arrived before them, as well as Riordan Rathbone – the head of the Saoirse Army. They waited closest to the door, murmuring good morning but otherwise muttering amongst themselves. Roxanne wasn't there yet, and nor was Caplin, so Skye and Dean remained a few yards further down the corridor, leaning against the wall and talking silently through Skye's telepathy.

Caspar arrived first, escorted by one of the new members of the Caplin Guard. His lips curved as he met Skye's gaze, and she returned the smirk, feeling Dean bristle at her side.

"Good morning," Caspar said warmly, his back straight but his hands in his pockets. He was dressed as pristinely as ever, wearing a silky grey waistcoat and matching trousers, his dark coat slung over his arm. The silver threaded pattern on his clothing glinted with every movement, and his hair and beard were trimmed and carefully styled. At the other end of the corridor, the Resistance Leaders hushed at the new arrival.

"A good morning indeed." Skye leaned a foot against the wall and gave Caspar an appreciative glance up and down, her mind flitting instantly to their recent bedroom activities and what lay beneath his expensive clothing. "And how are you, Mr Ronan? Enjoying your holiday?"

"I certainly am," he said, eyes glittering with amusement. "And I thank you and your family again for your kind hospitality."

"It's a pleasure," she replied, trying to ignore Dean glowering beside her. "And how is your niece? I see she's not made you grey yet."

Caspar laughed, the sound making her toes curl in her boots. "She's just fine. She sleeps a lot, and has a penchant for drinking games that I somehow keep getting roped into."

Skye suppressed a snort. Although the idea was ridiculous, if any uncle was going to play drinking games, it would be Caspar.

High heels sounded on the tiles then, and they all looked around to see two blonde women approaching. Roxanne was one of them, but Skye barely spared her a glance, her gaze drawn to another familiar face at her side. It was Lindsey Matheson, and Skye straightened, caught off guard by this new development. Lindsey was slender and willowy, her long blonde hair falling in a blow-dried cascade around her shoulders, her narrow face perfectly made up. Her clothes, too, were immaculate: cropped grey trousers and a peach blazer tailored to fit. And her *shoes*… Of all the things to pay attention to, Skye's focus went straight to her shoes, a pair of suede court heels in the same shade of peach as her blazer, the sort of shoes Skye wanted in her wardrobe. But as the two women drew nearer, Skye dragged her gaze back up to Lindsey's face. Lindsey herself was regarding them with cool indifference.

The women stopped in front of them, Roxanne smiling and chirping a sing-songy good morning, almost bouncing on the balls of her feet with nervous energy. But Lindsey said nothing for a long moment, then reached out a stiff hand.

"Lindsey Matheson," she said in clipped tones, and Skye shook her hand, pleased to find her grip was firm.

"Skye Bolton," she replied, unable to keep her lips from curling. "We were at school together."

"So we were," she said dismissively. "I recall I have *you* to thank for being the reason I wound up Tracing a non-existent crumb trail across half of Europa."

Skye was about to reply, but Dean cut in, reaching for Lindsey's hand. "Hello Lindsey." He beamed at her. "Do you remember me?"

Lindsey angled her head as she scrutinised Dean, then her face softened. "I do!" She gave him a small smile as she shook his hand. "You were Letitia's boyfriend."

Dean's face fell, and Skye resisted the urge to laugh as she realised he was checking Lindsey out.

Burn, she told him, *that will teach you not to flirt with the enemy.*

I wasn't flirting.

You were thinking about it. And believe me, none of the chat up lines you thought up would impress any woman.

Just because you don't like being flattered doesn't mean she won't think differently.

Just keep your jaw off the floor, we have work to do. But she was amused nonetheless, fighting hard to suppress her teasing grin.

Meanwhile, Lindsey had turned to Caspar, dismissing Dean entirely. "You too, huh?"

Caspar cast a small smile that gave nothing away. "Indeed. It seems we're both roped into this mess."

"No kidding." Lindsey looked at Roxanne then, who was smiling tentatively, glancing from one to the other. Skye thought back to the scandalous past she had lifted from Oliver's mind, where she discovered that her old rival, Amber Summers, was Oliver and Roxanne's love child. She wondered if Lindsey was aware she had a sister.

Silence fell as four more figures entered the corridor: Caplin, flanked by Ikarus and Irvine Sullivan in their

Guardian uniforms, with Skye's grandfather, Harlan Mason, a step behind. Caplin's gaze shot straight to Caspar, who tensed ever so slightly, but held his casual stance nevertheless. The two stared each other down as Caplin came all the way down the hall, then he swept past them, heading for Peter Sinclair and his fellow Resistance leaders by the door. Ike gave Skye and Dean a grim smile as he passed, but Caplin didn't spare anyone else a glance.

Harlan, too, shot Caspar a poisonous look, but he slowed as he drew level with Skye, clamping his arm around her shoulders. "Morning, sweetheart," he said gruffly, his walrus moustache tickling her cheek as he kissed it. Skye gave her grandfather a sad smile, tears threatening as his familiar scent of cigars took her back to a long-lost childhood.

She glanced around at the assembled opposing factions as they filed into the boardroom and spread out around the table. Everyone except the Guardians were wearing business attire, including Skye and Dean since they were still suspended from Guardian duties. Skye wore a generic navy trouser suit, while Dean was self-conscious in a shirt and trousers, his navy tie making him look out of proportion. For all his good looks, he couldn't pull off the formal style at all.

Skye chose a seat opposite Caspar, glad to have Dean and Harlan between her and Caplin. They had yet to make a decision about Camilla's offer, but even considering it made it difficult for her to meet Caplin's eye. Not that he looked her way much anyway. He hadn't said anything directly about her little visit to Oliver Matheson's house, but she knew from Sabine that he had had to do some damage control where the Resistance was concerned.

It was Sinclair who led the meeting, as always. "We have some surprising newcomers today," he began, glancing down the table towards where Lindsey looked bored and Caspar was smiling mildly, completely relaxed despite the tension in the room. "Some of you already know Riordan Rathbone, as well as Miss Matheson, who was a spy for the Saoirse Army until her father's surrender compromised her position. She is now able to speak more openly and is also here to represent Oliver Matheson today."

Skye blinked in surprise. A spy for the Saoirse Army? All that time? And then there was Oliver. She wondered what part he would play, and why he wasn't there to speak for himself. Perhaps he was still spending most of his time drunk.

"We owe Miss Matheson a lot," said Rathbone, his smooth voice gliding in before Peter could speak further. "She worked hard to keep her team of Tracers from rooting out too many of the Saoirse and Resistance hideouts, and is also responsible for founding and training the Ward Breakers who brought down the perimeter shields at Ronan Manor."

"That's amazing," Dean murmured at Skye's side, while similar utterances echoed him around the table. Lindsey kept her gaze trained on the table during Rathbone's speech, the blush on her cheeks deepening.

"It appears Ronan's Head Tracer has been a busy little traitor," said Caplin, his mockery cutting through the praise. "Which probably explains why she couldn't find me."

Lindsey's eyes shot up, narrowed as she pinned Caplin with her glare. "You can thank your superstar Mind Breaker for throwing Ronan off your scent. I knew you were hiding in the Highlands all along."

Skye stared, a hollow sensation settling in her stomach. "You knew?" she asked before she could stop herself.

Lindsey shrugged. "Of course I did. It was obvious Mrs Caplin's little sojourn into France was a ruse. But while the Ronans were busy with your lot, the Saoirse Army and the Resistance made pretty good progress."

Nausea replaced the hollow feeling, the smell and taste of burning invading her senses. Down the table, Caplin had also paled, Harlan grunted in disbelief, and Ike shifted behind them. Skye met her comrade's eye, his stricken expression matching her own shock. Beside her, she could feel Dean's eyes on her. She took a steadying breath, unsure what to do with the information, the knowledge that Darius's death and her and Jacob's suffering was almost for nothing, that it could have been ended at any time by the powerful Tracer sitting before her, for better or worse.

"We also have Caspar Ronan…" Peter Sinclair said, moving the conversation on, looking irritated by the interruption. "It is my understanding that the Nox has banished him, and he may have some useful information for us?"

Caspar nodded, looking so at ease that Sinclair might have just asked him about the weather. "Alessia is currently being accommodated by Brydon Marsden, and running her highly diminished court from Edinburgh. She wants you to believe her military might has been weakened considerably, but she has the backing of Marsden and Mason soldiers, as well as further troops hidden throughout Scotland and Ireland."

"And what's in this for you?" came Caplin's drawl from where he lounged in his seat. "You come here, selling out your niece. Why should we trust you?"

A smirk tugged at the corner of Caspar's lips as he held Caplin's stare. "Why Mr Caplin, I simply wish to avenge my dearly departed brother."

There were whispers from Nanette Ferries down the table, and Skye scrutinised Caspar, tilting her head, wondering how much he was about to reveal.

"Alessia thought she was being clever by keeping me in the dark about her plot to kill Doran. She and Ivor cooked it up between them, and gained the backing of many of the

Parliamentarians, including the Marsdens, Gerald Mason, and Oliver Matheson." He nodded towards Lindsey, but her expression was guarded. "But what Alessia didn't know is that the Telepath who Broke Farraday is a friend of mine, and when Farraday's memories confirmed Miss Bolton had no part in the poison plot, I asked him to take a peek into Oliver's mind too."

Skye struggled to keep a satisfied smile off her own face as she watched everyone else's expressions, the way they hung onto every word. Even Dean's eyes were wide as dinner plates.

"So it was Matheson?" Nanette asked, craning her long neck to get a better look at Caspar.

"Alessia ordered him to source and plant the poison, yes."

Murmurs broke out, and Lindsey was staring at the table again, jaw rigid, her clasped hands clenched.

Caplin butted in, drawing the attention back to himself once again. "So you want to avenge your brother, how sentimental of you." The last words were a sneer, but Caspar's expression remained carefully neutral. "And then what, you wish to take her place and continue the Ronan reign of terror?"

"I do not," said Caspar, and this time, there was no hint of a smirk. "I have no desire to inherit anything from my father's legacy, whether that be land or power. I simply wish to see my niece behind bars for her crimes, instead of having a Nox running rampant and turning what's left of this empire to ash."

To Skye's relief, Devan Harlow cleared his throat, steering away from Caplin's implied accusations. "I think we can agree that everyone at this table wants to put an end to the Nox. So the question is, where do we begin?"

"I can tell you where her armies are hidden," said Lindsey, examining her manicured nails as though they were more interesting than the conversation. "Disabling them would be a good start."

"You know where her armies are hidden?" asked Caspar, his surprise evident.

"Of course. My father was due to command one before he surrendered Blackwater. And I'm Head Tracer."

Caspar paled. "She didn't even tell me where most of her armies were hidden."

Lindsey had the audacity to look irritated. "Obviously, she didn't trust you."

To his credit, Caspar's lips curled faintly in amusement.

"So we disable the armies," said Sinclair, who then looked at Caplin. "Can we count on you for the manpower?"

"Of course," said Caplin lazily, as though he didn't care for the meeting either now that the daggers he was throwing at Caspar had been diverted.

"You can have some of my soldiers too," Harlan promised, courteously nodding to the Resistance leaders. "My army is small, but more than willing to fight against the Nox."

Skye sat up straighter, finally deigning to speak despite Lindsey's horrible revelation still roiling her insides. "Instead of fighting Alessia's armies, is there any chance we could turn them, get them to follow us instead?" She spoke mainly to Lindsey and Caspar.

Lindsey raised an eyebrow again, glancing at Caspar. Caspar himself looked thoughtful, his own brow furrowed. "I led some of those troops during the coup and gained their trust. They followed my father more than Doran, and it was no secret that he wanted me to be his heir, rather than my brother. Now they're both gone, and my niece… I suppose there are some who fear a future ruled by a Nox as much as we do."

Silence fell as Caspar's words sank in. Several people looked like they were trying to decide what to say. Skye beat them to it. "So if you step up as a leader, many will follow you."

Caspar shrugged slightly. "Some might. Many will refuse if I ally with Caplinites and the Resistance, and many would rather be loyal to the Nox. She is seen as sacred to a lot of my father's followers."

"So don't ally with us," Caplin snapped. "She's probably already told your people that you're a traitor, but no one knows you're here today except the people in this room. So declare yourself the new leader of the Ronan army and isolate your niece as much as you can. While you're at it, you can sober up Matheson and drag him out of his hovel to make it look more convincing, and rope his daughter in too."

"I'm sitting right here," Lindsey seethed, but Caplin ignored her.

The Resistance members shared a few glances. "That isn't a bad idea," said Harlow. "The Nox is our common enemy, but that doesn't mean we have to be open allies."

"It's worth a try," Caspar agreed. "Even if it means lying to 'my people', as you call them." He threw a sharp glance in Caplin's direction. "At least we have a shot at peace at the end of it."

"I doubt we'll ever have peace," Caplin said, "but at least we'll have one enemy less."

A chill went down Skye's spine as she heard Caplin echo words that Camilla had uttered just days ago. She glanced at Dean, who was thinking the same as he met her gaze: was it coincidence, or did Caplin know what Camilla had asked of them?

"Well then, Mr Ronan," said Sinclair, "how do you propose to win over the Nox's army?"

Chapter Twenty-Five

GLEN FARRADAY

Glen was used to a varied life by now. But if anyone had told him a year ago that he would be fighting for the Resistance, he would have laughed in their face. Yet here he was, running circuits around a training yard, surrounded by fellow nobodies who were determined to seek out a better life by putting their own on the line. Glen wondered if they would be so optimistic once they faced a real battle.

It had been a gruelling first week, but he was no stranger to pushing his body to its limits, and the physical and mental toll of the military training distracted him from recent events that he did his best not to dwell on. But it was during the quiet moments in between that grief crept into the pit of his stomach, when he lay awake surrounded by the snoring of his fellow recruits. He spent too much time going over those last fateful days at Castle Uaine and wishing he had done things differently, wishing Jemima had listened to him when he urged her and the others to join them in their escape.

"Reckon it'll be long before we see any action?" asked the man who had been running at his side for the past hour, guzzling water in the changing room. Glen thought he said his name was Steve.

"Probably not," Glen grunted, grabbing a towel and clean fatigues out of a locker. He had a delightful canteen lunch to look forward to, followed by an afternoon of target practice. "Apparently the Nox is getting her armies together up in Scotland."

"At least the Lux is finally stepping up. Can't say I'm too chuffed to be working with a Caplinite though."

Glen raised an eyebrow. Yet another one who seemed to think Skye was the Lux. Glen wasn't sure he believed the rumour himself. The idea was ridiculous. If the Lux existed at all, surely they would be someone good and virtuous like Roxanne, not Skye Bolton.

"Fancy a pint after training?" Glen asked hopefully. The guy seemed alright, and they had exchanged a few jokes during the morning's drills.

"Can't mate. The missus will give me a bollocking if I'm not home in time for dinner."

"Ahh right." Glen tried to hide his disappointment. It wasn't the first time he'd been palmed off with excuses. "Happy wife, happy life and all that?"

"Exactly. Gotta keep her sweet." Steve clapped him on the shoulder, then headed out. "See you at target practice."

Glen sighed and trudged to the showers. Twenty minutes later, he slumped down in the canteen, eyeing his lunch: mashed potato and grey mince dotted with carrots. It reminded him of school dinners, and he had never liked those much.

He ate without tasting it, not that there was much flavour to enjoy, and watched his fellow diners, his head rested on his fist. Aside from the first day when a few of his comrades had asked polite questions, he had spent every mealtime alone. He supposed he had his name to thank for that. He might be a Talentless working-class bloke like most of his fellow recruits, but his estranged father's name carried some weight in the history books.

Gavin Farraday had fought and died for Ivor Ronan, and bearing the same name tag on his uniform was probably why he wasn't winning many friends. He should have asked Devan Harlow to let him enlist with a pseudonym.

He was still trawling through his dull meal when his eyes were drawn to a tall, familiar blonde entering the canteen, with a dark-haired man and a young woman in a Caplin cadet uniform either side of her. Glen straightened in his seat, quickly forgetting his lunch and his loneliness.

It was Skye, wearing a suit similar to the ones he had stripped her out of on countless occasions. She looked glum herself, giving short responses and distracted smiles to the girl who chatted animatedly at her side. The last time he had seen her, she had been fleeing arrest in his stolen car, leaving a trail of broken glass and dead guards in her wake, mere hours after the argument that had been the nail in the coffin of their bizarre relationship – a relationship that Glen was also still losing sleep over, trying to find meaning amongst the meaningless.

It was when Glen wondered who her companions were that Skye looked up, her sharp brown eyes immediately locking on his gaze. He sat there, frozen in place by that look for a long moment, before Skye's lips curled and she crossed the canteen towards him, leaving her companions to get their food.

"I wondered where you ended up."

Glen watched her as she sat down opposite him, leaning on the table and crossing her arms, studying him with that all too familiar smirk. Glen set down his fork, holding her gaze. Her make-up was pristine, hair freshly cut and coloured, nails shaped and polished. And yet, despite her expression, there was a haunted look around her eyes that he hadn't seen since Blackwater. Glen had only heard second and third accounts of what had been going on in Skye Bolton's world, but seeing her now, in front of him, he saw through the brave face she was putting on. She looked like she had been to hell and back.

"It seemed like a good career move."

Skye's smirk grew, a glint in her eyes that he realised he had missed a little too much. "How was it being on the run with Phaedra Ronan?"

"She drank all my beer and kept beating me at poker." Glen wondered if she knew about the shooting, and the brief stint at Roxanne Summers's home. He was still wearing the obsidian pendant beneath his fatigues, a habit he decided was worth keeping up. "How are you?"

Her face faltered ever so slightly at his question, and she leaned back in her chair, holding his gaze. By the time she replied, her amusement was gone. "I've been better."

Her admission surprised him, and despite all the mess she had landed him in, despite how things had ended, his stupid, soft heart went out to her. "Any word on your dad?"

She shook her head, lowering her gaze to the table. "Did you hear about Cameron?"

Glen nodded. Roxanne had told him, bringing it up as a way to excuse her daughter's cold behaviour. "I heard you were with him when he died. I'm sorry."

She blinked, suddenly becoming very interested in scratching polish off her thumbnail.

"I also heard about you," he said, watching her reactions closely. "Is it true what they're saying?"

The smirk was back. "That depends on what they're saying."

He raised an eyebrow, impatient with her teasing. "You know what I mean."

She gave a cold laugh, eyes narrowing in the alluring way that had made him drop all professionalism in the first place. "Apparently so. You're all fucked if anything happens to me."

He waited, but before he could get a more definite answer, Skye's companions arrived. The man set a tray of food in front of Skye, then sat down beside her with his own lunch. The girl sat to Skye's left, eyeing Glen with open curiosity.

"This is my brother, Dean," she said, jerking a thumb at the man, who watched Glen with thinly veiled suspicion. "And this is Ombra, my delightful cousin. I hope you're not too attached to your ears. She'll burn them off with all her talk."

Glen blinked, examining the cadet more closely. And the more he looked, the more he realised this must be the same Ombra who Phaedra had been trying to protect, the Obscura behind the Mason kidnapping.

Oblivious to Glen's stare, the girl shot Skye a look sharp enough to cut, but Skye ignored her. "You two, this is Glen Farraday. He was my chaperone, and now he's working for the Resistance."

"You must have the patience of a saint, putting up with her all those months," said Ombra, taking off her crimson beret and slapping it unceremoniously on the table.

Glen tried not to laugh, immediately seeing why Phaedra had dated her. Remembering the promise he had made to Phaedra to keep his mouth shut about her identity, he picked up his fork as the others tucked into their meals. "Nice to meet you."

Skye's brother made a noise that could have either been a word or a grunt, still eyeing him between bites. Thinking the conversation was over, Glen took a mouthful of food, but it was cold and even more tasteless than before. Worse, hundreds of unsaid words felt like an impenetrable wall between him and Skye, who was studiously avoiding his gaze.

"Why are you working for the Resistance?" asked Ombra, a frown crinkling her forehead. She shared very few features with Skye, but her mannerisms and expressions were similar.

Glen shrugged. "Working for the Nox doesn't carry much appeal, especially not when she wanted to kill me."

"Is that because of Skye?"

Skye herself rolled her eyes, then popped another forkful of food into her mouth.

"Well, I let Skye get away, so yes, probably."

Ombra glanced between them, eyeing Skye with a puzzled look. Glen wondered if Skye had told her about their relationship, or if she was simply putting two and two together.

There was an awkward silence, and they continued to eat, Glen occasionally glancing at his unlikely dining companions and trying to think of something to say. Ombra still eyed him, and then, after a moment, her puzzled look was gone, replaced with a glint of mischief. Glen straightened, looking from her to Skye, trying to figure out what he had missed.

"You should come drinking with us," Ombra insisted. "Dean is more talkative after a beer, and you can meet my brother too."

Dean shot Ombra an irritated look, and then sat up, meeting Glen's gaze. "Sure. We can get a pint."

"I'm sure Glen has better things to do," said Skye, her tone casual, but Glen detected a hint of discomfort.

"Oh, don't worry, I think I can clear my schedule," Glen replied, and he couldn't resist giving Skye a smirk of his own as she looked up at him, the spark in her eye one of irritation rather than mischief this time.

Chapter Twenty-Six

Amber Summers

She had been expecting riches, and the house they approached met those expectations, but not quite in the way she had imagined. Yes, there was a security gate and armed guards that waved her and her mother inside. Yes, the house was large and expensive, but not as ostentatious as she had expected. It was a surprisingly modern house, and the lawns, which needed mowing, were minimalistic, stretching uninterrupted to the surrounding woods. Roxanne had explained that Oliver was being kept in the family summer house, but in all honesty, it looked every inch the bachelor pad, unlived in and uncared for.

Roxanne pulled up in the sweeping drive and turned off the ignition. Neither of them moved as Amber studied the façade and front lawn, nerves twisting her stomach. She already expected things wouldn't go well. They couldn't just brush twenty-two years of neglect under the carpet.

"Are you sure you want to do this?" Roxanne asked softly, her words punctured by the cooling of the engine and Amber's nervous deep breaths. "I can turn the car right back around if you don't."

Amber took another deep breath, but made no move to leave the vehicle. "I'm sure. Besides, he's waiting for me." *Not that you should care*, the harder part of her whispered, reminding her she owed him nothing. *If* he *cared, he would have made more effort to know you.* "Let's go." She let out her latest breath in a gust, then clicked off her seatbelt and thrust the door open before she could change her mind.

She forced herself to walk steadily across the lawn. The pale flagstones of the path leading up to the house had weeds between them, and some were cracked. The white marble of the front steps and porch needed sweeping, and a pair of potted cypresses flanking the entrance were in desperate need of pruning.

Roxanne took a set of keys out of her handbag and unlocked the imposing front door. The silver door knocker against the white lacquered wood caught Amber's eye – it was a coiled serpent biting its own tail, the only adornment she had seen so far.

There was more marble in the entrance hall, covering the floor and the wide staircase ahead. A rug in a tasteful shade of beige took up most of the space, and on each side of the hall were oval mirrors and side tables painted white with silver fixtures, the pots atop them filled with the desiccated remains of plants. Behind the staircase were double doors that were left open onto a dining room. A long white table and leather chairs filled the space, and behind them was a vast window that looked onto more lawns and some kind of water feature.

"Wait here while I see where he is," Roxanne said quietly, and walked to one of the white doors that lined the hall, her heels echoing on the marble floor. Amber did as she was told, clasping her hands and looking around as she took in another deep breath, trying to calm the butterflies that rattled around her stomach.

Despite the dead plants and the dusty smell, she found herself liking the hall in spite of herself. It was bright, the windows around the door behind her and the ones in the back of the house making the room a light and airy space, the sort of place that would be nice to retreat to in the warmer weeks of summer. She tried to imagine Cameron here, then let her mind wander to what it might have been like if she were acknowledged as part of his family too. But no, she couldn't let herself imagine that. Couldn't let herself think beyond the meeting today, which was sure to be a disaster. Her preconceptions of the man who had abandoned her and her mother left little room for redemption, never mind a positive relationship.

Roxanne was only gone a couple of minutes, and Amber's heart rate increased when the door reopened and her mother emerged.

"He's waiting for you." Roxanne gazed into Amber's eyes and tucked a strand of hair behind her ear. "Are you still okay to go in by yourself? Or do you want me to come with you?"

"I'll be fine," Amber breathed, glancing at the door, then back at her mother. "I know where the door is, if…" She was already prepared for the worst. She didn't dare hope for the alternative.

Roxanne nodded. "I'll be in the dining room." She inclined her head towards the room behind the staircase.

Amber braced herself, dipping her hand into the pocket of her cardigan and touching the wing of Cameron's paper sparrow for reassurance. As soon as Roxanne lowered her hands, she crossed the hall, heading to the room Roxanne had come from. She stopped outside the door, and her fingers trembled as she turned the doorknob. The door cracked open an inch, and she hesitated, taking a last deep breath before she stepped inside.

She found herself in a sitting room with more large windows dominating two of the four walls to her left and right. Expensive sofas and armchairs were arranged around a carved maple coffee table, all upholstered in more of those tasteful neutral shades. A bone china tea set had been laid out on the table, steam rising from the large teapot, a plate of assorted biscuits next to it. But Amber barely registered her surroundings. Not as her gaze went straight to the man who stood next to the table.

Oliver Matheson was not at all what she expected. For a start, she felt like she was looking at a ghost. He was what she imagined Cameron would have looked like if he had lived another twenty years. He had the same bright blond hair, styled in a similar way and carefully swept back off his face. There were the same clean-shaven boyish cheeks, the same large blue eyes. He was taller than Cameron had been, but he had the same slender build, though he held himself with more confidence and self-assurance than Cameron ever had. He was dressed simply but expensively in a pair of beige slacks and a cotton shirt in palest blue, his tan suede brogues new. As they stared at each other, Oliver smiled, but he was hesitant, wary.

"Amber," he said eventually, her name sounding foreign in his voice. "I'm so glad you came."

But Amber could only stare, still not quite believing her eyes. His accent was different to how she had imagined: a northern Irish lilt, nothing like Cameron's neutral English.

"Would you like to sit? I've made tea. Roxanne said you like tea." He gestured to the coffee table, and Amber realised he was also nervous, looking like he didn't know what to do with his hands. He was still smiling that uncertain smile, his eyes darting from her to the tea and back again. All these echoes of Cameron – his looks, his hesitation – made that kernel of grief that remained lodged in her chest ache.

Finally, she nodded, Oliver's suggestion jolting her into movement. She crossed the room, her arms and legs feeling too big, too foreign. She sat herself down on the edge of the sofa, smoothing the skirt of her dress and careful not to knock the table with her knees. Oliver poured tea into the two cups that had been laid out. The china was translucent white with silver around the rims. "Help yourself to milk and sugar." He gestured to the condiments, splashing a little milk into his own tea, then sat down in the armchair across from her, taking his cup and saucer and stirring carefully.

She didn't know what to say. What to do. So she did the obvious thing, busying herself with the milk and sugar, inwardly cringing at the fact that her *father* was probably watching her every movement. She did her best not to knock anything over, or spill her tea. When she was done, she left the cup on the table, not trusting herself to sip it without burning herself. Instead, she straightened and looked over at Oliver, her hands gripping her knees, palms hot through her tights.

They watched each other again, but after what seemed like an age, Oliver's smile faded and he spoke. "I'm sorry."

Amber waited, but when she realised he wasn't going to say more, she stammered, "W-what for?"

Oliver shrugged, his tea sitting in his lap, untouched apart from the initial sip he had taken. "Everything. For not being there, for not being a father."

Amber glanced away. The hard, angry part of her was silent now, leaving behind only the shy little girl who hated conflict. "Mum explained. I—I understand."

But he shook his head. "I appreciate that, but it doesn't make it right. And I know nothing I ever do will make it right, but… thank you for giving me this chance to meet you, even if after today you want nothing more to do with me."

Amber stared at her cup, and she crossed her arms, gripping her elbows with each hand. Eventually, unable to decide how to respond, she looked up at him. "Tell me about yourself."

Oliver raised his pale eyebrows in surprise. "Where would you like me to start?"

Amber raised her shoulders awkwardly. "Tell me… tell me what you like."

So he did. He told her he liked golf, and sailing. Rich man hobbies she had no interest in. But as he spoke, and Amber tried and failed to sound interested, he began to tell her about a solo sailing trip he had made before he was married, exploring the Norwegian fjords. And as he described the scenery and the sunrises, she found herself truly listening, and asking him questions.

"Would you like to go?" he asked when he had finished describing the aurora borealis and she said it was something she had always wanted to see.

Amber started, realising she had been talking normally, even smiling. Suddenly self-conscious again, she reached for her tea. It had grown lukewarm, but she gulped it down anyway. As she set down her empty cup, Oliver leaned forward to refill it.

"Help yourself to the biscuits. I didn't know what you would like, so I got a selection."

"Thank you," she murmured, reaching for a thin shortbread round and nibbling at the edge as she thought of how to respond. "We once went to France with my grandparents in their caravan. We went to Cornwall and Wales a lot too, but France was a real treat."

She paused, studying Oliver's expression, but he was only listening intently, his eyes trained on her face. Eyes like Cameron's. Eyes like… like *hers*, she realised with a pang. How had she never noticed that before? She and Cameron looked so alike, yet she had never seen the resemblance, hadn't even stopped to wonder. She sat frozen for a moment, the regret bubbling up again that she hadn't known what she and Cameron were to each other.

Then she started, realising she had trailed off in the middle of her story.

She fiddled with the biscuit on her saucer, absently crumbling bits off with the corner of her nail as she regained her train of thought. “We had to wait until the season was over, because my grandparents, well, they ran a B&B. So usually we went at the end of September, or October. Sometimes we were lucky and the weather was good. Normally it rained, but I didn’t mind too much. I read a lot, or we played board games.”

He gave her an encouraging smile, and she sipped her tea, unsure why she was telling him, but she babbled on regardless. Talking was better than awkward silence. “When I began secondary school, Mum started working at the hospital again. And she changed. She seemed… happier, like she was finally doing what she really wanted. And when I went home at weekends she had money for us to do things together. And then, for my eighteenth birthday, we went on a trip around Europa.”

Oliver was smiling, really smiling, his eyes crinkling at the edges. Amber stopped talking, his resemblance to Cameron haunting her yet again.

“I bet that was really special.”

“It was,” she said, a blush creeping across her cheeks at his enthusiasm. She wasn’t used to people outside her family having much interest in what she had to say. “I… I like reading, and I liked art history at school, and I’d read about all these places that I never thought I would get a chance to visit, at least not for a long time. But we went to the south of Spain, Italy, Greece. We went to Paris, which we couldn’t afford before, and Brussels and Amsterdam and Vienna… But we didn’t get to Scandinavia. We planned to go on another trip, but then… well, Mum joined the Resistance.”

Oliver looked down at his cup, his face hard to read. He took a long drink before speaking. "I know your mother and I have different political views, but it's an admirable thing, what she's doing. I'm proud of her, and you should be too."

"I am." Amber's voice came out harsher than she had intended, the defensive part of her finding its voice again. "Nobody is as proud of her as I am. Not just because of the Resistance, but because of how hard she works, how strong she is, how she… how she brought me up." She trailed off, realising her words could be seen as an accusation, a reminder of what he had turned his back on. But whether or not those words hit their mark, Oliver set down his cup, refilling it, and hers, before he changed the subject.

"She told me about you and Cameron," he said, stirring milk into his cup. "I'm… sorry you didn't know who he was."

Amber held her teacup in her hands, watching the bubbles spin on the top after she had just stirred it. That pang jolted through her chest again. "I'm sorry… that you lost him."

She glanced up to see pain flicker across Oliver's face. He, too, was staring at nothing, and Amber wondered what memory he was seeing in his mind's eye. "I haven't thanked her for what she did for him."

Amber sipped her tea, and was about to reply when he looked up at her and continued.

"I don't know if Cameron ever spoke about me. If he did, he probably had little good to say. But what Roxanne did for him… she was a better parent to him in a few months than his mother and I were throughout his entire life. He died young, but I truly believe he died happy, and that's the least a father could want for his son."

She blinked back tears, gripping the cup tightly as she held his gaze. But when his face began to swim, she looked down, drinking her tea, trying not to cry. It was true, Cameron hadn't spoken about him much, clamming up each time his father was mentioned. Amber had speculated that he was afraid of his father, and had expected Oliver to be abusive if he worked for the Ronans and interrogated people for a living. But the man before her didn't fit with what she had imagined. He seemed calm, kind, and was clearly grieving his lost son.

"I know what you think," he said, leaning forward in his chair, "that I've been prompted into wanting to meet you because of what happened to Cameron. And that may be partly true, but I've always wanted to meet you, always wished I could know you and be the father you deserve. And I know that while there is nothing stopping me now, you might not want that. But I can't go on without at least trying."

Amber nodded, still looking down at her tea. Her preconceived idea of him still floated in the back of her mind, and her Trace – that gut instinct deep within her – warned her not to trust him, not yet. But perhaps losing Cameron made him want to change his ways, seek forgiveness. In spite of everything, Amber found herself wanting to give him a chance to become the man her mother had fallen in love with once again.

"Well," she said in a small voice, finally meeting his gaze. "We have nothing to lose."

Hope and gratitude shone in Oliver's clear blue eyes, and they crinkled at the edges again, some tension leaving his shoulders.

They continued talking for at least another hour, Oliver asking her how she liked school and university, and what she wanted to do with her career.

"You must have been at Riverdene at the same time as Lindsey."

Amber nodded, swallowing the biscuit she had been nibbling. "Yes, she was the best in the school."

Oliver blinked. "You knew her then?"

Amber shrugged a little. "Not personally. She was a few years ahead of me. But she was head girl, and a great role model."

Oliver seemed to glow with pleasure at her praise of his daughter. "I don't think she realises this, but Lindsey is my pride and joy."

Amber gave him a small smile. "She was always kind. Not like her friends." For she remembered only too well the kind of company Lindsey had kept, the same kind of company the likes of Skye Bolton modelled herself on.

Oliver was quiet for a moment. "I always knew she was too kind for our line of work. She completed her training and worked her way up to become Ronan's Head Tracer. But it made sense when she confessed she's been spying for the Saoirse Army almost from the start. She's a better person than I could ever be."

She was shocked to hear that. The Saoirse Army were the closest allies of the Resistance, and had been fighting for Ireland's freedom from Ronan clutches since Ivor's conquest. Suddenly, Lindsey Matheson seemed a little less intimidating. "Can I… could I perhaps… meet her?"

Oliver's gaze shot to her in surprise. "I think that could be arranged." He studied her for a moment. "I would have to tell her, and… well, I don't know what she would make of it. But yes, I would like you to meet, if she's willing."

Amber couldn't hold in her hopeful smile. She didn't want to think of Lindsey possibly rejecting her. Losing Cameron before she had known what he was to her had rocked her to her very core, but the thought that she might have a sister out of all this when she had always been an only child… hope bloomed in her chest, as fragile as a porcelain flower.

There was a small knock on the door then, and both Amber and Oliver looked around to see Roxanne's blonde head peeking around the door. "I'm sorry to interrupt," she murmured, edging the door open a little more, "but it's been two hours and I just wanted to see if everything is okay."

Amber glanced at Oliver to see him beaming, and she couldn't help but smile too, realising that everything was more than just okay.

Chapter Twenty-Seven

PHAEDRA RONAN

"You're going to *steal* my sister's armies?" Phaedra asked her uncle. "She'll have a fit."

Caspar sucked his teeth, looking a little worried as he gazed at the ripple of sunlight on the lake before them. They had set down the pair of deckchairs they had sourced from Mrs Medley's shed close to the gently lapping shore. "That's the plan. She's already lost London. If I can win over most of the military, convince them to back me instead of her, we stand a better chance of winning the war."

Phaedra clutched her glass in her lap, a large whiskey on the rocks. She had known their short-lived, fragile peace was a lie, that her boredom at the lake cottage was a luxury. While she distracted herself from the darkness of recent months by spending time with her uncle and trying to build up the courage to tell him about her past with Ombra Medley, she was all too aware of her sister's threat still looming on the horizon.

"You think they'll choose you over her?"

He shrugged, ice clinking as he raised his own glass to his lips. "We can only hope fear of her ruthlessness will outweigh the Nox fanatics. The rumours are spreading about the patricide, and about her threatening you and I. She has killed and alienated her entire family, which means she would have no qualms about hurting or killing people who aren't of her blood. The ones with more sense will stay away."

"So she'll have a following of nutcases." She thought about Brydon Marsden back at Castle Uaine, how the old man seemed to follow her sister unquestioningly, his presence creeping Phaedra out as much as her grandfather had done. How many more twisted and power-hungry individuals were prepared to offer up whatever they could give and kiss her sister's boots, all just for the sake of a bit of renown and privilege if they and Alessia survived?

"What about Skye Bolton?" she asked, wondering if there were Lux fanatics too.

"What about her?"

"Will people follow her?"

Caspar was silent, sipping his drink for a long moment before he found his words. "Skye isn't your typical Lux. She's a Caplin supporter for a start, and after Caplin's ancestor seized control of Britannia and Ireland by claiming it was his divine right, we don't even know if the public would trust the next Lux. Skye has to tread carefully."

Phaedra huffed a sigh, then helped herself to more of her uncle's whiskey, the bottle lying in the grass between them. "Well then, here's to the Lux leading us out of the shadows," she said a little sarcastically, tipping her glass to her lips. But when she lowered her glass, she saw Caspar watching her intently, a faint frown between his brows. "What?"

"Aren't you… afraid for your sister?"

Phaedra twisted her mouth as she contemplated the difficult question. After what she had witnessed, and the things Alessia had done since killing their father, Phaedra wasn't sure how she felt about her anymore. Once, she supposed she loved her because she had been told that was what sisters did. But she didn't think Alessia loved her. She had always been cruel, playing tricks and mind games with her from as far back as she could remember. And then there were the death threats, and what she had done to Maggie and the others…

"Will she die?"

Caspar hesitated. "She doesn't have to. That depends on Skye. I've read that some Nox survived, but they were weakened considerably. But most of the time, the final battle was a fight to the death."

She tried to imagine Alessia without her Talent. Alessia weak, relying on others to protect her and take care of her. She knew what Alessia would prefer. She knew without barely knowing her at all: it would be all or nothing.

Pushing away thoughts of her sister being killed, she drove the conversation back to an earlier topic. "So Caplin and the Resistance have teamed up, you're going to try to win over the Ronan Army, and Alessia is stuck squatting in Edinburgh. Then what? Will you march on her?"

"If we have the manpower, then yes, it will probably come to that."

Phaedra suppressed a shudder, trying not to think of all the risks that would bring. "Well," she said, taking a deep breath and looking at her uncle with what she hoped was a fierce expression. "I want to fight."

She didn't miss the flicker of disbelief and amusement that crossed Caspar's face, although he worked quickly to school his features into a serious expression. "Oh?"

"Yes." She straightened in her chair, determined to prove his disbelief wrong. Determined to prove everyone who had underestimated her wrong. Including herself. "Everyone thinks I'm a waste of space. If you're all out there risking your necks so we might get some peace and quiet someday, I can't just veg around here and let you do all the work."

This time Caspar didn't hide his smile, and she hoped he wasn't laughing at her idea. "And how do you propose to fight?"

Phaedra held her head high, trying to act like she had given the matter some serious thought. "I want to join the Resistance Army."

Caspar raised an eyebrow. "Not my army?"

"Well, it wouldn't really be your army, would it?"

"True." He drained his glass, then poured them both some more. "Just… I would prefer if it didn't become common knowledge, for your own safety. I'll talk to Harlow, see if we can arrange something, and we'll double up on our training sessions so you can learn to fight with your Talent."

Phaedra stared at her uncle, not daring to believe that he was actually agreeing to her plan. "Seriously?"

"Of course, if it's something you want to do." He shrugged, then raised his glass to his mouth. But before he could drink, Phaedra darted out of her chair and threw her arms around him in a hug.

"Thank you!" she exclaimed, trying not to let him see the tears in her eyes.

***

Joining the Resistance Army cadets wasn't quite as glorious as she had expected it to be. They made her dye the blonde streaks out of her hair, tone down her make-up, and remove her chipped nail polish. They ran her through exercise drills that made her vomit, and once, she passed out. In her medical examination with Roxanne, the doctor told her she had to give up smoking, leave all drugs alone and drink no more than once a week if she expected to pass her fitness tests. If anyone else had examined her, she would have laughed in their face and called bullshit, but since it was Roxanne, she took it on the chin. She took her prescriptions for herbal remedies that would help curb her cravings, and drank bitter teas to calm her anxiety and volatile Talent. What was more, Roxanne had described the damage she was doing to her body in horrible detail, scaring her into changing her habits for her health as well as her military aspirations.

But while she was getting healthier and fitter, Phaedra hated every aspect of her training. It was not at all how she had imagined. She hated getting up early. Hated the drills. Hated being shouted at. She hated that she was expected to stay in the barracks most nights, even though she took a portal back to the lake cottage almost every night so she could sleep in privacy in a comfortable bed instead. She hated the disciplinary tasks that she was given the two times she overslept, and found herself missing Maggie more than ever when she realised the housekeeper's brisk manner had never been anywhere near as horrid as her officer's strict rules. And most of all, she hated the glamours and the fake name she had to keep up to hide her identity from her fellow cadets. But she supposed it was better than letting them know who she really was, and being hated for her name.

She was doubly grateful for her secret identity when the decision was made to train Resistance and Caplin cadets together, because if anyone hated Ronans more than the Resistance, it was Caplinites.

The first morning they were clumped together, the two factions refused to mingle, eyeing each other across the training ground, no one prepared to approach. By the afternoon, their officer was so frustrated with their aversion to each other that she paired them up with members of the opposite faction, instructing them to spar.

Phaedra trudged over to a corner of the gymnasium with her sparring partner, who turned to her with just as much reluctance, glaring down at her beneath dark bushy eyebrows. Phaedra raised an eyebrow of her own. He seemed to be around her own age, but that was where the similarities ended. She was sure he must weigh twice or three times as much as her, muscles bulging beneath his uniform. He immediately dropped into a stance much more practised than her own, which, added to his bulk, made her certain she was about to get her ass kicked. She glanced over at other cadets, convinced that Officer Munro had made a mistake in pairing her with this beast.

Cracking her neck, she took up a stance of her own, trying not to cringe at the thought of what this bigger, more experienced cadet was probably about to do to her. A whistle was blown, and within seconds she was on the floor.

"You coulda given me half a chance," she muttered, already winded. The boy said nothing as she got to her feet, nor did he offer her a hand.

He did give her a chance the second time around, but she still found herself stumbling to the side when he delivered a kick to her ribs, and then she was buffeted backwards with a few hits to her stomach. She yielded quickly, fighting for breath through the second winding.

"Could you go easy on me?" she complained, rubbing her stomach and taking as deep a breath as she could manage, the effort stabbing through her middle.

"I'm not supposed to," he shrugged.

She glared at him, tempted to tell this brute exactly where to shove his next punch, but Munro yelled her fake name across the gym.

"Reynolds, keep up!"

Phaedra glanced her way, unable to pretend she hadn't heard when she met the woman's furious gaze, and she looked back at her opponent, fighting the heat that was spreading across her cheeks. Dropping back into her sparring stance, they started again.

They had been sparring for no more than a minute when the boy's fist connected with her nose. She went down hard, and Munro's whistle sounded a moment later. Clutching her nose, she saw blood spattering the green mat beneath her, and a throbbing pressure built behind her eyes.

Munro herself hauled her up, grabbing her chin and turning her head this way and that, her face pinched. "It's not broken," she said, as though the blood pouring from her nostrils was no big deal.

But Phaedra couldn't speak, too blinded by the pain and choked by the blood. Glancing around, she found everyone staring at her, some even looking amused. Phaedra glared back, wishing she could bloody *their* noses for them, see how they liked it.

"Clean yourself up," Munro snapped. "I want you back out here in five minutes. Scott, spar with me." She turned her back to Phaedra, taking her place in front of the big guy.

Five minutes later, the bleeding having stopped but her nostrils still crusty, Phaedra exited the changing rooms, hovering on the sidelines of the gymnasium and waiting to be given new orders. About a minute passed before Munro spotted her and blew her whistle. Scott, she was glad to see, looked red, sweaty and breathless.

"Swap!" Munro shouted, heading in Phaedra's direction. Her short mousy hair was barely dishevelled from the sparring. "Reynolds, over here." She jerked her thumb at a girl who stood a few feet away, the direct opposite of Scott, smaller even than Phaedra. Glumly, Phaedra headed over to her, still sniffing and wiping her nose with the back of her hand.

"Hi," she muttered, looking at the floor.

"Hi," said the girl, sounding bored, hands in her pockets. But there was something about her voice that made Phaedra look up, and she froze when she recognised the person in front of her, her hand in front of her nose mid-wipe.

It was Ombra.

She looked different. Her hair was a uniform caramel brown pulled back in a tight bun. Her face was oddly bare without a scrap of make-up or her multitude of piercings. The bulky Caplin uniform made her look like a child wearing adults' clothing. But she was still as beautiful as ever, with those perfect, full lips and eyes in a shade of greenish-blue that Phaedra couldn't name, a few loose strands of hair framing her freckled pixie face.

Ombra raised an eyebrow as she stared at her, and it was then that Phaedra remembered she was wearing a glamour.

"Something on my face?"

"No, it's—" She stopped, wondering what she could possibly say, wondering how she could even begin to explain. She still wasn't entirely ready, her insides suddenly crawling with nerves, but perhaps the universe was sick of waiting and giving her the shove up the backside she needed. Besides, what if she didn't get another chance?

Munro blasted her whistle, making her jump. Ombra shrugged, dismissing her weird behaviour, then took her hands from her pockets and raised them in front of her, bending her knees slightly. Realising she had no choice but to get on with it, Phaedra followed suit.

Ombra wasn't as experienced as Scott, but she still beat her, bringing her to the floor with a well-placed foot hooked behind Phaedra's left knee. As Phaedra lay on the mat, winded for the third time in less than half an hour, she was torn between embarrassment and relief that she didn't have to hurt her. And at least Ombra had the decency to help her up, unlike her comrade.

As Phaedra stood, fighting for breath, she studied her former girlfriend again, close enough to breathe in her familiar sweet perfume, mingled with a tang of sweat. But as Ombra got ready to spar again, Phaedra held up a hand, then doubled over, putting both hands on her knees.

"You okay?"

She nodded, straightening again and meeting her eye. Ombra's forehead furrowed with concern. "You don't look good." And then, before Phaedra could stop her, she waved Munro over.

"For goodness' sake, Reynolds," said Munro after she looked her up and down and pressed a hand to her forehead. "Are you still smoking?"

"I'm trying to quit," Phaedra grumbled, her breath coming in sharp stabs.

Munro let out a sigh of frustration. "Medley, take her to the infirmary. She looks like she's going to pass out."

Ombra shrugged and stuffed her hands into her pockets again, turning towards the door after a glance at Phaedra. But Phaedra knew by her expression that she was only too glad to have a distraction from the exercise. She followed her, hurrying to keep up.

When they were out in the open, crossing the rapidly darkening training yard, Phaedra gulped down fresh air, the crisp evening cooling the sweat on her forehead. "Ombra," she gasped, and the girl paused halfway across the yard, turning to Phaedra as she caught up.

"Do I know you?" she asked, searching her face in puzzlement.

Phaedra couldn't help the grin that broke across her face, and she glanced around to make sure no one was near before muttering the name of the glamour sigil backwards, undoing its effects. As her face was revealed, Ombra stared, her pretty mouth dropping open.

"It's Phoebe." Phaedra blurted, words falling from her lips in a cascade. "Or… well… I'm actually called Phaedra."

Ombra blinked, her big eyes widening even more, and simply kept staring.

"I know it's weird. And I know I haven't been in touch… but I can explain."

"What happened to you?" she asked, her voice a pitch higher than usual. "And what do you mean, your name isn't Phoebe?"

Phaedra glanced around nervously. "Keep your voice down." She looked back at Ombra. "I can explain. Would you… maybe we can get out of here. I have so much I need to tell you."

But hurt slashed across Ombra's face, her eyes glazing. "No shit. I thought you were dead!"

The anger and disbelief in Ombra's outburst hit her right in her winded stomach, and suddenly, anything Phaedra wanted to say felt like too little to excuse her disappearance. They continued to stare at one another, a tear escaping the corner of Ombra's eye and trailing down the side of her nose as Phaedra struggled to find her words.

She glanced around the deserted yard again, speaking quietly. "You don't know who I am?"

Ombra let out a shocked gasp. "You just told me you've been using a fake name. How the fuck am I supposed to know who you are?" The fury was building, turning her dainty face scarlet.

"I…" Phaedra paused, heart hammering at the sight of Ombra's rage. She lowered her voice almost to a whisper. "I'm Phaedra Ronan."

Silence fell between them like a stone dropped into a well, and Phaedra held her breath, waiting for the inevitable sound of it hitting the bottom. But instead of words, Ombra's eyes darkened with suppressed shadows, and she turned on her heel, staggering off across the training ground.

"Ombra!" Phaedra choked, stumbling after her, reaching out.

“Stay away from me.” Ombra jerked a hand back, fingers splayed like a stop sign, curls of shadow trailing in her wake.

Phaedra froze, staring after her as she slipped into the gloom between buildings, disappearing into the twilight. She had never seen her like this, her anger so at odds with the cheerful, rebellious party girl Phaedra had loved and cherished. As she stared after her, wisps of shadow were all that remained, and a hollow devastation settled in her chest, the fear that she had lost her for good.

Chapter Twenty-Eight

SKYE BOLTON

"Are you nervous?" Skye asked, sitting at the kitchen table of the lake cottage in nothing more than a black lace and silk chemise, watching Caspar make coffee. It had been some weeks since she had last spent the night with him, but with Phaedra now staying most nights at the barracks, he had invited her for dinner the previous evening, cooking her a meal and fulfilling his promise to buy wine.

Caspar laughed. "Nervous about winning over an entire army? Soldiers my father recruited and commanded, and who were instructed to be loyal to the next Ronan president? I would be a fool if I wasn't." He poured the coffee into two cups, the rich aroma filling the rustic kitchen of her aunt's cottage, then brought them to the table. He, too, was wearing little, and Skye openly admired his shirtless top half. Honed muscle rippled beneath his lightly tanned skin – skin her hands and mouth had explored not an hour before. She bit her lower lip to resist smiling at the memory.

"Luckily for me," he continued, "they trust me. Which is just as well, considering how many times I had to step in and sort out whatever mess my Aunt Moira got herself into."

"She'll be glad to hand command over to you."

Caspar tilted his head. "Not quite. She's bound to know Alessia banished me. But she's old and never wanted power in the first place, so she'll cave eventually."

"What will Phaedra do while you're in Ireland?"

He shrugged. "She's not keen on staying at the barracks, so she'll probably make the most of having the place to herself for a week. I just hope I don't come back to find the house burned down, or I'll be even more in your aunt's debt."

Skye held in a grin. "With all her money, I would say she could just build another cottage, but she's sentimental about this place."

Caspar grimaced. "Then maybe I ought to leave her a chaperone."

They lapsed into an amused but comfortable silence, both drinking their coffee, grateful for the peace and quiet as they watched specks of dust drift in rays of sunlight.

"And how are things with you?" Caspar asked eventually, concern in his eyes as he watched Skye across the table.

"I'm fine," she said automatically, clutching her cup in both hands.

But Caspar raised an eyebrow. "You don't have to pretend with me, Skye."

She took a long drink, trying to hide from his scrutiny. "People want me to be some sort of hero. But to be honest, all I want is my father back."

Caspar nodded, lowering his gaze to the table, letting her have a moment to compose herself. She clutched her coffee cup too tightly as imagined images of what her father was going through spiralled out of control, mixed with the haunting memories she had seen in the butler's mind.

"You never told me how the meeting went with Camilla."

The images distorted, replaced with the memory of Camilla's sickly grin across the table. Caspar had told her he was in her debt, and yet, she knew how much she risked if she shared something as delicate as this. Even so, he knew Camilla better than anyone.

"She gave me a lot of food for thought."

Caspar winced. "What does she want from you?"

Skye gave him a grim smile. "I think you can imagine."

He studied her, his expression hard to read. "You don't know if you can trust me."

Skye glanced down at the table. "I don't know if I can trust anyone."

"Well..." He fiddled with his own cup, turning it slowly in his hand. "If I know Camilla at all, she wants reassurance that whoever wins this war, she will come out of it on top. If Alessia wins, it means a reign of terror which will likely last until the end of Camilla's natural life. So she wants to stay in Alessia's good books. She wants something out of whatever deal she's made with you to buy herself immunity from Alessia's wrath, but that gives her something to hold over you so she can control you. Right now, she has your father, and you want him back. But the price is some form of blackmail. Am I on the right track?"

Skye nodded and flashed a reluctant smile, enjoying listening to his musings.

"What is she holding over your head, Skye? Other than the obvious, what can you offer her that she wants?"

"She offered me my father's life and freedom, in exchange for someone else."

Caspar looked stunned. "She wants Caplin."

Skye bowed her head, fear and panic welling inside her chest.

"Well..." said Caspar, after draining the rest of his coffee. "If anyone can do it, it's you."

"Do what, exactly?"

He shrugged. "Kill him, capture him. Whatever it is that Camilla wants. And to be honest, after the past year, I'm surprised you're even debating this."

Skye let out a slow sigh. "It's not that simple."

"Isn't it? After the way he's treated you and your family, I don't understand why you're still loyal to him. If I were in your shoes, I wouldn't hesitate to hand him over."

"You would say that."

"Yes, I would. Maybe I'm biased – I don't like Caplin and I have no qualms about saying so. But I like you, and I can't understand why you're still letting him take advantage."

But she shook her head, her panic threatening to burst free at any moment.

"Look, Skye, ever since he found out what you are, he's been using you as a crutch, knowing that as long as you're loyal to him, he can pull your strings and steer you in the direction he wants. You may think you're in control, but I watched everyone very closely in that boardroom, and while you and Caplin might act like you don't care about each other, it's clear you do and he knows he can still influence you. He also knows that ultimately, the Resistance will follow you, because they have no choice."

Skye stared at her cup, her fingers shaking slightly with the effort of keeping her emotions in check.

Caspar continued. "Even if you don't believe he's taking advantage of you now, what about everything else that's happened? He won't help your father. He handed you over to my brother as a hostage for months. And he let you waste away in Blackwater after you sacrificed yourself to rescue him. I have a pretty good idea of what you went through while you were there. Don't think I don't know where the scars on your back came from."

She flinched, a prickle creeping its way across her scars. Glen had never mentioned the mottled discolouration that remained from the torture he had witnessed her endure at Blackwater, and on the occasions when she had worn revealing clothing, she had disguised the scarring with glamours. Caspar seemed to realise he had hit a nerve, for he lowered his voice, his expression softening.

"I'm just glad it was Doran in charge, and not my father. Ivor favoured Camilla for interrogations, and you know what she's like with a knife in her hand."

Skye could only sit in silence as sparks crackled in her clenched fists. Thoughts of what Camilla was doing to her father flooded her mind again, but she knew everything he had said was true. She had fought with Caplin over it just weeks ago.

"I know you don't want my advice, but for what it's worth, I wouldn't even think twice about handing him over. You owe Caplin nothing, Skye."

He seemed to be finished, his final words echoing through her mind. She sat there, letting them sink in, making herself see things from his perspective. Or any outsider, for that matter. Sabine had said it right from the start, as had her grandfather, and now even her fellow Guardians were considering someone other than Caplin to lead. But even so, handing Caplin over wasn't something she could bring herself to do lightly, not if she wanted to win the backing of his followers.

"You say nothing about this," she said eventually, her eyes snapping up to his again.

"You have my word," he said solemnly, pouring more coffee for them both. Skye drank deeply, barely tasting it. She felt his eyes on her for a long moment, until he brought up another matter she didn't want to discuss. "Are you preparing for your battle with Alessia?"

She shrugged. "What's there to prepare? I can already fight."

"Have you ever fought anyone with Obscurus powers?"

"I used to train my cousin, but we usually left Talents out of it. Neither of our parents wanted us to bring the house down." She tried to smile as memories of long-lost happier times drifted to the surface.

"Never in battle?"

Her hands tightened around her cup. "The warden at the prison… Ikarus and I had to tag team him."

He nodded. "You killed him."

"We did."

He shifted in his seat, drawing her gaze. "Will you fight with me? Today? I don't wish to overstep, but darkness powers are rare, and I trained Alessia myself. I can share everything I know, her weaknesses, her strengths."

She hesitated. She knew he meant well, that his insight would be invaluable. But sharing a bed with him was one thing. Letting him assess her fighting skills was a vulnerability she wasn't sure she was prepared for.

"I know your father is your priority, but if you are the Lux, Alessia could spring this final battle on you at any time, any place. You need to be as prepared as possible. And if you're not the Lux… well, there's no harm in ensuring you have the skills to make it out of a fight with her alive. None of us…" He swallowed, his eyes shuttering. "None of us want you to die."

Her gaze dropped to the scar on his shoulder, the black, spiderweb lines that Alessia's attack had left behind. Until Caspar had shown her the wound, the thought that she could lose a fight to the bookish little Nox hadn't even crossed her mind. She gritted her teeth, pushing away the horrific reminder that she had similar wounds coming her way sooner or later.

"You're talking like you doubt Vala's prophecy. I thought the legends say she's never wrong?"

Caspar released a slow breath. "I don't trust Vala, whatever the legends say. She let my brother walk into a trap, let him think your mother was the Lux. If Doran and Meredith had gone ahead and got married, that witch's nasty little prophecy wouldn't have played out."

"And I wouldn't be here."

The corner of his mouth tugged up in a grimace. "All I'm saying is, you could be a decoy. Just because we can't think of anyone else who fits the prophecy, doesn't mean it's definitely you."

She wanted to believe him, wanted to cling to the doubt and hope in his words. But she knew, in the eye of the storm deep in her chest, that Alessia was her enemy. She had known since she had first set eyes on her, the knowledge primitive, primal, as ancient as the earth itself. "Did you ever dream about Vala?"

Caspar raised an eyebrow, his surprise evident. "What makes you ask?"

Skye shrugged. "I dreamed about her for a long time. As long as I can remember. She didn't really say anything, she was just… there."

A muscle twitched in his jaw as he regarded her, his thoughts elsewhere. Finally, he blinked, drinking some coffee. "I dreamed about her. She promised death and heartache."

Skye's heart stuttered in surprise. "She gave you a prophecy?"

He nodded, but his gaze had drifted, his eyes glazing over as a memory haunted him. She waited, his expression setting her curiosity alight, that burning curiosity that would have tempted her to explore his mind if it weren't hidden.

She opened her mouth to apologise for prying, but heavy footfalls on the stairs drew their gaze towards the open doorway. Phaedra suddenly appeared, wearing a Resistance uniform.

"Oh, hello." Phaedra glanced from her uncle to Skye in surprise, then a smirk grew on her face. "I didn't know we had company."

Skye glanced at Caspar, who was running a hand through his hair in obvious agitation. She had never seen him embarrassed, but she supposed there was a first for everything. "Morning, Phaedra," she said with a smirk of her own, then crossed her arms over her chest, suddenly aware of how thin her chemise was.

"I thought you were at the barracks last night?" The irritation in Caspar's voice was evident.

"I had drinks after, then came home late. But it seems you were too busy to notice." She waggled her eyebrows at Skye, who resisted the urge to laugh. "I thought I heard some bumps in the night."

Caspar cleared his throat loudly. "Well, that cat's out of the bag, but please keep this to yourself."

Phaedra snickered. "Who would I tell?"

"Who wouldn't you tell, more like." His tone was casual, but the warning was there all the same. "If you're on duty today, you're rather late."

It was Phaedra's turn to scowl. "I know, I'm going."

"If you get kicked out of the army, I'll make you get a job."

"And I'll tell everyone what you're up to with the Lux," she said, then walked out with a last huff of laughter.

An awkward silence followed, broken only when Skye pushed back her chair with a scrape, picking up their empty mugs and depositing them in the sink.

"You could have warned me she had sneaked in."

Skye turned back to him, sheepish. "I was a bit distracted."

Caspar shook his head in exasperation, but she didn't miss the way his lips tugged up at the corners. He stood then, and her attention was immediately stolen by his toned abdomen, mischief glinting in his eyes. She held her breath as he prowled towards her and drew her close for a kiss, his teeth grazing her bottom lip and bringing her desire bubbling to the surface like molten lava.

"Care to distract me a little more?" she asked as his lips roamed below her jawline. She arched her neck as one hand tangled in her hair, while the other drew tantalising circles on her waist, his fingers warm through the thin silk.

"Didn't you promise me a fight down by the lake?"

She let out a frustrated exhale. "We have time for both."

His wicked laugh was hot against her throat, and the hand on her waist slid down, trailing to her bare thigh, then inching upwards, dragging the hem of her chemise with it. She let out another gasp, her focus clinging to that wandering hand, to his lips on her neck. As his hand in her hair made its way to the strap of her chemise, his voice reverberated through her as he murmured in her ear, "Is she gone?"

Skye inhaled a ragged breath, struggling to focus her mind, to sweep their surroundings in search of Phaedra. The house and grounds beyond were deserted. "Yes."

Wasting not a second longer, Caspar claimed her lips once more, and he pulled the strap from her shoulder, pressing her back against the counter as her chemise slipped down to pool at her feet.

***

Skye tried to feign reluctance as she strode down to the lake at Caspar's side, but she couldn't deny she was curious about his fighting style. She had never seen him in action, but there were plenty of witness accounts of his skill on the battlefield.

He chose a spot on the expansive lawn between the cottage and the lake, standing tall with his hands in his pockets as he weighed her up. She mirrored his stance, eyes sweeping him up and down, the anticipation of an attack transforming him from lover to foe. His simple shirt and slacks were black, the material loose, easy to move in. Able to camouflage his shadows. She wondered if Alessia preferred to wear black for the same reason. Considering Caspar had trained the Nox himself, it wouldn't surprise her.

"Your Talents are meant to match Alessia's in strength. Lightning cuts through the night, it's carried to its target by the darkness. The lightning can shield you from darkness, but if you let your guard down and Alessia's Talent hits you, you'll likely end up with a nice little scar to match mine."

Skye nodded, refusing to let him see her nerves at the reminder of his injury.

"I expect your Talent would be equally damaging to Alessia if you can bypass her attacks with a direct hit."

Without warning, Caspar raised his arms, feinting to the left then throwing a handful of shimmering darkness with his right hand, his movements fast and fluid. Skye slipped into a defensive stance, her heartbeat crashing and thundering in her ears as she lurched out of the path of the attack. He didn't wait before launching his next one, a double hit from both sides. She dodged one, shooting out at the other, light and darkness meeting and crackling in midair, then hurtling off course towards the lake.

Caspar straightened, his hands falling to his sides, no shadows curling around them now.

"The only Electricae I've ever fought are your parents." His voice was quiet, his expression guarded. Skye gritted her teeth, uncomfortable with the turn in the conversation. "Perhaps we should properly assess how our two Talents interact. You're not going to defeat Alessia by dodging her attacks, even if your reflexes are impressive."

Skye's lips twisted into a grimace, torn between pleasure at his compliment and unease at the reminder that, sooner or later, Alessia was coming for her.

"You dodged my Talent because you don't understand it, right?"

"Right," Skye confirmed, seeing no reason to pretend otherwise.

He slipped his left hand into his pocket, shoulders relaxing as he raised his other hand palm-up. Skye tensed as tendrils of shadow swirled from his fingers, ready for another attack, but he held the darkness in his cupped hand, a slice of night glittering and distorting in the sunlight.

"It's an odd Talent," he mused, watching his creation, his eyes bright with wonder. "There's a fine line between using it to blind and imitate the night, and causing damage."

The darkness grew, fanning out around him, above them, blocking out the sun. Skye watched intently, her own Talent prickling beneath her skin. But the darkness only drifted like a black cloud, the sunlight above it refracting into golden pinpricks of light, like stars in the night sky. Skye drew in a slow breath, torn between apprehension and awe. Caspar's creation was a thing of dark beauty.

Slowly, he drew the blanket of night back to him, raising his other hand to gather it in, shrinking it, shaping it into a ball.

"I was always told it's the most destructive Talent," Skye said quietly, still somewhat mesmerised by his seemingly effortless control over his power.

He tilted his head, watching the ball of darkness warp and ripple. "It is resistant to most of the elements, yes. It can swallow fire, destroy earth, metals, and flesh. Air can move it but not destroy it, and it merges with water. As for lightning…" He met her gaze then, his eyes darkened with shadow. For a brief moment, fear stabbed through her chest, but then he blinked, the shadows gone, his irises softening into the cool blue of the lake behind him. “Come here,” he said softly. The dark sphere in his hands expanded like a pair of lungs.

She hesitated, glancing from his face to the darkness he held, mistrust still lingering with the static in her fingers. Perhaps he saw her fear, because his lips curved into a small, encouraging smile. She approached slowly, her eyes never leaving his, her fingers clawed, ready to fight. She stopped a few feet away.

“Closer,” he murmured. “I have full control over my Talent. It’s not going anywhere without my say so.”

She gave him a half-hearted smile, narrowing the gap between them, stopping a foot away from the pulsing mass of darkness. It hummed slightly, like the purr of a cat.

“I want to see how it reacts to your Talent.”

Skye inclined her head as she met his eye again. “When I fought the Obscurus at Blackwater, our Talents merged.”

He nodded. “Let’s see if we can achieve the same now.”

She raised her hands either side of the sphere, her power crackling between her fingers, vibrating against her skin. She glanced between the darkness and his eyes again. He nodded further encouragement, and she willed the lightning to connect with the darkness. There was a buzz on contact, and she withdrew the electricity.

“I’ve never known you to be shy, Skye. Don’t disappoint me now.”

They exchanged a smirk, and she took a deep breath, trying again. This time, the lightning cut through the darkness, distorting it as the strands of bright white light met in the middle, creating a bridge between her two hands. Caspar’s fingers twitched, manipulating the cloud, a muscle flickering in his jaw as he concentrated on regaining the sphere formation. The two Talents buzzed and crackled as they fought for dominance, the darkness trying to wrap around the lightning.

"When they collide with force," Caspar explained, watching the two Talents closely, "they behave in a similar way to two Obscurae fighting: they merge and go off course. But if we concentrate, the darkness can also be used like a shield, manipulated into shapes around ourselves." As he spoke, the sphere stretched and warped, creating a wall between them. Skye took a step back, letting her current drop. "Attack me."

She took a further step back, then did as he asked. The shadow-wall buzzed as the electricity hit it, then branched out like lightning forking through the night sky. Caspar kept the shield up a moment, then twisted his hands, turning the darkness back into a sphere, the lightning still running through it. Then he turned, throwing the combined energy into the lake, where it hissed and dissipated.

"Let's see if it works the other way around."

Skye raised an eyebrow. "You want me to trap your darkness with my power?"

"Something like that. Ready?"

She bit the inside of her cheek, putting more distance between them, then settling back into a defensive position. She raised her hands before her, the lightning bridging between her fingers once again.

"I'll keep the intensity low, just in case."

"You think I can't handle a few shadows?" she teased.

Caspar didn't smile. "You've never had to endure my attacks before."

She scoffed, and his eyes glittered with mirrored mischief. "Some would say you think rather highly of yourself, Mr Ronan."

His smirk was back. "And many of my enemies would agree I'm right."

She let her mischief fade. "Go on then."

He aimed a handful of shadow between her hands, and she braced herself as it hurtled towards her. A deafening crack slashed through the quiet afternoon as the shadows hit her lightning, and she took a step back from the force. She added more energy to the current in her hands, willing the electricity to wrap around those shadows. It was a struggle, but she managed to contain them, taking a steadying breath as she balled the mass of dark and light in her hands the same way Caspar had done. Once she was confident it wasn't about to slip from her hands, she thrust it towards the lake.

"Good. So we know it's possible," he said, watching the light and darkness skitter across the surface of the water into nothing.

"Possible, yes, but that took time and effort that I can't afford in a fight."

"So we build up to it. We train every day. Unless you're already tired of spending time with me." He crossed his arms, another smirk gracing his lips.

"I'll have to check my diary."

"Mine is pretty clear."

Her lips twisted in amusement. "Fine. At least it gives me an excuse to see you." Her thoughts drifted to her family and their disapproving remarks. "And I don't have to sneak around now that Phaedra knows."

He laughed. "Silver linings. Now, let's try it again."

But Skye didn't budge. "How do we know Alessia's Talent will behave the same way?"

Caspar considered her words, lowering his gaze to a new ball of shadow in his palm. "When we fought before I left, the only difference was that she was stronger, and she could hurt me. If I fought with any other Obscurae, their shadows wouldn't affect me, just like an Ignis is unperturbed by flame, or you by electric shocks."

"If lightning cuts through darkness, why didn't it cut through your shield?"

"Because I applied more intensity. It's the same difference between blinding and hurting. Lower intensities simply remove the light and cause blindness, like your cousin did when she was involved with the Mason kidnap."

"Allegedly involved," Skye corrected, her lip curling.

"Sure." Caspar grinned, clearly not buying her lie for a second. "If Alessia isn't paying attention, your Talent could cut through hers and hurt her. But she's the Nox. You can't expect her to let her guard down."

"I don't underestimate her." Skye crossed her arms and raised her chin, masking her apprehension. "Not anymore."

"Good. You can rest assured she will be working tirelessly to prepare for her fight with you. I know that much for certain."

She swallowed, then adopted a fighting stance once more. "Let's go again."

Chapter Twenty-Nine

PHAEDRA RONAN

"What's got you so glum? Usually I'm the grumpy one."

Phaedra looked up from the depths of her murky glass of beer, peering at Glen where he sat across the narrow table from her in the crowded barracks pub. And before she could stop them, tears burst down her cheeks, and she buried her face in her hands.

It had been three days since her big reveal that had gone exactly how she *hadn't* planned, and Ombra hadn't shown up to training. Phaedra had spent the time going through the motions and doing her best to hold herself together, while a dull ache in her gut was a constant reminder that she had probably screwed it all up. On top of everything she had lost these past months, the hope that she might patch things up with Ombra had been the only shred of light that had kept her going.

A stunned silence emanated from Glen's side of the table, until she felt her seat creak with his weight as he sat beside her in the booth, wrapping his arm around her shoulders. "Hey," he said gently as she leaned into him, pressing the heels of her hands into her eyes. "What's up?"

He waited until she stopped shaking with sobs. "I found Ombra," she gasped, scrubbing her face with the sleeve of her uniform.

"And?"

"She hates me!" Her face crumpled as a fresh wave of tears fell, and she glanced around for something she could blow her nose with. "You don't have a tissue, do you?"

"Do I look like the sort of guy who carries tissues?" His light tone made her laugh in spite of herself, and he patted her back with a broad hand before getting up to grab napkins from the bar. She gave him a teary smile as she took them and dabbed at her face, then blew her nose.

They were quiet for a long moment, Glen sipping his beer and looking down at her with unveiled concern while she struggled to regain composure. "I'm sure she doesn't hate you. I mean, you can be pretty irritating, but you make up for it with your impeccable taste in friends."

She choked a laugh, shooting him an attempt at a filthy look. "Sure you're not talking to yourself there, old man?"

"Oh yeah, at twenty-eight I'm really looking forward to the retirement home."

She snickered, taking another napkin from the pile Glen had brought and wiping her eyes again. But despite his attempts to cheer her up, the tears kept coming.

"Did you tell her who you are?"

She nodded, twisting the soggy napkin between her fingers. "And then she just… stormed off." She gave a pathetic sniffle. "I haven't seen her either. What if… what if I never see her again?"

The frown lines between Glen's brows deepened as he regarded her. "You'll see her again. She's Skye's cousin, isn't she?"

She nodded, and hope bloomed in her chest. From what Phaedra remembered, Ombra and her cousin were close. "Skye comes every day. I could ask her."

Glen winced, and Phaedra clamped her lips together as she realised what she had thoughtlessly revealed. Judging by what Phaedra had walked in on earlier that week, any hopes that Glen might have of rekindling his relationship with Skye were well and truly off the table.

"What will you tell Ombra, if you see her?" Glen asked, his features smoothing into neutrality as he carefully skirted around the painful topic of Skye.

"I… I'll tell her everything." The spying, her dad's murder, her sister being the Nox. It was all too much, too overwhelming, still failing to make sense in Phaedra's own head. But she would tell her everything, if it meant she could win her back. "I'll tell her I love her."

"Maybe start slow," he advised, but his lips were curved in a small smile. "There's a lot to take in."

She nodded, but the tears threatened again, Ombra's anger and hurt echoing through her mind. "What if she doesn't forgive me?"

Glen shrugged. "Then we'll find you a rebound. I'll be your wingman."

She shoved his arm, but grinned through her tears as he playfully nudged her with his elbow. "I'm sure we can find you some other feisty blonde to boss you about."

"Who says I'm not the bossy one?"

She raised a sarcastic eyebrow. "Because we all know you're the secret teddy bear of the relationship."

He rolled his eyes, scratching the sandy beard that was gradually taking over his face.

"You should maybe get that trimmed before you start going on dates."

"Why, don't you think I suit the caveman look?" He drank deeply from his beer as she snorted. "Seriously though, Ombra probably just needs some time to get over the shock. Next time you see her, just ask her to talk, then calmly explain everything. You've been through a lot of shit recently. If she loves you, she'll understand."

Phaedra nodded. Right then, she couldn't imagine things ever being right again, but she hoped there was a second chance for them. She hoped Ombra could find some way to see past her name, to see *her* again.

"Isn't this your round?" Glen asked, setting down his empty glass.

"I'm the one crying here, doesn't that mean you should be buying me comfort drinks?"

"Seriously? Maybe we need to find you a new drinking buddy too. One who has really deep pockets."

***

Phaedra felt more nervous than she had done on any first date as she and Ombra crossed the park in silence, heading for the swing set where they had previously hung out on several occasions. Once, they had even spent an evening stargazing and talking until the early hours. Cheesy and cliché, maybe, but it was one of Phaedra's favourite memories with her. Now, instead of a star-filled velvety black, the sky was bright white, and every so often light rain fell in a mist.

When they reached the swings, Ombra slumped down on one, looking at the floor and chewing gum. She looked more like herself today, her usual dark eyeshadow framing her eyes and a few red and pink ribbons braided through her hair. She was dressed in baggy jeans and the patched denim jacket she had been wearing when they first got together. The sight of it tightened Phaedra's throat with nostalgia.

Phaedra sat down on the second swing, moving slightly back and forth, scuffing her trainers in the gravel. She had taken Glen's advice, approaching Ombra at the corner of the gymnasium when she finally returned to training, and asking her in the most mouse-like way if they could meet on their day off to talk. And to Phaedra's immense relief, she had agreed, even if she wouldn't meet her eye.

"I still don't get why you couldn't at least tell me your name," Ombra said after an agonising few minutes, eyes still trained on the floor. Her voice was cold, the bite in it sharp.

"How many Phaedras do you know?"

Ombra popped her gum, then continued to chew. "None, actually. It's not like you're the most famous Ronan or anything."

She had her dad to thank for keeping her out of the spotlight, making her use a fake name. The junkie party girl daughter was hardly a story Doran wanted the press to get hold of. "You would have figured it out at some point. And… well, I didn't know you were related to Skye Bolton. She's a Telepath."

"So, what *do* I call you?" Ombra asked, finally glancing up at her. Hardness still pinched her face, her eyes full of mistrust and accusations.

Phaedra tried a small smile, but Ombra's tone and expression stabbed like a knife through her heart. "You never seemed to have a problem with Phee."

Ombra looked away. "I asked Skye about you. She said you've been living in my parents' cottage." She let out a hollow, disbelieving laugh. "And you still couldn't pluck up the guts to speak to me. You just carried on, letting me wonder what the hell happened to you. I thought—" She swallowed, her voice cracking. "I thought I meant something to you."

A tear slipped down Phaedra's cheek as she stared at the ground, her anxiety over facing Ombra in the preceding weeks coming back to bite her. "You do. I—"

"All this time… all this time you've been keeping this a secret…" She glanced up at her again, her freckled face reduced to a look of despair. "I wish you had told me. I wouldn't have cared, you know? Just like you didn't care when you found out who I was."

"I know… I wanted to. I hated lying to you, O. I just… I'm a coward." She clutched the cold chains of the swing, feeling utterly wretched.

Whatever Ombra thought of her admission, she chose not to comment. Instead, she ploughed on with the rest of her pain, eager to get it out. "I was at the siege on your family's manor. I could have… I could have been fighting *you* that day. What if I'd hurt you? What if I've hurt or killed members of your family? Friends?" Her face distorted with fear. "How am I supposed to live with that?"

Phaedra grimaced. "I wasn't there. Neither was my family. I only… I only decided to fight recently, and only for the Resistance. I don't agree with what my family has been doing."

Ombra held her gaze for a long moment, then dipped her chin, biting her lip. "I just… I wish you could have come to me after… Or at least called. You… you don't know what you put me through."

Phaedra bowed her head, guilt twisting her insides as she recalled Ombra's countless texts and missed calls on the phone Alessia had taken from her. Phaedra hadn't slept the previous night, apart from several dreams in which today's meeting ended badly. She prayed those dreams weren't about to come true.

"I wanted to. Believe me, I did." Phaedra searched her face, hoping Ombra would meet her eye again, but she didn't. She blinked tears away, taking a moment to gulp down the lump in her throat. "I… I saw my sister kill my dad. I'm sorry, but… I was a mess. That's why I couldn't call you, and why I told Jim to cover for me. And then after, well, the shit hit the fan and I was stuck in a safe house with people watching my every move."

Ombra said nothing for a long moment, her head down, hair hiding her face. Phaedra also looked at the ground, swaying slightly back and forth, scratching nail varnish off her thumbnail. And then, to her surprise, Ombra leaned her swing towards hers, reaching out to take her hand. Phaedra looked up, her gaze locking with Ombra's, who looked more serious than she had ever seen her.

"I'm sorry," Ombra murmured, her sea-green eyes swimming with tears. "I'm sorry you went through all that."

Phaedra's own tears spilled over.

Looking away, she wiped her eyes, first with the edge of her hand, then with her sleeve, her cheeks soaked within seconds. And then Ombra stood and wrapped her arms around her, resting her head on Phaedra's, letting her cry into her T-shirt.

"I missed you so much," Phaedra said thickly, her voice a strangled pitch. Ombra only kissed the top of her head in reply, and held her closer, stroking her hair gently. If the world had ended right then, Phaedra wouldn't have cared. She was enveloped in Ombra's warmth and love, inhaling the familiar and comforting smells of sugary perfume, bubble gum and her own personal scent. She didn't know how long they held each other that way, Phaedra crying against her, but eventually Ombra leaned back, her own face stained with black-streaked tears. But in spite of their crying, she smiled, cupping her chin and pressing her perfect lips to Phaedra's. And Phaedra kissed her back, holding her tightly.

"Where do we go from here?" Ombra asked sometime later, huddled against her, Phaedra's head resting on hers. The rain had begun in earnest while Phaedra told her the full story, and they had migrated to the slide hut, the only bit of shelter in the park.

"What do you mean?" Phaedra mumbled, her stomach twisting as she expected the worst.

"Do we pick up where we left off? No secrets this time."

"No secrets," Phaedra agreed, kissing her hair.

"And we'll tell our families?"

Phaedra thought back to what little she knew about Ombra's family, and wondered whether they would be pleased or angry that she was dating a Ronan. And then there was her uncle Caspar. Of all her family, he had been the only one she had ever considered trusting with something like this. Walking in on him and Skye together had given Phaedra some hope that her own relationship might not be so forbidden after all.

"We'll tell our families," Phaedra finally agreed, and Ombra craned her neck to look up at her, capturing her attention with her dazzling eyes.

"Really?"

"Really," she replied, then leaned down to kiss her again.

They stayed like that for a few minutes, lingering on the kisses. Phaedra ran her fingers lightly across her cheekbones, her chin, the sweet spot on her neck that always made her shiver, while Ombra ran her own hands through her hair. Even when they parted, she continued to comb her fingers through it, taking in her appearance with a small smile.

"I haven't told you yet, but I like your new do," Ombra said.

Phaedra narrowed her eyes, trying to decide whether she was teasing. "Do you?"

"I do. It suits you. It sets off your ears. I never noticed before, but you have very pretty ears. They're dainty."

"I have pretty ears." Phaedra raised a sceptical eyebrow.

"You do. And a pretty nose." She ran her index finger down the length of her nose, then tapped the tip. "I'm glad that idiot Scott didn't break it."

"So am I. What an embarrassing way to re-meet you."

She huffed a laugh, now tracing her cheekbones. "It sets these off too," she whispered, leaning up to plant a kiss on her cheek. "And also this," she said, trailing her finger from beneath her ear, all along her jawline to her chin. Phaedra captured her hand in hers, kissing her fingertips one by one, and then her wrist, and then her mouth.

"So you like my new do," Phaedra said, shifting her weight and leaning down. Ombra moved beneath her, laying back on the floor, her hair splaying around her like a halo.

"I do," Ombra replied, running her hands up the nape of her neck and into her hair again, making her shiver.

"Good." Phaedra grinned, leaning down to kiss her once more.

Chapter Thirty

Amber Summers

Amber didn't know what to do with her hands, or her feet for that matter, as she waited in Oliver's sitting room, her heart beating so loudly that she could hear it pounding in her ears. Any moment, he would come back with the sister she had never known she had, the girl Amber had admired at school but never dreamed she was related to. Her heart rate only quickened as she listened to the muted voices in the hallway, then footsteps as they approached: the faint squeak of Oliver's shoes, and the echo of a woman's heels on marble.

Amber stood up, fighting the urge to wrap her arms around herself as the two people entered. She awkwardly clasped her hands instead, unable to take her eyes off the woman who stopped before her, studying her just as intently.

They were around the same height, but Lindsey's presence filled the room in a way that made her seem taller. Amber remembered she had been pretty at school, but what stood before her now was perfection: smooth skin subtly made up in powder and blush that gave her a peaches and cream complexion; thick blonde hair in varying shades of honey and gold that fell almost to her waist; light brown eyes the same shape as Cameron's and their father's;

bootcut jeans and a cashmere sweater in a shade of pink that complemented her skin tone perfectly, all of which must have cost a month's worth of Roxanne's salary. It didn't matter what Amber had chosen to wear or done with her hair or face. Next to this goddess, she knew she would always feel inadequate.

"Hello," said Lindsey, sticking out a hand. Flustered and aware that she was blushing furiously, Amber took it, shaking quickly, then letting go.

"Hi!" she said, her voice coming out more like a squeak. "It's so nice to meet you… again."

Lindsey nodded, tilting her head as she studied Amber a moment longer, then she took a seat opposite her. Having watched the exchange in calm silence, Oliver occupied the armchair to Amber's right. Feeling like her legs had turned to jelly, Amber sank back down on the sofa.

"I remember you," Lindsey said after a moment, her stare as intense as ever.

Amber nodded, not trusting herself to say something witty, or even normal.

"I gave you an award when I was head girl. I don't remember what it was for."

"Chemistry," Amber murmured. She had won the award for best project. It felt like a lifetime ago.

"Amber was head girl too," Oliver said, and Amber glanced at him, surprised and touched to see that he looked genuinely proud.

Lindsey gave her first hint of a smile, one corner of her mouth tugging up. "I suppose it runs in the family."

Oliver grinned. "You both take after me."

Lindsey glanced at him and her smile grew a little, but it was tight and tentative. Clearly this was as strange for her as it was for Amber.

"Am I right in remembering you were the one who almost got Skye Bolton expelled?"

"What?" Oliver exclaimed, his expression caught between shock and amusement.

Amber cringed. Her past with Skye wasn't exactly something she wanted to discuss with her new family. "It really wasn't as heroic as it sounds. She… she bullied me, and I reported her."

"She bullied you?" Oliver asked, his amusement replaced with a look of horror.

"I don't know why you're surprised," said Lindsey dismissively. "That school was full of bullies." The bitterness with which she spoke made Amber wonder if she, too, had been bullied, although she couldn't see how that would be possible. Lindsey had been one of the popular girls, always surrounded by friends at school.

"Well, I suppose she got what was coming to her…" Oliver's voice was strained. Amber knew that he had been Chief Warden while Skye was held at Blackwater, so she supposed he knew first-hand what the Lux had gone through while there.

"So, you were the ones who took in Cameron," Lindsey asked, changing the subject and sounding more eager.

Amber nodded, nerves rising in her stomach in anticipation of what Lindsey might ask her.

"Was he—?" Her voice cracked, and she glanced at her father, then back at Amber. "Was he… happy?"

She didn't miss the sudden flush of colour beneath Lindsey's flawless make-up, nor the sheen in her eyes. Whatever grief Amber may have felt for the odd, shy boy who turned out to be her brother, it was nothing compared to how Lindsey felt, who had known him all his life.

"I think so," she said quietly, glancing from Oliver to Lindsey. "Or as happy as he could be. I tutored him in medicine, and my mum took him to work with her. He…" She paused, taking a breath as a lump formed in her throat. "He planned to go to university, when the war was over."

Lindsey looked away, her eyes tearing up in earnest now. Oliver was silent, staring at his knees, his face unreadable.

"Thank you," Lindsey said eventually, carefully running a tissue under her eyes, trying not to smudge her mascara. "Thank you for what you did for him."

Amber didn't know what to say, but when a long moment passed and nobody spoke, she cast around for something to fill the silence. "I'm grateful I met him, even if I… didn't know."

Oliver shifted slightly, blinking and looking guilty. He avoided their gaze.

"I'm sure he would have seen you as a sister, if you were nice to him. He likes anyone who is kind." She trailed off, seeming to have missed the fact that she had referred to him in the present tense.

"I hope we did enough for him," Amber said, her hands twisting in her lap. She remembered the ease with which Cameron had fit into their routine once they got past the initial awkward days, his soothing, quiet companionship, his endless questions about medicine, and his eagerness to help her improve her Tracing skills. She blinked away tears of her own. "We got along really well, especially once we got used to each other."

Lindsey nodded. "I'm sure you did more than enough. I just wish… I wish he had known that he could have come home."

Oliver stood suddenly, then marched out of the room without looking at either of them. Lindsey paused, her head tilted to the door as though waiting for him to return, or else checking that he was out of earshot. When a door snapped shut somewhere in the house, she looked back at Amber.

"He's finding it hardest," she said quietly, fiddling with a silver ring on her third finger. "He blames himself for

Cameron running off. And I hate to say it, but he is to blame, partly. He didn't do enough for Cameron."

Amber watched her, completely still, but Lindsey was staring into space. Admittedly, she had known Oliver all of five minutes, but Lindsey seemed protective enough of Cameron that she would have taken care of him if he had wanted to return to his family.

"How is… your mum?" Amber asked eventually, praying she hadn't just put her foot in it by asking a taboo question. But Lindsey didn't seem angry.

"Not good," she admitted, still staring at a spot on the coffee table. "Unbearable, actually. I should probably be with her, but the arguments… we're all grieving, and the constant fighting and blaming wasn't going to help any of us get through this. So I left, then Dad told her he wasn't coming back even if he was released."

Amber couldn't imagine how awful Mrs Matheson must be for her family to abandon her at such a difficult time. Despite everything she had heard, a small part of her felt sorry for her.

"What's… what's your mother like?" Lindsey asked eventually, meeting Amber's gaze.

Amber stared, completely caught off guard. "Well… she's…"

"Sorry," said Lindsey, giving her a small, sheepish smile. "I'm just… curious. I'm twenty-five. I'm old enough to know things haven't been right between my parents for a long time. My mother is rotten, so I'm not surprised someone turned Dad's head. I've met your mum a few times, but I can't help but wonder what she's really like when she's not, you know, being a hero."

"Well," Amber began again, twisting her hands in her lap. "She's a doctor and a Resistance Leader and…" She tucked her hair behind her ear, realising Lindsey already knew as much. "She's kind and caring. And brave." She paused again, realising she sounded incredibly biased. "At least, *I* think she is."

Lindsey was silent again, musing over Amber's stuttered information. "She's not the sort of person I can imagine my dad with. I mean, he's an awful human being and she's like an earth angel, but I'm glad he had someone good in his life at some point."

Amber didn't know what to say to that, but she was proud that Lindsey thought highly of her mother even though she had been her enemy until recently. Roxanne and Oliver *were* an unlikely couple, but it seemed they had cared about each other at some point.

"Are you..." Amber murmured, trying to phrase her next question, unsure if she could even ask it. "What kind of work do you do? For the Saoirse Army?" Old anxieties surfaced as she finally gave in to her deep-seated desire to ask Lindsey Matheson about their shared Trace. Amber knew she was brilliant. Cameron and Oliver had both said as much, and her renown during their school days had clearly followed her into her career. Perhaps this was finally her chance to learn from the best.

But Lindsey was looking at her hands, uneasily twisting the ring around her finger again. "You know I was Ronan's Head Tracer?"

Amber nodded, clutching her elbows as Lindsey spared her a glance.

"I hunted people for Ronan. People like your mother. People for my father to interrogate." Lindsey swallowed, a haunted look crossing her face. "I led a team, trained them, figured out where their loyalties lay. Eventually, I recruited more people to the Saoirseans' cause, and our role was to sabotage manhunts as best we could, to steer the Tracers loyal to Ronan down the wrong path."

Amber stared, awestruck. No wonder Cameron had looked up to her. She wasn't just good at her job, she was working for a good cause.

"Don't look at me like I'm some kind of hero," Lindsey said firmly, eyeing Amber's expression, her jaw tight. "I wasn't the first turncoat to work for Ronan. The Head Tracer before me started it all, and promoted me before he was reassigned so he could ensure someone would continue his work. That's the real reason why I rose through the ranks so quickly."

Despite Lindsey's defensive tone, Amber's impression of her wasn't shaken. The work she did meant something. Amber could only dream of achieving half as much by the time she was Lindsey's age. "Is that why you joined the Saoirse Army, because of your boss?"

"No," Lindsey murmured, her gaze and voice trailing off as she fiddled with her ring. Amber waited, but squeaking footsteps approached beyond the door.

Lindsey started, and they both looked around as Oliver appeared in the doorway, a small, sad smile on his face. "How about lunch?" he asked, and Lindsey glanced her way, giving her an equally small smile.

"Why not? I could eat something."

Amber returned her tentative smile, realising the story of how Lindsey had joined the Saoirse Army would have to wait. She hoped she would get to hear it, someday. She hoped they would be able to have that kind of relationship – a friendship even. Taking a deep breath, Amber rose to her feet.

"I would love to stay for lunch."

Chapter Thirty-One

DEAN ROSWELL

Rain pattered the dusty ground of the barracks yard as Dean and Lorcan weaved between comrades and cadets. The scent of petrichor awakened his Talent, and he felt it rise through him, like branches of a tree reaching for the sky. Despite the unfurling in his chest, Dean was listless. His days felt wasted, his nights spent in agitation as he waited for his sister to come home, only to be met with slurred words and a reluctance to discuss their situation.

"Is Skye coming tonight?" Lorcan asked, hefting his gym bag, his reddish hair still damp from the shower.

Dean sighed, thumbing his silver connection ring and thinking his sister's name. A blunt silence was all he found at the end of their mental bridge. Which meant she was either sleeping, or she had taken her own ring off. "I doubt it."

Lorcan nodded, his expression unreadable. "Sabine asked for her. She has another crazy idea to share."

He grimaced, wiping raindrops off his forehead. "I'm not sure I can take any more of Sabine's crazy ideas." He knew she meant well, but after her ideas for an internal coup and commandeering prisoners, Dean didn't hold out much hope he would like the next one.

They rounded a corner, almost barrelling into a pair huddled beneath an awning, talking in low voices. Dean and Lorcan stopped just in time to avoid knocking into them, and Dean's heart stopped too as he was met with a pair of large, startled brown eyes.

His cheeks burned when he realised who it was.

"Hi Lindsey," he blurted, embarrassment and relief mingling at the sight of her. At her side, a bespectacled young man looked around, his face colouring as much as Dean's. "How was your trip?"

Lindsey's face was a beautiful mask as she glanced between him and Lorcan, her hair drawn back in an elegant chignon, the collar of her grey mackintosh pulled up against the rain. "Fine," she said flatly, and Dean immediately regretted his question. He knew she had been away with Caspar Ronan to locate the Nox's troops, but his curiosity and concern burned all the same.

"I… it's good to see you back." He gave her a small smile, examining her for any sign of harm. To his surprise, she returned it with the faintest curve of her lips. But she also stuck out her chin, holding her head high. Not for the first time, he was struck by how different she was from the Lindsey he had known at school, the Lindsey who had shrunk from people's gazes and barely said a word.

"Thank you," she replied, her voice even, cool. She glanced back at her companion, and Dean's heart sank as he realised he had interrupted something important. "If you don't mind, Jack and I were in the middle of a debrief."

"Oh, yeah," he said lamely, running a hand through his rain-damp hair. "Sorry." At his side, Lorcan watched the entire exchange in stoic silence.

"See you around, Dean Roswell," Lindsey said. But as Dean gave her another awkward smile, his heart stuttered again as she returned it, her pretty eyes fixed on him as he backed away.

Lorcan's silence continued until they rounded the corner. "What the hell was that?" he asked, cuffing Dean on the shoulder with a playful fist.

His face was aflame again, and he cringed as he replayed the whole meeting in his mind. "I think you need to bury me."

"Too right. She just turned you to stone."

Dean took in a tight breath, then huffed. "Please don't tell the others about this."

Lorcan laughed a little too loudly. "It's not the others you should be worried about. If that's what you call flirting, you're in desperate need of lessons."

He cringed again. "Who says I was flirting?"

His friend paused, green eyes glittering with delight. "Dean, my man..." He leaned towards him conspiratorially, laying a hand on his shoulder. "I haven't seen you look at a girl like that since school."

Dean scowled, shaking him off and trudging towards the pub where smokers milled around the door. Lorcan followed, the noise of their fellow soldiers swallowing his chuckles as they headed into the stuffy interior, the carpet beneath their boots sticky with spilled beer.

Despite the crowd, they quickly found their friends congregated around a central table. Sabine was sour-faced, Jacob was laughing, and Ike was, somehow, already drunk.

A flicker of relief crossed Sabine's face at their approach. "Sit down. I'll get your beer." Her tone sounded more like a threat than a friendly offer.

"Same again, Sab!" Ike announced brightly, waving his glass.

"You've had enough," she retorted, slipping into the crowd.

Ike pouted and stuck his tongue out at her retreating back, then his glassy gaze fell on them. "What's got you so cheerful?"

Lorcan grinned as he claimed the seat at the head of the table. "Dean needs flirting lessons."

"Shut up," Dean grumbled, dropping into a chair.

"Oh? It's not Matheson, is it? She had such a crush on you at school."

"No, she didn't." Dean buried his face in his hands, cursing Lorcan's big mouth.

"Dean needs to do more than be a football star and have nice hair if he wants to win her over this time," Lorcan teased, while Dean sank further into his chair. "She was pretty frosty with him just now."

"I dunno, mate. *I* wanted to run my hands through Dean's nice hair, never mind the girls," Ike claimed with a guffaw. "You should grow it out again. That floppy fringe gave you such a tortured poet look."

"Would you lot stop?" Dean complained, his face burning yet again.

"Still, with Ike around, Dean's got a lot more competition these days," Jacob added, while Ike puffed out his chest and flexed his biceps.

"What are you witches cackling about?" Sabine demanded, plonking down a tray of glasses. Despite her earlier comment, she shoved a pint towards Ike, who whooped and gulped down a mouthful.

"Oh, Ike was just regaling us with his new fitness regime," Jacob replied with a subtle wink at Dean, who nodded gratefully.

"Does it involve downing three pints in half an hour?"

"We've been here longer than that, Sab," Ike whined, slapping his glass against the others with a "cheers!"

Sabine hissed a frustrated sigh. "Would it kill you to say one more syllable?"

Ike shrugged. "You lot call me Ike."

"*Because you ask us to*," Sabine seethed, only to be met with more laughter and Ike waving her off.

"Right," Sabine began once they settled down, "there's something we've been meaning to put to you, Dean. We wanted to talk to Skye too, but since she can't be arsed to show, you'll have to relay the message."

"Oh, don't worry, Skye frequently swaggers into my mind like she owns it." Dean sipped his beer and managed to sound a bit more upbeat than he felt. The others chortled.

"Well, since half of us are still suspended from our duties despite securing Blackwater…" Anger smouldered in her golden eyes as she lowered her voice. "It's time we created a new Guard, one that will support the Lux instead of our lousy former president."

Dean swallowed his beer with difficulty, glancing around the noisy pub. "Here we go again with the treason."

She laughed, a wicked boom that set the hair on the back of his neck on end. "Caplin isn't head of state. He's just a man who commands an army, an army that could be easily swayed by the right person. Caplin's ancestor declared himself president because he was the Lux. What's stopping Skye from doing the same?"

"We've been through this," said Dean. "Skye doesn't want to be president."

Sabine narrowed her eyes. "What Skye wants isn't just her decision anymore. Once she stops wallowing, and she will, then she'll step up and sort this country out. In the meantime, we should be getting things organised so we can do our bit when the time comes."

"She's right," said Ike, tilting his glass towards Dean and slopping some beer on the table. "Skye knows how to get things done when she sets her mind to it."

"Yeah," said Jacob, looking at no one in particular. "She got us both out of that hell hole, even though her original plan changed when they decided to cancel my execution."

Everyone glanced at Jacob, who spoke so rarely about his own imprisonment, leaving everyone avoiding the topic too. Sabine let her brother's words hang in the air for a moment, then carried on.

"So, Skye will sort things out. At the very least, she will defeat the Nox. But for now, we have to prepare for war. We're some of Caplin's best soldiers, and he's put us on the bench because we threatened his authority. So let's do away with his authority altogether."

Dread crept in the pit of Dean's stomach, Camilla Linden's sickly smile echoing through his mind. Going along with Sabine's suggestions would be the quickest way to answer Linden's demands and free Victor, but that would just turn them into criminals.

"If we do this," Dean began, glancing around and lowering his voice even more, "we have to tread carefully. We have to make sure we have the Forces' backing before we make a move."

"People are already pissed off," Lorcan said, equally quietly. Even Ike was solemn across the table. "It won't take much to turn them."

"We could spread rumours," Jacob ventured. "That's what Caplin and the Ronans have been doing for years."

"And," Ike reminded them, leaning closer, "Skye's granddad Harlan still has a small army. He'll support her claim."

Dean took a deep breath, still dreading the idea of taking steps against Caplin, but feeling calmer with the new plan. "Alright, I'll talk to Skye."

"Good," Sabine nodded, satisfied. "And since Ike is the only one who isn't suspended, he can suss out who else from the Guard will support us."

"Sure, I'll be your recruiter, as long as I get to be captain," said Ike with a silly grin.

"Skye's the Lux. She'll be the captain."

“Oh come on.” Ike nudged Sabine with an elbow, at which she let out a low hiss. “You’re going to vote for your bestie over your favourite cousin?”

“Considering my other cousin is Caplin,” Sabine shot back, “you don’t exactly have much competition.”

Laughter rippled around the table, but they were interrupted by a voice looming just over their heads. “I thought I’d find you lot here.”

Ombra stood at her brother’s side, still in her cadet uniform. Dean still thought she looked strange with her hair pulled back in a strict, tight bun, her eyes almost small without the usual excess of make-up.

“Hey O, just in time to get us a round.” Ike shook the glass in his hand. But Ombra only shot him a sarcastic look, an eyebrow raised.

“I take it you haven’t heard the news?” She sounded haughty and utterly un-Ombra like. Dean wondered if it had something to do with her uniform, and hid his smile.

“What news?” asked Jacob, his eyes darting around in agitation.

“Caspar Ronan has declared war on the Nox. Stole her armies from under her nose.”

Dean’s stomach churned. So, the arrogant, younger Ronan brother had done it then. He had succeeded in winning over the bulk of the armies hidden in Ireland and Scotland, as they had secretly planned. Ombra’s gaze locked on his, her serious expression leaving him wondering what she knew. It was Sabine who spoke, however.

“Are we officially allied with Caspar Ronan, or is that still being decided?”

Dean avoided her gaze. Only Ike knew what had been agreed with Caspar, and he had been sworn to secrecy. He looked at Ike now, who watched him quietly, pale eyes holding a question.

“I don’t know,” Dean told Sabine, lying through his teeth.

“Skye would know,” Sabine said with a cold smile. “And if he’s on our side, that’s another voice in our favour.”

Ike let out a low whistle. “I never thought I’d see the day when we’d willingly side with a Ronan.”

Chapter Thirty-Two

Alessia Ronan

Their training sessions had become thrilling, exhilarating brushes with death. As she danced around the grounds with Lucien, getting better in her techniques, in her aiming, in her delivery of her dark attacks, the drills he ran her through became more and more dangerous… for him. Because Alessia didn't hold back. She made no secret of the fact that she disliked him and considered him disposable, and she was merciless in her attacks. After all, if she were to stand a chance against the rest of the country, she had to make sure she was more than a match for the best.

Despite her relentless onslaught and obvious hatred of him, Lucien kept his cool, unphased by the fact that she was aiming to hurt and kill rather than simply practising. The most ruffled he ever appeared was a slight shortness of breath following her heavier blows, which he recovered from quickly. And when he suggested breaks, he tried to make it sound like it was she who needed them, but she was satisfied to see that he was calling for them for himself. She didn't need breaks. She was the Nox.

"Can Skye Bolton fight this well?" she asked after Lucien called for one of those breaks. It was late afternoon, with watery sunlight filtering through hazy cloud. A light breeze whispered through her hair, bringing a hint of summer with it. It made a nice change to the endless drizzle that had fallen almost every day. It had been some weeks since Alessia had decided she hated Scotland. Not that she had been able to see much of it.

He shrugged. “I don’t know. I haven’t met her.”

“But she’s a match for me?”

“She’s supposed to be the only one who can defeat you. And she’s a soldier, so yes, I expect she can fight well. But as well as you? I don’t know.”

Alessia lapsed into silence, watching the trees swaying without really seeing them. She may have strength and power, but Bolton had been trained for combat from a young age, and had already proven her merit in battle. Alessia’s training had been sporadic, her instruction coming from people too old or too incompetent to deal with her. And she herself had been impatient. She had argued too much with her father and Caspar, and although Lucien was a successful instructor despite her dislike of him, a part of her worried that she was too late to catch up. Vala talked of a final battle, a fight between her and Bolton that would decide their fates. But how soon would that be, and how much time did she have to prepare for it?

Speaking of Vala, a dark figure in flapping skirts and shawls appeared on the top of the hill behind the castle. From a distance, Alessia couldn’t see her face, but there was something about the way she held herself that filled her with a sense of foreboding.

“You should go to her,” said Lucien quietly. Alessia’s eyes snapped to his face, and his expression was serious for once.

“What’s wrong?” she demanded, but he only bowed his head, turning away to go back to the castle. His reaction filled her with dread as she looked back at Vala. The Seer had begun to descend the hill, making her way towards her.

Grinding her teeth in frustration, Alessia set off at a brisk pace.

She met Vala halfway up the hill, barely winded despite the climb. But when she saw the look on Vala's face, she stopped dead. "What is it?"

Vala glanced around at the deserted grounds. The breeze whispered again, drawing waves through the grass.

"I have news," said Vala in a dramatic hush that made Alessia's blood boil.

"What news?" she almost snarled, resisting the urge to tell her to spit it out.

"It is your uncle, Alessia. I am afraid he has shown his true intentions at last."

"He already ran off to Bolton. What has he done now?"

Vala was silent for a long moment. The endless blue pools of her eyes held Alessia's gaze, infuriating her even more. "He has located your armies, turned them against you, and declared war on you."

Alessia stared. From deep within her heart, the icy rage began to spread through her body, her hands curling into fists and her chest tightening. "*He's done what?*"

Vala blinked, and her pale face became apologetic. "He went to your great aunt Moira first, telling her that you… killed your father and grandfather. And that your grandfather had named Caspar his heir, that you are a usurper. Moira was distraught. She likes Caspar, and trusts him too easily, despite what we told her about him deserting you. So she handed command of the armies over to him, and he convinced them that if they wanted peace then they must fight against the Nox, not for you."

Alessia felt like the ground had fallen away beneath her, like she was a leaf on the wind, being buffeted this way and that, caught in a storm. Caspar had stolen her armies. Caspar had lied to them, told them that she had killed her grandfather. Her *grandfather*. How could anyone believe him? But then, after all, she had always tried to stay out of the public eye, and kept her life as private as possible. Not like Caspar, who used his false charms and collected favours. He was doing the same with her enemies, even now. How could anyone trust Alessia if they didn't know her?

Kill him, whispered the breeze, the quiet voice sounding a little too much like her grandfather.

She struggled for breath. "What about Pierce? The Lindens?"

Vala cleared her throat. "Pierce is still loyal to you, but some of his division split when they heard about Caspar. He sent Oliver Matheson to try to convince Pierce, and he is already marching the soldiers he turned to a secret base in Scotland. Caspar is commanding the Irish division, and Lindsey Matheson has taken charge of the troops you had hidden in the south. As for the Lindens, they are still loyal to you. Arthur is working hard to root out spies and place your informants. Camilla still holds Victor Bolton and your other prisoners. You can trust them."

"How can I trust anyone?" Alessia spat, turning away and charging down the hill. She had to do something, but what? Caspar had taken the majority of her military power. Without an army, she couldn't wage war. All she could do now was try to win over the people, but with the opposition spreading lies about her, her family amongst them, she knew that, too, was a losing battle.

"Alessia," Vala said, more commanding than she had ever heard her. The tone alone forced her to stop. After a moment, she turned her head back towards the Seer, waiting. Vala approached her again, taking her time, her steps self-assured on the uneven ground.

Vala didn't speak until she was beside her again. "I have seen your fighting. You have full command of your enhanced Dark Talent. You will be a terrifying opponent in battle. But in light of what Caspar has done, it seems you are in need of a new army, an inexhaustible army that will answer only to you."

Alessia tilted her head, that ice in her veins stilling, waiting to hear her idea.

"I think it is time you put your new Talent into practice."

And with that she held out her hand, palm up, fingers curled elegantly. Alessia hesitated, then raised her hand to hers. The moment their fingertips touched, they were transported to a different place, a place Alessia knew too well: her family's mausoleum.

The white marble structure glowed in the warmth of the late sun slipping below cloud, the bronze two-headed dragon gleaming above the doors. A shiver of anticipation travelled down her spine as she realised why Vala had brought her to the cemetery. Without hesitation, she ascended the steps flanked by more dragons, the doors unlocking to her touch and swinging open. Her ancestors lay resting around her, their deathly presence causing the hairs to rise on her arms and the back of her neck. She had always had an affinity with death, but it was only since her ascension that she understood why: she was destined to control it.

Whispers followed her as she passed between her parents' final resting places – Ilaria's plaque decorated with vines and red roses, Doran's bearing the Ronan dragon. She approached her grandfather's tomb, running her hands over his name engraved in silver lettering on black marble. She remembered his dream, the one he had recounted with hope and passion in his eyes, the dream that she would rise as the Nox with him at her side. Neither of them had known that his dream would soon come true.

With a flicker of her dark power, the tomb cracked open. Another flicker, and the ornate marble fell away with a rumble, exposing the ebony casket beneath. Vala stepped forward, and with a flick of her own wrist, the cool air inside the mausoleum gathered to levitate the casket into the centre of the narrow space, laying it to rest on the low-raised platform between them. Vala's hands twisted, the clasps securing the casket clipping open, and she levitated the lid away.

Alessia stepped forward, taking in her grandfather's body, assessing how preserved he was. His features had become more skeletal than ever, but even so, his skin was intact, his lips and eyes closed, his thin grey hair neatly combed across his head. Alessia looked up at Vala, who nodded, a satisfied smile spreading across her lips.

As Alessia towered above her deceased grandfather, she raised her hands, closed her eyes, allowed the ice in her veins to surface, to overwhelm her senses and overflow. Frozen crystals formed at her fingertips, numbing her trembling hands, chilling her toes in her boots. She inhaled icy air, and the trembling stopped.

This was what she had been waiting her whole life for. This was what she had been born to do.

By the time her entire body was numb with cold, her breath emerging as frost rather than heat, she opened her eyes and looked down at her grandfather. Colour filled his cheeks, his chest expanded with a breath, and his eyes opened.

PART II

Chapter Thirty-Three

PHAEDRA RONAN

"You did it," she exclaimed, wrapping her arms around her uncle's middle in the hallway, relieved to see that he had made it back home in one piece. Ombra had spent the week with her, showing her all her favourite spots surrounding the lake cottage and helping her to improve control of her messy Talent. Picking up their relationship from where it had left off had been the best distraction from her anxiety over what Caspar might be facing in Ireland. But he had come out on top, and while she was terrified of how her sister would retaliate, she knew how much of a victory Caspar's achievement was.

"Did you really doubt me?" he teased, his eyes full of laughter.

"Of course not." She frowned in mock indignance, crossing her arms. "Tell me everything."

"Let me through the door first." He looked tired, but he was grinning as he hung his coat on a hook by the door. He then headed to the kitchen, Phaedra following eagerly.

"Was Aunt Moira happy to see you?"

"I think she was, actually," said Caspar, setting one of his bags on a kitchen chair and rummaging around in it.

"She had to pretend otherwise at first, of course. I think I almost gave her a heart attack when I showed up at her home."

"Because Alessia told her you betrayed her?" she asked, standing in the doorway and shifting from one foot to the other, the coldness of the tiles seeping into her bare soles.

"Yes. But I spun her a few tales, twisted the truth a bit, and she took my side by the end of it. She owes me a few favours anyway for all the times I got her out of a pickle."

Phaedra had hoped as much. She hadn't seen her aunt Moira since Alessia's inauguration, and hadn't spoken to her since a while before that. She wasn't the most talkative of women, but despite doing her best to appear cool and collected whenever Ivor had been around, she had in fact seemed quite… *normal*, by Ronan standards. And she had been kind to Phaedra all through her childhood and teens, even sneaking her sweets and little gifts when no one was looking.

"She asked after you," he said, drawing a bottle of amber liquid from his bag and setting it on the side. "And she gave us a present."

"Oh?" She drifted closer, interested in both her aunt's questioning and the bottle of booze.

"Ireland's finest malt whiskey. You won't be shooting this or mixing it with pop, you hear me?" he warned, but his lips were curled in amusement.

"I'm honoured you want to share it with me at all." She broke into a grin, watching as Caspar got out two glasses and ice. He was in a good mood, and he even whistled as he poured out the whiskey, handed her a glass, then brought the bottle into the living room.

"So, what did she ask?" Phaedra prompted, sinking down on a sofa and sipping the whiskey, making sure to savour it as Caspar had insisted. He was right, it was one of the best she had tasted.

"Just how you're getting along. She's been worried about you."

"Really?"

"Of course. You've been through a lot lately."

Phaedra fell silent, her nose in her glass. Ombra coming back into her life felt like she had finally regained a missing part of herself, and talking to her about her recent past had helped her to process some things and get them off her chest in a way that she hadn't been able to do with anyone else, not even Caspar or her best friend Jim. But she realised she had to change that.

Looking back at Caspar, she took a deep breath, her stomach squirming as she braced herself to finally tell the truth. "So… I have something to tell you."

"Oh?" said Caspar, looking mildly curious as he lounged in his seat.

"Yes," she said, setting her glass down and then pressing her hands between her knees, trying to decide where to start. "Remember… remember how everyone thought Jim was my boyfriend?"

"Yes," said Caspar, sipping his drink and waiting patiently.

"Well… he's not. Because… because I don't like men that way."

She let her words linger, watching his expression closely. He nodded slightly as he thought over what she was saying, swirling the whiskey and ice in his glass. "I see."

"Yeah, and… well, I have a girlfriend."

And Caspar smiled then, a genuine smile that made her breathe a sigh of relief. "And do I get to meet her?"

"Well," said Phaedra, realising she had said "well" a lot, but her head was spinning. Hope rose in her chest with the knowledge that he accepted what she had told him so far. "The thing is… well, her name is Ombra… Medley."

As she had feared, Caspar's smile did indeed falter a little, but he pasted it back on, sipping his drink again. "Ah. So that's why you're so worried."

Phaedra gave him a nervous smile of her own, her fingers twisting around each other in her lap. "Yeah, I… I know that's not ideal."

"It's not, but I can't talk."

Phaedra smirked. They hadn't discussed his relationship with Skye Bolton, and honestly, she didn't really want to know. "I'd like you to meet her. She's really cool."

"She must be. You wouldn't like anyone who wasn't cool. I mean, I'm your cool uncle."

She snorted, and they both laughed, releasing the last of the tension she was holding in her chest. There were no more secrets now. No more stress. Her uncle knew who she was and accepted her for it.

"You never told anyone? Not Doran, or…?"

"No," she murmured, her old fears flaring up, then ebbing away. She didn't have to worry about the rest of her family anymore. They were gone, and she was out of her sister's reach.

Pity and pain flashed across Caspar's face, and he downed the rest of his drink, then poured them both more. "Well," he said, handing her the glass and clinking his against hers. "I hope you never feel the need to hide yourself from me, or anyone, again. I love you no matter what."

Her eyes filled with tears as she drank, and then she stood and wrapped her arms around him, burying her face in his sleeve.

Chapter Thirty-Four

SKYE BOLTON

"This better be good," Sabine deadpanned at Skye's side, casting her golden glare around the crowded pub. "Solstice is the worst time to go out."

"Too many people for you, Sabine?" came Ike's cheerful voice across from them. His pale face was a picture of delight, grinning at Sabine's dark mood. "I suppose a crypt is more your scene."

"Haha," Sabine responded in the same monotone, sipping her beer. "At least corpses don't make dumb jokes."

Skye exchanged a knowing smile with Dean and Lorcan, trying to settle into the banter after so long away from her friends. But when Ombra had contacted her that morning and told her she was bringing her girlfriend to the pub – *and you'd better be there to meet her or else* – she figured it was time to finally stop isolating herself. Besides, from the conversations she had lifted from Dean's memories, Sabine was close to threatening another intervention.

"It will be good, trust me," said Lorcan, unable to hold in his delight.

"I can't believe you won't tell us who it is," Skye said, twisting her own pint glass absently and contemplating replacing it with whiskey. "The little madam has been wearing obsidian all day."

"It better not be the drug dealer," Sabine grumbled.

"Drug dealer?" said Lorcan and Dean at the same time. Skye glanced between her friends, glad she wasn't the only one who was confused.

"Yeah, she was way too sketchy."

"It's Ombra," said Ike with a shrug. "She's never been squeaky clean."

The pub doors swung open, and in walked Ombra, closely followed by two dark-haired people: a small, pale girl and a tall, lanky boy. Skye stared as they weaved through the pub towards them, Ombra grinning like a maniac. As they drew closer, shock eclipsed her curiosity as Skye realised who the girl with her cousin was, recognising the spiky pixie cut, the ripped jeans and heavy boots. Beside her, Sabine groaned.

"Hey, you lot," Ombra exclaimed, wrapping her arm around none other than Phaedra Ronan, pulling her in close. Behind them, the lanky boy stood with his hands in his pockets, eyes trained on the floor. "This is Phaedra. My girlfriend." Ombra's grin grew, if possible, even wider as she said the last word.

A stunned silence dragged on as everyone except Lorcan stared at the unlikely couple. But the more Skye stared, the more things made sense. The two girls were like peas in a pod, with the same taste for partying and obnoxiously loud rock bands, the same snarky attitude, and even the same eclectic fashion sense. The pair were so similar that Skye knew she should be worried about what kind of havoc they might create.

"Hi," Phaedra managed, fear and embarrassment mingling on her face. Her gaze fell on Skye, who was already beaming in response to her cousin's enthusiasm. The girl gave her a small smile in return, completely at odds with the sass queen who had teased Skye and Caspar on the last occasion she had seen her.

"Wait, *Phaedra*?" Sabine blurted, her forehead distorted in a frown. "You mean—"

"Phaedra Ronan, exactly," Ike confirmed, and then he began to laugh, breaking the ice and setting the rest of them off.

"How long have you two been dating?" Skye asked, still torn between disbelief and amusement.

Ombra shrugged, gazing up at Phaedra with the most moony look Skye had ever seen on her. "About a year."

A year?

Phaedra's smile grew as she gazed right back at Ombra, and then she seemed to remember the boy skulking behind her. "This is my friend, Jim."

There was a chorus of greetings, to which Jim only grunted in return, his ears going red.

"Maybe Jim can sit next to Sabine," Ombra teased. "They would get on *so* well."

Phaedra's smile faltered as Sabine glowered up at her, prompting Skye to silently tell Sabine to *be nice*.

"I can't believe you didn't tell me." Sabine was still seething five minutes later, as the trio took seats around the table with glasses of beer.

"How did you not realise she was Phaedra Ronan?" Ike demanded in mock seriousness. "You were supposed to be Ombra's bodyguard."

"*I don't know*," Sabine hissed. "I thought she was just another teenage delinquent. Ombra isn't exactly short of dodgy acquaintances."

"My friends aren't that dodgy, thank you very much." Ombra's words fired across the table. "Anyway, Phee isn't really a drug dealer. It was just a ruse to throw you off."

"Don't tell me *you* knew she was a Ronan." Sabine's voice dripped with fury, her golden eyes flashing.

But Ombra only smiled mysteriously, meeting Skye's gaze. *Don't tell.*

And ruin all your fun? This is the best trick anyone has played on Sabine in a long, long time. Skye raised her glass of beer, hiding her grin in it. Out loud, she said, "So go on, what did your mum say when you told her?"

Ombra bit her lip, visibly cringing. "Well, she didn't say much at all."

"Oh, she gave you the silent treatment? That makes two of us."

"She didn't say anything?" asked Dean, incredulous.

Lorcan laughed next to Dean. "Her words were literally 'oh, okay'."

"You're joking," said Skye, looking between Lorcan and Ombra. Phaedra smiled awkwardly at her side.

"What else can she say?" said Lorcan. "We're all on the same side now."

"More or less." Ombra shrugged, then gave her girlfriend a smile. Phaedra's eyes almost sparkled in return.

"Well, at least you're cute together," said Skye.

"Cute?" Ike exclaimed, raising his pale eyebrows. "Since when have you ever described anything as cute? Especially a couple."

Skye smirked. "Let me rephrase. You're *sickeningly* cute together. Stop looking at each other all gooey-eyed."

Ombra narrowed her eyes and stuck out her tongue. Phaedra blushed and lowered her gaze to the table. But Skye couldn't hide her own smile. She had never seen either of them look so happy.

"Here's to being sickeningly cute," Ike toasted, raising his glass. They all followed suit, clinking glasses, Ike even giving a whoop. "Some good news at last."

"I'll drink to that," said Dean, and he met Skye's gaze with a smile of his own. *It's good to see you laughing.*

Skye looked back at him, her grin fading into a close-lipped curve. *We have something to celebrate.*

Dean's concerned thoughts flooded down their connection, and Skye's telepathy shrank back, trying to stem the flow. Coming out tonight was her dipping her toe back into normal life – or as normal as it could get in light of everything. She wasn't ready to dive straight in, not while the thunderclouds of reality constantly rumbled at the periphery of her mind.

As the conversation bubbled around them, Skye's attention was drawn to a new arrival, and she locked eyes with none other than Glen. Unfinished business and unsaid apologies loomed like another storm cloud in her imaginary sky.

Glen gave her a grim smile and a nod as he shouldered through the crowded pub towards their table, then went straight to Phaedra. "Hello you," he said, ruffling her hair. The girl swatted his hand away in annoyance, then hugged him tightly.

"You came!"

"Of course I came. I'm your wingman, aren't I?"

Phaedra playfully punched his bicep, leaving Skye amused at their comfortable camaraderie. The teenager then put her arm around Ombra. "I can finally introduce you. Glen, Ombra. Ombra, Glen."

"We've met," said Ombra, getting up and shaking his hand anyway. "But it's nice to meet you again."

"Phee, you didn't tell me your missus was even shorter than you are," he teased.

"Oi, less of that," said Ombra, as loud as ever, but her eyes glinted mischievously.

"I want you to meet Jim, too." Phaedra indicated her friend who had been brooding at the end of the table, his expression as dark as his hair. "He's my best friend."

"Pleasure," said Glen, leaning over and offering Jim a hand. The youngster looked up from his beer, shaking Glen's hand and quickly letting go.

"Hi," he muttered, going back to his drink.

"Lighten up, Jim Bob," said Phaedra, and Jim glanced up at her, raising his eyebrow. "Don't be a party pooper."

He leaned back in his chair, clearly uncomfortable with so many unknown people.

"Anyone want a drink?" asked Glen above them. Most of them declined, but Dean drained his glass.

"I'll come with you, mate," Dean said, standing up and heading to the bar with Glen. Skye watched them go, sifting through Dean's mind, but it seemed he only wanted to make Glen feel welcome at a table full of strangers. He was a better person than Skye could ever be.

"So," she said after a moment, fixing her gaze on the young couple. "How has this been going on for a year and you didn't tell me?"

Ombra raised a haughty eyebrow. "Do I really need to remind you how occupied you were?"

Skye pursed her lips, struggling to avoid a grimace. "And you really didn't know…?"

The two girls shared another of those gooey looks, then a fearful shadow swept over Phaedra's face. "I found out Ombra was your cousin at some point."

Skye glanced between them, sensing the finer details of the story were best left for when she had Ombra alone. She switched to a lighter question. "How did you two even meet?"

"Clubbing," Ombra shrugged, reaching for Phaedra's hand. Skye had never seen her so comfortable with someone, and she wasn't sure she had ever referred to any of her partners as a *girlfriend*. Which meant things must be pretty serious.

"Well, that doesn't surprise me." Skye glanced at Jim. "And how about you? How did you and Phaedra meet?"

"Family connection," he said, his gaze a mixture of surprise and hostility.

"Oh, I see," she said with a knowing smirk. "And I suppose your family hates my guts."

Jim raised an eyebrow. "They hate Caplin, and anyone who associates with him."

"Don't listen to him," said Phaedra, rolling her eyes. "He doesn't even like the Resistance."

"Well I don't blame you there. They are a bunch of do-gooders." Skye wrinkled her nose in false disapproval. "So what now?"

"What do you mean?" asked Jim.

"Whose side are you on?"

Jim shrugged. "Nobody's."

"He just wants a girlfriend and a job." It was Phaedra again, nudging Jim with her elbow.

He scowled, but agreed with her. "Pretty much."

"You should go on a date with Skye," said Ombra, falsely casual.

Do you have a death wish? Skye silently asked her cousin, while her lips curled dangerously.

"You don't wanna go out with her," said Phaedra in a dramatic whisper. "She'll eat you alive."

Jim's ears turned red as he met her gaze, and then promptly dropped his eyes to the table, occupying himself with his beer.

I suppose he's too young for you, came Ombra's thoughts across the table. Skye's gaze snapped to hers, and she resisted the urge to roll her eyes when she picked up on the rest of her thoughts.

I see Phaedra's been blabbing.

I'm not judging. But I still think you should have stayed with the boxer. They looked up as Glen and Dean came back to the table. Glen's eyes met hers for a second, then darted away, a familiar blush colouring his cheeks.

Just keep it to yourself? It's a bit of a sore point with him.

Ombra only grinned as an image of herself with her lips zipped popped into her head. Satisfied, Skye turned her attention back to the conversation around the table.

The next hour went well, despite the eclectic mix of opposing factions. Jim seemed to warm to them the more he drank and started to take part in the banter. The tension that Glen brought with his arrival faded away as he chatted to her brother, Ike and Lorcan, although he exchanged a couple more awkward glances with her that she kept trying to avoid. Ombra and Phaedra kept them all entertained with their double act, Phaedra's temporary shyness dissipating. Skye nursed her drinks, eager, for once, to be present in the moment instead of trying to dull the fear pressing down on her chest.

Despite her failed attempts not to make eye contact, Glen drew Skye's attention when he stood, his chair dragging on the carpet. "I'm going for a smoke," he said to Phaedra. "Coming?"

"I quit, remember?" She frowned up at him. "Stop trying to get me back into bad habits, Glenny Boy."

"Glenny Boy?" he scoffed, pulling on his jacket. "Is that the best nickname you can come up with?"

"You should be honoured you're getting one at all."

Glen gave a snort of laughter, his eyes falling on Skye as she tried to suppress her smile. She looked away quickly, focusing on Dean and Lorcan, but she was too aware of his exit as he made his way out of the pub. After draining her glass, Skye plucked up the courage to go after him, feeling eyes on her back as she followed him out.

A light drizzle was falling, and the click of Glen's lighter drew her towards him, where he stood hunched beneath the awning. He raised an eyebrow as he watched her approach. "Didn't know you'd started smoking." His voice was gruff, but amusement lit up his features.

"I just need air," she said dismissively, stuffing her hands into the pockets of her leather jacket.

An awkward silence followed as they stood side by side watching the rain, the cigarette smoke clouding her senses. Finally, she looked up at him, struggling for words. "Listen, I…" She paused, stomach squirming as she swallowed the bitter taste in her mouth along with her pride. "I never apologised. For what I said. For how I—"

"You were drunk."

"That's no excuse."

He shook his head. "Let me finish. You were drunk, and you said things you probably didn't mean. But you were right. I know what went on between us – what I wanted from you – wasn't meant to be. Maybe if we'd met at a different time, under different circumstances, we would have had a shot. But I'm not going to waste whatever time I have left on what ifs." He sucked on his cigarette, exhaling a plume of smoke. "Anyway, you have a lot more on your plate than I do, being the Lux and all."

He met her eye, his lips curving around his cigarette. Skye breathed a sigh of relief, crossing her arms as her nerves began to subside. She had expected to have to grovel. After the way she had treated him, this felt almost too easy, but she wasn't about to complain.

"For what it's worth, I accept your apology. I know saying sorry doesn't come easily to you."

She shot him a dirty look, catching his teasing smirk in the glow of his cigarette. "Yeah well, it's not very often I'm wrong."

He snickered, and they lapsed into silence, Skye leaning back against the wall and resting a boot against it. The drizzle picked up, raindrops splashing back upwards on the road.

"Dean seems pretty sound by the way."

"That's because he doesn't know what went on between us."

"Oh? Protective big brother, huh?"

Her mouth twisted. "Let's just say I don't have a great track record with men."

"Ahh, it's all starting to make sense now." His new beard quirked as he looked down at her. "That's why you don't do *the whole dating thing*. Too many bad boys in your past."

She wrinkled her nose, trying not to laugh as his teasing came a bit too close to the truth. "Anyway, if you're looking for drinking buddies, Dean and the boys are always game. Although it looks like you fit right in with Phee and the cool kids."

"I dunno, Bolton. I don't drink the way those youngsters do." He finished his cigarette, tossing the butt to the damp curb. Slipping his hands into his pockets, he leaned on the wall beside her, eyes on the rain.

"How are you adapting to army life?"

He shrugged. "It's exactly as monotonous as you made it out to be."

"Enjoy it while it lasts. It won't be long before things get a bit *too* interesting."

He turned his face towards her, fear and questions in his eyes. "Has there been any news?"

"Not since—" She froze, snatches of thought drifting from inside the pub. She tilted her head towards the door, scanning the tumbling, jumbled thoughts, trying to make sense of them. "Looks like you just jinxed it."

"What?"

But she pushed off the wall, heading back inside. Glen followed closely behind.

The light-hearted hubbub of noise inside the pub had transformed into a charged sense of frightened anticipation. People were approaching the television screens dotted around the room, and the surrounding minds confirmed the headline she was too far away to see.

"The Nox has declared open war on Britannia, and is marching south, claiming and sacking the northern cities on the way. Citizens have been advised to remain within their homes—"

She and Glen came to a halt at their table, and she looked down at her friends and family, sombre gazes staring back at her. Phaedra and Ombra both got up to better see the television.

"Is it happening?" asked Ike, straining his eyes to see the screen across the pub full of heads.

Skye nodded, then relayed the announcement for them. "Alessia is marching south."

"With what army?" asked Dean, staring at her.

"That's what I want to know. Either someone is lying to us, or she had more hidden up her sleeve." She took a deep breath, surveying her comrades. "Well soldiers, drink up, looks like this is our call to arms."

They looked at each other, then at her, and did as they were told, slapping down their glasses and following her out of the pub.

***

The emergency meeting with the allies went on beyond midnight. Lindsey Matheson and her team of Tracers were dispatched to gather intel on the nature of the Nox's army, and announcements were sent out calling the allied armies to briefing the following morning. Whether they were ready or not, Alessia wasn't going to wait.

Despite her exhaustion, Skye didn't go to bed when she and her brother got back to the safe house. Instead, she slipped out of the cottage after Dean and Kerry had retired to their rooms and made her way down to the nearby beach, taking a half-empty bottle of scotch with her. It had been hours since the beers at the pub, so she figured a few swigs couldn't hurt.

She found herself a large, flattish rock and slumped down on it, breathing in salt air, a hint of sea spray from the high tide hitting her cheeks. Coloured lights bobbed in the dark waves, and the sky was full of stars overhead. The rain outside the pub hadn't fallen here. The night was balmy, perfect weather for a summer solstice celebration, if it weren't for the war heading their way. Skye pushed away thoughts of long-lost happy times, of drinking and dancing away the dark hours of the shortest night with her friends, of fire pits and barbecues on the beach with her family, of staying up to watch the sunrise. Instead, she concentrated on the lapping waves below her, unscrewing the bottle and taking a swig, savouring the burn.

She took another breath, willing herself to be calm as she reflected on the previous weeks. She had spent so long focusing on trying to help her father and drowning out her messed up reality as much as possible, but it was time to snap out of it and face the music. Alessia, it seemed, was done waiting. Caspar commandeering her army and declaring war was most likely what had provoked her, but it had only been a matter of time.

She fiddled with the silver chain around her neck as she mulled over the messy situation, grateful for its familiar, comforting links between her fingers. She was glad the opposition were making the first move. Maybe now the allies would stop squabbling over their own differences and get on with it. But still, the knowledge that she might have to fight Alessia sooner than she had anticipated weighed on her. She knew people would be looking to her, watching what moves she made in this war. She knew she would be expected to speak up tomorrow.

Skye kicked her heels lightly against the side of the rock, the alcohol warming her from the inside. The moon was out, a bright crescent that contrasted coolly with the dark sky. The breeze was almost warm, the temperature mild enough that she had been able to come out with just a light jacket. She enjoyed nights like this, and wistfully wished she got to experience them more often. But for all she knew, her nights might be numbered.

She didn't hear the footsteps as they approached, but she saw the shadow from the corner of her eye, and caught a hint of jasmine, damp earth, and another scent that she could no longer name. Skye looked up at the figure that she was sure had simply materialised from the night, taking another swig as she took in the dark, rippling fabrics, the hair swaying lightly, and the eyes that still shone sapphire blue even in the dead of night.

"Happy Solstice, Skye." Vala's voice whispered like the wind through ancient trees, sending a sense of foreboding prickling down Skye's spine.

"Hello, Vala," she replied, turning her gaze back to the black sea. So much for a bit of time to herself.

"It is not safe to be out in the night alone."

"According to you, I only have one enemy," Skye replied, setting the bottle down on the rock beside her with a dull clink. "I think I can manage."

Silence followed, Skye half wishing the Seer hadn't come, but she burned with curiosity. There was no peace to be had now, not as her heart raced, impatience and anticipation creeping through her chest. After a moment, Vala silently lowered herself to Skye's level, kneeling on the cool hard rock.

"You need to prepare your followers for the army Alessia is bringing."

Skye tried not to look at her, reluctant to give her the satisfaction of seeing her curiosity. But eventually, she tore her eyes away from the sea, turning her head slowly towards Vala. The Seer was watching her intently, threads of her invisible power unfurling around them and caressing Skye's cold cheeks. "Tell me."

Vala inhaled slowly, turning her own gaze out to sea. "A thousand years ago, a fearsome army tore through these islands like a plague, turning Britannia into a stronghold for the Nox."

Skye exhaled audibly, kicking her heels against the rock again. "I don't need a history lesson."

Vala pinned Skye in place with her fathomless gaze, her perfect lips curving into a smile from a dream. "Three Lux were destroyed by that Nox. In the end, only Lux Fire had the upper hand over her army."

Skye swallowed, a prickling awakening beneath her skin, cold fingers creeping up her neck and wrapping themselves around her throat. "That doesn't help me. Darkness is immune to fire."

"There are many kinds of darkness, my dear Skye," Vala replied, her smile growing. "Night and death, evil and ignorance, pain and suffering. You must embrace the light if you wish to drive it away."

Skye pressed her lips together, seeking hidden meanings in Vala's words. Searching for traps. "Well then, it's a good thing I've teamed up with our enlightened Resistance friends."

She gave a single nod. "Clouds do not form from a single drop, Skye. You need rain to make up your storm."

Skye exhaled, masking her creeping fear with frustration. She drew her feet up onto the rock, wrapping her arms around her knees. "Where did Alessia's army come from? She's not exactly popular."

Vala smoothed out her skirts, eyes lowered to her task. "You did not think the Nox would go up against a Lightning Carrier with only one weapon, did you, Skye?"

Skye glared at the moon without seeing it. The phantom hand around her neck was joined by others, wrapping around her arms, pinning her feet, threatening to drag her down between the rocks to be drowned beneath the foaming surf. She shook off the sensation, taking up her bottle of whiskey and swigging again.

"You're only going to feed me riddles, aren't you?"

Vala said nothing, a knowing smile on her face, the breeze swaying her hair. The scent of night-blooming flowers was overpowering, drowning out the brine of the sea.

Skye nodded at the non-answer, grimly resolving to examine what little she had been given after some sleep. She methodically screwed the lid back onto her bottle, then stood and left the beach without saying goodbye.

Chapter Thirty-Five

ROXANNE SUMMERS

When Roxanne arrived at the crack of dawn, the barracks were a hive of activity. Captains shouted orders, soldiers performed various exercises and drills, and when she stepped into the boardroom for the emergency war council meeting, the Resistance Leaders and their allies were stood around the table, talking over each other.

All her fellow Leaders were present, as well as Riordan Rathbone – the leader of the Saoirse Army – and Alistair Caplin with the captain of his Guard, Irvine Sullivan. Peter's voice was the loudest, as usual, with Nanette making snide comments in the background and Caplin looking like he was fast losing patience. As she entered, Devan and Darshana both nodded to her in greeting. Their eyes remained fixed on hers as she approached the group. Whatever they were trying to silently tell her, it couldn't be good.

"The army is bigger than we thought," Peter exclaimed, fear and disbelief battling on his ruddy face. "The Tracers said it's doubled since the first sighting."

"How can it have *doubled*?" Caplin demanded.

"I look forward to asking the Tracers that myself," Peter bristled.

Roxanne shivered, unable to shake the image of a marching army – death bearing down on them. "How far is she?" she asked, and Peter gave her a sharp glance as though she had no right to speak.

"Closer than we'd like," he snapped, turning back to Caplin.

"She's given us a battle location and two days to prepare," said Devan, cutting across Peter. "She knows she can't take Manchester, it's too big, so she wants an open battle at nightfall on Thursday."

The queasiness Roxanne had been feeling since last night churned in her stomach, and she froze, unsure if she needed to bolt for the bathroom. The last battle had been an attack on Ronan Manor. It had been small, yet devastatingly bloody. This time, the Nox was bringing an entire army. But before she could say anything, the door opened behind her, and she turned to see Caspar Ronan arrive with Oliver and Lindsey. She met Oliver's gaze, his cold expression churning her stomach again, then she swiftly looked away, focusing on Ronan instead.

"Good morning," said Caspar, his greeting less chipper and his jaw more rigid than usual.

"I'm not sure there's anything good about it," Peter muttered as they turned towards the new arrivals. "I trust your soldiers are on the way, Ronan."

"Of course," said Caspar, pulling out a seat at the table and sitting down. After some hesitation, Oliver and Lindsey followed suit. "Our troops are making their way here as we speak."

The door behind Caspar opened a third time, and Roxanne looked up to see Skye Bolton framed in the doorway, wearing her full Caplin Forces uniform. She didn't speak, didn't smile, but the room fell silent as she regarded them all coolly. She then stalked inside, making her way boldly to the head of the table. Her brother, also in uniform, quietly shut the door behind him.

"Good, you're all here," said Skye, looking at each of them in turn. Her gaze lingered on Oliver, as well as on Caplin, but aside from a dangerous glint in her eye, her face betrayed none of her feelings. "I suggest you all sit down. We've got a lot to discuss."

There were glances and a few mutters between them. Most people sat, including Roxanne, settling between Devan and Darshana. But Skye remained on her feet, as did Caplin.

"I don't remember revoking your suspension, Miss Bolton. Nor yours, Mr Roswell. Why are you both in uniform?" Caplin's voice was slick, carrying a strong dose of unconcealed venom. But Skye held his gaze unflinchingly, her eyes narrowed and her lip curling ever so slightly.

"Let's not pretend I still answer to you, *Mister* Caplin. You may have suspended me from your personal Guard, but this is an Allied battle against the Nox. Do you really think soldiers will put their lives on the line if they hear the Lux isn't fighting alongside them?"

Caplin blanched, blinking in surprise and horror. Roxanne cringed at the boldness with which Skye spoke to her superior, while Dean looked equally pained. Across from her, however, Caspar was openly smirking. Even Oliver looked amused.

"If you no longer answer to me, *Miss* Bolton," said Caplin, a slight tremor in his voice, "then why are you wearing my uniform?"

Skye raised an eyebrow, glancing down at herself. She looked first at her family name and medals on the right side of her chest, then at the Caplin crest above her heart, the black raven contrasting against the red shield. With a shrug, she tucked her manicured nails beneath the embroidered badge, tearing it clean off with an ugly ripping sound. A black expanse of fabric and a few loose threads remained. "I'll replace it later," she said, casually tossing it at Caplin, who simply stared as it came to rest at his feet. "Well, are you going to sit down? You really are going to want to hear what I have to say."

Roxanne swallowed at the blank fury on Caplin's face. After a moment of them glaring at each other, leaving Roxanne wondering if he was going to continue his fight, Caplin took a step back to lean against the wall and crossed his arms, still glaring at Skye but saying no more. Captain Sullivan retreated beside him, carefully expressionless despite the outrageous exchange. Skye gave another shrug, then turned to them all.

"Vala visited me last night."

A creeping silence followed, finally broken by Caplin's sneer behind Roxanne. "The charlatan, you mean?"

That curl graced Skye's lips again. "Just because she hasn't visited *you*, Mr Caplin, doesn't mean she's a fake." Her eyes slid to Lindsey. "She hinted at some secret advantage the Nox's army may have. What have your Tracers picked up?"

Lindsey's expression remained cool and unruffled despite the long night. "There is something odd about them. We can't get an accurate reading on their Talents and weapons, or even their numbers. Alessia has clearly employed some more competent Ward Weavers."

"Can your Ward Breakers bypass them?" Devan asked at Roxanne's side.

"Not without risking my team." Lindsey paled a little. "We had a close shave while scouting this morning."

Fear twisted Roxanne's stomach, and her Healing Talent awoke unbidden, seeking injuries Lindsey may have endured. But aside from shaken nerves, she was unharmed.

"When you have Marsden's Tracers to contend with," said Caspar, his own concern evident as he regarded Lindsey, "it's best you keep your team safe."

Lindsey nodded. "Thankfully, I know my grandfather's methods well, and we've been able to follow his team's tracks before they could cover them. Alessia is focusing heavily on fire defence."

Skye shifted. "Vala brought up an old Nox war. Mentioned something about a near-invincible army that only fire could defeat."

Old stories stirred in the depths of Roxanne's memory, but it was Caspar who voiced them, a frown forming between his dark brows. "A legend. It was said the Nox created the army, that she breathed life into stone."

"Much of the written records of that time were destroyed," Lindsey continued, picking up the threads of Caspar's musing. "The fragments that remain are based on oral tradition, varying from region to region. However the Nox created the army, she also controlled it."

"Does Alessia have that kind of ability?" Skye asked, looking at Caspar. "Does she have another Talent?"

"If she does, she didn't use it while I was there. She fought only with darkness."

"It would make sense if she has a second Talent," Roxanne dared to say, remembering Amber's research about the Nox and Lux tending to be Prodigies. "You have two."

Skye met her gaze, her expression unreadable, but it was Devan who spoke. "I'd rather bring the battle forward too. I'm not fighting Obscurae in the dark."

"I agree," said Caspar, eyes flicking to Caplin. "Better visibility for your Aeres Army."

Only frosty silence emanated from behind Roxanne, and she didn't dare to look around.

"Going back to the fire—" Lindsey drew their attention back to her as she fiddled with her silver ring. "I think it's worth ramping up our firepower. Our findings so far, Vala's hint, and my Trace are too many connections to ignore."

"My father had a penchant for filling his troops with Ignes," Caspar replied. "They are at your disposal."

"Weren't we working with Ignes to develop flamethrowers?" Peter asked, looking between Devan and Riordan.

"We've built up quite a cache," Devan confirmed. "We can equip at least a quarter of the Talentless soldiers."

"You can count on our resources as well," said Riordan. "I've already sent word to our headquarters in Belfast. We can get them here in time."

Devan nodded, unrolling a sheet of paper and weighing down the corners with polished grey pebbles. With sure fingers, he began to draw arrows and lines across it. "The Nox has chosen this expanse of fields just north of Manchester. It's mostly flat, surrounded by roads to get our soldiers and resources in and out. Alessia will attack from the north, so we can set up the Healers' facilities close to the southern road and arrange our troops between."

He looked up from the paper, sapphire blue eyes meeting hers. Roxanne clenched her hands in her lap, trying to settle her trembling. But if he saw her nerves, he only gave her a faint, encouraging smile.

"There's a hospital near that location," said Darshana in a level voice, pulling a pen from her bun of silver-streaked dark hair and writing the hospital name on the paper. "If you can spare some soldiers to help secure it, I can head there this afternoon and ensure it's staffed and equipped for surgery."

"I'll dispatch a team," Devan confirmed, making notes of his own. "Roxanne, I can send another team with you to start preparations at the site."

She nodded, taking a deep breath to ease her trembling. "Our fellow medics are preparing equipment as we speak."

Devan made further notes, but beneath the table, his free hand brushed her wrist, his warm fingers wrapping around her shaking ones. Roxanne looked up at him in surprise, and he gave her another gentle smile.

"I assume command of the individual armies will remain with their respective heads," Caplin drawled, and Roxanne glanced up to find him examining the paper, eyes narrowed.

"That would be wise, with the exception of the cadets," Devan replied. "If it's alright with you, I'd prefer to keep Resistance and Caplinite cadets under Officer Munro, for consistency."

Caplin gave a begrudging nod. "My Aeres Army will fly under my command. Sullivan will lead the infantry."

Devan dutifully wrote down the decisions while Peter and Nanette muttered amongst one another. As Devan set down his pen, Peter raised his voice. "What about you, Ronan?"

"Our division is split," said Caspar, picking up a pen and adding his own notes to a corner of the paper. "I'll lead the half in the field, and Oliver and Lindsey will launch the surprise attack from the north. Hopefully we can finish off Alessia when her troops are at their weakest." He looked at Lindsey. "We'll be relying on your Trace to time it."

"You're fighting?" Roxanne asked, glancing between Oliver and Lindsey.

Lindsey nodded, keeping up a poker face despite the curious glances Roxanne had caught her sneaking every so often. But Oliver gave her a hard stare and glanced briefly to her right, at Devan. Roxanne willed herself not to follow his gaze, all too aware of Devan's hand still holding hers beneath the table. "Since you were so kind to release me," Oliver said quietly, though Roxanne didn't miss the bite in his voice, "it was only fair I made myself useful."

"What colour are you wearing, Ronan?" Caplin interrupted, trying to mask the strain in his voice with mockery. "You can hardly don your family purple now that you're a turncoat."

"Grey," said Caspar, not even looking at him.

"You're re-kitting the entire army?" asked Nanette with a harsh laugh.

Caspar shrugged. "Nothing a few colour glamours can't fix. Besides, purple really isn't Matheson's colour." He glanced at Oliver with a half-hearted smirk.

A nervous laugh rippled around the room, but Nanette brought it to a halt with her next question. "What I want to know is, where will the Lux be in all of this?"

Heads turned to Skye, who still stood at the head of the table, silently surveying the foundations of their battle plans. She straightened at the question, her hands in fists at her sides. "Where every dutiful soldier should be: on the front lines, with my Lux Guard."

A tense silence followed. Skye crossed her arms, no doubt waiting for the inevitable challenge.

It didn't take long for Caplin to demand, "Lux Guard?"

Skye held his glare, her lips curving. "They chose themselves a new leader after you failed to recognise their efforts, Mr Caplin."

Caplin held his composure a little better than before, but Roxanne didn't miss the danger flashing in his yellow eyes. "And who might be in your little Lux Guard, Miss Bolton?"

The Lux tilted her head. "I'm sure you can guess."

Roxanne's queasiness returned as she witnessed the second showdown of the morning. She could well imagine what kind of trouble Skye's insurgence could paint for

Caplin, and it didn't sit well in her stomach. But after a long moment, Caplin looked away, his face a stony mask, no doubt saving the argument for when they didn't have an audience.

"Anyway," said Skye, finally pulling out a chair and settling into it. "We'll all be fighting against Alessia, whatever colour we're wearing."

It took a good ten minutes of breathing fresh air before Roxanne stopped feeling faint. Devan handed her a bottle of water, concern on his usually calm face.

"Thanks." She smiled weakly as she perched on a low wall at the edge of the barracks, obediently unscrewing the cap and taking a few sips.

"Are you feeling better?" he asked, scrutinising her face. "You've got some colour in your cheeks again."

Roxanne's cheeks grew hotter, fully aware that her blush was more to do with embarrassment. Not to mention his attentiveness at the meeting, the memory of his hand around hers beneath the table. "I'll be alright soon," she promised. The tension in the stuffy room and the talk of worst-case scenarios had made her excuse herself as soon as Peter suggested a break. It was bad enough looking weak in front of Devan, who was her friend, never mind the others. Peter already remarked too often that she wasn't up to the job.

"You don't have to be anywhere near that battlefield," Devan said after a few minutes. "No one would think any less of you. Hell, Peter and Nanette won't even be there."

Roxanne gripped the bottle tightly, the glass cool in her hand. "Darshana and I will be medics, just like last time."

Devan nodded, glancing at their surroundings. They were a good few yards away from the buildings, but he lowered his voice anyway. "I'm a bit worried about Caplin.

After that stunt Bolton pulled today, I wouldn't be surprised if he backs out."

She glanced around as well, ensuring no one was near enough to hear. "Where would he go?"

Devan shrugged, his eyes hard as he gazed out at the sunny fields, wheat swaying in a light breeze. "He doesn't have to go anywhere. He could just tell his Forces to stand down."

His words twisted her stomach. "Do you think Skye could convince them to stay?"

He sighed, taking a seat on the wall next to her. "Lindsey's had some Tracers keeping tabs on the sentiment throughout the armies, and there are quite a few who are unhappy with Caplin but hopeful about the Lux. Even before that, she was renowned, and she has leadership qualities. But… diplomacy isn't her strong point."

Roxanne huffed a quiet laugh, aware of Devan's hand close to hers again. "No, she's certainly not her father's daughter in that respect. But after the way Caplin has treated her, it was only a matter of time. He's made his own bed."

Devan grimaced. "Or she's made ours."

"I hope you're wrong." She shuddered, taking another sip of water.

"Did you eat this morning?" he asked, gently changing the subject.

She shook her head. She hadn't even been able to stomach a cup of tea.

Devan was silent a moment, long enough for Roxanne to look up at him. He was smiling, the brightness of his eyes making her momentarily forget her nausea. "Then let me treat you to breakfast. Maybe I can bribe the cook to make something other than lumpy porridge."

She let out another laugh, drank some more water, then got to her feet, taking a moment to check she wasn't about to keel over before she took a few steps forward. Devan touched her elbow as though to reassure her that he was there in case she felt dizzy again, then they both set off towards the barracks canteen.

Chapter Thirty-Six

ALESSIA RONAN

The scent of death permeated her every waking moment, but she breathed it in like perfume as she glided through the burning towns, the cries of the population rising over the din of gunshots and crackle of Talents. And always at her side was her greatest joy: her grandfather, Ivor Ronan, restored in all his cruel glory.

He was the way she remembered him in the years before he became ill, no longer suffering with pain, no longer plagued by that choking cough each time he tried to speak. And he regarded her exactly as she had always imagined whenever he talked about her ascension. When he stepped from that casket, he took both her hands in his, then knelt at her feet.

But she wouldn't have him kneeling now. No, the ones that knelt were all the fools who were beneath them, the fearful and the cowardly. The town square was full of people on their knees, begging for their lives. But not all of them were prepared to beg. Amongst the obedience, others stood defiant, ready to die.

"Nathanael," she commanded, addressing the Sicarius who towered at her side. His head was shaven, his skin the colour of polished bronze, and he stepped forward with deadly grace. The silver scythe brooch pinned to his black clothing drew the gaze of the townsfolk before them. Several of those still standing dropped to their knees, but others remained steadfast.

Without a word, the Sicarius raised his hand, then slashed it through the air. An invisible force passed through the five closest civilians who remained on their feet, stopping their hearts with a whisper. They crumpled like ragdolls, eliciting whimpers and gasps from the assembled crowd.

Nathanael turned his gaze towards her, a single question in the deep, dark pools of his eyes. She nodded, the sudden deaths now murmuring at her ears like a midnight breeze. He turned back to the crowd, repeating the killing cut. Another handful of civilians met their ends. Five more bodies to add to her army of Undead. Five more voices whispering to her as they passed through the veil.

Vala hadn't told her where she had found the silent stranger with his rare and deadly Talent. Just like she hadn't told her where she had found Lucien. Nathanael was another of her servants, it seemed. Another weapon she had collected from some unknown corner of the world.

Twenty more bodies lay sprawled on the floor within minutes. As three more dropped, the few who remained standing finally sank to their knees, their whimpers filling the air. But she felt no pity as she eyed those who had tried to resist her army, and no remorse for the lives the Sicarius had taken.

Nathanael stepped back to her side, his massacre complete. Thirty-three – she had counted. Thirty-three lives claimed by this man in a matter of minutes. Added to the number from the last two towns they had conquered, she had a hundred and sixty-six bodies to raise tonight, to add to her army. And by using Nathanael to stop their hearts, their bodies would be in the best condition to fight for her when they marched on the allies.

"Does anyone else wish for a swift death?" Her voice carried cold and clear across the assembled crowd. When no one answered, she nodded to Nathanael, granting him permission to leave. "In that case, you may return to your homes, where you will remain for the rest of today. Tomorrow you are permitted to resume your daily activities, but you may not leave the town limits, nor be out in the streets after nine PM. Anyone caught breaking those rules will be shot on sight. My soldiers are Undead; they feel no compassion, and will not respond to pleas of mercy. You have been warned."

Undead soldiers closed in around the kneeling crowd, their skin glistening pale and deathly in the gloomy light. There were squeals of protest as the civilians were dragged to their feet and herded out of the square. Alessia remained long enough to silently pass her intentions to her puppet warriors, then turned, heading towards the war tent. Beside her, silent as the grave, her grandfather followed suit, sadistic pleasure glinting in his glassy eyes.

She found her loyal followers waiting inside the tent: Jonathan Pierce and the two Marsden brothers, Lucien and Vala. All bowed to greet her.

"What news do you have for me?" she demanded, not waiting for them to straighten.

Pierce raised himself to his full height with a fluid motion, despite the fact that he was no longer a young man. The Marsdens, Andrew and Rupert, were not so graceful. She barely glanced at them, although her grandfather sneered as he beheld them.

"The opposition have accepted your terms, Madam President, with a slight alteration. They wish to begin the battle in the morning, instead of at dusk."

Alessia swallowed, looking down at the map covered in wooden markers which Pierce had spread out on the table between them. Someone had glamoured the markers in different colours – black for Caplinites, blue for the Resistance, purple for her own army. And amongst the black, a yellow marker drew Alessia's gaze, bearing a lightning bolt etched on the side. "They want to bring the battle forward?"

"Indeed."

She inhaled slowly, wondering how they had sniffed out her army's weakness so quickly. Or was it mere coincidence? Caplin's Forces were seasoned fighters, as was Caspar. They both knew full well that daylight provided better fighting conditions.

"What is the weather forecast for that day?"

Pierce hesitated, thrown off by her unusual question. "It's raining, Madam."

She nodded, pleased with that outlook. Rain would dampen the fires of any Ignis. "Then tell them morning it is. Nine o'clock."

"Yes, Madam," Pierce confirmed, nodding to one of his officers, prompting him to leave with the message. But as he slipped through the tent flap, her head of intelligence, Arthur Linden, stepped in, bowing before he spoke.

"Madam President, we have new information from the opposition."

Alessia's lips curved, hoping Linden's carefully placed informants had brought something useful. "Do tell, Mr Linden."

"I'm afraid they have discovered the Undead's weakness, Madam. I can only assume those scouts we spotted early this morning were Matheson's Tracers."

Alessia's eyes slid to the Marsden brothers. Rupert looked sheepish, but Andrew, the eldest, held her gaze, his cool expression unreadable. It was only for the Marsdens' sake that she had hesitated instead of ordering for the scouts to be hunted down. A foolish mistake.

"Next time Tracers come snooping around, shoot them on sight," she ordered, casting her cold glare on Pierce. The general nodded, and her grandfather's thin lips bore a proud smile. She didn't bother to check the Marsdens' reaction. Their niece and brother-in-law were traitors, and would meet a traitor's end if she got hold of them.

"I do have some good news, however," Linden hurried on, eager to paper over the cracks. "We have details of where every Ignis will be placed in their ranks, as well as the nature of their weaponry. The allied army is being kitted out with flamethrowers, and Caplin will launch the first attack with his Aeres Army. They will be dropping explosives."

She nodded, looking to Pierce again. "Obscurus powers can cover us from an aerial attack."

"I have some plans for reducing visibility for our flying friends," came Vala's voice from a shadowy corner of the tent, a predatory smile on her face. Ivor took a seat beside her, his expression echoing the Seer's.

"I don't remember the last time Alistair Caplin deigned to fight his own battles," came Ivor's harsh voice, a voice that she still couldn't believe she was hearing again. "This may be your only chance to kill him."

"I'm afraid our informant brought a warning," said Linden, drawing Alessia's attention back to him. "Caplin has been in touch with Gerald Mason and confirmed his Guard were the ones ordered to capture his son and nephew back in October. Caplin promised that the prisoners will be executed if anything happens to him during the battle."

Her deathly Talent trickled like melting ice through her veins, twining with her darkness. "Why should I care about a pair of Masons being executed?"

Linden glanced at Pierce, who stepped forward. "A large proportion of our remaining live army are Gerald

Mason's troops, Madam. If his son is killed, it's possible he could withdraw his support for your campaign."

Alessia turned away, placing her hands on her hips, letting out a hiss. Why did it always come down to these blood traitor Masons? She could never understand why her grandfather had allowed Gerald to remain close after his older brother let his daughter marry a Bolton. She looked at her grandfather now, who sat in his chair like a king upon a throne.

"Nobody gives a damn about Magnus Mason," Ivor confirmed, the cruel sneer still on his face. "He's just Harlan's abandoned sprog. But Primus is Gerald's only son and heir. Let him be killed and Gerald will have nothing left to fight for."

She nodded. Her grandfather knew people's weaknesses too well, and the mistake she had made with Oliver Matheson echoed yet another warning in her ear. Her followers' loyalty had a habit of crumbling when their offspring were killed. "Then Caplin isn't a target. What about the Lux?"

"The informant confirmed Bolton intends to fight on the frontlines," said Linden, meeting her gaze, then dropping his eyes to the floor. "As will your uncle."

Of course, Bolton wanted glory. She didn't need to be the Lux for it to go to her head. Still, Alessia knew what seeing the Lux fighting amongst them would do for the allies' morale. She may have been an odious human being, but it seemed she knew how to work her charm and win people's loyalty when it mattered. And then there was Caspar, whose intention didn't surprise her. He had always fought amongst the soldiers he commanded in the past, eager to appear as a man of the people. Perhaps it was only a matter of time before his ego became the death of him.

"They are both targets," she confirmed, looking back at Pierce. "Inform your soldiers they have free reign to end their lives, should the opportunity arise."

Pierce nodded, moving the yellow lightning marker to the front of the wooden army. Ready to be crushed.

"There is one more detail," said Linden, looking between her and Pierce. "The allies intend to launch a surprise attack from the north – the Scottish troops Oliver Matheson was sent to commandeer."

"Thank you. We will be ready for them." She held her head a little higher, refusing to show her lingering hurt over her stolen armies. "Now leave us. I wish to speak with Vala and Lucien alone."

There was a chorus of "Yes, Ma'am", then Pierce, Linden and the Marsden brothers filed out. She looked at Lucien, who had spent the entire time lurking in the shadows behind Vala, his hands in his pockets. When Alessia's gaze fell on him, he stepped forward, curiosity filling his flashing eyes.

"You will watch Bolton on the battlefield. Glamour yourself as an Undead soldier."

"Of course, President Ronan." His tone held that hint of mockery that made her lip curl in distaste. "Should I engage her, if the possibility arises?"

"No. There is still a chance that she will survive the battle. If that is the case, I want you to incorporate your findings about her fighting style into our training plan."

"Yes, Madam." He bowed his head, the pale light filtering through the tent flap glistening blue on his dark hair.

"Now go. Make yourself useful by finding some Talentless who are viable for receiving power."

The man only smirked, then sauntered out of the tent.

"You ought to have him flogged for such blatant disrespect," said Ivor, getting out of his seat and approaching a small drinks cabinet in the corner. It was the only request he had made, and all Alessia had seen him consume. And yet, he never seemed to become intoxicated.

"I can assure you, dear Ivor," came Vala's honeyed voice as she stepped to Alessia's side with a rustle of skirts, "Lucien is of more use to our Nox's cause if he remains unharmed."

Ivor only snorted, knocking back a measure of amber liquid. Alessia met the Seer's deep blue gaze, lowering her voice so her grandfather couldn't hear. "Will it happen then?"

Vala shook her head. "Oh no. Fate will bring you close, but not that close. You both still have far too much havoc to wreak before your final battle takes place." She gave a tinkling laugh, sounding more like she was talking about some upcoming festival rather than contemplating Alessia's potentially imminent death. Vala seemed to sense her discomfort, for she took her hand, her fingers even colder than Alessia's. "You will know when it is time. For now, do not waste your strength worrying, sweet Nox. Save it for raising the dead."

She leaned forward, planting the lightest of kisses atop Alessia's head, then swept from the tent, leaving Alessia glaring furiously at her retreating back.

Chapter Thirty-Seven

PHAEDRA RONAN

Phaedra adjusted her slippery grip on the machine gun in her hands, resisting the urge to wipe the bead of sweat that trickled down her face like a crawling ant. The late afternoon sunlight stung her eyes as she squinted at the target. She took a deep breath, then let it out as she fired, gritting her teeth against the recoil that vibrated through her right shoulder into her chest.

She set down the gun and rotated her shoulder, finally wiping her sweaty face with her sleeve as she inspected her handiwork. "*Shit*," she swore under her breath. The battle was tomorrow, and her aim still hadn't improved.

"Shit indeed."

She jumped, looking around to find her girlfriend standing beside her, arms crossed over her chest, her expression sceptical as she surveyed the target across from them.

"You could at least pretend to be supportive," Phaedra half joked, quirking an eyebrow.

Ombra didn't smile. "This isn't a school test, Phee. Encouraging you to fail at this will only get you killed."

Phaedra winced at her hard words. She knew Ombra could be blunt, but it was rare for her to be harsh. Perhaps

Ombra noticed, because her tone softened slightly as she continued.

"I just don't get why you're wasting your time with this instead of honing your Talent."

She grimaced. "I've been training with Caspar."

"Great, so you're a weapon of mass destruction. You don't need a gun."

Phaedra slipped her hands into her pockets to hide her suddenly trembling fingers. It was true – she had been training with Caspar. But as always, her control was next to none. He had coaxed her, encouraged her, told her to trust her power, but it had still emerged from her body in frightening volumes, requiring her uncle to absorb her outbursts or shield their surroundings with his own shadows. She wasn't ready. She would never be ready.

"Mass destruction indeed…" she muttered, absently rubbing her aching shoulder as images of a half-collapsed roof and dismembered Ronan soldiers loomed in her mind. She fought a shudder.

"We're having dinner with my family tonight," Ombra reminded her. Phaedra swallowed, unsure she was prepared for another meal with Alma Medley. The first meeting was intense enough. "After that, we're having another training session."

"Another training session?" Phaedra echoed, her trembling now adding a wobble to her voice.

But Ombra was already heading towards the barracks to shower.

***

"You're not wearing the Bolton crest on your uniform, Ombra, and that's the end of it," said Ombra's mother hours later, her words bearing a tone of finality that had

Phaedra concentrating very closely on the last of her roast potatoes.

"But Lorcan is wearing the Medley crest," Ombra replied hotly. "The whole Lux Guard are ditching Caplin's raven."

"Against my advice and their better judgement," Alma replied, setting down her knife and fork across her empty plate and fixing Ombra with her hawk-like eyes.

"Why the Bolton crest, anyway? What's wrong with the Medley one?" asked Ombra's father, Jackson, beside his wife. Phaedra liked him better than her mother. He had a kind, freckled face, thinning red hair, and laughter in his voice. According to Ombra, he had also worked in the courts alongside his wife before the coup, but Phaedra had long forgotten what he did.

Ombra wrinkled her nose. "It has *violins* on it. The stormbird is way more badass."

"George is learning to play the violin," said Sebastian, one of Ombra's younger brothers, from the end of the table. "It sounds like cats screeching."

"It does *not*," George retorted, scowling at his twin.

"It does too," Ombra replied under her breath. Phaedra used her napkin to hide her smirk.

"Are you fighting tomorrow, too?" asked Sebastian, staring down the table at Phaedra. The twins had their father's carrot red hair, growing thick and curly around their ears, and their freckles and green eyes echoed Ombra and Lorcan's. Their nine-year-old faces were angelic, but mischief often danced in their eyes.

"I am," Phaedra confirmed, forcing a smile as she set down her knife and fork. She hoped Mrs Medley wouldn't be annoyed that she was too full to eat her last potato.

"Mum doesn't want Om to fight," said George, somewhat more solemn than his brother.

“I wish I could fight,” Sebastian exclaimed, awe lighting up his eyes.

“Gods help us,” Alma muttered, beginning to stack plates.

“Phee and I need the garden for training,” Ombra said casually, handing her plate to her mother.

Alma froze, eyeing her daughter across the table. “Haven’t you done enough?”

Ombra shrugged. “Just a bit of fine-tuning.”

Phaedra smiled awkwardly as Alma turned her glower on her, then almost sighed in relief when her eyes went back to Ombra. “You’re not using Talents, are you?”

There was a pause, pink blooming in Ombra’s cheeks. “We’ll be careful.”

“Can we come?” Sebastian asked hopefully.

“No,” Ombra said firmly, slipping out of her chair.

Phaedra gave the disappointed brothers an apologetic smile as she got up too. “Thank you for dinner, Mrs Medley.”

“I didn’t make it,” Alma said briskly, as Jackson picked up the stack of plates. “But I’ll pass on your compliments to the cook.”

Phaedra wasn’t sure if she was making a joke, but before she could ponder it further, Ombra tugged her outside.

“Ignore her,” Ombra murmured after she slid the glass door shut behind them. “Moody is her default mood.”

“Trust me, after my sister, your mum is a golden retriever.”

Ombra snorted, hands in her pockets as she led her through a long garden, flanked either side by hedges and ending in a low stone wall. The murky river streamed lazily past beyond it, and wards glistened along the perimeter, keeping out intruders and prying eyes. They trailed past a swing set, discarded action dolls and dragon toys, and a haphazard hut tucked between the branches of a tree, a pirate flag hanging limply from a glassless window.

"Have the boys manifested their Talents yet?" Phaedra asked quietly, glancing back at the house to see Sebastian forlornly watching them beyond the glass doors.

"They're Terra like Dad and Lorcan," Ombra replied, leading her to the end of the garden, beyond a small guest house with hanging baskets that overspilled with red flowers. "That used to be their sand pit."

She pointed at what Phaedra had mistaken for a flower bed near the swings. Vines, wildflowers, and toadstools overflowed from it.

"Dad had to rein them in, or they'd have turned the whole garden into a jungle."

"That's pretty cool." She wished she had a Talent that could create instead of destroy. It must be beautiful to grow flowers instead of sowing fear. "What's your mum's Talent?"

Ombra came to a standstill at the end of the garden, then sat down cross-legged in the grass, facing her. "She's an Electrica, like Skye."

Phaedra raised an eyebrow, settling down opposite Ombra, the grass cool beneath her legs. "I thought electric Talents were pretty rare."

"They are, maybe even rarer than Obscurae. The Boltons and Masons are the only families in Britannia to have them, as far as we know. But enough about them." A teasing smile tugged at her lips, recognising Phaedra was stalling. "This is about you and your Talent."

Phaedra took in the determination in her girlfriend's eyes, the sinking sun bringing out the gold tones in her hair. For a wistful moment, she wished she could freeze time, stay trapped in this evening forever, with Ombra, and not face her sister's army tomorrow. Caspar had tried to mask his fear when he asked her to change her mind about the battle. But if Officer Munro deemed the cadets ready to fight, she wasn't going to sit it out, even if her stomach squirmed with dread.

"I can't risk it, O," she finally admitted, her voice barely above a whisper. "I almost killed Glen. I *did* kill my sister's men. I can't… I can't unsee what I did to them."

Ombra was silent for a long moment, watching her. When she spoke, her voice was as quiet as Phaedra's. "You can't feel guilty about killing people who wanted to hurt you, Phee. Tomorrow will be the same. Your Talent is the best weapon you have. *We* could be some of the best weapons the allies have. Anyone can learn to shoot a gun, but you could cause ten times the damage with just a thought. You just have to trust yourself."

As Phaedra shook her head, Ombra lay her hands on her knees, palms up. Shadows unfurled from her fingertips, flickering like dark flame in the waning light. "Copy me," she said gently, her sparkling eyes distracting Phaedra for a moment as she caught her stare. Lowering her gaze to her own hands, she tried it, struggling to focus. After a moment, her own shadows sputtered to life.

"But right now is fine," she protested, avoiding Ombra's scrutiny. "I took my sedatives."

"Don't take them tomorrow."

She shook her head again. "But then I won't be able to control it."

Ombra cocked her head. "What if you take half the dose?"

"Then I guess I'll have half the control."

She let out a huff. "I really wish we had more time to sort you out."

"Thanks for making me sound like a total mess," Phaedra replied, unable to keep the hurt from her voice.

Ombra's face fell. "I didn't mean that. You're not a mess." She took her hands, threading her fingers through

Phaedra's, their shadows dancing around one another. "You're just… scared. You shouldn't be scared of what's part of you, Phee."

"I don't want to hurt people," she said, tears stinging her eyes. "Not the wrong people."

"Look…" Ombra's grip on her hands tightened, and Phaedra met her fierce gaze. "When I was a kid, I couldn't control it either. Mum used to give me sedatives too, because she had no idea how to deal with it, and eventually Caplin found an Obscurus to tutor me. He told me that if I was scared of my Talent and tried to suppress it, I wouldn't learn to control it. I had to accept it, embrace it, let it become my friend. That's when I realised that each time my darkness surged, it was only trying to protect me. You need to let yours do the same."

"But Caspar couldn't teach me—"

"Maybe Caspar's way of learning control is different to yours. Maybe he never feared his Talent the way you do."

Phaedra let her words sink in, watching as Ombra's shadows twined above their joined hands again, coaxing Phaedra's to the surface. She let them rise, let them overflow and join Ombra's in a dance once again. Ombra had always had this calming effect on her, allowing her to turn her Talent into something beautiful, so different to the untamed power that normally raged out of her.

"Talents work on instinct, Phee. They're not like guns and blades. Our fears and emotions dictate how they manifest. Tomorrow, please promise me you will use it to keep yourself safe. Promise me that if you find yourself in a situation where your gun won't cut it, you won't hesitate to use your Talent."

"But—"

But Ombra shook her head, cupping Phaedra's face in a hand. "Promise me you will stay near me, so I can help you contain it if it gets out of hand."

"Okay…" she breathed, pinned by her gaze, leaning into her touch. "I promise I won't leave your side."

Ombra gave her a small smile, pressing her lips to Phaedra's. Phaedra's shadows quivered as Ombra's hair tickled her bare arms, her fragrant shampoo mingling with the scent of the wildflowers growing on the riverbank. "Good. Now let's give my brothers the shadow show they've been waiting for."

Phaedra grimaced, glancing towards the house and seeing the boys watching intently, both cross-legged on the floor, elbows on their knees, chins on their fists. "I'm surprised the kissing didn't put them off."

"You didn't see the faces they were pulling."

Chapter Thirty-Eight

DEAN ROSWELL

Dean sat at the corner of the war council table next to his sister, painfully conscious of the grey and yellow stormbird crest that Skye had persuaded him to add to his uniform. But while Skye wore her family crest with pride, he shrank a little more each time Caplin's cold stare slid his way. At least the rest of the table paid him little mind as the strategising dragged on.

"My Trace says we're too thin on Ignes and flamethrowers here." Lindsey's voice drew him out of a reverie, attracting his gaze like a magnet. She was tapping Devan Harlow's carefully drawn up battle plans, and her confidence as she met her superior's eyes filled Dean with awe.

"There will be plenty of fire on that battlefield tomorrow, Miss Matheson," Caplin cut in coolly, eyeing the plans with distaste. "And my Aeres army is well-equipped with explosives."

"We're not prepared enough for subsequent waves," she replied, holding her head high. "We need more firepower in the reserve units."

Sinclair raised his eyebrows as he looked between Caplin, Lindsey and Harlow. "Can we move people around?"

Harlow considered. "We don't have enough flamethrowers to equip the cadets, but it's not too late to transfer some of the Talentless. Ronan, can you hold back some Ignes?"

"Of course," said Caspar calmly. "I'll have the final numbers for you tonight."

"Happy with that, Lindsey?" Harlow asked, making some notes on the plans.

"That should help, yes." She glanced around, her doe-brown eyes meeting Dean's. He quickly averted his gaze, willing his cheeks not to heat. When he dared to look her way again, she was listening intently to Harlow as he reiterated a few more points.

I won't be home tonight, came Skye's silent voice when Sinclair closed the meeting and wished them luck for the following day. He glanced around in time to catch her sharing a look with Caspar, a hint of a smirk on both their faces.

Dean resisted the urge to wrinkle his nose. *So?*

But she only flashed him a wry smile as she got to her feet. *Have fun and don't stay out too late.*

He glared as she headed towards the door, catching up with Caspar as they slipped out together. Caplin and Sullivan left too, shortly followed by most of the Resistance Leaders. Dean glanced down the table to see Oliver and Lindsey still talking to Harlow and Rathbone, fine-tuning some last-minute details about the ambush from the north. However, Lindsey had pushed out her chair and looked like she was waiting to leave. Realising he looked out of place, Dean edged out the door, then leaned on the wall outside, slinging his jacket over his arm and silently talking himself into asking Lindsey the question he had been trying to muster the courage for in the past weeks.

As he had hoped, Lindsey stepped out of the building alone, and turned towards him with her groomed eyebrows slightly raised. He pushed off the wall, admiring the way the late afternoon sun glimmered in her blonde hair and warmed the graceful sweep of her delicate cheekbones. For a brief moment he forgot his intentions, then offered her what he hoped was a winning smile.

"Thank gods that's over," he said, then inwardly cringed at how ridiculous he must sound. Whatever he had planned to say, it wasn't that, but all he could do was hurry on. "A few of us are meeting at the pub. I think we could all use a drink after that. Would you like to join?"

Lindsey tilted her head, staring him down like he was insignificant. As the moment dragged on, Dean began to wish the ground would swallow him up, trying to think of a way to retract whatever stupid thing he had said. But then her severe expression softened, and she even gave him a small smile. "That's nice of you, but I'm not sure your friends would want me there."

Dean shrugged, putting his hands in his pockets, then wishing he hadn't, but it was too late to take them back out without looking even more like an idiot. "Don't worry about them. I'm inviting you because I want you there."

Her eyes narrowed a little. "You're not one of those dickheads who invites a girl to hang out with his friends and then ignores her, are you?"

Dean's cheeks warmed as he stared at her, wide-eyed. "No chance," he said, taking his hands out of his pockets and holding them out, palms towards her. "Why, has someone done that to you?"

But Lindsey only drew herself to her full height, not deigning to reply. Just then, the remaining people from the war council stepped into the yard, and Oliver stopped next to his daughter. "Coming?"

Lindsey hesitated, glancing at her father, then looking back at Dean, her hair shimmering in the breeze. "Actually, Dad, Dean has invited me for a drink."

If Dean was intimidated before, it was nothing compared to how he felt as Oliver's hostile glare zeroed in on him. He could do nothing but give a small, awkward smile, trying his best to stand tall. "It's just with a few friends. You could join, if you like."

But Oliver said nothing, only continued to disdainfully look him up and down. Finally, he looked back at his daughter. "Fine. I'll see you tonight." And with that he turned on his heel and trudged off across the yard, leaving Dean to exhale a shaky breath.

Lindsey looked back at him, her eyes almost as cold as her father's. "So, where to?"

When they arrived at the barracks pub, Dean couldn't decide if he regretted the decision to bring her there. The pub was noisy, crowded, and smelled too much like spilled beer and sweat. He should have taken her somewhere more upmarket, a wine bar or even a restaurant. But then he reminded himself this wasn't technically a date, but rather something he hoped would lead to a date once they got through the hellish day that awaited them tomorrow. Still, as he glanced at her to gauge her reaction, she crossed the pub with her usual expression of indifference, then stopped at the bar, casting an eye over the overhead boards bearing lists of beers and ales.

"Anything you recommend?" she asked.

Dean hesitated, glancing from her to the board, at a loss. Lindsey didn't look like the kind of girl who drank beer, but he knew better than to judge a book by its cover. "What do you like?"

She shrugged. "Nothing too fancy. What are they, *craft* beers?" she said with a hint of a sneer.

A sheepish smile curved his lips at her comment. "They have the usual fare on draught too. That's what I'm getting."

She glanced at the tap he was pointing at. "I'll have that then."

Once they got their beers, they found a table in a booth, but it was big enough to accommodate at least four other people if his friends did indeed show up. He mostly hoped they wouldn't, and deliberately chose to sit in a corner so they probably wouldn't notice them. They clinked their glasses to Dean's brief "cheers", then drank in silence. He tried to think of something to say, while Lindsey looked around the pub, taking in the crowd and the noise, the atmosphere oddly cheerful despite what awaited them the following day.

"So, your sister and Ronan, are they actually…?"

Dean stared, then lowered his gaze, grimacing. "I think so, but I'm not in the habit of taking much notice of my sister's… affairs."

Lindsey huffed a laugh. It was the most expressive he had seen her so far. "I mean, Ronan has always been a bit of a womaniser, but Skye? I didn't see that coming."

He cringed, not entirely comfortable with the topic of conversation, but at least they were talking. "Oh, don't worry, she has a habit of getting what she wants. She's no victim."

"No, looks like she's giving him a run for his money." Her lips twisted in amusement, then she drank her beer, delicately wiping the foam off her top lip with her thumb. "This is decent."

Heat rose in his cheeks as she met his gaze. "I'm glad you like it."

Another awkward silence fell, and the horrible realisation dawned on him that he was way out of his depth. Lorcan was right, he had no idea how he was supposed to flirt. His few relationships had fallen into place almost effortlessly. But now that he had Lindsey across from him, he realised he knew almost nothing about her.

As he struggled to decide where to start, she beat him to it. "So, what *have* you been up to since school, Dean Roswell?"

He let out a breath, relieved that her question was neutral and simple enough to answer. "This, mostly," he said, then realised his mistake, laughing nervously. "Not drinking, I mean – I joined the Forces when Skye joined."

She gave a small smile in response to his accidental joke, then looked him up and down, her eyes scanning him slowly. His blush deepened as he wondered what she was looking for. "I never saw you as the military type. I could have sworn you were going to study architecture."

"I was…" He let out a sigh. That had been a path he had started down, and a large part of him still missed it terribly. "It seemed like a silly thing to study while half my family were risking their lives on the front lines."

"I don't think it's silly at all." As she held his gaze, Dean became very aware of his pulse quickening. "There'll be plenty to rebuild once this is all over. But I get it. I did the same."

He nodded, appreciating her attempt to make him feel less ashamed. A kernel of what little he knew of the shy and studious Lindsey from school rose to the surface. "Weren't you planning to study medicine?"

She was silent for a moment, watching the crowd again. "I was, for a while. I wanted to be a lawyer too. Or a scientist." She shrugged. "Fate had other plans."

"I remember when we got paired up in that biology class." He paused, examining the memory and realising that fifteen-year-old Dean probably wasn't the best version of himself to remind her of, but it was too late to backtrack. "You must have thought I was clueless trying to build those cell models out of clay, but you… you were brilliant."

"You remember that?" she asked, and for the first time, her eyes lit up. "You weren't that bad. At least you did your share of the work, even if…"

He let out a chuckle. "Even if…?"

"Well… I think I had to re-label most of your part, and smooth over your fumbles in the presentation." She looked at her glass, suppressing a grin.

Dean flushed. "I don't think you told me about that."

"You were so pleased with yourself, I didn't have the heart to say."

His own heart sank into an embarrassed puddle, vaguely remembering the lumpy shapes and colours they had stuck together and labelled with toothpicks. "Was it really that bad?"

"You made up for it in other ways. Our models definitely looked the best after you worked the clay so magnificently with your Talent."

She met his eye, then looked away again, hiding her smile as she drank her beer. His blush deepened, and he busied himself with his own drink. "For what it's worth, I learned a lot from you."

Despite her lowered gaze, her smile grew, becoming more shy than teasing. He caught a glimpse of the sweet girl who had quietly guided him through the project, and even stayed up late helping him prepare his notes for their presentation. "It's good to know my efforts to teach you the difference between eukaryotes and prokaryotes didn't go to waste."

He huffed a laugh, not daring to admit that he had forgotten most of his science classes as soon as exams were over. "How did you end up becoming Head Tracer?"

She shrugged, her amusement fading. "I'm good at it. And Dad was always complaining about how useless Ronan's team was, so I suppose I took it upon myself to sort them out."

His awe from the meeting welled up again. “You were a spy for the Saoirse Army too…” he ventured, aware that the topic was probably delicate. “Why did you decide to do that?”

She hesitated, her warmth dissipating as she absently twisted a ring around her finger. It looked old, with tiny scales etched into the silver, a snake biting its own tail. “Remember Carey Shanahan?”

“Of course. I heard he got himself killed during that uprising in Ireland a couple of years ago.”

Lindsey winced, her jaw rigid. “He was my boyfriend.”

Dean’s face fell, ashamed of his insensitivity, although there was no way he could have known. Carey Shanahan had been in the year below him at school, and they had often played sports together despite their differing political allegiances. But now that he knew what Carey meant to Lindsey… suddenly her allegiance and espionage made complete sense.

“I’m sorry,” he said quickly, worried that asking her out had been too forward, too soon. Not to mention Cameron’s passing was still so fresh.

She hunched her shoulders, still fiddling with her ring. “He died for a cause he believed in. So, in his memory, I’ll keep fighting for that cause.”

Dean nodded, nursing his beer and silently kicking himself for being so thoughtless. Realisations over what this woman in front of him must be going through bubbled to the surface. He couldn’t even begin to imagine what kind of strength it took to walk out the door every day and continue fighting.

“Same again?” she said suddenly, raising her glass and looking up at him at last. He half expected her to be tearful, but to his relief, her eyes were dry.

"Er, yes, okay," he said, and she gave him a closed-lipped smile, taking her purse out of her bag and heading up to the bar.

When she settled back into the booth with their drinks, her smile was strained. "So, last I heard, you and Letitia were planning to get married."

Dean froze, though perhaps he should have expected his long-term ex to come up at some point. Lindsey and Letitia had been friends.

"Yeah, uh… the engagement didn't exactly last long."

Pity and curiosity mingled on her face. "I'm sorry it didn't work out."

He crossed his arms, reluctant to delve into Letitia's faults and hurtful actions. "I'm not. Not anymore. You… you don't need me to tell you what she's like." The pity in her eyes deepened, and he hid from her gaze, drinking deeply.

"To be honest, I could never really understand why you went out with her. You were… nice."

Right on cue, his cheeks heated again. "Nice?"

"Yeah, a decent bloke. As far as teenage boys go." Her lips tugged up, and her gaze lingered in that searching way that made him self-conscious again. "But I suppose she had her way of making herself liked. She didn't waste an opportunity to exploit her Talent."

"Well, if she hadn't been influencing my feelings, I probably would have left a lot sooner…" The relationship had lasted three years. Three years living under the hazy influence of her Empathic Talent, only to realise that Letitia had turned him into a shell of his former self by the time things ended. "Why did you two fall out?"

She stared at him, perhaps caught off guard by him deflecting. "I… well… everything and nothing really."

He nodded, giving her a weak smile. "Well, it's all in the past now."

Before she could reply, a loud voice boomed overhead.

"So this is where you're hiding!"

They looked up to see Ike and Lorcan, both holding a beer in each hand. Before Dean could say anything, they sat down, Lorcan next to Dean, Ike next to Lindsey. Ike set the beers on the table then stuck out his hand to shake hers. "Ikarus Arrowsmith," he said, and Lindsey shook it dutifully. "Or Ike, if you prefer."

"Hi," said Lindsey, looking him up and down as she no doubt recognised his name. "I'm Lindsey Matheson."

"I know," said Ike, and his smile faltered a little as he glanced at Dean. "I was guarding Caplin when you revealed you were spying for the Saoirseans."

"That's right." She paused, studying him. "Darius was your father, wasn't he?"

He nodded, then took a drink of his beer, his ears pink.

"I'm sorry about what happened."

Ike hunched his shoulders a little. "Not your fault." He offered her a faint smile, then bravely brushed off the difficult situation. "I can think of plenty of people to blame, but I'm not one to judge someone based on political allegiances. We're all on the same side now anyway."

"How was it today?" Lorcan asked Dean, dragging his gaze away from Lindsey.

Dean shrugged, trying to hide his disappointment that his private evening with Lindsey had been interrupted. Although considering she seemed adamant on bringing up the most embarrassing parts of his past, perhaps the boys had done him a favour. "We're as ready as we'll ever be."

Lorcan nodded, sipping his drink. "Did Skye have another bust up with Caplin?"

"No, actually. They both behaved, apart from looking daggers at each other every so often."

"Well, that's something. Still, Sabine has now convinced everyone to wear their own family crests on their uniforms tomorrow. That's going to be awkward fighting alongside the rest of the Forces."

"I know," said Dean, glancing down at his jacket. Any other time, he would proudly wear his adopted family's emblem, but not when it meant alienating his comrades. "At first it was only supposed to be the two of us, but getting Sabine involved… the pair of them are like a dog with a bone."

As though summoned, Sabine herself appeared with Jacob, and they both squeezed into the booth.

"Why are you all the way over here?" she grumbled, setting down her drink with a thud. And then her gaze settled on Lindsey. "Oh. Hello."

"Lindsey Matheson," said Lindsey, giving her a brief wave, too far away to shake her hand.

"I know who you are," said Sabine, not bothering to introduce herself. She then turned to Lorcan and her brother, acting like Lindsey wasn't even there. He couldn't really blame Sabine, although he had hoped she would be a little more civil.

He looked at Lindsey, smiling apologetically. To his surprise, she flashed the most genuine smile he had seen on her lips since they had become allies, the sight of it driving everything else out of his mind. She held his gaze until Ike reclaimed her attention, leaving him wishing he could invite her to get out of there. But they were trapped in the booth, and he knew he'd get an earful if they left now.

"Cheers, you lot!" Ike toasted loudly, shoving his glass into the centre of the table. "Here's to what might be our last beer."

"Lighten up," Sabine complained. "I don't know about you, but *I* certainly won't be kicking it tomorrow."

As the others burst into banter and bravado about the upcoming battle, Dean sought Lindsey's eyes again, her warmth and amusement igniting his butterflies. "Are you nervous about tomorrow?"

She lifted her shoulders, her voice just about audible above the ruckus. "How could I not be? Ikarus is right."

He took a deep breath and leaned closer, his butterflies flitting around uncomfortably. "And you're commanding. That's so brave."

Her lips curved teasingly. "We'll all be fighting the same battle, Dean."

"Exactly!" Ike butted in, raising his glass again. "Once she sees us lot tearing up the battlefield, Alessia can ride her little shadow cloud all the way back to Scotland."

Sabine snorted. "I'll be surprised if she even shows. She's too prissy to get her hands dirty."

Dean grimaced, but the conversation soon turned to lighter topics, with Lindsey even going as far as cracking a few dry jokes. Eventually, however, she announced that she ought to get home.

"I'll walk you back," said Dean quickly, gathering his things and exiting the booth while Sabine grumbled about having to let him pass. Lindsey didn't say anything to stop him, and as he glanced back at his friends to say goodbye, he saw Ike and Lorcan waggling their eyebrows teasingly. He gave them a mock frown, following Lindsey out.

"I hope they didn't overwhelm you," he said once they were walking at a steady pace, twilight casting long shadows across the road.

"Not at all." Hope bloomed in his chest at her upbeat tone. "I knew it would be awkward, being who I am, but they seem nice. Well, Sabine doesn't like me, but she doesn't have a reputation for being a people person."

"Sabine doesn't like anyone, so don't worry about her. Ike is pretty chilled though, and so is Lorcan. They're probably my best mates."

"Yes, I remember them from school. Ike hasn't changed a bit, and Lorcan was always quiet."

They walked in silence for a moment, then Dean said, "So were you."

He glanced down to find her smiling, trying to hide her reaction behind her smooth sheet of hair. "I was. With friends like the ones I had, it was hard to be anything but."

"But you've come out of your shell now." And he couldn't help but notice how much it suited her. Lindsey had always been pretty, but so quiet that she faded into the background. Aside from that shared biology project, he couldn't remember ever holding a conversation with her.

"And what about you, Dean Roswell? Have you come out of your shell?"

He shrugged, suddenly very aware of where he was putting his feet. "You tell me." But he knew the answer. He had lost too many parts of himself in the ruins of his relationship with Letitia, parts he was still searching for in the rubble.

She gifted him another rare smile, her gaze lingering a little too long again. He looked away first, just in time to turn a corner.

Their walk wasn't long, leading them to the row of private chalets reserved for higher ranking officials. Lindsey stopped outside the last one. Dean glanced up at the drawn curtains beyond the windows, the back of his neck prickling at the thought of Oliver Matheson coming out to interrogate him.

"Well, Dean, thank you for a pleasant evening." She turned to him, rising to her full height.

"Thank you for joining," he said, his stomach twisting with nerves as he met her gaze, her eyes bright in the gathering dusk. "I hope I didn't turn out to be one of those dickheads you mentioned earlier."

"Not at all," she said with a curve of her lips. "Quite the opposite, actually. It's been nice getting to know you again."

He gave her another awkward smile, painfully aware of the flush creeping into his cheeks the longer the moment dragged on. He didn't know where to look, nor what to do with his hands, so he stuffed them into his pockets again.

"Well?" she said eventually, inclining her head to one side and watching him from beneath thick, dark painted lashes. "Aren't you going to kiss me goodnight?"

He started, completely thrown off guard by her question. But before he could answer, she was already leaning towards him.

His hands moved automatically, brushing her hair away from her face while his heartbeat suddenly spiralled. As she tilted her head up towards him, he met her lips eagerly, expecting the kiss to be a simple peck. Just as he was about to draw away, she ran her hands up his arms and around his neck, fingers brushing through his hair. The kiss deepened into something much more passionate than he had dared to hope for, and he pulled her closer, his arms encircling her waist.

The kiss ended too soon, and she drew back with a smile. "Well, Dean," she said, her warmth and soft floral perfume leaving him dazed as her fingertips brushed his sleeves. "I hope next time you'll take me on a proper date. Goodnight."

Chapter Thirty-Nine

SKYE BOLTON

Skye awoke to kisses, and Caspar's hands trailing circles down her spine. She basked in his warmth and scent for some time, but when she shivered as his lips found the sweet spot beneath her ear, she curled around him, giving him full access to her naked body. He didn't waste the opportunity, kissing down her neck, and then lower, his mouth and hands exploring her freely. She gave him a sleepy smile as he looked up at her, dark hair tousled, his lips tracing a jagged scar above her right hip bone – a souvenir from her first battle.

He made his way back up with a mischievous gleam in his eyes, and his fingertips wandered along her thighs, sending shudders of pleasure down her spine. His lips found hers as he hooked her legs around his hips, and she melted into the kiss, burying her fingers in his hair and pulling him closer. He eased into her, moving slowly, teasingly, the pace much more lazy than the frantic sex of the night before.

"Good morning," he murmured in her ear after they finished, and she could hear the smile in his voice, his kisses hot against her neck. His ragged breath matched her own, and she caressed the planes and muscles of his back, her eyes closed as she savoured the final ripples of pleasure.

As their breathing slowed, she sought his lips again, the gentle patter of rain against the window the only sound as they lingered on the kisses. Finally, Caspar made to draw away.

"Stay," she whispered, tightening her arms and legs around him and drawing him back for another kiss. "Just a little longer."

He obliged, a shudder coursing through him as she ran her fingers through the hair at the nape of his neck. "It's already far too difficult to leave this bed when you're in it."

She let out a low laugh, luxuriating in the stroke of his tongue against hers, his touch light as he explored her hips and ribs once again. She didn't want to think about what kind of day awaited them when they left their bed. So she distracted herself a little longer, holding his warm body close.

When she entered the cottage kitchen sometime later, in full uniform and proudly displaying her own family's crest instead of Caplin's, the scent of cinnamon wafted from a pair of steaming bowls on the table.

"Porridge?" she asked, raising an eyebrow as she slid into her chair.

"Don't complain. You need it."

Her eyebrow rose higher in amusement, but she dutifully picked up her spoon, tasting nuts and raisins too. But as Caspar brought coffee to the table, she paused in her eating, her attention snatched by the change in his appearance. Awe washed over her as she looked him up and down, taking in his uniform.

For the first time since she had met him, he looked like the celebrated general he was reputed to be, rather than the dandy who gossiped and caused scandals at his brother's formal events. The shade of grey he had chosen to replace the traditional Ronan purple was formidable, and the only hint of his family was in the gold and purple dragon crest on his chest, beneath the golden epaulettes that marked his rank.

"It suits you," she finally managed, unable to stop herself from admiring the way his powerful body moved in his uniform.

"Thank you," he said, sitting down opposite her with his own breakfast. "I doubt it'll look so good in the middle of the battlefield when I'm covered in gore, but we'll all be in the same boat."

She caught a glimpse of darkness flickering in his eyes, the only hint of fear for the day ahead. But then it was gone, his irises returning to the icy blue that contrasted with his dark hair and beard, freshly trimmed and carefully styled to add to the air of a proud leader. In spite of her own fear, Skye felt a thrill of anticipation for witnessing him fight, eager to see if he lived up to the legends.

"Well, Caspar, here's to fighting for more than our lives," Skye said, lifting her coffee cup in a mock toast. Grinning, he bumped his own against hers, and they drank deeply.

"Sure you don't want some brandy in that?"

"Maybe we'll have one for the road."

***

Instead of heading straight to the barracks, Skye took the portal back to the Land's End safe house, finding Dean as he was finishing getting ready. When he saw her walk in, he turned and pulled her into a hug.

"You'll crease our uniforms," she grumbled, but didn't care as she held him just as tightly. She felt a little guilty for not having joined the drinks nor come home the previous evening, but by the time she had had dinner with Caspar, the exhaustion of the two days of planning had caught up with her. Besides, when she caught wind of his intentions to ask Lindsey Matheson out for a drink, it was another reason to make herself scarce.

"How did it go last night?" she asked, pulling away to let Dean finish buttoning his jacket. But he didn't need to say it out loud, for his thoughts were full of memories of the evening. Skye tried not to smirk.

"For someone so ridiculously good looking, you really are terrible at flirting, Dean."

Dean turned away to try to hide his blush, but she could see his reflection grimacing in the mirror. "Not everyone has a massive ego like you," he muttered.

"I heard that." But she was laughing. "At least she gave you a snog."

"Please don't start judging my kissing skills as well."

"Gross, Dean. I stopped watching when you went in for the smooch. I don't need that many details."

"No, just my failure at chatting up a girl." But he was trying not to laugh as well.

"Well, sounds like she found you charming, if she wants a second date."

"I'm sure she has guys lining up to date her. Even Ike could barely keep his eyeballs in his head last night."

"Make sure you're first in line then." She patted him on the shoulder, then went to collect her weapons from her room and began concealing them on her person.

"Anyway," she said as they headed to the door to leave. "After she sees you fight today, I doubt she'll care about your crappy flirting."

"Thanks Skye, you sure know how to flatter a guy."

***

The scene that overwhelmed them when they arrived at the battle site was an attack on the senses. Worse, a fine mist drizzled on the assembled armies, soon coating her with a damp film, and pearly fog rolled across the vast expanse of space. The grassy field would be churned into a dangerous mud bath within an hour of the battle starting, and visibility was going to be terrible. She wondered if the Nox's army would be less frightening if they couldn't see them coming.

"Morning!" Ike greeted, grinning as though they were about to go on a field trip, not fight a battle against the Nox. But as Skye neared and Ike puffed out his chest, she swelled with pride to see the Arrowsmith family crest embroidered above his heart: the sky-blue field decorated with crossed silver arrows.

"Ike, that looks so good," she said, glancing from his pale face to his crest.

"This was a great idea, Skye. It's another way to honour my dad."

"He would be so proud of you. He already was."

"Thanks," he said, his grin fading into a sad smile, and then he pulled her into a bear hug, his mechanical wings jostling her. She laughed in his ear, awkwardly avoiding the cold grey metal strapped to his back.

When Skye finally withdrew and turned, she found herself faced with Sabine's golden glare. "Where were you last night?"

Guilt flared in her chest again, but instead of letting it show, she stood straighter, sticking out her chin. "Come on, Sabine, I've spent every night with you lot."

"What happened to sisters before misters?" she demanded, but Skye didn't miss the faint curve on Sabine's lips. "Even Dean wanted to ditch us last night. For a *Matheson* of all people. Surely he could have taken his pick from the thousands of women on our side."

"I know, first Ombra, now him. But I can't really talk."

Sabine snorted, leaving the remainder of her disapproval unsaid. "Onto a more serious matter, I hope

Harlow has some more waterproof weapons up his sleeve, because it's really not the weather for getting a good hot blaze going."

"That's what I feared." The fog showed no sign of clearing.

"It's not going to be the bonfire you were hoping for," said Jacob, coming up from behind them and gazing at the damp, foggy field, "but I'm sure we can manage a barbecue."

Skye nodded, fiddling with her mother's chain around her neck and swallowing down her discomfort at the prospect of the amount of fire that was due to surround her today. As though sensing her fears, Sabine gripped Skye's upper arm, pinning her with her gaze.

"I tested the flame-retardant features on your uniform myself, Skye," she said quietly, her thumb rubbing her sleeve in a rare attempt at affection. "You could walk through fire, and it wouldn't burn you."

A lump formed in her throat, and she glanced towards the battle preparations, zipping the ring along the chain. When she was sure she wasn't about to burst into an embarrassing flood of tears, she looked back down at Sabine. "Thank you."

Caplin's horn blew then, making her flinch, and the Forces began to move into position. Sabine squeezed her arm, then rested her hands on a pair of ornate daggers sheathed at her hips. For once she had swapped her studded leather jacket for her uniform, her fiery heart crest emblazoned on her chest, matching Jacob's. "We're still fighting with them?"

"Afraid so," said Skye, glancing at the rest of the self-styled *Lux Guard* – at Ike and Lorcan, Jacob and her brother. Despite inciting Caplin's fury, Skye was grateful her friends had formally pledged their support.

"Then we're right behind you, *Lux*," said Sabine, looking Skye in the eye with more respect and admiration than Skye had ever seen her look at anyone. Skye blinked, touched, unable to find the right words to thank her.

"Let's go," Skye agreed, and they strode as one to the front lines ahead of the Caplin Forces.

Skye had never seen Caplin on a battlefield, but she supposed there was a first for everything. He must have led his army against Ronan at some point, but while she had been a soldier, never once had she seen him take command, despite him appearing in a Forces uniform on plenty of occasions. Yet there he was, imposing in a helmet shaped like a raven's head, a metallic beak sweeping down to cover his nose. His mechanical wings shone dark as obsidian, complementing the velvet black of his uniform. He stood amongst the Aeres specialist division, preparing to lead them in the aerial attack.

"About time," Sabine said bitterly, glaring at their former president. Skye silently echoed her sentiment, fighting to keep the sneer off her face.

In spite of everything, Caplin looked calm, standing out amongst the slate-grey wings of his fellow Aeres. But Skye knew exactly why he was there. She had heard the rumours, the whisperings of how she had stood up to Cowardly Caplin in the war council, and the hopes that she would step up as a leader now that she was the Lux. By showing up today, Caplin clearly wanted to rid himself of the unfortunate nickname. How he fought would truly cement his reputation and role in the war going forward.

"I'm not sure how much good an aerial attack will do in this fog, but it's got to be an advantage over Alessia," said Dean, clutching a flamethrower, fuel canisters strapped across his back.

"It's always been one of Caplin's special weapons against the Ronans," said Ike, coming up to stand beside them. "Maybe Alessia has learned from her family's mistakes and set up a flying division of her own."

"Let's hope not," said Skye, checking herself over one last time, making sure every weapon was in its place, every strap buckled, and her hair tied firmly back. She touched the silver chain which held her mother's ring one last time – partly in reassurance, and partly for luck – before tucking it safely beneath the high neck of her uniform. All around her, soldiers were moving into position, getting ready for orders. Skye would leave the pretty speech-making to Caplin. She may have people looking to her, but in these circumstances, she preferred to lead through actions rather than words. She was no politician.

Sure enough, Caplin blew his horn again, his second warning. He then spread out his mechanical wings with a hiss and took to the sky to hover before them, turning to face his Forces. Skye's insides bubbled with anger and hatred, remembering how Darius had done the exact same thing before they went in to rescue Caplin. And then Caplin had just let him die.

"Today, we fight alongside our former enemies. We fight with them for a common goal: defeating the Nox." His voice carried easily across the assembled soldiers' heads, helped along by the wind he was manipulating. "We are an army filled with people of various Talents, skilled and experienced in the art of combat. I have every faith that those of you who are loyal to what you hold dear will fight with everything you have, will fight until your last breath. Know that your fight and your sacrifices will not be in vain."

"Please excuse me while I vomit," said Sabine, watching Caplin with her nose slightly wrinkled. "All this sugar isn't mixing well with my breakfast."

"Let me get out of here before you hurl your guts up," Ike exclaimed, flashing his trademark grin and clapping Skye on the shoulder. "See you on the other side." And with that, he tugged on his own helmet and took flight with his fellow Aeres, rising into the low-hanging clouds until they were grey shadows, then becoming invisible through the fog.

Skye and her fellow infantry waited in the rain, three armies-worth of deep breaths and beating hearts. And then Caplin's horn crowed high above for the third and final call. A heartbeat later, an enemy horn echoed eerily through the fog.

She stood her ground, shoulder to shoulder with the comrades she had trained and fought alongside since the beginning of her career, bracing herself for the charge she could already hear coming beyond that wall of fog. Beside her, Dean's breathing had turned ragged, and she tore her eyes away from the mist, placing a hand on his shoulder. *We'll get through this.*

He met her gaze, placing his own hand gently atop her fingers. *I know*, came his reply. *I have you by my side.*

She gave him a small smile, which he returned, squeezing her hand before letting go. He then gripped his flamethrower once more, and they both looked back, hearing the enemy hurtle closer, war cries and pounding footsteps howling through the mist. Fear prickled up the back of her neck at the strangely inhuman tone of the cries.

Shapes erupted from the fog, a dark mass of soldiers unfurling towards them. Skye's breath caught, her heartbeat sped up, and her electricity surged.

"FIRE!" Skye yelled, aloud and telepathically, and the order echoed along the front line as the Nox army closed in. The space between the allies and the charging enemy lit up with bright fire, and Skye sent strands of her lightning into the fray. Some dropped, hair and clothing aflame, but to her horror, the majority leapt through the fire, and kept moving, flames clinging to their uniforms and trailing in their wake.

"What the—" came Sabine's voice as the flaming bodies continued their charge, screeching in pain but pressing forward regardless.

Skye sucked down a deep breath to calm her own welling panic, only to be met with a putrid stench of rot and smoke. She choked, confusion mingling with her fear. What kind of unknown weapon caused such a stink?

Unable to find the source of the smell, she allowed a ball of electricity to grow between her palms. Static rose in her entire body, and then she released it, the flash blinding for a fraction of a second before it forked out to several targets, bringing them down. Fire bloomed again, sending another handful of enemies to their knees, but many more pushed on, closing the gap.

Despite the flames and the lightning and their tightly held position, countless bodies bulldozed into the front line. Skye's heart skipped several beats as she sensed and saw her comrades fall, some killed, others trampled as opposing soldiers slammed into them, the rotten stench overpowering.

The crowd attacked and roared all around her, smoke and confusion thick in her throat. Dean remained anchored to her side while they fought first shoulder-to-shoulder, then back-to-back as the enemy buffeted them and forced their way through their defence. The soldiers' eyes were wild, mouths wide and screaming as they attacked. Human, but not quite.

"They're not dying!" came Sabine's frustrated shout, and sure enough, Alessia's soldiers closed in, almost fearless despite the fire.

Skye's lightning shook through them with almost no effect, and as the snarling enemies invaded her personal space, her back jostled Dean's fuel canisters, and the invisible hands of fear clenched around her throat.

She stared at the glazed eyes popping from grey, bloodless skin. The purple-clad soldiers moved with inhuman strength despite the grisly wounds and fire damage marring their bodies. Skye shot out, earning hisses and screeches, but her attacks didn't slow them down, didn't kill them like they were supposed to. And Skye realised, as the aroma of rot enveloped her, that the soldiers they fought were already dead.

Chaos reigned, with Sabine and Jacob battling viciously around them, setting the Undead soldiers alight without hesitation. Screams pierced Skye's eardrums, and the bulging eyes from burning faces were the stuff of nightmares. She cringed against her brother, the flames hot on her face and sending her reeling into terrified memories of her own skin on fire, the sights and smells stoppering her throat with panic.

I'm here, Dean reminded her as her frenzied thoughts crashed into his mind, his mental voice like a comforting embrace. *You're not trapped now.*

Skye forced a deep breath into her lungs, the smoke and stench coating her tongue with a heavy film. But she drew strength from Dean's shoulder brushing hers and called her power to the surface, relishing the buzz of electricity on her skin.

Finally, a body dropped from her attack, her lightning rattling through the corpse's skull. She attacked another, aiming for the head again, lightning singing as it found its mark. Another flailed towards her, brandishing ice shards that would surely impale her, but she aimed for the heart, and the body and ice thumped to the ground. Relief chased away her panic as she passed her findings to her comrades.

Aim only for the head or the heart.

Dean obeyed, aiming his flamethrower at faces, forcing fire down throats. Close by, Lorcan repeated the action, while Jacob and Sabine were mere blurs of flames keeping corpses at bay. Skye's hands vibrated as she aimed her lightning at more attackers, a myriad of Talents coming from every side. But cutting through the flames was mostly darkness – darkness pressing in, licking greedily at her exposed wrists and face, hissing as it came into contact with her electric shield.

A corpse hurtled in from the left, a mere smudge at the corner of her eye, and she spun towards it, shoving into Dean to save them both from a stream of bullets. Removing a hand from the flamethrower, Dean cast his own Talent on the machine gun in the corpse's hands, twisting the barrel to render it useless. Letting Dean deal with the attacker, Skye turned again, fending off another pair advancing on them. She didn't see the third coming in from the right, not until its dark power whipped at her unprotected ribs.

She stumbled into Dean again, who turned his flamethrower onto the two that had been in front of her, while Skye, slipping to one knee in the mud, aimed at her attacker's heart, lightning blasting them back. Before she could check her injury, Dean grabbed her beneath the armpit to haul her up, and she gasped as the movement pulled at the damage to her ribs. She pressed a hand to her side, finding her jacket torn, but the leather vest beneath her uniform was intact.

Something's not right.

There's not much "right" right now, Skye, came her brother's distracted reply as he cast more flames into the crowd. *Are you badly hurt?*

It's not that. She assessed her surroundings, beating off more attacks, not quite able to put a finger on what was bothering her. She felt as though her senses were muffled, like she couldn't perceive the incoming attacks the same way as usual. And then the realisation hit her: the corpses' minds were silent, with not even the buzz that accompanied hidden minds. *I can't hear them.*

But Dean had no time to reply, throwing up a spatter of mud to blind an Undead Aeres bearing down on them. The Aeres's wind slammed into them, sending soldiers staggering and fanning stray flames into an inferno that left Skye cringing again from the heat. And then Jacob slipped past, a stream of his fire engulfing the blinded Aeres, sending him plummeting into a knot of Undead. The blaze spread, flames roaring before them, surrounding them with smothering heat and the stinging scent of burning. Skye's unease was nearly unbearable, but she pushed on, focusing on her brother's presence at her side, on the corpses that continued to advance in waves, cutting them down without mercy. She couldn't afford to panic now.

Chapter Forty

PHAEDRA RONAN

As they watched the front lines take the first battering from the vanguard of her sister's army, Phaedra gripped Ombra's hand tightly, relieved that they were watching from a temporarily safe distance atop a small hill. But when the cadets surged to the edge for a better look and the pair were buffeted along with the wave, Phaedra's fear began to choke her.

"They're not *human*," Scott exclaimed, incredulous, and Phaedra followed her comrade's gaze, unable to comprehend what she was seeing. The distance spared her from the goriness, but even from far away she could tell that the enemy soldiers weren't dying like normal people, apparently oblivious to most injuries.

"They're Undead," Ombra confirmed in a terrified tone, drawing Phaedra's gaze. Her profile was outlined against the murky red glow of the fog.

"What do you mean?"

She raised her free hand, flashing a plain silver ring on her index finger. "Skye just sent me a message through our connection." She met her eye, and for the first time that morning, Ombra looked truly afraid. "Your sister's soldiers… they're Undead."

“A little louder for the rest of us, Medley,” Officer Munro demanded, bearing down on them.

Ombra repeated herself, tensing as another message came through. “Their only weak points are the head or the heart.”

If Munro was afraid, she didn’t show it as she adjusted her commands for their fellow cadets, the panic almost palpable. She then raised a radio to her mouth, no doubt communicating with other commanders. Phaedra tugged her collar, the air she breathed already acrid.

“It’s going to be fine,” Ombra reassured her, but her smile was half-hearted, the usual glint in her eyes gone, fuelling Phaedra’s own terror.

Shivering, she looked back at the battlefield. Directly across, flashes of fire lit up the fog, and she caught glimpses of the Aeres weaving in and out of the low-lying cloud, dropping their explosives on Alessia’s army. She wondered if her sister was amongst her soldiers. Somehow, she doubted it. Alessia was probably watching from an even safer distance, most likely disguised by a glamour.

“I wish we were down there,” Ombra said breathlessly, craning her neck to get a better view.

“You’re joking, right?” Phaedra looked from her girlfriend to the fight, the din of bombs and battle cries deafening. “It’s a bloodbath.”

Phaedra wasn’t sure how she was going to hold it together once they joined the fight. The machine gun slung to her back weighed on her, and beneath her skin, her darkness trembled as much as she did.

“You look like you’re about to shit your pants,” came a voice from above her, and she looked up to see Glen, dressed from top to toe in Resistance blue and gripping a flamethrower as though it were an extension of his arm. The amusement on his face was evident, but she didn’t miss the concern in his eyes.

“What are you doing here?” Phaedra tried to sound annoyed, but her voice shook. “I thought you were in the big boy ranks.”

“I drew the short straw. They don’t trust you cadets with flamethrowers, so they handed me this and sent me over here.”

“Don’t lie. My uncle asked you to check up on me, didn’t he?”

Glen frowned. “Your uncle hasn’t said a word to me since I left you in his care.”

Phaedra tilted her head. “Then…?”

He huffed. “Okay, *maybe* I volunteered. I’ve probably got half a chance of surviving today if I fight beside the most fearsome pair of Obscurae the Alliance has to offer.”

She snorted at his excuses, but gratitude warmed her insides, settling her trembling a little.

“Well, nice of you to join us,” said Ombra, grinning up at him, then looking back at the battle, hunger in her eyes as she watched. The heat from the flames was beginning to burn away some of the fog, improving visibility slightly.

“Will we actually have to join?” asked Phaedra, squinting to where Caplin’s explosives lit up the field. Alessia’s Undead kept pressing forward, more and more of them emerging from the fog to join the fray.

“Probably. They’re not going to be able to hold them off forever,” Glen said grimly. “They’ll send us later, fresh fighters to take on the enemy as they’re beginning to weaken.”

“At least, in theory that’s how it works,” Ombra butted in. “But they made that plan before we knew we were facing a bunch of dead blokes.”

“You think they won’t get tired?” asked Phaedra, looking between her friend and girlfriend, her stomach churning and throat still tight.

“Stay positive, Phee Phee.” Unable to ruffle her hair, Glen rapped his knuckles lightly on her helmet. “All we can do is hope we’re making it through this day alive.”

Phaedra grimaced, watching the way Glen’s gaze tracked the battle, lightning reflecting in his eyes. When he sensed her stare, he met her eye, colour blooming on his cheeks. “What?”

“She’s going to be just fine, you know.”

“Who is?” he asked, trying and failing to school his features into a neutral expression.

Phaedra grinned, glad of a distraction from the horrors she would soon endure. “You know who.”

He scowled, hefting the flamethrower and casting his gaze on another part of the battlefield, deliberately avoiding looking at the flashes of lightning. “I hope you wore sensible footwear,” he grumbled, drawing her attention back to reality. “That mud is going to be slippery by the time we head down there.”

Sure enough, an hour later when Munro gave the order to join the fight, Phaedra found herself sliding down that hill, gripping her machine gun and fighting to remain upright. Her heart was in her mouth as she searched frantically to find Ombra still at her side. Bullets and stray Talents whizzed past them before they had even reached the bottom, prompting Ombra to cover them with a sheet of darkness.

At the bottom of the hill a blur of bodies with freak strength surrounded her on every side. Every thought was suddenly swept from her mind, and pure instinct took over, leaving her unable to do anything but keep herself alive. Ombra wasted no time in joining the fray, blasting through their enemies with skill and control that Phaedra envied. Judging by the stream of flame that appeared somewhere to her left, Glen, too, had gotten started, and screams jolted through her that didn’t quite sound human. She hoisted her gun higher, then took aim and fired, missing her target as bullets sailed a foot or more above its head.

"Use your Talent." Ombra's voice was just about audible over the screaming, and she shot globules of darkness that slammed into the heads of grey-tinged Undead, sending their necks snapping and bodies crumpling.

Phaedra could only frantically shake her head in response. She wouldn't be able to forgive herself if she hit one of her comrades by accident, especially not after what she did to Glen.

After five minutes that felt like hours, Phaedra was amazed she was still alive, never mind anything else. Despite her heavy-duty boots, she slipped in the mud and gore, bodies jostling her. A yell attacked her senses, and she turned towards a corpse galloping towards her. She fired her machine gun on instinct, peppering the body with bullets. It fell, but another took its place, careening into her.

A screech tore from her throat, but the noise was lost to the cacophony as she plummeted to the ground, sliding several inches as the corpse bore down on her. She thrust her hands in front of her face, feet scrabbling for purchase in the mud. And then her darkness exploded from her, engulfing the corpse and tearing its skull and ribcage to pieces in front of her eyes.

She choked on the bloody matter raining down on her face, pushing herself onto her front and vomiting into the mud. She lay there, winded and gasping for breath, the cold, hard metal of her gun pressing into her stomach. She stared around herself in a daze, taking in her surroundings.

She was alone.

Panic numbed her fingers and closed around her chest. She sat up, scrambling around in a circle, searching for Ombra, for Glen. Not even a flicker of flame was visible through the fog and running bodies, and the soldiers' uniforms were indistinguishable, all tinged another shade of mud in the low light.

"Ombra!" she whimpered, hot tears streaming down her cheeks as she got to her knees. Mud and who knew what else was slick beneath her fingers, soaking through her trousers. "Glen?"

Her calls only brought more enemies. A pair of Undead paused in their running, then turned towards her. Their crazed eyes and snarling mouths were all she could see as they ran at her, hands thrust forward, unknown Talents erupting from them.

Phaedra crouched into a ball, burying her head between her knees, her hands clamped over her ears. She screamed again, and the darkness came funnelling out of her chest once more, knocking the breath from her body.

The sounds of the battle suddenly grew quiet, muffled somehow. Gingerly raising her head, Phaedra looked around, tears coating her lashes. But she could see only darkness, beautiful, glittering darkness that spun around her, shielding her, embracing her.

As Phaedra stared, a figure stepped through the spinning wall, hair whipping around her in a tangled halo, eyes black as midnight. And then the figure knelt before her, blinking the shadows away, those eyes becoming the soft green of calm seas once again. Phaedra sobbed in relief as the figure took both hands in hers, collapsing against her.

"I'm here," Ombra promised, her breath tickling her ear. "I'm with you."

Phaedra only held her tighter as the darkness continued to swirl around them, unsure if it was her shadows or Ombra's that protected them now. "I lost you!"

Ombra let go of her hands, cupping her face instead. "And I found you. I'm not letting you go again." She kissed her then, fiercely, sealing her promise as Phaedra clung to the front of her uniform, afraid to let go. "I saw what you did," Ombra said against her lips. "It was incredible."

Phaedra gave another sob, her darkness rising and falling in her chest like waves, unfurling at her fingertips.

"Come on now," said Ombra, standing and holding her hands firmly as Phaedra struggled to get her own feet under her. "Glen will think we've abandoned him."

Phaedra let out a hysterical laugh, and the shadows warped, no longer a spinning wall, but forming into something more flexible, enveloping them like armour and allowing them to assess the battle. Phaedra adjusted the strap of her machine gun, the metal banging against her hip.

They slipped and slid through the mud, avoiding heaps on the floor. Phaedra remained glued to Ombra's side, unable to breathe without inhaling smoke and a stench of burnt hair that stung her nose, trembling much worse than before. This was a bad idea. An idiotic idea. She had convinced everyone she was ready for this. Worse, she had convinced herself.

Something crunched beneath her boot, and she looked down instinctively, freezing in horror as blank eyes stared up at the smoke-filled sky. The dead soldier wasn't one of her sister's. The uniform was spattered with blood, but the three silver stars sewn above the heart were clearly visible, marking them as a Resistance soldier. Bile rose in her throat again.

Ombra yanked her by the hand and shouted something unintelligible in her ear, prompting her to move. Corpses were advancing on them again, three at once, and as Ombra sprang into action, Phaedra threw up her own hands, darkness blasting through an Undead soldier.

"Good shot," came a familiar voice behind them, and Phaedra whipped around to see Glen fire his flamethrower at a pair of soldiers who approached, his teeth bared in a grimace. The heat burned her face, but she managed a grin in spite of everything as Glen kept attackers off their backs.

Phaedra turned away, lifting her gun and shooting at yet another soldier who was running at Ombra. When the soldier cried out, blood bursting from wounds in her chest and shoulder, Phaedra froze in shock, realising the enemy soldier was a living human being, not one of her sister's reanimated corpses. But the woman looked up at her, anger in her eyes as she raised a hand and threw a fistful of ice shards her way.

Ombra shouted, sending a stream of darkness to intercept the ice, but it fell short. Phaedra stepped back, dropping her gun as she raised her hands instinctively. Her own darkness appeared as ordered between her outstretched hands, expanding before her face in shimmering black, disintegrating the shards into snowy powder. And then Ombra knocked the woman out with a sphere of darkness to her temple.

She hadn't expected any of the enemy soldiers to be alive, not after the sheer amount of Undead pouring down on them. But she remembered that Alessia still had a small portion of her army left. She approached the woman Ombra had knocked out, nudging her with her boot, then turned her over. Her eyes were closed and blood still seeped from the bullet wounds, staining the golden dragon crest with crimson. Phaedra couldn't be sure if she was dead or alive.

"Leave her," said Ombra, placing a hand on her shoulder. "There's nothing we can do for her. She wouldn't stop to help us."

Phaedra nodded, trying to bury her guilt as she turned away, jumping back into the fray with her girlfriend and Glen.

***

"Matheson has launched the surprise attack," said Ombra sometime later, but whether it was minutes or hours, Phaedra couldn't be sure. The fog had thinned, as had the fighters, but smoke still hung like a veil over the battlefield, the acrid smell of burning filling her nostrils. She did her best not to look at the ground, or at herself for that matter, unsure whether the dark spatters on her hands and uniform were mud or something more sinister.

"How do you know?" she asked, her voice dull with exhaustion.

"Skye. But she thinks your sister knew about the plan. She saved part of her army for him, and Matheson's already lost a chunk of his soldiers."

"Shit." Phaedra coughed a few times, trying to clear some of the smoke from her lungs. "How could she know?"

But Ombra only shook her head, continuing to tread carefully through the bodies. She froze suddenly, her darkness shooting out to rip apart a lone corpse that staggered towards them, its face bloody and a broken arm drooping uselessly. Phaedra looked away from the gory sight, its screech cut short as Ombra's destructive power rent through its skull.

"Maybe that was a bit overkill."

Ombra shrugged. "Just wanted to make sure it stays dead."

Not far ahead, Phaedra made out Glen's bulk, limping slightly. The fighting had thinned considerably, and Munro had passed a few minutes ago, shouting orders to rejoin the battle that still continued further into the field. Flashes and flames still flew back and forth in that direction, hundreds of soldiers fighting beneath the canopy of sooty smoke. Phaedra knew they should hurry, but her entire body ached, and her breath came with difficulty. She took advantage of the break in the fighting to get her bearings and take a few sips from the canteen strapped to her belt, wincing as cool water flooded her parched throat.

They trudged on, picking their way through the bodies. Phaedra did her best not to look too closely. In the distance, she spotted people in the white medical uniform moving amongst the dead and injured, stopping every so often to help someone, picking them up and carrying them off. Phaedra paused, watching, and after a moment Ombra realised she was no longer following and stopped too.

"Maybe we should help them," Phaedra suggested, trying to sound indifferent. But after the chaos and gruesomeness of the fighting, she secretly hoped Ombra would agree.

Her girlfriend glanced between her and the medics in the distance. Her face was splattered with brown and red and black, her hair sticky with sweat and less pleasant matter. Ombra didn't speak for a long moment as she considered, and Phaedra became afraid that she thought she was a coward.

"Maybe you're right," she said finally, looking back at the white-coated figures. "I doubt we're going to make a huge difference to the fighting at this point. My Talent is running low."

Phaedra gave a small smile, relieved that she wasn't judging her. At least not to her face. Inhaling a deep breath through her mouth, she yelled Glen's name, and he paused, turning to meet her gaze across the heaps of dead. She waved him over, and he limped towards them, fatigue weighing on his broad shoulders.

"All good?" He was frowning, eyes searching them both for any sign of injury.

"We're going to help the injured," Phaedra said breathlessly, gesturing towards the medics in white. "Wanna come?"

Glen followed her gaze, considering. Then he lifted the flamethrower he still held, examining the contents of his fuel canisters. "Alright. I'm nearly out of gas anyway."

"I'm sure you could still suckerpunch a few dead blokes if you really wanted to," said Ombra, but her voice lacked her usual teasing spark.

They all exchanged tired smiles, then began to walk in the direction of the medics, scanning the ground for injured soldiers as they went.

Chapter Forty-One

SKYE BOLTON

As Skye and her new Lux Guard fought on, still in the thick of it, the battle felt far from over. Caplin's aerial attack had long since ceased once they ran out of explosives and the allies and Nox army became too mixed up for the Aeres to fire without risking their own. They now fought low to the ground, while some flew back and forth, carrying injured back to the medics and bringing supplies and messages, or else scouting out the extent of Alessia's remaining strength. At some point, Alessia would have to withdraw, her already low numbers dwindling by the minute, but it was obvious she wanted to inflict as much damage as she could before they forced her off the field.

You should take a break, she told Dean, hearing his exhausted thoughts. They had been fighting for hours, and she was beginning to lag herself, her own electric Talent guttering. *Maybe you could get Ike to fly you over to where Ombra is helping the injured.*

I'm not leaving you, came his reply, as stubborn as ever. There wasn't much she could say to that. She would keep fighting until Alessia called off the attack or she dropped from exhaustion, whichever came first.

Sabine and Jacob came into view, blood-splattered and smoke-smudged, their golden eyes reflecting their many fires. Despite the fine rain that still fell in intervals, the flames burned bright.

"Any chance of this ending soon?" asked Sabine, flexing her ringed fingers, cracking her knuckles and her neck.

"It shouldn't be much longer—"

Jacob snarled at an enemy at Skye's back, sending a ball of flame over her shoulder, the heat crisping loose strands of her hair. Skye staggered aside, pivoting to see a purple-clad soldier hurtling towards them, skirting around the fire. With a flick of a wrist, the corpse Terra hurled rocks towards them, moving fast despite limping on a torn and bloody leg. As Skye and Jacob ducked out of the rocks' course, Dean stepped in, calling on his own Talent to crumble the rocks into harmless dust. Jacob delivered a fatal blow, and the body crumpled back to the afterlife.

A forlorn horn sounded, reverberating through Skye's chest. She looked around, focusing her telepathy in the direction of the noise to find out what was happening. She skipped through exposed minds, searching for an appropriate viewpoint. The headache that had slowly been mounting protested at the extra effort, and blood trickled down her top lip not for the first time that day.

"What is it?" Dean asked, fearing the worst.

But Skye gave a tired smile, a wave of exhaustion sweeping over her. "Surrender."

The remaining Undead soldiers withdrew like the tide creeping away from the shore. Breathing a sigh of relief, Skye leaned forward, bracing her hands on her knees. Her legs were like jelly, and pressure stacked in her lower back, begging her to sit down. But if she allowed herself such a luxury, she wouldn't get up again, and there was still so much more to do.

Straightening, she took in her surroundings. Aeres flew back and forth, their mechanical wings cutting through the lingering smoke. Her fellow soldiers were already approaching the injured, helping them to their feet or signalling for help. The sky was tinged a dirty, reddish brown, but a smattering of sunrays pierced the smog for the first time, bringing some hope with it.

Turning to her brother, she asked a question that she hoped wouldn't cause an argument. "Mind if I check on Caspar?"

Dean held her stare, soot and stubble shadowing his face. "Would it make a difference if I said I do mind?"

She tried to smile. "Probably not."

He raised an exhausted eyebrow, shaking his head in disbelief and, she was relieved to see, amusement. "Go on. We'll be here."

She nodded, setting off in the direction of Caspar's soldiers, rubbing her nosebleed on her already filthy sleeve. Despite her overexertion, she checked in on other parts of the allied army. The Mathesons were heading back to the main camp with what little remained of their troops, as battered and bloodstained as the rest of them. Devan Harlow moved through a sea of dead and dying, sorrowfully searching for survivors. Roxanne and Darshana instructed their team of medics to carry the injured back to a tent. Glen was amongst them with a bleeding soldier slung over his shoulder, powering on despite his limp. She had kept tabs on him and the girls during any snatched moments of reprieve throughout the battle. She had seen glimpses of his fight through Ombra's eyes, his actions and reflexes flowing as though it was all he was ever meant to do. She breathed a sigh to see the three of them safe.

As she approached the cluster of Ronan soldiers in grey, Caspar's eyes met hers the moment she was close enough to make out his face, relief and concern warring in his expression. He bent his head back to the soldier he was helping, tying a tourniquet around his leg with deft fingers. He spoke words Skye couldn't hear to the injured man, then commanded an Aeres to escort the soldier to safety. Once the pair took to the skies, he got to his feet, moving with less agility than usual, his shoulders a little slumped.

"Hey," he said softly as she came to a stop before him. They looked one another up and down, searching for injuries. Skye let out another sigh once she confirmed he was relatively unharmed. "You're alright?"

"I'm alright." She managed a smile. She wanted to reach out for him, wanted to press her lips to his, but eyes tracked them closely, some expressions hostile. Skye felt a trickle of foreboding. No matter how Caspar felt about her or who he chose to ally with, some of his soldiers clearly still mistrusted her. After glancing at a few of the soldiers, she returned her gaze to Caspar's exhausted face.

"Would you check on Phaedra for me?"

"She's fine. It turns out she and Ombra are quite the powerhouse on the battlefield."

He nodded, his chest deflating as he took in the devastation around them. "She wouldn't let me talk her out of it."

"You were hoping she would bottle it."

He huffed a half-hearted laugh, running a hand through his dishevelled hair. Beyond his shoulder, Skye glimpsed one of his soldiers approaching him, a blue band on his sleeve marking him as an Aqua. And then the Aqua's arm snapped back as though to swing a punch, picking up speed.

Skye cried a warning, gathering her own Talent. Caspar's eyes widened in shock as he staggered to avoid her attack, but she didn't aim at him. Her lightning collided with the wave of boiling water that was thrown into the air where Caspar had been a split second before. The water conducted the electricity into the Aqua's hand, straight up his arm into his heart. But as the Aqua dropped, his death throes were trampled by an onslaught of more grey-clad Ronan soldiers bearing down on them.

Any signs of Caspar's fatigue were swept away as he cut through the attackers with a wave of darkness, felling them with brutal force. His merciless attack thrilled Skye, and she fought to stay near him, covering his back as the traitors pressed in. But she and Caspar weren't the only targets. Screams of shock and agony joined the sounds of battle further afield. Everywhere she looked, Resistance and Caplin soldiers in blue and black were being cut down as well.

The attackers buffeted her, separating her from Caspar, and her weakening legs fought to keep her upright. As she met her attackers head on, she caught another glimpse of Caspar overwhelmed by enemies. His eyes glared with icy fury as his darkness swirled around him, snaking out with fatal lashes.

The mutiny, if that was what it was, sucked her power reserves almost dry. Skye found herself on her knees, with legs, flailing arms, and crackling Talents sweeping overhead and coming in from every angle. Her arms ached, her chest felt hollow, and she knew she couldn't keep using her Talent. She couldn't afford to render herself completely powerless, not when it was unclear how much fighting still had to be done. Dodging kicks, she slipped a knife from the sheaf in her left boot and relieved her handgun of its holster. She slashed the blade at the backs of knees as she forced her own trembling legs to stand, and pulled the trigger of her gun as she pressed it to the underside of an enemy's jaw. Her bruised body screamed in protest as she cut and shot and kicked her way through the crowd.

More had joined the fray. Dean and Lorcan hurled discarded metal and blinded with splattering mud. Sabine wielded her twin daggers with deadly grace, her own Talent as spent as Skye's. Jacob fought on with the dregs of his fire, knuckles aflame as his fists connected with crunching bone.

When the last wearing grey uniforms dropped in a heap amongst their fallen mutineers, all eyes turned to Caspar. He stood alone in their midst, his breath coming harsh and ragged, blood staining the right side of his own grey uniform. His eyes sought Skye's. Only shock filled them now.

"For gods' sake," Sabine exclaimed, knives still raised and teeth bared. "Someone arrest him."

"It wasn't him," Skye said firmly, shouldering her way through the Caplin and Resistance soldiers who stood between her and Caspar. She came to a stop at his side, turning to the allies, her knife and gun still clenched in her hands. "They attacked *him*."

"Then why is he wearing the same colour as the attackers?" It was someone else who spoke, an unknown Resistance soldier.

"Whatever this is," Caspar said, his voice strained, "I had no part in it."

"Oh really?" Sabine shot back, her voice full of venom. "So it's just a coincidence that they waited until the Lux was amongst you to attack?"

"Sabine," Skye seethed, unable to believe this was happening, like they thought she was some fool being taken for a ride.

"She's got a point, Skye," said Dean, his liquid eyes swimming with fear. Skye looked at him, her heart plummeting. "He could be plotting with the Nox."

Skye's hands around her weapons tightened, and she felt Caspar tense beside her. She took a deep breath, her telepathy rolling towards his mental shield like the smoke that still surrounded them.

Let me in.

She felt his gaze on her face. *You don't trust me?*

I can't help you if you don't let me do this, Caspar.

A ripple of anger emanated from him, then he let his mental shield drop. The gates to his mind screeched open, beckoning her into its dark depths. She lingered on the threshold as a cold sense of foreboding drifted from the gloom of his mind, and a whisper of stale air and flakes of ash caressed her telepathic tendrils. She reached blindly into the murky shadows, shuddering as she touched upon harrowing memories lying dormant beneath stones she would rather leave unturned. She withdrew, returning her gaze to the tangible world.

"Caspar has just opened his mind to me," she told the assembled soldiers. Dean's and her comrades' expressions faltered. She took a step forward. "It wasn't him. So if you could stop throwing around accusations, I would appreciate it if you could search this pile of bloody traitors and arrest anyone still alive. They are the ones who hold the answers, but I think you'll find the Nox herself is responsible."

Caspar's gaze pinned her as she turned back to him. His face was a frozen mask, but fury lingered in his blazing eyes. *You didn't even look, did you?* Despite the anger, there was a hint of amused disbelief in his thoughts.

I didn't need to.

He blinked, the ice thawing. *Thank you.* The simple thought floated towards her, and she gave him a tight-lipped smile, suppressing another shudder at the thought of what dark secrets he carried behind his charming façade. Shoving her gun back into its holster, she turned away, casting her eyes to the bodies on the ground. Whoever had given the mutineers the command, it was clear Caspar's soldiers weren't as loyal to him as they had all hoped.

As she sought out any grey-clad soldiers still clinging to life, a ripple of activity on the enemy side of the field caught her attention. Skye straightened up from the body she had just turned, her eyes drawn across the dark expanse dotted with trampled bodies that had been left behind. In the distance, she could just about make out a lone figure who emerged from the retreating crowd. It was barely a black smudge, but there was something about the way it held itself that made her certain it was Alessia. And then another figure drew her gaze, a lone person standing in the midst of the sea of dead. Smoke drifted around them, but in that moment, shards of sunlight pierced the low-hanging cloud. The light fell on a blonde head, illuminating a Healer's uniform unblemished by fire and blood.

Nobody stopped Skye as she staggered towards the figure, a horrifying certainty clenching around her chest and dragging her forward. Any shouts of her name were lost to the wind as she reached out towards the Healer with her mind, finding only deathly silence shrouding them. She left the allied armies behind as she traipsed across the blood-stained, body-strewn field, eyes fixed on that lone figure who stood unmoving between her and the Nox.

She reached the halfway point between her and the Healer, then broke into a run, a name heavy on her tongue. And then, when she was finally close enough to call out, the brightness of the Healer's uniform melted away, leaving behind a figure with iron grey hair, resplendent in Ronan purple and gold. She stopped dead as the figure turned, revealing a face that had haunted her family for generations.

"Hello, Bolton. I had hoped we would meet sooner or later."

An old man stood before her, epaulettes and brass buttons glinting in the filtered sunlight. His face was wrinkled and pinched, his skin deathly pale, his cheeks hollow with age. Eyes like chips of ice regarded her from blackened sockets, and his thin lips were drawn back in a cold sneer. Skye had never met the man, but any thoughts of her imagined Healer were swept from her mind as she recognised the monster before her. It was Ivor Ronan, back from the dead.

Dread flooded her, pooling in the absence of her depleted Talent, leaving her with the cold realisation that she had walked into a trap. She thought she had gotten off lightly when the Ronan patriarch died before she had been forced to meet him. But now… now she would have to face him in death, when he was stronger and less destructible than ever.

She stole a glance over her shoulder, spotting a handful of Caplin soldiers that had started to follow her. But a row of corpses had risen between her and them, some staring at her with dead eyes, most facing towards her comrades and preventing them from coming to her aid. She was alone with her family's greatest enemy, and her Talent was barely sparks.

"You're not real." She looked back at him, her voice not letting her down as it carried across the space between them. "You're dead."

"Oh," he said with a laugh that chilled her to the bone, "I may be dead, but I'm very, very real."

And with that, he launched into an attack, his reflexes faster than she had believed an old Undead man could possess.

Skye leaped away from the tendrils of darkness snaking towards her, reaching deep within herself for the last reserves of strength. Ivor left her without time for anything but raw survival instinct, circling around her and lunging back and forth, moving more swiftly than she could, her body like lead as she forced it through the motions. She tried to avoid using her Talent, saving what little remained for when she was sure she could get a hit in. But at this pace, it felt unlikely. Ivor's skills far exceeded Caspar's.

Ivor landed the first blow.

His darkness whipped at her foolishly exposed left side, hitting her ribs and leaving a twin to the injury she had received on her right side earlier in the battle. But this was much worse, leaving her gasping through the pain, stars flooding her vision. Ivor took the opportunity to get in another hit before she could see it coming, this time knocking her legs from under her. The thick leather of her boots took the damage from his dark power, but she fell heavily, the impact jolting through the arm that she threw out to break her fall.

Ivor advanced quickly, and she rolled onto her back, hitting him with electricity that didn't quite meet its mark. Ivor shook off the pain once she let the current drop – if it had hurt at all. She scrambled back, putting enough distance between them to give her chance to get back to her feet. And then they went back to their dance, lunging and dodging and side-stepping.

Exhaustion seeped in, weighing her down and making her movements sluggish. In the distance, she spotted Alessia, still watching. Perhaps she was waiting for Ivor to weaken her enough so that when she came in for the kill, there wouldn't be much of Skye left.

She took a breath that sliced through her injured side and dodged another hit.

"How long before you give up, Bolton?" he leered, effortlessly evading a throwing knife aimed at his throat. "You're tired. I can see it. I know when a soldier is reaching breaking point."

"But you've never fought a Lux before," she spat, and then ducked beneath his whipping power, shoving her hand up against his chest. The bang that sounded as her palm connected with him left her ears ringing, but she watched with satisfaction as he was blasted back, landing heavily on the floor with a bone-crunching crash. He lay there, dazed, staring up at the sky for all of five seconds, and then he jumped back to his feet, laughing.

"The last Necromancer Nox killed three Lux before finally meeting her end. Don't overestimate your chances, Bolton. Being the Lux doesn't mean you will survive."

The dread and fear flared up again, and she stepped back just in time to avoid another hit. She hadn't seen Alessia in action. In fact, she hadn't seen her at all since she ascended, until today. How likely was it that she could defeat Skye in single combat? Could she use her Undead grandfather as her puppet, or would she face her herself?

Another step back, but this time the darkness whipped across her neck, just close enough to leave a scratch. Skye put a hand to the wound, and a smear of blackened blood lay across her palm when she pulled it away, leaving little doubt as to how close she had come to death in that split second. She thrust forward with her lightning again, aiming for Ivor's heart, but instead she hit his arm, sending an almost useless shockwave through him.

"Sloppy, Bolton," he taunted, lashing out with his power again. He caught the arm she threw up to protect herself, tearing through her sleeve and leaving her skin bruised and bloodied. A yelp of pain escaped her, and she held her arm close to her body. She ducked out of the way of another attack, dropped to one knee, and stayed there. Ivor closed in on her, and all she could do was hit him with another shock, anything to keep him at bay.

He drew closer, shaking off the feeble shocks she sent at him, or dodging them entirely. And then a tendril of darkness drew back and slapped her across the face. Blinding stars erupted in her eyes again, and then her cheek smacked into the cold, muddy earth. She tasted blood and dirt, and had to blink the wet and mud from her eyelashes as she stirred, forcing an elbow beneath her and raising herself just enough to spit out the muck.

A cold laugh sounded above her, and icy, hard fingers closed around her neck, lifting her half off the floor and forcing her to look into those cruel eyes.

She gasped, but those fingers pressed down regardless, crushing the air from her throat, blood streaming from her nose and filling her mouth. Skye flailed, scratching at his face and hands, but he was oblivious, lifting her higher, his dark power drifting around him like clouds gathering to strike. And so, after a moment of struggle, she let her arms drop, going limp, closing her eyes and concentrating on trying to keep breathing despite the pressure on her windpipe and the agony in her left side. Ivor began to laugh again, the noise harsh, pitiless. As the laughter grew, she seized her chance.

Her fingers curled around cold metal at her thighs, withdrawing a pair of slim, sharp knives. Ivor lifted her higher, and she opened her eyes, met his gaze, and then raised the knives in her fists, slamming them into his eye sockets with a flash of silver. Ivor screamed and released her throat, collapsing to the floor beneath her weight. But before he could reach up to pull the knives from his eyes, white strands of electricity shot through Skye's veins and into the cold silver. Ivor Ronan's flesh sizzled and smoked as the last of her lightning lit up his skull from within. His corpse shook beneath her, and when she let go of the knives he grew limp, his head lolling back with a dull thud. Skye slumped to the ground, gasping for air, her breath coming in strangled wheezes. She clawed at her neck, willing the air to enter her lungs, not caring that it smelled of blood and smoke and Ivor's burnt hair and flesh. Beneath her, the corpse twitched, and she crawled away from him, not knowing for sure if he was dead once more.

Across the battlefield, Alessia began walking.

Chapter Forty-Two

ALESSIA RONAN

Alessia felt her grandfather's pain and his struggle to hold onto the second life she had gifted him. That was when she knew it was over. She had watched the fight, half from her own vantage point and half through her grandfather's eyes, and had seen how close he had come to killing the Lux. But Skye Bolton had a survival instinct that Ivor no longer possessed, and that had saved her at the final moment.

Unable to contain her fury, she set out across the battlefield, her darkness swirling and gathering around her, ready to do her bidding, ready to attack.

"It's not time," came a warning voice somewhere behind her, but she didn't heed it until a hand clamped on her shoulder.

She turned with a hiss, her darkness whipping out and ripping the hand away. Lucien staggered back, his eyes still flashing silver, though his face was distorted, grey-tinged beneath the glamour. A dark welt marred his wrist.

"Touch me again, and I will tear you to shreds," she snarled, her shadows poised like vicious serpents awaiting her command.

"It isn't time," he repeated, raising his other hand to heal the damage she had dealt. "If you face her now, she could kill you."

"Kill me?" she scoffed. "She's practically a corpse herself."

She rose to her full height, shoved away strands of hair that blew in her eyes, then swept back towards where her enemy lay, stepping over bodies and charred bones like they were nothing.

And then she stopped, watching her chance being snatched from her. An Aeres swept across the battlefield from the enemy camp, wearing the black Caplin uniform and dark, outstretched metallic wings that buffeted smoke out of his path. The pale-faced Aeres swooped down over Bolton, lingering for a moment to examine her, then gathering her in his arms and taking to the sky once more, going back the way he had come. Alessia gritted her teeth, icy rage rising in her throat, threatening to release a scream of frustration. She had been so close, ready to deliver the final blow that her grandfather had almost made, ready to end this war by destroying the one person holding her enemies together. But she would have to wait some more. There was no way she could get to Bolton now.

Watching the Aeres fly further and further away with the Lux, Alessia continued on, her grandfather's body distinguishable from the other corpses only by the gold epaulettes that decorated his uniform. When she finally arrived, she looked down at him, assessing the damage. He was still alive, but barely, his pulse beating feebly in her ears, eyes a blackened wreck around the knives. She looked away, unable to see her grandfather maimed in such a way, her insides bubbling with hatred. She took in a slow breath, the scent of burning and blood irritating her nostrils, accompanied by a hint of jasmine. She looked around as Vala approached, glamoured in a similar way to Lucien.

"There will be other opportunities," she said, seeming unconcerned that Bolton had got away.

Alessia disregarded her comment. Her biggest concern was now her grandfather. "He's dying again."

Vala looked down at the twitching body, her expression unreadable as Alessia waited, worried that her grandfather was suffering while she hesitated. "You can reverse the damage."

"Can I?"

The Seer looked up at her, those eyes still the familiar unnatural blue even in the changed face. "You brought him back to life. Of course you can heal him."

Alessia looked back down at her grandfather, then knelt by his body. She wanted to ask for further guidance, but she was too proud, too reluctant to appear weak or unknowledgeable. There was nothing stopping Vala from switching sides and supporting the Lux instead, after all. Instead, she trembled as she withdrew the knives, avoiding looking at the dark blood that coated the blades as she flung them as far away as possible. She then placed her hands over Ivor's eyes, closing her own. She allowed the ice to fill her veins, let it take over her body and overflow into her grandfather. When her limbs were numb and her chest was tight, she opened her eyes again. Sure enough, the damage the Lux had caused had faded away, and his eyes were whole once more, looking up at her. And then he smiled.

"I dreamed this moment," he whispered, reaching a gnarled hand up to rest on her cheek. She placed her own hand on his, her fingers still numb. "I knew it would come true."

Her throat tightened, and she swallowed the lump, taking another deep breath and helping Ivor to his feet. All around them, the bodies lay, bodies that wore the uniforms of four different armies. But she would make them her own. Closing her eyes once more, she spread out her arms, summoning her strength, letting the ice overtake her. As the power rippled outwards, travelling across the field full of dead, she let out a wail, overwhelmed by the force that passed through her as though she was a mere vessel. When she could stand it no more, she dropped to her knees, looking up in time to see the first of her new army rise. Gasping for breath, frost cracking on her lips, she stared around her, seeing more Undead soldiers than she could count, all of them getting to their feet and turning towards her. And then, as she stood, helped up by her grandfather, they knelt as one, every head bowed, every right hand resting on their newly beating hearts.

Chapter Forty-Three

AMBER SUMMERS

The clamour of the battle that raged beyond the canvas of the medics' tent seemed to be coming to an end at last. Amber turned from the injured soldier she had been dosing up with Veto and looked towards the sound of approaching footsteps, hoping to see her mother and Darshana coming back. But it was the man who had been staying with them along with the Ronan girl for a few days – Glen, was his name?

"Hey Amber." He gave her a strained smile and adjusted the unconscious Resistance soldier slung over his shoulder. "Got a spare stretcher for this one?"

"Sure." She nodded, indicating the nearest one. Glen crossed the space and lay the unconscious body down as carefully as he could, struggling a little to avoid dropping the dead weight. Amber hurried over, assessing the damage. The bloody wounds still bothered her, the sickly stench of blood, smoke, and Veto mingling in the air, but she had managed not to throw up or pass out while assisting her mother and Darshana by cleaning implements and running back and forth for stock. She had even managed to clean and bandage some wounds, and was feeling pretty proud of herself. This one needed stitches, but he looked like he wasn't about to bleed out. It felt safe to wait for someone trained to get back.

More noise approached the tent entrance, and two small, gore-spattered soldiers staggered in, supporting a groaning woman between them.

"Hi Summers!" said one of the soldiers brightly, and Amber stared at the muck-covered face, taking a moment to recognise her as Ombra Medley. The last time she had seen her, she had been a mouthy fourteen-year-old always getting into detention. "Got another one for you here. She got into a fight with a Terra's fancy knives."

"Hi," the other girl said, her smile as strained as Glen's had been. It was Phaedra, and her face was, if possible, even filthier than Ombra's.

"Let me help." Glen stepped forward, reaching for the injured woman and settling her onto another stretcher.

"We'll get more!" Ombra announced, her voice as loud as Amber remembered it, and the pair scurried off. Amber turned back to Glen and the two soldiers, glancing between them.

"Need any help with these?" he asked, eyeing her uncertainly.

Amber chewed the inside of her cheek, approaching the woman, taking in the slashes on her face and body. Blood still seeped from the cuts, and she held her hand tightly against a particularly nasty wound on her abdomen.

"I can manage until Mum gets back." She gave him a weak smile of her own, wheeling one of the drip bags over to the woman and taking a deep breath to ready herself for what she was about to do. "Thanks."

"Sure thing. You're doing great." He threw her a last, reassuring smile, then limped out.

Amber turned back to the injured woman, wishing she had as much confidence in her abilities as Glen did. "I'm going to insert a cannula and hook you up to some Veto. It will keep you comfortable until Dr Summers comes back."

The woman nodded, rolling up her torn sleeve with shaking hands. The raven crest above her heart was slashed in two, marking her as a Caplin soldier.

Amber scrubbed her hands for the millionth time that day, the rubber gloves she pulled on irritating her, but she hoped it wasn't something she would need to do often. She took steadying breaths, trying not to shake as she cleaned the woman's arm and unpacked a fresh needle, then felt around for a vein like Roxanne and Darshana had taught her to do. They had guided her through the process several times already that day, but this was the first time she was doing it alone.

Her mother hadn't wanted her to come. Had tried every excuse to get her to stay home. But after what had happened at the last battle, she couldn't sit this one out. Especially not when her new-found family were also out there today. Lindsey was even *commanding*. There was no way Amber would be able to look Lindsey in the eye again if she couldn't muster the guts to help in even this small way.

She set to work cleaning the slashes on the woman's body, starting with the one that still bled. She did her best not to look too closely at the wound, cleaning around it, then wadding clean gauze and instructing the woman to keep pressure on it. "The medics will be back shortly. They'll stitch you up."

"Thank you," the soldier said through gritted teeth, and Amber increased the Veto dosage. With a sigh, she let her head fall back, her muscles gradually relaxing, allowing Amber to continue her work.

A boom sounded outside, sending Amber knocking into the drip stand with a clatter.

She had barely looked around when a roar of flame erupted along the wall of the tent, licking up the canvas and rapidly burning through it. Amber grabbed the drip stand to steady herself, unable to believe her eyes as she took in the spreading fire, unaware of her breath tearing through her chest. The injured soldier jumped into action, ripping the cannula from her arm and staggering off the bed, raising her hands before her.

"Get them out, I'll keep the flames under control!" she yelled, prompting Amber to dash around to the bed on which one of the unconscious soldiers lay. She grabbed the rails, the wheels catching on something as she dragged it. But whatever Talent the woman possessed, both she and Amber realised the problem at the same second. The woman looked back at the drip bag of Veto. "It's not working!"

Tugging faster, Amber felt cool air from the tent entrance at her back. "Get the others out!"

The soldier half fell across the tent to grab one of the two remaining unconscious people. But as Amber dragged the stretcher and its occupant into the middle of the small clearing ringed by supply crates and ambulances, a second explosion sounded, engulfing the remainder of the tent.

Amber knew she screamed, but she couldn't hear herself as she sank to the floor, her ears still ringing from the blast. And then she saw him: a man over six feet tall, with cropped grey hair and cruel eyes the colour of flint, dressed in Ronan purple and adding more fire to the blaze, trapping the patients inside. As she struggled to her feet, he looked her way, eyes snapping between her and the soldier she had managed to save, a cruel leer twisting his features. Amber didn't know what to do as he approached, her knees buckling beneath her. She put her hands on the railing of the stretcher, knowing she wouldn't get very far with the semi-conscious patient. But the Ignis made the decision for her. He took several strides in their direction, his right hand on fire, then he shoved that hand against the patient's face.

Amber couldn't watch. The smell and sound were horrific enough, and she stumbled back again, bile rising in her throat as she found herself on the floor, crawling backwards, the tears from the smoke and the fear almost blinding her. She kept going, the man finishing whatever he had done to the patient's face and strolling leisurely around the stretcher towards her. But as he approached, she bumped into a pair of legs, and looked up just as a redhead with scarlet lips wrapped her fingers in Amber's hair and curled them into a fist.

"This pretty one is for me, Jenkins," said the woman, smiling down at her with those waxy red lips. As Amber met the woman's gaze, pain like she had never felt coursed through her entire body, taking up every inch from her fingertips to her toes, occupying every last bit of space in her mind. And then, just as she thought she couldn't stand the pain any longer, she blacked out.

Chapter Forty-Four

ROXANNE SUMMERS

Roxanne watched in terror as Alessia Ronan raised the dead once again, her fear like a rock wedged in her stomach. She stood there trembling, her skin covered with icy sweat, her breath coming in short, sharp gasps as she waited for the new army to turn their way and begin the fight anew. But as they waited, the Undead began to move away as one, marching in unison towards their new mistress. She couldn't understand it. Surely it would make more sense to wipe them out while they were weak? Alessia had the numbers now, she could do it easily, surely.

But then a figure swooped towards her, an Aeres she recognised as Ikarus Arrowsmith, carrying Skye Bolton in his arms. Of course. All Alessia wanted was to kill the Lux. If she managed that, she wouldn't need to keep fighting – the allies wouldn't stand a chance. But instead, after the fight Roxanne had craned her neck to watch over the heads of other soldiers, Skye had got away, picked up by Ikarus. The Nox knew she wouldn't get another chance today.

"She's in a state," said Ikarus as he landed amongst the exhausted and wounded soldiers surrounding them. He tried to get Skye to sit on the ground, but she refused, getting her feet under her, determined to stand. She swayed dangerously, and Ikarus kept a hold on her, preventing her from falling.

"You should sit," said Roxanne. Skye's eyes were out of focus, rolling this way and that, with blood and mud covering half her face and bruising around her neck. More concerning were the injuries she could see on her abdomen. The torn fabric and leather of her uniform exposed bloody and bruised wounds, stained with the sooty residue of darkness.

"No," Skye blurted, her voice hoarse, swaying again as she tried to take a step. Ikarus held her firmly, and her brother Dean arrived, looking frantic.

"What were you thinking?" he exclaimed, staring at his sister, clearly wanting to check her over himself, but he stayed out of Roxanne's way. "You've been fighting all day, did you really think you could go up against them?"

"Well I did," she spat, but finally looked down at Roxanne, who placed a firm but gentle hand on her chin, holding her face steady.

"I'm going to heal you, then you can be on your way," Roxanne said, already starting on her neck. Skye finally did as she was told, staying still enough for Roxanne to do her job, but she quivered with adrenaline beneath her touch. "You need to rest for a couple of days," she told her, starting to heal the injuries on her arm and sides. Skye gave a sharp intake of breath as Roxanne gently prodded her ribcage. "You've got broken ribs."

"That explains why it hurts like a bitch." Skye gave a hysterical laugh, then gasped again.

"All the more reason to do what the doctor says," said Dean beside them, glowering at his sister. "Do you know how close we were to losing you, and the war?"

But Skye was deaf to Dean's tearful reprimand, looking around. "Where's Caspar? I have to tell him—"

"He saw what happened," Dean said, and then his voice faltered. "But Caplin… Caplin arrested him."

"*What?*" Skye lurched forward, prompting Roxanne to place a steadying hand on her shoulder. Ikarus exclaimed her name, pinning her to his side. "But I already—"

"Harlow agreed." Dean's voice was a little firmer now. "The mutiny needs to be properly investigated."

Skye swore, but allowed Ikarus to hold her still. Roxanne continued her work as quickly as she could, anxious to get back to the other countless injured who were in a much worse state.

"All done," she said, stepping back and looking up at Skye's face again. She still looked dazed, but less than before, and she was no longer swaying where she stood. "Remember, you need to rest."

Skye nodded, then tore away from Ikarus, heading to who knew where. But as she staggered into the crowd, an explosion made Roxanne jump out of her skin. They all turned to see fresh flames leap into the air, and her heart rose to her throat as she realised that the blaze was coming from the medical tent. Roxanne broke into a run, her legs working before she even realised she was moving. Her only thought was of Amber, her daughter, who she had left alone in that tent.

Darshana was already there when she arrived, and Roxanne screamed her daughter's name, scanning the blazing wreckage of the tent and surrounding area for any sign of her.

"Where is she?!" she shouted, staring around, seeing the dead patient on the stretcher before the tent, but no one else. She was vaguely aware of Steven and Dale – two of her fellow medics – arriving, as well as others coming to see what the damage was. But when she was certain Amber was nowhere in sight, she looked at her friend. Darshana was frozen in place, her face a mask of horror.

"Someone took her," she murmured, meeting Roxanne's gaze. "A woman, and a man."

"Who?" she asked, looking from Darshana to the tent, then back again. "Ronans?"

"Yes," she gasped, also glancing around, looking at the dead man on the stretcher. "They wore purple."

Roxanne didn't hear the strangled cry that escaped her, nor did she remember falling to the floor, wrapping her arms around herself, trying to hold herself together as the worst fear she had ever experienced threatened to consume her. She didn't feel Darshana's arms around her, or hear the words people were saying. She didn't know how much time had passed when they sat her down on a box of supplies, wrapping a quilt around her and trying to coax her to drink something. At some point, Darshana disappeared, saying something about helping more injured, and Roxanne became vaguely aware of Devan taking her place, peering at her with eyes full of concern, his touch gentle as he brushed hair out of her face and wiped away her tears with a clean tissue.

"We'll get her back." His tone was determined, but Roxanne heard the emptiness of his words all too clearly.

"Why would they take her?" she asked, her voice sounding nothing like her own. "What could they possibly want with her?"

"They must have known whose daughter she is," said a voice above them, and Roxanne looked up to see Oliver approach, bloodstained and limping, but furious. Lindsey was behind him, looking just as bedraggled with soot and mud covering her face and braided hair. She stared at Roxanne, her features distorted with shock.

Devan wrapped his arm protectively around her as Oliver came to a stop, bearing down on them. But Roxanne could see the terror in his eyes, the same helplessness she felt. He had already lost one child in the past months. To lose Amber too…

"Who was it?" he asked, searching her face for answers. "Did anyone see?"

"Darshana saw," she said, then looked around as she saw her friend reappear, helping Dale put an injured soldier in the back of one of the ambulances. When the patient was safely in the vehicle, Darshana came over.

"What did they look like?" Oliver demanded, turning to Darshana.

Darshana's eyes narrowed a little as she looked up at him. She was one of the few people who knew the whole story of what went on between him and Roxanne all those years ago, and she disliked him just as much now as she had then. "It was two people. The man was an Ignis, grey hair, probably late fifties. The woman was short, with red hair and a long purple coat. They took Amber through an untraceable portal. I tried to follow, but it was already closed on the other end."

Oliver swayed, and Lindsey stepped forward to support him, looking up at her father with concern. He met her gaze, the look of horror on his face causing panic to surge inside Roxanne's chest again. "Camilla has her."

"Camilla?" Roxanne jumped to her feet. "That… that crazy woman who tortures people for fun?"

But Oliver wasn't looking at her. His eyes were on Lindsey, almost pleading. "You have to find her. Try to Trace the portal, take the team and scout out all the places she might have taken her. We have to get her back."

Lindsey only nodded, placing her hands on her father's shoulders, holding him as he swayed on his feet again. Roxanne burst into fresh tears, pressing the tissue to her mouth, while Devan drew her into his arms, holding her close as she cried.

Chapter Forty-Five

AMBER SUMMERS

Amber awoke in a dark room, with only a couple of gaps in the boards across a window letting the daylight in. There was something sticky on her face, and her limbs were heavy, her eyes and lips gummy, her mouth dry. After a few moments of disorientation, she managed to sit up and take in her surroundings.

The space was empty except for a bed in a corner with a bare mattress on top, and a pile of something in another corner that looked like broken furniture, but she couldn't tell in the gloom. There was also a door, dark panelled wood against the pale wall, and she scrambled over to it. It rattled, but wouldn't budge. "Hello?" she croaked, then swallowed to clear her throat. "Hello?" She rattled the door again, but got no answer.

She sank down on the floor next to the door, her back against the wall, and carefully explored the stickiness on her face with her fingers. Immediately, she assumed it was blood, from the smell and the feel, dry and crumbly in some places, sticky in others. She tried to trace the source, finding her nostrils crusty and blocked with it, but there was another trail, one that led into her hair.

She didn't know how long she sat there on the floor, the fear pressing down on her chest, her eyes adjusting to the dimness. The room she was in had crumbling plaster on the walls, and floor-length curtains in a dark material covered in dust. The floorboards creaked, and a stain on the floor over where she had been lying further confirmed the fact that she had been bleeding. Her surroundings were mostly silent, but her fear increased when she heard a scream in the distance, and muffled voices, followed by more screaming. She wanted to call out, to ask for help, but that scream made her hesitant, worried that someone would come and make her scream too.

The light coming through the blinds was dimming, deepening the shadows in the room. Was it her eyesight, or was it getting dark? She shivered, wrapping her arms around herself. Some parts of her were numb, others felt the chill. She rubbed her arms, trying to get some warmth into herself, wishing she had a blanket, instead of the thin cardigan and light cotton of the medic's uniform her mother had brought her from the hospital. Her white tunic was covered in blood, mud, dust and who knew what else. But when she heard footsteps approaching, she soon forgot the cold.

She waited, frozen in silence, listening as the footsteps drew closer. She realised there were two pairs, a lighter step, and a heavy stomp, and they stopped abruptly outside her door. Muffling a gasp, she shrank away, huddling in a corner as keys jingled, the lock rattled, and the door swung open.

Two figures entered, one tall and hulking, the other small and thin. There was a brief pause, and then a light was turned on. Amber cringed, trying to see through her fingers as she shielded her eyes from the sudden, harsh light.

"Well, how is our little guest?" said a honeyed voice. Amber trembled, recognising her as the woman who had filled her with so much inexplicable pain outside the wreckage of the medical tent.

As her eyes adjusted to the light, she squinted up at her visitors. The man who had attacked the tent shut the door, then leaned against it.

"Where am I?" she managed to say, her voice small and shaky.

"Why, you're in my home," said the woman, holding her arms wide as though to welcome her. "Or at least, that's what everyone thinks. It's far too dusty and draughty for me to stay here."

Amber said nothing, looking from one to the other, afraid of what they wanted to do to her.

"Are you hungry?" the woman cooed, eyeing her with feigned concern.

Again, she stayed quiet, aware of the gnawing ache in her stomach. She thought back to her mother and the safety of their cheerful kitchen, swallowing a sob. She hadn't eaten anything since that morning, when Roxanne had coaxed her to eat half a bowl of porridge. But the way the woman asked made her sure it was a trick question.

"Well, sweetie, hungry or not, in this house you have to sing for your dinner."

Amber flinched, staring up at her, waiting to hear what she was going to ask her to do. The man, standing half in shadow, folded his arms in front of his broad chest, watching her. She had seen what he could do, but even without his fiery Talent, he was terrifying, his leer setting her off trembling again.

"People say I like to play with my food," said the woman, and she reached beneath her coat and drew out a long, thin, slightly curved knife. It was sheathed, but she lifted it in front of her, drawing the dagger out slowly, the metal polished to a high shine and glinting in the light. "I like to chop it up into tiny pieces, maybe save a bit for later.

Sometimes the food isn't for me, but you see, it's bad manners to bake a cake and not let everyone take a slice."

If Amber's mouth had been dry before, it was nothing compared to now. In fact, her throat felt like it had closed up, her breath came with difficulty, and her pulse raced so fast she was sure she would pass out. "What do you want?" she asked, her voice a strangled gasp as she shrank further against the wall, eyeing the blade.

"Oh, just a little fun until your Mummy comes to pick you up. I'll leave your pretty face, but as for the rest of you… well, I'm sure Mummy will fix you if she doesn't take too long to find you."

Amber whimpered, and then, to make things worse, she heaved, leaning over as her stomach threatened to expel its contents. She pressed a hand to her mouth, but as she heaved again, only bile rose in her throat, and she coughed and spluttered.

"Oh, darling, don't be making a mess of the floor now," said the woman, pretending to look aghast. Amber looked up at her, eyes streaming as she braced a hand against the dusty floorboards.

"Perhaps it is a little early for playing," the woman continued thoughtfully, twirling her fingers around the knife. "I should let you get settled in first. But a little taste won't hurt." She smiled then, scarlet lips stretching over narrow teeth, and bent down, caressing Amber's face with a touch that made her skin prickle. Her fingers ended in talons painted a dark red, the colour of old blood. When those fingers reached her chin, they gripped, the talons digging into her skin, forcing her face up. Amber whimpered again and closed her eyes.

"Please," she said, but stopped there. Please what? Don't hurt me? Don't kill me? What could she possibly offer to stop them? She had no secrets to tell, no money to pay, no favours to give. She wasn't even important. But all thoughts were driven from her mind as the woman gripped tighter and that inexplicable pain ripped through her body once again.

"I know," the woman crooned as Amber screamed in her face, gripping her bony arm with both hands, anything to hold onto as the agony tore through her. "You let it all out." She laughed at her screaming, and then the pain stopped as suddenly as it started. The woman let go of her chin, patted her cheek gently, then let her slump to the floor. Amber could only lie there, exhausted as tremors rippled through her.

"I'll send your dinner soon. And there's a bathroom through there, in case you want to freshen up."

Amber opened her eyes to see her pointing, but she was too shocked to look around. The woman took a few steps towards the doorway and the Ignis framed in it. "I'll be back tomorrow, for more games. You be a good girl now and make sure you eat all your dinner. You've earned it."

Chapter Forty-Six

PHAEDRA RONAN

"Harlow said your uncle is allowed visitors."

Phaedra looked up from her half empty bowl of stew, seeing Officer Munro standing over her in the barracks canteen. She sprang to her feet, but as Ombra started to get up from her own chair, Munro barked, "Just you."

Phaedra nodded, grasping Ombra's fingers briefly.

"I'll wait here for you," said Ombra, fear clouding her eyes.

Phaedra pressed a kiss to Ombra's cheek, before hurrying after Munro, who had already started to march out.

She was clean and fed and looking forward to a bed, but her worry over her uncle's arrest weighed on her more than the exhaustion of the day, not to mention the other horrific rumours flying around. No one had even told her what happened, not until they had bumped into Dean and Lorcan while helping the injured. She had tried to see Caspar straightaway, but Munro had ordered all cadets to return to the barracks and wouldn't take no for an answer.

Phaedra struggled to keep up with Munro as she weaved through the darkening barracks, the place still teeming with activity despite the late hour. There was a lot of wailing, and outside the infirmary was a long queue of people with less threatening injuries still waiting to be seen. Phaedra and Ombra were mostly unharmed and had already cleaned and dressed their cuts for one another, but it was Veto that Phaedra craved, longing for the dreamless sleep it promised after a day she would rather forget. She still had some stashed in a drawer at the lake house. Perhaps she and Ombra could sneak back there to sleep.

Munro led her to a long, low building. After speaking to a pair of soldiers stationed at the main entrance, Munro beckoned Phaedra inside, and she found herself in a dingy corridor, lines of doors on either side. Barred windows were set in those doors, and a cluster of people were gathered around one of them partway down. Two of the people were guards, a third was Dean, and the fourth was Skye. The harsh glow of the fluorescent lighting cast the blood and injuries on their faces in horrifying detail.

"You shouldn't be here," Skye said fiercely, clutching the bars of the door she was looking through.

"I'll be fine, Skye." It was her uncle's voice, and Phaedra wrapped her arms around herself, the realisation that Caspar was behind bars bringing tears to her eyes. "I've slept in worse places."

"I *will* get you out. I swear it."

There was a brief silence, then Dean glanced at Phaedra. "We have to go, Skye."

Skye looked around at her brother, then spotted Phaedra. But before she could react, Caspar's hand reached through the bars, cupping Skye's face. "One more thing. Did you kill him?"

There was another pause, Skye's hand closing over Caspar's as she stared at him. Phaedra lowered her gaze, feeling like she was intruding on a private moment. "Pretty much. But what's stopping her from bringing him back?"

A colder fear closed around Phaedra's throat, the rumour she didn't want to believe: her grandfather, back from the dead. But if Alessia had raised all those other corpses, there was no reason why she wouldn't raise Ivor, too. She was twisted enough.

"When I saw you..." Caspar trailed off, his voice strained. "Never do that again."

Skye shook her head. "I won't."

Dean shifted, glancing at Phaedra again. "Let's go, Skye."

Skye nodded, straightening. "Try to get some rest."

"And you. You need to get better. Don't worry about me."

Skye still held his hand, turning her face to press a kiss against his palm, then stepped away, hunched as she followed Dean down the corridor. Phaedra felt Munro's hand on her shoulder, urging her forward. She approached the door.

Caspar looked exhausted, but his eyes lit up when he saw her. When he reached out to her, she took his hand. "Are you alright?"

"I'm fine," Phaedra confirmed, her tears already falling. "What happened? Dean and Lorcan said—"

"I don't know," Caspar admitted, squeezing her fingers. "I'm afraid the soldiers I converted turned on me."

Phaedra trembled. "Did they hurt you?"

He gave her a small smile, his face still covered with dirt from the battle. "I've been patched up and given Veto. It's nothing too bad."

She nodded, rubbing her tears away with her free hand. But her bottom lip still wobbled. "Is it true? He's... he's back?"

His smile faded. "He attacked Skye. She beat him but... I suppose you heard what she said."

A violent tremor shuddered down her spine. Caspar gripped her hand tighter. "Did you see him? For real?"

Caspar's face was grave. "I did."

More tears came. She wrapped her other hand around his. "What if she brings others back?" A gasp escaped her as a horrific thought occurred to her. "She might turn Dad—"

"Don't think like that," he said firmly, bringing his face closer to the bars. "I'll send word to have the mausoleum burned down if it puts your mind at ease."

Phaedra bit her lip, hesitating. "But Mum's in there."

"I think Ilaria is beyond caring whether her remains are bones or ashes, Phee." He swallowed, pain flickering across his features. "But put it this way, I'd rather she were ash than Undead."

She shuddered again at the thought of Alessia being insane enough to try raising their mother, and she did her best not to entertain the nightmarish images creeping into her mind. "Okay," she agreed, noticing the soldiers behind her fidgeting. "Let's do that."

Caspar looked up at Munro. "I know this is at the bottom of everyone's list of priorities, but could you ask General Harlow to have the bodies in the Ronan mausoleum cremated?"

Munro raised an eyebrow, glancing between Caspar and Phaedra. Then she nodded.

"Thank you." He let out a breath, his haunted face softening. "Now go and get some rest, Phee. You look like you're about to pass out."

Phaedra let out a half-hearted laugh, squeezing his hand one more time. "I hope you've got a bed in there."

"And a blanket." He smiled reassuringly.

"And food?"

"Even some food. I'll be fine."

"Okay. I'll visit you tomorrow, if they let me."

He nodded. "Sleep well, Phee."

She finally let go of his hand, backing down the corridor, holding his gaze until she stumbled and turned to walk forward. The lights went out behind her, and she wrapped her arms around herself, hating to leave him alone in the dark.

Chapter Forty-Seven

SKYE BOLTON

Kerry's sleep tea knocked her out for the entire night, but when Skye finally awoke, everything hurt. She hissed through her teeth when she tried and failed to sit up in bed, the injuries to her abdomen flaring at any slight movement. Eventually, she managed to get to her feet through a series of ungraceful rolls and shuffles, grateful for the heat of the shower to ease some of the pain and stiffness.

Roxanne had told her to rest, and as much as Skye would gladly dose herself up on Veto and sleep the pain away, she had no time for that. She strapped up her still healing ribs with tight bandages and donned some dark clothes that she didn't mind getting stains on. She had minds to Break, but there was always a chance things might get bloody.

"Here," said Kerry when she and Dean arrived in the kitchen almost at the same time. "I've made you both a big breakfast."

Skye tried to give her a grateful smile as she set down two plates laden with a full English. She was ravenous, but as soon as she swallowed the first bite, she realised that eating was going to be a slow and painful experience for at least a few days.

"Thanks, Kerry," Skye managed, straightening in her seat and struggling to breathe as her one swallow made its way down to her stomach. She rubbed her solar plexus. Dean, meanwhile, was eating his own meal without tasting it, his mind on the news Lindsey Matheson had told him yesterday. "Do you have any painkillers that won't dull my Talent?"

Kerry regarded her, eyes full of tears that she was trying not to let fall. It was the same scenario every time Skye and Dean came back from battle looking like they were at death's door. "I'll brew you something," she said, pulling bundles of dried herbs and jars of powder out of a cabinet.

"Is it your ribs?" Dean asked, still sullen over her apparent stupidity the previous day. She couldn't bring herself to tell him about the hallucination that had led her into the trap, too ashamed that she had fallen for it.

"I'll see Roxanne again today," Skye said, her voice strained after she swallowed a smaller mouthful of food.

"Can't she come here?" But he eyed her clothing – the high-necked black top and the plain black jeans – marking their significance. "You should stay home."

"Harlow said he'll let me Break the mutineers for the investigation."

"Surely it can wait," he said, his tone biting.

"I can't let Caspar rot in there, Dean. He didn't do it."

"Are you going to Break him too?"

"I don't need to," she said a little too sharply, drawing Kerry's scandalised gaze. Skye took as deep a breath as she could muster, but Dean cut across her before she could continue.

"Do you not think..." He paused, a pained expression on his face. Skye opened her mouth again to interrupt, but he hurried on. "Do you not think this could be a set up?"

"What the fuck could he stand to gain from staging a mutiny?"

"Language, Skye," Kerry muttered. Neither of them looked her way, too busy glaring at one another.

"I'm not the only person who thinks he might have been trying to have you killed," Dean continued.

Skye scoffed, then winced as it jarred her ribs. "I've been sharing his bed for the past two months, Dean. He's had plenty of chances to kill me."

Dean grimaced at her admission, then skimmed over it. "Just please, don't trust him, Skye."

"Oh, but it's okay for you to trust a pretty blonde who bats her lashes at you?"

"That's different. Lindsey was a spy."

"She's a Matheson."

Dean's face flushed with anger. "And yet you trusted Cameron. What's the difference?"

She hissed a warning, the figure in white standing alone on the battlefield flashing through her mind again. "Don't bring him into this. It's completely different."

"Is it?"

She held his glare as Kerry worked quietly in the background, their arguing setting her frayed nerves further on edge. Skye then lowered her gaze, managing another mouthful, her stomach rumbling for more. "I know Caspar had nothing to do with this, Dean. Please give me some credit."

Dean gave a small sigh, then went back to brooding on Lindsey and the news that Amber Summers was her half-sister. Guilt stabbed at her injured ribs as Skye tried not to imagine Roxanne's reserved daughter being trapped in a situation similar to what she had endured just a year ago. Clearly, someone was trying to bait Roxanne, as well as the Mathesons if they knew the truth.

"Roxanne and Oliver had an affair," she told Dean eventually, unable to hold her tongue any longer as she listened to his confused thoughts.

"How do you know?" he asked, eyeing her suspiciously.

"I found out when I Broke Oliver's mind. I think they're trying to keep it quiet though. Being affiliated with the enemy would probably hurt Roxanne's leadership prospects, even if we are allies at the moment."

"Yeah, she asked me to keep it to myself."

"She must be interested in you, if she's bothered to tell you why she's going to be so busy." She offered him a teasing smile, a peace offering.

Dean raised an eyebrow in irritation, refusing to comment, but his thoughts were full of hope.

"Just be careful, okay? Matheson—"

"I know, Skye. I know what he did to you. And I know she's close to him. But that doesn't mean she's her father."

She frowned, but then Kerry set a cup of steaming tea in front of her, the bitter, medicinal aroma wrinkling her nose. She set a pair of tablets down next to it, simple painkillers that would barely take the edge off.

"Drink that while it's still hot," Kerry instructed, glancing between them. "And stop arguing or I'm leaving you both here to fend for yourselves."

***

The mood at the barracks was subdued, devoid of the eagerness and anticipation of the previous days. A few forlorn soldiers nodded or saluted Skye as she passed, and she nodded back, the extra attention unsettling her. Did they truly respect her, or were they privately judging her recent reckless actions, just waiting for her to make one stupid move too many?

Squaring her shoulders and determined not to let her pain and discomfort show, she continued through the camp, heading for the main offices where the Resistance Leaders gathered. She found Harlow talking with Sinclair and

Ferries, but when he saw her approach, he excused himself and came to greet her.

"Morning Miss Bolton." He gave her a mock salute and a grim smile. He was dressed in a clean uniform, but his pale skin and shadows beneath his eyes were evidence of the previous day's battle.

"Just call me Skye," she said, nodding to him. "No need for formalities."

"Skye it is then," he agreed, falling into step beside her. "I suppose you can call me Devan."

They both nodded at passing soldiers as he led her through the barracks, towards the crumbling building where they were holding the prisoners – and Caspar. "Any news I might have missed?"

"Nothing from the other side." His voice was level, his strides even. "We've counted up to a third of our combined armies in losses, including the ones that died in the night."

Skye nodded bleakly, wondering how many of them were now living a second life as part of Alessia's Undead army. "What's the breakdown between armies, if you don't mind me asking?"

A muscle twitched as he gritted his jaw. "The Resistance took the biggest hit. But I expected as much. We're the least experienced."

"I'm sorry," said Skye, and she meant it. When Devan glanced at her, she could see the grief and uncertainty in his eyes, and even worse, the mistrust.

"Just do me a favour and remember us when you win this war, alright?"

Skye held his gaze for a few paces, knowing full well that she was not the Lux the Resistance would have chosen. "I don't know what sway I'll have when all of this is over," she said, turning her gaze back towards the building they were approaching. "But I know things weren't good under Caplin, and I don't see why they shouldn't be fairer."

"Well, I'm glad we've opened your eyes," he said as they arrived at the prison. At the top of the three steps up to the main entrance was a small brunette woman, standing somewhat apart from the pair of Resistance soldiers who flanked the doors. The woman watched Skye as she ascended the stairs, each step jolting her injured ribs. Skye gritted her teeth, doing her best not to wince.

"This is Dr Dooley." Devan indicated the woman, who took a tentative step forward, large, brown eyes staring up at Skye. "She's a Telepath who has been working with us for almost ten years."

"Hello." Skye reached out her hand, now fighting to hide her irritation as well as her discomfort. Devan had said nothing about working with another Telepath. "Mind Breaker?"

The woman shook her head, grasping Skye's hand, then letting go quickly. "I'm a psychiatrist."

"Ah." Even worse. She looked at Devan for an explanation.

"Jennifer has become quite adept at extracting valuable information from subjects, often without them even sensing her presence in their heads. Since we wish to make this investigation as unbiased as possible, Jennifer will sweep the prisoners' minds to corroborate any of your findings."

Skye nodded. "So basically, I get to do all the hard work." The corner of her mouth tugged up to make it clear she was joking. The woman didn't smile.

"I've already told the guards to let you in to see all the supposed mutineers," said Devan, "so you can do things in your own time. If you feel like you need to speak to anyone else we're holding, will you check with me?"

"Of course," she said, trying to bury her annoyance over needing to ask permission. "I must warn you, some people don't deal well with being Broken. I could damage them beyond repair, or even kill them."

Devan was silent a moment as they hovered outside the building, Jennifer standing between them. "Try to keep them alive, if you can. We don't want any unnecessary deaths on our hands. But if it's unavoidable… I'm sure you'll do what you think is best."

He led them inside, and Skye's gaze immediately went to Caspar's door halfway down the corridor. The hatch was shut, and a soldier stood outside it, back straight, hands clasped in front of him. She reached out telepathically, finding the familiar buzz of Caspar's mind within, still hidden, but alert.

"Do you need anyone to come in with you?" asked Devan, looking between them as a middle-aged soldier rattled a ring of keys before one of the doors.

"They're on Veto, aren't they?" Skye asked.

"Of course."

"Then it shouldn't be a problem. No need to waste valuable resources." She glanced down the corridor, seeing cadets and medics running back and forth with messages, food, and supplies. Her electric Talent was still replenishing, but she had enough to defend herself if any of the prisoners went for her.

Devan nodded to them both. "Then I'll leave you in Haversham's capable hands."

Haversham saluted, then finally shoved a key into the lock, glancing through the hatch before he opened it. Skye stepped into the cell, the combined smell of blood and sweat greeting her nostrils. The prisoner lounged on the bed, eyes flicking between Skye and Jennifer. The latter went to stand against the wall to Skye's left, head down, hands clasped in front of her, fading into the background.

"You're wasting your time," the prisoner sneered, blood and grime matting his hair and coating his neck. Beneath a crusty layer of blood, the golden dragon on his chest was barely visible.

"I'll be the judge of that," Skye replied coolly, then got straight to work, breaking down his defences with little difficulty.

His knowledge gave her nothing she didn't already know, and the second and third prisoners had the same story: their captain – the Aqua Skye had struck down – invited them to join the mutiny when he gave the signal, promising they would be rewarded for killing Caspar and supporting the Nox and true heir to Ivor Ronan. After each Break, Jennifer swept through the minds once Skye laid them bare, her telepathic presence as discreet as her physical tread. Aside from that, she stayed out of Skye's way, for which she was thankful. The last thing she needed was another Telepath trying to tell her how to do her job.

By the time she got to the fourth prisoner, Skye was beginning to lose patience, her frustration grating on her. Perhaps the information they had would be enough to clear Caspar's name, but she needed to know where the command had come from. The dead captain hadn't been acting alone. He would surely have been approached by someone on Alessia's side.

As they stood outside the fourth door, her ribs throbbing and head pounding from the effort of Breaking three already, Haversham hesitated.

"I can't really let you see this one," he said, jerking a sausage-shaped thumb at the door.

"Harlow said I can see all of them."

"This one is in a bad way. The doc said it's touch and go, and he needs a few days' recovery before they know for sure if he'll make it."

"All the more reason to see him now," she snapped, unable to keep the irritation from her voice. "He might be the only prisoner who knows what happened. If he dies, we lose that information."

Haversham paused, blinking and almost cowering beneath her glare. It helped that she was a little taller than him, and she stuck out her chin, waiting. With a sigh, he rattled the keys in his hand, searching for the one he needed and unlocking the door, which creaked as it swung open.

Skye crossed the threshold, the stench of blood and sickness overpowering. On a low cot lay a half-conscious man, blood staining his clothing and the bandages that were wrapped around his middle. Sweat gleamed on his face and neck, and his skin had a yellow-grey tinge. "What happened to him?" she asked Haversham, who lingered in the doorway behind her. Jennifer resumed her spot against the wall.

"Bullet hit some organ or other. They're having trouble keeping him stable."

Skye studied the prisoner, feeling a little guilty that she was probably going to undo the doctors' hard work to keep him alive. But she had to do this. It wasn't just Caspar who was at stake. There may be other traitors amongst them, waiting to turn on them at any moment. So as Haversham closed the door behind her, she set to work, reaching out with her telepathy, testing for weaknesses in his defence. Despite his injured state, the man's walls were stronger than those she had Broken before him, which made her all the more eager to get inside.

Jennifer jumped in fright when the man gave an agonised cry, and Skye let out a slow breath, placing a hand to her left side where her ribs ached. The man coughed, and the bloodstains on his bandages bloomed bigger. "I don't know anything," he said, opening his eyes for the first time. Those eyes widened when he saw her face. She knew that look. Her reputation as a Mind Breaker was well known. People knew it was game over when she walked in.

“You do,” she said, lowering her hand, not wanting him to see her weakness. “Or you wouldn’t be working so hard to keep me out.”

He coughed again, and this time blood dribbled from his mouth. Again, guilt squirmed along with the pain in her ribs, but she carried on, ignoring his groans as she dug away at his mental barriers.

“Please,” he said a few minutes later, the bloodstains on his stomach increasing further as he twisted feebly beneath her attack. But she didn’t relent, despite his protests, despite seeing Jennifer shifting uncomfortably out of the corner of her eye. And then she was through, ravaging through the man’s mind as he wheezed, a hand pressed to his stomach, his eyes screwed up against the ache that no doubt plagued his head.

What she found made her take a step back in shock.

He wasn’t a soldier in the Ronan army at all, despite the grey uniform he still wore. He was from Caplin’s Forces, and had served the former president for years before Skye had joined the ranks as a cadet. But as she waded through memories, his mind lurched, thoughts swirling into a frenzy, the pain and blood-loss forcing him into a panic. She knew what that meant. She had been inside dying minds before, and she searched more quickly, sifting through the chaos for the information she needed, the truth of why a Caplin soldier would be lying here in a Ronan uniform.

“He’s—” said Jennifer behind her, taking a fearful step forward, but Skye held up a hand, still searching frantically. He was fading rapidly, his mind clamoured with an eclectic mix of thoughts and memories that were irrelevant to her but important to him. And then, just as she reached an image of soldiers in grey being given commands in a dim room, the man’s body gave a series of jerks and his mind went blank, snatching the truth away from her before she could properly grasp it. Skye took a shaky breath, her hand going to her ribs again as she looked down at the dead man. The pressure in her temples pounded, and she stayed there for a long moment, trying to make sense of what she had seen in his mind. Finally, she looked at Jennifer, who was staring down at the man in horror.

"I take it you don't do much Breaking," Skye said, and those large brown eyes swam with fear as she looked up at her. Skye turned towards the door, rapping her knuckles on the wood to be let out. "Let's take a break."

"You shouldn't have wrapped your ribs," said a subdued Roxanne a short while later, making Skye gasp with every prod to her abdomen. She stood before the doctor with her top rolled up, gritting her teeth against the pain.

"I had to work," she said, the cool air of the surgery raising goosebumps on her bruised skin.

"I told you to rest."

"This couldn't wait." She hissed as Roxanne used her healing power on her, inspecting Skye's other wounds as she did so.

Roxanne didn't reply. There was a haunted look on her face, she wore no make-up, and had left her usually bouncy hair limp. She held herself in a hunched way, as though expecting someone to hit her. Skye had heard the rumour that it was Camilla who had carried Amber off, and her stomach roiled at the thought of what she was likely going through. The same ordeal that Skye's own father was going through, most likely.

"I'm sorry," she said quietly, but Roxanne kept her eyes on Skye's injuries, now starting on her arm which was already almost healed.

"They're your ribs. You'll be sorry if you keep exerting yourself."

"No, I mean about what happened."

Roxanne looked up at her then, those blue eyes searching Skye's. There was fear in her gaze, and sadness, and pain. Not for the first time since hearing the news, Skye felt that old flicker of guilt about her past with Amber, and knew she was fortunate that Roxanne seemed to have forgiven her. She didn't deserve to be standing here being healed by her, not really.

"Thank you," said Roxanne, looking back down at her arm, turning it this way and that, but Skye could tell she was no longer seeing it.

"I think I know where she is," Skye said quietly, and Roxanne's gaze snapped back up to hers with a glimmer of hope. "I know where Camilla is holding my father, so she might have taken Amber there too."

"Really?" she asked, her fingers tightening slightly on Skye's wrist.

"Yes," Skye murmured, although imagining Roxanne meeting Camilla terrified her. "If she took Amber, then she obviously wants something."

"What could she possibly want from me?" Roxanne let go of Skye, her expression bleak. "Is she hoping I'll convince the Resistance to back down? That's not going to happen. I'm only one of the Leaders, and they don't even take me seriously half the time."

Skye hesitated. Seeing that Roxanne was finished healing her, she pulled her top down, tucking it back into her jeans, then reached for her jacket. An idea occurred to her, something she was reluctant to do, but it could be some small way to redeem herself for bullying Amber all those years, and to thank Roxanne for her kindness. "I could meet her if you like. Find out what she wants. I worked with her, I know what she's like."

"You would do that?" Roxanne stared up at her with wide eyes. Skye shrugged, but then Roxanne was shaking her head. "No, I couldn't let you. She obviously wants something from me. Lindsey will check if she's holding Amber in the same place as your father, and then we'll take it from there."

"A word of advice," Skye said, taking a step towards the door, the knowledge she had gathered from the Mind Breaking making her eager to get back to her investigation. "Don't try to break her out of there, no matter how easy it might look. Camilla doesn't give empty threats. She'll kill her if she gets wind of you trying something."

Roxanne nodded, her eyes brimming with tears. "Thank you, Skye."

"It's nothing," said Skye, waving a hand. "I'll have a chat with Lindsey later."

She slipped through the door, the movement straining her ribs as she pushed it closed. Taking an experimental breath, she turned to walk down the corridor, and froze.

A hulking figure in a blue Resistance uniform leaned against the wall, hands in his pockets and a frown on his face. Skye waited for him to recognise her, but he stared unseeing at the floor, his thoughts far away. It was only when she worked her tongue into movement and managed a "hello" that he met her eye.

It was Glen.

He stepped away from the wall, moving with some difficulty. His eyes glued her to the spot, surprise giving way to concern as he looked her up and down. She tried not to shrink beneath his scrutiny. "Are you okay?"

"Are you?" she deflected a little defensively, but her voice faltered, worry and relief mingling at seeing him alive and whole. He was limping, and a bruise coloured his cheek above his sandy beard, while a dark red scrape marred his temple. The urgency of her investigation nudged her to keep walking past him, but his gaze rooted her in place. Despite her brisk tone, his hazel eyes were soft.

"I… I saw what happened."

She nodded, biting the inside of her cheek and taking a shallow breath, which sliced through her side despite Roxanne's efforts.

"You…" He swallowed, but the gravel remained in his voice as he spoke the next words. "You were incredible."

Ivor Ronan's cold, cruel laughter echoed in her ears. Her fingers twitched, remembering the way his skull shuddered and his eyes crackled as she landed the killing blow.

"So were you," she breathed, replacing the horror of her own fight with the glimpses she had seen of Glen's.

Uncertainty flickered across his face, along with a hint of colour high on his cheekbones. Her heartbeat stuttered, an ache of guilt and regret blooming in her chest that only aggravated the agony in her ribs.

"I have to go," she said thickly, struggling to keep her voice level. "Take care of yourself, Glen." She went to walk past him, pausing at his side. Glancing up at his face, she managed a close-lipped smile, and brushed his shoulder with the lightest of touches. "I mean it."

Chapter Forty-Eight

GLEN FARRADAY

He watched her walk away with a hand wrapped around her side, her footsteps more hesitant than usual. He had witnessed the battering she had endured, seen how she had almost met her end. His heart thumped in his ears now as it had then, when a field of dead and injured separated them.

I mean it.

Her words echoed. He could still see those dark eyes promising she cared, feel the imprint of her touch lingering through his sleeve.

Skye had tried to hide her hurt, as always, but Glen's heart clenched at the pain flickering across her face each time she moved. It had taken all his will power not to take her in his arms and offer what little comfort he could.

Stupid feelings. He shook himself as she turned a corner, not looking back. In spite of everything, he waited until her footsteps no longer echoed behind him. Taking a deep breath and squaring his shoulders, he pushed aside his thoughts and feelings for Skye, knowing he was wasting his time hoping something might be rekindled between them.

There was a long pause after he knocked on Roxanne's door, and the ache in his knee throbbed along with the damage to his face and left arm. When Roxanne's strained "come in" finally drifted out, he poked his head around the door, checking she was definitely ready for him.

"Glen! Come in." The Healer was flustered, eyes red-rimmed and glazed with crying. "Sorry, I was just…" She gestured vaguely, eyes darting around as she searched for words.

Glen hesitated in the doorframe, flushed at having interrupted a private moment. "I can come back."

"No, no… What do you need?"

He paused again, teetering on his decision to stay or leave. She looked like she needed a doctor herself. "Really, I can come back."

"No," she insisted, straightening and casting an assessing eye over him. "It's your knee, isn't it? Come and sit down."

He gripped the door a moment longer, then obeyed, crossing the room and lowering himself into the chair she pulled out for him. She sat in another chair beside him, and he leaned down to roll up his trouser leg, grimacing as the movement pulled the bruised tendons taut in his arm.

"I'm so sorry about Amber," he said as she got to work without a word, her fingers cool but gentle against his knee.

"Thank you," she mumbled, her eyes on her task.

"If there's anything I can do…" If he had just stayed behind in the Healer's tent a few minutes longer, perhaps he could have prevented the entire awful ordeal from taking place.

She nodded, her lip wobbling as she gave him a watery smile. "That's very kind of you."

He watched her work in silence, tensing as his knee spasmed. Once the cooling sensation stopped tingling across his skin, she pressed the pads of her fingertips to the indentations and joints around his knee, the pressure tender, but not as painful as before.

"What happened to your knee, Glen? I know it wasn't an accident." She looked up at him, her face completely serious, eyes seeing right through him.

Glen dropped his gaze, shame creeping across his cheeks. "It's… it's not a nice story, Roxanne."

She waited. When he didn't speak, her hand found its way into his, her fingers cool and soft against his calluses. He finally looked up.

"Have you told anyone?"

He gritted his teeth, trying not to crumple with anguish. "My ma… she had a good idea what happened. But no, I haven't."

She nodded, her hand squeezing his reassuringly. "Don't you think it's time to share the burden?"

Her voice was gentle, an open invitation. His face burned at the thought of sharing his shameful story, but perhaps he could trust her with this. After all, it seemed she had figured out most of it for herself.

"It wasn't an accident."

She nodded again, her expression neutral, holding no judgement. Glen bit his lip, unsure where to start. "I suppose… I guess you know who my father was, what my name means."

"He fought for the Ronans, yes."

"Yeah… well… Doran sponsored me when I boxed professionally, and made no secret about it. I didn't think anything of it. I was young, just doing what I loved…" He trailed off, caught up in bittersweet memories. "I didn't realise at the time how much weight my name carried."

Roxanne said nothing, waiting for him to find the words.

"I… I don't want to blow my own trumpet, but I was good. I was on a winning streak. I made a name for myself. And then… then I won a highly publicised match against a guy who was backed by Caplinites."

Roxanne's cheek dimpled as she bit it, and Glen raised his free hand to his mouth, chewing a nail. "Things might have ended there, but… I injured the guy. Ended his career, and that didn't sit well with his sponsors."

He froze, spiralling deeper into despair as he took himself back to the most harrowing moments of his life. What came after was so ingrained in his memory that he could still feel it in his bones: that initial punch from the shadows of a doorway as he made his way home after celebrating his win; the jeers and his clothes tearing as he was dragged into an alleyway; the fists and booted feet from every angle, bruising flesh and breaking bone until he blacked out. They waited until he was awake and sober for the worst part. They waited until they were alone with him, locked in a cellar he still didn't know the location of.

"Let's just say they made sure I would never box again, or forget who my father was, even if I can barely remember him."

Roxanne swallowed, squeezing his hand again. "They destroyed your career too."

"Not just my career," he said bitterly. "They… they used a hammer." He winced. The memory of that swinging hammer coming down repeatedly on his kneecap still rocked through him even now. "That's how they wrecked my knee. My hand too, but I managed to splint my fingers. It turns out finger bones have an easier time healing." He gave her a grim smile. She didn't return it, her face stricken.

"Didn't… didn't Doran get Oliver to see to you?"

Glen was silent, doing his best to concentrate on his breathing instead of the darkest moments of his life. "Oliver got me walking again, but even that was touch and go… They… they made sure that by the time a Healer got to me, I would be too far gone. They kept me locked up for a week. Maybe longer. It felt longer."

She pressed a hand to her mouth, tears glazing her eyes. It was Glen's turn to squeeze her hand, guilt roiling through him.

"I shouldn't have told you this. Not while Amber…"

"Don't be silly. I'm glad you told me. But Glen…" The tears welled over, slipping down her cheeks. "I'm so sorry this happened to you."

He shrugged as his walls came up again, flexing his leg, the pain eased considerably thanks to Roxanne's miraculous Talent. "It's in the past." But he had the reminder of it during every waking moment.

"I shouldn't have pushed you to work with us. Not while we're allied with Caplin."

He shrugged again. "Luckily I've learned they're not all bad." *I mean it.* Skye's words in the corridor echoed through his mind again, cutting through the horrific memories haunting him. He tried a small smile.

"If you need to talk to someone else… one of my colleagues, Jennifer Dooley, is a Telepath. She's currently supporting the Resistance in any way she can, but she's a psychiatrist by profession. If you ever need a specialist, she wouldn't hesitate to help."

His smile twisted. "Thanks, I'll think about it." The last thing he wanted was someone poking around his head and making him relive those moments anew. They were better in the past, where he did his best to leave them.

"I hope she can help you find peace, Glen." She gave his hand one last squeeze, then let go, standing and picking up a cotton pad. "Let me sort out that scrape on your head before you go."

Chapter Forty-Nine

DEAN ROSWELL

After what Lindsey had told him the previous night, he hadn't expected to see her at the council meeting late that afternoon. And yet there she was, sitting between Roxanne and her father, all three of them pale and drawn. Dean gave her a small smile as he took his seat, and she met his gaze, her lips curving ever so slightly. Skye loudly dragged out a chair next to him and sat down, looking tired and irritable.

He tore his attention away from Lindsey and met his sister's eye. *Did you find anything?*

I'll tell you all in a minute. The grim look on Skye's face filled him with nausea. He glanced back at the people gathered. Caspar Ronan was still locked up, and they were waiting on Caplin. But when the latter didn't show up after five minutes, Sinclair cleared his throat.

"Perhaps we should start without Mr Caplin. We have two representatives of his Forces, after all."

Skye gave a short nod. "Go ahead."

Sinclair nodded back, clearing his throat again, shuffling some papers. "How did your investigation go today? Harlow told us one of the prisoners died."

"I'm afraid so," said Skye, giving away no emotion. "Unfortunately, that was before I got the full story from him."

Down the table, Roxanne shifted uncomfortably. Dean knew how it must look to her – the knowledge the man held was more important to Skye than his life. But his sister had always been pragmatic.

"Dr Dooley told us an interesting story," said Sinclair. "She said the man who died was in Caplin's Forces, not Ronan's. Care to explain how he came to be wearing a different uniform?"

Dean's heart sank. No wonder Skye looked so agitated.

"That's what I was trying to find out," said Skye through gritted teeth.

"I thought I smelled a rat," said Lindsey, eyeing Skye. "They were too well-organised for a bunch of random traitors."

"So Caplin and Caspar Ronan are working together?" Nanette Ferries asked, wrinkling her nose.

"Caspar has nothing to do with it," said Lindsey.

"You would say that," said Sinclair, jotting down a note.

"Because it's true," Lindsey shot back, slapping a hand on the table.

Sinclair opened his mouth to retort, but Skye cut across him. "As I said last night, the mutineers were fighting *against* Caspar. So clearly the command didn't come from him."

"And yet you seem to be the only witness other than Ronan's own army," said Nanette, her hawk eyes glaring. "You are part of Caplin's Forces and friendly with Caspar Ronan, so why should we take your word for it?"

"Do you really think I would have spent my day Breaking prisoners if I was in on it?"

"It's awfully convenient that no one can Break *you* so we can know for sure," said Sinclair, and Dean straightened in his chair at the threat, his hands curled into fists beneath the table.

"Torture won't work either," came Skye's flippant reply. "Matheson already tried and failed with that."

Everyone's eyes snapped to Oliver, who lifted his own gaze from the table and gave Skye a dead-eyed stare. Skye only shrugged and picked at a broken nail.

"I think we can be satisfied that Miss Bolton is telling the truth," said Devan Harlow in his mild voice, clearly eager to settle the tension. "Did you Break all of the prisoners involved in the mutiny?"

"I did," Skye confirmed. "And since our dear departed friend wasn't a Ronan soldier at all, there are a few things I would like to ask Mr Caplin."

"Ask me what?" came a voice behind Dean, and he turned to see the former president sweep into the room, Captain Sullivan close behind him.

"Oh," said Skye, looking up at their boss with thinly veiled dislike, "about the fact that one of your soldiers was walking around in a Ronan uniform."

Caplin scrutinised Skye with a slightly raised eyebrow, calmly taking a seat opposite. All eyes followed him as he did so, waiting. "That's a question I wouldn't mind asking myself."

"You're in a room full of witnesses who don't trust you, Mr Caplin. It wouldn't do to lie."

Skye! Dean warned, his anxiety bubbling up at her careless tone.

"I would be more careful when throwing around accusations if I were you, Miss Bolton." Caplin eyed her coldly. "So, you found out one of the traitors was in fact one of my own. I hear the man died, so I suppose thanks are in order for giving him what traitors deserve."

A drawn-out silence followed, everyone waiting to see what Skye would make of the insinuated threat. Skye and Caplin glared at each other, the tension building between Dean's shoulders as he watched the standoff, but eventually, Skye's lips curled. "So, you're saying you had no knowledge of the mutiny before it took place."

"If I had known a band of soldiers were planning to turn on us, I would have had you interrogate them immediately, then put them to death."

"Me? Not Welch? I hear he's your favourite Mind Breaker once again."

"Oh, he's second best, as always, Miss Bolton. I didn't want to trouble you with such lowly tasks when you're busy being the Lux."

Skye glanced down the table at the assembled Resistance Leaders and the Mathesons. She appeared to be keeping her cool, but Dean knew how much Thorsten Welch got under her skin. "Caspar Ronan is locked in a cell because it was Ronan soldiers who carried out the mutiny. Now we know one of yours was involved, why shouldn't they lock you up too?"

Dean resisted the urge to cringe, although the same thought had already crossed his mind. Caplin's jaw twitched. "Because I give you permission to launch an investigation into any involvement my Forces may have had, Miss Bolton. You may Break any of my soldiers you see fit to interrogate, and I will instruct my team of Tracers to assist you. I'm even happy to let you collaborate with Miss Matheson and her team, and anyone the Resistance wishes to involve, so we can be sure we're all on the same page."

There was another silence, more waiting to see how this would pan out. "That would be very helpful indeed," Skye said eventually, bowing her head to Caplin. Dean let out a breath, grateful that the argument was over for now, but he could almost feel the anger emanating from her.

"We'll supply a team to assist you," said Devan, looking relieved that the matter seemed to be settled. "And so that we're all on the same page, as you say, Mr Caplin, we will question our own soldiers too."

"Surely we don't have the resources for such an investigation while the Nox is still ransacking her way through the country," said Sinclair, his voice booming through the room. "None of our soldiers are suspects."

"None of Mr Caplin's soldiers were suspects either, until Miss Bolton made her discovery this afternoon. We can't rule out blame."

"What about Caspar?" Skye said, looking at Devan pointedly.

Devan cleared his throat. "We held a Leadership meeting this afternoon to discuss Mr Ronan's situation following your discovery, and we agree that we prefer to keep him in custody until there is no doubt about his innocence – or guilt. But perhaps we can put him under house arrest while the investigation is ongoing."

Skye drew herself up in her chair, looking like she was about to argue. *Let it go, Skye,* Dean told her silently. *At least they're not leaving him to rot in a cell.*

Skye's jaw flickered, her eyes trained on Devan. But eventually, she relaxed back into her seat. "Fine."

"Well, if that's settled," said Caplin, pushing back his chair with a scrape, "I have an investigation to arrange." He didn't wait to be dismissed, despite Skye's continued glare, and a couple of the Leaders looking at him as though they had more to say. Caplin simply got up and left, Sullivan on his heel.

"I suppose that is all then," said Sinclair. He gathered up his papers and left with Ferries. Dean looked at those who remained seated – at Roxanne's stricken expression, at Oliver whose knuckles had gone white from gripping the edge of the table, and at Lindsey who was glaring at the door. Devan still sat there too, lost for words. Dean got up, moving to the chair in front of Lindsey.

"I have the address of where they're holding Victor," said Dean, taking Lindsey's pen and notebook from in front of her and jotting down the details. "I believe Skye already said Linden might be holding Amber in the same place."

Lindsey studied the address on the notebook after Dean handed it back, then looked up at him. "Roswell Manor?"

"That's right," he said, knowing how that must sound. "The Roswells let her keep it after she murdered my uncle. I'm afraid I don't know the full story, I've never met any of my mother's family."

There was a faint frown between Lindsey's brows, and she looked back down at the address, running a thumb beneath his writing. "I'll look into it. If she's there, we'll know as soon as we've scouted it out."

"Just be careful," said Skye, still sitting at the other end of the table, her face hard. "Camilla doesn't take kindly to people snooping around."

"We know who we're dealing with," said Oliver dismissively, getting to his feet. Lindsey looked back at Dean as her father left.

"Thank you." She reached across the table, laying warm fingers against his hand. Dean's heart stuttered as she met his gaze, her soft brown eyes glazed. "This will help a great deal."

Without thinking, he placed his other hand over hers, his thumb brushing her soft skin. He felt Roxanne's and Devan's eyes on them, and hoped Lindsey wouldn't be annoyed at his forwardness. "If you need anything at all, I'm here."

Lindsey visibly swallowed, then lowered her gaze to their joined hands, blinking away tears. "Thank you," she repeated, squeezing his hand, then withdrawing slowly. She then lay her hand on Roxanne's shoulder instead. The two women shared a tearful look, and it warmed Dean to see their relationship seemed to be a positive one. Devan supported Roxanne from her other side, and the three of them filed out.

When the door snapped shut, leaving them alone, Dean met Skye's gaze. *I know what you're thinking.*

If we can prove Caplin's involvement in the mutiny, we've got him, Dean.

Anxiety churned his stomach once again. *And then what? We arrest him and send him packing to Linden?*

Skye's jaw was rigid with uncertainty. *I don't know. We'll have to cross that bridge when we come to it.*

You're playing a dangerous game, Skye. If we move against Caplin, no one will trust us. We'd be breaking the vows we took to protect him. Things look bad enough as it is.

Fuck everyone else. She rose to her feet, hands curled into fists. *Fuck the Forces. Fuck the alliance. As long as we get Dad back, do you really think I care about this shit show?*

Dean winced. *You don't mean that.*

I do. I'll slit the Nox's throat for them if I have to, but once that's done, I'm out of here.

He stared at her, taking in her bared teeth, the pain flickering across her face as she folded her arms in front of her chest. The thought popped into his head before he could stop it. *What happened to the Skye who wanted to be a hero?*

She snorted, a cold smirk twisting her lips as she turned towards the door. *Fuck her, too. Caplin let that idealist idiot die on a scaffold along with Darius.*

Chapter Fifty

Alessia Ronan

"The mutiny has sown the expected discord, Madam President, although I'm afraid the few soldiers who remain alive have been taken prisoner. Word is the Lux is Breaking them to discover who gave the command."

Alessia glowered as Arthur Linden gave his report, sitting uncomfortably in a chair in the draughty parlour of Castle Uaine. She felt far from victorious, and the exhaustion from the battle still weighed on her, although the discord between the allies was some consolation. "Is my uncle still stewing in a cell?"

"They plan to transfer him to house arrest."

Alessia worried her lip, her gaze lost in the patterns of the ugly brown and green rug at her feet. She had hoped the Resistance and Caplinites would cast him out or execute him for treason, but it seemed they were more gullible than she gave them credit for.

Remembering she had an audience, she pressed her bitten lips into a thin line and raised her head. Either side of her sat her grandfather and Vala, while the three Marsdens occupied a pair of sofas in her peripheral. Lucien lurked behind Vala's chair, and General Pierce stood near the door, waiting for his turn to give a report.

"What else has your informant told you?"

"Roxanne Summers is working with the Mathesons to locate her missing daughter. My sister is expecting their visit any day now."

She nodded, struggling to sit straighter in her chair. The tension that had been gradually tightening her chest all day left her a little short of breath. "Tell Camilla not to kill any hostages without my instruction."

"Yes, ma'am."

"If my granddaughter is being sent to scout out Roswell Manor, would it not be beneficial to keep her there?" Brydon Marsden interrupted. "Lindsey took my best Tracers with her when she switched sides. Disabling them would be to our benefit."

"That way you can control Oliver too, eliminating him from the alliance along with your uncle, Madam," said Brydon's son, Andrew, boldly holding her gaze.

"As much as I would like to make your traitorous granddaughter one of my puppets, Mr Marsden," she said, then paused to take a sip of water, her throat dry. "I have other plans for the Mathesons."

If Brydon was uncomfortable with the threat, he kept his face neutral, while his sons eyed her with unveiled curiosity. Ignoring their searching looks, Alessia looked at Pierce.

"General—" she began, but her voice cracked. She gave a small cough, reaching for the water once more. Spending the previous day exposed to the elements clearly had her coming down with something. "General Pierce, your report?"

Pierce stepped forward, launching into a full account of the dwindling number of live soldiers and the increased amount of Undead. But Alessia had stopped listening. She coughed again, and the next swallow of water went down like shards of glass, leaving her retching.

"Alessia?" came her grandfather's voice, etched with concern. But it was faint beyond the ringing in her ears, the panic rising like a balloon in her chest. His dry fingers brushed the back of her hand, and she leaned forward, extracting a handkerchief from her pocket and pressing it to her mouth as she was overcome by a series of coughs that wracked her abdomen.

"Is everything alright, President Ronan?" someone asked.

A coppery taste filled her mouth, and her stomach churned as a cold realisation stole over her. Lowering her handkerchief, a scene from a nightmare stared up at her: scarlet blood blooming against the white.

She sat frozen, transfixed by the horrific sight in her hand. The ringing in her ears increased, drowning out the rest of the room. The longer she stared, the more other memories rose like bloated corpses to the surface: her grandfather's blood on countless handkerchiefs; red spots on pristine sheets; her mother's life pooling on white tiles.

She dropped the handkerchief.

"Everybody out," she said hoarsely, gripping the arms of her chair, torn between staying and bolting.

Nobody moved.

"I said out!"

There was further hesitation as everyone glanced between Alessia and the bloody handkerchief.

"Should we call a doctor?" asked Brydon mildly.

"GET OUT!" she yelled, finally rising to her feet, shadows bursting from her fingertips. There was no further hesitation. Pierce twisted the door handle and stepped out, closely followed by Linden. The Marsdens scrambled to join them, still casting confused glances back at her and her curling shadows. Vala and Lucien both moved towards her, while her grandfather wheezed quietly at her back.

"Do not be alarmed," Vala said when the door shut behind the men. She reached for Alessia's elbow, but when she came into contact with her, Alessia pulled away, turning and stepping backwards, her shadows writhing before her as a warning.

"What is happening?" she blurted, glancing between Vala and her grandfather. Ivor leaned forward with some difficulty, picking the offending handkerchief up from the floor. When he raised his bloodshot eyes to Alessia, his expression was full of fearful certainty. "No!" she gasped, stepping back again and pressing a hand to her chest. A small part of her still tried to dismiss it as an oncoming cold. But it seemed the truth was a whole other matter.

"Alessia, we can resolve this."

"No." She shook her head at Vala's words, snatching the handkerchief from her grandfather and flinging it into the fire as though it was a snake ready to bite her, the scarlet on white blackening to ash. Nothing could fix it. She had seen the disease consume her grandfather. Even Matheson's Healing Talent hadn't been able to reverse the damage in the end.

The cold, solid wall slammed into her as she stepped back too quickly, and tears sprang to her eyes. She clutched her shoulder, gasping, then coughed again. More blood coated the edge of her hand as she drew it away, and with a strangled sob, she rubbed it against her black skirt, desperate to hide the truth from her own eyes.

"Alessia—" Vala took another step towards her, but Alessia turned towards the door, struggling in her haste to turn the handle.

"Stay away from me!" she shouted, then finally wrenched the door open, breaking into a run once she was inside the corridor.

She stumbled on her skirt as she ran, catching herself on a side table and knocking the vase on top of it to the floor.

The porcelain shattered, and with another sob of rage, she took hold of the side table with both hands and flung it against the opposite wall. Whirls of shadow clung to it, and hateful tears streamed hot down her face. She heard footsteps in the corridor behind her, and she bunched her skirt in a fist and carried on running, her boots rubbing at her toes, breath stabbing through her constricted chest.

By the time she burst out onto the rooftop battlements, she was gasping for air, coughs spluttering out of her. She heaved as a cold wind hit her face, and doubled over, dropping her skirt and tripping again, a hand pressed to her tight chest. Spots of blood spattered the grey stone floor as she coughed again, and she let out a frightened moan, afraid of her own body.

She lurched towards the edge of the terrace, shadows snapping out at the empty air, then she finally stopped, panting for breath through her sobs as she collapsed against the parapet. The cold stone seeped into her hands and cheek, and the wind chilled the tears on her face.

It wasn't right. She was supposed to be at her strongest, supposed to be stepping into the power that had been promised to her since before her birth. Instead, she was a sobbing wretch, afraid that her body could betray her at any moment, stealing her plans from her grasp before they had barely begun to play out.

As she dwelt on the cold reality pressing like a dead weight on her chest, she became aware of a presence behind her long before she quieted, but she didn't straighten until her crying stopped. Pushing herself upright, she leaned against the parapet as she dried her face with her sleeves, ashamed of her outburst.

"I said I wanted to be alone," she said firmly, folding her arms across her chest. Green hills rolled as far as her eyes could see, and the sun shone weakly through a hazy veil, clean and pale compared to the dirty, reddish sky that had loomed above the battle the previous day.

A wisp of cigarette smoke reached her on the wind. "Let me help you."

It was Lucien, and for once, he sounded earnest. Alessia took a shaky breath, then turned to see him smoking beside the open doorway.

"You can't help me."

"I know why you're sick."

"I'm not sick," she denied, turning back to the emerald green view.

He said nothing, finishing his cigarette, then coming to stand beside her. She refused to look at him as she felt him scrutinising her face. Her breath was more even now, but her chest and throat still hurt.

"You overexerted yourself yesterday."

"Everyone did. Do you see them coughing blood?" The tears threatened again, and she angrily blinked them away.

"It seems you inherited your grandfather's condition. At your age, it's perfectly manageable, but using too much of your Talents will aggravate it. The same thing happened to your grandfather, but he still managed to live a long life."

"If I want a doctor, I will consult someone qualified."

"I can mirror the Healing Talent. I can easily reverse yesterday's damage, but you need to be more careful going forward."

Alessia sniffed, trying to hide her trembling hands in the crooks of her elbows. Then finally, she lowered her arms, curling her hands into fists instead. "Fine."

He gave her a small smile, which she didn't return. "Let's get out of the wind."

Without a word, she turned away, stalking over to an alcove with a crumbling stone bench nestled within it. Moss crept up the stout pillars that held it up. She perched on the edge, smoothing her skirt, then clasped her hands in her lap, waiting.

Lucien hovered above her, hesitant. “Are you sure you don’t want to go indoors? The healing works best on bare skin.”

Alessia scowled, then unbuttoned the high neck of her collar, avoiding his gaze as she revealed her throat and collarbone. Her fingers began to tremble again as she fumbled on the next button, shivering from the air against her exposed skin.

“That’s fine,” he said, shifting to block the wind. He raised his hand, then stopped, perhaps remembering her warning to him yesterday. “May I?”

She nodded, eyes on the opposite wall. She stiffened as she felt his fingers brush her throat, his touch uncomfortable, alien. The cooling sensation began, a feeling she had experienced only once before, long ago, when she had fallen from a horse at the age of seven and her father called Oliver Matheson to mend her broken arm. She hadn’t gone near another live animal after that.

The itch in her throat subsided, and his hand moved gradually lower, coming to a stop an inch below her collarbone. If he felt her heartbeat pounding against her ribcage, he didn’t comment.

“All done,” he said eventually, withdrawing his hand and sitting down beside her. Alessia re-buttoned her dress in a hurry, then crossed her arms again, hunching further into the alcove. “I’ll instruct the staff to prepare an infusion for you each night. Herbs to alleviate any further symptoms.”

She inhaled a careful breath, finally looking at him. There was no amusement or mockery in his face, although his silver eyes swirled like mercury. “Why do you always wear a glamour? It’s a waste of energy.”

He shrugged. "Why do you always wear black?" A smirk grew on his face when Alessia refused to answer. "We all wish to be perceived a certain way. You want to remind everyone you're the Nox. I want to remind everyone I have abundant power. Enough that I don't mind wasting some on looking a little bit threatening."

Alessia glared, and Lucien's eyes twinkled with mischief. "You're little better than a peacock," she said haughtily, turning back to the wall.

He snickered. "I'd like to see a peacock do half the things I can do."

"What, like preening?"

"Is the Nox making a joke?"

She side-eyed him, catching that irritating smirk again. But for all his faults, she did feel a lot better. Even some of her fatigue had ebbed. If she had indeed inherited her grandfather's illness, perhaps she could order Lucien to give her some of that Healing power. But so far, she hadn't been too impressed by his ability to pass on Talents.

"Vala told me you've experimented with thirteen Talentless so far."

"I have," he confirmed, burying his hands in the pockets of his leather jacket. "Only one has been a success."

"You have him locked in a padded cell because he sends everyone and everything flying across the room, how can that be a success?"

He raised an eyebrow. "Could you control your Talent when you were a child?"

She pursed her lips, remembering the explosions of darkness each time her father chastised her, or an infant Phaedra wouldn't stop screaming. She remembered the maid whose accidental death had to be covered up, the countless toys and books that had wound up ripped to shreds when her temper got out of hand. But at least she had gained control, unlike her useless sister.

"I visit our newest Aeres every day to teach him control. But I must warn you. If you're planning to create weapons out of the Talentless, it will be years before they're ready to fight for you."

Perhaps she wouldn't have years – a horrifying possibility she hated to entertain. "I would still like you to try. It… interests me."

They lapsed into silence, Alessia straightening and taking a deep breath. The air went down without difficulty, but she wouldn't give him the satisfaction of knowing what a difference he had made.

"Does it not bother you?" she asked, hands gripping the rim of the bench. "Where you come from?"

"Why would it bother me?"

She glanced up at him. "You descend from evil."

He studied her face, a frown knitting his dark brows together. "Do you consider yourself to be evil?"

She turned her head the other way. Lucien's gaze held an intensity that made her feel laid bare, and he was sitting too close. "Sometimes I try to fight it. The… the impulses. The desire for destruction."

"You want to remain in control."

"Of course." She looked back at him, absently worrying her lip with her teeth, then realised what she was doing and stopped. "What happened downstairs… I couldn't hold it in."

"Emotions are perfectly human, Alessia."

She raised her head and pushed away strands of hair blowing in her eyes. "What lives inside me is far from human."

Lucien finally released her from his scrutiny, studying his right hand as he flexed it. A shimmer of indistinct power unfurled in his palm. With a sigh, he placed it flat against the stone bench, the power winking out.

"It's not human," he agreed, molten silver smouldering in his eyes. "It's godlike."

She shivered, fingers tightening on the cold stone of the bench. Her grandfather had implied the same, over and over again, reminding her that to be the Nox was to be divine, holy. A sacred honour to restore balance to a corrupt world. But with today's discovery, her deathly Talent no longer felt like her own. It felt too strong, too wild, not something she had been born with, but a power that had been bestowed upon her, like some unknown force was testing her, waiting to see if she was strong enough to wield it. She had worked hard to keep her body and mind healthy, determined to earn the honour of being the Nox. But the sight of blood against white cotton taunted her again, taking her back to a childhood when her father and doctors had whispered that she was sickly. Frail.

At her side, Lucien tensed, and she saw his eyes had darkened to dull steel, glazed with an absent mind. She watched, waiting for him to return to his body, and when he blinked, a sly curve graced his lips.

"Linden's informant is here to see you."

She pursed her lips. "Surely Linden can take a message."

"Trust me," he said, those eyes glittering, "you really want to meet this one."

Chapter Fifty-One

GLEN FARRADAY

Glen worked methodically as he cleaned and organised the weaponry with three of his fellow soldiers, the monotony of the manual work leaving his mind with too much space to dwell. Because beyond the drills and labour they were ordered to do, Glen knew Alessia's Undead army waited for them. When it suited the Nox, he would be facing that army again, fighting former comrades who had lost their lives at his side.

The clock on the far wall of the warehouse read a quarter past two. He glanced at the gun parts spread out before him, still waiting to be cleaned and reassembled. *Over three more hours of this*. He buried his groan and looked around at the two men and woman seated around the workbench. His companions were subdued, each lost in their own heads.

"Farraday," came a faintly familiar voice above his head. He looked up to see Lindsey Matheson, wearing the grey Ronan uniform and a cool expression. "Are you busy?"

He shrugged, lost for words as to why the infamous Matheson Ice Queen had deigned to speak to him of all people. His companions watched with mild curiosity on their faces.

“I need guards for a scouting mission. Roxanne told me you’re trustworthy.”

“Sure,” he said, glancing at the two men behind Lindsey: a spotty youngster with glasses who looked like he was barely out of high school, and another who was closer to Glen’s late twenties, nodding to him beneath a shock of black hair. The pair wore uniforms that matched Lindsey’s. “When?”

“Now.”

He glanced down at his own clothing, a vest and army fatigues. “Should I change?”

She lifted a shoulder, a hint of impatience flickering across her features. “What you’re wearing is fine. I’ll glamour us anyway. Bring a gun.”

He stood and shrugged on his jacket, then chose a rifle from amongst the ones he had just cleaned, slinging it across his back. The trio paused long enough for him to pack ammo, then turned on their heels and set off, leaving Glen trudging behind them.

After they had put some distance between themselves and Glen’s fellow soldiers, Lindsey held back and fell into step beside him. “We’re going to look for Amber Summers. Camilla Linden kidnapped her during the battle.”

“It was Camilla?” Glen silently cursed. “I didn’t know.”

“Well now you do.”

“Do you have a lead?” he asked, ignoring her sarcasm.

“Roswell Manor. It’s in Devon. Up for the drive?”

His knee twinged and he resisted the urge to grimace. But when he glanced down at Lindsey, he saw her dusk pink-painted lips curved slightly.

“We’ll take a portal partway. The drive should be an hour and a half at most.”

They arrived at a hangar where the allies kept vehicles and equipment for the war effort. Beside a dull grey four wheel drive stood another soldier in the Resistance uniform, clutching a twin of Glen's rifle. He nodded to them as they approached.

"Johnson," Lindsey greeted the soldier, halting between them. "You might already know Farraday. These two are Tracers from my team: Seth Galloway and Jack Humphries."

"Hi," Glen grunted. He had never met any of them, although he had seen Johnson around the barracks.

"Today's mission is secret. No sharing with anyone outside this circle." She glanced at each of them in turn, her light brown eyes narrowed as she pinned them in place with her stare. She looked at Glen last. "Farraday is driving. Let's go."

Glen dumped his gun in the boot while the three men piled into the back. Lindsey claimed the passenger seat next to him as he slid behind the wheel. "Where to?"

"Head for the nearest public portal."

He did as she asked, the car silent as he drove. It wasn't the first time he had guarded Lindsey, having briefly been assigned to chaperone her family when he had worked for the Marsdens, but it was the first time she had commanded him. She was a far cry from the sullen girl who had sat between her mother and brother at the elder Mrs Ronan's funeral five years ago, the siblings unspeaking while Sheridan Matheson had something nasty to say about every mourner present.

"It's good of you to do this for Roxanne," Glen said later, tentatively attempting conversation. His passengers had been painfully silent until they had gone through the portal guarded by a small team of Resistance soldiers and emerged at a connecting one outside Exeter.

"It's not just for Roxanne," Lindsey said briskly, her eyes on the road before them, rolling hills rising either side. "Keep this to yourself, but Amber is my half-sister."

Glen's jaw dropped. He couldn't help himself. It was all he could do to keep driving straight. "I… didn't know."

"Well now you do." But there was no amusement in her voice this time.

He couldn't imagine it. Roxanne and… Oliver Matheson? Not only was it unlikely, it seemed downright impossible. And he wasn't sure how old Amber was, but he had a feeling she was between Lindsey and Cameron in age. If Oliver and Roxanne had had an affair, Glen wondered if she had something to do with Oliver quitting medicine.

"Our visit today will be brief," Lindsey cut into his thoughts, loud enough for those in the back to hear. "We'll get close enough to the manor to confirm if Amber is there, get numbers and an overview of the security measures in place. Then we go. I don't want to bump into Linden if we can help it."

Glen let out a breath, nerves grating at the thought of coming face to face with the psychotic interrogator. He had met her on occasion, and always did his best to avoid her.

"Turn left here," Lindsey commanded.

Glen glanced doubtfully in the direction she requested. "The moors?"

"Exactly."

They trundled along, natural beauty unfurling around them the further they got from the main road. The men in the back struck up a murmured conversation about the battle losses, but Lindsey didn't partake. Instead, Glen felt her eyes on his face.

"How come you joined the Resistance?"

He bit into the side of his cheek, unsure how to answer. Unsure of the answer himself. "I suppose Roxanne convinced me."

Lindsey nodded, musing over his words. "She comes across like butter wouldn't melt, but she can be quite persuasive when she wants to be."

"Well, I'm sort of in her debt."

"I doubt she considers saving your life a debt to be paid, Farraday. And neither do I."

His eyes slid to the side. "What do you mean?"

"I suppose they didn't tell you. It was Seth and I who picked you up."

His eyes widened, and he glanced between her and the road. The faint flickers of memory from the aftermath of the shooting were unable to fully materialise in his mind. Absently, he pressed the heel of his hand to the tender scar tissue at the centre of his chest. "Well then," he managed, finding his words with difficulty, "consider this my thanks."

Lindsey offered the smallest of smiles, and they lapsed into silence, Glen stealing glances at her every so often, as well as at Seth in the rearview mirror. Eventually, however, he couldn't hold in his curiosity. "How *did* you manage to orchestrate your spy ring?" He knew Marsden's and Ronan's Tracers overlapped, knew Lindsey had led them for a few years.

Lindsey shrugged. "I knew which ones were trustworthy enough to recruit to the Saoirse Army."

"And no one suspected you?"

"Some did. That's where threats and blackmail came in handy. It's a cutthroat game when everyone knows who's lying."

He whistled. "Remind me never to get on the wrong side of you."

"Don't worry, Farraday," she said with an amused twist of her lips. "I always knew you were one of the good ones."

Heat flamed across his cheeks, and he kept his eyes locked on the road, unable to find a reply to her compliment, wondering what else this talented Tracer had figured about him. But his embarrassment and wondering were short-lived as she gestured to a small car park at the mouth of a walking trail.

"Pull over here." Her hand was already on the door handle.

They exited the car, shutting doors quietly. Glen took in the expanse of moorland, the smell of damp grass and the buzz of insects flitting lazily back and forth in the watery sunlight. It was a peaceful scene, and as he drew his rifle out of the boot, he felt like he should be holding a dog leash, or the hand of a lover, not clutching a weapon and swivelling his head around in search of danger.

"Come on." Lindsey murmured a string of sigils, and a glamour settled over them that drew in the colours of their surroundings, making his companions blend into the sky and undergrowth.

They set off up a small hill, moving quickly but quietly. When they crested the hill, Glen spotted their destination: a crumbling old house surrounded by overgrown gardens, one wing completely obscured by creeping moss.

They descended the hill, the ground levelling out again. Glen squinted against the sunlight streaming in his eyes, but he could see no one for miles, the surrounding moors deserted. Halfway between the hill and the manor, Lindsey stopped, holding up a camouflaged hand to halt them. Silence followed as she angled her head towards her two fellow Tracers, their faces rippling in and out of view, full of uncertainty.

"She's in there," she said, her voice barely above a whisper, "and there are others."

"Another eight?" Galloway ventured, leaning towards her.

"I'd say six," the younger, spotty man corrected. "Two dead."

Glen's heart sank at the mention of the dead. "Can you tell who?"

Jack shook his head. "The others are strangers to me."

"It's going to be quite the rescue mission," said Lindsey, then fell silent as they surveyed the manor. The back of Glen's neck prickled, and he grasped the rifle tighter, resisting the urge to rub it.

"The building is wide open though," Jack breathed. "No locks."

"It's like she's tempting us in," Lindsey whispered back. "Daring us to come and get her."

"Clearly a trap," Seth said firmly, and Glen was inclined to agree with him.

"Any wards?" Lindsey asked, her head a flicker of shadow against the sky. But another movement caught Glen's eye, and he pivoted towards it, aiming the rifle. But it was only a whisper of wind through the undergrowth. A bird called somewhere nearby, and an itch crept at the back of his neck.

"Only alert wards," Jack replied, scanning the manor.

The other guard, Johnson, shifted on the opposite side of the group, his movement catching Glen's attention. "We should go."

There was a pause, Seth and Lindsey exchanging a glance. "She knows we're here," Seth confirmed, hefting his own gun and moving closer to Lindsey. She hesitated, but before she could give an order, something moved to Glen's right again.

Glen spun around, their glamour dropping away as a misshapen figure materialised from the shade of a tree, hurtling towards them. He flinched in terror, shooting on impulse, the gunshot sending birds flapping from their hiding places.

"Watch out!" Lindsey yelled close to his ear, and their group pressed together back-to-back, elbows bumping and feet stepping on one another. But the figure had disappeared following the gunshot, leaving him wondering if he had imagined it.

A blanket of tension settled over them as they stood frozen, eyes cast outward, breath sawing through their throats. Jack trembled at Glen's side, his glasses slipping down his nose. Glen shifted the rifle against his shoulder, searching for any sign of the vision that had jumped out at them.

And then the second attack came from all sides.

Furniture hurtled towards them. *Furniture.* They pressed tighter together, ducking to avoid the chairs, tables and cupboard doors that zoomed out of nowhere. Glen shot again, bullets bringing some of the items down, but a chair sailed over their group, one leg glancing off his temple. Another wound to add to his growing collection.

"What the fuck," one of his companions let out, as a third wave of random pieces of furniture materialised out of thin air. Lowering his gun, Glen lifted his left arm, batting a dismembered table leg off course before it could hit Jack. The impact jolted through his wrist.

"What do we do?" Jack moaned at his side, cringing against him as another chair swung low towards them. Glen kicked it to the ground.

"Back to the car," Lindsey gasped, and their little group lurched, stumbling back the way they came. But before they had taken three steps, dread filled the hollow in his stomach.

Corpses rose from the undergrowth, with missing limbs and rotting flesh. Jack let out an unintelligible garble at his side, fingers clawing at Glen's elbow.

He aimed the gun again, fighting to keep it steady despite the bodies knocking into him and the horror closing around his chest like a vice. "Don't suppose any of you are Ignis?"

"No," Lindsey stammered, the fear in her voice infectious.

The Undead moved towards them as one. Jack dropped to the floor, scrambling into Glen's legs. Glen staggered away, crouching into a defensive position and shooting the nearest corpse as his fellows did the same. His bullets passed right through as though it was smoke.

What the…

Jack screamed, and Glen shot at the corpse advancing on the fallen Tracer, but again, the bullets shot through it without causing damage, and the Undead kept moving. Fear clenched around his throat now, his voice lost amidst the rushing in his ears as he cried out a useless warning. The corpse collapsed onto Jack, clawed hands thrashing, jaws open in a soundless scream. Jack flattened himself against the ground as Glen approached to haul the corpse away from him. But his fingers grasped nothing but Jack's clothing, and the Undead disappeared before his eyes. Only Jack stared up at him, terror and tears splashed across his face.

Glen straightened, looking around at his companions. Seth was glued to Lindsey's side, his own rifle sweeping as he aimed at the approaching corpses. Lindsey held a handgun in her shaking hands, while Johnson flailed, punching at the air as more of the phantom corpses ran through him.

They're not real.

Yet despite what Glen's eyes were telling him, fear still tore through his insides, forcing him to lower his gun and take several steps back from their circle. He flinched as a snarling cadaver stalked towards him, and he stepped away again, unable to get breath into his lungs.

"They're just glamours," Lindsey confirmed, sidestepping as another phantom ran at her. "They can't hurt you."

But his instincts told him otherwise, pushing him back towards the car. He hesitated, his nerves prickling with the need to escape.

"The fear isn't real either," Lindsey said, even though her own voice shook.

A cackle invaded his senses. "Oh, you should see your faces!"

Glen blinked, the corpses melting away to reveal a pair standing in their place who were very much flesh and blood: Camilla Linden, and a tall, thin man wearing a tailcoat.

"Good show, Tony," said Camilla, barely reaching to clap the man on the shoulder. "We'll definitely do that one again."

The fear released its chokehold on him, but his arms still trembled as he leaned down to haul Jack back to his feet. Glen struggled to regain his composure as they edged back towards Lindsey and the other two.

"Be glad I didn't ask Tony to conjure actual Undead," Camilla said, her sharp voice cutting through the peaceful afternoon. "Lucky for you, only the Nox can do that."

"What do you want," Lindsey demanded, rising to her full height, "in exchange for the prisoners?"

"Are you sure you want the answer to that, Lindsey dear?" Camilla simpered, knives glinting at an ornate belt around her waist. "What if I want you in return? Would you like to be my latest guest? How about one of your hunky companions?" The woman's eyes swept over them, and when she reached Glen, her gaze pinned him in place. His fear melted into something unexpected: bashfulness, curiosity, and another emotion he was ashamed to admit – desire.

"Stop toying with my guards," Lindsey snapped, and the mixed feelings withdrew like an invisible caress. Glen's cheeks flooded with heat, and when he glanced at the other men, he saw similar expressions on their faces.

"Oh, but I've grown so tired of my playthings."

"Already?" Lindsey's head tilted, her tight braid slipping over her shoulder.

"Oh yes, your little sister is a bit of a bore. No wonder Oliver never bothered with her."

Lindsey hissed. "What do you want?"

"Come back with Roxanne, and I'll tell you."

Glen gritted his teeth as a shudder trickled down his spine. The idea of someone as caring and harmless as Roxanne being held prisoner by this monster didn't bear thinking about.

"So you can take her too?" Lindsey echoed his thoughts. "I don't think so."

"No Roxanne, no deal. I'll wave a white flag if it makes you feel better."

Lindsey stood her ground, but as the seconds dragged on with no further words being exchanged, she sagged. "We meet somewhere more public."

"You're really not in the best position to negotiate, sweetheart. One word from me, and the little bird dies."

"A pub," Lindsey offered, taking a tentative step towards her.

Camilla considered. "Only if you're buying. I have expensive taste, you know."

"And about as much class as a sewer rat," Lindsey spat.

A cruel smile spread across the woman's thin lips. "Careful, darling. You've already lost so much this year."

"The pub we passed down the lane, we meet there. I'll send word with the day and time."

Camilla bowed her head, and with a sigh of relief, Glen itched to get going. But Camilla wasn't finished.

"Tell Roxanne to bring whoever she wants, but make sure she trusts them. She doesn't want everyone listening to my offer. As for Oliver, don't bother bringing him. If I set eyes on him, I'll take you both, and make him watch while I rearrange your lovely face."

Seth snarled, stepping towards Lindsey and lifting his gun in warning. But Lindsey only lifted her chin. "What makes you think he won't return the favour? Not that you have much to ruin."

Camilla chuckled. "I suppose that's true. Oliver has more to lose than I do. He always liked pretty things. Delicate little dolls that are easy to break."

Lindsey sneered, finally stepping away. Glen and the others followed suit, only too eager to escape.

"And Lindsey?"

Glen bit back a groan as they turned back towards the vicious creature.

"Don't come snooping again. Or I'll return your sister to you piece by piece."

Chapter Fifty-Two

ROXANNE SUMMERS

When Lindsey came to her surgery, visibly shaking, Roxanne imagined the worst. At first the girl could barely speak, and her breath came in short gasps. Despite her eagerness to get the story out of her, Roxanne sat her down, then poured her a cup of the herbal infusion steeping in her teapot. Lindsey quieted a little, taking a sip.

"She's there," she confirmed eventually, staring into space, the cup shaking in her hand.

"Drink more," said Roxanne, unsure whether she felt relieved or more afraid.

"Linden caught us." Lindsey obediently took another sip of the tea.

"What did she say?"

"She wants to meet you."

Roxanne nodded, also sipping tea, her own limbs beginning to tremble. "Did she say why?"

"She wants to negotiate."

"I see," she said, wondering what Camilla could possibly want in exchange. Probably a prisoner swap, or to lay down arms against the Nox. "I suppose she wants me to go alone?"

"She said bring whoever you want, but to make sure you trust them. She said something like, 'You won't want everyone hearing what I'm asking you to do'."

Roxanne gulped the last of her tea and set down her cup, taking deep, calculated breaths in an attempt to calm herself.

"I'll come with you," said Lindsey, lowering her own cup. "I can't sit back and let you go alone. That woman is…"

The gratitude she felt towards Lindsey in that moment warmed her. "Thank you. You don't have to, but I appreciate it. And I appreciate what you did today. It means a lot."

"Don't mention it," she said with a shrug, calmer now. "I know I've only just met her, but she's my sister, and after what happened with… Cameron…" She spoke his name with difficulty, taking a deep breath before she continued. "Well, she's a blessing I didn't realise I needed, and I'm not going to let that psycho bitch take another family member away from me."

Roxanne blinked away tears, touched by Lindsey's fierce protectiveness over the illegitimate sister she never knew she had.

***

"I'll come with you too," said Devan later that day as he drove her home.

"I don't want you to—"

"To what, put myself out?" he glanced at her as he drove. "You could never ask too much of me, Roxanne."

She bit her lip, trying to keep it from wobbling with fresh tears as she shrank further into the passenger seat, her arms wrapped around herself. She didn't know what she had done to deserve so much kindness. First Lindsey, now

Devan. Even Skye and Dean had helped, and offered more help besides.

"Linden might ask too much of both of us," she said quietly, trying to keep the fear from consuming her. "Lindsey said she wants to strike a deal."

"Whatever she wants, we'll figure something out. I won't let her keep Amber from you for long."

She sniffed, blinking away tears. She had barely stopped crying since finding out her daughter was gone. It was worse when she was alone, but Darshana had spent the past two nights in her guest room to keep her company, and promised to spend tonight with her as well, as soon as she finished her shift. As she tried to stop herself from crying, Devan reached out, squeezing her shoulder gently.

"Would… would you like to come in?" she asked when they pulled up in her driveway. She was looking at her knees, embarrassed about asking him, but she hated the thought of going into that cold, empty house alone, even if it was only for a few hours. "I could make you a cup of tea. Or… I might have something stronger."

Devan gave a quiet laugh. "I'm driving, but tea is fine."

She looked up to see him smiling at her, his blue eyes glinting like gems in the low sunlight. His kindness momentarily chased away the exhaustion still etched on his face, and she held his gaze, allowing herself the luxury of connecting with him in that moment. She took in his cropped dark hair, the bruises still healing along his jawline, the gentle curve to his lips. Finally, she took a deep breath and managed a watery smile of her own.

She took her time getting out of the car and leading him up the path, fumbling in her bag for her keys. She unlocked the door, suddenly a little nervous about inviting him into her home. She couldn't lie to herself. She had considered inviting him for a social visit on plenty of occasions, despite reminding herself that she ought to keep their relationship professional, but the time had never seemed right. The time wasn't right then either, but at that moment she needed a friend to keep her company, nothing more.

"Oh, you don't have to take your shoes off," she said as he started to unlace his boots in the hallway, copying her.

"You have cream carpets, Rox. I can't walk on them with these on."

She smiled nervously, twisting her fingers as he removed his boots, secretly relieved. "I have some coffee if you prefer," she said, leading him into the kitchen and opening a cupboard. "Instant, I'm afraid."

"Instant is fine." He picked up the kettle and began to fill it for her. Roxanne's cheeks grew hot.

"You don't need to do that."

He shrugged. "It should be me waiting on you. But since I know you won't let me do that, I can make myself useful by helping."

Roxanne managed another wobbly smile as she took the kettle from him, their hands brushing and Devan's eyes twinkling. A little flustered, she put the kettle on the stove, lighting it, then busied herself getting cups and teabags and coffee.

"You have a lovely place," said Devan, approaching the window. "Do you do the gardening?"

"Mostly." She cringed a little at his scrutiny, goosebumps prickling at the back of her neck. "It needs tidying."

"It looks nice," he said, and she was sure he was just being polite. "Is that a vegetable patch?"

"It is," she confirmed, approaching the window as she waited for the kettle to boil. "My dad helped me get it started a few years back. We actually manage to grow most of our vegetable intake. We make a lot of soup."

He grinned, the expression making him look much younger than his late thirties. "Good way to get your vitamins."

Roxanne drew away as the kettle began to whistle, trying to push away thoughts of better times with her daughter before they made her cry again. She hated being in that house, surrounded by happy memories while Amber was in so much danger. She had spent an hour crying on the floor outside Amber's bedroom door the night before, unable to bring herself to step inside, until Darshana heard her and sat with her, then coaxed her back to bed.

After stirring the drinks, she handed him his cup and led him into the living room. To her surprise, he settled next to her on the sofa, and they sat side by side for a moment, Roxanne awkwardly clutching her cup and staring at her knees.

"How are your folks?" he asked eventually, breaking the silence.

"Good," she said without thinking. Her mother had been on the phone for hours the night before, her father talking in the background, both of them alternating between crying and pleading with her to let them come and help. But she had refused, not wanting them in danger on top of everything else.

"Are they still getting a lot of refugees?"

"Quite a lot more in recent weeks, yes." She sipped her tea, immediately regretting it as she burned her tongue. But as they lapsed into silence, another problem played on her mind. She wasn't sure how to tell him the secret hanging between them, not even sure if she should tell him. But he had seen and heard Oliver after Amber's disappearance, and she knew he had questions, even if he was too polite to ask. "Listen, Devan… I owe you an explanation about Oliver."

"You don't owe me anything, Roxanne."

She dared to look up at him, and he met her eye, his expression kind but serious. He reached for her hand again, a firm anchor that she didn't realise she needed. She swallowed down her tears, lowering her gaze to her tea. "Oliver is Amber's dad."

Devan said nothing, only squeezed her hand reassuringly.

"We were at university together," she managed, unable to look at him. "We dated, and... He wasn't working for Ronan then."

"Even if he was working for Ronan, it's not my place to judge who you dated, nor who you had a child with. All I care about is that you're safe, and ensuring we get Amber back."

"Thank you," she whispered, tears welling. She drank her tea, the warmth easing her tight throat.

"Anyway," he continued, letting go of her hand and getting her a tissue out of the box on her coffee table. "With the Mathesons' help, we might get Amber back sooner. Lindsey and her team have been invaluable to us these past months."

She nodded, dabbing her eyes as her mind spiralled into questions that had plagued her all afternoon: what was Amber going through? What did Camilla want? What would they have to sacrifice to get her daughter back?

"Would you like me to cook something?" Devan asked suddenly, interrupting her reverie. She looked up to see him watching her closely, concern on his face again.

"Oh no, don't be silly," she said, laying a hand on his arm and then withdrawing it again. "Unless... are you hungry?"

His eyes twinkled in amusement again. "I wasn't asking for myself. But you didn't have lunch, and it's already dinner time."

She glanced at the clock, seeing he was right.

***

"Something smells good," said Darshana when she entered the kitchen a few hours later, looking from Devan to Roxanne as they washed and dried the dishes respectively. They had finished eating the casserole Roxanne had defrosted, and a portion for Darshana was keeping warm on the stove.

"It tasted good too," said Devan, shaking his hands and then taking the towel Roxanne handed to him to dry them. "Thanks again, Rox."

"I didn't do anything," she said, a little flustered as Darshana eyed Devan, the unspoken question evident on her face.

"Well, you cooked it in the first place."

"Perhaps you two can have dinner again sometime," said Darshana, falsely casual.

Roxanne hid her blush by busying herself with relaying the table for her friend. "There's plenty here for you too."

"Great, I'll wash my hands," she said, pointedly making herself scarce.

Roxanne looked back at Devan. If he noticed Darshana's hints, he didn't show it.

"I'd best go," he said, studying her with that concern in his eyes again, but he was smiling.

"Thank you for staying."

"It's a pleasure." After an awkward moment of hesitation, he held his arms out, inviting her for a hug. Roxanne blinked in surprise, unsure if this was a boundary they shouldn't cross. But as Devan's arms faltered, uncertainty and embarrassment flickering across his face, she returned his sheepish smile and stepped up to him. She wrapped her arms around him as he enveloped her in his warmth, holding her close and resting his head against hers.

She stayed there, the tension between them dissipating as she clutched his jacket, scrunching her face against his shoulder and wishing for everything to be right again.

The hug continued until Roxanne heard the toilet door open in the hallway, and she drew away from him, her sheepishness returning.

"Goodnight, Rox," he said, planting a gentle kiss on her forehead. His fingers brushed her cheeks, and his touch was rough with calluses, but not unwelcome. She met his eyes one last time as he released her, and then he was gone, wishing Darshana goodnight as he let himself out.

When Darshana re-entered the kitchen seconds later, she had a silly smile on her face. "Nice dinner?"

"It's not what it looked like." Roxanne pursed her lips, trying not to laugh at Darshana's implication, sure that she was just trying to take her mind off things. Outside, she heard Devan's engine start, then rumble away down the drive.

"Oh really? So I've just been imagining you two flirting for months, have I?"

"Don't be daft." She turned back to the stove, dishing up the casserole for Darshana. "We've done no such thing. Devan is just polite. And… kind." Her cheeks heated.

"And handsome," said Darshana knowingly, grinning at Roxanne as she set the bowl of casserole on the table in front of her. "And he has quite the soft spot for you."

"You *are* imagining things." She went back to the sink, beginning to put away the dishes he had helped her wash. "And anyway, I'm far too old for him."

"You're not that much older. A few years maybe. He doesn't seem like the type who would care."

Dishes away, Roxanne leaned against the counter, folding her arms as she watched Darshana eat. It had been a long time since she had been on a date. A long time since anyone had given her the kind of butterflies that Devan did.

But any romances after Oliver were short-lived, her ability to trust long gone.

"When all this is over," Darshana said quietly, stirring her food with her spoon, "give Devan a shot. I think he'll be good for you."

Roxanne gave her friend a sad smile. The idea that things could ever be right enough for romance felt like too much to hope for. "Let's get Amber back first." A fresh wave of tears threatened, the prospect of another night without her daughter safely in bed already crushing her beneath its weight.

Chapter Fifty-Three

SKYE BOLTON

The moon loomed like a pale wolf on the horizon, encircled by a halo of misty light. It was larger than Skye had ever seen it, turning the lake into a rippling pool of liquid gold. She shivered, taking in the eerie beauty, the night alive with a chorus of summer crickets and the hoot of an owl in a lonely willow tree. She wrapped her arms around herself, watching the moon watching her, lake water lapping near her boots.

A scuffle in the undergrowth dragged her eyes away from the ethereal view, and she caught a glimpse of a shadow disappearing into the woods, moonlight limning silver hair. A flash of recognition drew her into the darkness, following.

She weaved through the trees, the silver-haired shadow drifting in and out of view. Skye reached for her voice, but her tongue was heavy in her mouth, her heartbeat lodged in her throat.

Wait! she said silently, trying to pick up speed, but the trees stood closer together, the undergrowth slowing her pursuit. The shadow carried on, hair like a flickering, fading flame in the distance.

As she followed, she became aware of more shadows walking at her side, faceless, soundless, almost shapeless in the gloom. No moonlight reached so far into the woods, the comforting glow left behind.

Skye pressed on, eager to leave the shadows behind, determined to catch up with the flickering figure that led her deeper into the woods. Except these were no longer woods. This was a forest, ancient and holy. Branches snagged at her hair and clothes, while roots tangled around her feet and leaves caressed her face as she passed.

As she stumbled into a clearing bathed in moonlight, the figure she pursued glowed with otherworldly light. Finally, it stopped, turning towards her.

Skye froze in her tracks.

She knew that face. It was the face of a boy she had last seen dead on a battlefield, blue eyes bleached silver in the dark. He said nothing as he stared at her, only smiled, those eyes twinkling like stars.

Skye fought against the weight of her tongue, swallowing down her disbelief.

"Cameron," she whispered, then found her voice. "Cameron!"

But the shadows either side of her slipped into the clearing, stealing his attention, draining his face of hope and replacing it with dread. "They're going to take me with them, Skye. They're going to make me fight you!"

"No!" Her voice was a choke of anguish, and she broke into a run, reaching for him. But grey hands wrapped around the white healer's uniform he wore, dragging him back amongst the trees.

Fear distorted his features, his face twisted in a cry. He reached out, trembling fingers outstretched towards her. "Help me, Skye!"

"Cameron!" His name tore from her throat, and she put on a spurt of speed, brushing his icy fingers with her own. Sparks crackled where their skin met. With a horrific cackle, the hands crept over his face, dragging him back into the shadows.

"Cameron!" she screamed, then a root caught her boot, sending her flying through the air, arms flailing, her heart in her throat.

She bolted upright, wrenching more screams from deep within her chest. She scratched at the tightness of her throat, kicking her legs to rid herself of the bindings tangled around her. The trees were gone, replaced by pitch dark, shadows and deeper shadows pressing on her retinas. Somewhere to her left, a door slammed open, a figure framed in the faint light beyond it.

"Skye!"

She choked, scrambling across the bed, kicking at the sheets again. The figure approached, and she snarled a warning, lightning flashing in her hands and blinding the intruder. And then she froze, letting the light die in her palms. It was Dean.

Dean was here. In her bedroom. With her. Her breath stabbed through her tight throat again as she gasped, slumping against the mattress as tears flooded hot and heavy down her cheeks. After a moment of shock, Dean sat on the mattress beside her, gathering her to him.

"She raised Cameron," she sobbed against him, arms wrapped tightly around his neck. "She brought him back from the dead."

Dean rubbed her back with soothing strokes. "It was just a dream, Skye. A nightmare."

"But what if it's not? What if she sent me the dream?"

"She can't send you dreams, Skye. You're the Telepath here."

"Not Alessia." She shook her head, meeting his eyes through the gloom. "Vala."

His hand paused on her back, uncertainty battling on his face. His thoughts went to Lindsey, and then spiralled into a chaos of horrific scenarios.

"Don't tell her about this," Skye murmured, seeing the doubts and dilemmas in his mind. "It would just upset her."

"She might know. She could use her Trace. Check the cemetery."

Skye shuddered, sitting up, angrily wiping her tears away with the back of her hand. "The cemetery is in occupied territory. There's no way for us to know." She took another struggling breath, rubbing her chest to try to relieve the tightness. She hoped it was just that, a dream. But her thoughts went back to the glamour Ivor Ronan had chosen to lure her onto the battlefield. The enemy knew what Cameron had meant to her, knew his death had triggered her rage. And as for Vala… the Seer had sent her prophetic dreams before. Did it have the same artificial shimmer? She wasn't sure. But one difference from all the other Vala dreams was that Vala hadn't been there. It was just herself, Cameron, and the faceless Undead.

"Don't tell Lindsey," she said, her voice firmer now. "And if Alessia has brought Cameron back, it won't be him. Not really." But her voice sounded more convincing than she felt.

***

Skye's head pounded, and she was getting nowhere. The Caplin soldiers waited outside the door in clusters, trickling in and out of the makeshift interrogation room one by one. Some were cooperative, even wanted to help, but most were hostile, their thoughts full of disgruntled inconvenience. No one wanted an intruder in their head, Skye could understand that. But the first Caplinite she Broke the day after the battle weighed on her, leaving her desperate to unravel the mystery of why he had wound up dying in a Ronan uniform and taking the truth with him.

Chairs and tables cluttered the space – it was normally some kind of classroom for fledgling cadets. Against the wall to her left, ever silent, sat Jennifer Dooley, shadowing Skye's gruelling routine and occasionally making notes. Most of the minds were unprotected, needing no Breaking, and Skye had gone through them quickly in the morning. But now, after her nightmare had torn her from much-needed sleep and her body and mind couldn't recover fast enough from the previous days' events, her Talent was beginning to lag. The double shot of whiskey she had sneaked in at lunch time to dull her headache and the throb of her still-healing ribs probably wasn't helping matters.

You could help me, Skye impatiently suggested between soldiers. Dooley cast her dark gaze on Skye.

I'm under strict instruction to check only the minds you check. There was a pause, and Dooley's straight mousy hair fell across her eyes. *Besides, Breaking minds is against my moral code.*

Moral code? Skye scoffed, putting her hands on her hips and taking a steadying breath. But she was in no mood to get into an argument with a do-gooder on her high horse. Instead, she glanced at the door. *Next.*

Another Caplin soldier skulked in, his jacket tied unprofessionally around his waist, the vest he wore sweat-stained. Skye frowned as he slumped down on the chair in front of her, hands in his pockets. Fuzz glistened on his top lip, and his blonde hair was buzzed short. He was eighteen at a push.

"Were you even on the battlefield that day?" she asked doubtfully.

The youngster shrugged, staring at the floor.

Skye's temper growled. "You either were or you weren't."

"I was." His voice was haughty.

Skye took a deep breath, counting in her head. "Do you behave this way in front of your commander?"

"Not really."

She ground her teeth, then dived into his mind, quickly gathering the information she needed, including his name and rank. She had half a mind to report him for his disgusting attitude, but she couldn't be bothered with the paperwork.

When she withdrew from the brat's mind, the door swung open behind her, and Skye turned her irritated gaze towards the interruption. But when she saw Thorsten Welch – Caplin's second Telepath – sweeping towards her, her stomach churned and a sour taste flooded her mouth. She straightened, her hands in fists at her sides.

"Hello, Bolton," said Welch, casting an imperious glance over the room, his telepathy brushing against hers like nails down a blackboard. "Made much headway today?"

Skye bared her teeth and took in the smug look on his chiselled, square face. He held himself loftily, oozing arrogance and power. "Why are you here?"

"Nice to see you too." He stopped at her side, running a hand through his tawny curls. "Caplin thought you could use a hand."

"Did he now?" Skye stuck her chin out, turning her head away to avoid breathing in the citrusy scent of his aftershave. Of course, Caplin had sent her old rival to check up on her. She knew full well it was part punishment, part mistrust.

He shrugged, muscle rippling beneath his cream-coloured shirt. "Two heads are better than one."

"Dr Dooley and I are doing just fine." Dooley remained silent in the corner, watching the exchange with her large, liquid eyes.

"Ahh, but why deprive our fellow Telepath of the chance to learn from the Dream Team?"

Skye bit back a sneer, while a blush warmed Dooley's face.

"I'm not a Mind Breaker, sir," said the quiet woman, her voice thin.

"I can tell," said Welch dismissively, turning his gaze back to Skye. "So go on, Bolton, what's the situation?"

She met his assessing stare, the malicious glint in his honey-coloured eyes all too familiar. She looked down at the soldier before her instead, who was watching them as silently as Dooley had been. "All loyal protectors of our esteemed president, so far."

"Good news then," he said, slipping his hands into his pockets. "It would be such a shame to have to execute soldiers when Alessia Ronan's corpse army still ravages the country."

"Send the next one in," Skye told the soldier before her, and the kid slipped off his chair without hesitation.

"The next two," said Welch, and the soldier paused. "We can tag-team."

"I said I don't need you."

"Don't you, Skye?" Sly charm dripped like syrup, eyes glittering dangerously. "What, scared I'll do a better job?"

"In your dreams," she shot back, folding her arms. Welch knew full well he was Caplin's second Telepath in practice as well as in theory. And she would never let him forget it.

Despite her protests, Welch remained in the room, his jibes grating on her already rattled nerves. But in her exhaustion, she gave up trying to resist him, agreeing to get through them two by two. But the competition gave her a spur of momentum, and she refused to let him outnumber her even if he hadn't been at this all day. And it gave her some cold satisfaction to make Dooley work double time as well, especially after her judgemental comment earlier.

A siren rang somewhere in the building, the signal for the end of the training day. Skye turned away as the last soldier slipped out the door, carefully dabbing a tissue at her threatening nosebleed before anyone else could notice. She was all too aware of movement behind her as Welch sauntered around the room, and she fiddled with the silver chain around her neck as she sipped slowly from a bottle of water, coating her dry mouth.

"I can train you," Welch said to Dooley, his voice heavy with self-importance. "Telepathic Talents shouldn't be wasted."

"I already have a career, sir," said Dooley, and Skye glanced around to see her gathering her notebook and her own water bottle. Despite her small stature, she stood straight, meeting Welch's eye. "I can assure you, my Talent is not wasted."

And with that, she left the room, the door snapping shut behind her. Skye couldn't help her smirk at the put down. But when Welch's gaze found Skye's, she quickly lowered her own, feeling seventeen again as she screwed the lid back onto her bottle and set it down.

"You need to let this go," he said, his presence stealing the air from the room. "It's a waste of time."

"I suppose Caplin told you to say that?" She forced her voice to stay light, shoving chairs beneath the table to give herself something, anything else to concentrate on.

"Be careful, Skye. You're on thin ice with Caplin."

She took a tight breath as she continued her tidying, playing for time. Then, with no more excuses to avoid his scrutiny, she finally turned to look at him. He was leaning against a table, arms crossed over his broad chest, his sleeves rolled up to his elbows. He was watching her with that infuriating curve to his lips, and a spray of curls fell over his forehead, curls she had once lovingly run her fingers through. *Lovingly*. She sneered at the memory, at the way he had gone from making her feel like she was everything, to treating her like she was nothing.

"Unlike you, I don't need Caplin."

He laughed, flashing a wolfish grin that had once had a very different effect on her. "You think the Forces will follow you just because you're the Lux? Don't kid yourself, Skye. They're not going to lay down their lives for a drama queen."

"That's rich, coming from the guy who threw a hissy fit when his student surpassed her master."

The grin faltered, and a muscle feathered in his jaw. "A student who forgets the master taught her everything she knows. Before me, you wasted your Talent on gossip and manipulation. I made you what you are, Skye."

"Keep telling yourself that." She tilted her head, her mouth twisted in a cocky smirk. But in many ways, he was right. He *had* taught her, trained her, shown her every way to break down a person's mental defences and fight her way into their mind. Aside from herself, she knew of no other Telepath with strength and skill like his. He used to be Caplin's favourite for a reason, until Skye came along and toppled him off his pedestal. And when she wounded his pride, he repaid her by breaking her heart.

"So, what's your plan when you realise Caplin had nothing to do with the mutiny?"

"I'm sure the Nox won't keep us waiting around too long before she launches her next attack." She gave him a disdainful glance up and down, crossing her arms. "Perhaps you'll join us on the battlefield, use those muscles for something other than flexing them in the mirror."

He tossed the curls from his eyes in cold amusement. "I don't need to wave a gun around to feel useful."

“No, I suppose licking Caplin’s shiny shoes is keeping you pretty occupied.”

“Someone has to, since you’re so busy sleeping with the enemy.”

Skye’s smirk grew. “I prefer to call it diplomacy.”

His jaw tightened, eyes boring into her, his telepathy a possessive caress. “So it’s true then? A Ronan of all people is getting my sloppy seconds now?”

Her rage spiked at his choice of words, and she prowled towards him until she stopped an inch from his face. “I’m no one’s sloppy seconds, *Thorsten*.” She spat the name that had once rolled like a poem off her tongue. “I’m a feast to a starving man.”

He scoffed, his breath warming her face. The citrus and spice of his aftershave clouded her senses once again, a scent that drenched the countless memories she kept locked in cages in the fortress of her mind. “I suppose he’d have to be starving, to go near toxic waste.”

She gave a hollow laugh. “It must be so nice inside that deluded small mind of yours.”

Welch’s lips curled, but his eyes were hard. He held her gaze as he boldly lifted a hand to cup her cheek, his thumb brushing her cheekbone. Skye’s jaw set beneath his touch, her fury rearing in response.

“Just remember, Skye: it doesn’t matter how many hearts you break, or how many men you string along. I will *always* be your first.”

Her teeth ground together as memories burst from their cages and hurtled unbidden down the hallways of her mind – secret looks and stolen kisses, days out to new places and nights alone together in his apartment, endless conversations and laughter and hope, all tinged with a longing so all-consuming that it ached. And with the good came more of the bad: the shaming, the sneers, the broken promises, and the final straw that brought her pride and self-esteem crumbling to the ground – a whisper of love in the dark that he never returned. But she buried her pain with anger, raising her own hand to the one that held her face, wrapping her fingers around his wrist and pressing down on the thin bones beneath his hand. Hard. She was pleased to see his jaw twitch with a wince.

"And you remember *this*: if you ever lay a finger on me again, I'll be the last woman you ever touch."

A soft warning snarl escaped him, and he tried to pull his arm back. Skye's grip only tightened, nails digging into the soft flesh of his wrist as she held his glare in a challenge, then she let him go, sauntering towards the door.

"Is that a threat?" His voice was as cocky as ever, but as she threw him a last glance, he was rubbing his wrist.

Her smirk was back, dangerous and deadly. "It's a promise." And with that, she twisted the doorknob and threw open the door, letting it slam behind her.

Chapter Fifty-Four

ROXANNE SUMMERS

"Darling," said Camilla, waving a cigarette at them across the table in the crowded pub garden. "I've waited so long to meet the famous Roxanne. Tell me, how do you keep your skin so youthful and glowy? I bet it's that Talent of yours. Oliver looks ten years younger too."

But Roxanne could only stare in horror, her every nerve ending screaming at her to flee from this woman who had committed so many atrocities. This woman who may have been committing such atrocities on her daughter, who might have made her little girl – no, she couldn't think that way. If she imagined what horrors Amber was enduring at this woman's hands, there was no way she could get through this meeting with a cool head. She wanted to scream, cry, wrap her bare hands around Camilla's neck, snap that bony body into pieces, but she knew she wouldn't get within an inch of her without losing her life, or Amber's, for that matter. So she endured it, the fear barely letting her hear over the rush in her ears, or see through the fog that clouded her mind. And Camilla Linden knew it.

"We're not here for niceties," snapped Lindsey. "Tell her what you need to say."

“Hello to you too, Lindsey dear,” said Camilla, her cruel gaze darting to her. “Tut tut, you used to be such a nice, polite child. What happened?”

“People like you happened,” Lindsey retorted, but Camilla’s smile only widened.

“I’m sorry you feel that way, dear. Your mummy and I used to be such good friends, and I know she would be so upset to hear about you acting this way.”

Lindsey’s hands curled into fists, and Roxanne reached out, laying a hand atop Lindsey’s to soothe her. They were sitting in a quieter corner of the garden, glamours surrounding them to disguise their faces and distort their voices, but she didn’t want to draw the patrons’ attention even so. “Please,” she said, fighting to be polite to the monstrous woman, “how can I get my daughter back?”

Camilla leaned back in her chair and smoked, watching with that cruel smile and shrewd eyes, looking from one to the other. Finally, she pointed at Devan with the hand that held her cigarette. “You sure you want me to tell you in front of Handsome here?”

“I’m going nowhere,” said Devan in that calm and level voice of his.

“Roxy, dear? It was you I was asking.”

“He’s staying,” said Roxanne, cringing at the nickname.

“Suit yourself,” said Camilla with a shrug, before taking a long drink of her gin cocktail. She took her time setting the glass down, then finished her cigarette and stubbed it out in a glass ashtray. “I want the Lux.”

Roxanne sat there dumbfounded. It had crossed her mind that Camilla might demand exactly that, but hearing it aloud made her already churning stomach give a series of painful backflips. She looked at Devan, who was doing his best to hide his concern, then glanced at Lindsey, who was still glaring at Camilla. And then Camilla herself began to laugh.

"You should see your faces," she exclaimed, making a show of wiping tears of mirth from her eyes, smudging her thick mascara. "As if any of you could come close to tricking Skye Bolton. Don't get me wrong, I'm not her biggest fan, but I know she's not that much of an idiot."

"This isn't funny," said Lindsey, her voice cutting through the laughter.

"Perhaps not to you," said Camilla as her chuckles subsided. "But I know that's too much to ask. Your sweet daughter might be worth the Lux to you, but I doubt all your little friends would agree."

"So what do you really want?" asked Devan, still calm.

"I'll tell you what," she said, stirring the toothpick and olive around her glass, then taking it out and waving it at Roxanne, "I'll offer you the same as I offered our friend the Lux. I want Caplin dead. Or handed over as a prisoner. And to show you just how generous I am, I'll release all the prisoners I hold, whether it's you or Bolton who carries out the deed. I can't say fairer than that."

Roxanne sat frozen, mulling over Camilla's words. Skye's behaviour towards Caplin finally started to make sense. She wasn't sure exactly how Skye intended to reach the goal Camilla had set her, but it certainly seemed like she was trying to alienate and isolate him. But how could Roxanne get to him? Aside from shooting him across the table at the next council meeting, Caplin was untouchable.

"How would that benefit you?" asked Devan. "And why only Caplin? What about others, like Caspar Ronan?"

"How it benefits me is my business," she said, popping the olive into her mouth. She then gave a wry smile. "As for Caspar, we have other plans for him."

She felt another stab of dread at the mention of plans for Caspar, wondering whether they were plans for revenge, or else to turn his loyalties around again. They had been in the same friendship circle as well as political allies since youth, after all.

"Do we have a time limit?" Roxanne asked, finding her voice with difficulty.

Camilla shrugged. "Until your daughter kicks the bucket, I suppose."

Roxanne's entire world spun, and she gripped the edge of the table as the bench seemed to slide beneath her, her vision blurring. Beside her, Lindsey half jumped out of her seat. "If you're hurting her…" she said, her voice low and dangerous.

The woman laughed, apparently unphased by Lindsey's threat. "I told Bolton I'll honour the deal unless we get to Caplin first. And then, well, maybe we'll make a new deal, or maybe we'll execute our prisoners. We're at war after all, our resources only stretch so far." She then took another drink, holding Roxanne's gaze over the rim of her glass.

"What about a prisoner exchange?" asked Devan after Lindsey sat back down.

Camilla gave a snort. "You have no one of value. We might have considered your father," she said, nodding at Lindsey, "before he stabbed us in the back."

Roxanne swallowed and looked at Lindsey, whose expression was unreadable. She knew exactly what the opposition would do to Oliver if they got hold of him.

"We will need to discuss the matter amongst ourselves," said Devan, and Roxanne didn't miss the hint of strain beneath his calm exterior.

"Oh, I wouldn't share this information with too many ears. You never know who might stab *you* in the back," Camilla said as she took another sip. "And you might want to remember that before you take too long deciding what to do about Caplin."

"Is there something you want to share with us?" asked Lindsey, eyeing Camilla suspiciously. Roxanne wondered if her Trace had picked up something the rest of them couldn't detect.

"Oh, just some friendly advice," said Camilla with her feline smirk. "Don't trust anyone who isn't family. And even then, well, you only have to look at the Ronans…"

They all continued to eye the woman as she snickered and drank, until Devan finally placed a hand on Roxanne's beneath the table. "We'll be in touch," he said, getting up. Roxanne followed suit, her legs shaky. Lindsey glared at Camilla for a long moment, then got up too.

"One more thing," said Camilla, and Roxanne's head whipped back around, meeting that malicious gaze. "Don't drag your heels too much. Sweet Amber doesn't take too well to imprisonment."

If it weren't for Devan's hand on her elbow, Roxanne was sure she would have fallen as her world swayed dangerously again.

Chapter Fifty-Five

Amber Summers

Time didn't mean anything. Not when they left her in the dark, starving, cold and numb. The only indication that time passed at all was the fragments of daylight that glowed through the gaps in the blinds, and the occasions when Amber stumbled to use the bathroom. The water from the taps tasted rusty, but it was all she had to drink, and the meals were few and far between, leaving her insides still gnawing with hunger even after she finished whatever scant morsels they brought her.

But worse than the cold and the dark and the hunger was when the red-haired woman walked through the door.

The torture had been that inexplicable pain deep in her bones at first. Amber could only assume it was the woman's Talent, causing pain with no trace of injury. And then there was the Ignis. When they pulled off her shoes and socks and he put his burning palms to the soles of her feet, she had vomited a watery bile that soaked into the floorboards, and no one came to clean up afterwards. Her feet had hurt until she fell into a fevered sleep, and when she awoke, they were numb and cold. In the dark she couldn't inspect the damage, but perhaps it was better that she couldn't see what they had done.

She always heard the footsteps before they arrived, *her* high heels and *his* heavy thud. Sometimes they didn't come for her, and she heard others screaming through the walls. But today, when they stopped outside her door, she scrambled to the other side of the room, whimpering as she curled up in the corner.

"Hello, little bird," came the saccharine voice that chilled her to the bone. "Are you ready to sing for me today?"

The light came on, blinding and bright, and Amber shut her eyes, pressing her arm to her face. The woman clucked.

"No need to hide, I bring news. Your mummy came to see me today."

Amber's trembling stilled for a moment, and she tried to open her eyes, squinting through her filthy hair. As she looked up, she found the woman looming over her, a dark shadow except for the orange glow of her hair in the stark light. The man remained motionless by the door, watching and waiting.

"She's very worried about you, but I told her we're getting along just fine, and you're looking forward to seeing her again."

The woman spoke as though she were a child, in that voice a pitch or two higher that people used when speaking to babies. Her captor crouched down before her, brushing Amber's hair out of her face and lifting her chin with one finger. Amber shrank back from her touch, but her head bumped the wall.

"There there," she said, stroking her cheek with that same finger. Amber's breathing turned ragged, afraid of the pain that was sure to come at any moment. "Mummy knows what she has to do to get you back. And I made a special bargain with her. If Mummy isn't brave enough to get me what I want, well, I asked the Lux to get it for me instead, since she wants her daddy back so badly."

"What?" Amber murmured, struggling to make sense of the woman's words.

"That's right. Mummy and the Lux will have to work together to get me my prize, and then I'll let all of you go free. Or… what's left of you, at least." She grinned down at her, red lipstick stains on her teeth, and her fingers gripped her chin tightly. Amber whimpered again.

"You know, your new sister told me not to hurt you," she said, and Amber could only stare, torn between confusion over how the woman could possibly know she had a sister, and hope that Lindsey was fighting for her too. "But I don't think I need to worry too much about her. She's all bark and no bite, that one." She laughed, a cruel, merciless sound, and then reached down to the belt around her waist, drawing a short, shiny knife from amongst a deadly assortment. "I think it's time you got properly acquainted with some of my friends here, since we probably won't get to play together much longer."

"Please no," Amber gasped, fear closing around her throat. She instinctively put out her hands as though to push the woman away, but was too afraid to touch her.

"Where should we start?" she said, still gripping her jaw, turning her head to the side to inspect her profile. "It would be a shame to ruin your pretty face. You look so much like your mother, you know? I'm not surprised Oliver went off with her. *Sheridan* let bitterness make her ugly."

"How…?" she murmured, unable to form the question in her fear.

"How do I know?" the woman cooed, turning her head the other way, caressing her cheek with the cold blade. "Hmm, I suppose you could call it women's intuition. Dear Lindsey was far more upset than a mere acquaintance would be, and I know how cosy your parents were back in the day. Oliver might think he's a private man, but he can't hide his emotions from me."

So, she was an Empath then. Now that Amber could see the clues, her own Tracing ability confirmed as much. This stranger was controlling her fear, her anxiety, her pain, and increasing them to an agonising level.

"I'm surprised Oliver hasn't come knocking himself, which makes me think Mummy and Lindsey haven't told him about our little meeting today. Then again, he never did have much backbone." She ran her hand into her hair then, stroking through the knots for a moment, and then gripping tightly and pulling her head back. Amber flinched as she felt the knife against her throat, but the blade didn't press down, only drifted slowly lower, until the point reached her collarbone, and then travelled along it. "As I was saying, I won't touch your face. But your arms… you don't really need both of those, I suppose. Are you left or right-handed?"

Amber began to cry. She couldn't help it. Her fear was rising again, along with a twisting in her stomach, bile threatening to come up. She watched as the woman dragged the knife down her left arm, the point snagging on the thin wool of her cardigan. Was she going to cut her arm off? Would she really do that?

"Well? Left or right? Or should I choose?"

She couldn't speak, the tears blinding her, sliding down her face, the choice impossible to make. The woman was going to hurt her regardless, what difference did it make?

"Fine. I'll assume you're right-handed." And with that she grabbed her left wrist, shoving up her sleeve to her elbow.

"Please—" Amber yelped as the cold knife pressed against the tender flesh of her forearm. But the woman was done teasing her. The knife sliced in, slowly and deliberately, and she screamed as it cut through her skin.

She couldn't look, turning her face away and biting down on her fist as her tormentor cut away more of her flesh. The tang of copper filled her nostrils, and the woman's quiet laughter bled into her ears. She began to feel faint, and she let it wash over her, preferring to be unconscious than endure this torture. But suddenly the woman stopped, lowering the knife and lifting Amber's arm up to her face. After a moment of stillness, Amber looked too, finding her arm slick with blood.

"You're a Healer?" said the woman, looking her in the eye. She wasn't laughing now. She wasn't even smiling. Her act was replaced with a look of disbelief.

"No," said Amber, looking from the woman to her wounded arm, unsure why she was being asked the question.

The woman wiped away the blood, but although Amber braced herself for the pain as she touched her cut, none came. And then she dropped her arm, grabbing her ankle instead, standing to inspect her burnt foot.

"You're a Healer," she confirmed, her eyes narrowed at Amber, the statement like an accusation. She let her leg drop too, and Amber sat up, taking her foot in her hands and turning it upwards to see the sole. Sure enough, only pale, unbroken skin stretched across her foot, unblemished except for a coating of dust from the floor.

"But I'm not," she said in confusion, looking at her arm as well, rubbing away the blood in search of the injury. The skin was tender, pink like scar tissue, but even that was fading before her eyes. Had she imagined the injuries, or was she hallucinating now?

"Clearly you are," said the woman, and Amber looked up to see she was smiling, the kind of smile that knocked her sick to her stomach. "Well then, there's nothing stopping me from cutting your pretty face now."

Chapter Fifty-Six

ALESSIA RONAN

It was a bright morning, full of golden sunlight accompanied by the scent of wet grass and wildflowers. The temperature was still cool, but finally carried a long-overdue hint of summer. Alessia stood on the terrace behind the castle, surveying the emerald lawns and trees that swayed in a light breeze. Inhaling deeply, she savoured the air that expanded her lungs.

Five days had passed since her mortifying outburst in front of her allies and advisors. She had shut herself away from the humid chill that had lingered in the air, receiving her visitors and informants in Brydon Marsden's stuffy parlour. Pierce had continued her conquest on her behalf, now claiming territories in the Midlands and chipping away at the shaky borders that the allies struggled to hold onto. The big cities still had yet to fall, but he promised her it was only a matter of time.

She had spent her time dwelling on the increasing number of bodies Nathanael had collected for her, ready to be raised little by little to add to her army. And when she wasn't dwelling, she was plotting with Arthur Linden and his informants, putting a plan in place that she was certain would crumble the alliance at its foundations. But she had foundations of her own to lay.

Alessia stepped down from the terrace, her boots crunching on the gravel path that led through ornamental flower beds. Lucien's eyes glittered from where he sat on a stone bench beneath a tree.

"Good morning, Madam President," came his greeting. For once, his face held no amusement or mockery as he studied her. On his lap, he held a gnarled length of wood that ended in a twisted cluster of roots. His hands stroked slowly over the pale grain, using his mirrored Terra Talent to smooth it. "How are you feeling?"

"Much better, thank you," she replied, caught somewhat off guard by his concern, not to mention his unusual activity.

"Do you require another treatment today?" His ever-changing eyes continued to scrutinise her, and she swallowed at his uncharacteristic display of kindness. No pain or irritation plagued her now. His daily visits had eased the condition considerably, as had the infusion that a maid brought every night.

"I feel fine, thank you." She watched his hands move across the wood, mesmerised for a moment as it transformed from rough to polished, his fingers passing over it inch by inch. "What are you doing?"

He held her gaze for a moment longer, then his eyes dropped to the twisted root. He continued his work, his movements almost sensual. "Vala instructed me to make her this staff."

Alessia crossed her arms as ice trickled into her stomach, twisting into a knot which she hated to realise was jealousy. Vala had sourced Lucien to train *her*, yet here he was, creating a beautiful gift for the Seer, his hands and eyes drifting over the wood with unmistakable reverence.

"What is it for?" she asked, fighting hard to keep her voice even.

"It's a root cut from the oldest willow tree on this island. Once it is polished, the cluster will hold quartz and obsidian." His fingers brushed the twisted end, where the roots intertwined like an elaborate cage. "I will then engrave it with runes to mark its intention. Once that is done, it needs to be bathed in a running stream for the three nights of the full moon, to activate its power."

Alessia blinked, staring as she made sense of his words. He spoke of Old Craft magic, the sort most scoffed at nowadays. And as he sat there, with his expensive jeans, leather jacket and slicked back black hair, he looked for all the world like one of those modern people who would scoff at it too. Yet here he was, practising it.

"But what is it for?" she asked again, impatience adding a bite to her words.

He finally looked back up at her, and held her gaze for a long moment. "It's to strip the Lux of her Talents."

A hush filled her ears, drowning out the chittering of birds and whisper of the wind. Only her heartbeat thumped, low and fearful, deep in the hollow of her chest. The moment dragged on, keeping Alessia trapped in the intensity of his gaze, his eyes now tinged violet. She finally found her tongue. "Why would you do that?"

Lucien let out a sigh, turning on the bench and carefully lowering the staff to the grass at the foot of the tree. "Skye Bolton is a Lux. Vala wishes to harvest her power."

A frown creased Alessia's brow, and her heartbeat picked up speed. "I intend to kill the Lux. What use could her Talents be?"

"You aren't the only one who is curious about the transfer of Talents. Have you never wondered at Vala's power? You know the Sight isn't her only Talent."

He spoke the truth. Alessia knew Vala could heal, move through space without the aid of portals, and plant dreams in people's sleeping minds. She had yet to find out what more she could do. "So, she wants the Talents for herself?"

"Perhaps," said Lucien, bracing his elbows on his knees, casual once more. "Or perhaps she will keep it for a viable Talentless to wield. Or give it to you. The staff will be able to store Talents as well as mirror them."

Alessia gritted her teeth, repulsed by the suggestion. "I have no wish to possess that woman's Talents."

The corner of his lips tugged up in a cold smile. "Regardless, those Talents are not to be wasted. Lux do not come along very often."

She raised her head higher and narrowed her eyes suspiciously. "How will it work?"

"Vala will wait until she is at her weakest. Before you land the killing blow, she will step in and take the Talents. Mirroring normally requires physical contact for a Talent to be harvested, but this won't. The crystals will enhance its reach."

Alessia let herself indulge in a fantasy for a brief moment: Skye Bolton on her knees, panting through the agony of broken bones and bleeding wounds. Perhaps even begging for her life. After the way she had defiantly stood up to her grandfather, Alessia wanted nothing more than to see her brought so low. "What if I kill her before Vala can use the staff?"

He shrugged. "I suppose we'll have to see if Talents can be harvested from Undead."

Her own lips curled as another image entered her head: the ghost of Bolton's mind trapped in her reanimated corpse, a slave to Alessia's bidding, forced to watch the destruction of everything she held dear. If all went according to plan, both fantasies would come true. Preferably sooner rather than later.

"Anyway," said Lucien, rising to his feet in a fluid motion. "We have *a lot* of work to do if you intend to defeat the Lux."

The icy knot in her stomach tightened with fear this time. She narrowed her eyes as he loomed above her, standing too close. "What do you mean?"

"I did as you asked. I watched her fight. Took note of her strengths, her weaknesses. I hate to tell you this, but she is powerful, Alessia."

She held his gaze, noting no amusement dancing in his eyes. Only the harsh truth that she didn't want to believe. "More powerful than I am?"

He inclined his head, a predator assessing an opponent. "In terms of Talents, she is your equal." He paused, and Alessia was all too aware of her pulse pounding in her ears. "But with her experience and physical strength, she has an advantage over you."

Another twist clenched her gut. Without a word, Lucien held out his hand to her, his fingers slightly curved, inviting her touch. Remembering the way Vala had made the same gesture, Alessia tentatively pressed her fingertips to his.

The sunny morning melted away, replaced with the oppressive haze of the battlefield, smoke hanging heavy in the air. From a vantage point close to the ground, hidden behind a pile of bodies, Alessia witnessed the Ronan mutiny through Lucien's eyes. She saw Skye Bolton slash, stab, and shoot her attackers like a savage. There was blood everywhere. *Everywhere.* Far away, back in her body, Alessia took a sudden step back, breaking her connection to Lucien's hand, unable to keep watching.

She turned away from him before he could see her distress, clenching her eyes shut and curling her hands into fists to hide the trembling. Scarlet was still imprinted behind her eyelids – spraying across faces, dripping down a knife hilt, pooling in the mud to be trampled through. And the person who was the source of so much bloodshed was stronger than her, more experienced than her, and much, much more vicious. Alessia fought a shudder, gulping down air.

"If you expect to defeat her, you can't let yourself be beaten down to the dregs of your Talent," said Lucien at her back. "Because when her Talent is spent, that is what she will resort to, and if you have no darkness left to fight her, she will kill you with her bare hands."

She wrapped her arms around herself, taking steadying breaths to try to push the violent vision from her mind. Deep within her, the ice of her deathly Talent crept through her gut. Whether it was in fear or challenge, she wasn't sure. "So, I need to kill her quickly."

"Yes."

She raised her head high and turned back to Lucien. "What did you gather about how she fights with her Talent?"

Lucien grimaced. "I get the impression she's been training with your uncle. She was familiar with the way darkness reacts with electricity, and some of her moves echo his."

Alessia hissed in disgust, and her darkness riled up beneath her skin. Another stab to her wounded pride. It was bad enough that Caspar had taken the Lux's side, but to *train* her? She suppressed another shudder, afraid of what weaknesses of Alessia's her uncle was sharing with her enemy. "Then you will teach me everything you know about Electricae. Everything I need to know to beat her."

"Of course," he said silkily. Bright strands of light crackled between his fingers, drawing Alessia's gaze. She watched it for a moment, until another question reared its head.

"If you never set eyes on Bolton until the battle, from whom did you mirror the lightning?"

An unknown emotion flickered in his eyes, but before she could decipher it, he masked it with his usual amusement. "My mother."

Alessia frowned. "I always thought you never knew your mother."

He shrugged, watching the electricity buzz between his fingers. "I can't say I got to know her much in the minutes before she died. That's when I took her Talents."

Her confusion mingled with curiosity. "You watched your mother die?"

But the light in his hand fizzed out as he closed his fingers into a fist and buried it in his pocket. "I do have some good news about the Lux's Talents." His eyes flashed as he changed the subject, and Alessia bristled. "Bolton relies heavily on her telepathy when fighting, almost like a sixth sense. But she cannot sense the Undead, meaning she's less aware of their approach. We can consider this a handicap."

Alessia took a deep breath, her darkness ebbing a little in relief. "So I incorporate Undead when I face her."

He nodded as his lips curled. "You should employ every weapon in your arsenal, Miss Ronan."

She held his gaze, the enormity of everything he had told her weighing on her. Slowly, she stepped into a practised fighting stance. "And are *you* part of my arsenal, Lucien?"

His smirk grew as he fell into a stance of his own, electricity zapping once more between his curled fingers. "You don't even need to ask."

Chapter Fifty-Seven

PHAEDRA RONAN

Phaedra shivered as shadows whipped around her, tugging her long dark hair into tangles and stirring her black skirts, hissing like serpents. She wrapped her arms around herself, her embroidered sleeves too tight, tapering to long, delicate hands. Her nails were no longer bitten and covered in chipped polish, but elegant and buffed to translucent perfection. And she was taller, so much taller, power emanating from her on waves of darkness and death. But as she stared at the shadows unfurling like smoke from hands that weren't hers, the creak of snapping twigs dragged her gaze upwards, and fear dropped like a lump of ice into her stomach.

Her father and mother stood before her, tattered clothes draping their skeletal figures, grave dust clinging to their faces and hair. Phaedra gasped as they moved towards her, and close behind them stepped Maggie and Kiaran, Sally and Jemima, all staring at her with glazed eyes. Unbidden, her shadows unravelled towards them, embracing them, welcoming them.

Beyond the shuffling corpses of her loved ones, a glow drew her gaze, and Caspar stood, his shoulders wreathed in flames instead of shadows, fire licking at his skin and turning him slowly to ash. His eyes, too, were glazed, black ice glistening in his grey face. As she stared in horror, his features continuing to burn and disintegrate, another figure came up behind him, placing gnarled hands on Caspar's shoulders, a cruel leer painting his pale face: her grandfather.

"You're dead," she whispered, a violent shudder tearing down her spine.

"No sweetheart," came a woman's voice, and Phaedra looked up to see her mother reaching out with bones for fingers. Her dark hair trailed past her waist, drifting with the shadows. "*You* are dead."

"Welcome to the afterlife…" came her grandfather's chilling voice as he stepped through the crumbling ash that had been Caspar, "*Alessia.*"

Phaedra jerked awake with her heart pounding through her chest and a face full of Ombra's hair. Twitchy with fright, she sat up, her surroundings barely visible in the faint light from the moon. At her side, Ombra's breathing hitched and she turned, giving Phaedra a glimpse of her sleeping face. Phaedra studied her for a moment, making sure that she was, indeed, alive and well, not a corpse like her Undead family in her dream.

Shivering and reassured that they were both safe, Phaedra lay down again, curling up close to Ombra's warmth, an arm around her waist. The images from her nightmare hadn't quite faded. She still saw the echoes layered over the moonlight slanting through the curtain, still heard her grandfather's words chilling her to the bone.

She shivered again, her chest tight at the thought of what Alessia could now do, at what she might do with that power. At her reaction, Ombra's breathing changed, and next moment she laced her fingers through Phaedra's.

"You okay?" she mumbled, her voice thick with sleep.

"Hmm," was all Phaedra could reply, planting a reassuring kiss on her girlfriend's bare shoulder.

Ombra paused, waiting for more. But when Phaedra didn't elaborate, she turned, facing her and wrapping her arms around her. She could just about make out the glow of the moonlight reflecting in her eyes as she studied her. "What's up?"

"Just dreams," Phaedra murmured, tightening her arms around her. On several occasions since the battle, Ombra had woken up thrashing with nightmares too. It had been comforting to know that Phaedra wasn't the only one struggling with recent events, but she hated seeing Ombra in such a state.

"Same again?"

Phaedra nodded, brushing hair from Ombra's face, kissing her cheeks and her nose. Already, the horrific visions of her dream were fading, chased away by Ombra's presence.

"At least Caspar's back now," Ombra said, sleepily returning her kisses. "One less thing to worry about."

Phaedra tried not to think of the crumbling image of him in her dream. It was a relief to have her uncle back at the lake house, even if the perimeter was heavily guarded and any visitors had to be signed in by the soldiers.

"Let's sleep," Ombra said, stifling a yawn and running her fingers gently through Phaedra's hair, the action soothing her. "Or you'll be grumpy at training tomorrow."

"Speak for yourself," Phaedra mumbled, snuggling up to Ombra again and waiting for sleep to claim her.

***

Phaedra frowned at the soldiers through the living room window as the sun sank towards the horizon, casting their long shadows across the garden. There were four of them: two from Caplin's Forces, and two from the Resistance. And they changed four times a day, one soldier from each army watching the house, the other two guarding the perimeter in case anyone tried to come in.

"Watching them won't make them go away," Caspar called, the smell of chicken and garlic filling the warmly lit kitchen and living room. Phaedra peered through the archway at him, noting the amusement on his face as he stood at the stove.

"It's just so stupid how they still think you did it. It's obvious it was Alessia's scheming." She entered the kitchen and leaned on the counter, watching Caspar toss greens into a steamer. To her immense relief, he was the picture of health aside from some lingering tiredness, not the ashen, crumbling corpse from her dream. She shivered, then pushed away the memory of her nightmare, frowning at the greens. "I don't like broccoli."

"Did Maggie make you eat it?" he asked with a raised eyebrow.

She wrinkled her nose. "All the time."

A nostalgic smile curved his lips as he set the steamer on the stove. "She used to tease me for leaving my broccoli."

"Did she tell you that you wouldn't grow up big and strong as a tree trunk if you didn't eat it?" She tried to put on a mock scowl, but tears stung her eyes, thinking of all the silly things the housekeeper used to tell her.

"I was almost your age when she started working for us, but yes, she did." Caspar was silent for a moment longer, his eyes glazed with distant memories, then he let out a sigh, giving her a sad smile. "Dinner is nearly ready. Could you set the table?"

Phaedra nodded, blinking back her tears as she grabbed cutlery and glasses and took them into the dining room, laying the table and lighting candles. They were soon tucking into roast lemon chicken with garlic potatoes and greens. Phaedra even gobbled up the broccoli when Caspar said there was chocolate mousse for dessert.

"Has Skye been in touch today?" Phaedra asked as she spooned the last of the mousse out of her bowl.

"She has. Same old."

"Gee, I thought Telepaths could just jump into people's heads."

"If only it were that simple. Soldiers are trained to withstand mental attacks and invasions when they reach a certain level. If the person responsible is still alive, they're hiding their mind pretty well."

"Will they train me?" It sounded like a pretty cool skill to have.

"If they want to trust you with secret information, then yes, probably." Her uncle smiled at her enthusiasm as he drank the last of his wine. The evening was mild, the window ajar to let some air flow through, bringing with it the scent of summer. Phaedra hoped the warmer weather was here to stay, after what felt like months of drizzle. Occasionally a moth wandered in, and then proceeded to flit around the candles on the table and Welsh dresser behind Caspar.

"Well, they might," she said, waggling her eyebrows. "I am an experienced spy, after all."

"And what if they ask you to spy on me?" His eyes twinkled with mischief, but Phaedra's own amusement faltered.

"I wouldn't. You're not like Dad and Alessia." They hadn't spoken much about her traitorous past since she had first told him, the topic making her fidget in her seat.

Caspar's face turned grave. "I might not be like them, but I'm not going to pretend with you, Phee. I still worked for them. Still did things or obeyed orders I'm not proud of. So I don't blame the allies for not trusting me."

Phaedra nodded solemnly. "But the way you've been since we left Alessia… I know you're a good person."

He was silent for a long moment, his face a neutral mask. "I try my best. But if protecting you means I have to fight someone else, I wouldn't hesitate. Evcn if it means fighting your sister."

She swallowed, thinking back to the wound Alessia's darkness had left on his shoulder and the spiderweb scar that remained. She hoped it would never come to that. She hoped he would never have to face Alessia again. If she could hurt even him, there was no guarantee he could walk away a second time.

"Anyway, enough doom and gloom." Caspar got up, gathering dishes. "I suppose you want a second helping of dessert."

"There's more?" Phaedra exclaimed, jumping to her feet and snatching up her dessert bowl.

But before she could take a step, any thought of more dessert was blown from her mind by an explosion that pierced her eardrums and shook the floor beneath her.

Phaedra landed in a heap on the floor, smashing crockery loud in her ears. She lay winded, her heart hammering and her ears ringing. She stared around, unable to comprehend why there was suddenly a gap in the wall, the wallpaper torn away to reveal crumbling bare brick, the air thick with dust and… and…

"Phaedra, get out!" Caspar choked. She looked around frantically, then finally spotted him through the table legs. His features were crumpled with pain.

"Caspar!" she gasped, scrambling around the table, barely noticing that her hands were bleeding. But the sight she saw stole any further words she had been about to say, as did the dust and smoke that filled her throat.

Through the inexplicable gap in the wall, flames flickered on the ceiling, smoke billowing into the dining room. And on the floor, crushing Caspar's legs, was the fallen Welsh dresser.

Phaedra spluttered, but not before dropping to her uncle's side, broken crockery crunching beneath her trainers as she flapped. The vision from her nightmare suddenly felt very, very real: Caspar consumed by flame, reduced to ash.

"Get out!" he urged, his shirt pulled up to his mouth so he could speak. He fumbled with something in his pocket and handed her a plain silver ring. "Call Skye."

"But you—"

"I'm trapped. Get help."

"I can't—"

"Out the window. Go!"

Deaf to her uncle's commands, she pocketed the ring and stepped over him, trying to lift the dresser. But it wouldn't budge, not even a fraction, and as she breathed in, her lungs filled with smoke again.

"Phaedra! Go!"

She began to cry, but he was right. She couldn't help him, not alone. She tried to suppress her coughing as she looked at the half open window. There was only darkness outside.

"Get help," Caspar said again, and she looked back at him, taking in the fear and agony twisting his face. "You have to leave me, Phee."

Her own face crumpled, but he was looking at the hole in the wall once more, shadows spooling from his hands to cover the gap – a shield to keep the flames at bay. Determined that she would find a way to help him, she pulled the window open further, heaved herself onto the windowsill and jumped down onto the grass, the impact shooting through her calves. She saw no one as she cast a wild glance at her surroundings, then pulled the ring out of her pocket and stared at it.

She held it between her thumb and forefinger. How did it work? Did he just have to say Skye's name?

"SKYE!!!!" she yelled at the top of her lungs, hoping against hope that yelling would draw the Telepath's attention. "SKYE!!!"

And then, miraculously, she heard Skye's cool voice in her head, asking the most bizarre question.

Is the shed on fire?

What shed? were Phaedra's panicked thoughts of reply.

The shed with the portal in it, is it damaged?

No.

On my way.

Chapter Fifty-Eight

SKYE BOLTON

Skye had never activated the portal so fast in her life. She spilled salt everywhere as she poured the circle, the crystals were slightly wonky, and she stuttered the names of the sigils, having no time to draw them out. But sure enough, she found herself stepping into the shed, then burst through the door into the cottage garden.

An inferno greeted her, burning hot enough to peel the skin from her bones. For a second she was back in an interrogation room, breathing in fire, inches from death. She stood frozen on the threshold, staring at the flames roaring inside the cottage, then lurched into movement, taking three steps before she tripped over something that shouldn't have been there.

Or rather, *someone*.

A corpse lay prone on the floor, eyes staring blindly up at the night sky. Three silver stars were sewn onto the soldier's blue uniform. But Skye had no time to wonder how the dead soldier had got there. She frantically scanned her surroundings, seeing and sensing no sign of anyone else outside, until she hurtled around to the other side of the cottage and found Phaedra screaming and crying, crouched low to the ground.

"Where is he?" she asked, a hand on the terrified girl's shoulder.

Phaedra started to speak, but her loud, frenzied thoughts were all Skye needed. And then her telepathy locked on Caspar himself, his mind unshielded, his panicked and pain-stricken thoughts flooding their connection. He was still alive, still fighting, but trapped.

She pulled her shirt up to her face as she ran to the front door and forced it open, thick black smoke billowing out of the hallway. Panic threatened to overwhelm her again, panic she had only ever felt as her torturers burned her alive. She cringed as she forced herself to run inside, letting out a startled whimper as a window smashed somewhere nearby. Through the archway into the living room, fire roared over the walls, the space unrecognisable, the smell and heat unbearable.

Her eyes stung as she took in the burning wreckage, then she tore her gaze away, focusing on Caspar once more. She saw his fight through his eyes, saw him keeping the flames at bay with his Talent.

She continued down the hallway, doing her best not to breathe in the smoke, keeping her shirt pressed tightly to her face as she let her telepathy guide her towards the dining room.

She paused in the guest bathroom beneath the staircase, soaking a towel in water from the tap, then pressed it to her mouth and nose. It muffled the acrid smell filling her nostrils, helping her to think more clearly.

Caspar.

You came!

I'm coming in. Keep your darkness away from the door.

She waited the second it took him to obey, then crossed from the bathroom to the dining room doors, shoving them open.

Caspar was sprawled across the floor, leaning on one elbow as he kept flames away from the gap in the wall. She hurried to his side, taking in the furniture and crumbled brick crushing his legs.

Cover me while I get this off you.

He did as she asked, doubling his efforts to hold back the flames as she approached the Welsh dresser and tied the towel around her face. She then crouched, gripped the edge of the wood firmly, and tried to lift. The dresser itself was solid oak, and the bricks that had fallen on top of it weren't helping matters. She should have brought Dean with her.

She grunted, her legs trembling with effort as she pulled, her back and knees buckling, her recently healed ribs protesting, threatening to undo all of Roxanne's careful work. Caspar's thoughts clamoured in her head, the fact that he had already resigned himself to dying, and his fear that Skye might lose her life too.

"Shut up!" she growled, followed by more grunting and groaning as she threw all of her strength into lifting the damned dresser.

With a final tug and an agonised yell, she lifted the dresser just far enough from the ground for Caspar to crawl backwards out of the way. She let the humongous piece of furniture drop, then struggled to her feet as her vision filled with stars. After a deep breath through the soggy towel, she bent over Caspar, sliding an arm around him and hauling him up.

Lean on me.

I'm not sure—

Lean on me or I'll carry you out like a damn baby!

He did as he was told, letting her pull his arm around her shoulders, and she heard his reactions to the pain as he put weight on his less damaged leg. She didn't waste any more time as she half dragged him to the window, panic flooding her again as she heard cracks overhead. She didn't want to be around when the ceiling fell in.

She braced one foot on the windowsill, looking out. The distance to the ground was a bit too high to be jumping with injured legs, but they didn't have much choice if Caspar was to live. She grabbed him beneath the armpits and hauled him over the windowsill, doing her best to ignore the chaos of thoughts going through his mind – the panic, the fear, the embarrassment at being thrown around like a rag doll. She lowered him as carefully as she could to the floor, but he still landed with a bump and a groan even so. But Phaedra was there before Skye had even jumped to the ground, and together they dragged him across the garden and into the trees beyond.

Skye collapsed to her knees, ripping the towel away from her face and gasping down a lungful of air. Phaedra was still sobbing beside her, fussing over Caspar, who lay in the grass, convulsing in pain. It was then that she looked at him properly, seeing the damage down one side of his shirt, the burn holes and the blood. He hadn't just been knocked down by the dresser, but he had also received part of the blast.

"We have to get him to Roxanne," Skye said, noting some of the wounds were particularly nasty, blistered burns glistening in the firelight. She didn't dare to move the fabric of the shirt. "Help me carry him to the shed."

Phaedra nodded and stood up, looking from Caspar's head to his toes, trying to decide which end to carry.

"I'm sorry, Caspar, but we're going to have to manhandle you a little more." Skye bent down and grabbed him beneath the armpits again, pulling him up so his back was to her chest. She did her best to avoid putting pressure on his injuries, his head bumping her shoulder.

"Be my guest," he said through gritted teeth, and Phaedra gingerly hooked her arms beneath his knees. His breath came in agonised gasps as they lifted him between them. Phaedra struggled a moment, then straightened her back, managing the weight better.

"Back to the shed," Skye commanded, giving the cottage a wide berth. As they crossed the front lawn, a screech of wood and breaking glass pierced her hearing, and the beams of the thatched roof crashed down. A flare of flames and a shower of sparks exploded in its wake, stark against the night sky. "Faster," Skye hissed, and Phaedra stumbled a little. Skye spotted another body, this time dressed in a Caplin uniform, but when she reached out telepathically, the lack of any mental buzz confirmed the soldier was dead. She could sense no one else in their surroundings, but the fire wasn't the only thing she was afraid of. She had no doubt it had been started deliberately.

Bursting into the shed, Skye blurted the names of the sigils as soon as the three of them were within the salt circle. They were back in the kitchen at the Bolton safe house within a split second, the cool and dark a welcome contrast to the blaze they had left behind. Skye allowed them a moment to catch their breath, kicking gaps in the salt to break the connection with the portal, then backed into the living room towards the sofa, easing Caspar down onto it. The lamplight shone on the slick sweat coating his skin, and his face contorted with every jolt to his injuries.

Kerry burst into the room, her grey hair dishevelled as she stared at the commotion. Skye turned to her, the sight and sound of Caspar's pain overwhelming her senses.

"Get them some water and make them comfortable. I need to fetch Roxanne."

***

When Skye slipped into her bedroom shortly after dawn, exhaustion and sorrow weighed down her every step.

Caspar was lying awake in her bed, watching the trees swaying in the red-gold sunlight beyond the window. His eyes lit up as he saw her, and he smiled. But Skye couldn't bring herself to return it, too full of concern and bad news.

"How are you feeling?" she asked, drawing up a chair beside the bed, floorboards creaking beneath the faded blue rug.

"Not as bad as I expected. The Veto has got me feeling more legless than too many glasses of bourbon."

Skye managed a small smile at his joke, glancing down the length of his body tucked under the sheets. Roxanne had made quick work of the burn wounds, as Skye had expected she would. In fact, she healed him even more quickly than Oliver Matheson had ever healed her. But his legs were another matter.

"I hope you like reading. I'm afraid you're going to be stuck with your feet up for a few days."

"I've already been eyeing your bookshelves," he said with an amused glance towards the sagging bookcase in the corner. It held an abundance of history books, with a few adventures and fairy tales that she hadn't cracked open since her early teens. The shelves were also home to shells, pebbles and bits of driftwood, mementos from half-forgotten days bleached with sunlight and childhood nostalgia.

Skye let her mind wander as she followed his gaze. But instead of seeing her bedroom tinged with the softness of dawn, she saw Caspar's face contorted in agony as she and Roxanne forced his bones back into place, the cracking and his untethered yells still echoing at the back of her mind. At least the shot of Veto Roxanne had given him had taken the edge off.

"How are you?"

She looked around at him again, taking in the concern in his eyes and thoughts. "Caspar…" She paused, the heavy blow she was about to deliver holding her back. "I have bad news."

Caspar nodded, and his warm hand found hers, clasping around it and easing the stiff chill from her fingers. Skye took a deep breath before continuing.

"Alessia sent us a communication. She… she had the soldiers guarding the cottage killed, and tried to assassinate you both with that explosion."

Caspar exhaled the breath he had been holding and turned his gaze back to the window. Skye tried not to listen too closely to his thoughts as she stroked the back of his hand with her thumb, but he had been expecting it, especially after he stole her armies. It was only a matter of time.

"I get her feelings towards me, but I could never understand why she would want to hurt Phaedra. That's… that's just evil."

Skye didn't know what to say, and the anguish that flooded his thoughts made her withdraw from his mind completely. They sat in silence, until she fidgeted, deciding she should probably give him some privacy. But just as she withdrew her hand from his, Caspar began to speak again.

"She's too far gone, isn't she?" The fear in his eyes froze her in place. She had never seen Caspar look so afraid, not even the night before when their deaths had been a strong possibility. "There's no kindness left in her."

"Was she ever kind?" Skye asked quietly.

He swallowed. "No, not really. Only to her grandfather. But still… to try to kill her own sister…"

Skye couldn't imagine ever wanting to kill a family member. And Dean wasn't even her blood, yet the bond they had… she knew nothing could ever break it, no matter how much they might have argued lately. Yet Alessia… perhaps that was what it meant to be the Nox. No one meant more to her than power. “Is… is that why you chose Phaedra over her, in the end? Because she threatened her?”

Caspar’s face was unreadable as his eyes bore into hers. “I have always put Phaedra first. Surely… surely you’ve seen that in my head by now.”

Skye frowned in confusion, and in her curiosity she tapped into his mind again, bracing herself to delve further into the dark depths of his memories where she had been reluctant to tread. But she didn’t need to go that far. The thoughts floating on the surface were far from what she expected, and her eyes widened as the truth was laid bare before her. She could already hear the words on his lips.

“I chose Phaedra because she’s my daughter.”

PART III

Chapter Fifty-Nine

DEAN ROSWELL

The view that greeted Dean and Skye when they arrived at the destroyed lake cottage tugged at his heartstrings, bringing the emotions he was trying to keep at bay threateningly close to the surface. He knew he shouldn't feel so sentimental – the cottage had only been bricks and mortar. But when Skye shared the horrible news, the attack felt like the destruction of something sacred, a violation of happy, innocent memories of childhood.

It was a sunny day, at odds with the charred skeleton of their aunt's cottage, and the horrors that had taken place the night before. Dean had come home late from an evening training session to find the safe house crowded. Cries of agony and the stench of smoke and Veto had been thick in the air, with Kerry trying to soothe a sobbing Phaedra. Once they had Caspar in Skye's bed, dosed up with Veto, she had shared the ordeal with him mind to mind, then left with Roxanne to instruct the Tracers to investigate the scene.

Those Tracers scurried back and forth across the sprawling garden now, wearing rubber gloves and white overalls, collecting samples and searching for evidence.

Lindsey was overseeing the proceedings, dressed in a dove grey blazer, the sun gleaming on the tight braid hanging down her back. Her face was rigid as she raised her sombre eyes to them.

"Thanks for joining," she said as they came to a stop at her side. Her gaze held Dean's with an intensity that set off butterflies in his stomach, distracting him momentarily from his sorrow.

"How's it going?" Skye asked. Her jaw was clenched and her voice was somewhat hoarse from the smoke the night before.

"Our findings so far are leaving us with more questions than answers." Lindsey glanced between them with foreboding in her eyes. "And with the answers we have found, the situation doesn't look pretty."

"What do you mean?" said Skye, her question sounding like an accusation.

Lindsey appeared unphased by her demanding tone, and looked instead at a familiar, dark-haired Tracer who approached them. "You might remember Seth Galloway. I believe you worked together to take over Blackwater."

Dean nodded and shook the man's hand. He didn't miss Seth's glance between them, his gaze lingering on Lindsey in a way that made Dean feel like he had crossed some unknown boundary.

"The autopsy reports on the dead soldiers just came in. Seth, would you do the honours?"

Seth nodded, his expression as grim as Lindsey's. "The Caplin soldiers were already dead when they were brought here."

Dean and Skye exchanged a puzzled glance, and his stomach churned, the back of his neck prickling.

"Not just that," Seth continued, "they were dead before they were even dressed in the Caplin uniform. Whoever they were, they weren't on guard duty last night, and they were dead considerably longer than the Resistance soldiers, who were killed on site."

Dean looked around, taking in the destruction of the cottage and scorched grass. Tape encircled the areas where the bodies were found, and two Tracers crouched near one with some kind of testing kit open between them.

"If the Caplin soldiers weren't on duty," Dean asked, "where are the ones that were?"

Lindsey was silent for a moment, surveying the garden with hard eyes. "I hate to break it to you, but a lot of the evidence points to Caplin's Forces being involved somehow. If Alessia's soldiers were acting alone, why would they plant Caplin bodies? Why not just kill them on site?"

He glanced at his sister. A muscle feathered in Skye's jaw, and Dean could well imagine the battle that was going on in her head.

"Alessia claimed the assassination attempt," said Skye, stepping towards the cottage, taking in the blackened and crumbling brickwork. "So she's either trying to frame Caplin, or Caplin or his soldiers are helping her."

"Looks like it's either of those options, yes," said Lindsey. She nodded her thanks to Seth, then followed Skye with her hands in her pockets.

"I suppose Caplin does have revenge as a motive," said Dean, staying close at Lindsey's side.

"Or he's trying to get back at me," Skye said bitterly.

They walked on, circling around to the side of the house. "Regarding the cause of the fire," Lindsey continued, "we found remnants of an explosive with remote detonation. Looks like it was thrown through this window."

"They probably thought they were in the living room," said Skye, as they all looked up at the gaping hole.

"Exactly," said Lindsey, stopping a short distance away from Skye. "Otherwise, they would have thrown it through the dining room window. Phaedra said it was open."

Dean whistled. "They were pretty lucky then."

"Extremely. The blast would have killed them at close proximity, or at the very least injured them beyond repair."

Dean suppressed a shudder. He didn't care much for Caspar, but Phaedra was only a teenager. And when he thought about how much time both Skye and Ombra had spent at the cottage recently…

"Based on that assessment," asked Dean, hoping he wasn't about to sound like an idiot, "is there a chance that it wasn't actually an assassination attempt, but rather the perpetrator just wanted to scare or injure the Ronans?"

Lindsey cast her calculating gaze on him once again, scrutinising him long enough that he felt the embarrassment creep up his neck. But then her painted lips tugged up in a satisfied smile. "Are you looking for a new job, Dean Roswell?"

Dean gave an uncertain smile of his own, and out of the corner of his eye, he saw Skye tilt her head in teasing amusement. Before he could say anything, Lindsey continued. "What Alessia has said and what we see don't add up. That said, if she's truly responsible, maybe someone screwed up the job, or the Nox still has a shred of humanity left in her and wanted to give her uncle and sister a fighting chance."

Skye was lost in thought at his side, her expression unreadable. Lindsey's suggestions were plausible, but it still didn't explain the evidence around Caplin's potential involvement. Skye's eyes flicked to him as she caught onto his train of thought. She turned back to Lindsey. "Any more clues as to who planted the bomb and the bodies?"

Lindsey exhaled slowly and looked towards the lake. "We found footprints and the remains of an untraceable portal at the lakeside." She paused, her face grave. "The footprints matched the standard issue boots worn by the Caplin Forces, four sets of them coming back and forth. It looks like they were carrying something heavy, probably the bodies."

Dean felt sick as he saw the scene playing out in his head. Caplin soldiers murdering the Resistance guards that had been on duty, then planting two bodies to make it look like their own had also been slaughtered. "Have you identified the Caplin bodies?"

"Not yet, I was hoping perhaps you or Skye…"

"I'll do it." Skye turned away from the wreckage of the cottage, her expression guarded. "I'll go now."

Lindsey nodded as Skye walked away, heading in the direction of the portal that the Tracers had set up for their investigation.

"Skye, wait—"

Don't follow me. Her thoughts were firm as she strode away.

Let me come with you. But he could feel her close her mind off from him, withdrawing and leaving him with a cold sense of dread. He took a few steps towards her, but hesitated. He knew that tone meant she didn't want him getting in her way. As Skye disappeared through the portal, Lindsey placed a hand on his arm, making him jump.

"Walk with me," she said, giving him a meaningful look, her face close to his. He was too aware of the brush of her fingers through his sleeve, the floral scent of her perfume setting his butterflies circling again. So he followed her, glad to leave the charred wreckage behind. He didn't know if Aunt Alma was aware that her cottage had been destroyed, but his next stop was to visit her and tell her the bad news. The cowardly part of him hoped that she had already heard about it elsewhere.

"There's something I need to tell you." Lindsey led him towards the path that circled the lake, away from the cordoned off section which was no doubt where they had found the footprints and portal. She remained cool as she stared at the sunlight glittering on the rippling water. "I know about the bargain Camilla Linden made with you and your sister."

Dean blinked, scrutinising her profile as his stomach squirmed with uncertainty. "How—?"

"She made the same deal with Roxanne."

Dean froze, and after a few paces, Lindsey turned to him. "What… what do you think about it?"

Lindsey sighed as her gaze drifted back to the cottage. "I think we need to work together. Cooperating is the only way I can see this working out."

Dean nodded. So far, he and Skye hadn't shared the details of the bargain with anyone, as far as he knew. "Who knows?"

"Roxanne and Devan Harlow," she said, looking back at him.

"Not your father?"

"Telling him would be a bad idea."

Dean nodded again. Oliver Matheson was another loose cannon they really didn't want to contend with.

"I'll speak to Roxanne, convince her to meet with you and Skye. We need a plan."

He took a deep breath, trying to settle his ragged nerves. "We do."

"And maybe… maybe speak to your aunt. Alma is it? She's part of Caplin's inner circle. If you trust her to take her family's side over Caplin, she will probably have some valuable information to share with us, like weaknesses, how to get rid of him."

“You must sense she’s trustworthy.” Dean eyed her, his awe blooming as he wondered just how accurate her Talent was.

Lindsey gave him a knowing smile that set the hairs on the back of his neck tingling.

“One thing I don’t get…” Dean mused as his stomach squirmed. “What could Caplin possibly gain from the explosion?”

Lindsey shrugged. “There’s always been bad blood between Caplins and Ronans, so it was probably only a matter of time before he tried to screw over Caspar.”

Dean grimaced, realising how naïve he had been to hope they might have a peaceful alliance. “Do you trust Caspar?”

She turned, pinning Dean with her gaze once again. The sunlight brought out flecks of gold and green in her light brown eyes, and he found himself lost in them, almost forgetting his question until she answered.

“I do.” A pause. A blink. A deep breath. “Do you trust me?”

Dean stared. He wanted to say yes, the word bumping against his lips. He wanted to trust this amazing person who had walked into his life when he had least expected it. Wanted to follow her and throw caution to the wind. But a voice in the back of his mind that sounded an awful lot like Skye warned him to tread carefully. He had been burned before. He couldn’t afford to let his guard down so easily now.

As if seeing the thoughts written all over his face, Lindsey’s lips curved into a wistful smile, her eyes softening. “I don’t blame you. You would be a fool if you did.”

She placed a hand on his upper arm, squeezing lightly, her touch sending his heartbeat fluttering into overdrive. She then slipped her arm through the crook of his elbow, inclining her head towards the lakeside path that trailed into the trees. Smiling uncertainly, he let her lead him on, happy to delay the dreaded trip to his aunt's if it meant he could spend a little longer with her, too aware of every point where their bodies joined.

***

Alma poured herself a large glass of red wine, and then sank into a plush plum-coloured armchair, staring at the floor. Dean sat on the edge of the matching sofa, the coffee her maid had brought him going cold on the table between them. He couldn't stomach anything, not after the news he had just shared, which had left his aunt stone-faced.

"My grandparents built that cottage," she said bleakly, then promptly downed half her glass, cold fury igniting in her dark eyes. "I'm going to kill that little madam."

Dean assumed she meant Skye, and his stomach squirmed again.

"Where is she, by the way?" Her tone cut through the room.

"She went to identify some bodies," he said, gesturing vaguely.

"And that takes all afternoon, does it? So she sends you to do her dirty work instead?"

Dean glanced at the clock on Alma's mantelpiece. Sure enough, it had been hours since Skye had gone through the portal. He dreaded to think what else she was up to.

"I need to… ask you something," Dean ventured, studying Alma's face, trying to gauge her reactions. "You know how Camilla Linden is holding Victor?"

Alma's jaw set, a muscle feathering just the way Skye's had done earlier. "Yes."

"She offered us a deal."

Alma raised the glass to her lips and drank deeply. Dean didn't miss her hand trembling ever so slightly.

"She… she wants us to hand Caplin over. Or…" He lowered his voice. He knew there were servants roaming the big house, and her twin sons played somewhere in the garden. Their childish voices carried. "She wants him dead."

Alma stared at him, then knocked back the rest of her glass and poured herself more. The wine splashed a little as her hand shook again. She was silent for a long moment, sipping her wine, one arm wrapped around her middle as though holding herself together.

Just then the door opened, and the maid reappeared. "Your niece, Miss Bolton, Madam."

Skye walked in, her eyes on her aunt. Dean didn't miss the defensive way she held herself, her hands curled into fists. Alma waited until the maid had taken her leave before she spoke. "I didn't think you'd have the nerve to show your face."

Skye remained standing, glancing at Dean. He felt the familiar brush of her telepathy as she searched his mind, coming up to speed with what she had missed. If she was surprised about Lindsey's revelation, she didn't show it. "I'm sorry, Auntie," she said, looking back at Alma, her voice uncharacteristically small.

Alma only drank again, then waved an imperious hand at the sofa Dean occupied. "Sit."

Skye did as she was told, crossing the room and lowering herself next to Dean, looking as tense as he felt. Dean tried to silently ask her where she had been, but she didn't reply.

"So, Dean told you."

"He did," said Alma, swirling the wine in her glass. "I suppose you want me to help you kill Caplin off."

Dean glanced fearfully at the door.

"Don't worry about them," Alma soothed him. "Even if Skye couldn't read every thought that crosses their minds, they wouldn't dare tell anyone anything they hear in this house."

He nodded, then slowly leaned back on the sofa, trying to calm his nerves. Even if Caplin was no longer the most powerful person in Britannia, all the talk of treachery wasn't good for his stress levels.

"I think he's responsible for the mutiny during the battle, and the Tracers found evidence that points to Caplin soldiers carrying out the assassination attempt last night," said Skye, a quaver of fear in her usually firm voice.

"Oh, the mutiny orchestrated by Ronan soldiers you mean?" said Alma, an eyebrow raised. "And what Tracers? More of Ronan's people?"

Dean grew cold. The thought had crossed his own mind, and the fear that getting close to Lindsey may have been a mistake, for this potential reason.

"Tell her what Lindsey told you today, Dean," said Skye, looking at him pointedly.

Dean glanced between his sister and their aunt. "Camilla holds Roxanne Summers's daughter, and she made the same bargain with her."

Alma nodded, her lips pursed. "Seems like everyone wants a piece of Caplin."

"Don't forget that one of the mutineers was a Caplin soldier, and today I Broke a few more minds that suggested the Forces were indeed involved in the attack on the cottage last night."

"You Broke more minds?" Dean asked incredulously. "Did Caplin give you permission?"

What do you think?

Skye, that's dangerous. If Caplin—

"I still haven't gathered enough evidence, but so far, a lot points to Caplin or his soldiers being involved with the Nox, or at least working against the alliance," said Skye, cutting across Dean's protests.

Alma shrugged. "So Caplin wants to bump off a Ronan. Nothing new there."

Skye laughed humourlessly. "But working with the Nox? Come on Auntie, you surely can't condone that."

"Who says I'm condoning it?" Alma shook her head. "Regardless, if getting rid of Caplin is the only way to get my little brother away from that mad hag, we need to build a case against him. If you can't prove he's involved with the Nox, you at least need to come up with enough evidence to condemn him."

"Condemn him?" said Dean, glancing between the two women.

"If you betray him, you'll have a riot on your hands, Lux or no Lux. But if you can prove he's betrayed you…"

"People will take my side," said Skye.

Dean stared as Alma's suggestions unravelled before him. As Caplin's High Justice, Alma had condemned people for a living. He was sure that no one had ever expected she would have to condemn Caplin.

"Are you prepared to lead the Forces once Caplin is out of the way?" Alma asked, her sharp eyes pinned on Skye.

Skye tensed at his side, and she began scratching chipped paint off a nail. Dean held his breath, waiting for her decision. Finally, she met Alma's eyes, looking unusually young and vulnerable, her voice soft. "You really think that's a good idea?"

If Alma noted Skye's fear, she gave no comfort, her manner as brisk as ever. "They won't accept anyone else, Skye. The only people who may have a right to inherit Caplin's power by blood are Ikarus and the Van Zantens. But when his own heirs are openly backing the Lux, it makes sense for you to be the one to overthrow him. You have us in your corner as well, of course, and you know Harlan won't hesitate to support his own granddaughter's claim over Caplin."

Silence followed, and Skye looked at Dean, fear still glazing her eyes. He took a deep breath. *I know you can do it, if it's what you want.*

She blinked, scratching her nail again. *But I don't want it. I never wanted any of this.*

His mouth twisted in pity, but Alma interrupted before he could reassure her further, clearly disgruntled at being left out of the conversation. "So, Summers needs Caplin out of the way too. That works in our favour – we'll need the Resistance on our side for this to work. Get me a meeting with her."

"Of course," said Dean, glad that Lindsey had already suggested as much. "And the others?"

"What others? Not that Sinclair..." said Alma, her lips pressing together in distaste.

"Just Harlow and Lindsey," Skye interrupted, glancing at Dean, her frightened demeanour already fading. "Like your girlfriend says, the fewer people who know, the better."

"She's not my girlfriend," Dean retorted, his cheeks growing hot at her sneaky betrayal.

Alma glanced between them. "What girlfriend?"

"Dean is dating Lindsey Matheson."

Alma looked incredulous, then drained her second glass. "Not you as well. Do your generation all think with what's in your underwear?"

"I resent that," said Skye, smirking as Dean sank into the sofa, wishing it would swallow him up.

Chapter Sixty

SKYE BOLTON

Skye's nails dug into her palms as she stood before Caplin's desk. The air was incredibly stuffy in the small office, and she struggled to draw a breath into her tight lungs. The former president glared at her from where he lounged in his chair, absently curling the dull yellow silk of his tie between thumb and forefinger. To his right stood Captain Sullivan, still as a statue, while Thorsten Welch occupied the space to his left, oozing smug satisfaction. Skye purposely ignored him.

"I said you could Break willing soldiers for the investigation, Bolton. I never gave you permission to go on a rampage through my Forces, intimidating and interrogating staff who weren't even on the battlefield."

Skye took in a slow breath, trying to quell her bubbling anger. "This isn't just about the mutiny anymore, Caplin."

While Caplin stilled, movement rippled through the room, their audience reacting to her disrespect. Sullivan's eyes widened ever so slightly, Welch's lips curled, and Dean shifted on his feet just behind her, her name drifting towards her on his thoughts. As the tense moment dragged on, Caplin dropped his tie and straightened in his seat.

"Roswell, you are dismissed. This matter does not concern you."

Skye crossed her arms. "Dean's not leaving unless your pet slings his hook as well." She jerked her chin towards Welch, whose cold smile only grew.

I thought you enjoyed an audience, Bolton.

She raised her head higher, meeting Welch's gaze for a fraction of a second, refusing to rise to his taunting thoughts.

"Welch, you may go," came Caplin's steely command.

Welch's disappointment flickered towards her with more taunts. *Pity, I would have enjoyed watching him fire you.* With his smirk still pasted in place, he shouldered past her on his way out.

Skye stood tall, refusing to look at him a second time, but she couldn't stop herself from firing a parting shot. *I'll enjoy watching you eat shit when I'm in charge.*

Silent laughter lingered in his wake as he left the office. After a moment's hesitation, Dean exhaled, also taking his leave. *I'll wait outside. Please be careful.*

Behind Caplin, Sullivan adjusted his stance, hands twitching near the gun at his hip. Skye tracked the movement, electricity prickling down her arms at the thought of a fight breaking out.

"Right," Caplin said, barely contained fury sizzling in his eyes. "How about you explain whatever little fantasy you've dreamed up?"

"Were you involved with the assassination attempt?" Skye asked, seeing no reason to beat around the bush.

"As much as I'd like to see the Ronans pay for their countless crimes, I wouldn't jeopardise this alliance, Bolton. Your lover still has something to offer in this war, and I still need to keep the peace with the Resistance."

"The minds I Broke today confirmed explosives were secreted out of the Forces armoury two days ago. What were they used for?"

"We carried out a secret operation to prevent the Mason army from advancing further into my territory," said Caplin without missing a beat.

Skye knew about the operation and had been expecting the excuse. "I'll warn you, Caplin, the Resistance don't trust you, and your support amongst the Forces is crumbling. You might try a little harder to keep this alliance going."

"Don't insult me with feigned concern, Bolton. I know your end game far better than you know mine."

"You think I want to take your place, just because your ancestor seized power?" Her fingers tightened on her arms, bracing herself for her half-hearted lie. "I don't care about ruling, Caplin. I just want my family safe and well."

Caplin scoffed and leaned back in his chair again. "And yet your *Lux Guard* are working so hard to discredit me. Don't think I don't see the little games your friends are playing. If it weren't for the Resistance, I'd have had you all executed for treason by now, Lux or no Lux."

Skye forced her lips to curl, her gaze locked on his. She didn't doubt his threat, as much as the truth hurt. She had seen his lack of sentimentality plain enough when it came to her father. "Is it treason to rise up against a ruler who doesn't give a shit about his subjects? And what about your soldiers? Why should they lay down their lives when you deem them worthless?"

"A good soldier expects to sacrifice themselves for the greater good, Bolton. Didn't you accept as much when you swore to serve and protect me?"

Skye tried to ignore the ringing in her ears. "There's quite a leap between fighting for the greater good and being cut down on their leader's orders."

Caplin stilled again, his glare boring into her. A warning breeze rifled through the space, crackling the papers on his desk. "You don't seriously still think I ordered the mutiny just because you found one of my soldiers had turned coat?"

She held his glare, willing her voice to remain even despite her pulse picking up speed. "After the incriminating evidence the Tracers found at the scene where your so-called ally and his niece were almost blown to smithereens, I can't say I'm all that willing to serve and protect *you* anymore."

The breeze whipped past her again, tugging at her hair and jacket collar. Skye stood her ground, her eyes narrowing. "What are you implying, Miss Bolton?"

Taking in a deep breath, she straightened and lowered her arms to her sides. "I formally renounce my position as a member of your Guard."

Her statement hung suspended on a precipice, and Skye clocked the tightening of Caplin's jaw, the curling of his hands into fists. Her heartbeat hammered in her chest, thrilled and terrified all at once.

"Only I can dismiss you from your post, Miss Bolton. To renounce it is to desert."

She forced herself to shrug. "So hang me. Good luck defeating the Nox without me." Before he could say more, Skye turned towards the door, reaching for the handle.

"Skye—"

Whatever Caplin had been about to say, he cut himself off, his angry breeze settling.

Skye waited, fingers brushing the doorknob. When he didn't speak, she turned her face towards him, an eyebrow raised.

His gaze stabbed through her yet again, but an unknown emotion flickered across his face, perhaps pain, or fear. The moment lengthened, tense with unsaid words. But eventually, Caplin hunched his shoulders, picked up a pen, and began to write. Realising the conversation was over, Skye fled the room.

Dean waited in the corridor, his features tight with worry. Welch, she was relieved to find, was nowhere in sight.

"What happened?" he asked, hurrying to keep up with her as she strode towards the exit.

"I resigned." She couldn't bring herself to look at him. The words sounded incredulous even to her own ears.

"You… what?"

She could see his aghast expression from the corner of her eye, and wished she didn't have to face it. *At least now I don't have to tolerate him sticking his nose into our investigation.*

"You— but you—"

I know, she thought a little more softly, and ground to a stop, her breath ragged. What had she just done? Her mind whirled, fear and disbelief battling in her chest. *I wish there was another way, but we're running out of time and I need to start making moves.*

Skye… He echoed her fear, worst case scenarios bleeding into his thoughts as he looked down at her. *You're not untouchable.*

I know. She sighed a deep breath, swaying on her feet for a moment, then marched on towards the exit. *But once we get Dad back, Caplin will either be dead or a prisoner, and when the Nox is gone, Britannia is going to look very different.*

Dean walked beside her in silence, but the buzz of his frenzied thoughts increased in volume. *You think The Resistance is the right choice to rule?*

I don't know, she conceded, thinking on everything she had seen these past months. *But maybe it's time for a change.*

The safe house was dark when they got in, with Kerry asleep in her room, while a slice of golden light and whispers emanated from the bedroom Ombra and Phaedra were sharing. Skye's eyes itched, and her nerves were still jangled from the argument.

"Sleep well, Dean," she mumbled, giving him a small, sad smile before heading to her bedroom. He gave her no reply, but she could hear the whorl of fears and doubts in his mind, how he was certain she had made a huge mistake. She hoped she wouldn't think the same after sleeping on her rash decision.

She squeezed through her bedroom door as quietly as she could, where the sound of Caspar's even breaths reached her through the darkness. She stripped out of her uniform, concealed weapons hissing in their sheaths as she dropped her discarded clothing in a chair beside the door, then slipped between the sheets of her bed.

Caspar's warmth seeped across the mattress, and she moved gratefully towards him, eager to be held and forget about the insane events of the day. His soft breathing faded away as her fingers caressed his bare skin, and he pulled her into his arms.

"How did it go today?" he murmured sleepily, his lips nuzzling the hollow beneath her ear.

"Not well," she whispered, nestling against him and tracing the planes of his chest with her fingertips. "Let's talk in the morning."

He tensed a little, knowing full well that she would probably slip out of bed before he awoke. Guilt flared through her exhaustion, but a heavy talk with Caspar on top of everything else was something she couldn't face right now. She still had yet to come to terms with his secret past.

"Tomorrow," he agreed, his fingers returning to tracing her bare arm as he pressed his lips to hers. She welcomed the kiss, running her fingers into his hair and relishing the feel of his hand trailing down her side, until he was cupping her against him. She hooked a leg around him, mindful to avoid his injuries as she tucked her face into the warmth of his neck and waited for sleep to drag her into its dark depths.

***

It was a relief to be alone. Away from Lindsey, Jennifer Dooley, and the chaotic minds she spent her days inside. Her Lux Guard brought a constant stream of updates, including confirmation that Caplin was keeping quiet about her resignation. And on top of everything else, the safe house was full of Ombra and Phaedra's incessant chatter, Kerry's coaxing to eat at regular intervals, and the suffocating resentment between Dean and Caspar.

With another crazy day's events whirring around her head, Skye poured herself a generous amount of whiskey, then went out to the little garden, choosing a bench that had a view of the coast. The late afternoon sun enhanced the colours in her surroundings, and she drank in the inviting blue of the sea, the golds and greens of the landscape, and the cheerful blooms bobbing in Dean's flower beds.

She tried not to entertain the memories flooding her mind, of games in the garden, racing Ombra down to the beach, of getting drunk with her father and other family members… She couldn't think about those things without being reminded that her father was currently sitting in a cell somewhere, alone, probably in pain. She swallowed a mouthful of the whiskey, the liquor going down with difficulty as a lump rose in her throat.

But her peace was short-lived. Long before she saw his dark head bobbing up the path, Skye sensed Caspar's approach. His mind was hidden, but his buzz was familiar to her by now, and she watched him come into view. He was struggling, walking on crutches that Roxanne had brought from the hospital, and from his grimace she could tell that he didn't like her to see him in such a state. She could understand why. She would feel the same if their roles were reversed.

She waited for him to near the gate, then went to open it for him. “You went out alone.”

“Don’t lecture me,” he said, but he gave her a small smile, his mouth twisted with what could only be pain.

She waited patiently for him to enter the garden, and they avoided one another’s gaze as she closed the gate. “Sit down. I’ll get you a drink.”

Moments later, Skye returned to the bench where Caspar had seated himself, looking more like himself now that he didn’t need the crutches. She handed him a glass, poured him a large measure, then topped up her own. They drank in silence for a moment, eyes on the shore where Skye assumed he had just come from. Walking down to the beach had become his only exercise since he had begun to regain the use of his legs, although Phaedra was usually with him.

“If you and Phee want to stay here long-term, Dean and I can go elsewhere.”

“No, you’ve done enough,” he said, not unkindly. “I can’t hide here forever, as beautiful as it is. I still need to speak to Phaedra about… you know… But when we know where we stand with one another, we’ll make a decision and find somewhere else.”

Skye mulled over the situation. The truth was, Caspar and Phaedra, especially Caspar, seemed to be safe from no one. The Nox and perhaps Caplin wanted him dead, he didn’t know if he could rely on his remaining soldiers, and the Resistance was split on whether they trusted him. Skye was beginning to wonder if she and Phaedra were the only ones who wanted to keep him safe.

“Don’t sweat it, Skye. I’ll be out of your hair soon enough, and once my legs are back to normal, I’ll be able to keep myself safe.”

She looked up at him sharply, then reached across the space between them and took his hand, gripping his fingers firmly. "You're not a burden to me."

But Caspar only gave her a small smile, the look in his eyes telling her he didn't believe her. In all honesty, she didn't entirely believe it herself. Trying to prove Caspar's innocence had become secondary to her need to prove Caplin guilty, and having him sharing the safe house was a distraction she could do without.

"So, you're going to tell her then," Skye asked eventually, letting go of his hand to top up their glasses. She knew Phaedra's parentage was another difficult topic to discuss, another complication she could do without being involved in, but since he had mentioned it, it was as good a subject as any to change to.

As she had expected, Caspar winced a little. "She needs to know. And it doesn't feel right having you know and not her."

Skye silently agreed. She couldn't bear carrying that secret around while interacting with Phaedra. "How do you think she'll take it?"

Caspar took a deep, thoughtful drink before answering. "I hope she'll understand. Explaining my feelings for her mother will hopefully soften the blow."

She considered his words for a moment, unable to rein in her curiosity. "You loved her then?"

He nodded, his gaze trained on the horizon. "She was the love of my life."

"I wouldn't have known," she said after a pause, surprised by his honesty. Surprised he was telling *her*, of all people. "You hold yourself together pretty well."

"Compared to Doran, you mean?" Caspar laughed darkly and met her eye. "I'm not my brother, Skye. Of course, I did my fair share of grieving, and after some whopping fights with Doran I barely spoke to him for years.

He knew Ilaria and I were close, suspected it was more than friendship, and he knew her suicide hit me hard. But he never knew outright that Phaedra was mine. Ilaria made me promise not to tell, for her sake."

"Well, that explains a lot." She chewed her lip, unable to shake the feeling that she was intruding on secrets she had no business knowing. She shoved her own confusion of feelings down, knowing she had no right to feel anything about his past, a past she had nothing to do with.

"The only reason I stayed in touch was for Phaedra," he continued, eyes distant with memories. "My father was the most despicable human on the planet, Doran had and neglected everything I've ever wanted, and Alessia… well, I had to protect Phaedra from her."

"What do you mean?"

Caspar gave another bitter laugh. "I should have known Alessia was evil from the beginning. Let's just say she wasn't the most loving sister."

Skye nodded, respecting his decision not to elaborate. She then hesitated over the next question, not wishing to pry, but unable to contain her curiosity. "If… if she had you, why did she take her own life?"

Caspar fell silent and absently turned the glass in his hands, long enough for Skye to think she had asked too much and begin to regret her question. But eventually, he spoke again, his voice quiet. "She wasn't treated well, Skye. She was raised to be sold to the highest bidder. My father terrorised her, Doran barely noticed her. Worst of all, she had a lover before the marriage was arranged, but he wasn't a good match so her family… had him killed, and her involvement with him kept secret. They… they made her watch."

Skye sat in horrified silence, not knowing what to say, and kicking herself for having asked and made him tell her such a distressing tale. She was quiet for so long that

Caspar eventually looked up at her, giving her a small, sad smile. "Don't worry, Skye. She's at peace now. I just wish I could have made her life worth living."

"I'm sure you made a difference," said Skye, turning her own gaze to the sea. The sun glittered on the waves, turning them silver and gold.

"I hope so." His voice was strained, his usual charming mask nowhere in sight. The realisation struck her that this was a side to Caspar that the world rarely saw, a vulnerability that she was privileged to witness. Without hesitation, she laced her fingers with his again, and he gratefully squeezed her hand.

"Listen, Skye," he said quietly, tense as he met her eye. "I don't think I can do this – us – anymore."

A hush settled over her mind – an ending. A pang of loss tightened her chest at his words, and she lowered her gaze to their joined hands.

"It's... a messy situation. Even after everything she's done, Alessia is still family, and I can't pick sides when the time comes."

She nodded, managing a faint smile. She had never expected their relationship to last beyond one or two casual encounters. But the fact that it had, the fact he had helped her and supported her, even going against his blood to do so... he had already given her more than enough, more than she could ask for. And he had never asked for more than she was willing or able to give in return. She hadn't let herself think of what they could be if they weren't who they were – old enemies with a blood feud standing between them. Perhaps things could have worked out differently, but she couldn't afford to hope. So instead, she buried her tangled feelings, taking a deep breath to ease her tight chest.

"Maybe this was a mistake, but... I'm grateful for what you've done. What we've had."

He smiled sadly, tucking a strand of hair behind her ear and planting a gentle kiss on her forehead. Letting out a sigh, she leaned her head on his shoulder, his hand still enveloping hers. An insect buzzed lazily past, and the sun sank lower, warming that last, stolen moment.

"Skye?" he asked after a while, the sky gradually turning a deep pink, the sun almost kissing the sea. She looked up at him, surprised to see fear in his eyes. "I know I don't have a right to ask you this, and ultimately it's your decision…"

He trailed off, leaving her waiting, impatient for more. As he struggled for words, she eventually prompted him. "What do you need?"

The corner of his mouth tugged up in another grimace. "When the time comes, please don't kill her. I know that's a lot to ask, but she's Ilaria's flesh and blood, and in her memory, and my brother's…"

Skye blinked, shocked to see the pain and fear so evident on his face, the way his words sounded like a plea. Selfishly, she hadn't thought about how her killing Alessia would impact him, or Phaedra for that matter. She thought there was no love between them, but she realised now that she was wrong. Alessia may have been the Nox, but Skye had taken for granted that she was unlovable.

"I'll do what I can," she said, not wanting to make any promises. "But… is keeping her alive even possible?"

He sighed. "As tempting as your collection of pirate adventures is, I haven't been idle while stuck in bed." He exchanged an amused grin with her. "Since I don't have access to the library at my home, your cousin was kind enough to lend me her laptop."

"Ombra?" Skye raised a bemused eyebrow.

"Oh yes, she's even started calling me Cas now."

Skye snorted, half wishing she had been around the last few days to witness it.

"Anyway, I had to trawl through a lot of rubbish and conspiracies, but I gathered some research on theories for defeating the Nox without killing them. It has happened, in the past. The Nox Queen Itis was defeated by her granddaughter. The Lux used some kind of magical device to strip her of her Talents, and then exiled her to the Outer Hebrides, where she lived until her death."

"Queen Itis?" Skye asked doubtfully. "Wasn't that in the fourteenth century?"

"Around then, yes. There were others, here." He tugged the obsidian from around his neck, squeezing her hand in invitation. She delved into his mind, his research coming to her as his thoughts touched on everything he had found over the last few days. When she reached the end of his train of thought, she was frowning.

"That's a lot of Old Craft mumbo jumbo."

He huffed a laugh. "Don't underestimate the Old Craft, Skye."

"Even so, it could take years to find all that stuff. Mystical horns that suck Talents out of people? Magic mirrors?" She struggled to keep the smirk off her face, even though she knew he meant well. "If it even exists. We know no one with the Mirror Talent does, that's for sure."

"They have existed." His eyes took on a faraway look as he descended once more into memories. "One of the legends around the origin of the Nox mentions a Mirror who collected Talents, hiding them from the Gods in powerless individuals, one day to be inherited by the Nox and the Lux."

This time, Skye couldn't hide her smirk. "Sounds like quite the fairy tale."

He grinned. "Stop teasing."

But her amusement faded, at a loss of how she could achieve what he was asking of her.

"I'll do what I can to help you," he said, as though *he* was the one reading *her* mind. "There must be a way, and I'm not afraid to dabble in the Old Craft if I have to."

She gave him a wistful smile. "Like a wise old wizard."

"Maybe with a bit less of the old, thank you."

She snickered, and he caught her gaze one last time, the ice blue of his eyes twinkling. But she could no longer look at those eyes the same way. They were too much like his father's, and the murderous cruelty with which Ivor Ronan had glared at her still haunted her dreams. Perhaps it was just as well things were ending between them.

Chapter Sixty-One

ROXANNE SUMMERS

The meeting with Skye, Dean and Alma Medley was as nerve-racking as she had expected. And she was ashamed that she had had to let Lindsey and Devan do most of the talking. But she was also in awe at how Lindsey had held her own beneath the former High Justice's scrutiny, while Mrs Medley ruled the discussion and cross-examined them as though they were in court. The meeting had left Roxanne feeling even more fearful than before, but at least they had a plan in place, and powerful allies in the game they were about to play.

"Here," said Devan, pushing a glass of Peter's brandy into her hands when they reached the Resistance meeting room.

"Thanks," she murmured. She must have looked how she felt, because he was eyeing her with visible concern.

"Do you think we'll have to fabricate evidence? Alma gave me the impression it might come to that," Devan asked after a moment.

"I doubt it," said Lindsey, glowering at the table. "Bolton and I have already found too much that points to Caplin being involved. And even if we hadn't, my Trace tells me he's dodgy. There's bound to be more evidence, and we'll find it."

"Could Bolton's resignation from the Guard jeopardise things?" Devan asked Lindsey. "Caplin's pretty angry about her going behind his back with interrogations."

Lindsey narrowed her eyes. "You locked up Caspar because you suspected him of treason. What's stopping you from arresting Caplin so we can continue our investigation without him sticking his nose in?"

Roxanne met Devan's gaze. "That's a good point."

But Devan looked uneasy. "We've already lost most of the Ronan army's support. Those that have stuck around have only done so because of you and your father. If we lock up Caplin..."

"We'll lose them anyway if we sentence him," said Roxanne, the brandy settling her nerves and helping her to think more clearly.

"Besides, the Ronan army was split to begin with," said Lindsey, "but Bolton is the Lux. People are already looking to her. Instead of letting her go rogue, convince her to step up and take command."

Roxanne glanced at Devan again. The Resistance Leaders had already discussed the pros and cons of Skye proclaiming herself the head of Caplin's Forces. And since the battle, she had heard of more people joining the self-styled Lux Guard, proudly displaying their own family crests on their uniforms instead of Caplin's. It disturbed her how easily people were swayed, but right then, it was what they needed.

"Skye herself is reluctant." Roxanne chose her words carefully. "Her chief motivation is getting her father back. But this might tip her mind in our favour."

"Anyway, with Caplin out of the way, we're more likely to get a democracy instead of another dictator," said Lindsey bitterly.

"As long as Bolton doesn't follow in the last Lux's footsteps, I think you're right," said Devan.

Roxanne sipped the brandy, praying Devan's words weren't a premonition. It was true that her goals were aligned with Skye's where their loved ones were concerned, but none of them truly knew what went on inside her hidden mind, what plans she might have once her father was free. "Do you think we can trust Skye to help us get Amber back, as well as her father?"

Lindsey twisted the ring on her finger. "I believe so. She stands to lose as much as we do if the secret gets out, and she feels guilty about what went on with Amber. She'll consider this some kind of redemption."

Roxanne nodded and took a deep breath. "And Dean?"

"Dean will do whatever Skye asks of him." Lindsey paused then, a hard expression passing her face that reminded Roxanne a little too much of Oliver. "He will also do whatever I ask him."

Roxanne swallowed. There it was. The reminder that Lindsey was not someone to be taken lightly. She might care fiercely where her loved ones were concerned, but she was still half Marsden. She suppressed a shudder.

"Don't hurt him. He doesn't deserve it."

"This is war, Roxanne. Sometimes collateral damage is inevitable." Lindsey's jaw tightened. "You should know that, after what happened to my brother."

Tears sprang to Roxanne's eyes, and she lowered her gaze to the glass in her hands, her guilt over Cameron flaring up. She hadn't missed the hint of accusation in Lindsey's tone.

"How long do you think the investigation will take?" Devan asked, tactfully changing the subject. "You heard Camilla, Amber is struggling."

"That could just be Camilla trying to scare us, but—"

The door banged open behind Lindsey, and Oliver stood framed in the doorway, his face pink with fury. Lindsey stopped speaking and looked around, her own face turning an equivalent shade of pink. Slowly, quietly, Oliver let himself in, then closed the door behind him with a resounding click. "What's this?" he said in a voice that sounded more like a threat than a question.

"Nothing, Dad," said Lindsey bluntly, turning back to Devan and Roxanne with fear in her eyes.

But Oliver looked between them, fixing each of them with a stare that made Roxanne fidget. "I heard you talking about Amber, and Camilla."

"We were," said Lindsey, while Roxanne, to her shame, sat lost for words, not trusting her voice.

"She's my daughter too. Did you not think to include me?" Oliver said, stepping to his daughter's side and looking down at her.

To her credit, Lindsey didn't shrink beneath his glare. Instead, she sat straighter, the fear in her eyes replaced with defiance. "I didn't think you were in any fit state—"

"And she is?" Oliver interrupted, jabbing a finger towards Roxanne that had Devan tensing beside her.

"Camilla invited me," Roxanne began, her voice coming out in a pitch that made her sound far from brave.

"Did she now? Did she invite your new boyfriend too, or did you just take him along to rub my nose in it?"

Roxanne was certain any colour that flooded her face had drained from it just as quickly. And then Oliver advanced, making to walk around the table towards her. Devan jumped up and blocked his path. Her heart jumped into her throat as she watched them stare each other down, Oliver standing an inch or two taller than Devan. Lindsey sprang up too, placing a firm hand on her father's upper arm.

"Dad, that's *enough*—"

But Oliver shook her off, making to shove past Devan, who grabbed his shoulders to stop him. There was a scuffle, and Roxanne knocked her chair over in her haste to get up too, hovering awkwardly as the two men wrestled. Oliver lifted a fist, arm snapping back for a punch, before Lindsey grabbed him and jerked him back.

"This is why we didn't include you," Lindsey shouted, her face contorted with anger and the effort of keeping her father from lunging at Devan. "You're a mess right now."

"You can't expect me to sit back and let you lot have your secret little meetings while Camilla tortures my daughter!" Oliver snarled in Lindsey's face.

"Oliver," Roxanne began, but he was shouting again.

"*He* doesn't even have anything to do with her," he yelled, pointing a trembling finger at Devan, who remained in a defensive stance.

"Who Roxanne confides in is none of your business," Lindsey spat back. "You lost that right when you walked away from her."

Oliver grabbed the front of Lindsey's jacket, pushing her back until she lost her balance and planted a hand on the table to keep from falling. Devan stepped forward to pull Oliver back, but then the latter let go, turning away and pressing his hands to his face in shame. After a moment, Lindsey stepped away from the table, straightening her jacket and tucking hair behind her ears.

"You should go," she told Roxanne and Devan, her expression inviting no argument. Oliver collapsed into a chair, elbows resting on the table, his face still buried in his hands. Obeying Lindsey's request, Devan placed a hand on Roxanne's shoulder, gently nudging her to leave.

"I'm sorry," Roxanne heard Oliver murmur to his daughter as she closed the door behind them.

Chapter Sixty-Two

PHAEDRA RONAN

Phaedra felt a bit strange having Skye Bolton trailing them at a distance as she and her uncle strolled along the beach, but after the assassination attempt, she knew they needed protection, especially while Caspar was still healing.

Their progress was slow, and Caspar's expression was strained as he struggled along with his crutches. Eventually he stopped to sit on the rocks along the coastline. But Skye walked on, making her way towards the tideline. Phaedra looked between them with a frown, finding their parting a little too tactical.

"Please sit with me, Phaedra. There's something I need to tell you."

She stared at him while a hundred worst-case scenarios jumped to mind. No doubt her sister had done something, or someone had been killed, or there was to be another battle. Caspar's eyes were on the sand, clearly trying to find words for whatever he had to say. She waited impatiently, fiddling with the hem of her jacket and kicking her heel anxiously against the rock she sat on.

"I… I have wanted to tell you this your whole life. It killed me to keep this secret, but… but I promised your mother. And I had to keep you safe."

"Safe from what?"

He looked up at her, his eyes haunted, and her fear doubled.

"You know your mother and I were close."

She frowned. "Yes. You were friends."

Caspar gave a slight smile. "We were more than friends, Phaedra. I loved her, very much. And she loved me."

Phaedra's eyes widened, even though she had suspected for some time now that her uncle's feelings towards her mother weren't entirely fraternal. She had seen the way he looked at her portraits. She had heard the comments he had made to her father when he thought no one was listening. But still, hearing it confirmed surprised her more than she expected.

"Did my dad know?"

A shadow passed over Caspar's eyes at the mention of her father. "I think he suspected. But I don't think he really cared. It was an arranged marriage, as you know."

She nodded, fiddling with her jacket again. "Then why does it matter? If my dad didn't care, why did she make you promise not to tell anyone?"

Caspar took a deep breath, looking out to sea with a pained expression, then turning back to her. "Phaedra... Doran wasn't your father."

She blinked, the words hanging in the air between them, causing her whole world to tilt. Everything she thought she knew suddenly slid off the edge. "Then..." she murmured, trying to figure out what that meant.

"I am," he said gently, his face pale and full of fear. Phaedra could only stare at him, her limbs turning numb as she struggled to make sense of her thoughts. She didn't know how long had passed before she managed to form a shaky, whispered question.

"How do you know?"

A muscle in his jaw flickered as he gave that grim smile again, the smile she came to realise appeared whenever he had to say something difficult. "After Alessia, she and Doran never..." He trailed off, leaving it up to her imagination. "I'm not proud of it, stealing my brother's wife. But we were young, and her world was so devoid of affection. I knew deep down that being there for her, making her feel safe and loved was the right thing to do. And I did love her, I never stopped. So we grew close. We thought we were being careful, but when we found out she was pregnant, I urged her to leave with me, go into hiding and become a proper family. But there was no way my father or Doran would let her leave with Alessia, and she didn't want to be parted from her. So... so she went to Doran, told him she wanted to try for another baby."

Phaedra dropped her gaze, the truth churning her insides. So Doran wasn't her father. Caspar had no doubt about it. The man who had raised her, loved her, the man she had watched murdered and grieved for, he wasn't her father. She gripped the rock beneath her, her world tilting again. She didn't know how she felt, couldn't fathom whether she was angry or horrified or relieved.

"Do you know how many times I wished I could live with you instead of them?" she asked, glancing up at him for a moment, then back down at the ground, her frenzied feelings prickling up her neck.

"Believe me, I wanted to claim you, to take you away. But Ilaria made me promise. We knew Ivor wouldn't stand for it, he was dead against scandals. You weren't safe if he knew the truth."

She curled her hands into fists, taking deep breaths. "My... Doran... he did his best, but..."

"I know," he said, then reached out a hesitant hand, laying it over her closed fist. She relaxed her fingers against the rock again, but didn't take his hand. "For what it's worth, he loved you very much. And I love you too. It doesn't have to matter who fathered you."

Phaedra gritted her teeth, her stomach lurching again. She had loved Doran too, for all his flaws. She didn't like him, but she loved him. But now, knowing that her father and her uncle had switched places, she didn't know how she was supposed to feel. "Things could have been so different," she said bleakly, unable to stop herself from resenting the way things had turned out, mourning the lost childhood she could have had, instead of living in fear of her sister and grandfather.

"I know. I wish they could have been different. I know Doran wasn't the perfect father, but he cared for you and provided for you and was as fair as he could be. If I had thought for a moment that you would be in more danger staying with him than coming with me, I would have stepped in."

She nodded, still looking at the ground, unable to put her feelings into any semblance of order. But she turned her palm upwards, curling her fingers around his. She was angry and hurt by the secret, still not quite able to understand why he had thought she was better off living in that manor than with him, but a big part of her was glad. Glad that the one family member she was closest to was her real father, even if he had lied to her throughout her entire life.

"I understand if you need time to let this sink in. I won't be offended if you need to… get away for a while."

She squeezed his hand. "I'm going nowhere," she said fiercely, glaring at the sea. She *would* need time, but she wasn't going to leave him, especially not after her sister's attack.

He squeezed back, and they lapsed into silence, watching the sun glittering on the rippling waves. Her chaotic thoughts jumped through her mind, and she tried to sort through them. One thought that kept coming back was that of her sister poisoning her father, and how it had been

Doran's only child who had killed him. The thought somehow disturbed her even more than it had done before, and she drew her knees up to her chest, hunched on the rock.

"Does anyone else know?" she asked eventually, the numb shock having subsided enough for her to feel the chill of the wind.

Caspar hesitated, then glanced over to where Skye paced at the edge of the water, the sun gleaming on her blonde head. "Skye saw the truth in my mind, but only recently."

Phaedra gave him a sharp look. "And you trust her?"

He met her gaze, looking sheepish. "I think so."

She bit her lip. Despite Skye's relationship with Caspar and her kindness in taking them in, Phaedra knew what kind of currency this secret could be if things turned sour.

"What about Alessia?"

Caspar was silent again, and he gripped her hand a little tighter. "I don't think she does, but... Camilla always suspected. She knew what Ilaria meant to me."

Phaedra shivered at the mention of Camilla. She had rarely come into contact with her, but she had a pretty good idea of what her job entailed. "I guess it doesn't matter now, if Alessia finds out. She hates me anyway."

She met Caspar's eye, and realised she no longer cared what her sister thought of her. She had all the family she needed.

"I'm proud of you, you know," he said suddenly, and the look in his eyes told her he meant it. Her throat tightened, and she blinked away the tears that suddenly sprang up.

"No one has ever told me that before."

"I know, and I'm sorry for that. I should have told you every day, every day since I watched you take your first steps. You are everything to me."

The tears fell in earnest then, and she lowered her head, pushing the heel of her free hand into each eye. Before she knew it, Caspar had wrapped his arms around her, and she gripped his jacket, knowing that wherever he was, she had a home.

Chapter Sixty-Three

AMBER SUMMERS

A cat was staring at her, and Amber stared right back as she drifted in and out of consciousness.

Each time she awoke, the cat had moved around the room. At first, it sat in a sunspot slanting through the boards across the window. Then it perched on the stained mattress that sagged on the bed. Another time, it clawed at an invisible fly a foot above its head. And now it lay beside her, paws pressed primly together, watching.

Amber stirred feebly, her limbs stiff. Her entire body was numb with cold, with only a dull ache in her shoulder and hips from where she had lain too long on the floor. She didn't know how many hours it had been since she had passed out from her latest torture, but as she peered at her arms, there was no sign of the damage the woman had inflicted except for the dried blood flaking from her skin. Was she hallucinating it all, or was she somehow, miraculously, a Healer as her captor claimed?

With a groan, Amber sat up, leaning her back against the wall. The dress she wore was the only change of clothes she had been brought – black velvet with short sleeves and a skirt that reached her knees. The material had been soft as cat fur at first, a luxury at odds with the situation she was in, but it was now stiff with blood, itching her skin.

Moving as though she were in a dream, she withdrew Cameron's paper sparrow from her pocket. The folded bird was crumpled, but miraculously free of the blood and grime that coated the rest of her, the sunshine yellow paper gleaming in the light slanting into the room. Clutching it close in both hands, she curled her legs against her chest, longing for a blanket.

She dozed off again, her head nodding towards her knees, then jerked awake to a soft flickering against her palm. She looked down to find a small brown bird flapping in her cupped hands. She blinked in surprise and dropped the bird, but it took flight before it could fall, darting around the room. The cat sat beside her, pearlescent eyes tracking the bird. Tentatively, she raised her hand, trying to stroke the cat's head, but her fingers passed right through as though it were smoke. A dream, then. Still, she took comfort in it, managing a small smile as the cat glanced between her and the bird, its fur a light, striped grey, like Mischa's. It was better than the nightmares that had plagued her. Better than the reality that greeted her each time she opened her eyes.

"Amber…" came a purr, and she blinked, meeting the cat's intense stare. "I know what you are."

So a cat was talking to her now. Perhaps she was finally cracking up.

"The stormbird and the dragon are flying into a tempest. The end draws near."

"End?"

"The phoenix cannot see the sparrow quivering in her cage."

Amber frowned, staring at the talking cat, then glancing at the sparrow still flitting above their heads. "All this talk of birds," she said in a thick, dazed voice, "you must be hungry."

The cat's eyes gleamed iridescent in the thin shards of light.

"At the end will be the second beginning."

She coughed, rubbing her arms to rid the chill and numbness. "Okay…" she murmured, dismissing the ramblings as a convolution of her dream.

"When the end comes, let your Trace guide you. It is older than you are. As old as the earth."

Amber rested her chin on her knees, let the purring voice lull her eyes closed. The purr grew louder, then faint as the cat padded away. Amber watched it through her lashes, but she couldn't find the words to ask it to stay. She shivered, letting sleep reclaim her.

"Follow me," said the creature, and when she opened her eyes again, golden sunlight streamed into the room. The cat was walking towards a forest path where the window had been, leading into summer green trees, deeper into the dream. "I will show you the end." And with that, it headed down the path. The sparrow chirped, swooping down to land on her shoulder, feathers tickling her cheek. As the bird chirped again, Amber staggered to her feet and trailed behind like a sleepwalker.

The path took them into the depths of ancient woodland, the trees growing denser, a canopy of leaves casting them in an eerie green light. Shafts of sunlight pierced the gloom, like the light peeking through the cracks in the boards across her prison window. Beneath her bare feet, the terrain grew rougher, loose stones to make her stumble, roots snaking across her path. But she felt nothing, not even cold now. Somewhere to her left, water trickled unseen, and various birds called, creatures rustling invisible in the undergrowth.

"Where are we going?" she whispered, afraid to disturb the peace. Her voice was swallowed by the quiet, as though the trees breathed in the noise. On her shoulder, the sparrow's wings flickered every so often, the movement loud against her ear.

The cat only let out a low purr in response, a comforting sound. It stalked on, tail high in the air, weaving through roots and brambles with ease.

They came to the edge of the forest, where a meadow stretched before them. Long grass rippled like waves in the breeze that tugged at Amber's hair. Sunlight flooded the area, and insects drifted back and forth, wings sparkling like jewels in the bright light.

The cat sat down at her side, its head high, ears alert, watching. The sparrow, still on her shoulder, was silent.

"Death comes on dark wings," purred the cat, and Amber followed its gaze. Sure enough, the sky faded to red as black clouds loomed on the horizon, chasing a raven across the sky, its cry shredding through the rapid beating of Amber's heart.

Night fell as the soaring raven became one with the dark, but something else approached now, bright white light illuminating the clouds, the low growl of thunder rolling towards them. As the lightning drew closer, so did the wind cast by titanic wings, and two godlike creatures descended from the clouds. One was a snarling dragon scaled in blood and gold and wreathed in shadow, and the other was a great bird the colour of a storm cloud. The snap of its beak rumbled like claps of thunder, and its lightning split the night sky into shards.

Amber shivered, watching the battle rage on, leathery wings and grey feathers cutting swiftly through the air. Keening cries reverberated through Amber's chest as claws flashed, beak and jaw snapped, darkness and lightning danced. Blood fell from the sky like rain, black and red and gold.

She crouched low beside the cat, wrapping her arms around her knees. "Who will win?" she whispered to it. Its ear twitched towards her. She didn't want the creatures to see her there. She feared what would happen if they did.

"It is not known," the cat purred back. "Those with the Sight cannot see such outcomes. The Nameless Gods do not will it, for it affects the fate of us all."

With an otherworldly scream, the winged creatures plummeted together to the ground, the impact shuddering through Amber, through the world.

Other creatures emerged from the darkness then: a great, hulking wolf with eyes like emeralds, hackles raised; an ethereal being of unknown size and shape moving like a shadowy cloud, drifting like it floated in water rather than air; a giant serpent slithering like a silver stream through the grass, with teeth as long as Amber's arm, as sharp as any sword. And amongst them, approaching the fallen creatures, was a woman, crowned in starlight, cloaked in midnight.

Amber trembled, praying that the creatures would not see her. But one did. While the others froze in conference, one broke away from the group and slithered towards her, the grass parting for the silver serpent. Amber staggered to her feet and backed into the shadow of the trees. The cat and sparrow had disappeared. She had not seen them go.

"You have come, my child," hissed the serpent, the voice trickling through her, ancient and deathly, yet full of life. "You have come to witness the beginning and the end."

Amber quaked as the serpent encircled her. She turned with it, keeping her eyes on the serpent's head, its eyes like glowing moons looming through the darkness.

"My silver blood runs in your veins. You will know when the end and beginning are one."

She shook her head, reaching for her voice, but it was buried deep within her, small and terrified. She gasped as something smooth twined around her arms, and she looked down, seeing tiny, twin silver snakes writhing around her wrists. She jerked her arms, trying to shake them off, but they held firm, biting their own tails, heavy as shackles, coiling tight. As she shuffled in a circle, more serpents curled around her ankles, bright in the darkness.

Let me go, she longed to say, but she could only stand there, breath ragged, tears blurring the moon eyes and sabre teeth of the giant creature.

"Do not be afraid, child. The sacrifices of your brothers and sisters will not be in vain. Their end is your beginning."

And as Amber dropped to her knees, weighed down by the shackles, she found her voice at last.

Chapter Sixty-Four

ALESSIA RONAN

A sea of stars blanketed the sky over the castle battlements, constellations and galaxies visible in the still night. Alessia's hands were buried deep in her pockets, her soft woollen coat keeping the slight chill at bay. These nightly walks on the castle rooftop had become one of her few remaining pleasures, but tonight, a visitor disturbed her peace, a visitor who insisted on further testing her patience.

Alessia didn't even give the man beside her the courtesy of looking at him as they stood side by side beside the parapet. Twice he had made her a promise. Twice he had failed to deliver. And yet he had shown up again, somehow finding the nerve to ask for another chance.

"The assassination may not have been successful," came the voice beside her, speaking softly as though afraid to disturb the peace… or afraid to provoke her. "But the cracks in the alliance are showing. Your uncle knows he can trust no one, and the Resistance and Bolton are pointing the finger at one another."

"Last you told me, the Lux is my uncle's lover. So the Resistance believes it's an act?"

"Whatever the truth may be, none of the rumours are favourable. Some believe she and your uncle plot to overthrow the Resistance. Others think she is behind the assassination attempt. My people are fuelling those rumours. If she intends to win over followers, she will find she won't have many."

Alessia remained silent, but her Talents swirled inside her chest, her lips curling a little in satisfaction. And even more satisfying was watching the games that played out between her secret informants, waiting to see which one would get caught in their tangled web of lies first. Her grandfather had already said his money was on the man at her side, after her other visitors that day offered their own perspectives of the crumbling alliance.

"And does anyone suspect *you*?"

His hesitation gave her the answer. Finally, she turned her head and met his gaze. Beyond his shoulder, two silver orbs watched from the gloom – Lucien, his eyes a pair of stars cloaked in shadow, the glamour he had donned each time her informants came with their secrets and promises.

"If they suspect you, you have exhausted your usefulness to me."

"The Matheson bloodhound likes to throw around accusations, but she's nothing I can't handle."

"You're a fool if you underestimate Matheson. She even tricked her father for years."

"Unless Oliver was in on it. Let's not forget it was his son who helped Bolton escape your father's clutches."

And my father's blind stupidity, Alessia thought darkly.

"What if I have Miss Matheson… eliminated?"

Alessia scoffed. "You failed to eliminate my uncle. Twice. And the Lux remains alive and free. Give me a reason why I shouldn't eliminate *you*."

If he was ruffled by the threat, he kept up a mask of cool indifference. "Because Vala has foreseen that I will deliver the Lux to you."

"Then you ought to get a move on. If you do indeed deliver me the Lux, I will give you a role in my inner circle, honour and privileges beneath my rule. But you had better be prepared to bow, Mr Caplin."

The fallen president's yellow eyes narrowed, the sly smile still pasted on his lips. Whatever secrets he shared, however much he massaged her ego, she didn't trust him. But he still had his uses, and until the breadcrumbs she had left for the Tracers and Camilla's twisted games lured him to his death, she fully intended to exploit him.

"Has Vala shown you this future, by any chance?" Caplin asked then, turning his gaze back to the stars. A sudden breeze tugged at her hair that felt a little too unnatural. Alessia glared his way, but his face held only mild curiosity.

"Why do you ask?" The truth was, she hadn't. Vala claimed not to know the outcome of the final battle. Yet.

"Oh, I just wonder if knowing what we're fighting for would make it easier to choose a side." He cast her a sideways glance. "Take Vala, for example. She has always been known to back the victor. And yet, she advised the Lux on how to defeat the Undead, giving your opponents an advantage during the battle. That sounds a lot like betrayal to me."

The ground fell away beneath her feet, ice creeping up her neck, closing her throat. Alessia's gaze shot to Lucien, who blinked, eyes of quicksilver swallowed for a split second by the night. The wind nipped at her hair again. She resisted the urge to bat it away.

"Vala knows her place. As should you. But if you would rather back a spoilt brat who shows you up in front of your followers and allies, be my guest."

Caplin's amusement still graced his lips, but the wind dropped, leaving only stillness in its wake.

"One last chance," Alessia said, crossing her arms as she surveyed him imperiously. "Prove you're still useful to me. Or the next time you show up here without the Lux, I'll have Camilla tear you apart."

His yellow eyes glinted defiantly, and then he bowed his head, turning on his heel and striding off. He was oblivious to Lucien's shadowy presence as he passed him. The door opened, letting out a slice of buttery light, which promptly extinguished as he closed it. Lucien waited a heartbeat, then the glamour warped, the night gathering into a man.

"You're worried," he said, withdrawing a cigarette and igniting it with the gleam of a silver lighter and a flicker of flame.

"He's baiting me," she said dismissively, turning back to the parapet. But despite her façade, doubt twisted with the ice in the hollow of her chest. Caplin descended from the last Lux. If anyone knew the legends, it would be him.

"Whether or not you meant it," he ventured, coming to stand beside her, "an alliance with the Caplinites would bring unity after you kill the Lux. Caplin's de facto heir is Ikarus Arrowsmith. He's unattached, and just a few years older than you. He might be a suitable match if you wanted to… seal an alliance the old-fashioned way."

"I'm not a broodmare," she snapped, wrinkling her nose in disgust at his suggestion and the cigarette smoke. "I have no intention to marry." And after her father had executed Darius Arrowsmith, she doubted his son would want anything to do with her even if she was interested.

He inclined his head, a ghost of a smirk on his face. "Nox have been known to love, you know."

She stepped up to him, seething in his face. "Love is for the weak."

He held her gaze, eyes still flashing like the stars overhead. And then he lazily lifted his cigarette to his smirking lips. She stepped away before he could blow a plume into her face.

"Love is what your enemies fight for, Alessia," he said as she began to walk away, his voice raising the hair on her forearms. She paused halfway to the door, turning back to his outline blocking out the stars. "Remember that in the coming days."

She sneered, watching him drag on his cigarette again, the smoke curling around him like mist unfurling across a frozen field. "I look forward to seeing how love leads my enemies to their doom."

And with that, she stepped towards the stairwell, leaving him with his ridiculous notions behind.

Chapter Sixty-Five

GLEN FARRADAY

"You look like you could use some company," said Glen, stopping beside Skye's brother, Dean, who looked like he was about to start crying into his beer. It was lunchtime, and Glen had escaped the canteen in favour of a burger and a non-alcoholic pint at the pub instead. "Mind if I join?"

"Sure," said Dean, blinking like a nocturnal creature that had emerged from its burrow to find it was unexpectedly light. He gave Glen a distracted smile and swirled the beer in his glass.

Glen settled into the booth opposite him, setting down his lunch and drink. "Help yourself to chips if you want," he said politely, while secretly hoping Dean wouldn't want any.

"Oh no, you're alright. I ate earlier," Dean said, rubbing his temples. "Cheers though."

Glen surveyed him as he munched on a chip, taking in the ashen pallor to his skin tone, the strain around his jaw. Realising this guy clearly needed cheering up, he tried to put on a brighter demeanour than he felt. "How are things?"

Dean shrugged. "Could be better. How about you?"

Glen nodded, cheerfulness promptly failing. "Same. I feel like I'm just waiting for the next storm to hit."

"Are they keeping you busy at least?"

"Mostly just drills, training, the usual. I'm guarding Nanette Ferries this afternoon though, breaks up the monotony."

"Sounds about as riveting as what I'm doing most days," he said with a bitter laugh.

"Oh? I thought you'd be at the centre of the action?" asked Glen, sipping his beer.

"Nah, I just feel like Skye's sidekick most of the time."

Glen grimaced. He hadn't spoken to Skye since the day after the battle, and when he had glimpsed her from a distance, she had usually looked stressed or pissed off. Neither mood invited conversation. "How is she?"

"Honestly?" Dean stared bleakly at his drink. "I don't really know. She doesn't tell me."

He raised an eyebrow. "From the way she talked about you, I always thought you two were close."

"We are. We were." Dean winced. "The thing is, Skye doesn't like feelings, so she does her best to avoid them by pretending she doesn't have any."

Glen stifled a laugh, the description of Skye far too accurate. But he couldn't help the concern that crept up for his former flame. And judging by how miserable Dean looked, he wasn't talking to anyone either.

"At least you have each other's backs, even if she doesn't talk. I'm sure she knows you're there for her."

"Yeah…" Dean gave him another half-hearted smile and drained the dregs of his beer.

Just as Glen bit into his burger, a blonde woman slid into the booth next to Dean, and he recognised Lindsey Matheson. There was a small frown between her brows, but she otherwise looked as pristine as ever.

"Hey, Farraday," she said, giving him the smallest of smiles as she scrutinised him.

He gave an awkward wave, his mouth too full to speak. But he quickly realised her unlikely presence wasn't a social visit when she turned to Dean, their faces close, leaving Glen feeling like he was intruding. Instead, he busied himself with his food, conscious he didn't have long of his break left.

"We've been looking for you," she said to Dean, who flushed as he met her gaze and seemed to melt like a puppy dog. *Poor guy*, Glen thought to himself. Clearly he was smitten, although Lindsey came across as even more emotionally unavailable than Skye. But considering how recently Cameron had passed and everything going on with Amber, he couldn't really blame her.

"Has something happened?" asked Dean, fear injecting his face and voice.

"Your aunt is here. She wants to go over… details." She glanced at Glen out of the corner of her eye, but he simply took another bite of his burger.

"I'd better go," said Dean, looking at Glen apologetically. "You're welcome to join us any time you want some company in the gym, by the way."

"Will do," Glen grunted. He had spotted the members of the Caplin Guard in the gym several times, but since Skye and the scary Ignis – Sabine – were usually with them, he had avoided them.

"Safe journey, Farraday," said Lindsey, eyeing him as the pair slipped out of the booth.

Glen's attention returned to his burger as he dwelt on his afternoon's mission. But before he could swallow his next bite, Phaedra dropped into Dean's vacated seat, a frown on her pale face.

"I can't believe you were going to leave without saying goodbye," she said, pouting as she glared at him.

Despite her mock fury, Glen swallowed and broke into a grin, her presence chasing his gloom away. "I'll only be gone a couple of days."

"Anything could happen in two days," she grumbled, then swiped a couple of chips, her eyes still narrowed as she gobbled them down.

"You've been so busy with your girlfriend, I didn't think you'd notice." He surveyed her as she stuck out her tongue and stole another chip. Her face was drawn, with dark shadows under her eyes, her tufty hair flat and unstyled. "Are you still staying at the Boltons'?"

She shrugged, glancing around the pub in agitation. "Mostly. My unc—" She paused, frowning at the table. "Caspar's still recovering."

Glen took a sip of his beer, watching her closely. Caspar could take a long walk off a short pier for all he cared, but hearing that Phaedra had been caught up in the assassination attempt had made him all the more eager to carry out his upcoming mission. Even if he was only reprising his role as a driver and bodyguard.

Phaedra stuck out her hand to grab another chip, and he tsked. "Do you want me to starve?"

She raised an eyebrow at his physique, nibbling her chip. "It's not like you're wasting away."

"Order your own if you're hungry," he grumbled, finishing off his burger.

"When you come back, can you teach me to punch properly? There's this other cadet who needs his face rearranging."

He snorted, almost choking on his food. "You're lethal enough as it is, Phee Phee."

"A soldier can never have enough weapons." Her lips tugged up at the corners, and before he could stop her, she grabbed his beer and took a gulp.

He let out a sigh. "How about I bloody this kid's nose for you, and you buy me lunch when I'm back? I'm pretty sure you're good for it, you Ronans are practically royalty."

Her sly grin grew. “Deal.” She jumped up then, play-punching his arm and sneaking one last chip. “See you when you get back, Glenny Boy.”

***

The drive up to Scotland was agonisingly monotonous, and rain began to fall more heavily the further north he got. The only break so far was the untraceable portal they took to skip a couple of hours and avoid the blockades that Alessia Ronan had set up through occupied territory. Once beyond it, they had a clear road up to Glasgow.

His fellow guard, Johnson, said little, flicking through the channels on the radio every ten minutes, to Glen’s endless irritation. In the back of the darkened vehicle, behind a soundproofing screen, sat Nanette Ferries and two of her political aides.

When Roxanne and Lindsey had recommended him for the job of escorting Ferries to a meeting with underground Resistance members in Glasgow, he had been honoured and all the more determined to prove they were right to put their trust in him. What was more, it was a break from the mundane tasks and training he had to endure each day. The driving itself was far from fun, but he was looking forward to seeing who Ferries would meet with, to get to know the brave people who continued the Resistance’s work in secret, despite the iron grip Alessia and the Marsdens held over Scotland.

Although sunset was hours away, the sky was as dark as twilight by the time they reached Glasgow, with rain hammering on the windshield at intervals. He slowed the car as they entered the outskirts of the city, meeting traffic. But they had accounted for it, having deliberately chosen rush hour to draw less attention to themselves, surrounded by other cars on their commutes. Their destination was a college, another method to avoid raising suspicions, and their meeting would be posing as a book club. Each of them were dressed in plain clothes, with Glen and Johnson concealing weapons on their person. Personally, he felt that he and Johnson looked like the most unlikely book club attendees, but he doubted anyone would notice they were even there, except perhaps after-hours cleaners or security guards, if there were any.

As they pulled into the car park, he clocked two inconspicuous cars, and saw Johnson's head swivelling in search of intruders. Roxanne and her fellow Leaders had briefed them fully and provided pictures of the other Resistance members. Anyone else who might show up couldn't be trusted.

Once parked, he and Johnson got out of the car, again checking their surroundings, then opened the back doors for their passengers to get out. Ferries and her aides looked different, disguised by glamours, but the way Ferries held herself made her unmistakable regardless. The glamour made her look older, her pointed features softer and more wrinkled, her hair grey instead of raven black. But those hawk eyes still swept over their surroundings, as shrewd and sharp as ever. Without a word, she smoothed down her emerald green skirt suit, adjusted the handbag strap on her arm, and stalked towards the college. As Glen and the others hurried to keep up, she pushed open the unlocked side door they had been told to enter by, then headed down a corridor, sensible court heels tapping on the tiled floor. They didn't have to go far before someone popped their head out through a doorway, a bald man with a big friendly grin on his face.

"Nanny!" the man exclaimed, stepping out into the corridor and grasping Ferries's hand in both of his. He was tall and thin – a beanpole was the term Glen's mother would have used – and dressed in a shirt, tie and sleeveless grey jersey.

"How are you, Bert?" said Ferries, leaning up on her tiptoes and planting a kiss on each of the man's cheeks, leaving behind a smudge of red lipstick.

"Oh, just fine, just fine. How was the trip?"

The two chatted animatedly as they stepped into the room Bert had been in, leaving Glen and the others to follow. Inside was a library, full of shelves of what looked like scientific and engineering textbooks, and in the centre were several clusters of tables and chairs where two others rose to greet them. One was a woman who looked to be around fifty, with long dark hair and the air of a schoolteacher, whereas the other was a much older man, with curly grey hair and glasses that slipped down his nose when he shook their hands.

"This is Grace Jones and Michael Bellamy," said Bert. Ferries introduced her aides in return, but didn't bother to name Glen and Johnson, not that he was expecting the courtesy. Getting the message, he retreated to the entrance, standing in the doorway where he had a good view of both the library and both ends of the corridor, his hand within reaching distance of the gun in his pocket. Johnson took up a position near the windows, the rain pelting the glass.

"So, how have things been?" asked Ferries after they had sat down, dropping her voice and getting straight to the point.

"Not great, I'll be honest, Nanny," said Bert, his grin fading to a serious expression. "We have Marsdens sitting in every city hall in Scotland, and when she's not slaughtering civilians for her Undead army, the Nox herself holds parliament in Edinburgh."

Ferries nodded, but she had her back to Glen. "How are the infiltration plans going?"

"Slow," said the man called Bellamy, speaking for the first time. "I've managed to bag the role of interviewer, but Andrew Marsden wants me to run every potential new recruit by him before I offer the job, so of course he discards any CVs that indicate the applicant might be linked to us."

"I was one of them," said Grace, her voice low. "Marsden called me up for a surprise phone interview, wanting to know why a college tutor wanted a job filing and answering phones for Glasgow City Council."

"What did you tell him?" asked Ferries, her back straightening.

"Told him I was sick of teaching rowdy teenagers. Didn't get the job though."

"Well, your real reasons make much more sense," came a horribly familiar voice from the back of the room, and Glen reached for his gun just as a shot rang out.

Glen's body spurred into action as his mind reeled from shock. Because the voice belonged to Andrew Marsden, and four soldiers in Ronan purple emerged from amongst the bookcases, shooting at the six Resistance members seated in the middle of the room. Most of them made it to the floor, but Grace Jones half collapsed against the table, dark red blood staining the blue blouse she wore.

Glen shot at the attackers, hitting one of them in the arm, making him drop his gun. Johnson was shooting too, but he took a bullet to the chest almost immediately and crumpled to the floor. Fear jolted through him as he realised he was the only one left to defend the Resistance members, and he advanced into the middle of the room, aiming to kill.

Ice sprang from the floor, hurtling straight at Andrew, whose narrow face distorted in a snarl. Scrambling from beneath the table with her lacquered hair sticking up in every direction, Ferries threw another handful of glittering ice at the attackers. She coated one of the Ronan soldiers, his face a picture of shock as his hands froze on his gun. The one who shot Johnson turned his gun on Ferries as Andrew backed behind the bookshelves, and the woman screeched as blood splattered down her side, a bullet lodged in her arm.

Glen fired shots of his own while they were distracted by Ferries's attack, bullets pinging off the metal bookcases or embedding in books. But then a gust of air whooshed him off his feet, sending him slamming into the wall. A heavy blow wracked through the back of his head, his gun slipping from numb fingers as he crumpled. All he knew was pain as his left arm and jaw connected with the floor and black stars flooded his vision.

Dizzy moments followed as he stirred feebly, struggling to remain conscious. Between table legs, he saw Ferries on her knees, screeching and snapping like a wild animal, frost still glistening across the grey carpet.

"Give up, old lady," came Andrew's snarl, followed by a crack as he thrust Ferries's arm down. She yelped, her free hand still scrabbling at Andrew's chest, leaving bloody handprints on his white shirt. Glen grunted, trying to get his elbows and knees beneath him to push himself up, but then Andrew hit Ferries over the head with the butt of a gun, and she fell to the floor with a thud.

All went still.

Glen froze, his cheek stuck to the rough carpet, the tang of blood filling his mouth as unconsciousness still threatened at the edge of his vision. A steady pounding sent pain shooting from the back of his head, and his face and arm hurt from where he had fallen. As the fuzz clouding his mind gradually cleared, he concentrated on the voices, willing his body to stop betraying him and let him fight.

"She's dead. You weren't supposed to shoot to kill."

"I thought—"

"You're lucky you didn't kill Ferries, you idiot. Ronan wants them alive."

"I'm sorry—"

"Consider this your last field job, Richardson. From now on you can do the admin work *she* applied for."

It was the same voice that had spoken earlier, Andrew Marsden. They must have already been waiting for them when they arrived. They had walked into a trap.

"You killed Farraday too?" came another familiar voice, similar to Andrew's, but with a hint of playfulness to it. Footsteps approached him, and he pressed his eyes closed, feeling a shoe nudge his stomach. When he wouldn't budge, someone leaned down and lifted his eyelid. Realising that playing dead was game over, Glen flinched back, bumping into the wall again. He grunted at the jarring through his shoulder, scrambling to his knees. But the face that looked down at him broke into a grin.

"Mate, we thought you were dead for a minute."

Glen stared, perplexed. Because the face and voice belonged to the other Marsden brother, Rupert. His dark hair was the usual untidy nest, and his tie was undone. It had been a few years since Glen had been his bodyguard, since they had drunk beers in the pub after Rupert's meetings, but he knew that face anywhere.

"I'd offer you a hand, but you'll probably pull me over."

"S'alright," Glen managed, glancing around. The Marsdens and their men had just attacked them. Why on earth was Rupert talking to him like they were still friends? Nearby stood Andrew and one of the guards, both looking down at him. Andrew and Rupert were very alike, but where Rupert was untidy, Andrew was pristine, his black hair slicked back, his face clean-shaven and his three-piece suit immaculate aside from the blood that stained it. Behind them, beneath the table, Grace Jones lay flat on her back. And, judging by the amount of blood around her, she was dead, or very close to it. Johnson was still lying by the window, also unmoving. As he took in their appearance, guilt dropped like a stone into Glen's stomach. This was his fault. He had failed them.

More Ronan soldiers entered the room behind Rupert, at least ten, carrying guns. If Glen tried anything, he would be peppered with bullets within seconds. So instead, he watched as they lifted the unconscious Resistance members between them.

"Where are you taking them?" Glen asked, looking back at Rupert.

"To Linden." Rupert grinned, standing back as Glen got heavily to his feet. "She'll make them sing, that's for sure."

"Sounds like they've got plenty of singing to do," said Andrew, glancing down at Jones's body with distaste. "I knew there was something fishy about Bellamy."

"You've done us a huge favour, pal," said Rupert, clapping Glen on the shoulder. "Sorry about the headache."

Glen blinked in further surprise, still not sure what was going on here. Did they think he was still on their side? That he had planned the trap? When Rupert indicated his head, he placed two fingers to his scalp. There was no blood when he pulled them away, though his scalp was tender, a dull thud still pounding rhythmically through his skull. As for his face, nothing seemed broken, although his tongue was sore and taking up too much room in his mouth. He must have bitten it when he fell. "No worries," he said thickly, but his thoughts strayed back to the mention of Linden. Whatever had happened here, whether he had known about the trap or not, he had delivered Ferries and her fellow Resistance members to the psycho that was Camilla Linden. The guilt in his stomach quickly turned to nausea.

"Don't know about you, but I need a beer," said Rupert, clapping Glen on the shoulder again.

And Glen, not knowing what else he could do, went along with them, drowning in shame and confusion.

Chapter Sixty-Six

DEAN ROSWELL

"You did *not* write poetry at school," said Lindsey, her laughter making Dean flush with embarrassment. He immediately regretted his confession when she asked him to tell her something people didn't know about him. They had just finished dinner at the pub, a late meal after an afternoon full of investigations and meetings. They had invited Skye to join them, but she was exhausted after a day Breaking minds and had excused herself to go back to the safe house to sleep.

"Only for English class," he said quickly, although it was a lie. He still had the little black notebook scribbled with half-finished verses drenched in teenage angst, but the only other person who had ever set eyes on it was Skye. And she had teased him far more than Lindsey.

"What were they about?" she asked, wiping tears of mirth from her eyes and smudging her make-up a little.

"The usual crap," he said dismissively, trying to think of a way to steer the conversation away from his embarrassing confession.

"Anything about *girls*?" she asked, narrowing her eyes in mock intrigue.

"Some," he admitted, trying to keep a straight face while his skin prickled beneath her scrutiny.

She chuckled, the most lively he had seen her since before Amber was captured. "Well, if it makes you feel any better, I wrote about you in my old diary."

She fixed him with a stare, as though daring him to judge or laugh. But his blush only deepened as he looked at her in surprise. "You did?"

"Oh yes. Quite a lot actually."

"What did you write?" he asked, struggling for a moment to form the question. He wasn't even sure he wanted to know.

"I can't really remember. And don't ask to read it, I burned it." Her words were matter of fact.

"Why?"

She shrugged. "I didn't just write about you. I wrote about everything. But I don't like who I was back then, so when I decided I wasn't that person anymore, well… I suppose I didn't want the reminders." Another shrug, and then her face smoothed into indifference.

"That's fair," said Dean, thinking back to times he himself would rather forget. Like his relationship with Letitia. If only he could burn memories as easily as notebooks. "But from what I remember, there was nothing unlikeable about you." He thought back to the sweet girl she had been, the shy smiles and soft-spoken words on the brief occasions they had interacted.

She avoided his gaze now as she had back then, fiddling with the snake ring around her finger. "I had no backbone, Dean." Her voice was low, and her eyes flicked up to his for a heartbeat, then down again. "I didn't protect my brother as well as I should have done. I… didn't protect myself."

An ache tightened his chest, Lindsey's regret echoing his own. How many times had he let his own family down? And it wasn't just Skye. The only father he had ever known rotted in a cell, while Dean plotted to condemn a man he was sworn to protect.

"I can't be that person anymore," she said, and the devastation on her face made him reach instinctively across the table, closing his fingers around her clasped hands. She took a deep breath. "If I have to kill for Amber, I will."

It could have been interpreted as a throwaway comment, but the fury blazing in her eyes confirmed she meant it. As he stroked the backs of her hands with his thumbs, a question bubbled to the surface, a feeling that had haunted him since the bloodbath that was the Ronan mutiny.

"Does it not bother you, what our hands have done to our enemies?"

Lindsey's expression grew hard. "Of course. But I keep reminding myself of what their hands would do to me if I let them. Of what they would do to my loved ones." The same anger still filled her light brown eyes. An anger that made him want to shield her from whoever had stolen the softness he remembered from their school days.

"I wish we didn't have to think like that," he said quietly, his old longing for a better life unfurling deep inside. "I hope… I hope the damage we have to do now will lead to a time when we only need to create, not destroy."

He lowered his gaze to their joined hands, afraid that she might interpret his words as cowardice, or a fool's wish. But she turned her hands palm up, curling her fingers around his. "I would love to see what beautiful things you create someday, Dean."

He dared to look at her again, the tenderness in her gaze softening the painful knot in his chest. As he sought a way to prolong that tenderness, he glanced at the remnants of their meals, spotting the poppy seeds from Lindsey's bread roll peppering one of the discarded plates. "Do you like flowers, Lindsey?"

A bemused smile lit up her face. "What girl doesn't like flowers, Dean?"

Without a word, Dean pressed his finger against the plate, a seed clinging to his fingertip. He gently smoothed Lindsey's hand flat and dropped the seed into her palm. He cupped his hand over hers and called on his Talent, coaxing life from the seed. As he slowly lifted his hand away, roots and stems shot out, spreading and growing, curling around the cradle of Lindsey's hand and intertwining with her fingers. He sneaked a glance at her face, thrilled by the awe and delight softening her features.

The tiny plant continued to grow, fern-like leaves springing free from the stems, a green bud swelling into being before their eyes. And then scarlet petals peeked out between the green, unfurling into a delicate flower that quivered in Lindsey's hand. A genuine smile parted her lips, and the look she gave Dean was pure wonder. And he realised, in that moment, that this was all he wanted: a way to make that look shine on her face every single day for as long as she would have him.

He smiled back at her, his hands cupping hers once again, the poppy bright between them. He tried to find a way to put what he was feeling into words, to confess that all he wanted to do was bring beauty into her life. His heartbeat stuttered as he lost himself in her gaze, her eyes as bright as the night he had kissed her. But before he could find a way to express himself, Lindsey's smile faltered, her attention snagged by Jack Humphries hurrying towards their table.

"Lindsey," said the pimply Tracer who looked barely old enough to have a job. The young man glanced between them, his face colouring as he took in the flower and their joined hands. "Dr Summers has asked for you. She said it's urgent."

Lindsey looked Jack up and down, her nostrils flaring as though scenting what was wrong. She glanced at Dean, reluctance and fear mingling on her face. "I'd better go."

"I was told to invite you too, Mr Roswell. And Miss Bolton if she's present."

Dean nodded, drawing his hands back, momentarily distracted as Lindsey carefully folded the flower into a napkin. Trying not to dwell on what her action might mean, he thought of his sister's name, but only silence responded at the other end of their connection. She was sleeping, then. "Miss Bolton isn't present," he replied, standing up. "But I'll come and pass on the info that concerns her." He glanced back at Lindsey, who nodded, pocketing the napkin inside her jacket. She gave him a last, tentative smile as they followed the young Tracer out of the pub.

The faces that greeted them in the meeting room immediately filled him with dread. Roxanne's grief and fear-stricken face was no longer unusual, but the rest of the Resistance Leaders looked like they were at a funeral, too. Peter Sinclair was agitated, a hint of fear lingered around Devan Harlow's eyes, and Darshana Sahay was there. It was a rarity to see both her and Roxanne in the same room, since they usually took turns attending to medical duties. Riordan Rathbone was also with them.

"Matheson, Roswell," said Peter Sinclair, his voice trembling ever so slightly. "Thanks for coming."

"What's wrong?" Lindsey's voice cut through the heavy atmosphere as she and Dean took seats opposite the Resistance Leaders. Any hint of the tenderness she had let Dean see moments before was replaced with a cold, hard demeanour once more.

"We've had some news…" said Sinclair, but he faltered, lost for words for the first time since Dean had met him.

"As you know," Devan continued, looking at Lindsey, "Nanette went up to Glasgow this afternoon to meet with some of our Resistance representatives."

Lindsey nodded impatiently. Devan took a deep breath before saying his next piece. "We've just received word that she's been captured."

Dean's dread flared, and Lindsey grew pale. "By whom?" she asked, her voice barely above a whisper.

"The statement came from the Nox herself," said Devan, and he pushed a piece of paper a few inches across the table – a typed letter with an elaborate, curling signature and a purple wax stamp. Lindsey reached across the table and picked up the paper with slightly trembling fingers, holding it up for her and Dean to read.

"How did they know?" asked Lindsey after a moment, a hint of anger adding a bite to her tone.

Sinclair shrugged. "Aside from those who were at the meeting, the only people who knew about it are in this room."

"Not all of them," said Lindsey, and she glanced at Dean. "Caplin was here with his Guard yesterday. The meeting was discussed in his hearing, if only briefly."

Sinclair shot his fellow Resistance Leaders a sheepish look. "Where is Caplin?"

"I saw him before dinner, with Captain Sullivan," said Dean, sickened at the thought that his former president might be involved.

"We need him here," said Lindsey, eyes narrowed. "I'd like a word with him."

"So would we, but we can't just haul a man like Caplin in for questioning," said Sinclair, but Lindsey cut across him, speaking directly to Devan.

"He's a suspect. What do we do with suspects, General Harlow?"

Devan was silent for a long moment, before finally glancing at his comrades. "By that reckoning, everyone in this room is suspect. Except Mr Roswell, who knew nothing about the meeting."

"It's true," said Dean, but he knew what Lindsey was getting at. It was yet another potential crime they could pin on Caplin for the case Alma was building against him.

"My Talent isn't screaming at me that any of you sold out Nanette's plan," said Lindsey, the sharpness in her tone increasing. "I can't say the same for Caplin."

"Considering the evidence pointing to his involvement with the mutiny and the assassination attempt on the Ronans, it seems to me that you have enough reason to question him," said Rathbone, his tone level. "If Caplin has nothing to hide, surely he won't object."

Silence followed as Rathbone's words sank in.

"Where's Skye?" Roxanne asked then, speaking for the first time as her bloodshot eyes met Dean's. Dean thumbed his connection ring and thought his sister's name again, but her silence continued.

"Unavailable," he said simply.

"Just our luck to get such an unreliable Lux," Sinclair muttered.

"Even the Lux deserves a break sometimes," Dean said before he could stop himself, surprised to hear the bite in his own voice. Aside from a narrowing of his eyes, Sinclair chose not to comment further.

"Let's see if he'll talk to us, at the very least," Devan said. "And if he won't answer our questions, we may need your sister's help after all."

"You're going to arrest him?" Lindsey asked, straightening hopefully.

"I hope it won't come to that. But if he resists, then yes, perhaps we'll need to resort to force." Devan stood up, no hint of fear or nerves on his face now.

It was a twist of fate that Caplin happened to still be at the barracks, holding a meeting with several high-ranking members of his Forces. Lindsey and Jack's Trace located him, and they led the former president and Captain Irvine Sullivan into the room half an hour later.

As they entered, Caplin and Sullivan eyed them all warily. Some of them had left and returned, but the tension in the room hadn't eased, and Dean was sure that the threat they posed was evident.

"Evening all," said Caplin coolly. "To what do we owe this late pleasure?"

"Please excuse our intrusion," said Devan, looking almost relaxed despite the atmosphere in the room. "But there has been an incident we would like to speak to you about."

"Incident?" said Caplin, looking faintly curious.

"Our fellow Leader, Nanette Ferries, was captured by the Nox while meeting with Resistance members in Glasgow this afternoon."

Caplin only stared at Devan with an eyebrow slightly raised, then finally glanced around at several of the others. "Oh. I'm sorry to hear that."

"No, you're not," Lindsey muttered at Dean's side, and he hoped he was the only one to hear her words.

"Mr Caplin—" Devan paused, a hint of uncertainty making his calm mask falter. "We don't like to make accusations, but you and Captain Sullivan are the only people aside from Resistance members who were aware of the meeting. For that reason, we wish to request your cooperation in assisting us with the investigation."

There was a charged silence, heavy with fear and threat. Finally, after several agonising moments, Caplin spoke. "What kind of cooperation do you require, General Harlow?"

"We wish to carry out a formal interrogation and—" another pause, during which Devan took a deep breath, "we may also employ a Mind Breaker."

Another silence followed, and while it did not go on as long as the first, Dean found it even more agonising. "Would this Mind Breaker be Miss Bolton, by any chance?"

Several people shifted uncomfortably, and Sullivan tensed at Caplin's side, drawing himself to his full height and curling his hand around his gun belt, dangerously close to the gun itself.

"Miss Bolton is the best Mind Breaker we have at our disposal," said Darshana, giving Devan a moment's reprieve.

"Forgive me, Dr Sahay, but Skye Bolton is at no one's disposal but her own. And I note she is not even here at present."

"Miss Bolton is at present indisposed, that is true," Darshana continued, unphased by the interruption. "But since she is leading the investigation into the mutiny of Caspar Ronan's soldiers and the subsequent assassination attempt on the same, we will ask her to investigate today's events as well, since evidence points to your involvement with all three."

"What evidence?" said Caplin, now with an injection of anger in his tone.

"In other words, we've got you cornered, Caplin," Lindsey said loudly, and Caplin's face turned to her, not bothering to hide his distaste.

"Are you going to present me with this so-called evidence before you hand me over to the Lux?" he asked, holding each of them in turn with his glare.

"Miss Matheson, if you will," said Devan, although he still looked faintly embarrassed by her outburst.

"You already know that a soldier of yours was disguised as one of Ronan's," said Lindsey without a moment's hesitation. "We also believe you, or at the least members of your Forces, conspired in the assassination attempt on Caspar and Phaedra Ronan and murdered Resistance soldiers in the process."

Caplin only raised his eyebrows at Lindsey as she paused for breath.

"There were supposed to be two Resistance soldiers and two Forces soldiers guarding the Ronans that night. But forensic reports show that the men wearing your uniform were already dead before they arrived on the scene, and until now we haven't been able to identify them as being members of your army. A full report can be presented at trial."

"Trial?" Caplin echoed, fixing Devan with his gaze again.

To his credit, Devan held his composure. "A formal trial has been suggested for Mr Ronan, but also for yourself, Mr Caplin, since it appears that both of you were involved in the mutiny, and Mr Ronan would like to press charges for the assassination attempt and damages."

But Caplin began to laugh, a cold, humourless laugh that made the hairs stand up on the back of Dean's neck. "Did Bolton put you up to this? She's trying to get rid of me. Can't you see history is repeating itself? A Lux overthrowing their ruler to claim power for themselves?"

"We're aware of your personal strife with Miss Bolton," said Darshana. "But the evidence that has arisen is independent of her. Yes, she Broke the soldier that was linked to you in the first place, but our own Telepath confirmed her findings. As for the evidence surrounding the assassination attempt, they were reported by Resistance Tracers working alongside Miss Matheson, who is a loyal member of ours."

"A loyal member who still fights in a Ronan uniform," Caplin said, shooting a glance Lindsey's way.

"Mr Caplin," said Devan, steering the conversation away from Lindsey, "as reluctant as we are to submit you to a formal interrogation, it would help us indeed to dispel any blame and put our minds at ease regarding your involvement. The longer these concerns go on, the more risk we put on our alliance. The Nox could attack again any day, and we don't wish to have these concerns driving a wedge between us."

"Your accusations are driving a wedge between us, General Harlow," said Caplin. "I do not wish to be interrogated."

"Got something to hide, Caplin?" said Lindsey, and the look Caplin gave her was so venomous that Dean was tempted to move in front of her.

"I'm the former President of Britannia. I have plenty to hide, but nothing that would be useful to your trial."

"Mr Caplin," said Devan after a sigh, "I'm afraid that due to the seriousness of the charges brought against you and the nature of the evidence, we have little choice but to arrest you. We arrested Mr Ronan based on less evidence."

Caplin stood up then, and Sullivan stepped forward, his hand going to his gun, but he did not draw it, not yet. Dean felt adrenaline course through his veins, and his Talent tingling at his fingertips, ready to stop bullets in their tracks should Sullivan decide to use that gun. Across the table, Devan also stood up, as did Riordan Rathbone.

"We don't want a fight, Mr Caplin," said Rathbone. "We're not armed."

"You'll get a fight if you arrest me," said Caplin, and his glare settled on Dean then, who rose slowly to his feet, realising that openly betraying his boss had finally become inevitable. "Your sister might be the Lux, but my Forces are still loyal to me."

"Not all of them," said Dean, sounding more confident than he felt. "And if the trial finds you guilty, you'll have even fewer followers than you do now."

But Caplin's eyes flicked to his captain, and Sullivan's gun was out of its holster, aimed carefully and steadily at Dean, who was nearest. "Don't come any closer."

Dean lifted his hands up beside his head, his Talent surging at the threat, his fingers almost vibrating with tethered power. Devan also raised his hands, but everyone else froze, fear evident on Roxanne and Sinclair's faces. Even Darshana looked nervous.

"Let's go, Captain," said Caplin, retreating a step towards the door. Sullivan gave the slightest nod, also taking a step, but moving in front of Caplin. The tiny break in his concentration was all Dean needed, and his Talent claimed a hold on the gun, the metal responding swiftly to his call. As the gun was tugged from Sullivan's grasp by Dean's invisible, magnetic Talent, Devan and Rathbone moved forward, advancing on the two would-be prisoners. But Dean was there first, grabbing the gun that swooped to his hands and stepping before the door, aiming at his former superiors. To his relief, Sullivan knew better than to try anything, and aside from stepping in front of Caplin once again, shielding him, he took no further defiant action. A sudden gust of wind sent Rathbone staggering into Sinclair, but Devan ducked out of the way. Within seconds, he was locking cuffs around Caplin's wrists, then did the same to Sullivan.

"You're making a huge mistake," Caplin drawled, his wind Talent rifling threateningly through the room again, stinging Dean's exposed skin. Dean only adjusted the gun to aim between Caplin's eyes in answer. Caplin gritted his teeth in grim acceptance, knowing full well that he wouldn't miss.

As others began to stand, Lindsey came to Dean's side, her arms crossed in front of her chest. "Oh no, Caplin. The mistakes are all on you."

Chapter Sixty-Seven

SKYE BOLTON

Alistair Caplin was awake and waiting for her when she stepped into his cell, and the smirk that curved his lips mirrored her own. He said nothing for a long moment, deathly still and silent in the dimly lit room. His straw-coloured hair and fine clothes were somewhat dishevelled, and his yellow eyes bore into hers, slightly glazed with Veto. They had secured him to a chair with handcuffs, unnecessarily. Even with his Talent, they both knew that Skye could overpower him easily. And now that he was her prisoner, with no one there to stop her should she lay a finger on him, she no longer had anything to fear from him.

"You must be loving this," he said eventually, giving a humourless laugh. "Lady Bolton finally got her way."

Skye didn't return the laugh, nor did she bother to rise to his goading. Whatever her smirk might tell him, she drew little pleasure from the prospect of what she was about to do. Since she was old enough to consider a career, working for this man, protecting him, had been all she had wanted to do.

The door opened behind her, and Skye didn't look around as Jennifer Dooley slipped into the room, assuming a position in a shadowy corner. Caplin's eyes followed the quiet woman, but soon snapped back to Skye. Of course, the Resistance wanted to be sure she wasn't embarking on a personal vendetta against Caplin. But considering all the evidence that had surfaced in recent weeks, she was certain that what she was about to find in his mind would be more than enough to condemn him.

"I suppose you had better get it over with," he said bitterly, his smirk replaced with a hard glare. In spite of everything, guilt twisted her stomach as she saw a hint of fear in his eyes.

"It doesn't have to be painful," she said quietly, drawing herself to her full height as she prepared to begin. "You could just let me in."

"And make it easy for you?" He snorted. "I'm not letting you in without a fight."

That was all she needed to hear. Without further hesitation, she dived straight for his mind, coming at him with an attack so strong that he physically flinched back. If he wanted a fight, he would get one.

Caplin's eyes flashed with fury, and his shields tried to shove her back. She withdrew, then went in again, harder than before, unnecessarily aggressive. Caplin had watched her Break minds, had seen what states she could reduce people to, but whenever he had asked her to test his shields, she had been cautious, holding back so as not to hurt him. But this, he had never experienced this before, and she unleashed every bit of anger and fear and frustration that she had been keeping in check all those months since her father was first arrested. All the betrayal she had felt since learning that he didn't do anything to help her and her comrades when they were held at Blackwater, all the bitterness that had eaten away at her since he had handed her over to Ronan like she was nothing but a bargaining chip.

To her left, Dooley shifted uncomfortably, wrapping her arms around herself as she witnessed Skye attack

Caplin's mind. Skye knew she was going over the top, knew that Dooley would report that she had tortured Caplin more than she had needed to. But when she thought about her own suffering, the torture she had endured, she couldn't stop herself. It took enough of her restraint to prevent her from unleashing her electricity on him.

She didn't stop until Caplin slumped forward with a groan, strands of yellow hair falling into his eyes. Skye withdrew from the edges of his mind, giving him a temporary reprieve as she drew in deep breaths, willing herself to calm. For a moment, she wished she had a drink to dull the ache that was beginning in her temples. It was four in the morning by the time she awoke from her exhausted sleep, and to her surprise, Dean was still awake. Which was why she had immediately gotten the full story of Caplin's arrest from him and hightailed it to the barracks without eating. Resistance guards had had to prevent her from storming straight in to Break Caplin, making her wait until Devan had woken and met her to discuss the interrogation.

When she felt calmer, she began again, holding Caplin's mind with a vice-like grip as she chipped away at his shield. He continued to resist, but she was more concentrated now, the pain she was causing less of an attack and more of a drawn-out ache as she peeled away his layers the way one slowly pulls off a scab. She barely acknowledged his reactions to the pain as she worked, aware only of the fact that she needed to be careful not to cause damage. Whatever she discovered, he still had to stand trial. If she killed him or damaged his brain beyond repair, the Resistance couldn't protect her. She, too, would be considered a criminal.

"Do you really think you're going to find what you're looking for?" he asked after some time, breaking her concentration. He knew she was getting close. Knew he was running out of time. No thoughts had slipped through his shield yet, but it was thinning, the frantic buzzing of his mind growing louder.

"Whatever I find, I'm going to have answers to all the questions I've been asking myself this past year," she said, letting him have another moment, allowing herself a break too. "Like why you've been such a prick to your followers."

He gave a small, exhausted laugh. "Self-preservation, Skye. When you get to the top, you have to put yourself first if you're going to stay there. You might want to remember that if you decide to act on your delusions of grandeur."

Skye scoffed. "It seems you underestimated your followers' sense of self-preservation, Mr Caplin. When the leader no longer has the people's best interests at heart, they rebel or look elsewhere for leadership."

"You're starting to sound like your Resistance friends. Tell me, are they going to make you another Leader, or are you just going to take my place once you've thrown me in jail and defeated the Nox?"

"Oh, I've been in your place, Caplin. You let me rot in your place. I'd like to see you fight your way out the way I had to."

But before he could reply, she shot out at him again, catching him off guard as she pierced through his defence, his first thoughts tumbling out as he reeled from the agony. Curling her telepathic fingers into the gap she had made, she clawed at his shield, tearing it apart with a final wrench. Caplin gave a drawn-out yell of pain, but she barely heard him with her ears, barely saw him with her eyes as she dived into his mind, his thoughts engulfing her. She didn't know where to look first, so rich was the information he held. But Caplin's mind was strong – there was no sign of him passing out or going mad, not yet. She could take her time, and she did.

Despite her purpose for Breaking him, she had never felt more like an intruder, seeing things in his head that no one was ever meant to know. She became aware of Dooley's telepathy probing Caplin's mind as well, reaching out now that Skye had laid him bare for her. Resisting the temptation to delve into thoughts that would satisfy less urgent curiosity, she focused on the reason she had been granted permission to Break him in the first place, looking for the truths that Dooley no doubt searched for as well.

Silence fell, and her senses became dulled to the world around her as a familiar face flickered in his memories – a face that raised hairs on the back of her neck and made fear clench around her chest. A face she had seen smiling mysteriously as she delivered unwanted prophecies.

Skye latched onto the memory, needing to know why the Seer from her own dreams had met with Caplin. The cell melted away around her as she stepped into the recent past.

"Bolton will be busy investigating red herrings for a while, so you needn't worry about her rallying any troops for the time being," said Caplin, his voice smug as he stood across from Alessia Ronan. Through Caplin's eyes, Skye noted Ivor sitting on Alessia's right, much more quiet and glaring since his second death, while Vala simpered on her left. Vala.

"Good," said Alessia, her tone far from enthusiastic. "And I suppose she doesn't suspect you?"

Caplin's arrogant smile faltered just enough to make Alessia narrow her eyes. "Of course not," he said confidently, pasting the smile back in place. "Everyone is looking at your uncle."

"Don't lie, Alistair dear," said Vala in the honeyed voice Skye knew too well, smiling at Caplin and fixing him with her fathomless blue gaze. "I saw the vision. Skye

Bolton Broke your soldier, the one who was supposed to die before *discovery."*

Caplin blinked, looking from Vala to Alessia, and back again. There was a pause as he swallowed. "Yes, that was an unfortunate oversight."

"So now Bolton knows you're involved," said Alessia.

"And a Resistance Telepath confirmed it," said Vala, her smile growing.

"They know he was one of my soldiers. They can't prove he was acting under my orders."

"Just kill him, Alessia. He's exhausted his usefulness," came Ivor Ronan's dark words.

"Not yet," said Vala, placing her slender hands in her lap and clasping them. "The Resistance suspect Skye and Caspar may be in on it together. Another suspicion is that you are in league with them as well. At this point in the game, the Resistance still have the larger numbers and the backing of the Saoirse Army, so if Skye loses that, she is on her own."

Hope rose in Caplin's thoughts, and he looked back at Alessia. "And Caspar? She seems pretty cosy with him."

Alessia gritted her teeth, disgust flickering across her face. "Well, Mr Caplin, how would you like to help me get revenge on my dear Uncle Caspar?"

Caplin's lips curled as he studied her. "If revenge is what you desire, Madam President, I would be happy to assist you."

"Killing one Ronan is better than none, eh Caplin?" said Ivor, venom in his voice.

"I trust you know where he is being held, and you have some of your soldiers guarding him as well?" said Alessia.

"Indeed," Caplin replied, glancing between them. "To keep everything fair, the Resistance and my Forces are both responsible for guarding your uncle and sister."

Alessia blinked, but if she had any qualms about her sister being collateral, she hid it well. "And are you willing to sacrifice any of your soldiers in your quest for revenge?"

Caplin took a long, deep breath. "All my soldiers are dispensable."

"Good," she said, before presenting him with her proposal. After a short discussion and a few adjustments from Caplin, they had a plan in place, and Caplin stepped forward, holding his hand out to shake Alessia's. She accepted the handshake stiffly, letting go quickly.

"I will see Mr Caplin out." Vala rose to her bare feet, long grey skirts brushing her ankles. She then crossed the room, linking her arm with Caplin's. Repulsion injected Caplin's memory, but he let Vala guide him out nonetheless. She was silent as they walked down the corridor.

"Indulge me, Alistair," she said as they reached a staircase, talking to Caplin with what appeared to be a flirtatious tone and mannerisms. "Have you ever wondered how you will die?"

"Let me guess," Caplin replied in clipped tones, "you've foreseen it."

Vala halted, forcing Caplin to stop with her.

"I have indeed. It will be quick, but you will know it is coming."

"Better that. At least I can curse my enemies before I leave this world."

Vala gave a tinkling laugh. "Your enemies will suffer more than you will. You need not worry about that."

"Then I thank you for that comforting knowledge," said Caplin, looking down at the Seer.

"You should tread carefully with your plans to deliver the Lux," said Vala, placing a cold hand on Caplin's face and preventing him from looking away. "You could lose more than just your life if your intentions are discovered."

"There is little else in this world I care about, my dear Vala," he replied, his arrogance all too audible.

"Are you sure? I see your desires. Your hunger for power, for control, for renown. I see how your pride has been hurt by Skye Bolton's actions."

There was a pause. "I don't believe you can see anything at all, Seer," Caplin sneered.

But in the moonlight drifting through the window, Vala gave him a knowing smile. "I have seen your heart, Mr Caplin, and it is black."

Skye took a step back as she slammed back into her body, blinking as Caplin's face materialised in front of her eyes, his lopsided smile prickling the hair at the back of her neck.

"I decided to back the winning team," said Caplin, his satisfaction only growing.

Instead of attacking Caspar for the sake of the old blood feud as she had expected, he was attacking him for the Nox. And his ultimate plan had been to hand Skye over to her, one way or another, dead or alive.

"Well?" His cruel laughter echoed through the cell when he saw the shock on her face. "Have you got what you need to lock me up and throw away the key?"

Skye's panic and nausea sent her pulse into overdrive, and the knowledge that Vala was backing the Nox clawed at her like vicious, invisible hands. She stared at Caplin, noting the hysteria she had unleashed by Breaking him. He would recover, after some rest, but now that she knew the truth, she couldn't help but feel some sick pleasure at the pain she had caused him. And that pleasure only grew as she said her next words. "Certainly, Mr Caplin. In fact, I think we have enough evidence to sentence you to far worse than a life in jail."

She left her words hanging as his face fell, and then she exited the room, leaving him in the grip of the fear that flooded his exposed mind.

Chapter Sixty-Eight

ALESSIA RONAN

"Alistair Caplin has been arrested," came Vala's gloat at Alessia's side. "The conclusion of Camilla's trap draws near."

But Alessia couldn't share the Seer's pleasure that Caplin had fallen into the sticky net they had laid out for him. Not as her throat seared, her chest tight with irritation once again. The smoke from the flames consuming the town hall did little to help. The arsonists now knelt Undead in the square before her, executed for their defiance and attempts to overthrow her latest conquest.

"Should I continue, Madam?" asked Nathanael at Alessia's other side, his liquid eyes surveying her. Alessia spared him a glance, then looked back at the rest of the townsfolk kneeling behind the Undead arsonists: adults and children, parents clutching babies to their chests, some whimpering, others simply staring with wide-eyed fear. But Alessia saw only fodder.

"Kill them all," she said hoarsely. "I will raise the suitable ones for my army tomorrow."

And then she turned away, leaving the screams behind as she coughed into a handkerchief made from black silk. Tears stung her eyes as copper filled her mouth.

"Perhaps Lucien could raise them for you," Vala suggested, falling into step at her side. "You need rest."

"No!" she hissed, casting her glare on the Seer. "It is *my* Talent. *Mine*. Lucien can keep his mirroring to himself."

If Vala was phased by her outburst, she masked it well. Instead, she tried to slip her arm through Alessia's, but she shied away from the Seer's touch, turning a corner into a side street. She staggered down it far enough to leave behind the smoke drifting in from the square, then braced her hand against a brick wall as she coughed again, each spasm wracking through her body.

"Let me heal you."

Alessia turned, leaning her head back against the wall, closing her eyes as she took shallow, agonised breaths. After a moment, she unravelled the felt scarf wound tightly around her neck, giving Vala access to her throat. The Seer's fingers were cold against her skin, and Alessia fought a shiver.

"I have seen a vision," Vala murmured as she worked. "One you will not like."

Alessia's eyes snapped open. Vala's face was close, her unnatural blue eyes drinking in the light, the scent of jasmine and death washing over her. This time, the shiver could not be suppressed, and she turned her head to the side, coughing into her handkerchief again.

"Tell me."

Vala blinked, her hand going lower, fingers curling around her neck. Alessia swallowed as she held her gaze, her shadows unfurling at the threat at her throat. Vala's lips flickered upwards, but was that reassurance or cruelty in her expression? Caplin's warning that Vala was helping the Lux floated up from the depths of her memory.

"Your grandfather has written a letter. He will ask you to give it to Caspar."

Alessia's shadows quivered in her periphery. As Vala's hand crept lower, pressing against her collarbone, her momentary fear gave way to fury. "What does the letter say?"

Vala's smile faded, her gaze as cold as her fingers. "Your grandfather will tell you. Tonight."

Alessia frowned, waiting for Vala to continue the treatment. The cold imprint of her hand descended through her ribcage, replacing the air in her lungs with ice. "Take me to him," she demanded as Vala withdrew her hand, her voice less hoarse.

The Seer only nodded, holding out her hand to Alessia once more. Alessia took it, and they stepped through time and space together.

Alessia found herself in the draughty parlour back at Castle Uaine, the fire in the grate doing little to keep the evening chill at bay. Her grandfather sat in an armchair next to it, his face haggard, his breath coming in wheezes. He surveyed her from blackened eye sockets, but no smile graced his lips as it usually did when he saw her. Only grief swam in his eyes. The expression didn't suit him.

"I will leave you," said Vala at her back, and she crossed soundlessly to the door, shutting it behind her.

"Vala said you have something to tell me." Alessia didn't miss the tremor in her own voice. Balanced on the mantelpiece was an envelope of heavy, cream paper, with Caspar's name looping across it in shaky handwriting. Alessia spared it a glance, the sight of it sparking an ache of foreboding in her chest, then looked back down at her grandfather.

"Take a seat, my dear," he said, gesturing at the armchair opposite him. After a moment's hesitation, she lowered herself to the edge of the seat. Waiting.

"There is little I regret, Alessia. And I did not regret this, not at first." He paused, coughing into his hand. When he resumed, his voice was tight. "But when I saw your grief, I knew I had made a mistake."

Silence ensued, and dragged on. Alessia held her breath, her heartbeat frantic in her chest. There was only one person she had grieved, aside from her grandfather. One hurt that ran so deep it would never heal. Her voice was barely a whisper when she finally dared to ask, "What did you do?"

Anguish crumpled his deteriorated face, an expression she had never seen on him before. "Your mother… didn't commit suicide."

Silence again, like the hush in a forest at the presence of a predator. Inside her, her Talents grew still. Alessia was still, her senses taut like a coiled spring awaiting release. And then the realisation struck her, and her Talents became a tidal wave crashing against the inside of her chest. She gripped the arms of her chair, leather groaning as her fingers and shadows dug into it. "*What did you do?*"

"I'm sorry, Alessia. But she… they were going to take you away."

"*Who?*"

"Your mother… and Caspar."

"*Why?*" The threat of tears tore at her throat now, and eloquence failed her. It was all she could see – blood on the bathroom tiles, her mother's glassy, lifeless eyes, the ornate hilt of a dagger sticking out of her chest. And he had done it. *He* had taken her mother away from her.

Her grandfather's expression held the distress she felt coursing through herself, his bloodshot eyes glistening. "Because they were having an affair, and they were afraid Doran and I would find out."

Alessia took a shuddering breath, air searing through her throat once more. The tears finally slipped down her cheeks, and she leaned back in the chair, fingers trembling against the leather. "So you killed her."

Ivor only held her gaze, eyes silently pleading as his breath rattled in and out. She wanted to scream, wanted to fly at him with her shadows, tear him apart. But she forced herself to remain calm, the ice tingling through her limbs. "Why not kill Caspar, if you were so scared he would run away with us?"

A tear trailed down his cheek, the strangest sight she had ever seen. "Because I loved him."

Alessia blinked, releasing more of her own tears. All those years, she had thought she was the only one he had ever loved. The only one he cared about. She knew he had preferred Caspar as his heir over Doran, but by the end, even he had been written out of the will. But none of it mattered now. Alessia had only ever loved two people, and one of them had killed the other.

"Why are you telling me this now?"

Ivor paused, coughing again, the sound like the dry cracking of logs in the fire. "She haunts me, Alessia. You hear her too, when you visit her tomb, don't you? She will not rest until I share the truth. She will not let *me* rest."

A quiet, deadly rage settled over her at the thought of her mother's spirit unable to be at peace. All those years, Alessia had grown up thinking that Ilaria had preferred to die rather than be trapped in an unhappy marriage. When all along, she lingered like a shadow, waiting for Ivor to come clean, to finally see her truth laid bare.

And Alessia would mete out her mother's revenge.

She rose suddenly to her feet, glaring down at her grandfather. "Outside," she commanded, not trusting herself to speak above a whisper.

Obeying the tether she had on his Undead life, her grandfather stood and stepped towards the door. There was no fear in his expression, only sadness. On opening the door, Alessia heard the scrambling of bodies, and saw Camilla and Brydon pressed against the wall, watching them with a mixture of sheepishness and fear. But Alessia only cast them a disgusted look, then stormed down the hallway, leaving her grandfather to follow.

She thrust the front doors open, then descended the steps, her boots echoing on the stone. Her grandfather staggered in her wake as she crossed the lawns, heading for the Marsdens' mausoleum nestled amongst a cluster of trees. The dead called to her, raising hair on her arms and bringing her icy necromancy Talent to the surface. She came to a halt before the doors of the mausoleum and turned to Ivor.

"Open it."

Ivor glanced between her and the doors, a flicker of fear clouding his eyes. But then her tether on him dragged him up the steps, and he pushed the doors open, stepping inside. Alessia followed, letting the doors swing shut behind her with a noise that echoed through the quiet space. Dust and silence fell, and only the sounds of their ragged breaths and the dead whispering from the grave reached her ears.

"Downstairs."

Her grandfather obeyed, taking jerky steps down into the vault below the mausoleum, faint lights bursting into life as they descended. The voices of the dead grew louder, but only one corpse held her attention, and her eyes remained pinned on the back of her grandfather's head as he walked beneath the arches, runes and sigils carved into the ancient stone.

At the end of the vault, they came to an ornate sarcophagus embedded in an alcove, the name on it so old it was barely legible.

"Open it."

Ivor looked at her uncertainly. "Alessia…"

"Open it." She let the ice and fury enter her voice, compelling her grandfather to obey. He braced his hands against the lid of the sarcophagus and pushed. It moved, but slowly.

Alessia watched his struggle, let it drag on until her patience wore thin, then gathered her shadows and sent them hurtling at the lid. It grated half off the tomb, teetering dangerously.

"Get in."

Her grandfather's eyes widened. "Alessia—"

"Did you think I would thank you for your honesty and forgive you?" She shook her head, shadows swirling around her, the ice lurking vicious and hungry beneath her skin. "You killed my mother. *Killed her*, and let us all think she had taken her own life. A slow, rotting death won't even begin to redeem you for stealing my mother from me, but I do not have the time nor the inclination to think up a worse torture. Get in."

Unable to resist the power she had over him, he climbed up the plinth that the sarcophagus rested on, then swung a trembling leg into it. A crunch of bones was macabre music to her ears.

He swung his other leg into the tomb, then turned to her, pleading dread flooding his features.

"Lie down."

He sank downwards, tears running down his hollowed cheeks as he drifted out of sight. Alessia stood stock-still, cold vengeance closing around her heart, then gathered her shadows around the lid of the sarcophagus, shoving it back into place with a heavy thud.

"Goodbye grandfather," she said, her voice cracking. But as she sank into a pool of dark skirts at the base of the sarcophagus, a whisper of warmth kissed her icy skin, and a scent of roses drifted through the dusty dankness of the vault. She pressed a hand to her mouth, failing to hold in the ragged sobs that escaped her lips.

Chapter Sixty-Nine

DEAN ROSWELL

The trials took up the next two days. Caspar's was over and done with by the end of the first morning, the evidence condemning Caplin absolving him from any blame. But Caplin's dragged on, countless hours blurring into one another as Dean sat with bated breath at Skye's side, watching and listening to the proceedings in the floodlit auditorium. And the country watched along with him, cameras trained on them, showing the world that the former president of Britannia was receiving a fair trial.

Skye and Jennifer Dooley presented their findings first, followed by Lindsey and her team of Tracers sharing their damning evidence. They even had Caspar and Phaedra in the witness stand, giving their accounts of the mutiny and the assassination attempt at the lake cottage. The teenager visibly shook beneath the glare of the floodlights, stumbling over her words as she was cross-examined by Caplin's defence.

As the second day came to a close – all of the evidence and witness statements shared with a jury made up of a mix of representatives from each faction – all they had to do now was wait for the verdict. With a heavy heart, Dean gathered in a meeting room with Alma, Skye, Roxanne, Devan and Lindsey. Alma drew sigils on the door with a piece of chalk, soundproofing the room so they could speak without risking eavesdroppers.

"I strongly believe they will rule in our favour," Alma announced, taking a seat with them at a large, rectangular table. Her brown eyes twitched behind her glasses, her chestnut hair swept back in a severe updo. But more formidable than that were the black velvet robes of the High Justice. Alma was no stranger to harrowing trials and condemning high profile criminals, but Dean knew she had never overseen a case quite like this one.

"Even the Caplinites on the jury can't deny what's in front of them," said Lindsey, but her nerves and exhaustion were evident despite her clipped tone.

At Dean's side, Skye was quiet, her eyes distant as they drifted on the table before her. Dean reached for her hand, curling his fingers around hers. She squeezed them in return, glancing up and giving him a sad, tired smile.

It's all for Dad, he told her, returning her smile. *Just focus on that.*

I can't bear to imagine what he's going to say when it's all over.

Dean's smile faltered. The same thought had crossed his mind. How would Victor feel when he discovered they had damned his life-long friend? Would he grieve Caplin, or be glad once they told him about his betrayal?

Across from them, wedged between Devan and Lindsey, Roxanne trembled in her seat, her blonde curls limp, her face drawn. Dean wondered if she, too, felt just as guilty. But while Dean feared for Victor, he feared for Amber even more. Victor knew the risks he was taking by publicly allying with Caplin. But Amber was just an innocent girl, having no part in this war except a desire to help those in need.

"There's just one thing I can't get straight," said Devan, interrupting the fearful silence that held them all in its grip.

"There was no concrete evidence about Caplin's involvement with the ambush in Glasgow."

Dean looked at him, then to Alma. Her face was unreadable, but he knew her calculating mind was working behind her glasses. After a moment, she glanced between Skye and Lindsey. "Why didn't that come up?"

Skye held her aunt's gaze, her thumb absently stroking Dean's. "Now you mention it, I saw no memories of planning the ambush in Caplin's head."

Dread dropped into Dean's stomach, curdling with a wave of nausea. Confusion tainted all their faces. Except Lindsey's, whose face had grown pale.

Devan turned to the Tracer. "Did your team pick anything up?"

Lindsey shifted in her seat, her eyes on the snake ring that she twisted around her finger. And for the first time, Dean realised what dishonesty looked like on her face. His heart sank as she spoke.

"Caplin wasn't involved with the ambush." Her voice was small as she avoided everyone's eye.

"He wasn't?" Roxanne squeaked, casting her terrified gaze on Lindsey.

"Wait a minute," Devan said, his voice level despite the growing tension between them. "The only thing that led to his arrest was your Trace telling you he was guilty of the ambush. Now you're telling us you've made a mistake?"

To Dean's shock and horror, tears flooded Lindsey's eyes, and her expression was almost pleading as she looked at Devan. "I'm so sorry. They weren't supposed to be harmed."

"What are you talking about?" asked Alma, her voice low and dangerous.

Lindsey cast her tearful eyes on Alma, her face blotchy. "We needed a reason to arrest him, and we were running out of time."

"Are you saying…" said Skye, sitting up straighter, her hand clenching around Dean's, "that you set up the ambush?"

Everyone waited with bated breath, but the answer was written all over Lindsey's face. Dean's stomach churned, and he was suddenly overcome with a feeling of falling, plummeting down into the cold, hard truth. Lindsey had done this. Lindsey had led their allies to their doom.

"Lindsey…" Devan choked out, leaning around Roxanne to look at her with a dread that matched Dean's. "Is this true?"

Lindsey looked wretched as she met Devan's eye, and gave a single nod.

"Oh, well this is just fantastic," Alma snapped, but Dean barely heard her as his free-fall came to an abrupt end, slamming into a reality that closed over his head and forced the breath from his lungs.

"Lindsey…" Devan's face crumpled with anguish and disbelief. "People died."

And the Lindsey that sat before them, the Lindsey that buried her face in her hands as she burst into floods of tears, became a stranger to him. At Dean's side, Skye released his hand, slamming her palms onto the table as she rose to her feet.

"Did Glen know about this?"

But Lindsey only shook her head, hands shaking as she unfolded a tissue. At her side, Roxanne had also begun to cry, eyes wide with shock, a hand pressed to her mouth.

There was a buzz of electricity close to Dean's ear as Skye's hands curled into fists. "So, you plotted with the Marsdens, and let Glen walk into a trap without briefing him?"

"Glen isn't stupid." Lindsey's voice regained some of her usual bite as she met Skye's furious gaze. "He knows who he's dealing with."

"He could have blown his cover!" Skye snarled, and the lightning crackled again, prompting Dean to wrap his hand around her wrist.

"Skye, calm down."

But Skye ignored him, leaning on the table again, glaring at Lindsey. "If he's killed because of you..."

And then Lindsey was on her feet too, teeth bared as she stared Skye down with a look that tore Dean in two. "Then what, you'll fry me? Go on then."

"Enough," Alma said, her voice steady despite the tension around the table. She cast her imperious glare on Skye and Lindsey in turn. "Sit."

With a last filthy look at one another, the two women sat back down, but Skye's fists trembled in her lap. At her side, Dean sank into his own despair, his heart aching, unable to meet Lindsey's eye. Skye was right. Her actions had been reckless, her words from the pub taking on a whole new meaning: *If I have to kill for Amber, I will.*

"Do I need to ask my niece to Break your mind, Miss Matheson?" Alma asked.

Lindsey crossed her arms, her shoulders hunched. "My uncles and grandfather think I'm still a double agent. But I swear, I only convinced them for this ambush, and told them Farraday was in on it. I..." Her voice cracked, and she swallowed. "I have met with the Nox, fed her lies to gain her trust. But I swear on Amber's life, I'm not working with them. My loyalties lie with the Resistance and Saoirse Army."

At the mention of Amber, Roxanne whimpered, "Oh gods, this cannot be happening." She leaned into Devan, who put an arm around her.

"I approached the Nox when I realised the Caplinite bodies at the lake cottage were planted by her to link Caplin to the crime. She clearly wanted us to mistrust Caplin. I know he wouldn't have been so careless as to leave such obvious evidence behind, so the only other explanation was that Alessia has been playing us all against each other."

"A ruse to crumble the alliance," said Devan, his features pained with the realisation.

"Skye can Break me if that's what it takes to regain your trust," said Lindsey, then she cast her pleading gaze on Dean for the first time since her confession. He held it, the truth still crushing him. "But I did what I had to do. For Amber. For your dad."

Skye snorted, and Dean averted his eyes. He couldn't look at her. Couldn't see her in the same light as he had just minutes ago. The tender hopes he had been nurturing for some kind of future with her disintegrated, like rubble crumbling into a churning sea.

"We'll take your willingness to cooperate as proof of your allegiance, Lindsey," Devan said in resignation. "But I'm afraid we need to suspend you from allied meetings. As for the trial, could this jeopardise things?"

They all looked at Alma, whose face was a mask. She let out a sigh. "As long as none of you speak a word of this, I think the lack of evidence regarding the ambush might be overlooked. But if the jury find Caplin guilty, I recommend his sentence is a swift execution so the verdict can't be overturned if the truth comes out later."

Devan nodded, squeezing Roxanne's shoulders as she heaved a shaky breath. "Thank you, Mrs Medley, for all your support. I'll see you for the verdict tomorrow." He stood then, coaxing Roxanne to her feet. Skye got up too, storming out after throwing a last poisonous look at Lindsey, the static in her wake raising the hairs on the back of Dean's neck. After a sigh, Alma followed the others out of the room, leaving Dean alone with Lindsey.

With great difficulty, he met her gaze. She had stopped crying, her expression a mixture of guilt and defiance.

"I know what I did was wrong. But I can't let Amber die when the price is the life of a traitorous liar."

"It's not just Caplin though, is it?" His voice was strained, the truth weighing heavily on his tongue. He had admired her determination, but where did it end? What else would she risk for her family?

She held his gaze unflinchingly, her voice barely above a whisper. "No one was supposed to die. But if this saves her, I would do it again in a heartbeat."

Dean swallowed. As long as her lies weren't discovered, it might just be enough to give Camilla Linden what she wanted. But he still couldn't accept the lengths she had gone to, the people she had sacrificed for Victor and Amber. Why were their loved ones' lives worth more than the Resistance members who were killed and captured?

"I…" He struggled to find the words, barely able to meet her eye. "I don't think I can trust you again, after this." His voice cracked as he spoke, and he stood, a lump rising in his throat. "I know why you did it, but I can't condone it."

A flicker of hurt crossed her features, but it was quickly replaced with anger as she jutted out her chin. "Did you really think, after what happened to my brother, that I was going to stand by and let Amber be killed too? I'm done with obeying men in suits who don't give a shit about my family."

Dean stood there, not knowing what to say, what to think. The horrible truth enveloped him, and the harsh reality of what this cold hard woman was capable of gripped his heart, threatening to rip it from his chest.

"You'll thank me," Lindsey said, rising to her own feet, a hard edge sharpening her voice. He willed himself to meet her glare. "You both will, when you get your father back. You might think what I did was wrong, but you know I've only done what you didn't have the guts to do."

Her words were like a stabbing knife, the look in her eyes the wrenching twist. Maybe she was right. He was a coward. He had stood by and let her and his sister do all the running around, done nothing while his father endured whatever Camilla was putting him through, too afraid of actively going against Caplin to stand up for his loved ones. He turned to leave, unable to face his shame. But there was one more question clawing at him, one more truth he steeled himself to ask.

"Was any of it real, what went on between us? Or did you just use me?"

Lindsey was silent so long that he made himself look back at her, surprised to see her eyes glazed with yet more tears. She drew a shaky breath, wrapping her arms around herself. "I wouldn't manipulate you that way, Dean. Not after what Letitia did to you."

He froze, the mention of his ex bringing up feelings he really didn't need to dwell on right now. And the fact that Lindsey had even an inkling of what went on… clearly Letitia had told her some of it, perhaps even all of it. It wouldn't surprise him if she had even gloated about it. But he didn't linger any longer to find out more. Instead, he nodded, wrenching the door open and letting it click shut behind him.

In the gloom of the corridor, a shadow flickered to his right, and he saw Skye leaning against the wall. He grimaced. She was probably waiting to drop an *I told you so.* Without a word, she pushed off the wall and tilted her head towards the exit, her expression unreadable as his eyes still adjusted to the low light. Dean hesitated. All he wanted was to be alone, to lick his wounds in peace, but he could feel her telepathy silently lingering at the edge of his mind. Reluctantly, he followed her out of the building.

Outside, Skye stopped abruptly and turned to him, drawing him into a hug. He wrapped his arms around her, tucking his chin against her shoulder, his throat tight as he tried to push his argument with Lindsey to the back of his mind.

I'm sorry, Dean. If I'd known what she was planning, I would have—

His arms tightened around her, willing her to hold her thoughts. *You don't need to protect me, Skye. That's my job.*

She huffed a laugh, looking up at him, a hand cupping his cheek. *No one gets to hurt my big brother. Say the word and I'll kick her arse for this.*

He smiled weakly. *After the sparks flying back there, I don't doubt you would.*

The moonlight lit up her grin, and she pressed a kiss to his cheek. *You deserve a beautiful life, Dean. When all this is over, I hope you can have that.*

Her words sent another stab through his aching heart. He didn't know how far she had delved into his mind, how much she had seen of his hopes for a relationship with Lindsey and his blooming feelings for her. Regardless, he wasn't ready to discuss it with everything else they had going on. So instead he deflected, like always.

You deserve a beautiful life too, Skye. Even if you don't believe it yourself.

Her lips pressed into a thin line, her false cheerfulness gone. He swore tears glistened in her eyes, but she lowered her gaze, stepping out of his embrace. *Let's go home. I think we both need a drink.*

He rolled his eyes at her suggestion, but let her lead him across the darkened barracks, eager for the solace of his bedroom.

Chapter Seventy

GLEN FARRADAY

The days that followed the ambush felt like some bizarre fever dream. Glen went through the motions as Rupert's reinstated bodyguard, which was a twist of fate that had come about only after Rupert had argued with his brother that his current guard was useless, and he would rather stick with someone he knew. He drove Rupert around in his fancy sports car, stood behind his chair at a parliament led by Brydon Marsden in the Nox's absence, and ate and slept in the staff quarters at Rupert's lavish Edinburgh townhouse. He did his best to avoid Rupert's wife, Marigold, who was Arthur and Camilla Linden's youngest sister. And while she wasn't unhinged like Camilla, Marigold still ruled the household with an iron fist, ordering everyone about, including Rupert. Meanwhile their two children, a boy and a girl both under ten, ran rampant through the house with all the arrogance and privilege of spoilt little heirs.

Glen waited. Waited for the moment when the Nox would inevitably set eyes on him and turn him into one of her corpse soldiers. Waited for the Marsdens to realise he was not a double agent like their niece. Waited for this web of lies that he had taken no part in to collapse beneath him, no matter how carefully he tread. The story came out, piece by piece: Lindsey, the former renowned Head Tracer and secret spy for the Saoirse Army, was still up to her old tricks. She had orchestrated the trap for the Resistance representatives, and she had let Glen walk right into it.

The betrayal stung like split knuckles, and his shameful stupidity draped heavily across his shoulders, another burden to smother him beneath its weight. He had actually started to like Lindsey. Trusted her even. And yet she had sat there smiling and wishing him the best for his mission, all the while she had been planning the ambush behind his back.

As he stood next to the door in Rupert's living room, watching him and Andrew discuss Caplin's trial while they drank whiskey at eleven in the morning, Lindsey's words in the car on the way to Roswell Manor echoed from the depths of memory. *It's a cutthroat game when everyone knows who's lying.* And she was the biggest liar of them all. What a snake. And yet, inexplicably, Lindsey had twisted things so he would be spared. Was it a favour to him, some kind of concern she felt, or was it just another of her games? He knew how it would look to the Resistance. If he showed up alive and unharmed, they would think he was in on it.

And then there was Dean. Glen hadn't missed the way he had looked at her, completely smitten and taken in by her false charm. Was she trying to get to Skye through Dean? Helpless despair filled him at the thought of Skye getting hurt by this double-crosser, and he could do absolutely nothing to prevent it. He could only hope Skye would see through her lies.

As the Marsden brothers' conversation began to rise into another heated argument, there was a rap on the door at Glen's side. Before he could react, Rupert's butler opened it from the other side, and a stranger crossed the threshold, bringing a wave of power with him that filled Glen with yet more dread.

The stranger's unusual silver eyes shot straight to him.

"Good morning, Mr and Mr Marsden," said the stranger. His tone was light, his stance casual, but there was something about him that invited no argument. Glen took in the gleaming black leather jacket, the designer jeans, the blue glow of late morning light in his dark hair. He stood slightly taller than Glen, with his hands in his pockets and the same cocky kind of arrogance as the countless rich people he had been paid to guard, but the invisible power that drifted from him in waves… that was what told him the moment of truth had come.

"What does she want now?" Andrew asked dismissively, concentrating on lighting a cigar.

"If by *she* you mean the president…" The man's drawl carried just enough threat to remind them who they were dealing with. "The Nox has an appointment with your guard."

His flashing eyes found Glen again, and it was all he could do to remain steady as his knees buckled beneath his weight. A buzzing began in his ears, and a rush of panic swept through his chest.

"What?" Rupert exclaimed, setting his whiskey glass down a little too hard on the glass tabletop. "What the hell would she want with him?"

The man raised an eyebrow, staring at Rupert with a feline smirk. After an agonising moment, Rupert sagged, waving a hand that quivered ever so slightly. Glen didn't miss the blush on the back of his neck, which he rubbed sheepishly a moment later. "Fine, but if I could get him back by tonight, I have an event to go to."

The man's eyes darkened to threatening storm clouds as they flicked to Glen, his expression unreadable as he looked him up and down. "You might need to make other arrangements, Mr Marsden. Our President may decide to keep Mr Farraday for herself." Another curve to his lips, a dark promise. Glen's stomach plummeted.

He followed the man out to the street, feeling like each step was leading him to the chopping block. Sure enough, a van idled on the curb, and the stranger opened the back door, his gaze pinning Glen with cruel satisfaction. Glen glanced inside, taking in the benches lining either side of the van, the restraints dangling from the wall. He was a prisoner, then. He swallowed his protests and stepped into the vehicle.

The door swung shut at his back, leaving him in the gloom. The front of the vehicle was blocked out, obscuring the driver from view, and when he heard the passenger door open and shut seconds later, the van rumbled into movement. Glen stumbled to a seat. No restraining. No locking. But with the power that had emanated from his collector, he knew better than to try anything stupid.

The drive wasn't long. When the van pulled up and the stranger opened the door, waiting impassively for him to get out, Glen blinked in the light to find himself at a prison. It wasn't a high security fortress like Blackwater. There was a barbed wire fence around the car park he found himself in, and armed wardens guarding the doors, but the building was relatively small – a city holding bay for low security prisoners on their way to more sinister locations.

Taking a deep breath and surprised they weren't clapping cuffs around his wrists, Glen followed the stranger into the building. A warden fell into step behind him, and as Glen glanced around, he noted a gun pointed at his back. His captors weren't that blasé then.

No words were spoken as Glen was led into a corridor flanked on either side by numbered doors painted a primary shade of blue. The scent of paint and urine lingered in the air, along with a whiff of aftershave and cigarette smoke that the man with the flashing eyes left in his wake.

Doing his best to keep his nerves in check, Glen glanced side to side, noting hatches in the doors, the heavy locks and sigils reminiscent of Blackwater. Cells then. Fear of the unknown prickled at the back of his neck, his stomach continuing to churn. He couldn't imagine he was about to meet the Nox. He doubted she would deign to visit a place like this. No, she had most likely sent this guy to do her dirty work, or else they were going to leave him here until she doled out whatever gruesome punishment she had thought up.

Memories of prisoners being tortured at Blackwater trickled into his mind, Skye amongst them. He had watched Jenkins burn countless prisoners, watched people half drowned and electrocuted as Telepaths cleaved their way into their minds. Even worse, he remembered the stink and stain of blood that coated Skye each time he picked her up from working with Camilla. His chest grew tight, wondering which of those fates awaited him.

Halfway down the corridor, his captor stopped by an open door, turning to Glen, those inhuman eyes tracking him. With a slight incline of his head, he directed Glen inside. Glen took another deep breath, then stepped inside a dingy cell. A small, barred window set high in the whitewashed brick wall let in light across from him; to his left was a seatless toilet and a sink, and to his right was a bed with a rubber mattress. Not as bad as Blackwater, but it was still prison.

He took it all in with a glance, then turned back to the stranger, hoping for further explanation. But before he met his gaze, invisible hands grabbed him, dragging him backwards and pinning him against the wall.

"What the hell?" he gasped as the impact echoed through his bones.

The stranger's unknown power filled the small space as the door swung shut behind him. "It's just a bit of wind, Mr Farraday. Never hurt anyone, right?"

Glen lurched forward, but the unseen tethers dragged him back again. "Let me—" Before he could get the words out, a final tether slotted into place: an invisible gag between his teeth, snapping his head back against the wall and jarring his skull. He groaned, stars exploding before his eyes, the sight of the cell sliding and blurring.

Through the dizziness, he saw the stranger's dark outline prowl towards him, and Glen's right arm moved upwards against his will. His knuckles pressed against the wall beside his head, fingers splayed and stiff like a butterfly pinned for display. He tried to speak, tried to move, but the invisible force held firm.

"I watched your matches. You were quite the skilled boxer back in the day."

Glen could only stare as the stranger's weird eyes assessed him.

"Such a shame those Caplinite bastards smashed your knee to pieces and left you to rot. Although it could have been worse. They could have smashed in your skull instead."

Glen's breath caught as his most terrifying memories burst into the forefront of his mind. The days spent in agony in the dark. No food, barely any water, the stink of blood and his own waste the only distraction from the pain that became his entire world for an undetermined amount of time. How could this stranger know what he had gone through? With a snarl, he arched his back away from the wall, but his limbs remained pinned.

"I remember right is your dominant hand," the stranger continued as though nothing had happened. "Your right hook was pretty lethal."

And then, inexplicably, the man pressed his left hand against Glen's splayed fingers, palm to palm. He fought against his bonds, trying to curl his fingers into a fist. With a pulse of power, his bindings held firm.

"This could go a lot more smoothly if you don't struggle."

Glen tried to speak again, wanting to ask what he was doing. And then the cord holding the obsidian around his neck snapped, and something whispered at his left temple, a feeling both familiar and strange: telepathy. The man smiled as Glen's mind caught onto the realisation.

"You're quick. Most people write it off as a headache."

Glen bared his teeth as telepathic fingers prised his mind open, sifting through his inner sanctum with more force than Skye had ever done, more ruthless than the Ronans' Mind Breaker had been. He arched his back again, and an invisible punch to his gut left him winded, gasping through the gag.

The man pressed his hand even more firmly against the wall. "To answer your question, Miss Ronan wants me to conduct a little experiment. Some punishment for pissing her off, I believe. Hold still, this might hurt."

And without warning, water flooded from the man's fingers, soaking Glen's hand and sleeve. And then Glen's eyes widened as he fought his tethers to see what was happening. The water wasn't just soaking him. It was *flowing into* him.

He groaned again, his body rigid as the water entered his veins like a flood raging through a tunnel, flowing through his arm, pooling at his bent elbow, then rushing up his upper arm and crashing into his chest. He jerked forward, and the man's right arm shot out, a hand shoving his shoulder back against the wall. His face flickered, a glamour slipping, his strange eyes becoming the transparent gleam of clear water.

Glen gasped for air as the water flooded his chest, ripping through him like a tsunami, a tidal wave clenching around his heart. This was some rare kind of torture, torture he never could have imagined. He slumped in his bindings as his chest expanded, the water claiming every crevice, leaving no room to breathe.

Hang in there, came a whisper of telepathy, the voice even more smooth and liquid than when he spoke out loud.

The invisible gag withdrew from his mouth, and he greedily drank down air, but the water was still in his chest, pressing down on his lungs like the weight of a river threatening to cave in on him. Waves crashed against his heart again, trying to find a way in.

The man's hand pulsed against his, and more water trickled into him, the current running through his arm and swirling in his chest.

Stop this, Glen wanted to say, but he was still choking for air, unable to do anything except keep breathing through the tension and the panic.

Let it in, came the silent command, and after a heartbeat of resistance, Glen let his head fall back against the wall, let his body go limp, obeying without understanding why. The water lapped against the shores of his heart, the floodgates holding firm. And then they flung open, inviting the water to fill his heart until he felt like he would burst.

The stranger held him in his watery grasp for another minute or so. Black stars gathered at the corners of Glen's vision, like sirens trying to claim him, threatening to drag him down into the depths of unconsciousness. And then the stranger stepped back, releasing him. Glen fell forward, the cold hard floor slamming into his knees. He grunted at the sharp stab through his old injury.

It was like a bath being unplugged.

He choked down a deep lungful of air as water spurted from both his hands, forcing the flood from his chest, his body draining as liquid rushed through his arm back the way it came. He stared at the puddle forming around his knees, the water slowing to a trickle, and then a drip.

But there was still something wrong. Something very, very wrong.

"What the hell?" he blurted, chest heaving as he panted for breath, his heart still feeling too full, pounding frantically like it might explode from his chest. "What did you—?"

"Congratulations, Glen Farraday. You are now an Aqua."

"What?" Glen choked out, unable to make sense of the words. He was coughing and spluttering as though he had just been drowned, but his throat was dry. It was his chest that was raw. His lungs that protested against the watery invasion. His heart that struggled to beat with the weight clogging it. He pressed his hands to his chest as though he could rip open his ribcage and drain the remaining water. "What did you do to me?"

The stranger stood over him, eyes pitiless. "Didn't you always want a Talent, so your estranged daddy might acknowledge you?"

"But…" he blurted, drinking down more air. And then the realisation dawned on him as the water swirling in his chest pulsed, sending a wave of it spurting from his fingertips again. He stared at his splayed fingers, unable to believe his own eyes. "Why water?" he asked, dumbfounded.

His captor slipped his hands into his pockets. "It was Gavin Farraday's Talent. If you were viable for anything, your genes would likely play a part."

Glen blinked, his thoughts slow and sluggish as he stared up at the stranger. "You didn't ask about my mother's Talent."

A cold smirk slowly spread across the man's face. "I didn't need to. She was Talentless. Isn't that why your daddy walked out? Couldn't deal with his boy being as useless as the woman he married?"

Glen's breath caught, a pain stabbing through his chest that had nothing to do with the water churning within him.

"So he found himself a flashy new wife with a flashy Talent," the stranger continued, his voice casual. "Except his only Talented children were a pair of twin daughters who have preferred to marry and procreate instead of carrying his name to the battlefield. Still, he died when you were all kids. Imagine how he would take it, seeing his son fight for the Resistance. He must be rolling in his grave."

"You seem to know a lot about a man who died twenty years ago," Glen retorted, trying and failing to push away the hurt that pierced his heart with every revelation.

"Let's just say I have an affinity for history." He crossed his arms, eyes flashing through a spectrum of colour in the dingy cell. "I also have an affinity for the future."

Glen wheezed, pressing a hand to his drumming heart as more water seeped from his fingers into his T-shirt. "Oh really? You're going to give me some twisted prophecy now?"

The mysterious smirk grew. "You're going to get everything you want, Glen Farraday. Once you've learned how to control the water, that is."

"And how would you know what I want?" he asked, a defensive bite to his voice. *I don't even know what I want.*

"You'll figure out what you want, very soon." He raised his hand to the door handle. "I'll see you back at the van once you've... soaked in your new situation a little."

"Wait!" he gasped, trying to get his feet beneath him and slipping in the water. "You're not handing me over to the Nox?"

He shrugged. "President Ronan has enough toy soldiers to play with, for now..." He paused, amusement playing around his lips again. "It looks like you get to live another day, Glen Farraday."

Chapter Seventy-One

ROXANNE SUMMERS

Roxanne couldn't remember the last time she had slept, and her eyes itched and body ached as she sat in the makeshift courtroom. She tried not to sweat in her Resistance uniform beneath the glare of spotlights and the scrutiny of cameras, fully aware of all the lives that hung in the balance. Most precarious of all was the life of the man sitting cuffed to his chair on the stage – the former president fallen from grace.

Roxanne wondered if the Nox herself was watching the trial, if Camilla was sitting somewhere gloating over their efforts to make their end of the bargain not look like the farce it was. Everyone else around her seemed to be keeping their cool, despite Lindsey's lies that had come to light the night before. Alma Medley, standing on the stage in the black robes of the High Justice, certainly seemed to think the jury would reach a guilty verdict, but until she heard it, Roxanne was preparing herself for the worst.

There was a ripple of activity as the jury got to their feet over on the right side of the audience. A spindly man cleared his throat, the spotlights gleaming on his sparse grey hair. "Madam High Justice, the jury have reached a verdict."

Alma nodded, her shrewd eyes flicking to the pair of Resistance soldiers flanking Caplin. "Would the defendant please stand for the reading of the verdict."

Caplin looked calm as a soldier unlinked his cuffs from the chair, then relocked them at his front. He stood with his back straight, head held high, hands clasped as he stared at no one in particular, waiting for the decision. The jury representative cleared his throat again, lifting a piece of paper in both hands.

"The jury find Alistair Tobias Caplin guilty of all three charges brought against him: guilty of inciting the mutiny which claimed allied lives on Thursday, twenty-third of June; guilty of conspiring to assassinate Caspar and Phaedra Ronan, as well as the murder of the soldiers on guard on Friday, first of July; guilty for conspiring with the Nox and the Marsden brothers to capture members of the Resistance on Monday, eleventh of July."

Roxanne swallowed as the final crime was spoken aloud, and Devan's hand found hers, settling her trembling and squeezing reassuringly. Below, on the stage, Alma's face remained a severe mask, but Roxanne didn't miss the exhale of breath from her companions sitting around her.

"Thank you, representatives of the jury." Alma's voice rang out clearly, and she turned to Caplin. Despite the damning verdict, his face remained impassive. "Alistair Tobias Caplin, the jury finds you guilty of the charges brought against you. As determined by the laws of the empire which you yourself, as President of Britannia, approved, the sentencing for such acts of treason against the people of this land is exile or execution." Alma paused, her eyes sweeping the row where Roxanne sat with the allied leaders. "Would the Allied Board please stand to vote on the sentencing."

Despite the jury ruling in their favour, Roxanne knew the worst was yet to come, and she shook from head to toe as Devan released her hand and they got to their feet. They stood in tense silence until Alma continued to speak.

"As agreed at the commencement of the trial, the Allied Board is made up of the leaders of each allied faction. As the leader of the Caplin Forces and the Lux, Skye Bolton, please provide your vote."

If Skye was nervous about condemning her former employer and claiming his leadership title, she didn't show it as she spoke. "Mr Caplin plotted to hand me over to the Nox. Not only would this have put my life on the line, it also risked putting the fate of the empire in a tyrant's hands. For such treason against the people he once swore to lead and protect, I vote execution."

A series of mutters followed. Roxanne's stomach churned from the ease with which Skye seemed to deliver her decision, though she didn't miss the murderous way in which the former president and the Lux glared at one another across the courtroom.

"As leader of the Ronan Army, Caspar Ronan, please provide your vote."

"Mr Caplin is in part responsible for mine and my niece's near-demise, and the corruption and deaths of many of my soldiers," said Caspar, speaking as calmly as ever. "As a consequence, I also vote for execution."

Two votes. Two votes for a man's death. But considering the people who cast them, Roxanne was hardly surprised. Riordan Rathbone came next, as leader of the Saoirse Army. His steady voice carried through the room. "I vote exile."

"Exile," Darshana agreed, and then Peter was speaking before she had barely finished.

"Mr Caplin is responsible for many heinous crimes, not just throughout the course of this war, but also throughout his dictatorship. He let the country fall into poverty while he and his inner circle sat comfortable in their mansions, raising taxes and passing laws that allowed their law enforcement to oppress and brutalise citizens fighting for their rights. For years of constant cruelty, a life lived in comfortable exile does not seem like a severe enough punishment. I vote for execution."

Another series of mutters followed, the discomfort evident. Even Alma looked ruffled, for she was one of the few who had benefited from Caplin's regime. But then Devan spoke up, his voice silencing everyone once more.

"I vote for exile," he said. His words were simple, but Roxanne felt a stone drop into her stomach, her chest tighten in anxiety. She knew he was trying to do the right thing, knew he was trying to be fair, but his vote had left her with a terrible decision.

She had the casting vote.

She felt Devan's gaze on her face, felt other eyes glance her way, expectant. But she looked only at Caplin, at the one person standing between her daughter's safety and her death. And Caplin looked right back, waiting. In fact, the more she watched him, the more confident he seemed, sure of what she was about to say. Could she condemn him? Could she justify killing a man in exchange for her daughter? What right did she have to place Amber's life above his? She was a Healer, not a killer.

Devan's warm fingers brushed hers as she hesitated, and she flinched away, clasping her hands before her, wringing them. Somewhere in the audience a throat cleared, but she could only continue to stare, unaware of the expression on her face, unaware of anything except the decision she had to make. Sentence this man to death and guarantee her daughter's life and freedom, or send him into exile, risking Camilla's rejection?

"Dr Summers, your vote, please," Alma prompted, her voice cutting through the fog of indecision threatening to drown her. The woman's words from the previous evening drifted from the depths of her memory – *I recommend his sentence is a swift execution.*

Roxanne drew a shaky breath, holding Caplin's gaze as she said, "I vote for execution."

Caplin swayed as she spoke that final, damning word, his composure slackening. Around her, noise erupted, and she was distinctly aware of Peter's surprised exclamation of "Bloody hell!" But she couldn't look at them. Couldn't look at anyone as she ducked her head, not wanting them to see the tears that sprang to her eyes. As people got to their feet, obscuring her from view, she slipped away and exited the courtroom, heading to her surgery and locking herself in.

She sank down to the floor with the door at her back, sobbing in self-disgust. The awful noises escaping her were pierced only by the din still emanating from the courtroom and spilling into the rest of the building. She had condemned a man to death, *she* had, when her entire existence had been dedicated to saving lives. How could she live with herself after this? How could she let her daughter or her parents look at her again?

A soft knock jolted her from the spiral of self-hatred, and she hiccupped, lowering her soaked hands from her face. A pause followed, tension flooding her as she waited to learn who was standing just the other side of the door. Another knock vibrated through the wood, followed by a voice that normally sent her heart fluttering. "Roxanne, it's Devan."

She drew in a tight breath and blinked tears from her eyes. Through the bubbling disgust at her own actions, a spark of anger flared at what he had done. But no, said her more rational voice. What did it matter who delivered the final blow? The result was the same.

"Roxanne, please let me explain."

His voice was pleading, apologetic. Not the confident leader she had come to know. With difficulty, she got to her feet, suddenly aware that the cold from the linoleum had seeped into her limbs, leaving her stiff and shaky with needles. She unlocked the door with a click, then went to stand in the middle of the surgery, her back to the door.

There was further hesitation, then Devan let himself in, closing the door quietly. For a moment, there was only silence behind her.

"I'm sorry if my actions hurt you, Roxanne. That was never my intention." He sounded genuine, almost tearful. But Roxanne still couldn't bring herself to look at him.

"With the discord amongst the Caplinite followers, I didn't want to make it obvious we had conspired to kill their leader. It would have only added more fuel to the flames, and we can't risk further deserters."

She drew in a sharp gasp and pressed a hand to her solar plexus, the betrayal gripping her. "So why didn't you discuss it with me? You must have planned this, you and Rathbone and—" She stopped herself, realising she was spiralling, letting paranoia bleed into her thoughts. She struggled down a breath through tears and tightened lungs. "You knew my daughter's life is at stake, and yet you left me with a terrible choice."

Silence followed, and dragged on. Only the sound of the plastic clock ticking behind her and the distant uproar of celebration and dissent reached her ears. Finally, she heard Devan's intake of breath. "It was a choice I knew you would make."

She sniffled and wrapped her arms around herself. She couldn't get Caplin's look of horror out of her mind, the echo of his expression sickening her. Death was terrifying as it was, but to know it was coming…

“I’m sorry,” he said quietly. But it was too late. He shouldn’t have gone behind her back, excluding her in exactly the same way Peter and Nanette had always done.

“Please go.” More tears slipped down her face with the words, and she reached for a tissue stowed in her pocket.

“Roxanne…”

But she could only shake her head as she angrily wiped her eyes. She heard him sigh behind her as he waited a handful of heartbeats. And then, without another word, Devan retreated, letting the door click shut behind him.

Chapter Seventy-Two

Alessia Ronan

"We have news," said Vala as soon as Alessia entered the war tent. The Seer sat alone, looking at her with colour in her youthful cheeks and a satisfied smile on her face. "Alistair Caplin's execution has been announced for tomorrow."

"Tomorrow?" Alessia sank into her chair, painfully aware of the empty seat next to her, usually occupied by her grandfather.

"At ten o'clock," said Vala, giving a slight nod. "And what is more, soldiers of the Caplin Forces are deserting in droves. They're not happy they had no say over Skye claiming the leadership role."

But despite the good news, Alessia felt no pleasure. "How many?"

"At least a quarter of the army. I foresee more will follow tomorrow after the execution goes ahead."

"Good." The ice in her veins stirred, her shadows twining up her arms and curling around her shoulders like an embrace. But her chest was still tight with grief, and sickness pressed down on her, crushing her lungs. Even miles away, she could still sense her grandfather's agony as she left him rotting in the cold, dark sarcophagus, slowly wasting away as he dangled from a thread of life.

"We should march on the allies soon," said Vala. "Once Alistair is dead, the allied army will be overwhelmed with chaos. We should take advantage of that."

Alessia nodded, staring at the wooden armies laid out on the table before her. The enemy's troops were already significantly depleted after the last battle, and with the Undead she had raised that day, along with the further soldiers she had killed and resurrected since, she didn't need Pierce to tell her the allies were outnumbered. The next battle would surely wipe their threat off the face of the earth, and then the Lux wouldn't have many places left to hide, no matter how many Aeres friends she managed to cling to.

"Tell Pierce to prepare to march," she said, her gaze snagging on the yellow Lux marker that stood alone before the wooden allied army. "And tell Lucien he must train with me. Now."

Lucien's forehead shone with sweat as he panted across from her, his leather jacket discarded, his usually pristine hair falling in his eyes. But despite his obvious fatigue, Alessia didn't stop. She advanced on him through the tall grass of the hillside, ignoring the sharpness in her chest as she gulped down the thick humid air. Moisture coated her brow, and her dark training clothes stuck to her, like a film coating her limbs.

"Let's take a break," Lucien instructed. His glamour had slipped, showing drawn, pale skin and faded grey eyes that now only flashed when lightning flickered in his palms.

"I don't need a break," she hissed, throwing all her anger and frustration behind her attack. Lucien yielded a step as her snaking shadows collided with his dark shield.

Alessia coughed into the crook of her elbow, then hurled another attack at him, determined not to let her condition slow her down. There were many things she was once glad to have had passed down from her grandfather. His sickness was not one of them, and now she wished she could rid herself of the rest too.

"Don't hurt yourself," said Lucien, his shield of darkness rippling with her latest blow. He spoke with just enough condescension that her own riled darkness surged to the surface, overflowing in a torrent of more attacks that had him stepping back again.

"Miss Ronan," Lucien warned, but his grey eyes widened with shock for a fraction of a second, and Alessia ploughed on. He side-stepped, letting out a gasp as her latest stream of darkness glanced off his sleeve. She pressed on relentlessly.

"Alessia," he said firmly, but his shield faltered at her next blow, and her name became a cry as her darkness grazed his cheek. "Stop!" he shouted, fear evident on his face for the first time since she had met him, his arm raised to defend himself.

Alessia brought down her next blow, gouging a deep, dark cut along his forearm.

The explosion that followed rattled in her ears as she was thrown backwards, landing heavily on the grass. Dazed and winded, she fought for breath, blinking in the sunlight that shone down on her. She rolled onto her elbow and shook her head to clear the drawn-out whine in her ears. Lucien stood some eight yards away, his fear replaced by a look of fury. He held a fireball in one hand, a spinning twister in the other. As he braced himself to attack, determination on his features, Alessia got her legs beneath her and stood. A ball of darkness was already growing in her hands as Lucien lunged at her.

"STOP!" came a furious bellow that neither of them heeded. They ran headlong at one another, until a cloud of darkness deeper than any Alessia had ever conjured materialised between them, sending them blasting back to the ground. With the breath knocked out of her a second time, all Alessia could do was choke, clutching her chest as she fought for air. When she finally looked up, Vala towered above her, anger emanating from her in waves that made her suddenly afraid.

After a few moments, Vala reached out a pale hand. Alessia hesitated, then took it. The Seer hauled her up easily, as though Alessia was no heavier than a rag doll. Behind her, Lucien had also risen, blood trickling from his nose, hair falling into his eyes.

"Well?" Vala demanded in a tone Alessia had never heard her use before. "Are you going to explain why you were trying to murder one another? You are supposed to be training, not fighting to the death."

Lucien glared and spat blood onto the grass. Alessia jutted out her chin, then turned on her heel, trying not to let on that her body was as wounded as her pride.

But as she trudged down the hill towards the portal that would take her back to Castle Uaine, cold satisfaction twined with her Talents. The fight had given her hope. She could have killed Lucien, she was sure of it. And if she could kill him, she could kill the Lux, because there was no way Skye Bolton was as strong as Lucien was with his mirror.

"I will not have Lucien come again," said Vala sometime later, after waiting for Alessia to finish eating a solitary meal of grilled chicken and greens. Alessia masked the hint of guilt she felt with a smile of satisfaction as she delicately wiped her mouth with a napkin. She didn't let herself think about the fact that she had lost one of the few people she could talk to so soon after imprisoning her grandfather.

"Are you afraid I'll kill your pet?" she asked instead, her voice dripping with the same false sweetness Vala tended to employ. She thought she saw Vala wince ever so slightly.

"I believe you and Lucien are too closely matched. I value both of you, and want to lose neither."

But whatever Vala said, she had bested Lucien today. She at last felt ready for the final battle, ready to don the battlewear that had been designed especially for facing the Lux, woven with protection sigils and obsidian. Now she just needed the tightness in her chest to subside.

"How long before the end?"

"Not long," Vala promised, remaining in the shadowy corner of the dining room. "And with the loss of so many allies and followers, perhaps it is better to put her out of her misery sooner than later."

"I want her miserable," Alessia said darkly, pouring a cup of infusion from the pot a servant had brought her. But she knew that whatever misfortune befell Skye Bolton, she would not suffer anywhere near as much as Alessia had done these past days. "I want her crawling at the end."

"She will crawl," Vala confirmed, the emotion in the bottomless pools of her eyes unreadable. "And that is when we will strike."

Chapter Seventy-Three

SKYE BOLTON

The jangle of the key turning in the lock was loud in the dimly lit corridor, but it was nothing compared to the hammering of her heart. The guard looked at her, silently asking once more if she wanted him to come inside with her. She shook her head, then entered the gloomy room. One bare bulb hung from the ceiling and flickered every so often, dull enough that the corners remained half in shadow. But the cell would only be occupied for one more night.

Skye's gaze snapped to Caplin, seated at a rickety table, his back straight, eyes on the wall opposite him. He didn't greet her as she let the door snap shut behind her, didn't acknowledge her presence. She couldn't blame him. She and three other people had sentenced him to death, and in spite of everything, guilt chewed up her insides.

"Come to gloat?" Caplin asked eventually, after letting Skye stand watching him for several minutes.

"A part of me is satisfied," she said, no humour or malice in her voice. "In many ways, you deserve this. But I take no pleasure in it."

Caplin was silent for a moment longer, and she didn't miss his hands curling into fists on the table. "You should," he said with a grim curve to his lips. "I know what I've done to you and your family, Skye. If the tables were turned, I would like nothing better than to see your head on a spike."

He glanced at her for a fraction of a second, then looked away again. Skye breathed deeply as she watched him, drawing herself to her full height.

"I wasn't going to hand you over to the Nox, you know?" he continued in the same monotone. "I know you don't want to believe it, but I only said what I did to win over her and the Seer."

"Whatever your intentions towards me, it doesn't change the fact that you tried to assassinate Caspar. Twice."

"What was I supposed to do, Skye? You let yourself be seduced by a Ronan. In your father's absence, I took measures to protect you."

She snorted at the condescension. "No one seduced me, Alistair." She made herself say it, say his name. Hold his gaze. "Except you, with your false promises."

"I delivered on those promises, Skye. You had glory, renown, a prestigious position in my Guard and all the financial and political privileges that brought. What more could you want?"

Skye gritted her teeth as her anger clenched around her heart. "You don't get it, do you? Power and privilege mean nothing if my loved ones aren't safe. Your inaction put us in this position, Alistair. You made your bed."

He nodded, his smile bitter. "I thought we were the same, you and I. I used to think ambition drove you the way it drove me, and I took advantage of that by pushing you to be Ronan's hostage, convinced you would see it as an opportunity. But since Victor was captured… I know where your priorities lie."

She returned his nod. She had seen as much in his head, his understanding that she had turned on him because of his treatment of her and her father. Some part of him cared that his friend was being held prisoner, like some part of him felt sorry that Darius was dead, and that she and Jacob had suffered in his place. But he felt no guilt, no feelings of regret that what had happened to them had been his fault.

"I was the bargaining chip, wasn't I?" he asked then, and Skye was jolted from her reverie, locking her gaze with his again. "Linden, or the Nox. They want me dead in return for your father."

"What makes you say that?" she asked, careful with her words, fearing that he could find some way to overturn his sentencing.

"They must have offered Summers the same for her daughter. Why else would a soft sop like her sentence anyone to execution? And why would Alma work so hard to get rid of me after spending her entire career serving me?"

Skye didn't know what to say. What could she say? It was no use lying. Caplin took her silence as an answer, nodding his head slowly. "Like I said, I would have done the same in your place."

"I would say I'm sorry. But I'm not."

Caplin huffed a humourless laugh. "That's my girl." He surveyed her then, looking her slowly up and down, his expression difficult to read. "You know, if you can manage to keep your temper and recklessness in check, you could be a great leader someday. I might have even made you my heir."

Skye scoffed quietly, flashing a wry smile. "I suppose you would have preferred that, rather than me being your usurper."

He laughed again, then grew serious. "Tell Victor I'm sorry."

"Really? I thought you were incapable of apologies."

"I'm at death's door. I'm allowed some regrets."

She swallowed, taking a last, long look at him, committing his sly features to memory. "Any other last words?"

Caplin was silent for a long moment, his head bowed, his fists relaxing as he flattened his hands on the table again. He stared at his hands for some time, then finally looked back up at Skye. Perhaps she was reading him wrong, but for the first time ever, he almost looked proud of her. "I would wish you luck for your final battle, Skye. But I already know you will win."

Skye felt hollow as she crossed the darkened barracks, snippets of the conversation replaying themselves over and over in her mind. Questions plagued her as she filled in the gaps between his words, trying to make sense of his intentions and her feelings. Was he trying to lower her guard with compliments in the hope that she would change her vote? What if his knowledge that she and Roxanne had conspired to execute him might somehow overturn the sentencing? She would warn Alma before heading home. Her aunt would know what to do if Caplin opened his mouth.

But there was something else she had to do first. She stopped outside the chalet where the Mathesons were staying, rapping loudly on the door.

Lindsey opened it, wearing a grey hoodie and tracksuit bottoms, her hair pinned up in a messy bun, completely at odds with the way Skye was used to her looking. She raised an eyebrow, clearly pissed off to see her there.

"Is your father here?" Skye asked, not bothering to apologise.

Lindsey opened the door wider, giving Skye a glimpse of Oliver sitting at the table, nursing a glass of liquor.

"I need to speak with him," said Skye, loud enough for Oliver to hear her. He met her gaze across the room, then jerked his head, inviting her in. Lindsey stood back as she stepped inside.

"What d'you want?" he deadpanned, already somewhat intoxicated. He had been at the trial and was still wearing the tailored grey waistcoat and trousers she had seen him in earlier, but he had removed his tie and left his top buttons open, the sleeves of his shirt rolled up.

"I want the Sicarius you used to execute Darius." She wasn't sure why. The decision had come to her when she left Caplin in his cell. Perhaps it was justice for Darius, or because she had seen his work and knew he was swift and clean.

"Why?" asked Oliver, raising his eyebrows.

"That's my business," she said, jutting out her chin. "You can get him, can't you? I assume he worked for you."

"Yeah, I can get him. But before tomorrow?"

"Yes, before tomorrow."

Oliver scoffed, then leaned back in his chair, sipping his drink. "Why don't you execute him yourself? Electrocution will stop his heart almost as effectively as a Sicarius."

Skye snorted. "Execute him myself? You know how that will look?"

He shrugged, surveying her over the rim of his glass. "Not my problem."

Skye inhaled through gritted teeth as static buzzed in her veins. "Then I'll make it your problem. Once the execution is over tomorrow, I'll be paying dear Camilla a visit and leaving with the prisoners. But if you don't do as I ask, I might have a mind to leave your daughter behind."

"Watch what you're threatening," Lindsey snarled, taking a few steps towards her.

Skye didn't bother to look around. Instead, she stared Oliver down, waiting for his decision, praying he wouldn't perceive it as an empty threat. Finally, he knocked back the rest of his drink and set the glass on the table with a resounding click. "Fine. His name is Horowitz. I'll have him here tomorrow."

“Thank you.” Skye gave him a small nod, then retreated towards the door.

Oliver snorted. “Skye Bolton, thanking *me*? What is the world coming to?”

“Let’s get through tomorrow and we’ll find out.”

***

Beside her, Dean felt sick. And for once, Skye’s own stomach echoed his, guilt and fear and dread battling within her. All around her, people chattered quietly, but their minds were louder. There were some that were angry or dreading Caplin’s pending execution, whereas others were celebrating, excited to see the spectacle of their former president meeting his end. They were crammed into the auditorium they had used for the trial, and even more cameras had been erected on stands, more unnatural light flooding the stage.

Skye scanned her surroundings. Devan, Sinclair and Rathbone all stood nearby in their respective uniforms. Neither Roxanne nor Darshana had shown up, but Skye wasn’t surprised. She knew they were both opposed to the execution, even if Roxanne had had to cast her vote for it. Further away stood the remainder of the Caplin Guard, Skye’s former comrades, with Irvine Sullivan amongst them. They still wore their uniforms, proudly displaying the red shield and black raven that formed Caplin’s crest, but they were surrounded by Resistance soldiers, heavily guarded. The new self-styled Lux Guard was also present, as near to the front as Sabine could get them. As Skye looked, Sabine’s golden eyes met hers, and she nodded to her, a satisfied smirk on her face. Her brother Jacob stood next to her, alongside Lorcan and Ikarus, whose pale face was tinged with grey. Skye wondered what thoughts were going through his hidden mind.

As the minutes ticked closer to the scheduled time of the execution, Skye's attention was drawn to the arrival of Caspar and the Mathesons. They each wore formal suits the same as Skye and Dean had chosen to do. Caspar held her gaze as he came to stand beside her, brushing the small of her back with his comforting touch. She resisted her body's urge to lean into his warmth, respecting the new boundaries between them, and they exchanged a small smile in greeting. But his expression was guarded, leaving her unable to gauge his feelings. Oliver ignored them and stood next to his leader, whereas Lindsey nodded tentatively towards them, holding Dean's gaze longer. Skye didn't miss the whirlwind of torn thoughts that went through her brother's mind, and withdrew, giving him privacy.

They brought Caplin out then, and a hush fell as he crossed the stage. Guards in Resistance uniforms flanked him, and his hands were in cuffs once more. He was in full military dress, all his medals and regalia bulking up his body and making him appear taller than he truly was. Or perhaps that was just the way he was holding himself, proud and defiant to the end. Skye's own spine straightened, and his eyes briefly locked with hers as he scanned the crowd with his usual air of superiority, taking in the faces of those who had come to either mourn or celebrate. When they reached the centre of the stage, the guards either side of him drew back several feet, clasping hands behind their backs and fading into the background.

It was Sinclair who got up to read the death sentence, a more elaborate version of the one Alma had delivered the previous day. For once, everyone was glad to let Sinclair have centre stage, no one willing to do the honours. As he spoke, Skye heard a whimper near the stage, and she looked to see a small brunette woman standing front and centre with a handkerchief pressed to her mouth. It was Irma, Caplin's wife. Another stab of guilt shot through her gut, and Skye chewed her lip as she watched the husband and wife look at each other across the few feet that separated them. She hadn't even considered Irma's feelings in all of this. Perhaps Caplin didn't love anyone except himself, but his wife clearly cared for him. She took a deep, painful breath, vowing to ensure Mrs Caplin was provided for, if Caplin's will didn't do so. She couldn't let the poor woman be left destitute.

"Any last words, Mr Caplin?" Sinclair asked after his little speech was over.

Caplin nodded, taking a small step forward and raising his head high as he addressed his audience. "My bloodline ends with me, and I know many of you will not be sorry to see the end of it. I know my rule hasn't been what many of you hoped for. The blood of the last Lux runs through my veins, but the Caplin dynasty has not brought the light that the Lux normally promises. That said, you have a new Lux now." He paused, searching for her face in the crowd. "I will not be around to see my legacy, but I hope she leads you out of the shadows that I leave behind."

Skye held his gaze, willing her face to remain expressionless. But after an agonising couple of breaths, Caplin's gaze drifted elsewhere.

The executioner stepped onto the stage then, dressed head to toe in plain black, a silver scythe brooch glinting on his chest. His face was pale in the floodlights, his dark hair contrasting sharply with his complexion. Sure enough, it was the same Sicarius who had ended Darius. Horowitz, Oliver had called him. Sinclair began speaking again, reciting some final words from a paper he held before him. Irma's crying increased in volume, and the look on Caplin's face seemed frozen in place as he stared at an invisible point in space, waiting for the end that was seconds away. The Sicarius raised his arm, filling Skye with déjà vu as Darius's execution flashed through her mind's eye. She knew what was coming next, and the taste of blood filled her mouth as she bit her lip too hard. Like a coward, she turned to leave, unable to bring herself to witness the death she had helped to orchestrate.

Chapter Seventy-Four

DEAN ROSWELL

Dean had never felt so ill at ease, and the atmosphere surrounding him wasn't helping. There were angry jeers and weeping, but many celebrated, the depravity of their cheers sickening him. Some even cracked open bottles of champagne after Resistance guards threw a sheet over Caplin's body and carried him out. Dean hadn't witnessed the killing blow. Skye's departure had distracted him and – he had to admit – spared him from it. But seeing the man he had always worked to protect lying there dead churned his stomach, and it took all his willpower not to throw up in front of everyone. He stayed just long enough to find out if his presence was needed, and then made his escape after Skye.

She wasn't hard to find. She leaned against a wall in a nearby office, drinking from a hip flask with a shaking hand while she zipped her mother's emerald ring along the chain around her neck with the other. She avoided his gaze, but didn't resist when he took the flask from her and then pulled her to him, holding her tightly and squinting his eyes shut against the top of her head as he, too, drew the strength he needed from her in return.

He held her until her trembling stopped, breathing in her scent of shampoo and subtle perfume. "We're expected," she said thickly, and sure enough he could hear voices in the corridor as people emerged from the auditorium. Skye started to pull away.

"Wait," he urged, unable to miss the uncertainty and tears swimming in her dark eyes. "Are you alright?"

She hesitated, her expression softening. "I will be, when we get Dad back."

He nodded, giving her shoulder a reassuring squeeze. "Then let's go and get him."

He stepped away, but Skye stayed where she was, her eyes taking on that faraway look that meant she was scanning minds. "We need to talk to Harlow. The Tracers have news."

"News?" he asked, dread prickling beneath his skin.

Skye took a deep, steadying breath, then crossed the room and waved him towards the door. "Alessia is marching."

Lindsey waited for them near the doors to the auditorium, the fear on her face making his heart plummet in spite of everything that had happened between them. But before Dean could ask any questions, she closed the gap between them. "The Nox is on the way with an army of Undead. It's larger than the one we faced outside Manchester."

Dread gnawed at his churning stomach, echoing the terror in Lindsey's wide eyes. The pain of their last conversation no longer seemed so important in the face of what approached them now.

"The Leaders and Caspar are in the meeting room," Lindsey continued, tearing her eyes away from him to look at Skye, who was almost crackling with nervous energy.

Skye took in a resigned breath. "Let's have a chat with them then." And with that she strode off towards the meeting room. Dean exchanged another glance with

Lindsey, a glance loaded with words they were running out of time to say, then followed.

Inside the boardroom the atmosphere was mixed. Caspar and Oliver sat smug-faced at one end of the table, and Dean couldn't help his surge of anger at their satisfaction. At the other end of the room stood Roxanne and Darshana, both wearing their blue Leader uniforms. Roxanne was pale and looked like she might faint, and Darshana's hand hovered at her elbow, as though she feared the same. The rest of the Resistance Leaders sat at the table, along with Seth and Jack from Lindsey's team of Tracers. Lindsey slid into a seat next to her father, but Skye remained standing, as did Dean. The twisted knot in his stomach rose to his chest as he took in the bleak expressions.

"How long do we have?" Skye asked, and to her credit she had regained her usual composure, not betraying even a hint of the trembling wreck Dean had walked in on just minutes before.

"A few hours," said Jack, swallowing and lowering his gaze.

A painful silence followed the Tracer's words, and Dean glanced from face to face, praying that someone would look more hopeful than he felt.

"There's no running from this," Caspar said, his tone grim. "She'll have the country and our lives sooner or later, and I'd rather go down fighting."

"We don't have the numbers," said Devan weakly. For once his calm demeanour had given way to a look of exhausted fear.

"Don't we?" Caspar replied. "Caplin's Forces answer to Skye now."

"What's left of them," said Lindsey. "About half of them have deserted since we imprisoned Caplin."

"Will you lead the rest?" asked Devan, looking up at Skye hopefully.

"I can't," said Skye, and Dean saw several people wince as her words cut through the room. "I have an appointment with *Camilla*."

The people at the table looked at one another, some of them confused. But then Roxanne stepped forward, still unsteady on her feet. "We both do," she said in her small voice. Devan looked up at her, clearly torn. Sinclair was frowning, as was Rathbone.

"Can't it wait?" asked Rathbone, his voice strained.

"What the bloody hell do you need to see Camilla Linden for?" boomed Sinclair.

Skye shifted at Dean's side, meeting his gaze.

I could go, he offered, noting her worry and indecision. *I can take a small team and bring Dad and the others back.*

Her jaw tightened, veins of suppressed lightning streaking through her irises. *I'm coming. If Camilla has set a trap, I'm not losing you to her too.* Without letting him argue further, she turned back to the others. "One hour," she conceded. "I'll talk to the troops, find out if they really will fight for me. And then I'm going to get my father back."

The Lux Guard waited for them as they strode across the barracks to the cluster of black-clad soldiers. Both Skye and Dean had changed into their own uniforms, although Dean was certain Skye felt as uncomfortable as he did wearing the colours of the man who had just been executed by their arrangement. Sabine turned to them as they approached, standing proudly with the flaming heart crest on her own jacket, golden eyes blazing and a confident curve to her lips.

"I've got them ready for you," she said in her deep voice. "I even convinced some of them to stay. They're waiting for you."

Ike stepped forward, managing a small smile in spite of what they had witnessed not an hour before. "You should have seen her," he said, clapping Sabine on the shoulder, which only earned him a glare. "They're terrified of her."

"As they should be," said Skye, but her voice was full of pride as she looked down at Sabine. "You deserve to lead this army, not me."

"I'm not the Lux," Sabine said, raising her eyebrow with more than a pinch of sass.

"You'd make a better Lux than I do."

"So, they'll fight?" asked Dean, anxious to skip the small talk.

"Of course they will," said Sabine, her eyes flashing. "They know Caplin was a prick."

Dean winced, but he knew there was no love lost between Sabine and the former president after what happened to Jacob. And he could only imagine what kind of strength it had taken for Jacob to be standing beside his sister, looking just as determined.

Skye glanced around, then jerked her head to one side, gesturing for Sabine to follow her. Silently, Skye invited Dean to join them.

"I need to ask a favour," said Skye quietly once they were out of earshot of the others. "I can't explain properly right now, and you can't repeat this, but I made a deal with Camilla that meant I could get my father back once Caplin was dead."

Sabine blinked once, her only reaction.

"If I don't get back with him before this battle starts, I need you to lead them for me."

Sabine shifted slightly, raising her chin higher as she fixed Skye with that golden stare. "You're leaving."

"I…" Skye's voice broke, her eyes glazing. "I have to, Sabine. She might kill him, especially if things go south for us today. I wouldn't ask this of you otherwise."

Sabine pursed her lips slightly, still looking like she wanted to argue. So Dean stepped in. "You would ask the same of Skye, if it were Jacob."

That golden stare snapped to him, and she narrowed her eyes. But her anger banked as the tension left her shoulders. She looked back at Skye. "Fine. But talk to them first. I didn't bust a gut for you to just ditch us."

If Skye felt nervous, she didn't show it as she stood before the remaining troops of the Caplin Forces assembled in the training ground. Her features were solemn as she surveyed the soldiers. *Her* soldiers.

"I know I'm not the Lux anyone expected," Skye began. Despite her modest words, her voice carried every drop of her usual confidence. "And I know I'm not the heir Caplin would have chosen. But what marches towards us is bigger than a dispute between me and your late president. The Nox not only raises the dead, she brings death. We cannot let her reduce our homes to ash or turn our loved ones into Undead enemies."

She paused, and fear rippled through Dean as it did the rest of the army. Soldiers exchanged glances and mutters, and Skye's spine straightened a little more.

"I'm not asking you to fight for me. I'm asking you to fight for what you hold dear. Fight for your families. Fight for those who cannot fight for themselves. Let us have something left to come home to after we have defeated the Nox."

"The stormbird will lead us out of the dark," came a voice in the crowd, and Dean looked to find Ombra amongst the cadets, her narrow face fierce, the stormbird resplendent in its halo of sunrays on her chest.

Skye curled her hands into fists, her voice gaining strength. "Lightning cuts through the night, but so does hope. So does unity. Will you join me in carving a path through the dark?"

There was a heavy silence, a storm cloud about to break. And then, like the first rumble of thunder, another soldier added their voice, echoing Ombra. "The stormbird will lead us out of the dark."

More voices added to the gathering storm, repeating the slogan. The chant rose to deafening levels, replacing the doubtful expressions in waves. Skye sought Dean's gaze, a hint of surprise in her eyes, the faintest smile on her lips. Dean returned it, swelling with pride.

Skye looked back at the crowd, her voice ringing out and quieting the cheers. "Since you've granted me the honour of leading you, my first official act is to make Sabine van Zanten my General. She will be my voice in the event of my absence."

For once Sabine looked shocked, staring at Skye with her eyes wide and her mouth slightly open. But she quickly closed it, smoothing over her expression with her usually cool demeanour, and nodded her thanks, stepping up to Skye's side.

As the final cheers erupted, Skye turned away, nodding to her Lux Guard. "Ike, you're leading the Aeres Army."

"Aye aye, captain," Ike joked with a mock salute.

"Stop being ridiculous and get them ready," Sabine growled, but amusement danced in her smouldering eyes. Ike only grinned and slipped off to rally the Aeres.

Skye turned to her cousin. "Lorcan, I need you with me…"

"Where are we going?" he asked, surprise and curiosity on his freckled face.

"We're going to get my dad. I'm sure we'll be back before the fighting."

With a last glance at Sabine, who gave a curt nod, they headed back to the main building of the barracks, Lorcan following close behind.

Back in the boardroom, they found Lindsey kneeling at the edge of a salt circle, drawing sigils in its centre with chalk. Her eyes met Dean's as they entered, fear and tears swimming in them. Roxanne, Devan, and her Tracers hovered around her.

"The troops are arranged," Skye said bluntly. "We'll be back as soon as we can."

"I'm coming with you," said Roxanne quickly, trembling from head to toe. "You might need a Healer."

"We *will* bring your daughter back." Skye bristled with thinly veiled impatience. But Roxanne only shook her head, curling her dainty hands as she took her place at Skye's side. Seth, Lindsey's fellow Tracer, also stepped up next to Roxanne, clutching a machine gun.

On the floor, Lindsey drew the last sigil – a protection symbol, allowing through only those who meant them no harm. "I've just called Camilla. She said the connecting portal is ready, and she's waiting," she confirmed, brushing chalk off her hands. As she made to stand, Dean reached out automatically.

She gazed up at him, her light brown eyes as uncertain as Dean felt. But as he held his stance, unable to be unkind to her despite her lies, she took his hands, the chalk on her fingers soft against his.

"I'll bring her back," he promised when she was level with him, inhaling her floral scent. He took in the fear tightening her jaw, the terror widening her eyes. His heart gave a pang, and he had to stop himself from taking her into his arms, reminding himself that trusting her was a mistake. "And the others. We'll bring them all back."

Lindsey nodded and tentatively squeezed his fingers. "If I don't make it off that battlefield today, I want you to know I'm sorry. I shouldn't have lied to you."

His breath hitched, her fear shredding through his own attempts to hold himself together. "You're fighting?"

But she only gave his fingers one last squeeze, then ran her hands up his sleeves. "Come back safe, Dean Roswell."

Her eyes were glazed as she stepped away, and she lowered her head, clutching one elbow, an echo of the shy girl she had been. Before Dean could say anything, Skye strode up to the salt circle.

"Let's go," she said, her voice laced with anxious impatience.

And before anything more could be said, she stepped through the portal, leaving the rest of them to hurry after her.

The late morning sun shone brightly on the moors, staining their surroundings yellowish green. Dean squinted after the dimness of the room they had left, spotting the manor looming like a dark stain at the bottom of the hill.

"I'll guard the portal," said Seth, dark eyes glowering beneath bushy eyebrows as he clutched his gun.

Skye nodded her thanks, her own eyes fixed on the manor, and they set off down the hill. The dread in Dean's stomach had not gone, but now he felt hope too – hope that soon they would have Victor and the other prisoners, and would have one thing less to worry about. He could only imagine what Roxanne was feeling as she walked at his side. She kept stumbling, like she wanted to break into a run.

They approached the building, finding Camilla sitting at a wrought iron table on the porch. She was wearing a scarlet dress that left much of her pale skin exposed, smoking and drinking a red and orange cocktail. Her butler,

Tony, stood at her side. She didn't smile as they approached, only watched them as she puffed her cigarette.

"Where is he?" Skye demanded once they ascended the porch steps.

"Inside," she said, gesturing dismissively with her cigarette.

"Well, are you going to bring them out?"

Camilla drank deeply, keeping them all waiting, before she said, "You can go in and get them."

A short silence followed, and Dean could hear the anger in Skye's voice as she said, "Camilla—"

"Go in and get them or don't get them at all. Makes no difference to me," said Camilla, and with that she picked up a newspaper that had been lying on the table and began to read.

Skye looked at Dean, uncertainty evident in her eyes. He couldn't blame her, his own unease growing. Was it indeed a trap? What if Camilla locked the doors on them as soon as they were inside? Skye looked at Roxanne and Lorcan then, and Dean suspected they were speaking telepathically. Sure enough, Roxanne gave the smallest nod, and she and Lorcan retreated back down the steps.

Let's go, she thought to Dean, and they stepped through the half-open double doors coated in peeling, dark green paint.

The entrance hall they found themselves in smelled damp and dusty, and was as cool and silent as a crypt. Their footsteps echoed on the marble floor, and mould crept across the walls. Across from them was what had once been a grand staircase, but now the steps were broken and caved in, the carpet torn in places. At either side of the staircase, both on the ground floor and the landing above, corridors led off in two separate wings.

"My telepathy is being blocked," Skye whispered, and the fear Dean heard in her voice only increased his own.

"Wards?" he murmured back, glancing around.

She only nodded. "Which way?"

Dean glanced down the corridor to his left, then to the one on the right. "We could… split up," he said reluctantly.

Skye nodded again. "I think we need to. The quicker we can get out of this place, the better."

He looked back at her one last time. "Shout if you need me."

"I will. Meet me back here." She gave him a grim smile that was far from reassuring, then strode off towards the right-hand corridor. Taking a deep breath, Dean headed in the opposite direction.

The left-hand corridor was in an even worse state than the entrance hall. The carpet beneath his feet was heavy with dust and pockmarked with frayed holes, and some of the doors at either side of him hung off their hinges, or had no doors at all. But even the closed doors were unlocked, and he looked in each room, finding parlours, lounges and some bedrooms with en suite bathrooms. Most of the rooms were shuttered or had boards nailed over the windows, but were just about light enough for him to see that they were empty.

He was about halfway down the corridor when he found the first occupied room. A bald man lay on a narrow bed, his feet dangling off the end of it, but he quickly scrambled into a sitting position when he saw Dean, fear distorting his face. There was slightly more light in here, a thin slant of bright sunshine cutting through the room, and Dean could see the mottled bruise across the left side of the man's face.

"Are you a prisoner?" Dean asked, and the man blinked in confusion.

"I'm… yes…"

"We're here to get you out," said Dean with as much reassurance as he could muster.

"Really?" said the man, and he swayed slightly as he stood.

"Do you know where the other prisoners are?" he asked, a little more urgently.

"There are some here, nearby. I've heard them."

Hope and fear tightened his throat, and he looked to his left, already heading to the next door. The man followed. The next room was also occupied by a small man with a mess of grey hair.

"Bert!" the prisoner exclaimed, staggering to his feet and crossing the room with a limp. The two men embraced, but Dean was already looking in the next room. The third prisoner was unconscious, another stranger Dean didn't recognise, but he wore a stained and faded Resistance uniform.

"Help him while I look for more," he said, frantically moving further down the corridor.

He found three more prisoners: another man who was babbling and missing three fingers, a woman who refused to move from the corner of the room until she recognised the one called Bert, and the third was dead, and had been for some time, judging by the smell and the flies. Dean tasted bile as he gagged, but after a deep breath, he moved to the next room.

The air smelled in there too, of sickness and old blood. And the specks of light that fell across the bed were barely enough to make out the body that lay in a heap on the mattress. Dean crossed the room, the wheezing breaths assuring him that this one was still alive, and he tentatively nudged the man's bony shoulder, pushing him back so he could see his face. One eye was swollen and purple, blood crusted beneath his nose, and the dark hair and beard were a tangled mess, obscuring most of his face. But as Dean leaned over him, trying to revive him, the good eye opened, and Dean shrank back when he recognised him, that brown eye the same as Skye's.

"Victor!" he gasped, and then got down on his knees, examining his stepfather more closely. Victor tried to speak, but only a cough came out as he grasped Dean's arm with weak fingers. Tears of relief and horror stung his eyes as he took in the state of him, his clothing torn, his skin coated with dried blood and grime.

"Can you stand?"

Victor coughed again, and shook his head, falling back against the filthy mattress, his breath loud and uneven. Dean tried to pull him into a sitting position, but Victor groaned in pain. At a loss, he got to his feet, then scooped him up in his arms, shocked to find that he was almost as light as a child.

"Skye is here," he murmured, and Victor's breath rattled out of him in a gasp as he clutched Dean's shoulder with trembling fingers. "She's looking for you too." He tried to smile, but Victor's good eye flickered, hazy with pain.

"We've found all the prisoners in this wing, sir," said the one called Bert from the doorway.

Dean nodded grimly and adjusted his hold on Victor. The sight of his father's agony wrenched his racing heart. "Hang in there, Dad," he soothed, his voice cracking. "We'll get you to a Healer very soon."

Chapter Seventy-Five

PHAEDRA RONAN

Alessia is marching.

The warning rippled through the barracks, and Phaedra struggled to breathe. *A few hours,* some warned. *She's already here*, others exaggerated. *This is the end.*

She found Ombra in the sleeping quarters, waiting at Phaedra's bedside. She was already dressed in her black Forces uniform, hair braided in a crown around her head and fully equipped with all manner of weapons. Her green eyes were wide and bright with nerves, tracking Phaedra as she hurried towards her.

"I figured you'd come back here," Ombra said, pulling her into her arms the moment she was close enough, ignorant of their comrades scurrying around them. "Are you okay?"

Phaedra nodded, knowing full well it was a lie. She was far from okay: unprepared, uncertain, terrified. "They're saying we're outnumbered."

"All the more reason for us to join the fight. Did you hear Skye's speech?" Excitement shot through Ombra's nervous expression, lighting her features for a moment.

Shaking her head, Phaedra reluctantly extricated herself from her girlfriend's arms and began to change into a battle uniform. The trio of silver Resistance stars embroidered on the blue fabric glinted in the morning light. As she pulled on the garments, Ombra babbled enthusiastically behind her.

"She's rallied the Forces, and made Sabine her general. How awesome is that?"

"Sabine?" Phaedra asked distractedly, remembering the scary Ignis who would probably sooner incinerate Phaedra with her glare than be pleasant with her. "Isn't Skye commanding?"

Ombra hesitated, a hand on her gun belt. "She's gone to get Uncle Victor."

"Oh…" Phaedra drew her own weapons out of her locker: the array of knives she barely knew how to wield, the standard handgun and ammo, a truncheon. She lay them on the bed, gazing at them doubtfully. Her darkness swirled uneasily in her chest as Alessia's imposing figure loomed in her mind's eye. Soon, she might be facing her in person. The objects in front of her and her unreliable Talent felt insignificant against her sister's threat.

She picked up her knife belt anyway, slinging it around her waist and fumbling with the cold metal buckles. As she struggled to feed the strap through the fastener, it slipped from her trembling fingers. The belt – heavy with steel – fell with a dull thud, dangerously close to her boot.

"Let me," Ombra murmured, leaning down to pick up the belt before Phaedra had barely acknowledged what happened. Her thin face was tight with suppressed worry as she drew close to Phaedra, embracing her hips with the belt and tugging the straps tight with sure fingers. Phaedra's face burned with her clumsiness, but she let her senses reach for her girlfriend's comforting presence, let herself inhale her soft, sugary scents of wildflowers and vanilla, and feel her touch brushing against her through the rough fabric of her uniform.

Without a word, Ombra reached for the other items on her bed, strapping on the gun holster, then filling her canteen and securing it in place along with the knives and pistol. Phaedra could only watch, moving her arms out of the way and breathing raggedly as she tried not to let her imagination wander to what was marching towards them.

When she was done, Ombra leaned up to her, cupping her face with both hands and pressing her forehead against Phaedra's, her skin warm. "Breathe with me," she whispered, her breath tickling her lips. Phaedra let her eyes close and clung to Ombra's shoulders, hanging on for dear life. Because Ombra was her life, had been her rock these past months, and a shelter against the raging storm of confusion, truths and lies that Caspar's reveal had left in its wake.

"You don't have to go out there," Ombra murmured after ten deep breaths.

"I'm going nowhere without you." She opened her eyes to find Ombra already gazing at her, her expression gentle. Ombra's light fingers brushed her cheek, and she leaned into her touch.

Ombra nodded, doubt flickering across her face. But instead of responding, she wrapped her arms around Phaedra's neck and pulled her into a deep kiss. Phaedra melted into her, lips parting, tears springing to her eyes. She did her best not to think that it could be a kiss goodbye.

"Stay close to me," Ombra whispered against her lips, kissing her again.

"Always," Phaedra whispered back, her fingers lingering on the tight braids Ombra had arranged around her head. She leaned back then, taking in her appearance: the way the sunlight slanting through the high windows brought out the gold in Ombra's hair, how a flush clouded around the freckles high on her cheekbones, and the way her eyes never left Phaedra's, the colour of a calm, sun-kissed sea. She imprinted her face in her memory. Just in case. "I love you."

Ombra's answering smile made her breath catch. "And I love you." She pressed one last kiss to her lips, smoothing her hair, her touch sending a shiver skipping down her spine. She then reached for her helmet, handing it to her. "Let's go."

Continuing her deep breaths, she dangled the helmet from its strap and followed her girlfriend out into the streaming sunlight, the barracks electric with anticipation. Fully armed soldiers were already piling into jeeps and vans to carry them to the battlefield, and Phaedra heard Officer Munro shouting orders before she could even see her, handing out machine guns to the cadets. But before she could approach her commander, she heard her name shouted behind her.

She turned to see Caspar striding towards her, formidable in his grey uniform. He had barely two hundred soldiers left to command, and yet he looked as confident as ever, refusing to let any fear show.

Phaedra froze as he approached her, and the cacophony around her dimmed beneath the blood rushing in her ears. This man was her father. She still hadn't come to terms with that fact, the truth hitting her in the gut each time she remembered, her mixed feelings bubbling to the surface: the stolen childhood, the web of lies, the resentment that he hadn't claimed her and saved her from eighteen years of fear and misery. But he was here now, and she was willing to face the challenge of accepting the past and rebuilding their ruined lives together.

"Phee," he said quietly, his gaze gentle as he looked her up and down, a small smile softening his severe expression. "I'm glad I caught you."

“It’s really happening?” she mumbled after a moment, as though the troops rallying around her didn’t give her the answer. “She’s coming again?”

He nodded, then stepped closer, cupping her head with one hand as she looked up at him. For a split second, fear flashed through his eyes, before settling into grim amusement. “I can’t convince you to sit this one out either, can I?”

She shook her head, and his fingers smoothed the hair at the nape of her neck. More conflicting emotions skimmed across his face. “Your mother said you were strong when you came into this world,” he murmured, lowering his voice so only Phaedra could hear him. “She was right. You’ve done us both proud.”

More tears sprang to her eyes, and she wrapped her arms around him. He returned her hug, holding her tightly and planting a kiss on the top of her head. “If anything happens to me today,” he said against her hair, his voice reverberating in his chest, “go with Ombra. I trust that she and the Medleys will take care of you.”

She nodded, tightening her grip around him, not wanting to let go. But when they finally drew apart, she schooled her face into a fierce expression. “Nothing is going to happen to you. You’re going to live forever and be my cool dad.”

He laughed, taking her helmet and fitting it carefully onto her head, securing the straps. More mixed emotions warmed his features – some combination of pride, delight, and nostalgia. “That sounds like a plan to me. Be careful, Phee.”

“General Ronan?”

Phaedra glanced around to see General Harlow waiting a few feet away, looking as menacing as Caspar had done a few moments ago. But when his gaze settled on Phaedra, he nodded to her, giving her a small smile. "May I have your support assessing the lay of the battlefield?"

Caspar nodded. "Of course." He glanccd down at Phaedra one last time and squeezed her shoulder. "Stay close to Ombra. And stay safe."

"You too," she said, a pitch higher than usual. She watched his retreating back as he and Harlow disappeared into the crowd, then turned to find Ombra talking to Sabine. She approached them, the sight of the Ignis fraying her nerves once again.

"We have an advantage over the Undead while the sun's out," Sabine was saying, sparing Phaedra a glance as she came to a stop at Ombra's side. "But I have a feeling the Nox will have Obscurae turning down the brightness. Reckon you could commandeer the shadows?"

"I can try," Ombra replied, head high and back straight in determination. Pride flowed through Phaedra at her girlfriend's fearless stance – and a little bit of envy that she couldn't act so bravely herself. "I can't take control of someone else's darkness, but I can probably… push it away." She shrugged.

Sabine gave a sharp nod. "That's something. Me and the other Ignis will get a good hot blaze going. It hasn't rained for days so we won't have the problems we had last time."

A trickling sense of foreboding crept down Phaedra's neck, something tugging for her attention. It didn't make sense that Alessia was choosing to attack now instead of waiting for nightfall. If her Undead were weak to heat and light, what tricks did she have hidden up her sleeve? But before she could find the words to voice her worries, Sabine turned to her.

"You, help Ombra push away the shadows."

"You're not her commander, Sabine," Ombra teased with a grin.

But Phaedra's shadows were rallying in response, tingling at her fingertips. "I'll do what I can." She wasn't quite sure how. Blast the shadows with her own? Create a wall of darkness against the attacking Obscurae? She didn't doubt Ombra had an idea. They would figure it out.

"Can you command Munro to let us have flamethrowers this time?" Ombra asked, a tad too excitedly.

"Well," Sabine growled, glancing at where Munro was inspecting the cadets' preparations. "I'm definitely not *her* commander, but I could suggest it."

Sabine glanced back at Phaedra then, her dark painted lips set in a furious line. "Don't die," she said firmly.

Phaedra shrank under her golden glare. "Uh, thanks?"

"If you die, Ombra will be insufferable."

"Oh…" She wasn't sure what she was supposed to say to that, but Sabine was already moving away, squaring her shoulders as she stomped over to Munro. Ombra snorted, and Phaedra let out a slow exhale as she met her eye once more.

"Ready?"

"Not really," Phaedra confessed, taking a shaky breath.

Ombra slipped an arm around her waist, her eyes lighting with mischief. "Let's kick your sister's arse."

Air whipped at her clothing and bit her face where her goggles left her exposed. Far below, war cries, smoke and explosions trailed into the air, tainting her euphoria as she flew through the skies. Despite the harness cutting into her and the deaths happening beneath her, exhilaration bubbled in Phaedra's belly as the Aeres she was strapped to swooped and dove, bringing her close enough to push away the enemy's veil of shadows with her own.

The Aeres who held her was called Daniel Ravelin, a soldier in Caplin's Aeres Army that now fought for the Lux. Off to her left, Ombra flew with Ikarus, her own stream of shadows catching Phaedra's eye every so often. As the sun beat down, Daniel weaved to avoid the occasional gunfire and offensive Talents that hurtled their way. While Daniel took care of keeping them safe, Phaedra concentrated all her efforts on remaining in control of her Talent, her darkness shuddering out of her in billowing clouds that only grew more aggressive with each near miss.

"Any sign of the Nox yet?" came Daniel's yell in her ear as Ikarus and Ombra swooped by, his powerful arms tight around Phaedra's abdomen.

"Not a peep. Sabine reckons she'll be a no-show again."

"With all these zombies piling in, she doesn't even have to fight," Ombra shouted over the rush of wind and creak of the Aeres' metallic wings.

But fear prickled down Phaedra's spine either way, the knowledge that Alessia could show up at any moment twisting her gut. Phaedra knew she would be an instant target, as would Caspar.

"Maybe we should—"

But whatever Daniel was about to suggest, his voice was drowned out by a deafening clang of rock on metal, and he swerved dangerously, his grip on Phaedra slipping. She yelped as they tilted sideways, shouts and gunfire muffled by the ringing in her ears. Daniel's left arm tightened around her while he freed the other, manipulating the air to keep them upright, but they were still tilting, the fight below suddenly looming closer.

Another rock whizzed past her ear, piercing her hearing as it struck. This time, Daniel let go completely. She screamed as she fell, then jerked to a halt, the harness straps attaching her to the Aeres stretched taut. She craned her neck, looking over her shoulder at Daniel's terrified face. Sunlight gleamed through gaps in his grey steel wings.

And then, just as she heard Ombra scream her name, something heavy and jagged thumped her in the stomach.

The straps of her harness snapped on impact as the rock that hit her dropped away. Fibres gave way and unravelled, slowly at first, then thrusting her into a freefall.

She didn't even have breath to scream, the threads of consciousness thinning as she hurtled to the ground.

She was standing amongst the battling bodies, chaos overwhelming her vision, but no one touched her. No one even noticed her as she stood blinking, her body numb, her heart still.

Movement in her arms made her jump, and she looked down to find she was cradling an armful of shadows, warm softness beneath her fingertips. The shadows vibrated, shifted, pointed ears materialising, pearlescent eyes looming from the darkness. Her chapped lips parted in pleasant surprise as a pure black cat stared up at her, its presence eerie in the midst of so much bloodshed.

"Hello?"

"Hello Shadow Warrior," purred the cat, and Phaedra frowned, her fingers slipping in velvety soft fur.

"Am I hallucinating?"

"You tell me." The cat turned its gaze away, and she followed it to see a body lying on the ground, arms and legs sprawled like a bird in flight. *Her* body.

Phaedra watched, dumbfounded, as a furious wave of darkness wrapped itself around her body, warding off hissing corpses. Ombra scrabbled with her harness buckles and leaped out of Ikarus's arms, rushing to Phaedra's side. Not Phaedra's side, but her body's. Ombra's face distorted in a terrified shout, but Phaedra couldn't hear the word, only recognised the shape of her name on her lips. Within seconds, Ombra had pressed a hand to her neck, to her face, lifted an eyelid, then began administering chest compressions, her darkness still swirling around them, shielding them from the fight.

"Am I… dead?" She felt oddly calm, despite Ombra's panicked attempts to resuscitate her happening before her eyes.

"Not quite," said the cat, its tail flicking against her sleeve. "The Aeres slowed your fall, but you took quite a hit from that Terra attack."

"Will I… be okay?" And in that numbed in-between, she found that she didn't feel strongly about either option, simply an acceptance. Perhaps it was the comforting weight in her arms, or the knowledge that whatever happened, there were people who loved her on both sides of the void that yawned between life and death.

"That depends on how willing you are to keep fighting when death keeps taking."

Phaedra stared down at the cat's iridescent eyes. What kind of riddle was this?

"Will you fight for us, Phaedra Ronan? Will you embrace the darkness inside yourself to find the light?"

"I'm trying," she mumbled, the shadows around the cat curling curiously.

"This is the end of your first life and the beginning of your next, Shadow Warrior. You will be plucked thrice from the snapping jaws of death, and you will learn to bend it to your will. Do not squander the gifts you are given."

The cat was thinning into more curls of darkness, growing lighter in Phaedra's arms. "Wait! What do I have to do?"

The cat purred, barely a silhouette. "Trust your power, Little Dragon. Trust yourself."

The creature faded into nothing, the glint of its eyes the last to disappear. At her feet, Ombra was kissing the lips of her lifeless body, and as she kissed, breath blew into Phaedra's mouth, tickling her throat, expanding her chest.

And then she opened her eyes.

Chapter Seventy-Six

SKYE BOLTON

Skye's sense of foreboding grew the further she walked down the corridor. She looked in dining rooms, a library, studies and countless bedrooms, all coated in dust and damp and filled with the broken skeletons of what had once been lavish furniture. What if this was all some elaborate trick, and there were no prisoners here at all? With her mind muffled by wards, she could hear no mental buzz, no indication that there were living people beyond any of the walls or doors.

She opened another door, jumping with fright at a startled flap of wings. As her heartbeat gradually slowed, she surveyed the bird muck-covered room, eyeing the nest in the corner. The woodpigeons cooed nervously, then she left them to it, closing the door firmly behind her. She moved to the next room.

As she stepped inside, a foul stench attacked her senses, and she pulled up the collar of her jacket, masking her nose and mouth. But her heart sped up again as her eyes adjusted to the gloom and she spotted a heap on the bed. The person was shrouded in blankets, and she stepped carefully closer, noting the matted hair masking their face. She approached the prone figure, pulse pounding rhythmically in her ears, but as she reached out, touching the bony shoulder, she recoiled, noticing the flies disturbed by the movement, the wasted skin, empty eye sockets staring blindly.

A body.

She gagged, wanting to bolt, but she made herself study the haggard face, searching for any signs that this corpse could be her father, or Amber. Relief mingled with her horror when she ensured it was neither, and she staggered back, bumping against the doorframe on her way out. Out in the corridor, she braced a hand against the wall, taking deep, dusty breaths to settle her churning stomach and clear the stench of rot from her nostrils. She lingered just long enough, before her frantic fear pushed her on.

There was a body in the next room too, and she repeated the process, forcing herself to look for identifying features. The Tracers had said there would be dead, but she hadn't expected Camilla to just leave them here to rot. Perhaps it was just for Skye's benefit, to make her fear the worst each time she opened the door to a corpse.

She was nearly at the end of the corridor, and there were only three doors left. The smell as she opened the next door was also terrible, but different. She wrinkled her nose as an aroma of blood and vomit engulfed her, but as her eyes swept across the room, she gasped at the sight of a dirty blonde girl sitting against a wall, arms tucked around her knees and staring into space. Alive. Skye's heart leaped, and she stepped inside, glancing around to make sure no one else was in the room. She flicked on the light switch to her right, and the girl shut her eyes against the glare. But not before Skye recognised her.

"Summers," she said, stepping further into the room. She breathed through her mouth as she studied Amber, a confusion of emotions flooding her – nerves, shame, and concern. It had been a few years since she had last seen her, and Skye remembered her as a shy, skinny, baby-faced thing, not unlike Cameron. But the girl that sat before her was a bag of bones, her full cheeks replaced with skull-like features, her eyes sunken and circled with shadows. Her blonde bob was tangled with what was unmistakably blood, and she wore a dress that had once been black velvet, but was now matted with dirt and Skye didn't want to know what else.

"Summers," she tried again, stopping in front of her. The girl didn't move. "Summers…? Amber?" Her eyes snapped open and she finally looked up at Skye, her pupils dilating in recognition. Skye took a deep breath to calm the nervous static at her fingertips, then regretted it as she inhaled the foul smell of the room. Gingerly, she squatted before her, knowing full well that she was probably the last person Amber wanted to see.

"Your mother is here." She tried to sound gentle, but all she could manage was an urgent murmur. "She's waiting outside."

Amber blinked, but said nothing as she continued to stare vacantly at Skye. With a haunting sense of déjà vu, Skye realised Amber's eyes matched Cameron's. And Oliver's. She swallowed, lingering grief joining her mess of emotions.

Amber's wide blue eyes dropped to her hands, and Skye noticed she was holding a wrinkled piece of yellow paper. Skye studied the folds, recognising a bent wing, a wonky beak… an origami bird.

Skye looked back up at Amber's impassive face. "Can you walk?"

There was another pause, but Amber said nothing. Then finally, slowly, she got to her bare feet, the torn and dirty dress falling to her knees, and carefully placed the paper bird in her pocket.

"Good." Skye stood, casting another doubtful look over her. She could see no injuries, and despite a slight sway, she seemed unharmed. But the dried blood stuck to her had to have come from somewhere. When she was sure Amber wasn't about to keel over, she turned to leave. "Let's go. We don't have much time." She didn't know if that was true, but the longer she spent in that building, the more her dread increased, and the state of Amber and the room did little to reassure her. She opened the next door, the stink of rot overpowering, and the light switch wouldn't work. Skye summoned a handful of crackling electricity in her palm, filling the room with flickering white light. There was someone in here too, but Skye didn't need to approach to know that the body on the floor was long dead. She forced herself to look for any sign it was her father, then shut the door quickly.

Skye was relieved that the next room was the last one in the corridor. She glanced at Amber, who stood silently outside her room, staring into space. Shrugging off her weird behaviour, Skye opened the final door. One of the boards across the window was hanging off, filling the room with a ray of sunlight. And sprawled across the bed was Nanette Ferries, her silver-streaked dark hair half-obscuring her face, her green silk skirt suit stained with yet more blood. Skye crossed the room and checked for a pulse, which she found, but couldn't wake her.

"Summers!" she shouted, her voice eerie in the still building. After a few moments longer than Skye would have liked, Amber appeared in the doorway, head bowed to the floor. "Help me," she said, fighting off a pang of frustration. What the hell had Camilla done to her? "Help me carry her," she said when Amber didn't move, but finally she shuffled into the room as Skye heaved Nanette off the bed, staggering a little as she pulled Nanette's arm around her shoulders.

"Okay?" she asked as Amber slung Nanette's other arm around her. Skye took most of Nanette's weight and wondered if it would be easier to just carry her alone. But

Amber didn't answer, only stepped forward when Skye did, silently helping her drag Nanette out of the room.

Her heart sped up when she heard noises at the other end of the corridor, and her pace quickened too. As they burst into the entrance hall she saw other prisoners in varying states, some of them holding up unconscious bodies the same as Skye and Amber. Someone in a Resistance uniform rushed forward when she recognised Nanette, but when Skye's gaze locked with Dean's and she saw he was carrying a ragged prisoner, she handed Nanette over to the stranger without a word. Hope rose within her as she rushed over, hope that the man Dean carried was her father, that he was alive, that he was safe.

"Is it him?" Her voice was strangled, tears springing to her eyes as she approached. She peered down at the damaged face, barely recognising him covered in blood and bruises and tangled beard. But it was him, her father, and he was alive. She cupped his face in her hands, tears slipping down her cheeks. "Is he alright?"

"I don't know," Dean admitted, his voice thick with concern. Victor's good eye opened, and his breath was a wheeze as he focused on Skye, his hand reaching for her feebly. She took hold of it, his fingers thin and cold. To her surprise, he still wore his wedding ring, the band loose beneath a knobbly knuckle.

Her throat closed as she held his gaze, relief and love pooling in her chest. But as she tore her eyes away and examined the rest of him, noticing the festered wounds on his body and his legs twisted at odd angles, a deadly rage settled over her. She looked up at her brother, meeting his terrified gaze with a fierce glare.

"Get him out of here," she said, and Dean's eyes widened at the look on her face. "I have a bone to pick with Camilla."

"Skye," he warned, but she shook her head, pressing a kiss to her father's feverish brow, then glanced around.

"Is this everyone?"

"There are two dead. Five alive."

She nodded. "Three dead my side. Two alive. That's all of them then." She squeezed her father's hand one last time and met his eye. "You're safe now, and we'll have you healed very soon." He only breathed raggedly as she kissed his cold knuckles, then she stepped away, hating to let him out of her sight, but she couldn't let Camilla get away with this. "Let's go."

Skye swept past the other prisoners, heading to the front doors which, to her relief, remained open. The rage was building deep in her chest, the same rage that had exploded from her after Cameron's violent death. She would *kill* Camilla. She would break her scrawny neck.

But as she burst through the doors, she saw that what she had planned for Camilla would have to wait. Because in front of her, across the overgrown lawn that spread before the manor, a cluster of people waited for her. At the front were two figures clad in rippling black clothing, and behind them, Skye counted twenty-one Undead corpses, standing deathly still, waiting for commands. Her rage gave way to a fear that gripped her heart like an iron fist.

She barely registered Roxanne rushing past her. The world faded around her as she started at Alessia and Vala across the lawn. Camilla and her butler were gone, and Lorcan stood between them, glancing back and forth, fearful thoughts slipping through his mental shield. So it had been a trap, but not the kind she had been expecting.

Taking a deep breath, Skye walked with forced calm down the steps. *Get everyone out*, she ordered Lorcan as she passed. She glanced to where the portal was, relieved to see Seth still guarding it. At least they could still get her father and the others to safety.

The Nox and the Seer didn't move as she set off across the lawn. The fist around her heart tightened even further, but she closed her mind, blocking out Dean's panicked thoughts before they could bleed into hers. If Alessia was here for a fight, she needed all her concentration.

"Hello, Skye," said Vala in her honeyed voice once Skye was close enough. The Seer stood tall at Alessia's side, her tattered shawls swapped for an imposing cloak that was black as midnight, encrusted with crystal constellations that glittered in the sunlight. Her bony fist was wrapped around a gnarled, polished root that was almost as tall as she was, the twisted end encasing clouded quartz and shards of obsidian that drank in the light. Runes were carved into the shaft of the staff, weaving a story of life and death, light and darkness. Skye's lightning crackled beneath her skin as she took in the sight of it, then met Vala's fathomless gaze. She suppressed a shudder, curling her hands into fists.

She was greeted by the Nox's icy glare next. Alessia eyed her with cold defiance, clad in a black coat adorned with intricate swirls of embroidery and studded with shiny black buttons that were unmistakably obsidian, her mind well and truly obscured.

"Where's your army?" Skye asked, trying to keep her voice light and casual. She did her best not to look at the corpses arranged in a regimented row behind the two women.

"About to wipe yours off the face of the earth," Alessia promised, her tone severe.

She was probably right. And judging by the sight before her, her own battle would look very different. "You've been busy then. Maybe you should have been saving your strength to face me."

A muscle flickered in Alessia's tense jaw. Beside her, Vala's smile only grew. "We are sorry for springing this on you, Skye, but with the country so weak and divided, we felt it was time to end this quickly. Perhaps there will be no need for further bloodshed after this final battle."

Skye studied Vala, her sickly smile and ocean eyes betraying none of her intentions. She thought back to the memories she had seen in Caplin's mind, how Vala had sat at Alessia's side, leaving Skye with no doubt where the Seer's loyalties truly lay.

"So, is this a fight to the death?" Skye demanded, all too aware of the corpses looming behind her.

"I certainly won't spare you, Bolton," said Alessia in a dangerously quiet voice, her eyes narrowed in a cold promise.

Before Skye could utter another word, Alessia's shadows shot out in tendrils, weaving into a dark canopy overhead, blocking out the sun. Skye blinked in the sudden lack of light, glancing around in time to see the corpses lurching towards her.

Chapter Seventy-Seven

ALESSIA RONAN

Ice coursed through Alessia's veins as she watched her Undead servants advance on Bolton. Frost crackled on her lips and fingertips as she sent them at her in groups of three and four. Around and above the Lux, Alessia's veil of darkness kept the sunlight at bay, preventing its blinding rays from weakening her corpse soldiers.

Bolton's lightning crackled and hummed as she punched hearts and faces, the Undead screeching as they dropped back to their deaths. And when the corpses attacked, she threw up her hands, strands of lightning stretched into a shield between them.

Alessia gritted her teeth in concentration, willing an Undead Ignis to throw fireballs. Bolton's eyes widened in shock as flames slipped past her shield and licked at her sleeves. The Ignis seized the opportunity and tackled the Lux to the ground. But by the time Bolton thrust a fist into the corpse's mouth, knocking out teeth as its skull lit up from within, the flames on her clothes had already petered out, smothered by the flame-retardant sigils woven into her uniform. She struggled back to her feet before a pair of Obscurae drew closer, shadows tearing at her hair in an attempt to cleave the skin from her bones.

Beyond the fight, Bolton's allies gathered on the porch and front steps of the crumbling manor house, transfixed by what was happening. Alessia spotted a dark-haired young man handing the former prisoner he had been carrying over to another soldier, who headed towards the portal. As more corpses closed in around Bolton, the man sprang forwards in a run, fear evident on his face.

"Ah, ah," said Vala, and with a wave of her hand, a shimmer of semi-transparent purple flame flared between Bolton and the man, who stopped short, panting. "The Lux must fight alone."

"Dean, go!" Bolton shouted, and the distraction cost her. Alessia compelled her puppet to send a whip of darkness lashing across her face. She raised her arm just in time, but the gasp of pain as the darkness cut through her sleeve made Alessia's lips curl in satisfaction.

The foolish man did not go, and instead watched through the flickering flames in a horrified daze, flinching each time Bolton snarled and staggered. Alessia felt the echoes of every punch, kick, and vibration of the Lux's Talent, her heart stuttering each time one of her Undead was sent back to the grave. She had cut down six already, and showed no signs of tiring. Yet.

"Is this your tactic?" Bolton taunted, panting heavily in the seconds between opponents. "Get your puppets to do the hard work for you before you have to fight me yourself?"

Alessia said nothing, willing another pair to join the two attackers already engaging Bolton, ordering their next hits to be especially brutal. A yelp of pain escaped the knot of Undead around her, spots of blood tainting the overgrown grass, to be trampled on by five pairs of feet. Alessia tugged her gaze away from the sight of the blood and took a deep breath of the warm summer air. Another cry rent through the tangle of bodies, and then a flash blinded her for a split second, followed by a rumble of thunder as the earth shook beneath her feet.

The four corpses dropped to the floor, jerking in their death throes.

"Fight me," Bolton snarled, taking a handful of steps towards Alessia, runnels of blood stark between her white knuckles. Alessia held her glare, determined to stand defiant when her instincts screamed at her to run the other way.

The silent corpse creeping up on Bolton sent a pebble skittering in the dirt, and the Lux whirled, falling into the fight once again. Alessia watched her enemy side-step and circle, doing her best to keep the Undead before her, within her line of sight. Alessia sent two more to sneak up on her while the ones in front kept her distracted. The corpses responded to her silent pull on their tethers.

"Skye, watch out!" Dean warned beyond the flaming barrier. But before Bolton could react, two of the corpses at her back snaked their arms beneath hers, closing them around her chest like vices, fingers wrapping around her throat in a crude embrace. She screamed as they dragged her down to her knees, the sound making the ice and shadow in Alessia's veins quiver with pleasure.

Alessia stepped forward as the remaining Undead advanced, curling their fingers around the Lux's limbs and tangling in her hair, undeterred by her kicking and screaming as they pinned her to the ground. Beyond the purple flames, Dean was yelling her name as he struggled to keep her in his sight.

This was it. This was her chance.

She drew closer, close enough to see the fear flashing in Bolton's eyes as they locked on hers. That fear drew the darkness to her fingertips, shadows forming in her palms, growing into a lethal blow. Alessia raised her hands, aiming for those terrified eyes, for the teeth bared, breath hissing out of her.

As Alessia released the shadows, Bolton lurched against the arms that pinned her, jerking her wrist free.

Thunder cracked as lightning collided with the shadows between them, the Talents merging like a midnight storm. Bolton's screams of fear were replaced with a yell of defiance, and she threw another stream of lightning at Alessia before she could react, before she could even blink. She stumbled back a step as the current hit her left palm and coursed through her to the ground, every inch of her skin growing hot, a scent of burning invading her nostrils.

Alessia panted, the aftershocks thrumming through her limbs, her own Talents riling up to quash the invasion. Her clothing might have been woven with sigils to protect her from electrical attacks, but she had no armour on her exposed skin, and a red welt was rising on her hand where the lightning had connected with her.

The dark canopy above their heads dissipated into curls of shadow, and the Undead groaned as the sunlight half blinded them and seared their skin. Bolton roared beneath them, and another rumble of thunder shuddered through the ground. Her body lit up with lightning, sending the corpses staggering back with gasps and hisses, their pain Alessia's as she fought to regain her composure.

Bolton rose to a knee within seconds, strands of electricity still crackling over her body, vengeance blazing in her eyes. That look forced Alessia to take another step back as the Lux straightened to her full height.

The only two corpses that remained Undead ran at Bolton, but to Alessia's shock and horror, she made quick work of them with a pair of well-placed blows. And then she turned to Alessia and raised her hands, settling into a deadly calm as she returned to a fighting stance.

Alessia raised her own hands, drawing her shadows into a billowing shield of darkness as she assessed her chances. She could raise the dead again, but the scent of burnt hair and sizzled flesh filled the air, the condition of the corpses reduced dramatically. And she was all too aware of the ache that lingered in her chest, the tickle at the back of her throat that would no doubt worsen if she used too much of her power. Despite the onslaught of Undead, Bolton did not appear weakened, apparently unphased by the bleeding wounds obscured by her black combat uniform, a split lip only enhancing her vicious appearance.

Bolton gave her no chance to contemplate further as she launched into a fight, stepping to Alessia's left and then springing back to the right, lightning glancing off her shield. She stepped right again, then again, footfalls careful, eyes never leaving Alessia's. Alessia kept her in her sight as she circled her, and too late she realised the sun was streaming in her eyes. Bolton's shadowy figure lunged, dodging out of the way of Alessia's darkness, aiming at her head. But Alessia got her shield higher at the last second, causing Bolton to pull up short, then step back to put space between them once more.

They circled again, Alessia veering around to avoid the harsh light in her eyes. But a series of attacks came in again, this time absorbed by the shield and humming through it. Before Bolton could summon further power, Alessia thrust her arms downward, a snarl of frustration escaping her as her shield split into two attacks that she sent hurtling at her opponent. Bolton evaded one, but she caught the other in a net of lightning between her hands, working it into a thrumming ball that she threw back at Alessia. Alessia jerked out of the way, the combined powers scorching the ground where it crashed.

"Neat trick," she ground out, her lip curling in distaste.

"Thanks, your uncle showed it to me." Bolton flicked her tattered ponytail off her shoulder with a cocky jerk of her head.

Alessia sneered. She didn't need the reminder.

"He asked me not to kill you, you know," she teased, circling again, no doubt working to herd Alessia into an unfavourable position. "He still cares, after everything you did to him."

"Then he's a fool. He should save his worries for my traitor sister."

Bolton's gaze flickered over Alessia's shoulder towards their small audience, and Alessia took advantage of the break in her concentration. Her shadows snaked out, and Bolton stepped back, but the darkness caught her, skimming along the right side of her abdomen. Her counterattack followed soon after, a bolt of lightning that crackled harmlessly against Alessia's warded coat.

With her confidence boosted by the successful hit, Alessia lurched forward, throwing two more attacks at the Lux, her shadows humming through the air. Bolton braced herself for the attack, throwing up a lightning shield again, capturing the darkness, then throwing it back at Alessia. This time, with the smaller space between them, Alessia had no choice but to catch it with her shield. Vibrations ran through her hand as the shield grew heavy with combined power.

Before she knew what was happening, Bolton tackled her, lightning flashing before her eyes as a boot swiped at the back of her legs. Her knees folded, and her stomach rose to her mouth as she fell, the impact lancing through her lower back. The electricity veining through the ball of shadow in her hands burned painfully at her fingers, but as Bolton's shadow loomed above her, Alessia let out a yell. She reached inward for her power, then let the darkness explode out of her, throwing her opponent back and enveloping Alessia like a dome.

Somewhere to her left, she heard a thud and a grunt, but she was too occupied with her own searing breath, the rawness of her throat, and the tightness of her lungs. She had used more power than she had meant to in her panic, and the damage was already taking hold.

She couldn't afford to engage Bolton in hand-to-hand combat. Lucien had given her some training if it should come to that, but he had assured her she would lose. She didn't have the experience and physical strength that Bolton had gained through years of athletic and military training. And as Alessia slowly rose to her knees, struggling to keep her shield in place, Bolton was already standing, ready to resume the fight.

To Alessia's surprise, Bolton didn't smirk or taunt her as she rose unsteadily to her feet. Her expression was pure predator, face rigid, body tense, eyes assessing. Darkness stained the backs of her hands and the edge of her jaw, and no doubt there was damage to her body too, judging by the flicker of pain across her face as she stepped forward.

Alessia attacked again, the shadows bridging between them. With sure steps, Bolton dodged one, deflected another with a fist full of lightning, then dropped to one knee for a third, a glittering black ribbon streaming harmlessly over her head. Bolton took her eyes off Alessia for a second, head bowed, an arm crossing her abdomen.

A slice of silver shot towards her, and Alessia struggled to recognise the unknown power hurtling from the Lux's outstretched hand. She only registered it was a knife when it lodged in her right arm a split second later. A strangled yelp escaped her as the cold sharpness stabbed through flesh and tendon, but worse than the pain was the warmth of blood that seeped down her arm, the red that coated her left hand as she wrapped her shaking fingers around the hilt of the knife.

Bolton didn't wait. As soon as she saw that her weapon had met its mark, blinding strands of light exploded from her fingertips, connecting with the knife hilt and sending Alessia flying backwards with a bang.

Her body spasmed, her skin burning as she lay rigid in the grass, staring up at the cloudless blue sky.

Get up, came a cruel, ancient voice through her mind. Alessia wanted to obey, for her own sake much more than the Seer's, but the current still coursed through her, her feet still jerking in her boots. She was vaguely aware of Bolton advancing from her periphery. She seemed far – perhaps Alessia had been thrown further away than she realised.

Get up! the cold voice in her head repeated, and her Talents slithered through her veins, forcing the electric invasion out of the deeper parts of her body, swarming around her heart. She took a breath that sliced through her tight lungs, letting out a strangled gasp.

Before she could even think about getting up, lightning crashed into her again – crashed *through* her. She screamed. Her body was on *fire*, the lightning blistering across her skin, smoke rising from her body. As the current dropped, she reached for her darkness again, willing it to push the aftershocks from her body. Blood pooled at the back of her throat, and she choked. She pushed herself onto her front to cough it up, throwing another shield around herself as she did so.

Bolton stopped some feet away. Only her boots were visible as Alessia vomited blood into the grass.

Get. Up! Vala's furious voice entered her head yet again, at odds with the milk and honey with which she usually spoke. With a whimper, Alessia got a shaking hand beneath her and choked on the pain that lanced through her right arm, the same arm that struggled to keep up the shield.

Sitting up, she looked down at the knife still sticking out of her, the blade slick with blood. *Her* blood. Memories flashed unbidden through her mind, blood slick on another blade, scarlet on pale hands and white tiles. She let out another strangled whimper as she raised her trembling left hand, wrapping her fingers gingerly around the hilt.

It is just a little blood. Pull yourself together, Alessia.

She hissed in defiance at the Seer's chiding, pain wracking through her abdomen as she coughed. Bracing herself, she tore the knife from her arm, letting out another yelp. Blood splattered down her sleeve and dripped from the blade, and the tears that sprang to her eyes and the desperate sounds escaping her lips were not how she imagined this ending. The knife fell from her numb fingers, and a second later, her shield dropped, the pain obliterating her focus.

She coughed blood into an already bloody hand, then raised her eyes to the Lux. To her surprise, Bolton only looked down at her, the predatory intent gone, her eyes wide. There was only… only surprise and pity on her face.

And then a determined expression settled like a mask over Bolton, and she stepped forward. Alessia's shadows riled up, curling unbidden from her fingertips. But to her shock, the hand that Bolton held out was open, nails chipped, fingers stained with blood and dirt and darkness.

"Fight me," said the Lux.

Chapter Seventy-Eight

SKYE BOLTON

Skye knew she should just kill her. Knew she could end it now in one fell swoop. But when she saw the fear in her eyes and the blood spewing from her lips, she couldn't bring herself to finish her when she was down.

Alessia stared up at her in disbelief, and then her eyes narrowed, her voice coming out in a hoarse gasp. "Why?"

Skye shrugged, the movement tugging on the cuts and bruises Alessia and her corpse soldiers had inflicted. "You asked for this fate no more than I did."

They stared at one another a moment longer. Alessia still trembled from shock and injuries. Now would be a good time to strip her powers, if Skye had any idea how to do it. Instead, she took a deep breath, doing her best to bury the guilt and memory of Caspar's plea to spare his niece.

The Nox didn't take her hand, perhaps suspecting a trap, but Skye stepped back as she watched her struggle to her feet. The smell of burnt hair and fabric emanating from her was familiar to Skye, and lightning damage branched across her neck and the side of her face, her ear bloody, dark hair crackling with static. But to her credit, Alessia settled back into a fighting stance, raising her bloody hands, breath wheezing out of her. Despite her weakened state, she sprang back into action with surprising swiftness.

Lightning came almost unbidden to Skye's fingertips, crashing into the darkness and throwing it off course with a hiss. Alessia was quick with her second attack, but Skye was ready, flashing light and glittering darkness colliding between them. They fell into a dance, the Nox fighting with renewed vigour, determined not to waste this second chance Skye had granted her. She lunged forward with another attack, and then another, shadows unfurling around her with breakneck speed. Skye side-stepped and back-stepped and circled, studying her enemy's stance, her moves, her tactics. Someone had trained her well – not just Caspar – but Skye recognised that she lacked experience. Perhaps this was even Alessia's first real fight.

Darkness jabbed at Skye's side – a low blow above her hip that she barely saw coming. She hissed at the sting, pivoting to protect the injury from a second blow, and countered with another hit, this time catching exposed skin through a rip in Alessia's leggings. The Nox stumbled again, taking her next few steps with a limp.

Alessia closed the gap between them with bared teeth and snapping shadows. Before Skye could react, Alessia grabbed her arm, pulling it aside and then jabbing forward with her other hand. A fist full of darkness hit her in the chest, banging against her collarbone with a force that sent her crashing to the grass. Skye lay there winded. The shadows had cut through the protective layers of her uniform, and when she touched her torn skin, her fingers came away coated in blood and sooty darkness. She gasped for breath and that hurt too, but she hadn't heard anything crack. Filled with a glimmer of hope at that realisation, she halted Alessia's approach with another bolt of electricity, buying herself enough time to scramble to her feet. But the injury had her stooping, veering to her left, and it was only a matter of time before Alessia got in another hit, more shadows cutting through fabric and flesh above her right knee.

They continued to fight. Skye regained some strength as her breathing gradually eased. She regained ground as well, forcing Alessia away from the lawn. Thorns and twigs caught on her long coat as Skye herded her into the undergrowth. Considering the Nox had been aware she was heading for a fight to the death with a soldier, her clothing wasn't the most practical for the surroundings, and Skye did her best to use that to her advantage, treading through the undergrowth easily in her combat boots. Alessia tried to circle, but this time Skye stepped in her way and kept up her attacks, seeing the frustration grow in her narrowed eyes. As Skye sent another blow careening towards the Nox's face, Alessia fell back in the brambles to avoid it. She advanced quickly as Alessia fought to escape from a tangle of twigs and leaves that scratched at her sleeves and tugged at her clothes.

Alessia raised her arms to defend herself, but not before Skye's lightning enveloped her, lighting her up like an electric storm. But somehow, impossibly, Alessia sent her own power hurtling towards Skye. She was thrown back, caught out by her surprise that the Nox had been able to summon her Talent despite the agony she had surely been under. Perhaps she realised she wouldn't get a third chance.

Skye's moment on the ground gave Alessia enough time to disentangle herself and get back to her feet, coughing as she rushed through the undergrowth and back towards the lawn. Skye let her go, the Nox too far out of reach for Skye to land a decent blow, so she saved her strength as she followed, the electricity growing in each hand, ready to strike. She needed to finish this, and soon. She had expended too much concentrated energy fighting the Undead, her electricity reserves already running low.

Somehow, fighting Alessia's darkness with knives and fists didn't feel like a recipe for success.

She caught up to the Nox and lurched into a barrage of attacks. Alessia was also lagging, more defensive than offensive now, her reflexes slower, her stabbed arm bothering her. Skye began to hope, getting in more hits than she received, forcing Alessia back towards the undergrowth and circling around so the sun was in her eyes. The Nox yelped as another electric shock coursed through her damaged shoulder, her shield faltering again.

She batted off Alessia's frantic, desperate hits with much more ease now. They circled again, the sun slanting in at the edge of her vision as she did her best to keep Alessia in her sight. But just as she forced Alessia back around and blinked sunspots out of her eyes, another figure appeared just within her line of sight – a figure standing silently beneath the sunrays, a pale shadow wreathed in golden light.

"No," she gasped as she recognised the silhouette, her lightning flickering between her hands as she backed away.

Alessia only watched with icy, dead eyes as Skye stared from her to the figure half obscured by the blinding sunlight. But she knew that outline too well, knew the nervous shift from foot to foot, the gleaming blond hair, the white Healer's uniform – a nightmare becoming reality.

She stepped further back, shaking her head, fear and grief tightening her chest. The silent figure turned with her as she put the sun at her back once more, and tears slipped down her cheeks as his face came fully into sight.

And then Cameron stepped towards her.

"Please!" she cried, but Alessia's face was a cold mask, showing no emotion as she watched Skye fall apart. "Don't make me do this."

Cameron took another step towards her, his face gleaming like translucent marble in the sunlight – too pale, too perfect. His blue eyes held the same glassy sheen as the Undead that had pinned her down just minutes before, and on the right side of his neck, an inch below his jaw line, were neat stitches where the fatal gash that had taken his life had been. Skye was still walking backwards as his face crumpled with fear, his words echoing a dream. "Help me, Skye!"

"You're not real," she denied, aggressively shaking her head as the lightning between her hands sputtered. "This can't be real."

Her eyes found Vala then, a horrible truth slotting into place: a dream delivered, a twisted prophecy, a cruel warning. Vala's face was faint with the distance between them, but the pleasure in her expression was only too visible.

"They're going to make me fight you, Skye!" His voice was distorted with terror, and he lurched towards her, hands outstretched. Skye staggered back, lightning sparking between her hands, a half-hearted shield against the cruellest torture the wicked Seer and the Nox could dream up.

"I'm sorry, Cameron," she choked out, her tears falling in earnest now. "I should have stopped you. I shouldn't have let you join the fight."

Somewhere, beyond the rushing in her ears, her brother was screaming her name. But Skye could barely hear him. All her senses zeroed in on the impossible vision advancing on her, the anguish on Cameron's face so at odds with the predatory way in which he prowled towards her.

"Kill her," came Alessia's command, her voice as harsh as cracking ice.

"Help me, Skye," he whispered, his wide blue eyes locking her in place, pleading as his hands lifted towards her – hands that had once healed her, now reaching for her throat.

“You can’t be real,” Skye sobbed, stumbling backwards, willing herself to land a blow, to fight him, to defend herself. *It’s not Cameron*, she reminded herself. But her eyes and ears said otherwise, and as fear and indecision gripped her, the lightning in her hands buzzed and died out.

As she took another step away from him, a whip of darkness behind Cameron sliced through the air.

Cameron fractured, the darkness cleaving him into a thousand bright white butterflies that promptly dissipated into wisps of smoke. But before Skye could register that Cameron had been nothing more than a glamour, that same whip of darkness smashed into her left side, shattering the ribs that had so recently been healed.

Her knees and right hand stung as she hit the ground, but it was nothing compared to the agony in her side, nothing compared to her fear as she tasted blood. Where the vision of Cameron had been, the Nox now bore down on her, and a billow of shadows hit her in the chest with even more force than before. Skye collapsed, all too aware of the blood dribbling from her mouth, her breath becoming short, sharp gasps. But somehow, her heart was still beating, the sound of her pulse thundering in her ears. Out of the corner of her eye, she saw another figure approach behind Alessia, another figure in a rippling dark cloak.

“I’ll make a puppet out of your body, Bolton,” Alessia promised as she stood high above her, shadows spinning around her, gathering for the killing blow.

Chapter Seventy-Nine

AMBER SUMMERS

Amber was numb, standing at her mother's side as she watched the showdown between the Lux and the Nox, unable to feel anything, not fear, or hope, or despair. She hadn't even felt anything when her sobbing mother pulled her into a tight embrace, then desperately checked her over for the scars and injuries she wouldn't find. She wouldn't find them because they were no longer on her body. They only remained inside her head.

She was numb, but she watched closely, resisting when Roxanne tried to pull her towards the portal. She had to see this. She had to watch. Her Trace told her to, and so watch she did.

She watched as the two women fought, watched as they circled and side-stepped, dodged and landed blows. She watched as one of them went down, and then the other, and then the other. And she watched as the Lux went to pieces, staring wildly at an apparition invisible to the rest of them, then crumpled beneath the Nox's final attacks. But now her Trace told her to watch out for something else, and her eyes locked on the Seer, fear and hatred rising from deep within her numbed heart. And then she was running.

She didn't hear her mother shout and chase after her, didn't hear the outbursts of the others either, the stepbrother and the soldiers and the few prisoners that had hung back. She ran, weeds and nettles and burrs cutting into her bare feet, but it didn't matter. She was numb, and the skin would be healed in no time.

The Seer was advancing, and so was the Nox, both of them raising their arms, looming over the fallen Lux. Shadows unfurled above the Nox's hands, but instead of shooting towards the Lux, they were caught by invisible hands that dragged them towards the Seer, towards the staff in her pale grip. The Nox hadn't noticed, wasn't aware that she was the one who was the Seer's puppet, her shadows the strings. At her feet, the Lux lay sprawled and bleeding in the grass, strands of her bright white light crackling up and down her body.

The distance between them narrowed, and Amber leaped through the shimmering purple flames of the barrier between them, felt them burn, but adrenaline and her Trace spurred her on, her injuries healing over swiftly. She put on a final spurt as the Lux's lightning was also caught in the thrall of the staff, twining with the darkness. Amber drew on strength she didn't know she possessed as the glittering and flashing Talents were dragged towards the Seer's staff. The Nox had noticed now, was staring wide-eyed at the staff and the Seer, tugging her arms back, desperately trying to pull the darkness back to herself.

Amber shoved into the Seer, tackling her to the ground and grabbing for the staff. The darkness and light were still unravelling, thrumming through her arms as she tugged the staff from the Seer's shocked fingers, then smashed the twisted end against the ground. The Talents refracted, and a blinding light engulfed the four of them.

Amber heard cries of agony as an unknown force threw her flat on her back. It burst through her chest, slammed into her heart, then spread through her body, reaching the top of her head and the tips of her fingers and toes. She barely registered that one of the cries was her own, and all she could do was lie pinned to the ground, feeling the force sweep through her like a tidal wave. It surged against the limitations of her body, threatening to burst her like a bubble, before ebbing back into her heart. As she gasped air into lungs that struggled under the force of the unknown power, a vision swept Amber's consciousness away on the frantic fluttering of the wings of a small bird.

She flew high above a battlefield, her tiny heart beating wildly in a feathered chest. Smoke rose in a smog from raging fires, choking her lungs, veiling the sight of soldiers fighting and dying far below.

She swooped lower, spying a wounded golden dragon sprawled amongst the bodies, its chest barely rising and falling, embraced by shadows.

She flew on, her tiny wings beating away smoke, bringing her closer to the clash of alive and Undead, their shouts and screams deafening. Faces both familiar and strange sailed past, wielding fire and ice and wind and rocks. And amongst the fighters, a grey tabby streaked through the bloodshed, leading her on her frantic search.

She didn't know who she was looking for until she saw them: her new family, the father and sister she never knew she had. They fought back-to-back, brandishing flamethrowers, their fire barely keeping the press of burning corpses at bay. Ash and blood darkened their golden hair, soot smeared their skin, and terror twisted their faces.

She circled above their heads, fluttering helplessly as she witnessed their fight – a losing battle. Their enemy's numbers were too great, their bodies too tired, their fuel levels too low. Her sister's eyes lifted to her, just for a heartbeat, meeting her gaze. She then turned her weapon on the incoming corpses, pulling the trigger. The flamethrower gave a sputter and died.

Her sister let out a strangled yell as she backed into their father, a trio of cadavers hurtling towards her, eyes wild, mouths screeching, hands outstretched. And then, like a wave sweeping across the battlefield, the Undead dropped, silent and still, back to their deaths.

Amber's eyes were closed when she came back to herself, screams and running feet just about audible over the rush of unknown power in her ears. Grass tickled her twitching fingers, the cool hard ground seeping through her dirty dress. But it was what was inside that held her focus, like she had something in her chest that shouldn't be there, like her body was too small to contain the strange and invisible force. But the pulsating power gradually calmed, and after a moment, she sat up.

Alessia Ronan lay prone, glassy eyes staring at the sky, but Amber's Trace told her that the Nox was not yet dead. Bolton was thrashing, writhing in the grass and clawing at her own chest. Amber blinked, not quite understanding what she was seeing as the veins on Skye's neck, face and arms stood out dark, almost black, against her skin. Her eyes, too, were black as they bulged with terror, witnessing horrors invisible for the rest of them. As for the Seer, she lay in a heap of cloak and skirts, barely stirring, the stench of death emanating from her in waves.

And then there was Amber, whose mind was suddenly full of voices that were not her own.

Chapter Eighty

ROXANNE SUMMERS

Roxanne didn't know what she had seen, couldn't understand it. All she knew was that Amber had been caught up in whatever it was, and she rushed to her, the wall of purple flames disappearing with a whoosh once the Seer was down. She searched her daughter for any sign of harm, and then cupped her face. She flinched as she received a static shock from her, and then touched her again, more carefully, turning Amber's face towards her. But her eyes were glassy, and she was staring at the woman who had held the staff that now lay shattered in the grass.

"We have to leave," said Amber, uttering her first words. Roxanne shrank back, her daughter's voice strange to her, full of fear and foreboding. But then Amber was getting to her feet, taking Roxanne's hand. Another static shock jolted up her arm, but Amber held tight, pulling her towards the portal.

That was when Roxanne's gaze fell on Skye, taking in the sudden darkness of her veins, the blackness in her eyes, and the shadows that puffed from her hands in wisps. Dean was there, already lifting her in his arms, his back straining with the effort, but Lorcan was helping him. The other two women – the Nox and the Seer – lay unmoving, unconscious, but before her Talent could latch onto the damage they had suffered, Amber tugged her along with an urgency that frightened her.

Roxanne's head whipped around, and she saw the last couple of prisoners disappear through the portal that Seth still guarded. He waved them over frantically, his face full of terror. She gave a whimper of relief as they burst through the portal, and then pulled out a chair in the meeting room beyond for Amber to sit on.

"What happened, Rox?" said a voice with a thick Glaswegian accent above her, and she looked up to see Bert Lennox, one of the Resistance members who had been captured along with Nanette. He, too, had watched the battle and that bizarre explosion that Amber had somehow caused at the end.

"I don't know," she admitted, looking from Bert back down at Amber. She was staring into space again. Concern tore at Roxanne's insides. She could find no physical signs of harm, but what had Camilla done to her to make her behave in such a way?

Dean staggered into the room then, closely followed by Seth and Lorcan, who shut down the portal behind them. Dean's face was distorted in pain as he carried Skye, enveloped in the dark tendrils that still emanated from her. As Roxanne took in the shadows, and the scorches on Dean's arms and jacket that hadn't been there moments before, she began to piece together what had happened. Skye was still thrashing, and one of those tendrils lashed out and caught Dean on the side of his neck, eliciting a hiss of pain and leaving behind a dark gash. He let Skye down, and she slid to the floor, crawling into a corner and curling into a ball.

"Roxanne," he said, the urgency in his voice enough to pull her away from her daughter, however reluctantly. "Can you help her?"

She looked down at Skye doubtfully, who crouched against the wall, hands clutched close to her chest as she appeared to convulse. "I can heal her wounds, but I don't know… I don't know what that is."

"She absorbed the darkness," came an eerie voice from behind her, and Roxanne felt another stab of fear when she realised the voice belonged to her daughter. Amber was staring at Skye, her expression unreadable.

Roxanne looked back at Dean, then down at Skye. Everyone was staring at her, lost for words as she raved and whimpered, nothing like the warrior she had been just minutes before. Hesitantly, Dean knelt before her, taking hold of her wrists as though to soothe her, but quickly shrank back as the darkness burst out again. After a moment, Roxanne crouched before her too, setting to work healing the worst of the wounds, working quickly so she could get away from her before she lashed out again.

"If that's darkness, we should get an Obscurus."

"No!" Skye shouted, and Dean fell back in time to avoid the wave of darkness that shot from her hands.

"Or maybe Veto," said Dean, getting to his feet. "At least so we can get her home."

Roxanne gave Skye a shot strong enough to knock her out, and Dean arranged for an Aeres to take her home, wherever that might be, for they spoke in whispers. But Roxanne's work wasn't done. The aides that Darshana had left behind to help the injured prisoners led her to the infirmary, and Dean followed close on her heel.

"Will you see to Victor?" he asked, his voice full of pain and terror.

"I'll see to all of them," she said. She hated to be parted from Amber so soon, but she had refused to budge from the chair, so Bert and Lorcan stayed behind to keep an eye on her. "I'll see to you, too," she said then, casting her eye over Dean's wounds as an afterthought.

"I'm fine," he said, wincing with every step.

"They'll leave scars. I'll sort you out after I've helped the others."

To stop Dean from hounding her, she looked at Victor Bolton first. His wounds were numerous, and he slipped in and out of consciousness as she healed him, fixing his damaged eye and broken nose, the infected, half-healed stab wounds that she was shocked to find peppering his abdomen, carefully placed to hurt but still keep him alive. There were broken ribs too, pressing dangerously on his lung, and half his teeth were shattered, but there wasn't much she could do for the missing ones. He would have to have them reconstructed, and she told Dean as much. But the worst were his spine and legs. The bones had been broken. And broken again. And again. As she felt along his back, her Talent searching for the damage and trying to repair it, she realised the injuries were too old for her to fix entirely. The bones had tried to heal on their own and had fused together in a way that she would have to surgically break them again if she had any hope of repairing them, and even then, she knew the chances were slim. She supposed she had to be grateful that Amber appeared unscathed, because if this was the worst that Camilla could do…

"Dean," she murmured, taking his arm and drawing him a few paces away from Victor's bed. He looked down at her, dread in his eyes as he waited for what she was about to say. "I can't fix his bones. Not fully."

"Why not?" asked Dean, his voice trembling.

"The injuries… they happened too long ago." And so she explained her fears to him, and the anguish on his face made her regret what she had to say next most of all. "Wait until he's more lucid, but… you need to tell him he might not walk again."

She tore herself away from Dean's devastation, turning to the other patients desperately in need of her help. When she finally finished and headed back to where she had left Amber, she met Oliver storming up the corridor. Lindsey and Devan were just behind him, and all three of them looked anxious, exhausted and bloodstained. So the fighting had gone ahead after all.

"Did you get her?" Oliver asked, looking around, then back at Roxanne, his voice full of fear.

"She's in here," said Roxanne, gesturing to the door she had been about to walk through. "But Oliver—"

Oliver didn't wait, and neither did Lindsey. Roxanne was left alone with Devan, who stared at her, a question in his eyes. And as she met his gaze, the weight of her exhaustion crumpled her. She burst into tears as he crossed the space between them and drew her into a tight embrace.

"I'm sorry, Roxanne. So, so sorry."

But she could only sob against his shoulder as he held her, her relief tainted by her endless unanswered questions and the emptiness she had seen in Amber's eyes.

Chapter Eighty-One

DEAN ROSWELL

Alma encouraged Dean to bring Skye and Victor to her house, and they installed Victor in a spare bedroom, hooked up to Veto and antibiotics and who knew what else Roxanne had prescribed. The Healer informed them she would keep him unconscious until his infection was gone, by which time it would be safe to bring him around.

But as for Skye, the hours waiting for her to wake up were agony, the Veto keeping her under well into the evening. When Dean told Alma what had happened, she instructed him to put Skye in the guest house in her garden before the Veto wore off. "If she can't control it, I don't want her near the children," she had said, fear cracking her usually calm mask.

So, after ensuring that his stepfather was stable, Dean spent the afternoon at Skye's bedside, waiting and hoping that the darkness that had erupted from her earlier was now gone, or that she at least had control. It was twilight when the door creaked open behind him, and Lorcan stepped quietly inside, carrying a tray with food and water.

"No change?" he asked, setting the tray down on the nightstand, beside which Dean had long grown stiff in an armchair designed for decoration rather than comfort.

"Nothing," Dean murmured, rubbing his aching neck and returning his gaze to his sister. She hadn't moved apart from the steady rise and fall of her breaths. At least her skin had returned to normal, her veins no longer soot-black.

"Roxanne gave her a pretty strong dose," said Lorcan. "At least while she's asleep, she's healing."

Dean nodded, eyeing her bandages. One of Roxanne's medical aides had seen to Skye's wounds, dressing the worst of them, the stink of ointment filling the small room. But it was the internal injuries that worried them, the damage that the broken ribs had caused. Roxanne had shown him how to give Skye more Veto when the current dose wore off, urging him to ensure she rested.

"You should eat, mate," said Lorcan, nudging the tray at Dean's side. But the smell wafting from the bowl of stew only made Dean nauseous. "And maybe get some sleep. I can sit with her for a while."

"I'm okay," he mumbled. He picked up the bowl, spooning up a piece of carrot and some of the broth, but it lodged in his throat as he swallowed.

"Ombra is staying with Phaedra at the safe house. Apparently Camilla Linden called Ronan and told him the Nox isn't dead."

Lorcan's words reached him through a hazy fog, and he looked up at his cousin, taking in the worry in his green eyes. "What does that mean?" But he didn't expect an answer, and more questions flooded his mind.

"I don't know. Do you think they'll have to fight again?"

Dean shuddered at the thought and stirred the spoon in the stew, but he couldn't stomach any more. "I really hope not. I…" But he couldn't utter his fears aloud. There had been too many times during that fight when he was sure his sister was a goner. And to his shame, he had actually stood there and wished Skye had killed Alessia when she had the chance. At least he wouldn't be sitting here now, dreading what would happen when Skye finally awoke.

"Mum asked Kerry to come and stay too. Apparently the Ronans are moving out of the safe house as soon as Phaedra recovers from injuries she took today, so Kerry will probably be more comfortable here."

He nodded, comforted a little by the thought of a familiar anchor amongst all this upheaval. "Dad and Skye will like that."

Lorcan squeezed his shoulder, then settled into another chair, coaxing him to eat. But an hour or so later when Lorcan turned on the bedside lamp and left him for the night, he took the bowl with him, the stew cold and barely touched.

Dean was dozing by the time Skye stirred, but he jerked awake at the sound of her movements, a crick in his neck and shoulder. He leaned forward, taking her hand to reassure her, and was relieved when she opened her eyes and they were once again their natural brown, not the deep black brought on by the darkness.

"You're safe," he said before she could speak, brushing hair back from her face. "We're at Alma's."

She glanced around, taking in her familiar surroundings, then looked back at Dean. Grogginess and confusion were still etched on her face.

"How do you feel?"

She took a moment to answer, her voice a hoarse whisper. "I don't know."

"Are you in pain?"

Her eyes roamed their surroundings again. "Where's Dad?"

"In the main house. Roxanne said he needs to stay under Veto for a few days. He has a nasty infection."

"I want to see him," she croaked, then surged upwards. But before she could move off the bed, she gasped, her face crumpling, a hand going to her ribs.

"Stay," Dean soothed, taking hold of her shoulders and easing her back down. He glanced at the bandages puckering beneath her white vest, but saw no blood seeping through. "You need to rest too. Roxanne will see you both tomorrow."

She did as she was told, but she pulled him towards her and wrapped her arms tightly around him. Dean relented, letting her bury her face against his chest like they were children again, when she had climbed into his bed each time she had a nightmare. Breathing a sigh to clear the ache for simpler, happier times, he gathered her close to him and allowed sleep to claim them.

But when he awoke to a stinging sensation in the creeping light of dawn, a nightmare had bled into reality. Tendrils of darkness hovered over Skye – over both of them – and they burned where they touched his bare skin, eating through his T-shirt. He tore away from her with a yelp, fell off the bed, then scrambled across the room until he banged into a chest of drawers beneath the window.

Skye sat up with a strangled moan and rubbed at her arms, trying desperately to rid herself of the shadows spewing from her fingertips. "Stop it!" she gasped, whether to Dean, or the shadows, he wasn't sure. And as her panic grew, so did the shadows swirling around her, growing more restless, gathering like a storm. "Make it stop!" she yelled, tears bursting down her cheeks as her rubbing turned to scratching, drawing blood on her arms.

And then, as Skye curled in on herself, she convulsed, the shadows gathering close around her, and then exploding outward.

Dean buried his head between his knees and ducked low behind the armchair, the force ruffling through his hair as it passed above him – passed *through* the armchair, blasting it to smithereens.

When he finally dared to look up, his eyes widened at the destruction. The armchair was in pieces, the lamp smashed, and chunks of plaster dropped from the wall. Skye's veins and eyes were black once again, and she gripped her hair as though she was about to rip herself to shreds.

"Get away from me!"

"Skye—" he began, hesitating as he knelt behind the destroyed armchair.

"Get out!" she screamed, and convulsed again, the shadows already gathering around her for another attack.

Seeing no other option, he shot to the door, staggering through it and slamming it behind him.

"I could see her," said Ombra two hours later when she got back from spending the night with Phaedra. "It's darkness, she can't hurt me."

"I'd rather you didn't," said Alma, her hands shaking around her coffee cup. "Obscura or not, I don't want you seeing her in that state."

"I'm a soldier—" Ombra began.

"What about Caspar Ronan? We could give her more Veto and take her to him," Alma cut across her.

"He and Phaedra are going to look for Alessia."

"So she's definitely not dead?"

Ombra shrugged. "Apparently not. But she's lost her Talents."

"Yes, and somehow they're in Skye," Alma snapped, her voice dripping with frustration. She looked at Dean. "Will Ombra be safe with her?"

Dean chewed his lip and surveyed his cousin in her ripped jeans and brightly coloured T-shirt. Ombra was right;

she would merely absorb whatever darkness emanated from Skye. "I think so."

"Let's go then." And with that, Ombra marched out to the garden, leaving Dean and her mother to follow behind.

Skye was on the floor, leaning against the opposite wall in an exhausted heap when they entered the guest house, but she drew her knees up to her chest when she saw them, holding her hands between her legs and her body as though she could keep the darkness from escaping. Dean and Alma stayed in the doorway as Ombra approached, more careful and hesitant than Dean had ever seen her.

"Skye?" said Ombra, kneeling on the floor before her, closer than Dean would have liked. But Skye only looked at her cousin as though she were a frightened animal.

"Don't come closer," she said, and a flicker of shadow shot from her hands. She clutched them tightly to her.

"You can't hurt me," Ombra said gently, and she reached out a tentative hand, touching Skye's knee. "See? Hey, this is cool, we have the same Talent now."

But Skye only shook her head frantically, inching further along the wall.

"Here," said Ombra, and she turned the hand on her knee palm up, beckoning with her fingers. "Give me your hand."

Skye sat frozen for a moment, and then, so slowly she barely appeared to move at all, she placed her hand in Ombra's. The younger girl's fingers curled around Skye's. "See, that's al—"

There was a flash of light, and Ombra was thrown backwards with a bang, her hair standing up in a static halo. Alma rushed inside with a series of shocked exclamations, checking Ombra over, then hauling her to her feet. But before she could get her outside, there was a buzz as Skye's lightning lashed out again. Alma threw her hand up, her own electric Talent hurtling out, veering off Skye's and sending it forking across the ceiling. Plaster groaned, splitting into hairline cracks that travelled overhead. With the threat diverted, Alma grabbed her dumbfounded daughter and dragged her outside. Dean watched them long enough to see Ombra shake off her mother in exasperation, and then he knelt before Skye, oblivious to the plaster flaking from the ceiling in a rain of chunks and dust.

"You still have your lightning," he said, awestruck as small strands of white light buzzed and crackled up and down her arms. But the darkness also writhed around her wrists, making her flinch.

"It's fighting it," Skye blurted, and she buried her face in her hands, gasping and shuddering as the two Talents continued to roam across her limbs. "But the darkness is winning. It's like a parasite. It feels like ice creeping under my skin."

"You can't let it win, Skye." Dean reached out, but he was afraid to touch her.

Skye started to sob into her hands, but when she finally lowered them, her face was fierce. "*Get me Veto*," she snarled.

Sabine summoned him to the barracks that afternoon, demanding an update that Dean couldn't give.

"I need to know where we go from here. What do I tell the troops?"

"I don't know, Sabine," he said, running a hand through his hair. Exhaustion and stress weighed on him as they stood at the edge of a training ground, well out of earshot of anyone else. "Tell them to take a break. Go home to their families."

"I need Skye's orders. She's supposed to be their leader." Her voice was brisk, bordering on anger.

"Skye's in no fit state. She's… she's not herself right now."

Sabine stared at him, her face a subdued mask. "What happened at the final battle? Skye won, didn't she?"

The weight of her question crushed him, and he sagged before her, wrapping his arms around himself. "I don't know."

"What do you mean, you don't know?"

He shook his head. "Skye didn't win." He hated to say it. Hated to admit the horrible truth, even to Skye's best friend.

"But she's not dead."

He shook his head again, more aggressively. "Neither is Alessia."

Sabine took a breath, confusion slackening her usually hard exterior. "But Lorcan said Skye has her powers. That's good, isn't it? She's even stronger than before."

"I don't think so," Dean admitted, his voice sounding desperate even to his own ears. "She can't control them."

"Let me see her."

"You can't, Sabine, it's too dangerous."

Sabine began to argue, but Dean interrupted. "What happened here, with the armies?" Aside from Lorcan confirming that his friends lived, he had no idea how the battle had gone.

She hesitated, folding her arms across her chest. "The fighting started, and then about an hour in, all the Undead just… dropped dead."

Dean shuddered, trying to imagine it. "It must have happened when Alessia was stripped of her power."

"Does Skye have that too? Can she raise the dead?" For the first time that afternoon, Sabine looked almost afraid, echoing Dean's own fear. In all the commotion with the darkness, Dean had forgotten about Alessia's second Talent.

"I really hope not." He swayed on his feet, wondering how they could possibly find out. He needed to get back to

Skye. If he had measured her Veto right, she would be waking up around now.

But as he arrived back at Alma's a short while later, Ombra came rushing to greet him at the door, her face full of panic. "Skye's gone."

Chapter Eighty-Two

ALESSIA RONAN

Becoming powerless was never part of her agenda.

Death or victory, that was what she had expected when Vala came to her when she ascended and told her that her father had killed the wrong woman, that the Lux did indeed still live, and that the final battle would come sooner or later.

Whatever fear Alessia had seen in Skye Bolton's eyes during their battle, it was nothing compared to Alessia's devastation when she regained consciousness in the grass and found her powers gone. Almost as bad was the feeling of abandonment when she saw that Vala had left without a word, not even sticking around long enough to explain what had occurred. The betrayal left an unbearable ache in her hollow heart.

Only the Linden woman helped her, ordering her servants to carry her inside the rotting manor and leave her in one of the lesser decayed rooms. But there was no kindness in Camilla's actions. Alessia knew full well her mercy was most likely due to her hope that she could use the fallen Nox as a bargaining chip, and her intentions became clear when a soft knock at the door finally came.

Alessia didn't answer, remaining huddled in the moth-eaten armchair in a multitude of dusty-smelling shawls, staring through the window and biding her time until she recovered enough to get out of this place. It was only when a familiar scent of cologne filled the room that she knew who her visitor was, but she didn't bother to look around.

"Alessia," said Caspar, stopping in the middle of the room, just within her line of sight. He waited a moment, and when she didn't reply, he got down on one knee before her, reaching out a tentative hand. She flinched away as she felt his touch on her arm, withdrawing her hands beneath her shawls.

"Alessia, come home with us."

She heard the kindness in his voice – and hated it. Hated *him* for his distrust of her, his dislike of his father, his preference for taking Phaedra's side, his affair with the Lux and his betrayal. She hated his smirks and false charms and the fact that people worshipped him despite his lack of dedication and loyalty to the Ronans and their cause. The fact that they shared blood was no reason to come home with him, wherever his home may be now.

A shift in the doorway finally made her look around, and she narrowed her eyes as she spied her sister gripping the doorframe that she leaned against, her face as fearful as always. And Alessia hated even more that Phaedra was seeing her in this state. She knew how she must look: sickly and pale, a husk of the person she used to be, sitting there huddled in her layers, reduced to nothing. She took in Phaedra's appearance, noting the short hair and healing bruises on her face, her dark clothes that were slightly more demure but still as scruffy as ever. Once she was satisfied that Phaedra was the same as always, her eyes finally fell on Caspar.

There was no stupid curl to his lips or amusement in his eyes now. Instead, he looked at her with what could only be described as pity, and it made the ache in her heart twinge. Pity, it made her sick. She had never looked on anyone with pity, and she certainly didn't want anyone to look at her that way. She turned away, looking back through the window, unable to stomach that expression on his face any longer.

"Alessia, we want to help you."

"No, you don't," she said finally, her nails digging into her palms as she heard how hoarse her voice was, her throat tight. "You don't want anything to do with me. You're only here out of some sort of loyalty to my mother."

His silence confirmed she was right. Minutes passed before he spoke again, saying her name one last time. She ignored him, still glaring at the window.

Caspar sighed and rose, turning to leave. But before he reached the door, Alessia made a split-second decision – a last twist of her knife before he walked out of her life. Why shouldn't he bear some of her pain?

"Caspar?" She waited for him to pause and turn back to her, but she kept her gaze trained on the window. "My mother didn't kill herself."

There was a silence. Not even the sound of breathing interrupted it. And then Caspar exhaled, taking a step back towards her. "What?"

Finally, she turned her head, met his eyes – twins of her own, of her sister's, of her grandfather's. She forced every bit of hatred she felt towards her family and her failure into her words. "Grandfather killed her."

Caspar sagged, his face crumpling in horror and anguish. Behind him, Phaedra shifted in the hallway, her eyes wide, the colour draining from her cheeks.

"How could you… how could you know?" Caspar's voice shook, so at odds with the slick charm everyone knew him for.

"He told me," she snapped, then turned away to glare at the wall. "And then I left what remained of him to rot."

"Why?" he asked, taking another step towards her. "Why would he kill her?"

"Because she was going to run away with you," came Camilla's bitter voice from the doorway.

Caspar turned to her instead, his voice harder now. "Did he tell you too?"

"A few of us overheard. I suppose that's what happens when adulterers get caught. They get what's coming to them."

Caspar snarled, grabbing Camilla by the collar of her shirt and pressing her against the doorframe. Alessia glanced around, watching as Caspar seethed in the woman's face, like a wildcat cornering its prey. She had never seen him lose control before, except once, at her mother's funeral, when he had swung a punch at her father. Maggie had dragged her away before she could see the fight escalate.

"What else did you overhear, Camilla?"

But Camilla only laughed, a cruel, heartless sound. "Only that he killed the maid who snitched on you, so you wouldn't find out. Ilaria was as barmy as a box of frogs, who wouldn't believe she had topped herself?"

"Don't you dare—" he spat, shoving her against the doorframe so hard that her head cracked against it.

"Cas, stop!" came Phaedra's frightened squeak, and he froze, eyes wide, his grip loosening on Camilla. But the woman only laughed, pressing her fingers to her auburn hair, her hand coming away bloody. Alessia looked away, another image flashing through her mind: crimson blood on white tiles.

Caspar let out a shaky breath, staggering back against the opposite doorframe.

"Give him the letter," Alessia murmured, her voice barely above a whisper.

"Letter?"

There was a rustle of paper as Camilla withdrew a crumpled envelope from her pocket. She held it out for Caspar. “From your father.”

Caspar snatched it from her hands. “You opened it? It’s addressed to me.”

Camilla shrugged. “Didn’t think I’d ever see you again. Alive.”

There was a hiss, followed by more rustling and tearing of paper. Silence fell as he scanned the contents of the letter, then he screwed it up and shoved it into his pocket.

“Come, Phaedra.”

And then their footsteps began to retreat. Soon after, Camilla left too, and Alessia was alone again, just like she had always been.

Chapter Eighty-Three

PHAEDRA RONAN

The journey home in Caspar's estate car was saturated with distraught silence. Caspar drove himself, unable to trust anyone else to join them on this trip, and Phaedra sneaked peeks at him as they crossed the country. He stared bleakly at the road, knuckles white on the steering wheel, the speedometer creeping past the limit. It was just as well there were few cars on the road.

She sank further into the passenger seat, arms wrapped around herself. She hadn't wanted to leave her bed that morning, an ache still rippling through her abdomen each time she breathed, the thought of meeting her sister again only making it hurt more. But she couldn't let Caspar go alone. And after the ominous hallucination she had witnessed on the battlefield, she didn't want to let him out of her sight.

Caspar sped on, his jaw rigid with suppressed fury. It was only after they passed through a public portal and came out in Suffolk that he seemed calmer, and she dared to speak. "What did the letter say?"

Caspar didn't answer at first, shifting into a higher gear as they gathered speed, trees and fields whipping by. Phaedra waited, nervously twisting a loose thread on her black sweater.

"He confirmed Alessia's story," he said eventually, his voice tight with emotion. "And explained why he did it."

Phaedra let out her breath, tears threatening as she took in the devastation on his face. She had to swallow the lump in her throat before she could ask her next questions. "Is it true? You were going to run away?"

Another silence followed, but she closely watched his expression, saw the muscle flicker in his jaw. And then, after a long moment, she witnessed the lone tear escape the corner of his eye and disappear into his beard. It was another moment before he pulled over, switching off the engine, the silence broken only by the motor ticking and Caspar's shuddering breaths.

She waited, her own tears finally falling as she watched him brace his elbow against the car window, teeth clamped around a knuckle as he stared at the golden wheatfield beyond the windscreen. Not knowing what else to do, Phaedra reached over, taking his shaking hand in hers.

"It's true," he said eventually, his voice having regained some calm. "We planned to take you and your sister into hiding. Vala…" He trailed off, swallowing with difficulty, unable to meet her gaze. "Vala visited me in a dream on the morning of my twenty-first birthday. She showed me an image of your mother, stabbed with a dagger *I* gave her to defend herself should she need to. I hoped the dream wasn't a real prophecy, but I still feared it, so I put plans in place to run. I secured a secret home for the four of us, withdrew funds, and told Ilaria to pack. I had to go to Ireland for duty for a couple of weeks, and we intended to run as soon as I came back. But when I arrived at the manor to collect you…"

"She was gone," Phaedra whispered.

He nodded, another tear slipping down his face. He was silent again, chewing on his knuckle once more. Phaedra realised she had never seen him like this. Not even when he told her he was her father.

"When I found out what happened, I tried to take you. But Maggie… she found me in your nursery and talked me out of it. She was the only one who knew that I fathered you, and knew the consequences if that secret got out."

"How did she find out?" Phaedra asked, choking up again at the mention of Maggie.

"She walked in on us kissing when Ilaria was pregnant. She put two and two together and nearly wiped the floor with me." He smiled weakly at the memory. "We're lucky it was her and no one else. You know she practically raised your mother, not just you and Alessia?" He looked at her then, his smile growing through the tears.

Phaedra's eyes widened. "She came from Mum's household?"

He nodded, eyes returning to the wheatfield beyond the car window, shimmering gold in the breeze. "That's why we knew we could trust her. She would never have done anything to hurt Ilaria."

They lapsed into silence, the enormity of all these truths heavy in Phaedra's heart. Caspar's sadness was a testament to how loved her mother had been, as was Alessia's. Phaedra had never felt sorry for her sister before, but seeing her in that wretched state, sick and weakened… A small part of her wished Alessia had come home with them. Perhaps she still would, and they would have a chance to repair their broken relationship and become a proper family at last. But she knew it was unlikely. Still, she was glad to be alone with Caspar in that moment, to suffer the weight of their twisted, messed up family together.

As if reading her thoughts, Caspar squeezed her hand, giving her a smile that was much closer to his usual self. "Let's go home." He extracted tissues from the glove compartment, and they both dried their eyes before he turned the engine on. He swung back onto the road, his driving much steadier than it had been before.

Caspar's home soon loomed on the horizon, a white building with slate roofs – Caligo House. With the war over and the Resistance gaining control of most of the country now that Alessia's threat was gone, he finally deemed it safe to return to his estate, and Phaedra hadn't hesitated when he asked her if she wanted to live with him. After the hell of the past months, stability was all she craved right now.

The house was old, formerly belonging to the Blackthorn family, and had entered Ronan possession as part of her grandmother's dowry. Caspar had told Phaedra it was gifted to him when he came of age, but he had only started living there shortly before his mother died, when she had lamented that her ancestral home was going to waste.

"Why did you live in a pokey little apartment for years before you decided to move here?" she asked as they turned into the lane leading to the estate.

Caspar shrugged. "It seemed pointless having a big old house if I didn't have a family to fill it with joy."

Phaedra bit her lip, realising his reasoning was yet another reminder of all they had lost, of all the years of happiness and memories that had been stolen from them. "We can make up for that now," she murmured, and he gave her another hopeful smile.

But his smile faded when they pulled into the driveway to be greeted by an unwelcome sight.

A woman in a navy skirt suit stood between a large white van and a sleek green car, her black stilettos shining dully in the evening sunlight. She was slight, with legs so thin they looked like they might break like twigs if she was pushed over. She turned towards them, her sheet of long black hair swinging with the movement. Her light brown eyes were narrowed in a scowl.

Phaedra recognised the woman. She was Mrs Matheson, Brydon Marsden's daughter. For some inexplicable reason, she had been invited to the Ronans' formal events for as long as Phaedra could remember, even though nobody seemed to like her. Doran had always encouraged her to call her Auntie Sheridan, although the blood relation was distant.

She didn't want to get out of the car as they rolled to a stop beside the van and Caspar turned off the engine. Judging by the way he sat frozen with his hand on the handbrake, he felt the same. He eyed Sheridan warily through the windscreen, and the woman waited, cold amusement lighting up her sharp features. Finally, with a sigh, Caspar removed his seatbelt and got out of the car. Phaedra followed.

"What do you want?" Caspar asked bluntly, lacking his usual charm.

"Hello to you too, Caspar," said Sheridan, her arms crossed over her chest, her long nails painted red. "Surely you can manage a warmer welcome after I've come all this way."

Caspar stopped before her, looking down at her with an imperious glare. "Spit it out."

Sheridan wrinkled her nose, her chin jutting forward as she held his stare. Then she dropped her arms to her sides and stalked to the back of the van, nodding to the three men who accompanied her. Obeying the order, the men opened the van doors, then proceeded to pull out a long box made from rough, hastily clapped-together pine.

A casket, Phaedra realised.

"What the hell is this?" Caspar asked sharply, and he angled himself with his back to Phaedra, blocking the box from her view.

Sheridan crossed her arms again, her stance and tone haughty. "Your father."

Phaedra's stomach roiled. Caspar's hands curled into fists, his body becoming rigid. And then, before Phaedra could take a step forwards, shadows emerged from his fists like vapour, drifting into a curtain behind him and obscuring the casket.

"Open it," he said, his voice low and dangerous. Phaedra took a step back and wrapped her arms around herself. For a wild moment, she imagined her grandfather's corpse was about to spring from the casket and start attacking them. But after the horrifying scrape of wood as the lid was prised open, everything remained still, the truth hanging like a gossamer veil over the assembled people. And then, as Phaedra waited, a stench of rot reached her nostrils. She pressed a hand to her mouth, gagging and tasting vomit.

The lid scraped closed once more, but the stench lingered.

Sheridan lurched into movement as the shadow curtain faded, patting Caspar on the shoulder as she stepped towards the green car. "Give my regards to my daughter, won't you? And tell Oliver to burn in hell." With that, she got into the car, smoothing her skirt on her lap before one of the men shut the door and got into the front. Her other attendants climbed into the van, and with a crunch of tires on gravel, they drove off, leaving behind clouds of exhaust smoke and dust.

Phaedra looked back at Caspar. His shadows were thinning, drifting into the gathering night. Tentatively, she approached him, taking in the still-clenched fists, the tightly set jaw. And the cold fury blazing in his eyes. Words failed her as she watched him, fearing what that anger might drive him to do.

The butler stood frozen in the doorway, having witnessed the entire ordeal. After a moment, he approached, as tentative as Phaedra. "What should we do with the body, sir?"

Silence dragged on, thick and heavy as the stench that emanated from the casket. And then, just as Phaedra thought he wasn't going to reply, Caspar turned on his heel and headed into the house. The words that followed were in that same low and deadly voice.

"Burn him."

Chapter Eighty-Four

Amber Summers

Peace and sanity were a distant memory.

Amber was safe from the outside world. But she was not safe inside her head. Not when memories haunted her. Memories of a laughing woman tormenting her, waxy lips curved like a slashed wound, red hair hanging like blood-stained rags. But worse than the cruel laughter were the knives repeatedly cutting into her flesh, peeling the skin from her bones.

Amber didn't sleep. She spent all hours sitting in the armchair by her window, watching the days and nights slip by, just like she had done in her makeshift cell. She watched the world around her, refusing to let sleep claim her and drag her back into her prison of pain. If she could see where she was, she could believe she was safe, even as she rubbed the phantom pain from her arms and legs, even as she shuddered through the memories that tugged for her attention.

But almost as bad as the memories were the voices. Her mother's was loudest, a constant stream of worry and wondering what *that woman* had done to make her behave so strangely. And if it wasn't her mother, then it was her visitors: her grandparents, her father and Lindsey, Darshana and Devan. They all came, all taking turns to sit with her. Some held her cold hands despite the static that crackled between them when they touched, trying to talk to her, trying to get her to look at them. She endured their voices drifting towards her, the words they spoke without even opening their mouths. Her father's thoughts were the worst, his wondering full of images that looked too much like the ones she had seen with her own eyes, unspeakable acts that had been committed on her own body.

"We should get a Telepath to see her," he had said to Roxanne out on the landing. "That Dooley woman, the psychiatrist."

"NO TELEPATHS!" Amber screamed in reply.

That was the only time words had crossed her lips since she arrived home. The rest remained locked inside her head, and she remained locked with them.

Nobody knew what to do for her, and Amber didn't know herself. Her mother brought her food that she touched only to settle the gnawing in her stomach. Roxanne's eyes and Talent constantly searched her body for the damage she would never find. Her skin was pristine, glistening pale and perfect like the lie that it was. The wounds were only visible in the darkest depths of her memory.

The only conversations she had were with the cat in the dead of night, the cat that found its way to her lap. Sometimes it was Mischa, her warmth purring and reassuring, her velvety fur real beneath her cold fingers. And other times it was the cat from her dream – the cat that wasn't really there. The cat that spoke back.

They silently exchanged words, the cat's eyes shining pearlescent in the dark. It told her everything she needed to know, and coaxed her out of her chair, leading her through ancient forests to another time, another place, another self. The cat always returned her to her bedroom before the grey light of dawn trickled between the open curtains, where her mother lay sleeping fitfully on Amber's bed, her dreams bleeding into Amber's cold reality.

Rest, Amber, the cat silently ordered, pressing its warm nose to her hand before it faded from sight.

Chapter Eighty-Five

LUCIEN

Vala raged.

The creature that returned to Castle Uaine was no longer the woman he had known all his life, a woman who was almost always composed, sweet smiles and pleasantries, her voice barely rising above light, tinkling laughter. That façade was gone, replaced with a force of nature that both thrilled and terrified him.

Vala had changed her glamour. Or perhaps this was her true appearance, the appearance of a dark goddess returned to exact her vengeance on the world. Her hair no longer softly swayed like willow branches, but instead rippled like vines caught in a howling storm. Her youthful cheeks were replaced with sharp angles and planes, cruelty etched into every line of her face. And her eyes, once the deep blue of the ocean, were now black as midnight, flashing every colour of the spectrum when she cast her gaze his way. And if she had emanated power before, it was a shadow of what billowed from her now, a force greater than anything he had ever experienced. Britannia thought Alessia as the Nox was frightening enough. But the First Nox was close to ascending once more, the second coming that Vala had waited a millennium for, biding her time as she travelled through it.

But not all had gone according to plan.

The Nox was defeated, struck down and stripped of power. But before Vala could harvest that power, Skye Bolton had, inexplicably, absorbed a large part of it and was now on the loose, running from the world and, it seemed, running from herself.

It was hours before Vala quieted, her rage calming to a furious simmer. She came to him then, reaching out to him, and he let her. She caressed his jaw with long, cold fingers tipped in black talons, lifting his chin so she could see his face clearly. To anyone else, the caress would seem motherly, but Lucien knew it for what it was: possession. He was hers, her servant, as he had been since she plucked him from a cruel, loveless childhood.

"You always were my favourite," she crooned, her voice still dripping with some of her previous sweetness, but now it was laced with poison. "Ronan thought she was stronger than you, but what a little fool. The only being stronger than you is me."

Lucien only smiled, holding Vala's gaze, not bothering to hide his satisfaction at being called her favourite.

"I have a task for you. One last task before I make my final ascension."

"Anything, Vala," he said, knowing full well what her next words would be.

"You are the Lux Killer, Lucien. So find Bolton, take back the powers she stole from me, and end her."

She let go of him then, taking a step back, and he bowed his head.

"It would be my absolute pleasure."

The Last Lux concludes with Book Three:
The Curse of the Midnight Phoenix

Acknowledgements

In the year since publishing my first book, I've received such an overwhelming outpouring of love, support, and best wishes from my family, friends, work colleagues, and beyond. People I haven't spoken to for years reached out to support me and my little (big) book, relatives who don't usually like fantasy took their time to read The Stormbird in the Shadows, and complete strangers have added it to their shelves – virtual or real. I can't thank all of you enough, or put into words exactly how much your support means to me, but there are some extra special mentions I want to acknowledge in these final pages of my second book.

I am eternally grateful to my wonderful family for all your love, guidance, and support, not just when it comes to my writing endeavours, but throughout my whole life. Family love has been the biggest theme throughout this second book, and you've all inspired me to pour that love into my characters. Thank you for everything.

Karlein Kwong, thank you for being the first pair of eyes on Book Two! Your excitement, support, feedback, and encouragement has gone such a long way in helping me bring out the best in this book. You helped me capture all the feels, the romantic warm and fuzzies, the tension and the drama. I'm so glad to have you as my critique partner and fellow shadow daddy enthusiast!

Nick Burgoyne, thank you for being Team Glendra's biggest fan, for picking apart all those pesky plot holes that I hoped you wouldn't notice, for helping Dean find his bad boy side, and for all your honest and helpful feedback and line edits. You read my manuscript not once but twice (and some scenes even three times), and my writing wouldn't be what it is without all your writerly wisdom and encouragement. I'm so grateful for your friendship and everything you've done to help me grow as a writer.

To my beta readers, Tom, Holly, Sarah, Réka, and Nick (again!), thank you for all your time, comments, and suggestions to help my manuscript shine during the final stages. Your feedback has been invaluable and I appreciate every one of you.

To Joan Culum, my friend and incredibly talented cover artist — you've done it again! Thank you for yet another magical cover, this time with all those dark and lovely villain vibes. Alessia looks terrifying in all the best ways, and the colours and details are stunning, especially her very special battle coat. Thank you for your endless patience and determination to get it just right. What you have achieved is perfection.

Thanks to Helen Salsbury for all your kind words and marketing advice, to everyone in the Instagram indie author community for your endless expertise, tips and cheerleading efforts, and to my own personal promotions team – Mum, Lisa, Kelly and Réka – for telling everyone about my book even when I was too embarrassed to talk about it.

Finally, I want to say an extra special thanks to Angela. You were the first person to read The Stormbird in the Shadows from start to finish, and your excitement and encouragement did wonders in helping me bring my writing dreams to life. Sadly, I never got to send you the sequel you eagerly awaited, but as one book lover to another, I hope heaven has an infinite library. Rest (and read!) in peace.

About the Author

Naomi is originally from Cheshire, England, but she has lived in four different countries and lost track of how many languages she started learning. Aside from anything bookish, her obsessions include art, mythology, the passing of the seasons, and drinking too much tea.

Naomi studied languages and translation at university, but her core passion has always been to write. Her dream of seeing her name on the cover of a paperback novel finally came true in November 2023, with the release of her debut urban fantasy novel, The Stormbird in the Shadows.

To connect with Naomi and sign up for her newsletter, you can find her links here: https://linktr.ee/naomi_g_writes

Printed by Amazon Italia Logistica S.r.l.
Torrazza Piemonte (TO), Italy

65457652R00427